Hope on the Waterways

Milly Adams lives in Buckinghamshire with her husband, dog and cat. Her children live nearby. Her grandchildren are fun, and lead her astray; she insists that it is that way round.

Milly Adams is also the author of *Above Us the Sky*, *Sisters at War*, *At Long Last Love*, *The Waterway Girls* and *Love on the Waterways*. This is the final novel in her Waterway Girls series.

To find out more visit millyadams.co.uk or follow her on facebook: @millyadams2

Why YOU love Milly Adams

'As usual I have thoroughly enjoyed this author's book – it was absorbing and full of suspense at what Leon may do. The historical information was interesting too and showed a forgotten side of the war led by women. I look forward to the next instalment'

'I really enjoyed this – I had previously read a little about the 'Idle Women' and so was drawn to this as soon as I saw it. It certainly didn't disappoint – the characters and the way of life are all so very real feeling, and I am really pleased to see that there is a second book about these characters; so pleased, in fact, that I have already pre-ordered it :)'

'Excellent book what went on then was totally different they contributed so much to the war effort very interesting can't wait for the next'

'Excellent read, could not put it down'

'I loved this book, really good story, was sad when it ended'

'I enjoyed this and will look forward to the next. Fans of Nadine Dorries and Donna Douglas will find this worth a look'

'A good story about believable people, combined with fascinating history, and brilliantly accurate descriptions of life on board a narrow boat'

'Another book that you cannot put down until you have read about what the woman did you have no idea what it was like another great read'

Hope on the Waterways

Milly Adams

arrow books

1 3 5 7 9 10 8 6 4 2

Arrow Books
20 Vauxhall Bridge Road
London SW1V 2SA

Arrow Books is part of the Penguin Random House group
of companies whose addresses can be found
at global.penguinrandomhouse.com.

Penguin
Random House
UK

First published in Great Britain by Arrow Books in 2018

www.penguin.co.uk

A CIP catalogue record for this book is available
from the British Library.

ISBN 9781784756932

Typeset in 11.5/14.5 pt Palatino
by Integra Software Services Pvt. Ltd, Pondicherry

Printed and bound in Great Britain by Clays Ltd, Elcograf S.p.A.

Penguin Random House is committed to a
sustainable future for our business, our readers
and our planet. This book is made from Forest
Stewardship Council® certified paper.

Acknowledgements

My deeply felt thanks go to those who made the completion of this novel possible.

Of course, these are the usual culprits: those who have helped me with canal life, the books I have read and listed in *The Waterway Girls*, which was the start of this journey, and, of course, the lovely Cass, my editor. I want to thank her for her boundless energy and kindness in laughing at my jokes. She really shouldn't because it only encourages me. But she'll learn.

The people, though, who made *Hope on the Waterways* reach the bank were those who progressed the sale of our house, and the buying of another, throughout the writing of this novel. Their efforts were over and above . . .

'Him indoors' and I are enormously grateful to Wye Residential in High Wycombe, to Darrell and the girls, and especially to Ian. He must have made hundreds of phone calls on our behalf to keep the chain vaguely moving and is now surely bald, as we are now, from pulling out our hair. He is lying in a darkened room as I write this.

And then there's Joe de Silva, Anne Buckle, and Amy at our solicitors, Blaser Mills in High Wycombe, who did all in their power to solve everyone's problems, not just ours. Our estate agents, Jill, Patrick and Ben at Luke Miller & Associates in Thirsk were unfailingly patient and helpful. The removals firm, W.H. Cox of Amersham never wavered in their help and encouragement as completion date after completion date came and went, and a particular thanks to someone who offered up her allotment for one particular task I had in mind ... but let's say no more about that! Hayley, our buyer, and I bonded tighter than any buyer and seller in the history of human endeavour as we tried to navigate a way through the problems of the chain.

Hayley, of course, was gracious in the extreme, whereas I frequently used rude language (though in the privacy of my home). The dogs got upset, but 'him indoors' just ignored it. Not that any of this was directed at Hayley – it was at the chain. Lastly, huge thanks to Annie, Kris and Miss Delilah, aged one, who let us stay between moving out and moving in to our new home. It was massive fun.

And so, hope played quite a part as we all hung in together – much like Polly, Verity and Sylvia. We all finally made it through to a safe mooring. Will they?

I do so hope you enjoy the last in the series as much as I loved writing it.

Warmest wishes,

Milly Adams

To Hayley, Ryan, Zac and Zoey
We finally made it

And to Jo Bentley
Thanks for the fun

Map of the London to Birmingham Grand Union Canal

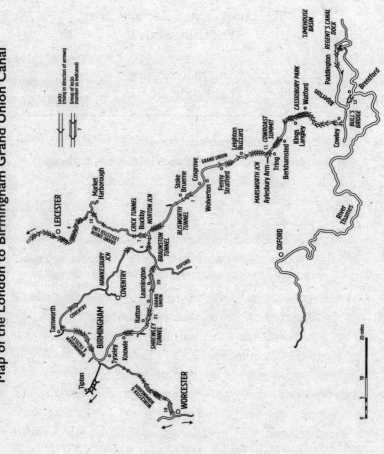

Broaden your waterways vocabulary ...

Basin – a partly enclosed area of water at the end of or alongside a canal, housing wharves and moorings

Bilges – the bottom of the boat

Butty – engineless boat towed by a motorboat

Canal frontage – land abutting the canal

Counter – deck

Cut – canal

Gunwale – inner ledge around boat

Hold – where the cargo is carried, both motorboats and butties have holds

Lock – the main means of raising or lowering a boat between changes in water levels on a canal

Long pound – a long length of impounded water between two locks

Moor – to secure a boat against the bank

Motorboat – a narrowboat with an engine

Prow or fore-end – front

Short pound – a short length of impounded water between two locks

Slide hatch – sliding 'lid' above cabin doors to keep out the rain

Snubber – long strong rope for towing a butty along a long pound

Stern – rear

Straps – mooring and lashing ropes

Wharf – structure built for cargo loading or discharge

Windlass – L-shaped handle for operating lock paddles

Bull's Bridge, Southall, is the location of Grand Union Canal Carrying Company's (GUCCC) depot

Limehouse Basin, also known as Regent's Canal Dock

Grand Union Canal **Paddington Arm** runs into Regent's Canal leading to Limehouse/Regent's Canal Dock

Tyseley Wharf, Birmingham

Chapter 1

Early January 1945, heading along the Regent's Canal, dodging V2s

Sylvia Simpson leaned against *Horizon*'s cabin, examining the grey looming clouds, and then the empty fifty-foot hold stretched out in front of her as they headed east along the Regent's Canal towards Limehouse Basin. *Horizon*, an engineless butty, was strapped alongside the motor narrowboat *Marigold*, with both boats under the control of Polly and Verity. All three girls had been recruited the previous year on to the Inland Waterways Scheme set up to replace the boaters who had gone to war.

Their task was to transport supplies from the London wharfs to where they were needed and then the same in reverse. This morning they were pat-pattering east as fast as they could, which, she sighed, didn't amount to much. After all, four miles an hour didn't exactly part anyone's hair. Sylvia scanned the skies again, but what was the use? The layer of swirling grey would hide any V2 streaking towards them. 'I just wish dear old *Marigold*'s engine could get a bit more of a head of speed going. I feel as though we're the ducks at a fairground shooting gallery.' She snatched a look at the other two standing on their deck alongside.

Polly replied, resting her elbow on *Marigold*'s tiller, keeping both boats to the centre of the canal, 'You're not alone there, Sylvia. It's an endless dog's dinner, but what can we do?'

Standing the other side of the tiller, Verity adjusted her green woollen hat and called, 'We duck, darlings, since Sylvia brought up our little feathered friends.'

The three girls laughed, and that summed it up, really; just keep laughing and get on with the job. So last night they'd moored up overnight at Alperton as usual and made an early start this morning to load up at Limehouse quick as a flash. What's more, the rabbit and parsnip stew was simmering in *Marigold*'s tiny cabin range, and who knew, Sylvia thought, they might even manage to gulp it down while the blokes loaded the holds. Then they'd head hell for leather back down Regent's Canal and finally on to the Grand Union Canal past Hayes to motor north for Birmingham, well out of the danger zone. Again, Sylvia snatched a look at the clouds, listening, always listening, but why, when it just made her irritated with herself?

She called, 'I need to break the habit of looking and listening because you can't hear the V2s, as you did the V1s. Which makes me ask, clever clogs Verity, how can we duck if there's no warning?'

'Don't be so picky, darling.'

Sylvia grinned across as Verity moved to lean against *Marigold*'s cabin, lighting a Woodbine, then waggling the packet at Sylvia and Polly. Polly took one, but Sylvia shook her head as she thought aloud. 'And, in fact, how can these rockets, or anything come to that, go faster than sound? I just don't understand.'

Polly, still with her elbow on *Marigold*'s tiller, replied, 'I've no idea either, and you're not the only one on edge; if we're not looking for the rockets, it's the wind trying to freeze off whatever we've left exposed.' So saying, she pulled her muffler up over her mouth.

The wind gusted, making Sylvia's nose run. Damn, she thought, wiping it on her sleeve, then feeling suddenly ragingly furious, she shouted, 'Oh Polly, and you too, Verity, I know it's winter but I'm sick, sore and tired of this weather, never mind that awful little Hitler sending his ghastlies over to blast everyone to kingdom come.' Sylvia stopped, scared that she was being sacrilegious; kingdom come? Did that mean our Lord's Kingdom? After all it was: 'Thy Kingdom come, thy will be done'.

The old uncertainty which was never far away tore at her just as fiercely as the wind. She could ask Sister Augustine next time she put pencil to scrappy paper, or perhaps not, because she didn't want to get into a discussion about kingdoms, or more importantly, now the words had entered her head, His will being done. She shifted at the tiller, feeling

3

guilty but even more angry, and now also upset because try as she might to ignore it, she was still in such a muddle about her future – to be a nun, or not to be a nun, as Shakespeare might have said. Her mouth dried, as panic began. Had she really been called as she had thought at the convent orphanage? Was she disobeying God's will by being here, choosing another path, for now at least?

Unable to bear it she jerked herself from this train of thought, elbowing her butty tiller a tiny fraction, which was pointless, but it might break the chain of agonising questions. When it didn't she shouted to the other two, 'I dream of the sun, only the sun, every night. Can you imagine being warm ever again on this wretched cut?' She even banged the tiller with her fist. It hurt, and she was glad.

Polly and Verity laughed from their deck, or counter as it was called by the boaters. Sylvia joined in, not sounding quite right, but muffled enough by her scarf not to cause comment. She began to feel calmer, keeping her thoughts on the cold, cold cut and pondering how working the canal boats had become such a different world that it required its own language.

'How many of the people we pass on the towpath know that a cut means a canal, and a counter is a deck?' she called.

Verity, wisps of blonde hair slapping her eyes, ignored her but asked Polly, with a wink, 'What's the daft girl going on about now, eh?'

4

The icy wind increased to the point where the waters of the cut rippled as they passed Camden. Sylvia felt her thoughts being left behind as she listened for rockets and Polly replied, 'Who knows, we're all as mad as a mad hatter's tea party after all.'

All three were hunched against the wind, which had ratcheted up more than a few notches. Sylvia called, 'You speak for yourself, Polly, and just answer me this: why does my nose always go red enough in the cold to rival Rudolf's?'

Verity called, 'Not sure, darling, perhaps to match your hair, but just think how useful you could be on a dark night. I'm surprised the RAF don't stick you on top of a Wellington and use you as a pathfinder.'

Dog, sitting on the roof of *Marigold*'s cabin, barked, wanting to be part of the laughter. Polly wagged a finger. 'No one asked your opinion, Dog, so settle back down or no treats for you when we load up at Limehouse.'

They pulled in to the bank and changed to a short tow to travel single file through Islington Tunnel after hooting their intention to any oncoming boats. Once into it and subsumed by darkness, Polly bellowed back to Sylvia, 'Come on, Rudolf, flash away and guide us through.'

'Shut up,' Sylvia yelled. Their laughter echoed.

When they were out into the light they lashed abreast again and Sylvia pulled her woollen hat further down over her ears, and her scarf, which had slipped, up over her nose. She squinted ahead while Verity eased herself up on to *Marigold*'s cabin roof, sitting alongside Dog, cuddling her. It was probably for warmth as much as out of love, Sylvia thought, then ticked herself off, knowing she was wrong; it was always out of love in the case of that particular animal, a love felt by them all for Dog, who seemed to sense their moods, and lighten them if need be. Poor creature, she was frequently overworked.

As Sylvia watched, Verity straightened, clearly struck by a thought. As the breasted boats pat-pattered along between the warehouses which lined both banks, and under a bridge, Verity called, 'As you've brought it up, lovely red-nosed Sylvia, remind me about this sun that so obsesses you? It is beyond memory as far as I'm concerned and seems to have given over its control of the skies. Quite frankly, darlings, there has to be more to life than freezing on a bloody narrowboat's counter hoping we're not going to be blasted to smithereens.'

Polly, steering lightly, grinned. 'Now, now, Verity, "bloody" indeed. If my mum was here you'd have to wash your mouth out with soap. Let *me* explain in language simple enough for even someone as daft as you, Lady Verity Clement: the sun is a little yellow orb which sometimes peers out between the clouds over Britain, but not nearly often enough, and is known to give off heat. Is it simple enough for you both to understand or shall I draw you a picture?'

At the mention of Polly's mum, Mrs Holmes, Sylvia grinned, but didn't answer because she was too busy silently thanking that wonderful woman for knitting all their hats, socks, mittens and scarves. Admittedly they were strangely colourful but if you had to pull out the wool from old sweaters bought from jumble sales, they would be, wouldn't they? It was still wartime after all, but surely it would end soon and then . . . what then? She saw the orphanage, the convent, the nuns. No, she pushed it away, but back it came, because now Harriet was there in her postulant's dress, as clear as day. Sylvia reached for *Horizon*'s tiller, needing to ground herself in the present, but slowly, inexorably, Harriet continued to force her way to the forefront of her mind.

Harriet who was her friend from their early days in the orphanage, Harriet who had the bed next to her in the dormitory and with whom she had talked and laughed when school was over as they walked back to St Cecilia's in the crocodile, hand in hand. The sisters on point duty, front and back, looked like penguins, one of the older children had mocked, only to be smacked across the hand with a ruler by Father O'Malley for being cheeky.

As the years went by their class grew too old for holding hands, or hopscotch, or skipping, but not too old for chatting. They would sit in the common room, talking of this and that, all of them. But when they were sixteen something happened, and Harriet grew serious, and in the darkness of the dormitory she began to talk to Sylvia, in a whisper so as not to disturb the others, of God, for she had had a dream and heard His voice, and knew she, Harriet Wilkes, had been called to serve.

In that dream, Harriet had said, Sylvia had been spoken of by God too. She had whispered on the longest day – June 21st 1942, 'He says we are to be postulants together, Sylvia. Just as we are now friends. We can stay here, in this convent, and devote ourselves to Him, and teach, or look after the orphans. But He said also that He will call to you, too. So, we must promise to enter as postulants, together, mustn't we? Won't that be good?'

So Sylvia had promised, because she was Harriet's friend and they would be so lonely if separated.

'Sylvia?' Verity called, jerking Sylvia back to the present. 'Polly Holmes is such a know-it-all, isn't she? And it was your fault that she lectured us, Miss Sylvia Simpson, for asking about the ruddy sun in the first place, so there.'

Sylvia swallowed, and breathed deeply, and as she replied Harriet faded, but would come back because she always did. She said to Verity, finding the words from somewhere, knowing that her reply would lift her back to *this* normality, 'I quite agree, and I suggest you ask Mrs Holmes to knit a solitary sock, Verity, to pop it into Polly's mouth in order to give us all a rest.'

She and Verity sniggered while Polly gripped her tiller more tightly and grunted, trying not to laugh. 'I might remind you both that you can go down into the warmth of your cabins if you feel the need to continue to behave like a couple of five-year-olds. That will leave Dog and me to martyr ourselves by staying on the counter, steering our lonely path. Remember, however, when it is your turn to do the honours, then you too will be the solitary . . .'

Verity bellowed, 'Oh, all right, we get the picture.'

Sylvia shook her head, unable to retain her staged silliness. 'I feel safer, somehow, with the three of us together, counter to counter, even though the rockets are still falling. We've been so lucky so far, not to be hurt.' There, she thought, I'm here, with my current friends, safe from memories, safe from decisions. It's just a question of going from day to day, on a mission. Yes, a mission to help everyone. She found herself looking up at the sky, and beyond, calling silently to Him that her mission, her war work, was surely enough, at least for now.

Polly murmured, 'You're right, Sylvia. We are lucky, much more so than all the poor devils who've been killed in the last months.'

Sylvia looked, as Verity said, hugging Dog again, 'I think it might have been two or was it three V2s that fell around here, today? I try to stop myself from counting but I just can't.' She squeezed Dog until she yelped. 'Sorry, darling girl,' Verity said, releasing her, and covering Dog's ears. 'But talking of numbers, Sylvia, you said we three girls together on the counter, but I believe you mean the four of us? Nod if you agree, and I will release our Dog's heartbroken ears.'

Sylvia laughed, and nodded so Verity stroked Dog, and crooned quietly to her, 'There you see, you *are* one of us, sweet Dog, so you must ignore daft Miss Simpson.'

Polly steered off centre to make way for a laden breasted pair motoring back to the Grand Union to head northward. It was Timmo, Peter and Trev, on *Venus* and *Shortwood*. ''Ow do,' Timmo called as the two pairs passed right side to right side.

'How do,' the girls replied, wanting to ask how the lads were doing after Thomo's death in a V1 explosion, but they didn't. They'd only be told, 'Fair to middlin', which was all the boaters ever said, because what was the point of saying anything else, when it changed nothing?

Peter called from *Shortwood*, 'Got the rabbits did yer, at Alperton? We 'ung 'em behind yer engine room when yer were in the land of Nod. Yer might let us win just one darts match in return, eh?'

The laughter of the men followed them as the girls continued on.

Verity said, 'Win at darts? The very idea. Anyway, as you were saying a while ago, Sylvia, about feeling safer counter to counter . . . Why not let's say cheek to cheek as the song says? Listen, we should find a dance at the end of this trip. It would do us good to step out, even if we have to dance with one another now the blokes are doing their bit over there.' She pointed towards Europe.

For a moment they all fell silent. Verity's Tom was trying to push the Germans towards the Rhine while Polly's Saul had left the Mulberry harbour and was frantically driving supplies to the front line. Sylvia broke the silence. 'I merely ask, would we be welcome at a dance with our boater smell and our callouses?'

Verity responded, 'Oh faint heart, we could have a proper wash before we go, pool our slap, and draw a seam up the back of our legs, then we'd be the belles of the ball.'

Polly piped up, 'Oh, come now, a bit of rouge and pretend stockings won't be enough. Besides, we'll be too cold with nothing else on.'

As Angel Lock hove into sight, they were laughing hysterically and Sylvia made it worse by shrieking, 'She's right, even a Ladyship couldn't carry that off, Verity, unless she wore a tiara. I suppose you have a few, or if not you, your mum will. Besides, we'd get chilblains in unmentionable places.'

Polly, still laughing, was pulling in to the bank just before the lock. 'Your turn to lock-wheel, Sylvia. Timmo's been through so it'll be ready for us.' She didn't expect a reply because it was all second nature now. Sylvia leapt for the bank while Polly steered the boats into the lock. Sylvia shut the gates behind them and opened the paddles to let the water out.

The boats sank to the lower level, and she walked the beams back with her bum, opening the gates, wondering how long it would be before her trouser seat had to be patched again.

She jumped back on to the butty as Polly pulled away. Dog barked in welcome as she always did, and they continued past the buildings which still loomed alongside the cut, casting shade across the water. There were gaps now, common to all the cuts in Britain's cities; a warehouse gone here, a factory there, absences that resembled lost teeth, jagged and dark. Some were old Blitz wounds where rosebay willowherb grew in spring and summer, but since the V1 and V2 rocket campaign over London and the south-east they'd also been passing new gashes, oozing with the smell of cordite, dust, debris and heaven alone knew what.

Sylvia longed for the northern passage, where they identified villages and distant towns from the spires and towers, not to mention the allotments which edged the towpath, and then there were the fields, the hedges, the birds ... They entered and left another lock, and motored on, hearing the calls of a formation of geese flying high up, probably heading for the Thames.

Sylvia allowed herself to look at them, and they gave her heart, for not all had changed with the war. Polly was watching them too, her elbow still resting on *Marigold*'s tiller, her face pinched with the cold. 'Thank heavens for nature.'

Verity muttered, 'Damn Hitler, the vicious little pipsqueak. He's lost his diabolical dream, so why doesn't he just surrender? These poor, poor people who put up with this murderous mayhem all the ruddy time while we just . . .' She fell silent.

There it was, Sylvia thought, one minute they saw hope in a skein of geese, the next they were back in the war. No one replied, and Sylvia contented herself with trying to work out yet again why the buildings lining the cut didn't protect them from the wind as they pat-pattered along. Even in the shadows beneath the bridges, where the cold was always deeper, there was wind of some sort. Still, she shouldn't moan, for beneath these bridges it was like an air raid shelter, and they felt protected for a few seconds. But yes, as Verity had said, what about the people out there, living in this hell?

They were approaching a bridge across which gallant red buses continued to pass, no matter what. Sylvia murmured, 'I thought I'd never say this, but I miss those perishing children who leaned over the parapets hurling abuse and manure at us boater scum. It's because they were a sort of normality. But they've gone, evacuated.'

Verity roared with laughter. 'So, our Sylvia, those heathens are our normality, eh? Crikey, just about sums up our Inland Waterways war work doesn't it?'

Sylvia laughed along with the other two. When she joined the scheme she thought she'd never be part of the team, never laugh as they did when everything was such a mess in her head, but . . . they had saved her reason, because – yes, all right – she was running away from the convent, the orphanage, Harriet, and the dream she, Sylvia Simpson, had finally experienced, just as Harriet said she would.

Polly called, 'You've got that look, Sylvia. How did your telephone call to Sister Augustine go? You did telephone her back, after she left the message with the depot office?'

Sylvia shrugged. 'Yes, I did. She wanted to know if I was going to accept the invitation to the orphanage reunion so they could get some idea of how many could come. I said that I didn't know where we'd be.'

Verity muttered uncertainly, for the two girls knew of her struggle to put aside her confusion about what she should do with her future, and whether, indeed, she should even be here. 'Ah, but we could manage the timetable somehow, if you wanted to go, but only if.'

Sylvia stared down at the water rippling away from the sides of the boat.

Verity repeated, 'We really can work out things if you want to go, dearest Sylvia. But only if. Don't let Sister Augustine badger you, or make you feel stressed.'

At this, Sylvia dragged herself away from the movement of the water and gripped her tiller and answered, 'She never tries to do that, quite the reverse, after all she supported me coming on to the scheme to try out the world, as she put it, but seeing her just makes the thinking and fidgeting increase.'

Sister Augustine had sat quietly in her study when Sylvia confessed that she had applied to, and been accepted for, the Idle Women scheme, as the Inland Waterways girls were called. But Sylvia had confessed she feared she was running away after being called in that dream she'd had a few months before.

To her surprise Sister Augustine had smiled that smile of hers. 'Is this sense of a calling imaginary, and the dream too? You have always told me you can't really remember it. Don't forget that I came to the dormitory when I heard you shout out loud enough to wake the whole orphanage. I too heard Harriet say you had called to God, but I also heard Rosemary from the bed opposite say that you had been talking rubbish. Dear Sylvia, it happens, you know, that girls who have lived with us wonder where their duty lies after we, with God at the helm, have enveloped them in love. I say to you, what I say to them – please, please experience life outside this world and be kind to yourself. Only you, and God, can decide what is the right path. We are your parents while you are here, and after you leave us too. You may return to stay whenever you need, but, dearest Sylvia, what we have done here at St Cecilia's does not imply any obligation towards us, or God.'

What could have been kinder, she thought; she had shared this with Verity and Polly, and also told them of the dream which she couldn't remember, and Harriet who had heard her call to God, but what she couldn't bring herself to share with them, or Sister Augustine, was any mention of the promise to Harriet, for she, Sylvia Simpson, was the betrayer, while Harriet was a postulant, for Sylvia had watched Harriet leave the dormitory to fulfil her calling. Her friend had looked back at her as she walked down the centre aisle and beckoned, but Sylvia had not followed. She just wasn't sure enough.

Verity was still waiting, and Sylvia said, 'I want to go and see them all, in a way but—

A piercing howl cut right across her words. She and Verity spun round to see Dog sitting bolt upright, ears pricked, the hair raised along her back, still making that dreadful sound, and then the boat lurched, and tossed in a buffeting sucking of air, different, harsher, much harsher than the wind. Hats were ripped from their heads, and scarves pulled from their mouths, and they gasped, trying to drag air into their lungs. They clung to tillers or cabin roofs, their ears popping, trying to understand, their minds in chaos. Nothing was firm, nothing was safe. Dog was howling, howling. Finally, Verity, still on the roof but lying flat, her voice strained, held Dog close, 'It's all right, it's all right.'

Sylvia was hugging the tiller, her ribs aching, as the boats rocked, just as Polly was doing. 'It's all right,' Verity repeated as their breasted boats were driven into the bank by some primeval force. The jerk almost knocked Sylvia off her feet, and Polly too, and after a while, it was almost all right, but Sylvia wished Verity would shut up, because her voice was rising, and rising, and now Dog was howling again. At last the world slowed to a fevered rocking as they looked from left to right, searching the area ahead for the V2 which had exploded. Polly pointed over to the south of the cut; Sylvia and Verity followed her arm, and saw smoke rising. The V2 must have scorched into the ground there, but the silent blast that had caught them was still taking down buildings near and far.

They spun round and saw that the warehouse to their left was cracking; would it crash on to the cut, and them? Was the cut going to burst its bank? They smelt cordite, and dust, and now they *heard* the blast – rolling on, and on, and on over the crashing of buildings. The warehouse nearest the bank collapsed on to the one behind, but the one to their left was still standing as it cracked from top to bottom.

Verity gasped. 'It *is* a damned rocket, isn't it?'

'Course it ruddy is,' yelled Polly, cutting the engine, to stop the *Marigold* from driving again and again into the bank. She was coughing, pointing ahead and to the right at the smoke which had turned black. It was perhaps a hundred yards away beyond the warehouses. Or was it much less? Sylvia wondered but what did it matter, for the blast was crashing on as the water bubbled and the boats rocked, tilting ever more fiercely. They fought for breath as the warehouse debris rose into the air, scattering bricks into the cut and into their holds.

'Duck,' screamed Verity. As they did, bits of brick hit the bank. 'Not us, not this time, it's those poor beggars over there,' Polly coughed, pointing to the smoke. 'And not for Timmo and the boys either.'

'Bet?' Sylvia groaned. 'She's a bit ahead with the new trainee crew.' She could taste blood in her mouth and realised she had bitten her tongue.

'She was well ahead. She must be at Limehouse,' shouted Polly. The cut was settling, the rocking becoming less violent but still enough for them to hang on to the tillers. Polly continued, 'If the girls handled the locks without mishap, that is. Come on, let's get out of here, what the hell did I cut the engine for?'

Verity and Sylvia checked the boats for damage but there were only superficial scrapes as the fenders had taken the worst of it. Verity restarted the motor in the engine house, and ran back across the roof of the cabin, doubling over, while debris still rained down. Within seconds they headed under another bridge, safe for those few seconds, then out again while Dog remained on the roof, dusty hair still standing up along her back, small bits of debris caught in it. She was sniffing the air, for they were heading nearer the black smoke that the breeze was carrying across the cut. It was pungent with destruction and mingled with the looming clouds.

Distant cries reached them, and the bedlam of rescue vehicles which set Dog barking, but there was no more of her unearthly howling. Polly yelled, as she motored on, 'Hang on to her collar and keep her with you on the roof, Ver. Sylvia, keep your eyes peeled for any warehouses about to fall, and for Bet, of course.'

Polly needed both hands on the tiller to steer them almost straight as the boats bucked against the unsettled water and they all peered ahead, and then there they were, Bet's breasted motor and butty crashed lopsidedly into the bank, both cabins damaged, and no sign of life. Verity wailed, 'Bet? Oh no! No, dammit. No.'

Dog leapt from the roof to the counter, barking frantically. Sylvia felt she could hardly breathe. Not Bet. Not their old trainer, their best friend. Please, God, not Bet.

Polly steered into the bank too, then cut the engine, her face deathly pale; Verity held back Dog. 'Wait, Dog.' Her voice shook. Sylvia leapt on to the towpath, her eyes fixed on the damaged boats. Were the girls hurt? Please no, Bet had just got over her latest chest infection, but how stupid, what was a chest infection here, now?

She moored up the prow while Verity hauled on the stern mooring rope, securing it on the bank stud as the bucketing cut slapped the boats backwards and forwards against the bank. 'Think it'll hold, Sylvia?' she yelled.

'It has to,' Sylvia called as Polly jumped from *Marigold*'s counter on to *Horizon*'s and then to the bank. They all began running along the towpath, desperately calling Bet as the smoke and dust thickened, engulfing them so that it stung their eyes; they choked and coughed. Still they ran, calling Bet's name, but there was no reply from the butty and motor.

Chapter 2

Does the waterway girls' luck run out?

They were still calling for Bet within a hair's breadth of reaching her butty *Sky*, when all three of the crew emerged from the prow's store, coughing and carrying brooms. Bet, her scarf up round her mouth and nose, hurried Mabel and Evelyn on to the bank just as Sylvia, Polly and Verity increased their speed. Dog beat them all and sat leaning against Bet's leg until the girls reached them.

'You're safe,' gasped Polly.

'No need to state the ruddy obvious,' Bet snorted over the sounds of the rescue services to the south. 'Just help us haul out a couple of the smaller tarpaulins, to sheet over what's left of the cabins.'

Polly took no notice and held her close. 'Stop being such a grump. I don't know what it is with you; if you aren't having a bad chest, you're bringing rockets down to destroy your boats. Are you after another bout of shore leave?'

Bet's grin was shaky as she shrugged free. She said something, but the girls struggled to hear her over the increasing noise of fire engines heading towards the locus of the smoke. Taking a deep breath, she began again. 'Enough of your cheek, my girl. Come on, everyone, we'll check *Sky*'s cabin first, and the hold, then nip across to *Hillview*. It bore the brunt of the blast, after all, but the butty was the one that crashed into the bank. First though the tarpaulins.'

She handed her broom to Verity and leapt back on to the prow. Dragging out a neatly rolled tarpaulin, she chucked it at Verity and Evelyn, who were standing on the towpath, forcing them to drop their brooms. 'So, aren't we going to sweep after all?' Evelyn called.

They all heard Bet clearly as she raged, 'I got them out to keep us busy and stop any fussing. So now we'll sort out the cabins, but collect and chuck the brooms back, Mabel, if you don't very much mind.'

Sylvia muttered to Verity as Mabel did just that, 'She's totally shaken, but who wouldn't be?'

The sound of whistles, screams, shouts, and the revs and clangs of the Fire Service pump engines was growing, carried on the wind that was pushing denser and denser smoke over them.

'Come on, girls, chop chop.' Bet was dragging out another rolled-up tarpaulin. She threw it to Polly, who hugged it to her. Then Sylvia caught the coiled rope that Bet had hurled from the store. Standing with her hands on her hips on the prow counter, Bet yelled, 'You never know, Sylvia, it might come in handy and we can't have you and Mabel toddling along empty handed like Lady Mucks as though you're out for an early afternoon stroll.'

Bet jumped to the bank, taking an end of Polly's tarpaulin, and said, 'The ruddy pheasant stew's in *Hillview*'s oven, so that's bound to be ruined. At least nothing caught fire, or we'd have neither boat any more, just a pile of charcoal.'

Sylvia hoisted the rope over her shoulder and linked arms with Mabel. The girl was shaking from head to foot as she tottered along, then she started shrieking, 'We heard nothing, just felt this suck. A great big suck that took all the air, then a sort of roar and a wind that shoved us over, tore up the cabin and I didn't know what the hell was happening.'

'It was a V2,' Sylvia soothed her, knowing that she was shaking too but that it must have been far worse to be closer still.

Mabel snapped, 'I know what it was, of course I do, now, I just can't get such a dreadful suck out of my head.'

Bet, who was lugging a tarpaulin ahead of them, stopped, turned and yelled a command, treating the sound of the rescue services as though it was a mosquito to be swatted. 'If you say suck again, young lady, into the cut you will go. We have more to do than have hysterics; we need to make a silk purse out of a ruddy sow's ear, then the *Marigold* girls must get on to the Basin to pick up their load.'

They continued along the towpath towards the stern of the boat, examining *Sky*'s hold as they went, though all Sylvia wanted to do was scan the skies for more rockets. Mabel, still at fever pitch, shrieked, 'Bet's a tyrant, that's what she is.'

Sylvia grinned. 'Of course she is, but she'll teach you to be a sort of boater, and then the boaters will teach you to be a good one.'

Mabel seemed unconvinced as she looked from the boat to Sylvia, then at the smoke and noise, and finally up to the sky. She was still shaking. Sylvia said into her ear to make sure she was heard, 'Best to think of something else, so check the hull as we're going along. You won't hear the V2, or see it if it hits you, anyway. It's going too fast. Only the survivors get that pleasure.'

Mabel looked appalled and shouted back, 'Well, thanks for that bit of information, I don't think.'

Sky seemed untouched except for the fenders which had been ripped off and flung into the cut, and into the hold where they lay shredded on the bilge boards. Sylvia squeezed Mabel's arm, as in front Verity shouted above the noise, 'A tyrant, you say, Mabel. Well, yes, but we found Bet doesn't often bite. Still, I dare say she – what's the word – oh yes, I know, she can't half suck.'

Polly, walking alongside their old trainer, slipped her arm around Bet, saying, 'I don't think anyone will say suck again. What do you think, girls? Anyone about to mutter the magic word – what was it again?'

Bet howled, 'Shut up' but was forced to join in the shaky laughter.

Reaching amidships, they saw that the right side above the waterline was completely caved in thirty feet from the stern and parts lay in the bilges. Verity looked over her shoulder at Sylvia. 'We were in such a rush to check on the grumpy old bag I didn't see this, did you?'

Polly and Sylvia were shaking their heads, as Bet stepped closer. 'Thank the Lord we were unloaded, or we'd have sunk and lost the supplies.'

Mabel muttered, 'Not to mention the three of us.'

Bet was peering closer. 'We're replaceable, ducky, the boats aren't – especially the motor.'

Mabel blanched. Sylvia grinned while Polly called, 'I don't think it will work to tarpaulin the hull, Bet. Best just to sort out the cabins and get back to the depot on your motor. If *Hillview* is still sound enough, that is.'

They set off again towards the stern. Reaching *Sky*'s cabin, Bet said, 'Too far gone. I reckon it was from being whacked into the bank by *Hillview*.' She kicked at the wood. Her precious pierced plates were smashed, and her horse brasses too, no doubt, were buried beneath the splinters. What about the hunting horn from Bet's father? He had two and Bet had given the *Marigold* trainees one. Sylvia nodded to herself. If Bet didn't find hers, they'd have to return theirs. It didn't matter a jot, because possessions in the face of all this were absurdly unimportant. They stepped across the counter, on to *Hillview*.

The breeze clutched at their sweaters as they examined the damaged cabin roof. Half was in place, the other half floating on the cut, drifting towards the far bank. Any approaching narrowboat would use boat shafts to force it aside, or barge it with the prow, so there was no need to do anything about it. Smoke was thickening now.

'Oh,' coughed Bet, dragging out her handkerchief and holding it over her face, having scooted along to the engine, giving the thumbs-up on her return. 'We can sort this enough to get back for the cabin and hull to be repaired, and if not, at least the motor's still useful. It's up to the company to decide what to do with the butty. Let's chuck the debris and one of the tarpaulins in the hold, then fix the cabin. Oh, bravo, the hunting horn.' She stooped, then brandished it at the smoke. 'There you are, you V2 buggers. Missed us, you did.' She hooted it once, and then again.

Sylvia caught Verity's grin and shrugged to herself. All right, so possessions weren't important, but it would have been hard for Bet to have lost something that had belonged to her parents.

Extraordinarily, the stew in the tiny stove was untouched, though the fire was out. They set to, creating a sort of tent over the damaged areas, obeying Bet's commands until Polly slapped her hands together. 'There you go, Bet, shelter from the cold, and should it rain as you toddle along to Bull's Bridge Depot, you'll stay vaguely dry. As for

Sky, I have to say you're not going to be Miss Popular, but it would have been worse if they'd had to scoop bits of you all out of the water. Just too messy for words, and it could kill the fish, if there are any.'

Everyone was relaxing – lightning didn't strike twice. They gobbled down the stew Bet was forcing on them, though each of the *Marigold* girls kept an eye on the time, until Polly said, 'Enough of this dawdling, we've got to get on to the Basin.'

They jumped on to the bank, with gravy-soaked pieces of bread in their hands for Dog. It was still freezing cold, and their eyes were stinging as Polly called, 'Dog, come on, playtime's over but we have a treat for you.'

They waited but she didn't come.

'Dog,' they called as the *Hillview* crew joined them on the bank. As they called again and again looking up and down the towpath, Mabel said, 'Damn, I forgot to tell you, I noticed her take off after a cat about ten minutes ago, heading over there; I thought she'd come back.' She pointed to the bridge across the canal, in the direction of the blast. 'I should have said. I'm so sorry. My head's such a mess.'

Polly snapped, 'For heaven's sake, Mabel . . .' She looked at the other two. Sylvia and Verity said together, 'We've got to go after her.' Bet yelled, 'She's got a good head start. Oh, really, Mabel.'

The girls, already running off down the towpath, heard Bet call after them, 'I'm so sorry, girls, Mabel

27

doesn't realise Dog's not just a dog. In fact, she doesn't realise very much.'

Polly waved, saying, 'Poor girl, I remember that tone, don't you? She's in for a right ticking off any minute now.' She called over her shoulder, 'Not to worry, Bet. Mabel wasn't to know. Be gentle with her.'

Bet bawled back, 'Blow that for a game of soldiers. Contact the depot for me when you see a phone box and tell Bob we're limping back if you will, but point out *Sky* needs rescuing. I'll leave her moored. Don't listen to his mithering. Just put the phone down. Never met such a grump.'

'Well, we jolly well have,' the girls heard Mabel and Evelyn shout.

Polly, Verity and Sylvia didn't laugh as they reached the bridge, because they were too busy calling for Dog. They left the canal behind, as they jogged through the billowing black smoke. Polly shouted to the other two, 'Damned cat.'

Verity replied, 'Damned Dog.'

Sylvia said nothing, because the same anxiety that had hold of Verity and Polly, in spite of their tone, had hold of her. Dog couldn't be lost, not really. Perhaps she was confused by the smoke. How long could they search? There was a war on and goods to transport. Oh Mabel, Oh Dog. Damn and blast the bloody V2.

They drew in to the side as an ambulance tore past, heading away from the centre of the blast. Polly sounded as despairing as Sylvia felt as she shouted, 'If they're careering around like that, they wouldn't see a dog in the road, would they?'

'Oh, shut up, Pol,' shouted Sylvia. They ran on, calling and calling for Dog as they passed houses with paper criss-crossed over the windows, and gaps where summer hollyhocks probably grew amongst the ruins. There were broken bricks in the street, and rubble where a house had been this morning, with rescuers now working like men possessed.

'Damned Hitler,' Sylvia panted, feeling real hate but it was just disguising the panic. Where was Dog? 'Dog, Dog.'

Polly nodded, calling, 'Dog, oh come on Dog, we've a load to collect. Don't do this to us today. Dog, darling, come back. Dog.'

Verity joined in, 'Chase whatever you like in the countryside, away from the rockets. In fact, do it anywhere you like, but come back to us.'

They had slowed and were crunching on debris. They passed a woman entering a terraced house. 'You looking for yer dog, are yer? There's one over there where the rocket came down. Helping 'em out, she is. A mongrel, brown and 'airy?' The woman, wearing a headscarf and carrying a string bag bulging with potatoes, pointed off to the left. 'Just got back from the air raid shelter, swapped me leeks for spuds with Mrs H, not that the all-clear's gone, but I need to get on.'

'Oh, thank you,' shouted Polly, almost hugging the woman, who just smiled, and kept pointing. They ran on, past more blast damage that had cut a swathe through houses, and a factory. They thought of Mabel's 'suck'. They could have lost Bet, and Dog was alive, and they could live here instead of the cut, so what had they to moan about? They ran faster.

In the heavy smoke-drenched air they struggled for breath, fighting stitches, wanting to bend over and take a moment, but there was no time. They ran even faster, the air increasingly hot and damp, the smoke so much thicker they could taste it, like a foul soup. They reached the centre of the blast, or so they supposed, because a tape had been stretched around a crater which was surrounded by destruction. A couple of policemen guarded the tape as neighbours and relatives waited, some swearing, some weeping, but most just watching. One of the constables, his arms outstretched, seemed to be daring anyone to break through, and yelling every few moments, 'Get yourselves to the shelter, the all-clear ain't gone.'

'Lightning don't strike twice,' an old boy shouted back. 'Reckon this is the safest place.'

Behind the policeman dust and smoke rose from the crater, and the rescue squads were digging steadily amongst the debris of ruined and damaged houses and shops, some of which were burning. Over these the firemen were playing water, their pumps roaring, the water hissing as the fire officer shouted directions.

The girls stood together, handkerchiefs to their faces, searching for Dog. A wall crashed to the ground behind them. They swung round and saw dangling floors, and fireplaces just like those in the bombed house in Birmingham they had passed for months as they headed for the Bull and Bush pub. There was an explosion on the other side of the crater and the crowd ducked. Strangers clutched one another as flames whooshed. More dust filled the air. A woman next to Sylvia gripped her arm. 'It's the Pig and Whistle's booze going up.'

'Please, let it not have fallen on Dog . . .' groaned Polly.

As the Heavy Rescue Service arrived, the woman next to Sylvia said, 'The Pig's got a basement. Maybe someone's down there? There're basements all over the bloody place, and poor buggers fall through with the blast, but sometimes the joists hold up the rubble. Saves 'em, it do.'

Shouts and whistles directed the firemen. The air grew damper and heavier with moisture.

It was pointless to run around like demented beings calling for Dog. So the girls questioned the watchers, working their way round the area circling the tape until they were at the other side of the disaster area. 'Have you seen our dog?'

'Please, she's brown and hairy.'

'Please look out for her, we'll be here until we find her. A lady said she was here.'

Polly was crying, clutching the arm of an old woman. 'She's our girl, you see.'

The old woman muttered, 'Reckon I saw a dog over there, see, through the spray from the hose.'

The girls peered between the rescuers, firemen and ambulance crews who were rushing backwards and forwards but couldn't see Dog. They moved a few yards to the right trying to see past the base of the turntable ladder – and there she was, digging frantically on top of a heaped pile of bricks and beams. They could see her barking, but not hear her. A small team of rescue workers looked on as a squad member sat on top with Dog, cupping his hands and shouting to the workers. As they watched, the man turned and gave a thumbs-up, patted Dog, and taking hold of her collar, eased himself from the pile, taking her with him. The squad took over.

The girls called, but Dog was being walked away from them. They looked at one another. 'Come on, we're not having that,' ordered Polly, and led the way towards a policeman who was busy arguing with a couple of old men. Verity stopped and said, 'Excuse me.'

The policeman put up his hand to tell them to wait. Polly said, 'Oh come on, while he's busy.' She ducked beneath the tape, and the other two followed, dodging past the firemen and workers and leaping the hoses, feeling the spray until they reached Dog.

Polly hauled her from the rescuer. 'She's ours,' she yelled. 'She ran off. We have to get to Limehouse to pick up our load. Come on Dog, come on.'

Dog followed. The man, his tin hat strapped on tight, yelled after them, 'Give 'er a bone, she's saved a good few today, just like she was born to it. Smells 'em, she do. Fancy leaving 'er with us? We could do with 'er. I'm serious, mind.'

The girls shook their heads and continued to back away, crashing into a fireman playing a hose on the warehouse. Sylvia lost her balance and fell backwards on to the ground. Dog barked and licked her face, then gulped water that was dripping from the edges of the nozzle as the young fireman looked down at Sylvia.

'No need to fall at me feet. I'm only doing me job.' He was laughing, but the tiredness in his voice was as heavy as the atmosphere.

The water dripped off Sylvia's clothes, and her bum was soaked. A yard away Dog barked at the fireman, and he snatched a look. Dog was straining against Polly, who now had hold of her collar. He said, 'A right good sniffer. We'll take good care of your dog if you leave it here.'

Verity muttered something. Polly nodded and told the fireman, 'We've already been asked that and if we could split Dog between you and us, we would, but we couldn't leave Dog. Do you agree, wet bum?'

'I think you should shut up,' Sylvia said. The fireman laughed and continued to play his hose on the building, but it was Sylvia he was looking down at, his eyes kind and full of laughter. As she began to scramble to her feet he hooked the nozzle beneath his arm and held out his hand. 'Grab hold, I'll give you a hand. Well, a lend. I want it back.'

She started to shake her head but slipped again. He grabbed her and hauled her upright. For a moment they stood close, and his smile was weary, but somehow . . . She realised she was still holding his hand. 'Thanks for the lend,' she muttered.

'Any time.' He let her go and took the nozzle in both hands, still looking at her, and for a moment she almost forgot the chaos and activity around them – then Dog barked and clawed at her trouser leg. Sylvia and the fireman looked down at her.

'Did Dog save that person over there in the ambulance?' Sylvia asked, loitering for a moment, unwilling to leave as Dog drank again from the dribbling hose. They watched the doors shut and the ambulance shoot off. The fireman replied, smiling at her, 'Yes, such a good 'un, the dog I mean, though I dare say . . .' He stopped, his face becoming serious as he looked at her, puzzled, and then confused. 'Sorry, I just meant.' He stopped again. 'Oh, I don't know what I meant.' But it was Sylvia now who muttered, 'It's all right . . .' She stopped, because she didn't know what was all right, just that she couldn't quite look away. It was he who did, directing the hose higher.

As Dog sat at Polly's feet, a fireman hosing further along called, 'Hey, Steve, try and get them girls to pass the hairy search expert over to us, will yer? Tell 'em he just took over when he got here, like he'd been popped from inside a cracker, God bless 'im. Tell 'em he saved that bloke who's just gone off to hospital, alive and kicking. Well, not kickin' but bloody angry 'e was. 'E had a nice bit of chop that's gone up in smoke, and not a lot left on 'is ration.'

'Do me best, Dodge. You just concentrate on hosing that lot down, eh?'

Sylvia watched Dodge, the other fireman, now, and the rescuers who were still working in a chain on the huge pile of rubble behind the girls. The people behind the tape were drawing closer together, chatting furiously. One man cupped his hands and bawled, 'That'll be old man Smeeth. Been saving up 'is coupons, 'e 'as. It's his birfday.'

A woman cackled, 'Well, 'e's alive, that's a pretty good present, if yer ask me.'

Sylvia, who still stood with Steve, looked at Dog, and back to the firemen, shaking her head. 'I'm sorry, Steve, I agree with the girls; if we could share her ... But we can't, so she stays with us.' The other two girls were fussing over Dog as Sylvia felt the sweat run down her face, just as it was running down Steve's face too. She watched as it ran over freckles and into his mouth, until he swung round, asking, 'You all right?'

Sylvia swallowed, and nodded, wanting to stay for just a minute longer. It was because she was tired, that was all. Of course it was.

She heard herself say, 'How strange, when we've been shivering in the cold, here we are, hot and bothered.'

When Steve laughed she was embarrassed. She stooped to help Polly brush the filthy dust from Dog's coat, picking out bits of brick. She said, 'Polly, you and Verity must be so proud, because Dog is yours, really. After all, you saved Jimmy Porter from drowning, which is why the Porters passed "our expert" to us.' Why was she chattering on?

Polly tugged Sylvia's hair. 'Dog's adopted you now, Sylvia, and she's as much yours as ours. But we need to get back to the boats, and what's more, find our hats. Not sure how far the blast threw them.'

Sylvia shook her head, only now realising that they no longer had them. 'We've got to phone Bob first.'

The fireman, Steve, was turning, and tucking his nozzle under one arm again as he held out a flask. 'Here, pour this in his mouth.' His hand was streaked with black from the fire, and water still leaked from the hosepipe's nozzle.

Sylvia took the flask. 'She's a her, and thanks.'

He laughed. 'Apologies to all four girls. What do you think, will you think again and leave her with us?'

Sylvia shrugged, pouring water into Dog's open mouth, then stroked her before handing back the flask. Polly and Verity shrugged too, Verity saying, 'We need to think about it. We've got to find a phone box, so might come back this way and let you know. If you don't see us, you'll know the answer. Thing is, you see, we need Dog when we go along the canal. She's part of us.'

Polly said against the ongoing bedlam, 'I suppose, if we were good people, we would leave her, but I don't think we could bear it. We all love her, you see, and she loves us.'

The fireman tipped back his metal helmet, revealing red hair damp with water or sweat. 'Ask for me if you come back, Steve's the name, and I hope you do, not just because you'd be giving us an answer.' He was directing his words at Sylvia, and for a moment he looked familiar. It was his hair, of course. It was like looking at a mirror image. He said, 'Yes, I really hope you do.'

Sylvia blushed, glad she was covered in the same sooty sheen as everyone else around them.

Polly, grinning at her, squeezed her arm. 'Come on, we have Bob to tackle. By the way, Steve, her name's Sylvia.' She kept a hold of Dog's collar as they headed for the tape, ducked down beneath it, and wove between the people. A woman stopped her. 'Thank yer dog for finding me Uncle Smeeth. If his chop weren't burned to a cinder, I'd make sure he let the dog share it.'

As the girls continued, they heard the clatter of boots, and turning saw Steve chasing them. 'Wait up, there's a phone box still working if you go left, not right.'

A man in the crowd called, 'Best to go right, young 'uns. You 'ear that, go right, the Coppernob is getting his hands muddled.'

Steve laughed. 'We passed it on our way here, and it *is* left, down past the bakery. Did you hear that, Sylvia? You just have to come back the same way to pass us.'

The bloke insisted, 'There are two, one to the left, and one to the right, but the right hand one is nearest.'

'Ah,' said Verity. 'If the right hand one is nearer, that's no contest.' As they threaded through those who were gathering to watch the proceedings, they heard applause starting. Someone called, 'Not for you gals, but for yer dog.'

Chapter 3

Decision time: left or right?

The girls hurried along the blasted streets, having turned left as Steve suggested, and not right as the man in the crowd had advised, but only because they had followed Dog who was straining on the end of a piece of rope they'd found.

Polly grinned. 'She's really pleased with herself, and who wouldn't be, helping to save lives.'

The three girls watched Dog leaping about the pavements, almost smiling. Verity crunched over the debris, which reminded her of heading towards Poplar with the other two girls a few months ago at the height of the V1s.

She felt Sylvia gripping her arm, as they slowed to get their breath. 'I just had a flash of our walk to meet your biological grandfather, Verity, it's the same sort of debris. Any regrets that you haven't tried to see him again?'

Verity shook her head, coughing, hating the moist, cordite-impregnated smoke. She pictured the seedy man, and his greed. She said, 'I was damnably glad to leave the memory of that family behind. If I'm honest, I'm relieved that my mum, or mother, or whatever I should call her, died young of pneumonia. I suppose that's unforgivable in your Catholic eyes, but it has simplified things. I just wouldn't have wanted to go on seeing him, but that might have made me feel guilty.'

She squeezed Sylvia's arm, felt the answering pressure and continued. 'I love my family at Howard Hall. Perhaps Father's affair had to come out, so Mother and I could understand one another better, because she *is* my mother, or had become my mother, really. Good heavens, she's had to put up with me for all these years . . . and with such grace.'

They were passing an untouched pub with an ancient yellowing menu showing through the windows and caught up with Polly. 'We must hurry, no more slacking,' Polly urged and they started to run again to Dog's barks of pleasure.

Verity was peering ahead, looking for the telephone box. Sylvia, who was doing the same, panted, 'Where is the wretched thing? I want to get away from here. Why didn't Bet tell Bob on arrival?'

Polly said, 'Because we're supposed to tell them what's what at the depot if anything like that happens.'

Verity grinned. 'Never mind all that. Much more important is our young fireman Steve, with eyes only for our own particular redhead. It's so apt, two little coppernobs together. I do think we should return that way, just to keep the flame flickering.'

Polly muttered, 'Very droll, Ver. He's the one that puts out the flames, remember?'

The girls stopped by the front door of a house where a woman was scrubbing the step, despite the smoke and devastation all around. Verity could have wept suddenly at the sheer valour of it but said instead, 'Excuse me.'

The woman, her hair tied up in a turbaned head-scarf, looked up. 'You all right, lovie?'

Verity smiled, 'Now I've seen you, yes. But we're looking for a telephone box that's around here, apparently.'

The woman dug her scrubbing brush back into the water and sat back on her heels. 'Yes, just carry on the way you're going and you'll come to it, outside Solly's second-'and furniture shop. But don't hang about, you never know what that 'itler is going to send next.'

The girls smiled and hurried on, passing a young woman cleaning her windows. Dog walked more calmly now. Polly said, 'Sylvia, our Sylvia, what *do* you think of Steve, then? We saw you blushing beneath your charming sooty sheen, but I doubt he could. Come on, let's decide whether to go back his way and say goodbye, and tell him where you currently reside, fair maiden. There's a war on, remember, you can't hang about waiting for a printed invitation if you like someone.'

Sylvia groaned. 'Do shut up. Let's just find the wretched phone box and get Bet sorted. We need to decide about Dog too.'

Sylvia led the way, knowing she couldn't bear to give Dog to anyone, even if it was the noble thing to do, and even if Dog enjoyed the work. No, she damn well couldn't. She felt like stamping her foot but then they turned a corner, and there was the telephone box by a row of terraced shops. The terraced shops were all boarded up, except for a 'Furniture Emporium', and a newsagent on the left hand corner of the square and a pub across the road, which was shut. Polly was pointing. 'Come on, it's almost midday and at this rate Bet will be back at the depot before Bob has been told, then we'll get it in the neck from both of them.'

As they neared it, they saw that the blast had caught the phone box – or was it some hooligan? The glass was shattered, and the telephone receiver yanked from its moorings.

'Blast,' Polly sighed, looking from it to her watch.

Sylvia covered Dog's ears. 'Don't listen, Dog, you've done your blast activity for the day, and for ever, as far as I'm concerned.'

Verity squatted by Dog, holding her face, and asking, 'What should we do, Dog? We know you're needed, but I for one couldn't bear to lose you.' She stood. 'I've voted, so has Sylvia. What say you, Polly?'

Polly kicked at half a brick, which immediately splintered into fragments. Sylvia shook her head. 'It's not your phenomenal strength, Polly, it was cracked all over.'

Polly looked from one to the other, and said,'It's a no from me too, of course.'

Then she added, 'But perhaps we should go back that way to avoid disappointing—'

Sylvia interrupted, howling, 'You really are the end, Polly Holmes I've—'

She was interrupted by an elderly man coming to the door of the shop and nodding towards the telephone box. 'What you girls up to? Yer shouldn't be 'anging about with these damned Vengeance rockets being a nuisance. Get on with yer, get on home, or wherever you're headed.'

Verity stood up. 'Well, we were headed to the telephone box but we'll have to find another. Sylvia's boyfriend said left and we should have tried right. Naughty Steve.'

Sylvia flicked a foot Verity's way, missing deliberately. The man said, 'Come in and use mine, then get yourselves on out of 'ere.'

Sylvia dug into her pocket and found a few pence. 'We can pay you, sir.'

'Never mind that, just don't yer bring that dog in 'ere, cos she'll be peeing on me furniture and then 'ow can I shift it?' The old man led the way into the shop, while Polly tied Dog to the lamp post. A knotted rope already hung there, but there were no children left to use it as a swing. Most had been evacuated. 'Sit and be good, like you always are, lovely Dog,' Polly crooned.

Inside the shop they looked around at the chairs and tables piled on top of one another. Had this old boy sold anything at all over the years? Sylvia wondered. He was standing by an old oak counter, tapping it, his fingerless gloves frayed. "Ere you are, give whoever you need to telephone a bell, and put yer money away. 'Tis a long time since anyone's called me sir. Me name's Solly Fisher, just yer remember that, cos yer might need to find yer way back to buy up me stock when one of you 'as a ring on yer finger and a bloke in yer heart.'

While he shuffled behind the counter, chuckling, and lowered himself into an ancient carver chair, Sylvia nodded at the phone. 'You know the number, Polly.'

'Coward,' Polly muttered, snatching up the receiver. She asked the telephonist to put her through, then, her hand over the mouthpiece, said, 'Bob doesn't bite.'

'That's all you know,' Sylvia and Verity muttered in unison.

Solly Fisher said, 'You look as though you've been down where the rocket hit.'

'Do we, Mr Fisher?' Verity asked. 'Please don't say I look like our Sylvia, all smoked like a kipper, and greasy.'

Solly laughed, pointing to the mirror hanging on the back wall of the shop. Polly put down the receiver. 'It's engaged.'

'Ah well,' the old boy said. 'Try again in a moment. I ain't rushed orf me feet, am I? But when you've done, I needs to phone me boy to tell him the rocket didn't get me, in case 'e's heard about it.'

Sylvia dragged Verity over to the mirror. Two greasy blackish faces looked back at them. 'My word, I thought I looked bad, darling,' Verity drawled, 'but not quite as bad as you.'

Sylvia giggled. Verity nudged her. 'Well, if Steve's seen the beauty behind the mask, he's a good man to cultivate.'

Polly muttered, 'He's not a plant, idiot.' She picked up the receiver again and asked for the number. As the telephonist tried to connect her, she looked at Sylvia. 'Or perhaps he is. He's a coppernob, so what could he be, a dahlia?'

Sylvia swallowed her giggles long enough to say, 'Shut up.'

Verity shook her head. 'No, a vegetable. Now, let me—'

Sylvia said, 'That's enough, for heaven's—' She stopped as the breath was sucked from her, the earth tilted and her ears popped. Polly dropped the receiver as Verity reached out to clutch Sylvia's arm. Then there was nothing.

As Steve Bates directed the jet of water at the diminishing fire inside the warehouse, his frozen hands were locked in position around the nozzle. Once, in the Blitz, he had held this position all night, and

45

never once run out of water because they were pumping it from the Thames; neither had he been able to do a pee, there just wasn't a chance. It was the same night after night, but so what? It had to be done. He smiled but his face felt almost too stiff to do so.

He thought of the cat, followed by that dog appearing from nowhere. Just as well they had, too, because the dog had sniffed around when the cat disappeared and started scrabbling at a demolished building as though it had found its life's work. Steve smiled again. 'That redhead would insist on "her",' he said aloud. 'Her', he repeated. Well, his voice was working anyway, sore though his throat was from the smoke. First the cat, then the dog, then the girls, just like that. Then her in particular. Yes, her, Sylvia, and he'd almost been crass, but then something stopped him, mid sentence because she was different, she was ... He shook his head. Don't be bloody daft, man. He rolled her name round his tongue. 'Syl–

Suddenly the world shuddered, sucked, then blew, the blast almost knocking him off balance. The flames in the warehouse died and burst into life again, then the roar reached them.

'Bloody hell.' he yelled, as the hose leapt from his hands and spun, writhing like a demented snake. Gushing water soaked the ground, not to mention Pete, who was clinging to the pump ladder. Pete yelled, 'I don't ruddy well believe it, we've got another one. So much for lightning not striking twice.'

Steve captured the hose, lifting it by the nozzle, but Sammy, the Sub Officer was bawling at him. 'You, Steve, on the first pump engine with Dodge and get over there.' He was pointing to rising smoke and debris about a hundred yards away, or maybe two hundred. Who knew until you got there? 'Take two auxiliaries with you, but you're in charge. Get going. God, how much worse can it damn well get? I'll get the Rescue Squad on to it pretty damn quick, and more of our blokes.'

An Auxiliary Fire Service bloke took Steve's place on the hose, enabling Steve to run as fast as his galoshes allowed. Dodge was on his heels. They leapt into the cab, Steve driving, with the two AFS already clinging to the outside on the foot shelf, poor buggers. The war meant that the service had to bring all the engines possible out of mothballs.

Dodge yelled, 'Sub reckons it's Watney Street. Know it?' Steve nodded, his foot hard down as they roared towards yet another billowing cloud. Thank God those girls hadn't listened to him, and instead had taken the right hand route to the phone box. He rammed through the gears. They had, hadn't they? Well, that's what they said, but he hadn't watched them go. Surely they had.

He didn't realise he had spoken aloud. Dodge yelled above the racing engine, 'Had what?'

Steve swung the wheel and they careered around the corner. Dodge shouted, his voice high, 'Take a right, a right, damn it, then another left.'

'I know, keep your bleedin' hair on.' Steve swung right, clipping the corner. The two AFS managed to hang on. An Air Raid Patrol bloke was running towards the blast, blowing his whistle. He probably didn't know he couldn't be heard, but at least it kept him busy.

One Rescue Squad vehicle was shadowing the pump engine, and Steve kept an eye on them in the mirror. They were bloody close, so he hooted and from his open window waved them back. They understood and slowed, creating a stopping distance between them. Steve half skidded on debris that shifted beneath his wheels as he swung round another bend. The buildings were now showing the blast and some were still tumbling, but where was the point of impact? They found it several streets further on.

'Ruddy, ruddy lightning doesn't know the bleedin' rules,' Dodge ground out. 'The boss's sent out the messenger lasses on their motorbikes, so we'll be getting other engines.'

'Right,' was all Steve said, as he drove slowly now, getting as close as he could to the area of flattened buildings, and then the crater, feeling a seething rage as they approached the damage. Bastard Hitler. Bastard.

They were forced to a stop by rubble blocking the road. The AFS leapt down, taking shovels, and working like Trojans, while Steve and Dodge hurled themselves from the cab, swearing and grunting as they hauled first one lintel away and then another. Then they were off again, careering towards the smoke and cries. There was the crash of a building to their left, but it had imploded and left the road clear. 'The Rescue Squad will deal,' Steve yelled.

'Another bloody building gone,' cursed Dodge, dragging out a cigarette and lighting it, making Steve laugh. How could he light up when there was so much smoke already? And there, ahead, was the epicentre with its smoking crater.

They screeched to a halt, the AFS hauled out the hoses, while Steve and Dodge ran forward assessing the situation. Dodge pinched out his cigarette and threw it to one side. 'Just in case,' he yelled, which was what he always said, daft bugger.

Steve bellowed to get the hoses on the flames which were licking the remains of what looked like a newsagent, judging from the newspapers flying about.

Dodge ground out, 'We'll need the rescue lot out sooner rather than later.'

'They're here, you daft old bugger. They followed us.'

Dodge shook his head as they ran. 'Too damned old and tired for this job.'

Steve grinned, 'You'll do another few years cos Enid won't want you at home. You'd only be sent to the allotment to stare at your cabbages, and all the while you'd be missing me.'

Dodge guffawed. They were rushing towards a terrace where Dodge remembered there were a few shops. '"Were" being the right damned word,' he shouted above the noise of approaching vehicles, for whatever had been was blasted into heaps of fractured bricks and beams. 'So, what's new, man?' one of the AFS men yelled, running up behind them. 'I've got the barrier tape.'

'Good lad,' Steve said. He stared around. 'Get it up here, quick as you can. The rescue boys are checking the houses, and debris?'

'Aye, that they are.' Tommy, who had been in the AFS since the beginning and was as good as any National Fireman, was setting up the tape as Dodge and Steve hurried on. Steve yelled to the other AFS bloke, 'We'll need to find the gas valve on each street, like always. It could be under the ruddy rubble. The pipes could be fractured.'

'Right you are.' The AFS gave directions to the new lot who were heading their way from another engine. Dodge and Steve carried on and could hear the crunch of bricks beneath their feet, the cries from who knew where. The Rescue Squad would help sort that out. Flames were licking from a block of flats. It would be all hands to the pump, again, with the Fire Service helping out the Rescue Squad, and the Rescue Squad helping out the Fire Service. Steve looked over his shoulder. 'The pump's got further in, and they're dousing the shops and flats either side of the newsagent's, putting 'em out, or damping 'em down in case they catch.'

Dodge wasn't listening but pointing. 'Would you look at him, poor lad.' A naked young man sat slumped against a lamp post, dead but seemingly unmarked. It wasn't the first time they'd seen such blast victims and it wouldn't be the last at this rate. A young woman was heading towards the bloke, with a blanket over her arm. Steve trotted across. 'You can't help him now, lass, but let's get you somewhere cosy.'

The young woman had curlers in her hair and a fag hanging from her mouth. She pushed Steve off. 'I know 'e's gone, and I don't know who 'e is, but the least I can do is cover the poor devil's crown jewels. As for cosy, the WVS will be along with their tea canteen any minute. Until then I'm checkin' me neighbours, in what houses there are standing. Me nan's probably still asleep, dreaming that the earth moved – at 'er age, for 'eaven's sake.'

Steve wondered if she was in shock. She took her fag out of her mouth. 'Don't look at me like that, we're bloody used to this, what wiv the Blitz and now this. Can't spend all me life in a shelter and you never know when the bleeders are coming, does yer?' She gestured to the surrounding chaos and the fug of blast, debris and the smoke over which hoses played. 'There was three girls, you know, with a dog on a rope walking along, they was talking to me neighbour while she scrubbed her step. Seems they was 'oping to telephone, but me neighbour didn't know some toe-rag 'ad robbed it and sent them on. Maybe Solly let 'em use 'is shop one. Or they was hit and just gone into dust? Poor cows.'

Steve felt odd. His head ached suddenly, and his mouth was dry. Three girls and a dog? Oh, they didn't deserve that, they bloody well didn't, and it was he who had said go to the left. 'Where's Solly's?'

She pointed to where the shops had been. 'The end one,' she said. Steve looked towards the debris, defeated, then furious, then could have bloody well kicked the bloody crazy world to hell and back. He yelled to Dodge, pointing, 'Come on, those girls and the dog were seen around there.'

Dodge leapt a fallen lamp post and headed back towards him. Steve turned to the woman. 'Get yourself to the WVS van when you've sorted out your nan,' he told her. 'Any problems, the Rescue Squad will be bringing up reinforcements. Don't go into any building yourself, you hear?' But the young woman was already on her way, calling back, 'Teaching your granny to suck eggs, is yer?' Her laugh followed him as he headed for the shambles that had been Solly's.

Dodge caught him up, and they slogged past damaged houses either side, intent on reaching the end of the demolished terrace. They were both sniffing for gas, it's what they always did because gas and flames didn't damn well mix. There was no gas, but the smell of cordite, blood and misery grew stronger and the air became darker from the smoke and spray as the hoses played. Steve heard more engines arrive, but now he could see a dog, the girls' dog. Yes, they had been here. But . . . Dog, yes that was her name, was alive, so perhaps they might be too.

He looked up and down the street for a sign of them, but there was none, except for Dog, who was running around from one blasted building to another with a length of torn-off rope dragging behind her, her tail down, as though demented and confused. Dodge said, 'Flippin' heck, the woman was right, they turned left, like you said.'

Steve repeated Dodge's words. 'Yes, like *I* damned well said.' It *was* his fault.

He headed towards Dog, calling, but she took no notice, and as they hurried he and Dodge checked for fire hazards. They gestured to a couple of AFS vehicles skidding to a stop behind their own pump engine that they should focus on the burning three-storeyed flats off to the left, from which he could hear cries. He cupped his hands. 'Bring your engine as close as possible. And Tommy, once the tape is sorted, you know to let the engines through. I want a two-man rescue team with me.' He saw the Rescue Squad officer in charge spin round. Steve yelled, 'All right with you, is it, Dave? We might have people buried here.'

Dave gave him the nod, and Steve caught up with Dodge and they jogged towards the terrace. All the time he was watching Dog, who suddenly stopped, crouched, and threw back her head and howled. Steve headed towards her. Were they there? But no, Dog was up, heading slowly now towards the end of the terrace, and it was then he saw the trail of blood Dog was following. He ran towards her, and then found that Dog was not following it; it was coming from her, pouring from a deep gash that gaped between her ribs and hips. He called her, but she took no notice. Instead, God bless her, she was clambering up on to the rubble that had been the terrace, working her way along. They must be under there. But where?

Dog reached the end, where the Furniture Emporium had been, or so Dodge said. She sniffed there too before clambering down the other side and into the road. She staggered, her head hanging, her tail down. Steve ran towards her but she turned from him and slowly sniffed her way back to the top and around the peak. She barked, then scrabbled with her front paws until they also bled.

As Dodge and Steve headed the last few paces to the rubble they never took their eyes off her, both of them calling quietly, 'Come girl, come Dog, come on down, let us help. Come on, lass.'

She merely lay down on the rubble, sinking her head on to her front legs, her muzzle stained red

54

from the blood of her paws. Steve felt he could hardly breathe as all around them the banging and crashing continued yet somehow here everything seemed silent. The two men were frozen to stillness as Dog howled, then barked once more before laying her head down, and Steve saw her tail wag. Then nothing.

He stared. She was listening, concentrating, that was all. She was hurt, but no more than that. She was having a break, like they all did. Just a bit of a pause before going on.

He yelled at Dodge, who stood by his side, 'She's having a rest, that's all. She's found them, and she's having a rest. I know that's all it is.' Sweat was running down his face and his eyes were stinging, and as he moved to the foot of the debris he called, 'You're such a good girl, Dog. We'll have you better in no time, and the same with your girls, don't you fret, our lass. Don't you fret.'

Dodge was still beside him, and they saw Dog's tail lift, then fall. Dodge said, 'Don't take on so, my old lad, she's done good work today.'

Steve said, brushing his face with his arm, 'Don't be daft, I'm not taking on. It's the sweat, that's all. She'll be all right, they all will.' He put a foot on the heap of bastard bricks, mortar, beams and God knows what, but Steve dragged him back. 'Let the Rescue Squad advise, lad, you know that. If they're under there, we'll get 'em out, but safely.'

Chapter 4

Beneath the rubble

Polly tried to open her eyes, but her lids were too heavy. She was so tired. No, they should be up, and at the tiller, feeling the boat pat-pattering on the water. They'd be late with the delivery. What was it – aluminium again?

She was on the narrow side-bed but she needed to turn over because the mattress was lumpy. She was half sitting – but why? She wanted to move, but there was a lump hurting her hip. She tried to open her eyes again, but gave up, too tired, just too tired, and her ears hurt. Bells were buzzing, but bells didn't buzz. And what bells? It was war and the bells didn't ring. Her mouth was so dry that her lips were stuck together. How silly. She jolted suddenly, as there was a loud crack from somewhere, then she rested. It was probably ice along the hull. They'd have to hack their way out. She should get up.

She tried to cough, but the skin on her lips tore away and she tasted blood, warm it was, because she was so cold. Her throat grated and her chest hurt. Was Dog lying on her again? Something heavy

57

was. Dog was getting fat. She smiled. Dear old Dog. She'd write that to Saul, but not say that she wished he was still on the Mulberry harbour instead of driving a lorry. Or that she wished he was here, with her on the cut, chugging along behind them on *Seagull* with Granfer on *Swansong* and how the hell had he learned to drive a lorry? Did the powers that be think because you could drive a boat, you could drive a lorry? Saul, my love, I miss you, every minute of every day, but I have this funny buzzing in my head and I can't move. I must be so tired, but I can't remember why, but I can remember you.

She tried to lift an arm to stroke Dog. Her beloved friend was too heavy, and pressing too hard on her chest, on all her body really, but she couldn't move her arm. Perhaps she was asleep and all this was a dream? Yes, that's what it was. She was asleep. Dreams were strange. Did Saul dream when he rested from his driving?

Was it Potty Thompson in the Ministry of War Transport, the one who had recruited the girls, who had come up with the daft idea that narrowboat 'steerers' could drive lorries? Why couldn't lovely Saul stay safe on the Mulberry harbour at, what was it? Shiny Beach, no, no. Gold Beach. But no, he had to take supplies to the men who were chasing the Germans, he had written, because he could write now. Her boatman could write.

She tried to move again, but everything hurt, and her eyelids seemed stuck together. Everything in her dream was stuck, and hurt, and heavy and now she must sleep again.

Verity wondered why her arm was wet, with a wetness that was running to her hand. Had they left the roof slide open a bit above the double doors into the cabin? She tried to move it. It hurt too much. She tried to open her mouth to call Polly. Then forgot who she was going to call. Her head was full of little bits that leapt and then fell. She opened her eyes, or thought she had but it was dark and no fire or ashes glowed in the firebox beneath the range. She tried to open her eyes wider, but it was still black as pitch. There were cracking noises, and creaking so the wind must be whooshing down the cut, but how strange that the boat was still.

Was it still like this where Tom was? Well, it would be if he was on land, and of course he was on land because he had gone ashore on D-Day. Perhaps he was crouching with his rifle in a ditch or charging across a field after the Germans, because at last the enemy were on the run. Soon they would be in Germany, and they'd better stay there and then it would be over. All of it, and Britain would be free of it. The world would be free . . . but now the words were falling about in her head. She listened for the creak but her head was buzzing, and she didn't know what she'd just been thinking, and she couldn't hear anything but the buzzing so she searched for a crack in her mind and dragged Tom through it,

'Tom', her lips had moved, but were clagged with lipstick, thick thick lipstick that was warm in her mouth, and gritty.

She made them work again. 'Tom.' She heard it cutting through the buzz in her head and she could see him, but he wasn't in Germany. He was wearing a cap, why? Oh, yes, he'd been their chauffeur, her mother, not her real mother, but someone who was better than that and who had adopted her and loved her all her life, hadn't liked him. She did now though, and wanted them to marry, wanted him to come home, but where was he? She couldn't remember. She thought she just had, but it had gone because something was lying on her, taking her thoughts away. Oh, Dog, yes Dog, but there was something else, and it was all so sharp and heavy. She hurt, and her head did too. It was the rain coming in through the hatch and running along her arm. She really should shut the hatch, but she was too tired.

She mustn't be tired, they had a load to deliver, but she couldn't remember what. 'Tom, do you know?' she asked, but it wouldn't come through the grit in her throat, and the grit in her lipstick. What grit? Why grit? Why did her lipstick hurt? She slept. Then woke, thoughts playing through the buzzing, and the weight, and the grit. Tom had written and told her that he had thought of the three of them as he struggled up the beach on D-Day, remembering how the waterway girls just kept on, keeping on. He said it had helped him endure.

Yes, she must get up. She couldn't. Dog, move, she thought. Dog didn't. So she must be asleep. Everyone was asleep so all this was a dream. But Dog had barked, earlier. Yes, and howled, she had. Just one bark or was it two? It was so far away, and yes, Verity had been frightened. So frightened because . . . She couldn't remember. It was all just a dream. Darling Dog. Should they let the firemen have her, or was it the rescue lot who needed her? It would be kind, but she was their beloved, she made a foursome. They hadn't decided, she was sure. She must call out to Polly on her side-bed, just to check on that.

She opened her mouth, but she was so dry. It still seemed so dusty and as she turned her head, something hurt her cheek and then there was nothing, again.

Sylvia called, or thought she did, but she couldn't hear the sound. 'Polly, Verity, Dog.' There was no answer. They were probably asleep. When she first joined the waterway scheme she thought it was so unhygienic to have a dog in *Marigold*'s tiny cabin, just nine feet by seven, and she, Sylvia Simpson, wouldn't have had one on *Horizon*. That was all so long ago. Then she had been alone, the new girl, and now they were all for one, and . . . She couldn't remember the rest. Her ears hurt, and sort of buzzed. Her eyes were sore beneath their lids and she wanted to turn over in her cross-bed. There was room to

61

turn on this big bed, but not on the side-bed. Polly slept on the side-bed in *Marigold*'s cabin. Perhaps she should offer to swap.

Swap what? She couldn't quite breathe. In and out she had to go. She tried. Of course, yes, in and out. That was better. Oh yes, she remembered now, the side-bed. In and out, but the air was so thick. Was it foggy outside, and creeping into the cabin? It seemed to cover her. They should be working, but perhaps it was still night. She listened for owls but there was another noise . . . a saw? Was that what was buzzing? It hurt her ears.

She should talk to someone in her head, she knew she should, but who, she couldn't . . . She slept. She woke and thought she heard Tom, inside her head, leaving the buzzing outside. He was a good boy. He'd had to stay on the butty or motor with her because of his broken leg while the girls wound the locks, and he steered as she'd talked. She had found herself telling him all about her problem with her Lord. She felt looser once she'd shared it but couldn't understand why she'd told him. He'd said it was like talking to a stranger on a train. That you tended not to talk to a friend, they knew you too well, but she had talked to her friends in the end. There should be a song. *I know you so well*, she thought. Someone else knew her inside and out. Who? She couldn't remember. Was it the Lord she was thinking of?

She did hope he was all right. Who was all right? She couldn't remember. Was it Tom? Ah yes, Tom.

And Saul too. Saul who was away from his Polly, and his beloved canal, his granfer, and Joe his nephew, Maudie's son. Joe was with Mr and Mrs Holmes who were evacuated to Dorset and staying with Lord and Lady Clement. Why? Oh that's right, because his mother had been hurt by his father, the dreadful cruel Leon, and had to get better. But he had hurt Joe too before Saul rescued the boy.

She lingered on Joe, dear little Joe, whose darkness had lifted now. They sent one another pictures, but his were better than hers. She tried to draw otters, and birds. Her kingfisher had been her best, but Joe's was better, and he drew the sheep, and the cows, and his pony, but she couldn't think of the pony's name. What was it? What was what? She couldn't remember. It didn't matter because lovely Joe wrote her notes at the bottom of his pictures, and she replied at the bottom of hers. He was precious, a dear precious boy who she loved, who must be kept hidden and safe from Leon. Yes, yes, all the thoughts were running so fast, chasing one another in and out of her ear. Why her ear? Oh, yes, they wanted to play with the buzzing.

She tried to open her eyes. When you were asleep things felt heavy, but why did they hurt this time? Granfer would know but he was at Buckby by Braunston Tunnel. Why was he there? She couldn't . . . Ah yes, it's where the old boaters lived. He was with Lettie. Lovely lettuce, no, no, Lettie. His sister. Everyone had someone, except her. God should be enough, but ... Ah, that's right, God. She slept because she didn't know if He was enough, because she was so lonely, and she hurt. She couldn't open her eyes, but it was only because she was dreaming.

Her mouth was so very dry and her throat seemed full of grit, but ... They should be casting off, not lying about in bed. Did they even have a load? She couldn't remember, and why was it so dark and so still? Why was she so tired, and her ears ringing? And why did she still hurt all over?

She heard Polly then. 'Where are we? What's happened?' And Sylvia jerked awake. What? What?

A man's voice quavered, 'It's dark, and I'm cold.'

A man? Here on the butty? Verity spoke now, her voice sounding faint beneath the ringing. 'What's happening? What the *hell* is happening?'

Sylvia forced her eyelids open, then shut them quickly because she was covered in dust, and now there was grit in her eyes. More was falling on her face and something hard was digging into the top of her head.

The man said, 'We're in the bleedin' cellar wiv the whole of the ruddy house on top of us, and I was supposed to telephone my boy to tell him the rocket ain't got me. Then we had another one, that's why we's 'ere.' He coughed, then groaned, 'Me chest don't 'alf hurt, and me leg.'

Polly spoke now, but there was darkness. Sylvia's eyes were sore, but she couldn't rub them because there was something on top of her, a blanket, with corners, heavy, and her arms weren't joined to her. Don't be stupid. Arms were always joined to you. Polly had spoken but what had she said? And Sylvia needed arms, because arms had hands and the three of them could hold one another's hands and feel better. But should they hold the man's hand too? She didn't know.

She heard Verity through the buzzing. 'I thought I was on the boat. I don't remember, but we tied Dog up, yes, I remember that, and we were using your phone, Mr . . . Mr . . . ?'

The man said, 'Solly Fisher.'

Verity said, 'But lightning doesn't strike . . .' she paused, wheezed, 'the same place twice.'

Polly's voice grew even weaker as she said, 'Patently it does, idiot.' Then she groaned, and they heard her cry, 'Mum.'

Sylvia listened. What did it all mean? She heard again, 'Mum.' And a sob. She experienced fear like nothing she'd ever known, because Polly was the strongest of them and now she was weeping.

The man said, 'Don't take on so, lass. I 'eard yer dog bark, I'm sure I did, but then I drifted orf, and I 'eard voices, men's voices, they was. They get the rescue lot 'ere pretty quick, and them was just down the road, wasn't they?'

Sylvia gasped, her voice croaky and clogged, 'Dog, oh Dog, I thought she was here, on me. Oh Dog.' Then her head began to clear and she began to remember. Her thoughts played around behind the buzzing and she knew they were beneath bricks, and Dog had done what she had done before, found those who were trapped. This time they were people who loved her. They were like a family, the four of them. Yes, that's right. She was tired, and closed her eyes, but then dust showered down on her. She jerked awake.

She listened, and tasted the dust, and felt the sharp weight, and said as she tried to move, 'I'm not on the boat, am I, we're buried, aren't we?'

There was creaking all around. Mr Fisher murmured, 'Best you stay still, lass. 'Tis 'ard, I knows, but as I said, I reckon we're in the cellar with a weight of stuff over us, most of it being held off by the shop floor joists, which 'ave broken but hitched themselves on summat. I got me arm loose from under a pile of rubble and stretched, couldn't reach anything so's I reckon they're more'n a few feet above us, but it's too dark to see anything. Thought I were dreamin' first off. Stay still, for Gawd's sake, don't rock the boat.'

Polly laughed then stopped abruptly, groaning, as Verity's hoarse whisper reached them. 'If only you knew how funny that is, Mr Fisher,' she said. 'We work on the canal at the moment, running the narrowboats up to Birmingham, and if I ever get out of this I'll rock the blasted boat as much as I like.'

Mr Fisher cackled. 'Nah, we're the blasted ones.' Then he too groaned, from deep in his soul Sylvia felt. It was then that she remembered what it was she should be doing – praying – but the words kept slipping away, and in the end she just said inside her head, 'If you're listening, thank you for letting us live, and Dog, and please stop me from hurting.'

Her breathing was strange, it was in and out, but not really proper breathing. Then she realised she had only asked for her own pain to stop, and wept silently inside her head, and still inside her head she said, 'Please stop everyone's pain, not just mine, everyone's.'

Verity said, sounding stronger for a moment, 'I hope he's listening, Sylvia. And I hope your fireman comes to rescue you, in shining armour, or . . .' She paused, then murmured, 'At least a tin hat. Was he a vegetable or a flower, Pol?'

So, she'd spoken and they'd heard, Sylvia thought. Good. Nothing mattered if they were together. All for one and . . . ah, one for all. That was it.

She tried to swallow but her throat was too dry and too clogged, so she made herself say, 'This is only a pause. It will pass.'

Polly said slowly, 'You're right, it's what we say, isn't it, and it had better do that sooner rather than later.' Her voice faded. Then it was as though she rallied. 'Coppernob's a dahlia, a deep red dahlia, isn't he Mr Fisher?'

Mr Fisher grunted, then said, 'You girls speak yer own language, but I'll say yes, to keep yer 'appy.'

*

Outside, one of the Rescue Squad had inched up the debris, noting the beams which emerged from the destruction. He spoke quietly, but wasn't heard against the hoses and the shouting.

Steve cupped his hands and yelled, 'Say again.'

This time the bloke shouted down to Steve and Dodge, 'There looks to be a lot of structural material in amongst the tiles, bricks and glass, and with luck the girls and Mr Fisher will've fallen through to the cellar, with the joists giving 'em a chance. The dog was digging, yer say? Well, she were right at the other site, so let's try and make contact.' He called to one of his mates who was poking around at the side of the rubble, 'The coal hole's blocked, ain't it?'

Another of the squad called back. 'Yep, no way in there, Stan.'

Stan seemed to be thinking. He nodded. 'It'll have to be through this lot, if we're going in after 'em. Hang on, I'll toss this down, so we can burrow in and try to make contact.'

He made to grab Dog and chuck her down, but Steve shouted, 'Don't you bloody dare throw that lass anywhere, Stan. You bring her down with respect, d'you hear.'

Stan just looked from Dog to Steve and nodded. 'I reckon you're right. That's what 'appens in this game, you just forget about decency. But she's the one good thing this bloody day has thrown up.' He lowered his voice. 'You know she's a goner?'

Steve nodded, 'Of course I bloody know, just bring her down.'

As Stan gathered Dog to him, her head flopped on to his shoulder, her clouded eyes looking up at him. He looked away, unable to bear yet another body, and murmured, 'You've done well, gal. You've done so well.' He inched down, and passed Dog to Steve, who carried her carefully, stepping over hoses and across puddles until he reached the pump engine. At the cab he wrapped her in a bit of tarpaulin and laid her on the passenger seat. 'You done good, Dog, and now we're going to get the other girls out, I promise you that.'

Back at the debris Stan had clambered carefully back to the top, easing bricks out and throwing them down, letting them shatter, while Dodge went to grab a hose and damp down a smoking pile near to the ambulance point. Steve yelled, as he hurried back to the demolished shops, 'There's one over to your left, Dodge, just looking as though it's smouldering. Keep an eye on it, eh?'

Stan called down to him when he arrived at the base of the rubble. 'I tried calling. One of those girls called back, they're all right, but weak from the sounds of it, and hurt. One asked if Coppernob was there? You I 'spect, Steve. Seems Mr Fisher's there with them, chap who owns the second-'and furniture shop. His son works at a firm in the City of London and he wants us to tell 'im, so we'll sort it as soon as we can. The girl says not to tell anyone about them, just get them the hell out of it, they have a load to pick up. Sounds a bit lardy-da, she does. What load she's talking about, gawd knows. A new frock with her coupons I 'spect.'

Stan continued to remove the bricks. 'We'll work from the top, creating a chain, so come up carefully behind me, Steve, if you're not needed on the pump. The rest of the squad are busy back at the first site.'

He yelled across to another of the Rescue Squad who was dusting off his hands after hauling out a body from beneath the shattered public phone box. 'Alfred, you get the other side, and get someone else too, then take down from the top to relieve the pressure. You all right to stay with us, Steve? We needs yer til the squad from Poplar gets 'ere.'

Steve checked around, but there were two AFS crews now, and another National Fire Service sub-officer was there too. Others were helping along the length of the terrace. He cupped his hands and yelled across, 'Sub, I'm needed here. All right with you?'

He received a nod, and the sub went back to directing his men as they fought fires in the flats.

Stan called, 'Brick by brick, Steve, with me, here, and let's get a tunnel started. Stop the moment you feel anything shift. The girl said the old boy thinks the shop floor joists have jammed a lot of the bricks just a couple of feet or so above them, but they're lying on some, and under some. Cor, a bit of luck, if you ask me. Now we have a chance – for one or two of 'em at least.' This last he said quietly.

Steve was clambering up, step by careful step, muttering, 'We just need the bloody rockets to keep their distance and the night to hold off.' It was only two in the afternoon, so they had a good chance of a daylight rescue, but with the heavy cloud and the smoke, daylight was a bit of a ruddy joke. But never mind that, they'd have to work like demons, because Dog wasn't going to be let down, if he had anything to do with it.

Chapter 5

Brick by brick as the day wears on

She really should say a prayer, Sylvia thought, waking again, but the words in her head were jumping and crumbling. 'You know what I mean, though, as Sister Augustine says you are all knowing. Please . . .' she finally whispered. 'Please . . . help.' Dust and grit were streaming down, and there were sounds like scratching. And creaking.

Solly said, 'I 'spect they's started digging us out, but careful like. I seen 'em do it so often, cos there've been so many bloody bombs, or rockets. I reckon me joists is strong enough, better'n me joints any'ow.'

Sylvia tried to laugh, but all she produced was a croak. The others did the same. She swallowed; her throat was so dry and gritty it just seemed stuck together, but the buzzing was fainter. She tried to speak, but she didn't know what was in her head, and what was escaping, so gave up. Verity was right, they had to get back to work. She had said that, but when? How long had they been here? She kept falling asleep: how strange. What would Bet say, and the depot? Probably that there was a war to win, and here they were, lying in bed. But no, they weren't, they were under the rubble and it was getting harder to breathe.

'Are you all right, Mr Fisher?' she asked finally, forcing out the words though they scoured her throat. 'Are you all right, Verity? And you, Polly?' There was no answer. Had the words come out of her mouth? They had hurt her throat, so they must have. But still no one had answered. She was too tired to try again. She tried to think about *Horizon*, her home. Her lovely home, the lovely cut, the sore hands, and the callouses that were their battle scars, they had decided, laughing. Oh, how they laughed, all the time. And Bet did too.

Her thoughts stopped. Bet? Her boats, so broken. She, Polly and Verity should have . . . ? What was it? She said, forcing the words from her mind and out through her mouth into the rubble again, 'What should we have done for Bet? What? I can't remember.'

Polly almost moaned, 'I can't either. What was it?'

Verity drawled, 'Darlings, we should have phoned the depot. Damn and . . .' She faded.

Solly spoke now. 'No blast, eh?' His words ended in a cough and Sylvia could hear his gasps for breath.

Silence had fallen again, then Verity said, 'There are mice pithering about or are the rescuers moving bricks? Perhaps we won't die today.'

Sylvia let the words tumble. They all listened to the quiet nothingness, then something, then the nothingness and perhaps they slept but then there was the coppernob's voice, calling: 'We're getting closer, girls. Just stay quite still.'

Solly muttered, 'Maybe yer posh girl's right, we're not going to die today, and me son's not going to have to say Kaddish for me.'

Verity hurt everywhere. She had to be right, they mustn't die today, they had a load to deliver. She tried to shout, but it was a whisper: 'We have a load, so we mustn't die.'

She wondered if she'd been rude to try to shout. These nice people were trying to get them out but did the rescuers realise they needed to get into Limehouse and out, on to the quiet of the Grand Union, with the spires and towers in the distance? Yes, those lovely spires, and the familiar locks, full of water, locks that she could drink dry; she was so very thirsty. Yes, a whole lock full of water.

Suddenly she heard a sort of laugh. It came from her because she hated opening and shutting the gates, filling or emptying them using her windlass to wind the paddles, or sluices as some people called them. But there they were, pat-pattering along in *Marigold* with Sylvia in the butty and Dog asleep by the stove. Heaven. Bliss, and it was there that she could breathe air into a chest that didn't hurt.

On the cut they were home and it wasn't just locks, there were the pounds: the long straight stretches, or even the short ones, which ran between hamlets, towns, the spires and the towers. Such lovely spires, so English, so much their home. And smoke from the village chimneys perhaps fed by coal they transported. She smiled. And what about the Aylesbury Arm? Now that was a piece of heaven. Maudie, Joe's mum, and Saul's sister, loved the Arm with its wild flowers and otters. She coughed, and forgot what she had been thinking. It was so hard to hold thoughts.

She tried to open her eyes, but they were stuck. What had she been thinking? Oh yes, the cut. There were fields which changed with the seasons. There were kingfishers that Joe had tried to teach Sylvia to draw. Oh dear, how bad the drawing had been. There were owls that called in the dusk, and bats that flew, and foxes that shrieked. And the pubs, don't forget the pubs where they usually won at darts. Sylvia wouldn't play darts when she first joined *Marigold* and *Horizon*. Lordy, she seemed such a sourpuss and crosspatch, but now she'd drink with the rest of them, and laugh. How wonderful to hear Sylvia laugh, but her battle wasn't over, they all knew that. To be a nun, or not. Gosh, what a problem. How on earth did God call anyone? In a dream, Sylvia had said, but she couldn't remember the dream, just what her friend Harriet had said she'd called out in her sleep.

She kept breathing, counting her breaths, pondering a call made in a dream Sylvia couldn't remember. How could she be so sure then? But she wasn't, that was the problem, and that was why she was here, wasn't it? Well, not here, here, below the bricks as they were now, but on the cut. To get experience of life, as Sister Augustine had said. She was all right, was that Sister, but that Harriet ... had she really heard dearest Sylvia call out? She didn't think so. The thoughts faded again, dipping in and out to the cry of the night-time owls, and the lapping of the water against the hull ...

She opened her eyes in a flurry, snap, just like that. All that she could see was darkness, all she could feel was dust in her eyes. She shut them again. Yet the snap was still in her mind, but why? Ah, 'The winnings kitty,' she gasped. 'It's in the cabin. What if it's taken and and, what if *Marigold* is taken?'

Polly's voice sounded over to her left, and then Sylvia's to her right, not far away. She hadn't realised they were so close. Polly croaked, 'Don't be such an idiot. Who'd run off with a boat?'

Sylvia just said, 'They wouldn't run off with a boat, they'd motor off in it, idiot, and don't be so selfish, it's not just *Marigold*. What about *Horizon*? They'd take her, too. Then Bob would have a lot to say, you mark my words.'

Suddenly the three of them were trying to laugh again, and Solly chipped in. 'Don't know what yer's talking about, but seems to me no one'll be running orf with a bleedin' boat, and won't yer dog stand guard?'

Verity let his words jumble and toss in her mind. The tiredness was dragging at her. She tried to clench her fists, so she could concentrate, but her left hand was slimy and gritty. She had to sleep, but she wanted a drink of water so much; cool cool water, and it was cold here. And getting colder. She tried to call, 'Tom'. But nothing came out, and she couldn't remember him, couldn't see him.

Polly tried to ease her hip. Solly groaned. 'Stay still, gal. I'm at yer side, it's just a piece of brick. I can just feel it wiv me left hand.'

She muttered, 'It might be a piece of brick to you, young man, but it's a ruddy boulder to me.'

He laughed, but said, almost in a whisper, 'It's cutting into me hand, yer see, that's 'ow I knows what it is.' Polly listened for the others to tell her she was an idiot, and to sympathise with Solly, but there was nothing. She shouted, 'Wake up, we shouldn't sleep. Wake up.'

A man's voice called faintly from above, 'Good girl, you tell 'em. Try and stay awake, keep breathing, talk a bit, we're coming for you. We won't give up, so don't you either.'

Polly's eyes began to sting. 'Don't cry,' she told herself. 'You can't afford to lose the moisture.'

She tried to swallow but couldn't. She whispered, 'We're so thirsty. So very thirsty. We could drink the cut dry.'

Solly yelled then, 'She says she could drink the cut dry, whatever the 'ell that means, but I could do with a slurp an' all.'

Polly heard a voice call back. 'Don't matter what it means, Mr Fisher, just as long as you're all still with us. Someone's telling your son. We're tunnelling through the rubble and sending someone in soon as we can with water, and then getting you all out. Or that's what we hope. Depends how it pans out, but if it doesn't, we'll try another way. You do your bit by staying – well, staying alive.'

Polly had stopped listening, because she was travelling along the cut, leaning over and drinking the cool water, drinking and drinking. Silence had fallen. She tried to call, and finally whispered, 'Is everyone all right?' Stupid, she thought. Of course they weren't all right, but she needed to sleep, that's all. Suddenly she wasn't even thirsty any more and for a moment thought she could hear the lapping of the water and the rocking of the boat and hear the pat-patter of the engine. Perhaps she was dying, but it didn't matter. Nothing did, and she could no longer see Saul's face.

Bet waited for one more minute on *Hillview*, ignoring the biting wind and looking at the smoke rising from the second blast. The two spirals had met, and mushroomed, and now the wind was sweeping them way beyond the cut. Where were the girls? Had they phoned? She should have left but had somehow not been able to, and then the second rocket landed, but of course it wouldn't hit them, not her girls. One set of boats was enough, one team almost wiped out was damned well enough.

But they weren't back. Why? She jumped on to the bank. 'That's it, I can't hang about here a minute longer.'

Mabel stared at her from the counter. 'Thank heavens for that. We could be hit any minute. But why are you releasing the mooring strap? It's usually my job.'

Bet stood there, hands on her hips. She should have limped back to the depot long ago when she turned the motor to head west again. But no. If she knew those girls, and she damned well did, if everything was all right they'd have scuttled back to the boats by now, full of their adventures, with Dog bounding ahead as though she'd had adventures too. She should take Evelyn and Mabel out of the danger zone, but she couldn't leave her four girls. Why oh why had she asked them to find a phone? How dare two rockets come down so damn close.

She looked at her crew. 'Get under that bridge,' she said, and pointed fifty yards further on. 'Get under there, it's as good as an air raid shelter. I won't be long, I promise, then we'll get out of here.'

Evelyn came out on to the counter. 'It's the after-noon, Bet. If we don't go now we'll be struggling along in the dark long before we reach the depot, and it's terribly frightening here. There might be more rockets, and it's so cold now that it'll be perishing. Just look at the tarpaulin over the cabin, it's going to break free in this wind, and we'll freeze.'

Bet swung round, shouting, 'Just leave the ruddy boat and get under the bridge and think of the girls. What if they were caught up with the V2? What then? I asked them to find a telephone box, after all. We'll just moor up when it gets dark as usual, what's so difficult with that concept, for God's sake?' To her own horror, and the girls', Bet's voice broke, and she ran desperately towards the smoke.

Bet slogged through the streets where front doors were firmly closed. Through some windows the occasional dim light showed on this murky smoke-drenched afternoon, now 'dimout' was in force. It was a London without children, but a bit of light, and it was this she concentrated on. The breath was jogging in her chest but at least she was free of infection, which was such an arse. Yes, that was more like her, not that snivelling idiot who had just put on such a ridiculous performance.

She followed the noise of shouts, engines, vehicle doors slamming and found the first crater. She shouted to a fireman sluicing down the road with his hose, 'Have you seen three girls and a dog?'

He gestured and shouted, 'Follow the smoke.' He sounded so exhausted she thought he was actually asleep on his feet, and there was probably another emergency on the way and he'd be called to somewhere else, poor bugger.

Bet ran on, and on, drawn by the rising smoke and the sounds of rescue work, passing newly damaged houses, but also others that were untouched. It was so arbitrary, this damned V2 and its blast. At last she reached a tape encircling a scene of bustling ambulance men, rescue workers and firefighters. A solitary policeman was patrolling the tape but Bet merely lifted it and strode towards the centre as though she owned the place. All the while she was searching for Dog; for where Dog was, the girls would be.

'Get back, lassie!' the police constable yelled. 'What the hell are you doing this side of the tape?'

He must have run after her and was now barring her way. Bet was staring past him at the huge piles of rubble on which rescue and firemen were working. 'Was there a phone box where any of this rubble is?'

She was gripping his arm. The police constable pointed. 'Aye, over there.'

Bet felt her heart almost stop. Her arm fell, and her legs gave way. The policeman reached out and held her up. 'Steady as you go.'

'Who's beneath the rubble?' Bet managed to mutter.

'A couple or so lassies, and an old boy, Solly Fisher or something like that. He had the second-hand furniture shop, which they were in cos the phone box had been robbed by scunners. They were talking to the fire crew back where the first one hit, the lassies were, just an hour or so ago.'

The policeman was old, his face smudged with sooty smoke. He followed her line of sight. 'We've got most of 'em out of the flats, now it's just the lasses and the old 'un, but it's a bad 'un, and they've gone awful quiet, so we hear.'

Bet drew herself up. 'But they're alive, as far as you know?'

'Couldn't swear to that. Gone quiet, they have as I just said, you see.'

'Of course I damned well see, but it means nothing, you hear. Nothing.' Around them the men worked on, shoring up fronts, clearing a route through, continuing to hose the road clear of the remnants of debris, or something far worse. A couple of ambulances waited near the rubble, for her girls.

The policeman saw her looking, and his voice was gentle. 'The ambulances'll stay unless there's another emergency in the area.'

She nodded. 'I am going over there, and I will give my girls an order, do you understand. I was their trainer, and we can't afford to lose a canal boat team.'

This time it was she holding *his* arms. He nodded. 'I'll come with you. Under the rubble, it's hard to stay hopeful, even if . . .' He trailed off. Then he looked into her face and shoved his shoulders back. 'Aye lass, it can't do any harm.'

Together they walked, and he said, 'Wipe your face, it's so cold your tears will create chaps.'

Bet's laugh was shaky. 'We can't have chaps created. Heavens, whatever next.' She accepted his handkerchief, wiped her cheeks. 'I won't blow my nose, you'll be pleased to hear.'

He grinned. 'It's the missus who'll be pleased.' He shoved his handkerchief, smeared with soot, back in his pocket, and together they stopped at the foot of the rubble, some of which had been Mr Fisher's shop. The policeman called out to the workers, 'Can we have a bit of hush for a moment? Got the lassies' boss here, to give a word of encouragement. All right with you, Stan?'

Stan nodded, his face dragged down with exhaustion. 'Give it a rest, lads. Let's get off on to the ground, and take a few minutes' break for any necessaries, and then top yer bladders up again with a drink of water. Mrs Walters from over the way said we can use her lav.' They eased back down to the ground, and a couple made their way to the house.

Bet stood, trying to sort out her words, but the background noise was chaotic. She couldn't think, so just tried to relax. Almost immediately she knew what she must do, and her furious dictatorial yell rose above all else.

'I'm not having you messing about down there, you girls. Get yourselves back on duty, we need you, the country needs you. We've aluminium or wood to be collected and delivered and darts matches to be won. We can't have Timmo and his team taking over the ruddy lead. So, chop chop, do you hear me.'

Stan, standing by the ambulances with Steve, looked shocked as her words roared across the site, and the policeman stepped back as though he was about to be hit. Bet nodded at him. 'They're my girls, I trained them for the canal work, they'll understand an order. I want nothing more than to stay and see them safe, but I have a duty to my new trainees and need to get them away from this hellhole.' By shouting Bet had jolted herself into her responsibilities; now she felt ashamed. 'And these girls,' she pointed to the rubble, 'have boats which are still serviceable, while mine are damaged. Now, where's Dog? I'll keep her on my boat till the girls are up and running.'

The policeman shrugged and called out to Stan, 'Reckon she's going to start giving orders to the dog too. He'd better be sitting when he's told, or she'll be yellin' at him. She's going to take it on to her boat, so she says. Better be quick about an answer or it'll be your turn for a bollocking.'

Bet snapped. 'Dog's not an it, or a he, Dog is a she.'

Steve Bates, standing next to Stan, looked up, shouting across, 'You're quite right, Dog is a she, your coppernob told me that.'

Looking from Bet to Steve, who was taking another sip from a flask, Stan muttered something, patting Steve's back. Steve nodded, and shook out the last drops as he crunched over the debris to Bet's side. 'I'll take you to Dog,' he almost whispered, his face sad.

Together they walked to the cab of the pump engine, and Bet heaved herself up into the doorway. She stared down at the tarpaulin. It took her a moment to realise, and the shock was like a blow. She wouldn't cry, of course she wouldn't. Good God, she'd blubbed more today than she had for years.

Steve said as he looked up at her from the road, 'She's been a great dog, sniffing at the rubble, finding people since the first rocket came down, but copped it herself when this bugger hit – but not before she'd found her girls. They were hers too, you know, not just yours. There's one with hair like mine, a coppernob too—' He kicked at a piece of brick as Bet looked down at him.

He stood straight, staring at her, full in the face. 'You can have Dog, but only if you treat her well. You've got to find a nice place to bury her, where they can visit, because we *will* get 'em out. If we possibly can.'

Bet eased herself down, removed her top sweater, and stepped up to the cab door again. Carefully she wrapped Dog in the sweater, crooning, 'A nice comfortable blanket for you, our lovely Dog.'

Steve helped her down and tucked up one of the sleeves around Dog, stroking her head. She was so cold. Bet ground out, 'It will be possible to save them because you will make it so, do you understand?' Steve smiled, and stroked Dog one more time, his grimy hand trembling.

Bet said much more quietly, leaning towards him, wanting him to really understand how grateful she was, and how important the girls were, 'Thank you, for all you've done and will continue to do. I don't *know*, but can guess how dangerous it is for you. Those three girls mean the world to me, and to many others. And this girl does too, so I thank you for keeping her warm, and safe for us.'

'But she's not . . .' Steve's voice trailed away as Bet looked down at Dog. Bet said, 'She has been wrapped up by you, so that will have warmed her soul. I will lay her down in our orchard in Buckby, which she loves, but we will not tell the girls, will we, not yet.' It was not a question, but another order. 'You will save them, they will be taken to hospital, and as far as they know, Dog will be with Fran at Buckby. It is not a lie, but we can't have them more hurt than they are already. No broken hearts on my watch, do you hear, no weight of grief too hard to carry, a weight that could take hope away and stop survival, and subsequent recovery. Remember the name, Fran, at Buckby. Now I must go.'

With that she walked away, and Dog was no weight to carry. Darling Dog. Then she stopped, and returned, standing at the foot of the rubble. She lifted her head again and raised her voice. 'Chop, chop, girls, there's work to be done. No lazing about taking a break when others are hard at work.'

She said to Steve, 'Tell 'em they're to get fit to run the boats without delay. Tell them to phone the depot when they reach the hospital, or perhaps you could phone for them to tell me the state of play. If I hear nothing, I will know . . .' She shrugged. 'I can't wait, I have to take my other girls to safety, and then get on with the job. There's a war on. You do understand?'

For a moment she thought she sounded as though she was pleading. Steve nodded, but didn't dare pat her arm. She might bite off his hand – or cry, and that would be worse from such as her. 'Of course, it's like us, we have to get the job done, in spite of . . . I'll make sure the depot knows, though what depot I haven't a clue. But the girls'll tell me. Or not. And if not, you'll understand what's happened.'

They stared into one another's eyes. Bet nodded. 'You're a good boy, and our coppernob is a good girl. She's lonely, though she doesn't know it, or I don't think she does. You and she would do very well together, and I say this because you mention that you noticed her.'

She spun on her heel and walked off, with Steve looking after her, aware he'd been given another order, but one of which he approved.

Sylvia had jerked awake at the sound of Bet's voice. 'Bet, Bet,' she tried to shout, but she couldn't speak for a moment. She tried again and heard movement from the other two; they also called, but the combined sound was little more than a whisper. Sylvia muttered, feeling some strength flowing through her at last, splitting her lips as she found she was smiling, 'She gets everywhere like a ruddy rash.'

Polly's laugh was stronger now as she croaked, 'Miss Sylvia Simpson, you so seldom swear. I will tell on you, and Bet will put you in the corner.'

Verity's voice was a bit stronger as she called, 'We need to get out of this hellhole first. I apologise, Solly, it was probably a lovely cellar, with a perfectly lovely coal hole, but there comes a time in the affairs of boaters . . .'

Sylvia and Polly croaked, 'Oh, do shut up.'

Polly continued, as Sylvia coughed and tried to draw breath. 'Let's all shout, so she can hear us, or someone can, just so they know we want to get out.'

Solly growled, 'I reckon they knows that, gal.'

Nonetheless, all four yelled, 'Hello, hello, we're still in here.'

There was no answer, but then they sensed movement above, and heard the scrabbling of feet. 'Oh, so Iron Drawers got your attention, did she? Woke you up, brought you back into the land of the living. Sitting to attention, are you? She's gone, got to take her girls and boats on, she says. Says you're to get a move on and pick up a load, soon as. Chop, chop, she says.'

Polly replied, 'That sounds like Bet. Is that Coppernob?'

'No, it's Frank. I've taken over from Stan, and Coppernob does as I say. Right now he's seeing your boss off the premises, so to speak, so we can all relax. The plan is, if you remember, that we're going to tunnel in between the joists to get water to you and make sure you keep awake. We'd thought of coming in through the coal hole but it's jammed with rubble and we don't want to disturb things more'n we 'ave to.'

Suddenly a joist cracked and crashed. They listened as rubble tumbled, then stopped. 'Some bricks must have slid along a joist,' Sylvia whispered. She gathered her strength and called to Solly. 'You all right, Solly?'

He grunted. 'Them bricks slid off to where the coal came in.'

Polly's voice was hoarse, 'Are you untouched, Sylvia, and you, Verity?'

'Broken but unbowed,' called Verity.

Polly croaked a laugh. 'A simple yes or no, drama queen.'

Sylvia called, 'It's too dark to see if the joists have moved closer to us, Frank.' She started coughing.

Frank called, 'Don't you worry, we know what we're doing. Just stay where you are and we'll get to you. Mr Fisher, we have your son, Jacob, here. He's worried about his inheritance, and says you can't pop your clogs till you show him where yer will is.' Frank's laugh was loud. 'I'll get him to shout to you, then I'll get the men back on the job.'

There was a pause and Verity muttered, 'Stay where we are? Where exactly does Frank think we might move to?'

The other two girls, and this time Solly too, said, 'Shut up.' Their laughter was weak, as were their voices and they were cold; they all hurt, and their strength was ebbing again. They wanted to sleep for ever, but they mustn't. Bet had said they must get back to work, chop chop.

A man's voice called, 'Dad, Dad, it's Jacob. I told you it was time you came to live with us. I'm pleased to see the V2 thought the same. Where's your will? Gone up in smoke, or at the solicitor?'

Solly was chuckling quietly. He said, 'That's my boy.'

'Dad, Dad, did you hear me? I love you, Dad. Stop buggering about and get out of there.'

Solly muttered, 'I will, my boy. I will.' He was quiet, too quiet. Sylvia shouted suddenly, 'Come on, Mr Fisher, you must set an example. Answer him properly, chop chop.' The shout exhausted her.

For a moment there was silence, then Mr Fisher rallied, saying, 'I love you too, boy, and you don't need my will, cos I'm coming out to spend all my money, just so you don't get it.'

They heard distant laughter, then Jacob called again, 'Dad, make sure you do. We've got to find Emmanuel, remember? You can't both get blasted by a rocket. I know he's my father-in-law but he's a nice old boy. Got to get the Red Cross onto it, and that was to be your job.'

Mr Fisher whispered, 'Gone missing 'e has.'

'So sorry,' Sylvia whispered back.

But then exhaustion claimed them all.

Chapter 6

The afternoon draws on

Frank was halfway up the pile of rubble searching for gaps where they could begin another tunnel. The one they were working on had collapsed and sent down a shower of bricks, not that they were about to tell those trapped that small point. Steve was on the other side doing the same. Both of them worked desperately, but carefully, because they couldn't find the gas valve to stop the flow of gas they were beginning to smell.

Frank was moving on up, investigating with a torch and gingerly withdrawing bricks until he eventually looked across at Steve and nodded. 'This'll do you nicely, Skinny Lizzy, come and give me an 'and. You'll have to do your usual bit, cos there's been another strike further south, and we've lost the rescue unit that were on their way. They've been diverted.'

Steve inched down to the ground, then back up to support Frank. They worked methodically, but quickly, testing stability all the time, bracing the side of the tunnel with planks but only when really needed. The weight could bring the whole lot down on top of those trapped. It was a miracle it hadn't done that when the first lot shifted. Steve eased his shoulders, aware of a headache starting. It was only tiredness and would pass when he could grab a couple of hours' rest back at the station.

On and on they went, making the girls shout not only to guide them, but also to keep them awake because the smell of gas was now more obvious. Finally, as the afternoon waned, they were ready. Steve threw his jacket down to Dodge, who was waiting on the ground, then tied the rope around his waist. Dodge had handed his hose to an AFS bloke, who held it at the ready in case there was a spark and the whole lot went up. Fat lot of good a hose would do, but it might just damp the flames for a crucial moment, and anyway it made them feel they were doing something. Dodge beckoned the two ambulances closer, but not too close, just in case.

Freezing in his shirt, Steve did what he had done many times before, and edged to the rim of the tunnel at Frank's signal, working his way down, headfirst, while Frank took up the slack of the rope. While Frank shone a torch into the tunnel Steve removed the bricks blocking his way as he went, placing them in a bucket on a second rope. The bucket was cloaked in hessian to reduce the risk of sparks, and he listened to the creaking of the joists as he made it wide enough to ease the girls and Mr

Fisher out when, not if, he reached them. They didn't deal in 'if', he told himself.

As he worked, Steve called out to the girls. 'I'm tunnelling in at a slant, but always downwards. I warn you, my face will be as red as my hair when you see me. I will pick a way through the final barrier to lower in flasks of water, and a torch, and then widen the hole. Then we'll haul you out. The alternative was to take the lot down, but this is quicker.'

He thought of the gas. Was it from this shop, or the one that had stood next door? Either way, time was of the essence. 'You're dehydrated, and this will help. Answer me if you understand.'

There was silence.

He barked, 'Chop chop, come on, pull yourselves together, stay awake, help me, and one another. What about you, Sylvia? Were you going to come back and see me, or just leave me with a broken heart?' He laughed. 'Come on now, concentrate, let's have an answer and put a man out of his misery.' He hoped the use of a name would penetrate as he checked the rope around his waist, tugged on the brick bucket, and used his own torch to see which way to go, because he was blocking Frank's. The bucket was raised. At last, there it was. 'Hello, hello.' It was croaky and weak, but it was a voice.

'And hello to you, Miss Sylvia. Nice to hear your voice. How are you getting on in there, eh? Having a nice nap while the rest of the world works. It won't do, you know.' Steve eased out the next brick as the bucket descended then cursed silently as he saw the way was blocked. 'Play your torch to the left, Frank.'

It was the end of a joist, and Steve daren't move it, so he angled behind it, praying the bricks above would remain stable. He thought he caught another whiff of gas; it must be rising through the rubble, so, he asked himself again, were the gas pipes fractured under Solly's shop or was it working its way through from the neighbour's? What the hell did it matter? It was here, so chop chop. He cursed Bet's words, they were too easy to use.

'Hello?' he heard again and realised he should have talked more.

'Is that you again, Coppernob? How is everyone? Try waking them up for me. I'm going to get water through to you soon, how about that?'

There was a sound. It wasn't a voice but a sob, and he pictured her as he had helped her up from the puddle, her hand in his, those eyes, that hair, her smile. She wasn't damn well going to die; none of them were. He said, 'I know, I know, you feel you could drink the canal, I expect. We had your boss here, as you heard, and she'll be back on it now getting the other girls to where they should be. However, what I need you to do is to keep the others awake, especially Mr Fisher, who is a year or two older than you, so not quite as strong, perhaps.'

Mr Fisher's voice was hoarse. 'I heard that, and I'm as spry as the next one, if you don't mind.' His voice faded and was lost in the coughing. Steve continued to work, listening to the creaks and the grating of the rubble. He stopped when he heard something crash. 'Everyone all right?'

This time it was the posh girl. 'Everything is bloody fine and dandy. Couldn't want for a better place to spend a few hours.'

Sylvia said, 'Oh shut up.' The pair of them laughed, but only for a moment.

Then it was Sylvia again. She was still sort of laughing. 'They're all right,' she said. 'We daren't not be, or Bet will worm her way in here and give us what for.'

'She wants you to telephone her at the depot, wherever that might be, when you get out and let her know when you're coming back to work. She said you're to make that quick.'

Sylvia's laugh was weak. 'That's our Bet.'

Steve continued to work furiously. The rope was digging in and chafing his waist but he kept his voice level, though his head was throbbing. It was hanging upside down that did it, he knew, so he had to put on weight then it would be some other bugger upside down getting sliced and diced by the ruddy bricks. But he was glad it was him, this time, because he had sent them this way. He drew in a breath and the dust caught him, mixed with gas. He coughed. He was so bunged up with dust he could barely smell it, and he hoped that the girls and Solly were too, so they'd never know if they went up in smoke. He tugged on the rope, and called, 'I need a word, Frank.' Somehow he craned his head so he could see the edge of the hole. Frank leaned over it. 'Out with it.'

Steve said quietly, so that those trapped couldn't hear, 'The gas is worse.'

Frank hung further into the tunnel. 'Get a bloody move on and I'll chivvy the lads I sent to help find the bloody stop valve.'

Steve carried on, furiously.

There was silence. He thought quickly, then said, 'So what's this about a boat? Strange sort of war work. Important, is it?'

Silence again.

'Hey, I asked a question, don't go to sleep on me, Sylvia, I'm not that boring, am I?'

At last she answered. 'Not a bit boring, unless it's you boring through the bricks. What do you say, Polly?'

At last he was getting used to the voices. Now Polly was replying, as though dragged from sleep. 'What I say is that was a dreadful joke, Sylvia, if it could even be called that. Agreed, Verity and Solly?'

Solly grunted, and Verity just about laughed. 'I agree. We're called the Idle Women, by rude blokes, Steve. Is that your name? I keep forgetting.'

Steve got his fingers around a stubborn brick and a jagged piece of steel. It was the steel he eased into the bucket first. No sparks, thanks very much, he thought. They were sounding nearer. 'Steve?' Sylvia called, suddenly sounding frightened.

'Yes, I'm still here, course I am. Not about to leave damsels in distress, am I? Why the Idle Women?'

'We are part of the Inland Waterways Scheme. IW, got it?'

'So you laze about on boats?'

The posh one shouted, 'When you get us out of here we'll thank you, then we'll slap you.'

Steve sort of laughed, but his throat was so dry he couldn't even swallow. Verity's voice had sounded louder, so he was close. Very gently he eased out the next few bricks, again reaching for his torch, which was tied to the bucket rope. 'I'm shining a torch, can you see it? I'm close, you see, very close.'

Solly said, 'God bless you, lad. I can see some light. Girls, it's there, shining through.'

Steve called up, 'Frank, get ready to haul 'em up when I've tied them on one at a time. But they've got to have a slurp first, they're about done in.'

The water flasks came down tied to the hauling rope. Frank called, 'I've Dodge here, and the ambulances at the ready. Hurry, you know what is building. I've got a whiff now.'

Steve eased out more bricks, relaxing when he saw the network of joists supporting the load. He lowered the water flasks and dangled down his torch. Sylvia said, 'I'll pass the water on to Polly, and she can pass it on in turn to try and reach the others. I think she's close to Solly. It's hard to see, even with the crack of light you've made. We're covered in bricks, you see.'

Steve's heart sank. 'Use the torch to have a good look, there's my girl.'

There was a pause, and then Solly called, 'No, it's all right, lad, there'll be space enough to get 'em out. The bricks don't go up to the joist, so they can be eased off by each of us. Just mean we have to do a bit of work, careful like.'

Steve yelled up to Frank, 'Lower me. I need to get into the space to help and I'll send up some more bricks, to make it easier.'

Frank yelled, 'Gotcha, but get a bloody move on, me tea'll be cold and the missus will give me 'ell.'

The girls laughed, and judging from the strength of the laughter, the water had revived them. There was no way Steve was going to tell them it wasn't Frank's tea the Rescue Squad bloke was worried about. He was lowered another few feet, into and through the hole. 'Afternoon, girls,' he said, hanging headfirst and grabbing the dangling torch, playing it over the scene. They were half lying, near but not on one another, covered in brick and plaster dust, drinking from the flasks, but also moving bricks.

'Do it very very carefully,' he said.

Solly was nearest. Steve left the torch switched on but hanging free, and asked the old man to try and shift a piece of wood that lay half over his legs while Steve helped. 'On three,' Steve said.

The activity didn't create an avalanche, but Solly groaned, and Steve could see the angle of his right leg. He tugged his rope and called, 'Let me right down, I need to be in the hole to help. Mr Fisher's coming up first. I'll tie him on.'

Frank let the rope out and Steve landed on all fours, with the joists just above him. He left the dangling torch on, and its beam swayed from side to side, highlighting the girls. He saw Sylvia was covered in dust, her face and hair grey with it. Is that how she'd look when she was Solly's age? For a wild moment he hoped he was at her side to see. What the hell was the matter with him? He'd only just met her. Must be the gas. But even as he thought this, he was dragging a smaller torch from his pocket and flashing it around. Then he propped it up on rubble so he had visibility from a different angle.

'Now, let's see if you girls mind the man going first? Not good manners, but Solly is nearest to the tunnel.'

Sylvia, who was moving a brick off her shoulder, looked up. 'We'll let it happen just this once,' she murmured, smiling. The dust coating her face like a mask cracked as she did so. Steve wanted to wipe it clear. Instead he smiled back, his gaze fixated on her as he crawled to Solly, and for a moment it seemed everything stopped, even in this hell, for the mask cracked further as her smile widened, the propped-up torch shining its beam full on her. Her eyes were green/hazel and they were kind and deep, and they brought him peace. Solly said, 'When you're quite ready, son.'

Steve turned back to the task, a brick in his hand, wondering what the hell he was playing at, but it had only been a split second, after all. He snatched a look back at Sylvia, and she was still watching him. Again they smiled at one another, but all the time he was easing the rubble from Solly, who grinned at him, his dust mask cracking slightly too, and winked. 'Not the right sort of place to meet someone like that, is it, son?' he said quietly. 'But in this world, in these times, you have to grab them moments when you can, cos yer never know what's about to happen.'

'Ah,' said Steve, equally quietly. 'But we've already met before, an hour ago, and I do know what's going to happen: you're all going to be rescued, that's what.' The pair of them laughed and now Steve removed the last broken brick, and said, 'Come on then, old timer, it's going to hurt like buggery but let's see if you can drag yourself to our escape hatch, and then I'll tie a rope around you. Keep your head down, though.'

Solly puffed and panted as he crawled to the hole, but never complained as Steve tied the rope around the old man's waist, then said, 'I'm going to tug, and they'll lift you, just keep your head down as you go up, and your arms in front. Trust them.'

Frank called down, 'Quick as you like with the others, Steve.' Solly was pulled up through the hole.

Steve moved into Solly's space. 'It's like dominoes,' he said to the girls. 'We'll take each of you in turn, letting the others all fall over to here, as it were.'

He undid his own rope and eased the bricks from over and around Polly, who winced as several, including a broken piece of joist, were taken from her arm. She opened and shut her hand, moving her arm a little. Her shoulder and top were stained with blood. Steve worked fast, freeing her from the last of them. Her trousers were torn and blood-stained too. 'See if you can crawl to the opening, when I've sorted this,' he told her. He wound a length of bandage around her arm, nodded, and she crawled off. He followed, catching the rope Frank had sent down, calling, 'Mr Fisher's safe, chop chop.'

Steve tied it round Polly. 'Tug on the rope,' he said, starting back to the others immediately. She did, and up she went as the other rope came dangling through the hole.

The blonde girl, called Verity as he now knew, was already easing free of her bricks, and the swaying torch glinted on a piece of metal overhead. Steve called, 'Let me. We don't want that crashing on to anything.'

Verity looked at him. 'I bet we don't.' Their eyes met, and she nodded. 'No sparks, eh?' she muttered.

Sylvia was also shifting the bricks off her body. 'I thought I smelt gas.'

Verity's arm was dangling and dripping blood. 'Broken?' Steve asked.

Verity shook her head. 'Numb. It's going to be the worst case of pins and needles anyone has ever had any minute now, darlings.'

'You're not wrong there.' Steve was on his knees, his head just below the joists, which were creaking. They had to get out, and soon.

He helped her to the tunnel, then tied the rope around her. 'Careful, now. Folded arms, head down. Trust 'em.'

Verity nodded. 'Thank you for everything, if I don't have time to say it later.'

Steve grinned, wanting to say, 'Just go.' Instead he said calmly, 'See you topside.' He wasn't a bit sure he would. Well, he thought, as the gas grew more pungent, that's what this job means.

He turned, to see Sylvia halfway through removing a mountain of bricks and wooden stays, but then she lay back, coughing, trying to grab a breath.

'Let me,' Steve said, inching towards her. He removed enough of the stays, and the final few bricks, and laid them down as though they were the most fragile porcelain. 'Thank you,' she said. 'We must hurry, and you must go first, because you've saved us all and it wouldn't be fair if—'

Steve stared at her, overwhelmed. 'It's my job to get you out. Hurry, now.'

Sylvia shook her head. 'No, it should be you.'

'Come on – over to the tunnel, the sooner you go, the sooner I can.'

She dragged herself along, with him in her wake. He tied the dangling rope around her, their heads close together. 'Thank you, Coppernob,' Sylvia breathed. 'But hurry, please.'

He looked at her. They were so close that he could see she'd split her lip and the blood had stained her dust mask, just as the cuts of the other girls had stained theirs, and Solly's too. He said, 'You're welcome, Coppernob yourself. Off you go.' He tugged, and up she went. He called after her, 'Head down, arms in, trust them.'

'Hurry up, Fireman Steve,' she called.

He watched as she went up. A second rope was thrown down. Good old Frank. He could tie it on while she was being hauled to the surface, and who knew, he might make it, they all might. He waited for Sylvia to be hauled clear, wondering how he could meet someone and so soon feel he had known her all his life, and want to live the rest of his life with her? Was it these times, as Solly had said? Probably. Everything was so different. At last Frank called, 'The girls are well clear. Up you come.'

But the smell of gas was bad now and behind him he heard a sound and turned. A steel joist was on the point of falling, and there would be sparks.

'Could be you and me, Dog, setting off on a journey,' he murmured, sadness enveloping him, because when he looked at Sylvia, he had thought there could be a future for them, and an end to his strange loneliness.

*

Once on the ground the girls had been offered stretchers but refused them. 'Bet would never let us live it down,' Polly said to the medic. He didn't understand but hustled them, limping and stumbling, to the ambulances. They were helped up into the back, and each in turn collapsed on to the side-beds, just as though they were in their cabins, and it felt like home, but smelt of disinfectant, not the cut. 'Solly?' asked Sylvia.

'In the other ambulance and just being taken off. A bit of a problem with his breathing and his leg. His son's with him,' said one of the two ambulance men, swinging himself up to check their pulses. The other one slammed the back doors shut, ran to the cab and set off. 'Call me Bert,' said the medic. 'We're heading west, away from the path of the rockets – with a bit of luck.'

As they swung round a bend, the girls began to relax, and the pain broke through in a way it hadn't in amongst and beneath all the bricks, dust and grime. It was now that they heard a massive explosion.

'The gas?' breathed Polly. Sylvia grabbed at the ambulance man's sleeve. 'Steve?'

'Just relax,' the man said. 'He'll be fine.'

'You've X-ray eyes, then,' snapped Verity.

The man looked at her and replied gently. 'No, just hope. You need it a lot in our game.'

As Sylvia jolted in the ambulance, the pain grew worse, and the guilt too. Had Steve been taken because of her? It was his voice she had listened to, his face she remembered while she was buried, unable to move. Yes, and the feel of his hand when she had fallen backwards into the water when he had helped her to her feet, and those eyes, so kind, that had looked into hers, and her prayers had been woven in amongst all that.

So there it was, Sylvia Simpson. After a lifetime of care in the convent orphanage it was not only her God she'd needed, but a red-haired fireman called Steve she barely knew, so what did that say about her?

The blackness came again, and she was glad.

Chapter 7

Hospital and visitors

Sylvia woke, tasting dust. She could feel sharp bricks and there was light behind her eyelids. Was it Steve's torch? She listened. Just clatter and low murmurs, and a smell which wasn't dust, or gas. She ached when she turned to try and see through the rubble, scared of disturbing the joists. She lay still and there was such a sadness in her heart. But why?

There was something cool on her wrist, and she opened her eyes to see a nun standing there. Was she a child, back in the convent? Had being buried all been a dream? She looked down at her arm: it lay on white sheets, and pale smooth fingers moved lightly on her pulse. She had had such strange dreams of hard hands, a red-haired man called Steve. And she had dreamed too of girls and boats, and bangs and someone calling 'chop chop'.

She must be in the sick bay. She checked to see which nun was looking after her, Sister Maria? Sister Cecilia, or perhaps Sister Augustine? No, it wouldn't be her, she was in charge of the orphanage. Sylvia blinked, and realised it wasn't a nun, but a nurse, with a navy uniform, a white starched apron and a white veil.

Sylvia said, 'I thought you were a nun.' There was no dust clogging her throat but it was still sore, and her voice was ragged.

The young nurse laughed. 'Hardly. I think Sister would have something to say about that remark, after she caught me climbing in the window after midnight. I've been gated.'

Sylvia heard a laugh, then a posh voice. 'A girl after my own heart.' But it wasn't a real laugh and it mirrored Sylvia's sadness. Ah, Verity, of course. And Polly, and Dog. 'Where's Polly?'

'Here.' Polly's voice was weak and tired.

Sylvia looked to the left. Verity lay propped up on pillows, her blonde hair washed. Her face was scratched and cut, with one cut stitched along her cheekbone, and her arm was bandaged and in a sling.

'You're clean?' Sylvia muttered.

Verity smiled. 'And so are you, sweet pea. I couldn't work out what the smell was when I woke, and that's because it wasn't dirt.'

The nurse, straightening Sylvia's bed before moving to Polly, murmured, 'Not dirt, rubble.'

Polly, Sylvia and Verity said as one, 'Boat dirt, we meant.'

The nurse tidied up the beds of the other two girls. 'You've been in and out of consciousness for a couple of days, believe it or not, during which time you've been stitched, bandaged, bathed, hair-washed and bedpanned. Your next of kin have also been informed, it seems, after someone notified the depot, whatever that is. We know because a Mrs Holmes telephoned the hospital, probably your esteemed mother, Miss Polly Holmes, and pointed out to our administrator that visiting hours were only for those living locally, and couldn't possibly apply to those coming from the West Country.'

Polly grinned at the girls, her chestnut curls almost back to being bouncy. But the smile didn't reach her eyes. She asked, 'Is there news from the site?' She paused, and Sylvia clenched her jaw. *Don't ask*, she wanted to shout. I don't want to know because I left him there, and he can't be gone, not with his smile, his copper hair, his . . . Polly was speaking again. 'There was an explosion as we left.'

Sylvia listened as the attractive Nurse Annie Newsome, or so it said on the label pinned to her dress, shook her head. 'No, no news but perhaps your parents can find out for you. It's chaos, you know, the damned V2s are having a high old time, that's why you were brought over west. They've evacuated a lot of the vulnerable hospitals.'

With that, she moved on to the other beds in the ward. Sylvia called after her, 'There was another person with us, Solly Fisher, how is he?'

'Causing mayhem in the Men's Ward.' The nurse's laugh was cut short as a sister swept through the double doors into the ward; they swung backwards and forwards in her wake, her shoes squeaking on the pristine floor. 'We do not allow shouting in the ward, Nurse Newsome, do we, so let's keep the noise level at a dull murmur, shall we?'

Nurse Annie Newsome did a sort of bob and busied herself pouring a drink of water from the jug on a patient's bedside cabinet further down the ward.

Sylvia's bed was between Verity's and Polly's. The three girls looked at one another. Verity muttered, 'Oh Lordy, another Bet.'

Polly simply said, 'He didn't deserve to die. It's not fair.'

Sylvia felt his hand leading her to the opening, his smile, the tiredness, his calmness, the rope rasping against her armpits as she was hauled up, and away from him. She stopped, looked from Polly to Verity. 'But who has Dog?'

The other two stared. Verity said, 'Just what I was beginning to wonder. But, look, after we heard her bark the men must have taken her away so they could get on. But where?'

As they lay back on their pillows, trying to gather their thoughts, Polly shouted, 'I know—' The sister at her desk in the centre of the ward looked up. 'Sorry, Sister,' Polly almost whispered. She beckoned the other two to come closer, which made them roll their eyes. 'Don't be absurd, darling,' muttered Verity. 'We're prisoners in the beds and my legs feel like water, or did when I was helped to the lav, having said no to the bedpan, so spell it out.'

'Bet was there, so she'll have taken Dog on. She'll have had to get Evelyn and Mabel back, and probably took them all on *Marigold* and *Horizon*, or even slogged along on *Hillview*. But it's Steve I feel so terribly sad about. We owe him our lives and now he's . . .' She fell silent.

Sylvia lay back on her pillows again, remembering Steve's voice, his hand as he helped her up, and a sob escaped. Her heart was so heavy she thought it would never recover.

Polly called, 'We've all cried, Sylvia. Let it go, just give in.' But Polly's voice was fading, and Sylvia's eyelids were heavy.

In the afternoon, the clatter woke them, and above that, the crisp tones of Mrs Holmes, Polly's mother. 'I quite understand your concerns, Nurse Newsome, but our girls need us, and I have already discussed an out of hours visit with your administrator and matron.'

Polly stared down the ward, torn between groaning and laughing as she watched her mother lead the charge past Nurse Newsome, Lady Pamela Clement, Verity's mother, following, with a bit of a blush to her cheeks. Polly wasn't surprised, her mother had that effect sometimes, but then everyone fell in love with her. Polly waved, checking that the other two were awake. 'Prepare to receive boarders, my hearties.'

Sylvia muttered, 'The thing is, can we ever raise our heads in this ward again?'

Verity was waving to her mother, Lady Pamela, but replied, 'I doubt it, and what's more we'll pay with enemas all round the moment they've gone, from the look on Nurse Newsome's face.'

The three girls groaned, but when the two women arrived, and showered them with hugs and kisses, and loads of fuss, it was all forgotten. Lady Pamela sat between Verity and Sylvia, and Mrs Holmes between Sylvia and Polly. 'To share ourselves equally between all three of our girls,' Lady Pamela said, clasping both her daughter, and Sylvia's hand.

Mrs Holmes was digging in her voluminous brown handbag, and drew out three woollen hats she had knitted, in an interesting combination of stripes. 'You will have discarded your old ones, or perhaps they're still in the rubble.' Her voice broke, but only for a moment, because it wouldn't dare to let her down at a time like this.

Lady Pamela said, 'We have contacted Lady McDonald, you know the mother of the IW trainee you dragged out of the lock a few months ago, girls. She's insisted her husband, he who seems to know a lot of people if you remember, ferret about to find out about Tom and Saul. You will be pleased to hear that they are together after Saul's lorry was hit whilst supplying the front line.' At the look of alarm from all three girls she shook her head. 'Calm down, it was empty, so no supplies were lost.'

Verity shouted, to a 'hush' from Nurse Newsome, 'Mother, it's Saul we're concerned with, not the ruddy supplies.'

Mrs Holmes and Lady Pamela shared a grin. 'Just our little joke we cooked up on the train journey here,' Verity's mother said. 'You owe me a bob, Joyce, it *was* Verity who wailed first. You see, girls, you've led us into bad habits and we seem to bet on most things these days. Anyway, Saul was seconded to Tom's company, and it seems he is now part of the PBI, which means—'

All three girls interrupted, 'The Poor Bloody Infantry.'

Polly grumbled, 'Why should that make me feel better? At least when he was driving a lorry he was in and out, not in the midst of things.'

Verity's mother said, 'Unlike you girls.' This time it was her voice that wavered.

As they all turned towards her, there was yet again a kerfuffle at the swing doors, and in glided Sister Augustine. Mrs Holmes sniffed and said, 'Nurse Newsome won't even attempt to stand in the way of the heavenly brigade.'

Polly hushed her. 'I think perhaps that's sacrilegious. What do you think, Sylvia?'

But before Sylvia could even consider the question Sister Augustine was upon them and had obviously heard. 'I'm not sure whether it is or not,

Polly; it is Polly, isn't it? But it has to be said, a religious habit works well to open closed doors at times, so one just has to use what one has.' Her smile was broad as she stopped by Sylvia's bed, then stooped and kissed her forehead. Lady Pamela moved to the chair on Verity's left, and Sister Augustine sat in her place, as though on a throne.

Well, thought Polly, here we all are, like starlings on a telephone wire. She was feeling exhausted suddenly, but pleased to see the mothers, and the orphanage nun. Was Sylvia pleased to see Sister Augustine, though? The poor girl felt a pressure whenever the orphanage, or indeed the convent, was mentioned, and who wouldn't, if you were in her shoes and thought you might have been 'called'. Polly couldn't imagine what that was like, but quite honestly, she wondered if it wasn't a sense of imaginary obligation, really, just as Sister Augustine had suggested to their poor conflicted friend, not helped by that Harriet, who sounded a manipulative kettle of fish.

There was silence around the beds but yet again this was broken by a man in a wheelchair being pushed through the doors into the ward. It was Solly Fisher and his son. Solly was waving his walking stick at Nurse Newsome, saying, 'The doctor said I could, didn't he, Jacob?'

Jacob nodded. 'Well, yes, but you did waggle your stick at him.'

Even Sister Askwell, who had followed them in, laughed, and so did the rest of the ward. One woman said to her neighbour, 'Wonder who's coming in next, it's like bleedin' Piccadilly, ain't it, and it's not even visiting hours. All down to these bleedin' rockets, it is.'

'Quite so,' said her posh neighbour. 'But one day it will stop.'

Solly had reached their bed. Jacob smiled at them all, and said, 'You look like a panel about to sit in judgment on a criminal. That would be you, Dad.'

The ice was broken, and everyone laughed as Jacob made the introductions. Sister Augustine's wimple shook as the giggles overtook her. Solly Fisher looked at her then said, 'We're on opposite sides of the fence, you and me – yer 'ave yer church, I 'ave my synagogue, but we both love these girls, don't we?'

Sister Augustine smiled. 'Indeed we do, Mr Fisher, and the fence isn't high, you know. What's more, the girls do a grand job on the canals.'

Jacob said, 'They do a reasonable job under the rubble too. We just hope that the fireman got out as well, because I gather there was an explosion.'

The girls fell silent, and left it to Jacob to explain to the women, whose distress was soon a mirror of the girls'. Again a silence fell, but not for long because a doctor called from the swing doors, 'I said one minute, Mr Fisher, and there'll be no stick waggling this time, if you please. I'm waiting.'

Jacob was already busy trying to turn his father's wheelchair round, and Solly attempted to help by issuing navigation instructions. Finally, Jacob, looking hot and bothered, shouted, 'Dad, shut up.'

Again there was laughter, and Sister Askwell didn't even try to hush them, because the whole ward was a party to the jollity. Solly said, over the laughter, 'I just wanted to say our time in the cellar wasn't a pleasure, but it would have been bloody awful without you three, and thank the Lord, yours and mine, for yer dog, girls. He's the one who found us. And God bless our fireman, and our eternal thanks to the lot of them. I'm to go and live with me boy, in Golders Green, but I know where to find you girls. The Bull's Bridge Depot, eh?'

Polly asked, 'Oh, it was you then, who phoned the office?'

Mr Fisher shook his head. 'Not me, doll, but me boy asked around about the boaters, and we know where the orders are given out now, so yer can't disappear into the ether cos yer'll be back at work soon as yer can. Types like you always is.'

He waved as he was pushed away, but there was a logjam at the double doors, as Polly saw Bet trying to squeeze past. They heard her say, 'I should have brought my horn, then you'd have known to wait.'

Solly's reply was rude, their mutual laughter loud. Bet marched down the ward. Sister Askwell just shook her head, then returned to her reports, leaving Nurse Newsome to lead the way to the girls.

Sylvia called, as Bet reached them, 'Oh Bet, you reached the depot safely. We wondered who let the parents know.'

Bet stood at the foot of her bed. 'Not me, I told the coppernob to do it if you made it out in one piece, and not to if you hadn't. The message got through before I could find a phone box to check myself.'

Bet looked tired, but who wouldn't, shepherding trainees about, Sylvia thought, as she hid her despair at the mention of Coppernob. She stared ahead, not at either of the girls, who were doing the same, trying not to cry. She took a deep breath and finally forced herself to show interest and asked Bet, 'So what's happened to your boats?'

'I'm running *Marigold* and *Horizon* while they sort it out.'

Polly asked, 'Still with Evelyn and Mabel, or have they thought better of it all?'

Bet smiled, 'They're good girls, and happy to start for Birmingham when I get back from here. The rockets can't go on for ever, and we'll make damn sure we'll get in and out of Limehouse like a dose of sa—'

Verity had been nodding, and she interrupted, 'And Dog, is she missing us?'

Bet seemed to falter for a moment and lose her smile. 'She's with Fran,' she said, 'out of the danger area. Ma Mercy took her up, on their way to Tyseley Wharf. But let's get back to you. The doctor says you'll all be ready for duty in a couple of weeks.'

The mothers and Sister Augustine looked shocked. 'Back at work?' queried Mrs Holmes. 'I rather think not. They've done their bit.'

Bet stared at Mrs Holmes, then at the girls. 'What say you?'

Sylvia said, 'Two weeks should do it, and of course we haven't done our bit, Mrs Holmes.' Verity added, 'The war is still going on. We're needed, or I am at least.'

Polly reared up on her pillows. '*You're* needed? You're a ruddy nuisance on the cut, steering this way and that, and throwing your fag stubs wherever you please, leaving someone else to stamp them out on the deck.'

Sylvia nodded. No matter how bloody everything got, the three of them were a team, and because of that, they were an unbeatable threesome. Yes, there was a war on, work to be done and no excuses, if you please. Just one foot in front of the other, until it was over. She said, 'I haven't trained, put up with these two day after day, Mrs Holmes, just to walk away. Good heavens above, yes, two weeks should do it. Besides, what would Dog do without us?'

The mothers and the nun looked at one another, silenced. Bet was biting her lip. The girls hadn't seen their trainer so downcast, ever. Polly said, 'What's up, Bet? Surely you don't want us back sooner, that really might be pushing it.'

Lady Pamela seemed to shake herself. 'Two weeks, Bet and not a day earlier, but they're to come to Howard House until then. Henry said he will drive up for you. Sister Askwell is happy to release them in two days, and so are the doctors. They need the space, sadly, because the injured from the rockets are increasing daily.'

Verity smiled at her mother. 'We'll come by train, because we don't want to stretch Dad's petrol coupons. It'll do us good to get back to normality.'

The mothers protested while the girls agreed with Verity.

Sylvia lay back on the pillows, thinking visitors were lovely but exhausting. Sister Augustine was chatting across her bed to Polly, and Lady Pamela and Mrs Holmes were laughing with Verity when there was a round of applause from the rest of the ward and someone called, "Ere comes another one, girls, and 'e's a bit of all right, 'e is.'

The girls looked up. Almost marching through the ward was Steve, his helmet under his arm, his boots crashing down on the floor. 'Steve,' breathed Sylvia, feeling faint with disbelief, and then overwhelmed with joy. 'Steve,' she repeated, reaching out before she remembered where she was.

He came, his red hair shining, and stood next to Bet at the foot of Sylvia's bed, *hers*. He grinned, eyes only for her, and said, 'Just wanted to check that the other coppernob was doing all right.'

Polly called, 'Oh Steve, we thought—'

Verity interrupted, 'We thought you'd copped it, Coppernob. Oh, it's so good to see you, it really is, and to be able to thank you. Mother, this is the man who saved our lives. This man who only has eyes for Sylvia, and she for him I might add, but then being under rubble does make one bond sooner rather than later.'

'Shut up,' said Sylvia automatically, heedless of it all because while the girls had been talking, Steve's eyes had not wavered from hers, and all the time she felt as though she had been saved from desolation, to arrive finally at somewhere she really belonged.

Sister Augustine stood up from the chair beside her, her habit rustling, 'Steve, well I never did.'

Steve noticed Sister Augustine, then, and clearly the shock made him step back. Sylvia stared from one to the other. Steve tried to smile. 'Well, I never did, too. Sister, what brings you here?'

Everyone in the ward was listening, and Polly and Verity looked from him, to Sylvia, to Sister Augustine, who stretched out a hand towards Sylvia, who suddenly knew the answer before she heard it. 'Sylvia Simpson is one of ours too.'

Steve looked at Sylvia, puzzled. 'But I don't remember you at the orphanage.'

Sister Augustine smiled, and came to him, taking his hand and patting it. 'You're a few years older, and you were in different houses, and different schools, so your paths didn't cross. But you have my undying gratitude for saving these girls, and all those others whose well-being you have put before your own. Ah, Steve Bates, I always knew that you would shine, always, just as Sylvia does, and will go on doing.'

Verity drawled, 'It's the hair, coppernobs are different.'

All the women shouted, 'Shut up.' Then laughed, and while they did Sister Augustine went on, 'So, young man, while you're here, let me remind you about the reunion, since you still haven't replied. It would be so lovely to have as many old boys and girls as can make it. It's in a month.'

While the others talked amongst themselves Steve looked at Sylvia, asking quietly, 'Are you going?'

'If I can. Depends on our orders.' But if he was to go, she knew she must, because where he was, she wanted to be. Did he feel the same?

Bet looked from one to the other, and while Steve came around to the side of Sylvia's bed, Bet moved to talk to Verity, but all Sylvia was really aware of was his dark blue eyes which were so tired, his smile which was more than tired. 'Thank you for saving our lives,' she said.

'It's my job.'

'But thank you. We heard the explosion, and thought—'

'I got out in time, and just after the lot went up they found the gas valve, and we doused the remnants good and proper.' He raised his voice.

'Someone was looking after us all. What do you say to that, Sister Augustine?'

She smiled, 'I will give thanks, Steve.'

Sylvia looked from Steve to Sister Augustine, thinking, *Please, Sister, don't fall on your knees here.*

It must have been written all over her face because Steve touched her shoulder, grinning. He bent down and whispered, 'She'll wait until she gets to her home ground, don't worry. She's a wise woman, and always has been.'

She felt his breath on her neck and longed to reach up and touch his cheek. She saw Sister Augustine watching. Sylvia said, 'I will give thanks too.'

And she would, for all their lives, but mostly because Steve was here, alive, and she couldn't think of anything, or anyone, else. All she could do was feel joy. Yes, that's what it was. Could one want to lay one's life at another person's feet in the sheer magic of their being? She realised she was thinking the words of the nuns, about God. Was it the medication? She was watching Steve as he moved back to the foot of the bed and as he lifted his head to smile again, she was aware that her joy must be love, for she could see it in his eyes too and it was the same as in the eyes of Saul and Tom when they looked at their girls.

For a moment she paused because it was different to what she felt for God, which was a belief, a trust, and, yes, a love, and she understood, as she had not before, what Sister Augustine had said and what her friends reinforced – there was no need for imaginary obligation.

She leaned back on the pillows, so tired, and with a mind clearer than it had been for months, years. God had led them to one another and saved them both and her conflict and confusion drifted up into the ether, and away.

Sister Augustine inclined her head towards Sylvia, her smile gentle, knowing and understanding, and there was a world of acceptance in that action. Sister Augustine whispered, 'Now, you must recover and take up your life, dearest Sylvia, free of its muddle of worries and obligations.'

Within twenty minutes, the mothers had gone, and Bet, and Sister Augustine too, but all would return for a short while the following afternoon. It transpired that the mothers were staying in Wembley. Steve remained, sitting where Sister Augustine had, and held Sylvia's hand. He ran his finger over her callouses, learning from the girls about their work and they about his. He could only stay for half an hour, as he had to leave then to get back on shift.

He stood at last, looking from one to the other, and said, 'I'm glad you're safe,'

'It's because of you,' Polly told him.

Steve said quietly, 'I repeat, it's our job. You remember that when you think of Dog, because she felt it her job too. We all do this because we need to, and want to. It's what we're trained for.' He turned on his heel and left. Sylvia watched. How odd. Did he not think that they knew how wonderful Dog was, and how glad they were she was having a rest with Fran? How could they possibly forget that in the short time before they saw her again? The double doors swung closed behind him. The girls talked together until exhaustion crept in. As they began to feel drowsy, Polly and Verity asked if Sylvia was nearer making a decision about the convent and her life.

Sylvia smiled. 'I think I'm beginning to understand that there are different kinds of love, so yes, I am nearer, or in fact, already there; now that Steve has survived. I felt so dreadful at the thought of him dead; guilty for thinking of him, not God, so sad too, sort of lost, and then he appeared, and suddenly it was all so simple.'

Verity nodded. 'It's what I felt for Tom. I saw him and I knew, and it was pretty much the same for you and Saul, wasn't it, Pol?'

Polly smiled, her voice soft. 'Oh yes, but could it be the war? We are under such strain that when we see someone and there's that "something" we are bold enough to grab at it, just in case . . .'

The others nodded, understanding what she was saying and happy to be together, knowing that somehow they had to stay this close for ever.

The next day Timmo, one of their favourite boaters, came outside visiting hours, by which time Sister Askwell had given up on them all, because Sister

Augustine, Bet and the mothers had already reappeared and were sitting by the beds. As Timmo clumped down the ward in his boater's boots they all smiled. He was now the steerer, or captain of his boats, after the death of his brother Thomo and would want to know when their darts-throwing arm would be back in action, Polly guessed.

''Ow do, lasses,' Timmo said, his hat under his arm, his face ruddy from the cold and his hands even more calloused than the girls'. He was wearing a bulky jacket, which was unusual for him. Normally it was a thick jumper, but he brought the boater smell with him, and with it the ripple of the water, the hiss of the oil lamp, the hoot of the owl and the flash of the kingfisher. ''Ow's yer throwin' arms, that's what them on t'cut need ter know. Cos we got to win our losses back off yer, so chop chop, and take 'eart.'

They all laughed, but then Polly wondered what he meant by take heart because they had survived and weren't badly hurt. She said, 'It's not too bad at all, Timmo, we're just bashed about a bit, and Bet's given us two weeks off, after which we'll thrash you.'

The girls laughed again, but the women didn't. Instead they shifted uncomfortably and Polly didn't understand. Neither did the others as Bet glared at Timmo, who didn't notice but said, looking puzzled, 'I 'ad thought to find you sadder, and I does feel that t'is good to be brave. But to take Dog's place, the boaters 'ave found you this little 'un.' From beneath his jacket he brought a little mongrel, white and grey, with a chaotic coat, and ears that pointed upwards.

The girls stared at Timmo, while the older women sat as though frozen. At last Polly said, 'What do you mean? Dog's with Fran at Buckby, only for two weeks.'

Timmo was confused, until a dawning realisation made his eyes widen. He looked at the older women, helplessly, then at the puppy in his arms. Mrs Holmes stood, saying gently, looking from one girl to the other, 'Dog is indeed with Fran, buried in the orchard, my dear girls. She saved you but was too badly hurt to survive. Steve carried her to the cab of his engine, and Bet wrapped her in her jumper and Ma Mercy took her to Fran. We didn't quite lie, but we couldn't tell you, just yet.'

Lady Clement continued, 'No one could bear to, all quite cowardly because we know how she was your fourth Idle Woman, so we must thank you, Timmo, for doing it for us.'

Polly was running the words through her head. Dog? No, not Dog? Sylvia was crying, Verity too, but Polly wasn't because of course it wasn't true. They had heard her bark when they were under the rubble. Ma Mercy had taken her to Fran's. She'd be there, sniffing about, missing them. It was Sylvia who said, her voice full of tears, 'Remember how Steve stood here and said when we thanked him,

126

"It's our job. Remember that when you think of Dog, because she felt it her job, too. We all do this because we need to, and want to. It's what we're trained for." He was preparing us, and he's right, Dog was doing what she has always done – which is to look after us.'

Polly's throat was too thick to speak, but she had no words even if she had been able to. She watched Timmo lay the puppy on Verity's bed, but Verity wouldn't touch her, she just cried. The puppy yelped, disturbed. Sister Askwell came rustling up. 'Not on the bed, even given the circumstances, young man, if you please.'

Sister Augustine lifted the puppy, which nestled in her arms, as though calmed by the nun's goodness. Mrs Holmes said, 'We will make other arrangements for her, and when you come to Howard House, girls, you will get to know her. Until then, grow stronger. We will meet you tomorrow at Sherborne Station if you will insist on making your own way.'

Polly sank her head in her hands, and just nodded. Her mother said, 'You will telephone us from Waterloo Station to tell us your expected time of arrival, and we'll work it out from there, because delays will occur. Do you understand, Polly?'

Again Polly nodded as she sensed Timmo coming close to her bedside. She looked up at him, barely able to see him through the mist. He was turning his hat over and over again in his hands. 'I am sorry for yer loss, for I remember the lass coming to me at the lay-by when Thomo had died. She did just sit by my side, and she did make it bearable for me, at that minute. I is sorry 't'were me that brought to you the truth of her loss.'

He walked away through the ward, to calls of, 'Nice thought, lad', 'Don't you take on, they'll thank yer for it.'

At the doors he turned, and Polly called, 'Timmo, please thank the boaters. And thank you very much, but you see, Dog was our . . .' Her voice became a sob, and Timmo left with Bet hurrying after him, to take care of him.

The mothers and Sister Augustine waited, holding their girls' hands until they were again asleep, while the puppy slept on Sister Augustine's lap. They then walked down the ward, with the puppy, and the other patients watched. One called, 'We'll look after the lasses, don't you fret.'

Chapter 8

Tom and Saul heading for the Rhine

Tom and Saul were dug in with the rest of their infantry platoon at the edge of a copse, near a village west of the Rhine. The ground was frozen hard but the company had managed to channel out trenches the day before for cover, while those 'above' who decided things bloody well got on and decided, or so the men hoped. The night had been painful; cold and long, and now it was nine in the morning, and there'd been no sun to warm their cockles, or that was how their pal Geordie had put it.

Tom muttered to Saul, squatting with his back pressed up against the side of the trench while Geordie took his turn on watch, 'To think you could have been in your nice warm lorry, Saul.'

Squatting next to him Saul drew the bolt on his rifle, fearing it had frozen in the cold. 'T'lorry be a bit too warm, Tom. It were up in flames last time I saw it, when I bailed out, just in time. Scorched me pants it did.'

Geordie looked down. He was chewing tobacco and spat, his spittle staining the snow a few inches from Tom's feet. 'Aye, man, I reckon I could do with a bit of scorching.' His voice was little more than a whisper, for Lieutenant Morris had said the German tanks could be coming, forcing their way through to the Rhine, and home, and there might be Nazi infantry fanning out ahead of them. What was certain was that there were Nazis hunkered down in the village and best they didn't know there were Tommies about with a load of chatter carrying across to them.

Tom laughed quietly. 'One day you'll hit me with your spit and I'll have to shoot you, so no need to worry about the Nazis cos if they don't get you, I will.'

Saul stood, then, staring around. No birds sang, there was no rumble of tanks but he bet there were some rabbits or a partridge out there he could trap. He thought of his Polly: was she bashing *Marigold* out of the ice before setting off for Tyseley, Birmingham, with a load? Or higher in the water, and lighter, motoring to Limehouse? There was them damned rockets over London now, so he hoped with all his heart she didn't linger.

He whispered, "As you 'eard from yer Verity, then Tom? I sees there was a mail drop, or a drop of something anyways at the last stop.'

Tom shook his head, still hunkered down, and said, 'Nope, but what I wouldn't give for a fag.'

Geordie, his place taken by Tony Moore, dropped down with them. 'Have a chew?'

Tom shook his head. 'Not the same, but I suppose the lieutenant's right, the smoke could be spotted.'

Saul laughed quietly. 'Don't matter whether 'e be right or not, our Tom. We does as 'e says.'

Tom grimaced. 'Talking of letters, bloody miracle, isn't it, that any comes through at all? We don't know where we are, so how do they?'

He was fingering his packet of Woodbines, his rifle stock resting on the ground, the barrel leaning on his shoulder. They were all shivering, their heavy khaki woollen gloves worn two thick, except for their trigger fingers, which poked through the holes they'd made. Saul slapped his hands together; Mrs Holmes had knitted the gloves, so it was extraordinary that they were one colour.

Tom shifted slightly, and his shoulder nudged Saul's. 'I remember being at Mrs Green's guest house in Birmingham, just me and the girls while you waited with Dog and Granfer on your boats at Tyseley. Mrs Green said to carry a white handkerchief, but only bring it out to surrender, or it'd be spotted and you'd be shot.'

Saul grinned. Tom had told him before, but they both liked to talk of times with their girls. Saul said, 'I just does 'ope them rockets is leaving 'em be.'

Geordie muttered, still chewing, 'Aye, that's what it comes down to, bonny lad: hope. We only know folks're all right when we 'ear. So best we leave that be, an' all.' He shifted his weight, as Tom muttered, 'Heads up, sarge is on 'is way.'

They eased up, and leaned against the trench wall, joining Tony on watch, their breath billowing. Tom looked up as Sergeant Williams approached bent double, giving a quiet word to his lads. When he reached them Tom said, 'Look at all this breath, Sarge, might as well be fag smoke.'

'On the other hand, lad, it might as well not, or you'll be on a charge, and that'd be worse than any ruddy tank, if I have my way.' He winked and moved on. They watched as he continued along all the men until he reached a couple of pine trees where Lieutenant Morris stood, poring over a map. He was smoking.

'Course he ruddy is,' muttered Tom.

Saul laughed slightly. 'I'd be smoking me 'ead off if I be 'im. Who wants to give an order and it be wrong? 'E were a farmer, so 'tis said, so 'tis my thinkin' 'e'll be right glad to be back on 'is land bothering about poachers like me.'

Geordie nodded, then said quietly, 'I lost Mam in the bombing at Heaton, Newcastle, so I come out o' the mines to get back at 'em. Now they're sending conscripts into the pits fresh from Eton and Gawd knows where, and I'm ruddy out 'ere. Right mad the conscripts are too, and the pitmen aren't that happy to have a load of likely lads doing naught but getting in t'way.'

Saul thought of Sylvia, who'd come from the convent orphanage, and been difficult for Polly and Verity when she had joined the boats, and no one knew why. It wasn't until she'd suddenly told Tom about trying to decide whether to be a nun that anyone understood. It was so like Geordie to suddenly say what he had just said about his mother, just like that. There was silence as they absorbed it.

When Sylvia had told Tom when she first knew him, and then said she didn't know why she'd told him, and not the others yet, Tom had said that people sometimes told a stranger, someone who wouldn't care, and wouldn't remember. But, thought Saul, he and Geordie and Tom were friends, and did care.

Perhaps Geordie'd suddenly said it because they were waiting for their own armoured division to get to them and help clear the village of Nazis who were hunkered down? Or perhaps it would be the Nazis' Tiger tanks that'd reach them first. Then they'd be gone in a puff of smoke – was that what had made Geordie blurt it out? To clear the decks, perhaps? Or just to hope they understood? Hope. Well, they all lived on that out here.

Saul sighed, but that made his breath billow even more. He stared at the snow frozen to the branches of the trees and in ruts on the ground. Thing was, he didn't know what his thoughts were doing, chasing one another like ferrets on a hot day. All the time he'd been ruminating he'd kept an eye on the group around the lieutenant, and suddenly the snow started falling from the branches, and on to their shoulders. The ground trembled beneath his feet: German Tigers, or their own armoured division?

He looked around, seeing all the other men appearing at the rim of their trenches, doing the same.

Tom's lips had thinned. They'd already suffered in the German Tigers' hands as they had headed east chasing after the Germans. Huge great brutes the tanks were, with exhausts belting out smoke, and guns which tore their company apart. The sounds and screams were such as he'd never want to hear again. Lieutenant Turner was killed, and Lieutenant Morris had been drafted in, and was a survivor of another cut-about company which had amalgamated with theirs.

Beneath the pines he saw the radio operator yanking off his headset, speaking urgently to the lieutenant. Morris stubbed out his cigarette, and Sergeant Williams came down the line at the double, giving orders to be at the ready because the ruddy armoured column was coming up at ruddy last, so they'd have to be up and out, ready to follow them into the village. 'Bit like clearing a hornets' nest,' the sergeant said as he hurried on.

'It's nothing like a bloody hornets' nest,' ground out Geordie. 'Hornets are from nature, this lot in the village are from 'ell, man, and they've lost so why don't they just wave their bleeding handkerchiefs?'

'Save your breath, Hughes,' the sergeant threw back over his shoulder. 'You're going to need it.' They hopped out of the trench, running at the double to form up under the pines. As their armoured column rumbled into view, they watched them use the high hedges for cover from the Nazis in the village as they crossed the fields, their tracks destroying overwintering wheat. Saul picked up the sound of an aircraft engine. He searched the grey tumbling clouds, and there it was, streaking out, and it wasn't one of theirs, but was reconnoitring like a fox on the prowl, damn it to hell.

He heard the lieutenant say, 'At ten hundred hours we move out in the wake of the column, Sergeant Williams, if you will.'

Saul heard the shake in the lad's voice, for he was just a lad; and no wonder the bugger smoked. The radio was being packed away and hoisted in its haversack on the back of the radio wallah, who snatched up his rifle and stayed at the ready.

Tom checked his watch. 'Five minutes, lads. Remember we promised ourselves that drink in Verity's club in Jermyn Street when this whole bloody lot is over, Saul. You and Sylvia can sing for our supper like last time. You come too, Geordie, if you haven't buggered off back to the pits.'

The three men slapped hands. They did this every time. So far it had worked. Saul wondered if he should ask Sylvia's God for safe passage, but it wasn't his God. His were the trees, the sky, the endlessness of nature, and the cut. Above all, the tranquillity of the cut, and the work. He pulled at his gloves, feeling his callouses beneath the wool. They were his scars, just like the scars his Polly had now, and Verity, and even Sylvia. Perhaps that churchy lass would have a bloke to love by now, but who knew? Who knew anything?

All the time the ferrets were racing in his head he was listening to the engines, to the aircraft, but then Sergeant Williams gave the signal, and they fell in some hundred yards behind the column which had almost reached the edge of the village, heading along the side of a turnip field. It was as well the 2nd Tank Division had arrived, because as the company approached the village they saw the bloody Tigers chuntering out of the side streets, their turrets swinging with their damn great guns. Tom groaned. 'The bastards slunk in under cover of the noise of ours, so here we go again.'

The company drew in close behind the armoured column as they neared the outskirts of the village. The German guns swung too far to the east, then steadied, and readjusted, as the 2nds engaged the Tigers, blasting, taking out a Tiger. But then the Tigers returned fire, overshooting.

'Take cover, Severns,' roared Lieutenant Morris. The men hurled themselves down into icy ground, well churned up by their tanks' tracks. Face down, Saul clung to the thought of Polly, safe. Be safe, be pat-pattering along the pounds heading to Tyseley. Watch the kingfisher, even though it be cold, cos it be there if you watch close, my Polly. Tell Sylvia to draw it again for Joe, do that, eh? Keep the lad hidden from Leon, if he still be alive.

Next to him he heard Tom, as the ground shuddered, the guns blasted, the tanks blazed, and men screamed as they bailed out of the turrets. 'Verity, you damn well stay safe, you hear. You get in and out of Limehouse, and no messing. Do you hear?' He was shouting against the noise. Geordie whistled silently, and then just swore, in a sort of chant when it got noisy. It's what he did every time, it was what he'd done when the pit props gave way and the seam ceiling crashed down, missing him by a bloody inch, he'd said.

Lieutenant Morris roared an order. With Sergeant Williams he waved their platoons to either side. Saul, Geordie, Tony and Tom followed their sergeant as they set out to flank the village to the east. In their platoon were Clive and Harry, carrying anti-tank weapons. Saul, Tom, Tony and Geordie were panting as they crouched over, running as though there was a roaring bull behind them. Others were running too. Tom yelled, 'Clive'd better aim bloody straight with his bloody toy, or our tanks are going to get slaughtered.'

Clive, lugging one of the anti-tank weapons, yelled to his mate Harry as they headed for the corner of a house, 'The buggers say to aim straight.'

'Tell 'em to mind their own bloody business and get their own rifles in order, or have they been allowed to play with a sub-machine gun?'

'Shut the noise,' yelled the sergeant in spite of the bedlam as the big boys hurled shells at one another.

Suddenly from windows, rifles and sub-machine guns were firing, taking down the Germans. 'Resistance,' yelled Geordie.

But then they saw the gun of a Tiger take aim at one of the houses. It fired. The building exploded. The firing stopped. 'Bastards,' shouted Geordie as they followed the sergeant, weaving, and crouching into the shadows of a high village building. Saul thought it looked like a convent, or how he imagined they looked with slits for windows and a cross on the top. Where were the nuns? There was an explosion, and the building was torn apart too. Saul felt the air being sucked from his body, his ears were about to explode and then he was thrown through the air, the rifle being shaken from his hands. It skidded along the cobbles.

The sarge was scrabbling to his feet, yanking at Tom, then Saul, then the next bloke, and the next. Geordie's nose was bleeding. No one was dead, everyone was dazed. The sarge yelled, 'No bloody time for fannying about like a load of daffy prima donnas, let's move.'

Shredded building stone was still whirling. 'Clive, get that bloody anti-tank bastard on your bleedin' shoulder just in case a damned Tiger sticks its 'ead round the corner before we get to the next junction. Come on, come on, you dozy lot.'

'I'll bloody swing for the sarge and his shoutin',' swore Geordie, as he wiped his nose, but the blood kept coming. 'I've broken the bastard thing, and it were my pride and bloody joy.'

Saul was laughing as he scooped up his rifle and ran, because Geordie's nose was like Bet's hunting horn, so damn big it could knock into things long before Geordie arrived. The dust was falling, choking them. Another blast, another wall, more rubble, but they scrambled over it, in a strange sort of world of their own, coughing on the dust and ignoring the grit in their eyes. God, he hoped he'd never be trapped under that lot. He couldn't bear the thought.

They ran on. The sarge sent Harry with his bazooka to circle round to the far side to join Corporal Jones and ordered Clive to head on with Saul's lot to the track ahead. Saul could hear Clive's breathing as he struggled with the anti-tank weapon but as they neared the bottom of the backstreet they were all waved down by the sarge. They knelt. Clive crept forward to the far end of the last house. They heard a whistle and looked up in surprise, for they'd never heard any of the Continentals whistle. It was a boy, at an open window, stabbing down at the street below and to the left, before stepping back. Sarge and Clive crept forward, while the platoon took up positions guarding the rear and side, with Saul and Tom searching the windows.

There was a blast, a whoosh, and a Tiger was disabled, the men bailing out as the back of the tank caved in. It had been waiting to catch the main armament column as they rumbled through the village. The platoon kept their defensive positions heading along to the main thoroughfare where they regrouped. They heard Harry's bazooka then, taking out another tank, but not completely because there was return fire. Another boy was at a window. He pointed to the houses down a backstreet, imitating rifle fire, and made a steeple shape.

The sarge saluted him, and stabbed his finger at the room, waving the boy back, then gesturing for the patrol to take five. They knelt, all senses alert. Five was not five minutes, it was five whatevers. The boy had gone, and Saul was relieved because the lad was about Joe's age, and at least his nephew was safe with Polly's mum and da at Howard House with Verity's parents. And he'd stay safe if his da, Leon, never found him. Joe's ma would be safe being hidden by Granfer at Buckby because that Leon was a vicious bastard, and though the police were keeping an eye out, they hadn't caught him yet.

The bastard should be out here, doing his best to win the war, but his type only gained from the suffering of others. He was probably flogging stuff on the black market again, now he'd escaped from custody after being charged with just that. Saul kicked at a broken tile, wiped his mouth, and drank from his flask, hearing the crunching of more broken tiles, and then Tom was beside him, kneeling in the smattering of snow. 'You doing all right, mate?'

'I is always all right, Tom. It's Geordie with 'is nose that's the problem. But at least now it's broke 'e won't give us away by sticking it out across the road long before we get there.'

Geordie, on the other side of him, muttered, 'Smug bugger, that's what you are, man.'

'But alive,' said Clive, wiping the sweat off his forehead. How could he sweat, Saul wondered, on a cold day like this? Clive saw him looking. 'It 'appens after I fire the bugger. Don't know why. Scared I'll miss, or scared I'll hit? Who the hell knows but I want to get 'ome to me missus, and that's that. No one asked them here, and now they won't go. Got t'do summat, or so I think.'

The sergeant said, seeing a signal from Lieutenant Morris who was further down the street, 'Time's up. Got to get these hornets out.' They could hear the rifle fire still going on, and the stutter of a sub-machine gun. The sarge said, 'Ready, are yer? Got to smoke 'em out, can't have 'em going on and on like they're doing. Got to get 'em over the Rhine, then maybe they'll stop sending them rockets over to us. I've 'ad just about enough, I 'ave.'

They all scrambled to their feet, Tom and Saul looking at one another, but there was no need for words. Their girls had to be safe, otherwise what was it all about?

The sergeant was edging to the corner of the building. He peered round, his fisted hand up. 'All clear,' he yelled against the growing gunfire. He scythed the air with his hand, 'On three,' he said. They listened, on three they tore across the cobbles, watching, watching every nook and cranny either side, then together Tom, Saul, Geordie, Tony and Clive forged ahead, to join up with Lieutenant Morris and his team, and Saul thought of the girls' words. 'All for one, and one for all.'

Chapter 9

Three days later, the girls prepare to head to Howard House, Dorset

Verity said, over the usual hospital clatter, and gossip, and groans, 'It's so strange to be dressed, darlings.' The bruises on her face had come out and were livid, her scratches more defined, and her arm was still in a sling. 'I know it's just cracked, not broken, or so they say, but it feels as though a ghastly clodhopper of a giant has given it a great big whack, and then another one for good measure. Quite frankly, a girl could do with a gin. Sister Askwell was quite right, we weren't ready when we told the mothers we would be. Still, a day or so late is better than no more days at all.'

Sylvia and Polly laughed as Verity gripped the bedside table, and Sylvia felt her own legs wavering. Polly muttered, 'I don't know about needing a gin, my legs already feel as though they've had one too many.' She and Sylvia gripped one another's hands as the ward swayed.

Nurse Meadowes, who was on her first day shift after a series of nights, bustled up. 'Hold on to the bedstead, girls. You should have taken your time, but what with your trainer insisting you chop-chop before I sent her packing, and Mr Fisher's son Jacob sorting out a taxi which is hooting outside the hospital, it's best you soldier on, and bugger off.'

All three girls gasped. Verity said to her, as she made her way to the other girls, 'Oh my word, and you seemed such a sweet little thing. Is it we who have driven you to this?'

Nurse Meadowes's laugh was long and loud. 'You, and especially Solly, who I insisted must wait in the corridor. You know, of course, that he is banned from the ward after causing such chaos yesterday. A sing-song indeed, and a rather rude one at that, just as doctors' rounds were starting. Sister Askwell was not amused.'

Sylvia looked back at her bed. She had left it unmade, and not even turned it back tidily. As though reading her mind, Polly murmured, 'They'll strip it, don't fret. Come on, girls.'

They followed Nurse Meadowes through the ward, shoulders back though they hurt, wearing the clothes from *Marigold* and *Horizon* that Bet had brought for them first thing that morning. They were in one of three carpet bags. She had muttered, 'You can wash and wear at Howard House. I'll be waiting at the main doors to escort you to the station and will look after the bags until then. The trainees have taken the boats on to Limehouse for loading, with one of the older trainees. They'll pick me up at the depot to head on up to Tyseley.'

As they headed towards the ward's swing doors, they waved to their friends, for that's what the patients had become. They stopped at the nurses' table in the middle of the ward, to thank Nurse Martin, the elderly woman who had come out of retirement for the war, and gave her the thank-you letter from all three of them, and the promissory note, courtesy of Sir Henry Clement and Jacob Fisher, who had come up with the idea of theatre tickets for the staff to show their gratitude.

Nurse Martin grinned. 'That's so kind, we'll use them I'm sure, though I'm not quite so certain we'll ever be the same after a few days with the waterway girls.'

Polly asked, 'Where are Nurse Newsome and Sister Askwell? We need to thank them, now that we can actually run from Sister's snapping teeth.'

The whole ward laughed. Nurse Martin looked down, smiling, then up again. 'Oh, never fear, Sister'll be at the main doors, making sure you leave the premises; Nurse Newsome is on another ward.'

'That bad, are we?' asked Sylvia, her head still swimming.

'Oh, you have no idea quite how bad,' muttered Nurse Martin. 'I think the repartee and naughtiness will go down in the annals of her behaviour diary, and not on the good side.'

She grimaced but her hazel eyes were alight with fun. 'You take care – in and out of Limehouse quickly from now on. We don't want you back again, do we, everyone?'

She conducted the 'Noooo'. 'Off you go now. Nurse Meadowes will escort you to make sure you don't visit any other wards and cause a riot.'

She stood up and kissed all three, whispering as she stepped back, 'Don't forget us. Keep in touch, let us know you're all right, eh?'

They carried on, with Nurse Meadowes beside them. The patients waved, and began to sing, 'Good-bye-ee, good-bye-ee, Wipe the tears, trainee dears, from your eye-ees.'

They left through the swing doors. Waiting for them was Solly in his dressing gown and striped pyjamas, hobbling on his crutches, his lower leg in a plaster festooned with signatures, including Nurse Newsome's, the girls' signatures and rude messages from many others. He hobbled along with them to the lift, chuckling. 'Taught 'em that trainee ditty, I did.'

Verity tucked her arm in his, careful not to become tangled in his crutch. 'Goodness, really, we would never have guessed. We will gloss over the fact that we are trained, not trainees.' But they were indeed on the point of wiping tears from their eye-ees.

At the lift, Solly pressed the button with one of his crutches. 'Thing is, the word "trained" don't scan, do it. So dig out some soul, gal, for Gawd's sake. Begging yer pardon, for the Gawd, Sylv.'

Sylvia raised her eyebrows. 'Sylv? Since when? Anyway,' she rushed on, not wanting to know. 'Please be aware, everyone, that this use of Sylv is solely a one-off, so Polly and Verity, don't even think of it.' As the lift doors started to close, Nurse Meadowes waved. They descended.

Once in reception they could feel the cold draught as the main doors opened and closed before and after the comings and goings of patients, visitors and staff. Waiting just inside the doors, as though on guard, was Sister Askwell, with a page of typewritten instructions for all three of them. She emphasised that they were to return in ten days to have their numerous stitches removed. 'They will become itchy, red, possibly sore. If you are worried and they appear septic, straight to a hospital in Sherborne or to your parents' doctor, who could, of course, remove the stitches if that was preferred. Is that clear, Lady Verity?'

Solly grimaced. 'Oh, don't call 'er that, Sister, or she'll be showing off all the way to the station.'

Sister Askwell opened the door and waved them through, putting up a hand to stop Solly. 'Just where do you think you're going, Mr Fisher? It is not your time, sadly. You are to be with this hospital for several days more, heaven help the lot of us.'

She followed the girls out, ignoring Solly's grizzles, and walked alongside them as they navigated the steps. The fresh air reminded Sylvia of the cut, their beloved cut, and she ached with homesickness, almost feeling the movement of the boat. Wouldn't it be better to go on to the boats to get well? But they couldn't because Bet, Evelyn and Mabel were taking *Marigold* and *Horizon* to Tyseley while the three of them were recuperating. Perhaps at the end of that trip the GUCCC would have a new pair ready for Bet, who they could see was waiting for them at the bottom of the steps.

She was wearing a coat, her old Harris tweed, which was strange. Idle Women usually only wore sweaters. Polly called, 'Getting feeble in your old age, then, Bet? What say you, Sylv?'

Everyone laughed, and Solly called from the top step, 'Short names be good, Sylv.'

Sister Askwell swung round and shouted up the steps, 'It's an enema for you unless you return to the foyer this minute, Mr Fisher. I've told you once to stay inside, and will not say it again. It's too cold for folks in their dressing gowns.'

At the word 'enema' he had already grumbled his way towards the doors. Verity whispered to Sylvia, 'Does she mean it?'

Sister Askwell, who had the ears of a bat, snapped, 'Indeed I do, it's the only thing he can't bear the thought of.'

'Can't say I blame him.' They turned at the sound of Steve's voice. He grinned. He was in mufti. He spread his hands. 'I have the morning off-shift and

Bet thought she might need reinforcements to make sure you behaved yourselves on the way to the station.'

Bet's smile was huge. 'But I bet you've just come straight off an all-nighter, Coppernob.'

Steve was looking only at Sylvia, when they heard Solly yet again. 'You behave yerself with our Sylv, Coppernob, and get her to the train on time.'

Sister Askwell set off up the steps. 'I've warned you, Mr Fisher . . .' Solly shut the door with a bang, but Nurse Newsome opened it again immediately and stepped out, calling, 'Well done, girls, you're an example to us all. Enjoy Sherborne, but the war still needs you, so don't do anything I wouldn't. I look forward to removing your stitches.'

Solly bellowed from the door, 'Wiv 'er teeth, I bet yer.'

The door shut behind Nurse Newsome, and Sister Askwell kissed them all. 'I'll see you off from the top step.' The taxi driver, grabbing the carpet bags and putting them into the cab, was scratching his head. 'She's a tartar that one, but salt of the earth. She'll give 'im one, I bet yer. An enema, I mean. In you get.'

Sylvia was torn between screaming and laughing as Steve took her arm and helped her into the taxi, taking the flip seat opposite; she sank into the seat, looking at him as he met her eyes. Somehow there were no words needed. He had saved her life, their lives, but it was more than that. He was here to see them safe to the station, in spite of having had no sleep. He was here for her, she knew it, just as he had been daily, slipping in just for a few minutes, when he could snatch the time. He nodded as though he could read her mind. *I want you safe and on that train*, he mouthed.

'Thank you,' she whispered in return.

'You're welcome, Sylv,' he smiled. She raised her eyebrows, knowing when to give up. 'How long's he been calling me Sylv behind my back?'

'Do you really want to know?' He grinned.

As the other two clambered in, she sat back, feeling content, although she'd thought that she'd want to be back in that nice clean ward or in the cabin the minute she left the hospital, somewhere familiar where she could lie down. But she didn't. She'd rather be here, with him.

When Polly and Verity were in, Bet followed and sat on the other flip seat. The taxi driver looked at her. 'Don't 'ave extra passengers in me taxi normal like but seeing it's for the war effort. That's what you said, ain't it, Missus?'

He winked, slammed the door, and hurried round to the driver's cab. He roared off. Bet said, turning away from the girls' stares, 'You need to put the meter on, driver.'

'Not for boater girls, I don't. I knows what they damn well do, day in and day out, and it ain't right they should be bloody bombed. I'll be dropping yer back to take the bus to Southall or Hayes, or wherever is best, Missus, and you, cocker, can pick yer Tube station and I'll drop yer there so's yer can get back on fire duty, 'ow about that? Jacob's a mate of mine, yer see. Started as a barrow boy and now's a, well, not rightly sure what 'e is, but he buys and sells and does right well too. Told me all about yer.'

He seemed to screech around the corner on two wheels, the girls clinging to one another while the carpet bags slid backwards and forwards along the centre of the floor. Polly said, 'What does he mean, extra passengers?'

Steve knocked up against the door, Bet's coat fell open and there was Timmo's puppy, nestled in the crook of Bet's arm, asleep. Sylvia stared. It was like some strange dream, all of this, and from Polly's and Verity's faces she knew they felt the same but their pain reflected hers, sharp and stabbing. Dog, oh darling Dog. Sylvia's mind and heart wept.

Steve said, into the stricken silence, 'So ruddy cold, isn't it?'

Sylvia wondered what the British would do without the weather but just as she was doing, the others seemed to hang on to his words like a lifebelt. He rubbed his hands together. The taxi driver called, 'That's cos yer not cosying up to one of your fires.'

Steve grinned. Verity, squashed in the middle between Sylvia and Polly, smiled back at him. 'You should have Sylv with you on your winter rescue work, you know. Look at her nose, she's worthy of the name Rudolf. You could send her down instead of a torch.'

Polly clung to the handle as they hurtled around another corner. 'Why didn't we think of that under the rubble?'

It was the first time they'd talked about it, and though their voices were jolly, they weren't quite right.

'Because we kept falling asleep – and I will in a minute, because, quite frankly, this is far too boring.' Sylvia was trying to smile, though, her eyes on the puppy. No, surely not, it was far too soon and besides, hadn't the mothers said they were taking it back with them?

Bet for once in her life was saying nothing as they proceeded through the traffic and into the station. She exited first, followed by Steve, digging into his pocket. 'Take a tip at least, driver.'

The cab driver shook his head. 'Get back in, I said I'd take yer two to where yer want to go.'

'I'll take the Tube, cos I have to get these girls to their trains, but thanks, mate. Really, thanks.' He jogged round the cab after Bet, who stood silently with the three girls. 'Are you going back with the cabbie to a bus stop, Bet?'

Verity nudged Sylvia's arm, and then nodded at Polly, whispering, 'A bob she makes a run for it.'

Steve was jerking his head at Bet, looking meaningfully at the puppy who had woken and was looking around. It had a collar and lead. Bet stepped forward, kissed the girls. 'I was going to come all the way, but Steve will see you on to the train and I will telephone Lady Pamela, to check on how you are.'

She spun away, taking the puppy with her. The girls dug in their pockets and each handed Verity a bob. 'Hey, Bet, thanks for running away, I don't think. Verity's won her bet,' Polly muttered, sighing with relief as Bet and the puppy disappeared inside the cab. It was too much, really it was, Sylvia thought. Too soon, too everything. Steve leaned forward and kissed Bet on the cheek, shutting the door behind her. She waved through the window at the girls, and the taxi shot off, revealing Steve with the puppy in his arms, looking at them helplessly, and three carpet bags in the road, where Bet had slid them out.

'What was I to do, say no to a woman who shoves this little thing at me, or just drop the pup on the ground?'

Polly shrugged. 'Don't be such a weakling, Steve.'

'Well,' he said, 'I didn't notice any of you saying very much to her, like no. I gather your mothers thought you would bond on the journey home but might not if you reached Howard House and this little mite was already there.'

There was another silence, until a taxi hooted at Steve, and the driver gestured to him to get out of the way as he worked his way up the rank. Steve joined the girls, who rushed to pick up the carpet bags. They made their way on to the concourse. He strode ahead. 'You'll miss your trains in a minute, and I'm supposed to get you on safely, so follow me, at the double.'

They did, looking at one another. Polly shouted so he could hear, 'You've caught bossiness from Bet, you know.'

He shouted back, 'I can see why she has to keep you in order. Hurry up, as fast as your little legs, or limps, will carry you.'

But he slowed a little so they could keep walking on their damaged legs without falling flat on their faces. Verity dug her hands into her pockets, her head down, a sure sign, Sylvia sighed, that she was sulking. Polly had their tickets in her shoulder bag, which she carried in her hand because her shoulders and upper arm were stitched. She looked as though she would bash someone with it, given half the chance.

As they reached their platform, they stopped. Steve was talking to the ticket collector at the gate. He nodded Steve through, and then the girls, calling after them, 'You have a good rest and do as your boss tells you.'

Polly gripped Sylvia's arm, then remembered the great gouge above her elbow and released her, saying, 'The world is suddenly full of people who know best, and bloody bosses. Well, I hope his fire-fighting watch are happy to look after a dog, that's all I can say.'

Steve walked before them, alongside the train, looking through the windows presumably for some seats, the puppy sort of sitting on his other arm. Polly said suddenly, 'I remember walking along this platform with Saul when we went on holiday to Burton Bradstock. Lord, I hope he's safe.' The longing in her voice was clear for all to hear, and Sylvia squeezed her hand; she reached for Verity's too, but it was still in her pocket. 'At least the two of them are together now, just like the three of us, if that's any comfort.'

Verity drew her hand from her pockets, looking curiously at the piece of paper she held, saying, 'It is, darling. It's what helps me sleep at night. I couldn't bear Tom to feel alone.'

Steve stopped and peered once more through the train window. 'Look, there are seats there. Hop in, the guard is blowing his whistle.' They heard it then, turned and saw his green flag waving. 'Just like it did when Saul and I went,' Polly whispered.

Steve opened the door, throwing in the carpet bag he'd taken from Polly. Beneath his other arm he still held the puppy. The girls clambered in. Steve held up the pup. 'Here you go, call her Pup, says Bet. She's not Dog's replacement, but a gesture from the boaters, or so Bet said to remind you. She wrote it down and slipped it into your pocket, Verity.'

Verity was still looking at the scrap of paper in her hand. The train lurched; the girls clung to the window rail. Steve yelled, the door swinging open as he moved with the train, 'Take her, or I'll have to throw her in.'

Sylvia grabbed Pup, Steve shut the door, and blew her a kiss. Sylvia leaned through the window, the puppy lying quite still in her arms, watching him, and he nodded at her. 'I will write. I have the address of Howard House,' he yelled, scribbling in the air in case she couldn't hear.

She heard and shouted, 'If you write I promise I'll reply.'

Her leg was aching, perhaps some of the stitches had torn? The puppy was too heavy for her sliced and diced arm, but what was she going to do. Drop her?

Verity pushed back the sliding door into the carriage and took the window seat, followed by Sylvia and Pup, and finally Polly, who heaved the carpet bags up into the luggage rack before sinking down. Verity stared at the poster exhorting a pilot to keep mum because the woman might not be dumb. When would it end? When would Tom be home? What the hell were they to do with a puppy? How bloody dare Bet.

She looked down at the note she had been given by Bet:

Girls, you must be smart, and accept a gift when it's offered. This little girl is a stray saved from destruction by the boaters, in memory of Dog, and just think of Pup's fate if you don't care for her.

She passed it along to the other two. Polly muttered, 'That woman is the absolute end. Pup's not a stray, she's one the boaters went out and bought, probably from someone in Buckby.'

Sylvia said, 'You realise you've accepted her name. We all have.'

'No, we haven't. It was Bet who named her,' Polly protested.

'But you've just used it,' said the woman opposite. 'So she's yours, and I reckon she needs to do a pee.'

Sylvia felt the wetness on her lap then and groaned. 'Too late,' said another woman, who was sitting by the window. 'Might be an idea to hop off at the next station and see if anything else is on the way.'

The three girls looked at one another in horror. 'I will swing for Bet,' Verity moaned.

Sylvia plonked Pup in Verity's lap. 'Stop being such a prima donna. It's your turn to do the honours, and you'd better hope the next station comes quickly.'

The woman opposite was unpacking her basket, which contained bags from some department stores along Oxford Street. 'Got any clothes in that carpet bag of yours?' she asked.

Polly sat forward. 'Yes.'

'All right,' the woman said. 'I'm getting out at Woking. You can have my basket. Put something along the bottom and let her sleep in that. She won't soil her own nest, or so they say.'

Verity tried to keep the panic from her voice as she said, 'For goodness' sake, Pol, jump to it, and thank you so much. Are you sure you can manage without the basket?'

Sylvia said, 'We must pay for it.'

The woman shook her head. 'No, take it as my offering to the dear little thing.'

Verity was stroking Pup and was gentle when she lifted her into the lined basket and held it on her lap. 'Don't know what Father will say.'

Polly sighed, 'Do you really think that the family mafia who assembled round our hospital beds haven't laid all their plans and told everyone what is happening? What we need to consider is what they would have said had we arrived without Pup.'

Verity looked at Sylvia now. 'You realise of course, Sylv, that Steve is totally in cahoots and when you next speak to him, you will have to deal very firmly and give him only one kiss and cuddle per evening.'

Sylvia blushed.

Verity reached down and stroked Pup. 'I don't quite know how it will work out, having her on the boats, but she'll just have to be chained to the chimney, like the young children, until she is old enough ... After all, we couldn't have Dog's ... well, Dog's what? Not a replacement – but how about protégée? – falling in the cut. Yes, that will do, because no one and nothing could replace our beloved Dog.'

She looked at Sylvia. 'You know, we can never thank Steve enough for saving our lives, but perhaps you can. He must have seen many things that leave him raw, and love after all is a powerful currency, and you, our lovely girl, can help to heal him should you ... Well, you know. I do think, as well, darling Sylv, that it is entirely appropriate for you to be saved by someone who knows all about the convent, because love you as we do, how can we understand what it is to be an orphan? Perhaps someone on high is looking after you both.'

Suddenly realising just where they were and the audience they had, she sat back. Sylvia was looking past her, out of the window, her face thoughtful, and Verity did so hope that the girl would allow love into her life.

Sylvia said, 'Am I to be called Sylv from now on, then?'

It was Polly who looked at the women opposite. 'Oh, I think so, when the boyfriend has also started calling her that, don't you, ladies?'

The women, agog at the discussion, all nodded. One brought out her knitting needles and

Chapter 10

Recuperation at Howard House

Lord Henry Clement met the girls, and Pup, at Sherborne Station that evening, to drive them back to Howard House. Polly thought she would collapse from exhaustion. One of her wounds, a great gash on her ribs, was seeping through its stitches and had stained her bandage, and her jumper. She sank on to the back seat, while Sylvia, smelling ever more strongly of Pup's urine, sat in the corner. Between them, in the basket which rested on the *Times* newspaper sacrificed by Henry Clement, slept Pup.

'I hope you've read your newspaper, Lord Henry?' called Polly.

'No, call me Henry, please. And yes, I have.' How strange to hear him insist on just his Christian name, thought Polly. He had always been so distant, and correct. Was it her parents' influence?

Sylvia said, as Henry pulled away from the kerb, 'So sorry about the pong. We learned our lesson and took her out at every station as per instructions from the other passengers. Naturally the other two girls managed to keep themselves spotless.'

Lord Henry burst out laughing and looked at his daughter, Verity, sitting in the front seat. 'Why am I not surprised? So, you let Sylvia bear the brunt, eh?'

Polly reached across and stroked Pup. 'Not quite all Verity's fault, just for once. The love of Sylv's life actually handed Pup to her.'

'Shut up,' muttered Sylvia.

Verity looked back at them. 'Poor Sylv, we do have a go, don't we?'

Her father said, as he drew away at a T-junction, his headlights still slitted in the dimout, 'That's what a team does.'

They drove along the narrow roads, the headlights picking out cock pheasants strutting across in front of them, while the moonlight revealed the cows grazing in the fields. Polly relaxed back, her hand still on Pup. It was almost like motoring along the cut, between fields, allotments and woods. Ah, woods, how she loved the beech trees of Cowley Lock. Homesickness pulled at her, as much as the pain of her injuries. They must get back to work, and help finish the war so their men could come back.

They were turning now to embark on the gravel drive up to Howard House, but the gates were closed. Verity moved, but her father said, 'No, let me. Injured warriors have some perks, you know.'

They watched as Lord Henry, limping slightly, clicked open the gates and drew each one back. It was then that Polly realised he was walking without his sticks. In the kerfuffle of the station it hadn't occurred to her. Verity and Sylvia noticed too, and Verity muttered, 'Good Lord.'

'He is, in every way,' agreed Sylvia. 'What on earth has happened?'

When he returned to the car, and drove through the gates, Verity asked, 'No sticks, Father?'

He laughed quietly, stopped and opened the driver's door, easing himself out. 'Must close the gates, to keep in the pigs.'

'Pigs?' queried Verity. But he was walking back to the gates. 'What in heaven's name is he doing with pigs? What's been going on?'

Polly thought she probably knew, but said nothing.

The gravel crunched as Henry returned then closed the door, which gave a subdued click, unlike the cabs they had taken. It was said the only sound in a Rolls-Royce was the ticking of the clock. However, the sound of the gravel beneath the wheels as they set off down the drive was a noise to bury any clock, let alone one in a Rolls-Royce. It was indeed such a noise that it brought back being buried. She felt sweat breaking out. But Lord Henry was saying, 'Blame Thomas, Polly's father, eh, Polly?'

Polly hoped he was smiling when he said that. Clearly he was because he went on to say, 'Thomas Holmes drew my attention to the waste of a natural resource. Apparently in years gone by pigs rummaged among the leaf litter when released into the woods and basically grazed *au naturel* all winter, and summer too. So next thing, we had obtained some and they are left to root about, though of course they are also given the kitchen scraps. Tasty our trotter friends are, too, when you can catch the blighters.'

They were passing the front of the house and heading on towards the garage, above which Tom, now Verity's fiancé, had had his quarters when he was chauffeur. Yes, that's right, she told herself. Concentrate on that, and Tom, and Saul. The almost silent engine of the Rolls-Royce ceased. Lord Henry opened her door, and Polly clambered out, wincing and holding her side as the pain caught, and its sharpness pushed aside the remembrance of rubble until the sweat cooled and she saw Lord Henry waiting, looking at her, puzzled. She groped for something to say, and finally asked, 'But what about your sticks, Lord— oh sorry, Henry?' Yes, it was all right. She was back here, safe.

'Ah, indeed. It's quite amazing how digging and delving in the vegetable garden in obedience to your father's commands loosens the old joints, my dear. The Holmeses are a formidable force.'

Polly faced him. 'Is it a problem having Mum and Dad and Joe evacuated here? I can always try and sort—' Lord Henry's hand gripped hers as he peered down at her, his face creased in a broad smile. 'Bless you, it wouldn't be the same without them. What we shall do after the war when they might want to return to Woking, I simply don't know. They are such friends of ours, now, just as you three are friends to one another.'

He walked round the other side of the car and helped Sylvia out. She carried the basket, with Pup asleep. Thankfully the puppy had not disgraced herself again. Polly found herself laughing slightly at the thought.

Verity was reaching into the boot to reclaim the carpet bags, but her father took them. 'We'll go in the kitchen way as Mrs B and Rogers insisted on preparing pheasant stew, feeling that it could wait for as long as necessary. We will all eat around the kitchen table, as we have taken to doing.'

The girls looked at one another, amazed. Was this stiff, unbending man who had made mistakes by having a mistress, Verity's real mother, in his early years of marriage, and who had withdrawn into arrogance in his shame, really talking of eating an evening supper in the kitchen?

They followed him across the cobbled courtyard, the four of them together, and Pup.

When they reached the steps down to the basement kitchen, Verity's father led the way shining his dimmed torch behind him so that they could descend safely. Verity let the others go first, because she wanted to absorb the changes in her father. Eating in the kitchen? Pigs? Digging and delving? Call me Henry? There had been such happiness in his eyes when they had scrabbled down on to the platform. She had thought at first that it was because he was happy to see them alive, but now she realised that bigger changes had been wrought, principally by having Polly's parents evacuated to keep them safe not only from the rockets, but also from Leon Arness.

Leon had been a brute of a boater married to Saul's sister, Maudie, whom he had abused, until she disappeared. He had also assaulted their son until Joe had been rescued by his Uncle Saul and Granfer, and then taken to safety with Polly's parents in Woking. It was in Woking that Leon had found them, after dodging a court case for trading on the black market, and had attacked Mr Holmes in an attempt to take back Joe, his son. He was now wanted by the police for grievous bodily harm. But would he ever stop tracking down his son as he had promised? They all felt that if he had a breath in his body he'd keep on.

She shivered at the thought. Heaven knew what he would do with Joe if he ever found him. More beatings, she supposed.

The others were already in the kitchen, and she hurried after them. In the bright kitchen, her mother and Lady Pamela Clement were hugging Sylvia, which Verity thought deserved a medal because of Pup's indiscretion, but her mother didn't flinch. She rushed to Verity when she saw her, and clasped her tightly. Verity whispered, 'Oh Mum, it's so good to see you, but now *you* stink of pee too.'

Lady Pamela stepped back, laughing. 'It's worth it to see you three, and Pup. Dear Mrs B has lots of newspaper, and Rogers has dug out your old playpen. Pup can spend some time in there while we work on her training. How does that sound? Can't have her wandering off and becoming lost.'

The Lady Pamela Clement of old would (a) not have eaten in the kitchen, and (b) certainly not have shrugged off a puppy's tiddles. Verity kissed her mother's cheek. 'It sounds splendid.'

Now Mrs B was with them, wrapping her arms around her, smelling of cooking as always. 'My, when we heard the news of your ordeal our hearts stopped, but we knew it would be all right because you three were together.'

Rogers was edging Mr B to one side. 'So, it was nothing to do with that young fireman who almost sacrificed his life, then, you dear old dumpling? You know, girls, the one who has taken a shine to Sylvia, and she to him.'

He was hugging Verity now, but gently, and whispering, 'You three get to bed as soon as these women have stopped clucking and feeding you. You look bloody awful.'

Just then there was the clatter of feet on the steps and a rushing sound as Joe scorched through the boot hall into the kitchen, all eleven or so years of him bursting with joy. He ran straight for Polly and hurled himself into her arms. 'Oh Polly, I were so scared that you be 'urt. If you was, what would our Saul do? It would fair break his heart, and Granfer's, and mine. It would 'ave broken Ma's heart too, if she knew you.'

Polly was hugging him, and as Verity looked she saw Polly pale, and tears slide down her cheeks. Verity sidestepped her mother, but before she could reach her beloved friend, Joyce Holmes was at her daughter's side. 'You sit down, my lovely. Thomas – fetch water, can't you see the staining over her ribs?'

Thomas had also paled, frozen in distress, and this man who could get Verity's father to dig and delve and buy pigs looked for a moment like a child that had broken the family heirloom. His wife's words unlocked him, and he rushed to the scullery and poured water into a glass. By the time he returned Mrs B had simply reached for the water jug on the table and done the necessary. It was Polly who grinned at her father, saying, 'Poor dad, but thanks.'

Mrs Holmes gave him no opportunity to answer, muttering, 'Well, sorry Thomas dear, I was a bit flummoxed myself.'

Polly sipped from the glass, her colour slowly returning. Sylvia was saying to Mrs Holmes, 'It's seepage, probably, Mrs Holmes. She's heavily stitched and we were warned it could happen. Perhaps we need to eat and get to bed?'

Rogers nodded at Sylvia. 'Quite right, bed is the answer, but all you girls must check your stitches. If some have snapped, or whatever they do, we must call the doc, who is at the ready – or so I gather, Henry?'

Verity's father nodded. 'Indeed he is. Come on, it's been a long day, so, chop chop, let's get on.'

The three girls looked at him in horror. Verity sighed, 'Good grief, you've become Bet, Father.'

Henry looked shamefaced as Joe came to stand beside him, leaning against him. 'Well, she has rung every evening and given her orders, hence the doc on standby, the bedroom set up with three beds to emulate – well, the cabins, I suppose, and the pheasant stew to make you feel at home—'

Verity interrupted, seeing things more clearly. 'Ah, and all of us eating round the table, like the boaters.'

All the Howard House occupants looked at one another, and then at Verity, as if she were mad. Rogers said, pulling out chairs, 'Certainly not, that's been the case for quite some while. Why heat that huge dining room, and even more so, the cottage? So we've amalgamated the families here under one roof. We all prefer it, anyway.'

Verity smiled across at her mother and mouthed *wonderful*, while Joe grinned at Sylvia, 'I's special glad to see yer, Sylvia, cos we's just tight friends. We can go out drawing together, and yer can tell me what it's like to be buried.'

Sylvia laughed aloud, and it was the first time the experience had seemed remotely funny. Joe looked offended, but she said, 'You're a tonic, young Joe, and there's nothing I'd like more than for you to show me where I'm going wrong, yet again.'

By eight the girls had retired to Verity's old room, where three beds had been set up. They looked around. Each had a bedside table, and light. Each had a jug of water, and a bell to ring. 'This could be my dormitory at the orphanage, though there were twelve in that,' Sylvia said, almost seeing it as she spoke.

Polly sat on the bed, trying to ease off her jumper. The other two girls helped. Sylvia checked the bandages, and slowly unwrapped the one from around Polly's ribs. The bruising was extensive but the stitches had held. Verity dumped the soiled bandage in the bag that Lady Pamela had given to them, while Sylvia dabbed the bruises with iodine, ignoring Polly's fuss. 'Bite on a bullet, why don't you?' she muttered.

Polly whispered through the pain, 'I would if I had one, Sylv, or is it Miss Bossy Boots?'

Verity peered at the wound. 'Doc Havers should have a look at it tomorrow, just in case. Can you imagine if we weren't up to taking the boats up the cut? We'd never live it down with the boaters. You know how they continue, come what may.'

Sylvia wound the new bandage round Polly's ribs to keep the dressing in place, tucked in the tail and patted Polly's shoulder. 'Tickety-boo, madam.'

After they had checked and dressed one another's wounds they collapsed into bed. Sylvia usually slept alone in the butty, except for the two weeks when Tom had needed to recover from his broken leg, and had shared *Marigold*'s cabin with Dog before reporting for duty. The girls had shifted into her butty cabin then and perhaps that's when they had really started to form their friendship, Sylvia thought now. Would Verity tell him that Dog was dead? Probably not; why distress him when he had his own problems? She tried to find a comfortable position, but it was impossible, and instead she looked round the room, feeling that at least she wasn't alone.

Verity called, 'Shall we turn out our bedside lights? We can use our bells to wake one another if there's a problem, and if it's a huge one we can yank the bell pull by the fireplace and it will ring through to Rogers's quarters.'

Polly murmured, half asleep, 'Yes, understood Lady Verity, over and out. We need to sleep.'

They all laughed, and turned off the lights. Within half an hour they were turning them back on. In the ward the nurses' desk had a light on all night. Here, the darkness was like being buried again. They plumped their pillows and tried to settle, leaving the bedside lights on, comforted by the soft pools of light. At last Sylvia's body loosened, her lids growing heavy as she heard the sound of breathing, of Polly coughing. But then, ouch, a moan, and the sharpness of rubble, the dust, the pain, the darkness. The loneliness, the sticky eyes, the sucking that had taken the breath from her body. She screamed and woke to find the other two sitting up, staring around the room.

Sylvia whispered, 'Sorry, so sorry I screamed.'

Verity shook her head. 'No, it was me.'

Polly eased herself up on her pillows. 'It was me. I was buried again.'

The girls heard knocking on the door, and it eased open. It was Lady Pamela and Mrs Holmes, both of whom had apparently kept their doors open, and lain awake, on alert. Lady Pamela rang the bell pull, ignoring the girls' protests. 'Mrs B will have my guts for garters if I don't let her know. She has the makings of cocoa all ready and will be bustling into the kitchen to brew up. Rogers will be bringing it up any second.'

The girls looked at one another. Verity asked, 'How on earth would Mrs B hear it in Rogers's quarters? Her quarters are upstairs.'

Her mother was busy folding their clothes, which they had just flung on to the chair. 'Oh do mind your own business, Verity. You young ones are not the only ones who . . . Well, who . . . You know what I mean.'

The girls were exchanging looks as Rogers appeared in the doorway, in a checked dressing gown and slippers, carrying a tray of cocoa, his grey hair awry. He set it down, and carried mugs to the girls, each of whom was wearing a pair of Verity's old pyjamas. About to leave the room, the silver tray tucked beneath his arm, he halted as though he was thinking hard. He turned, looking at Lady Pamela.

'If I may, madam?'

Lady Pamela nodded, 'Oh really, Simon, you know you may, just as you always do.' She glanced at the girls. 'We're long past all that butler nonsense.'

He addressed the girls. 'I saw many things on Flanders fields. I heard many things. Many things happened to me; hurting me, frightening me. On my return I had dreams, but they were more than dreams. It was as though I was there. I woke crying out. It is natural. Just remember that you are not there now. You are safe. Of course, you will have to go to Limehouse again, but you now know to go in and out like streaked lightning, though that might only be at four miles an hour.' He smiled at them all. 'I also killed, just as your father did, Verity, and yours, Polly, and perhaps yours too, Sylvia? That is also something one has to dream out, or think out, or work out, or talk out of yourselves somehow, just as your men will have to on their return. So trust in the fact that you are safe, and together.'

He nodded to them all, then added, 'Henry and I served together throughout the war, but we could talk. It helped. Even so, it took some years of peace to settle us down. You have experienced an afternoon. You will recover because you have one another.' He left.

They drank their cocoa, and Lady Pamela sat on the end of Verity's bed while Mrs Holmes sat with Polly. The talk was normal, desultory, homely. They kissed the girls goodnight, and suggested they might like to leave a light on. Verity explained about the nurses' desk. Her mother pointed to the lamp by the window. 'Why don't I put that on, then it is dark

Chapter 11

Their recovery continues

Sylvia heard shouting and dragged herself awake, seeing the other two girls asleep, and the curtained window through which light slid. There was a painting of bluebells above the opposite bed, and a fire glowing in the grate. But, she thought, confused, they hadn't had a fire in the dormitory. So where . . . She looked for Harriet, but no, she had done as she promised and become a postulant nun at St Cecilia's convent attached to the orphanage. Sylvia wished she didn't keep remembering how she had wept the morning she found her best friend dressed and leaving the dormitory. Harriet had held out her hand: 'Come on, it's meant to be, Sylvia. We've been called. I told you we had when you had that dream. I told you we owed it to the sisters, to God.'

Sylvia shut her eyes. The two of them had been a family within a much larger family yet she had let Harriet leave, alone, even though they were so close that there was no space between them, as one of the nuns had once said. 'No,' Sylvia had said to Harriet.

'Not yet, I can't even remember the dream, not really.'

Harriet had stood by her bed, leaned over and said, 'But I remember you calling out to God. One day you will remember and join me.'

She had walked silently to the door, and Sylvia had hid herself beneath the bedclothes, because—

'What on earth is that shouting?' murmured Polly.

Sylvia clung to her words, just as she had clung to the canal, a place she had run to – anything to keep busy, to escape her betrayal. She made herself listen to the sounds from outside.

Verity groaned. 'Good grief, someone's shouting. Is it Father?'

Polly was scrambling from her bed. 'No, it's my dad. Are they having a row?'

Sylvia joined her team, at the window, and while Polly pulled aside the left-hand brocade curtain, she pulled the right, and together they looked out on to the frost-glazed front lawn and gravel drive.

'Well, I'm blowed,' Polly sighed. They watched as about ten men, some with rifles on their shoulders, one with a musket, and another with a pitchfork, drilled to Mr Holmes's commands. They weren't in uniform, but surely . . . ?

Verity was opening the window, but Polly stopped her, grinning. 'The Home Guard may have been stood down, but clearly this lot want to go on playing soldiers, so let them. Look at your father with his sergeant's stripes on his arm.'

Sylvia wiped condensation from the window and said, 'They like being in a team too, it gives them a purpose I suppose, makes them feel useful.'

Polly smiled at her. 'You so often hit the nail on the head, oh wise one, but quite what foe they think they'll take on, Lord knows.'

Verity had turned away and was trying to undo her pyjama buttons. 'Quick, give me a hand, let's get up, heaven knows what time it is. Joe was going to show us how well he can ride Maisie, and then we can get to the bottom of the Howard House militia. I do just love that Father's taking orders from your dad, Pol.'

Sylvia said, 'More importantly, why haven't Rogers and Mrs B married? It seems so strange to . . . Well, you know.'

Polly said, dragging on her trousers, 'Nowt so queer as folk.'

The other two just raised their eyebrows, Verity muttering, 'Must you always come out with an idiotic saying?'

Polly picked up her folded jumper and hurled it at Verity, who returned fire with a slipper, leaving Sylvia to add to the mayhem with a pair of socks, and so it went on until they were worn out from laughing. They flopped on to Polly's bed and lay there exhausted but then they heard marching on the gravel, and Thomas Holmes bawling. 'Left, I said, Henry, I mean sergeant. Left.'

Galvanised, they threw clothes on and headed for the door, only to be stopped mid stride as Sylvia flung out her arm, insisting they tidy the room. 'Poor Mrs B. We're not in our cabins now, you know. Well, in your cabin, which is always a pigsty.'

They even made the beds and smoothed down the bedspreads, hearing the commands and the crunch of gravel, then Joe's voice, clear as a bell. 'Uncle Thomas, aren't them up yet?'

They rushed to the window as Henry Clement broke off in the middle of an about-turn, replying, 'They will be when they're ready.'

At that moment there was a chaos of falling bodies as someone bashed into Henry. Then a clatter, a curse, and a voice shouting, 'Sarge, he trod on me foot, cos you stopped, you daft bugger, mid-turn.'

At that, they tore down to the kitchen as fast as their injuries allowed, which was more of a staggered limp. Mrs B, who was busy chopping vegetables at the table, looked up. She pointed with her knife. 'Sit yourselves down and I'll bring tea and toast.'

The girls shook their heads. All had changed now at Howard House, with everyone mucking in. 'We'll sort out breakfast, you get on,' said Verity.

Polly went to the playpen, but Pup was missing. Fear clutched at Sylvia's heart. 'Where's our Pup?' they said together. Mrs B laughed. 'Rogers has her. One of our brave soldier boys has brought his sheepdog as usual; she will teach her manners. She's quite safe and they're both secured in a pen in the vegetable garden. Can't have Pup falling in the canal, can we?'

Verity slid up to Mrs B and put her arm around her. 'My, my, you have sorted things out.'

Mrs B seemed to smile at something only she could see. 'We've had your Bet on the phone quite a lot. She has many good ideas. It's quite tiring, really.'

The girls were chuckling as they ate their toast and gulped their tea. As they dragged on their boots in the hall Joe careered down the steps, carrying under his arm a metal helmet with earpieces. 'Oh do 'urry, all o' yer. The aunts won't let me start until yer come over to the schooling paddock, too. I'm so glad you came at t'weekend, so's I could see yer proper.'

'Right behind you,' called Polly, 'but give me a kiss first, because we're sort of aunts too.'

'I's eleven now, Polly. I doesn't 'old hands or give kisses. But cos yer is aunts I will give yer one tonight when me day is done.' He turned and stalked up the steps. The girls grimaced. Verity muttered, 'Darlings, I feel very old now we're labelled as 'aunts', and to be given a kiss appointment by an eleven-year-old just about takes the biscuit.'

Sylvia said, 'Oh, stop moaning, and get up the steps.'

They followed Joe through the yard to the sandy schooling paddock.

Verity and Sylvia leaned on the paddock fence, their arms folded on the top bar as Joe strode to his skewbald pony, Maisie. Verity said, 'It's a frisky little thing, but then ponies are. I remember cantering my own pony, Toby, across Father's fields, where sheep grazed – and what a handful he turned out to be. I hunted my mare, Star, later, but Mother set her at a fence on the hunting field and she died. It was when we were on the cut, do you remember, girls? What a fuss I made, but it was an accident. Lordy, I still miss her.'

Joe was standing by Maisie while Verity's mother tied on his helmet. He hated it, they could tell.

Verity went on, 'I can remember Father saying, as he did up the chinstrap for me, 'If you come off, you could crack your head open, so wear this or it's no riding, do you understand?'

She grinned as Sylvia whispered, 'It looks like a soldier's tin hat.'

'That's precisely what it is, from the 1914 to 1918 World War, made of steel, and with a leather chinstrap that Father tested and tested for me. Joe must wear it. Imagine if he came off.'

Sylvia, still leaning on the bar, shook her head. 'No, let's not imagine. Your father is a sensible man, you know, Verity. It must be wonderful to be cared for like that.'

The girls fell silent, and Verity put her arm around Sylvia's shoulders. Once Sylvia would have shrugged her off, but she had slowly dropped her guard and shared her thoughts with them, and it was such a relief, because her last friend had been Harriet. She remembered them playing cat's cradle in the playground with old parcel string. She looked at her hands and could feel it wrapped around them, as Harriet picked out the crossed strands with thumb and forefinger.

She dropped her hands to her side. She didn't want to think of the muddled strands of Harriet, postulancy, and the convent wrapping around and through her mind. She conjured up Steve instead, and the mere thought of him made her settle.

Polly said, 'I'm pretty certain that Sister Augustine and the nuns cared like that for you, and still do, though I can see that they share it amongst all the others in the orphanage, so it's not the same I—'

Verity interrupted. 'Oh, I think love can be shared far and wide, but I agree with Polly, which is why, our lovely Sylv, I think you and our other coppernob need and suit one another very well. I know I've said it before but you both understand where you have come from, and there's bound to be a sort of shorthand between you. And there's also the beginnings of love; it already sticks out a mile from you both, doesn't it, Pol?'

Sylvia smiled, because as she watched Joe, walking along as though he was braced against the world, leading Maisie around the schooling ring, she recognised Steve's walk. Did she walk like that, too, because, like them, she was braced against the world? Was that why she had grown to love this child so much? After all, Joe didn't know yet that his mother was still alive so he was almost an orphan. When would they tell him about Maudie? When she was better and remembered him properly, she supposed.

She sighed, because it was worse for Joe. To him his father was someone who hurt him, who was unmitigatingly violent to anyone who crossed or challenged him, while she and Steve just had a blank. Steve, with his red hair, his sooty, smiling face and the feel of his hand as he helped her to the opening of the escape tunnel . . . She relaxed. Yes, she thought, the girls were right, it *was* love. But she was suddenly frightened because it was all *too* wonderful, which was ridiculous, so she concentrated on Joe being given a leg-up now on to Maisie's back, settling himself, and walking her forward and round the ring. He grinned at them as he passed, proud as punch, and Sylvia wished she could draw him, and somehow capture that smile. But Joe and Saul were the ones with the talent. For her, it was pleasure, and much of that was the link it created with this lad who had every reason to be wary of her.

'Look,' Polly urged them. Joe was riding around the paddock, the walk changing to a rising trot. Verity called, 'Grip with the knees, Joe.'

'I is,' he shouted back. 'Isn't I, Auntie Pam?'

'I think you probably are, but a bit tighter, maybe.'

The girls shared a proud smile, and Polly said, 'Shows how much he's grown into himself. Saul would be happy, and Granfer too, not to mention Maudie. I do hope she is still recovering well. I must write to them, because they will have heard the news of our debacle.'

At the mention of Joe's mother, Sylvia wondered aloud when Joe would be told his mother lived. Polly shook her head. 'Mum told me last night that Granfer says not to, and he is her grandfather, after all. He says that Maudie is still not herself though she is improving. Leon must surely think she's dead, thank heavens, and that's her best defence against him.'

Their fathers joined them, leaning on the paddock fence, both of them puffing on their pipes. It was a comforting smell, and Polly said to her father, slipping her arm in his, 'Had a few spare coupons, did you?'

He took his pipe from his mouth and smiled. 'Mr Burton, your old boss at the solicitors', doesn't smoke, sensible fellow, so he sends down some he gets on his coupons. If Henry performs well in the garden, he gets half.'

Henry guffawed, and Sylvia asked, 'Does Mr Burton ever come to see Joe? He should, really, because he was so supportive with his legal advice when I mucked up and thought Joe'd burned our butty, when it was Leon's man all the time. I can't believe I could have been so stupid.'

There was a brief silence, then Mr Holmes muttered, 'That's all in the past and forgotten, so you should forget too, but as you're all topsy-turvy at the moment from the explosion, we'll forgive you.' He winked at her. 'Mr Burton will visit, with the missus, when they both feel better but it takes time when you lose a child. As you know, the lad was in submarines. His was sunk.'

The three girls looked at one another, shocked: there were so many hopes and dreams down the pan, and now Mr and Mrs Burton would never be grandparents. Thank heavens Mr and Mrs Holmes had Polly, Sylvia thought, otherwise they too would be without children, after their own son's death.

Henry had leaned forward, tapping his hand on the top bar in time with Maisie's stride, as Joe cantered the last few paces with his arms crossed. 'That's my boy,' he called, then swung round to the girls. 'Of course, our hearts stopped when Bet phoned with the news of the V2. We couldn't have borne to lose you all.'

Verity slapped him on the back. 'A great massive dollop of thanks goes to Sylv's Steve.'

'Oh, do shut up,' Sylvia said with a grin.

Polly and Verity reached across and squeezed her hands as they rested on the bar. Verity continued, 'I know I'm going on, but he's right for you, he really is, and he's special to us all. He's given you back your life, so you must live it, darling.'

Verity's voice was so serious that her father and Mr Holmes looked from Verity to Sylvia. Mr Holmes said, 'Of course she's going to live it, and he's saved you all, not just Sylv. What's more, you'll all get better and be back on duty on the cut, and before you know it, the war will be over.' He stopped, then looked at Henry. 'Well, we'll get on differently, I suppose, because we've all lived fuller lives these last few years, haven't we, Henry?'

Henry nodded, his eyes narrowing as he watched Joe. He called, 'Pammy darling, how about putting up a few poles spread about the paddock and see if Maisie and Joe want to try a few titchy jumps. What say you, Joe, and you, the "aunts"? We need the agreement of the bosses, after all, don't we, Joe?' Joe's laugh rang out in the frosty air. 'Yer so funny, Uncle Henry.'

As the two 'aunts' spread out the poles Joe waited while Maisie tossed her head. Harriet had tossed her head, thought Sylvia and wished she wasn't suddenly remembering her past so clearly. Mr Holmes was right, she was all topsy-turvy. Harriet had tossed her head as she turned from her that last time in the dormitory, accusation in her eyes, and left, walking from the room alone.

'Off you go, Joe,' called Joyce Holmes.

'Look at me, girls.' Joe flew over the poles. Sylvia clapped, harder, and harder, wanting the pain so that her memories would stop. Polly put her arm around her, 'Steady on,' she said, 'and dry your face, dearest Sylv.'

Joe called, 'Why are you crying?'

Polly replied, 'She's not, the wind is fresh and making our eyes run. You just mind your own business, nosy parker, or you'll fall off.'

His laugh rang out again as Lady Pamela sent him round the paddock for one last canter. 'I love it so,' he shouted as he drew abreast of them and then careered on.

The girls walked back to the stables with Lady Pamela and Joyce Holmes, while the men headed off into the garden to resume clearing the decks for their spring planting projects, while the ex-Home-Guard patrols continued around the periphery of the grounds. Polly muttered, 'I dare say the wives are heartily glad to get rid of their men for a few hours, but what enemy are they defending us from, or does it even matter? Perhaps they're just feeling worthwhile.'

Verity took the saddle from Joe and hoisted it on to the peg. Polly hung up the bridle, while Sylvia helped brush Maisie down. Joe said, 'I 'as finished my story about Lettie, the sheepdog, Sylv. But I 'as to start a new one for the class competition.'

Sylvia peered over the top of Maisie at the girls. 'Did you hear that, you two? Joe's writing something for a competition.'

Polly and Verity leaned on the stall door, arms crossed. 'Is there a particular subject?'

He shook his head. 'We 'ave to write about something that we does think is brave, or good, or interesting. But I is not tellin' yer, nor no one, cos it has to be just our own work. Yer can read me Lettie stories, though.' His smile was shy.

'Tell you what,' Verity said, as Maisie pawed at the ground and straw mites danced in the air. 'We're going in now and leaving you with the aunts who are about to bustle in from the tack room after doing who knows what, to what knows who—' Joe laughed. 'You're funny like yer da, Verity.'

Verity wagged her finger at him. 'So perhaps you'd bring it to our room, or into the sitting room and we can all share it. Have Lettie and Granfer seen it?'

He shook his head. 'You'll be the very first. I finished the last line last night, cos I want to get on with the new one at school tomorrow, all sort of fresh in me mind. Give me the brush, Sylv. I'll finish her.'

The girls waved, and walked, trying not to limp, back across the cobbles to the steps leading to the kitchen. Sylvia said, feeling every footstep as it jarred her body, 'I really do need to sit down.'

When they had almost reached the house they heard the clatter of boots on the flagstoned boot hall, then two men hurried up the steps, one carrying a pitchfork, the other a musket. They saluted, then hurried across the yard. 'Next shift for the patrol,' whispered Sylvia.

They walked, grinning, into the kitchen, which was when Mrs B told them that the patrols weren't aimless, they were designed to give warning not just of Germans, but Leon, should he discover Joe's whereabouts. At the first sound of whistles, the police would be telephoned and Joe would be gathered into the house.

Polly gasped, 'Have you heard something, then? Is he alive? Does he suspect Joe's here?'

Mrs B, making pastry, shook her head. 'Who knows to both of those questions with all the rockets but if he's survived, he found Joe at your parents' in Woking, so we're taking no chances.'

She went on to tell them that Joe was registered at school as Joe Clement, his address as Howard House, none of which would ring a bell with Leon, or so they and the police chief, a friend of Henry's, hoped. The problem was that Leon had simply disappeared after savagely beating Thomas Holmes almost to death when the wretched tyke found Joe living in Woking with Polly's parents, so was still a threat. People such as he seldom gave up, as long as they were still breathing, and he considered Joe to be his property; it was as simple as that.

Rogers entered, the *Sketch* newspaper under his arm. Mrs B said, 'I've lit the fire in the sitting room, so it's snug for you girls. Off you go and sit, and the doctor will be here –' she looked at the clock – 'ah, about now.'

'Doctor?'

Rogers was sitting down, his newspaper open. He peered over his half-moon reading glasses at them. 'I gave him a call half an hour ago, to tell him you were well and truly awake. It was always the plan, and I think you were told yesterday

188

evening, so best you do as the boss has just said, and go to the sitting room, to save him traipsing up the stairs to your bedroom. He has quite likely come from some farm or other, and his boots will be muddy, and his hands will be cold because he will ride that damn horse of his on his rounds. But then, petrol is still short.'

The girls made their way up the stairs and through the green baize door. They had just settled themselves on the settees which faced each other either side of the fire when Sylvia said, 'I can't believe Leon would ever find our lad—'

The doorbell rang. Verity hurried as quickly as she could to the green baize door and called down the back stairs, 'We'll get it.'

'Right you are,' called Rogers from halfway up the back stairs. 'Get the old sausage to wipe his feet on the doormat. He never sees the mud, somehow, treads it everywhere, he does.'

Polly was already answering the door. Into the majestic hall strode Dr Havers, his black medical bag in his hand and his stethoscope hanging round his neck. His jodhpurs were mucky, his boots indescribable, and his tweed hacking jacket had seen better days. Sylvia called from the sitting room door, 'Good morning, Doctor. Would you mind wiping your feet, or so said Rogers.'

The doctor, a grizzled old man whose cold red nose was competition for Sylvia's, laughed, 'Ghastly old nag, he is.'

Nonetheless, he had a go, then stormed ahead of Polly into the sitting room, where Sylvia and Verity were now sitting on one sofa. Polly followed him in. He plonked his bag on a rather nice antique side table and looked at all three of them. 'I received a telephone call yesterday from a Bet Burrows instructing me – I say again, instructing me – to check you three over, on pain of death if I did not. This hot on the heels of a call from your father, Verity. Half an hour ago, I had a further call, this time from Simon Rogers, to say you were up and about and before you got up to no good you were to be checked over and given your orders. I gather you've been playing with a V2. Nasty creatures, they are. You should know better.'

He had moved to stand with his back to the fire, but while he talked, he'd been looking at all three of them, his eyes keen. Verity stood. 'I'm really sorry, Dr Havers. Bet was our trainer, and still thinks she is.'

'Oh, come along, Verity. You should be pleased you have someone who will go out to bat for you – you all should. Now, this is what will happen.' He was rubbing his hands together. Sylvia presumed it was to warm them, though he looked so gleeful she wondered if it was because the examination would hurt.

'I will check you over now, and then, in seven or eight days' time, I will remove the stitches. That will hurt.' The hand-rubbing seemed to take on new energy. Sylvia watched as though hypnotised. 'Then you will be signed off to return to your boats. So not only do you have someone who takes care of you, but you can comfort yourself it is merely because you are useful to the war effort.'

Verity was smiling. 'You never change, Dr Havers. And how is Mrs Havers?'

He smiled in return. 'My dear wife is still making those dreadfully hard scones, dear Verity, that I have to secrete in my pockets until I can safely dispose of them. Thankfully Fred, my horse, still likes them. Now, who's first, unless you'd like to retire one by one to the privacy of a bedroom?'

Privacy? thought Sylvia. Since when did boaters need, or expect, privacy?

Dr Havers started with Polly, pursing his lips at the slash on her ribs. 'That hurt, but they've cleaned it well, there's no infection and the scar should heal.' He cocked his head at her. 'Mark you, you'll have your fair share of callouses from the hauling ropes, presumably. Those should go, or at least minimise once you are no longer playing silly buggers with it all, but the wound scars won't. My suggestion is to wear them as badges of honour.'

He checked her arm, her shin, and examined the others, still with desperately cold hands, and a stethoscope which felt even colder, all the time amusing them with a running commentary. Then he plonked himself on Lady Pamela's silk sofa next to Verity – Lady Pamela would not be pleased, thought Sylvia, and exchanged amused glances with the other two. He wrote out his notes, saying, 'I will leave dressings. You must keep the wounds as clean as is already the case, but you will be able to return to duties at the time prescribed by the esteemed Bet Burrows, though gently. Don't want to open anything up, do we?'

Verity smiled slightly. 'Gently isn't possible, but we'll do our best, because, no, we don't want to open anything up.'

Dr Havers made no attempt to leave, but sat there for a few moments, staring at the fire. 'Would you like a cup of tea?' Sylvia wondered.

He waved a no and started to talk. 'I dare say Verity's father has spoken to you about the mind, or one of the other "elders", or perhaps not. You see, something like this V2 event is most strange. You deal with it at the time, but the mind can't leave it alone, or other rubbish drifts to the surface. Don't be frightened, weather it, support one another, and if you feel the darkness reclaiming you too fiercely, talk to someone – perhaps your trainer, because it sounds as though she could frighten away a million shadows, or even a doctor. Finally, remember that each of you can always telephone me.'

He patted Verity's leg. 'There you are then. Must away. Dear old Fred will be wondering how long I'll be and we haven't finished yet. Perhaps I could just wash my hands before I go, some patients are so damned fussy. "You wash them 'ands before yer come anywhere near me, Lord knows where they been," they shout.'

He was off, across the hall, leaving mud on the silk rug between the two sofas, and more in the hall.

The girls clustered around the front door, with Polly looking thoughtful. 'Does anyone talk to Steve about his dreams?'

The doctor returned and shook their hands. 'Steve?' he said, opening the huge oak door.

Polly replied, 'The fireman who rescued us, hanging upside down to clear a way through, then joining us in the cellar under a weight of rubble, with the smell of gas becoming worse. He got us out, and we thought he'd gone up in the explosion, but he hadn't.'

Her voice was shaking by the end. Verity held her hand, saying quietly, 'He was so brave, Dr Havers.'

Dr Havers looked thoughtful. 'He's trained of course, but like our soldiers, sailors and airmen, policemen, ambulance men . . . everyone, really, there is a price to pay. So yes, he will have dreams, he should talk, and more importantly someone should listen. But on the whole, those whose job it is to be in danger will joke their way through it, and chat to their chums, who understand because they have been there too. A bit of shorthand, shared history, whatever you like to call it. I expect you three do that, if only to get through the misery of winter on the canal. I once had to deal with a boater. Lord above, tough? Could have beaten me at one-armed wrestling any day. Her husband could too.'

He left, almost skipping down the steps, untying Fred, mounting him, and trotting briskly down the drive. The girls swept up the mud, quietly.

Chapter 12

Steve and Dodge tackle more V2s

At the fire station mess table, Steve finished writing his letter to Sylvia. He hardly dared to think she really wanted to hear from him. Well, if not she could rip it up unread, and he would know where he stood when he received no reply. But by heavens, he hoped she did write back, because he'd love to have someone of his own, and a family. It must be strange to belong. Not that he would marry just anyone, it would have to be love. He paused . . . marry? He'd only just met Sylvia, but yes, marry, he realised, because this was someone he wanted to spend the rest of his life with. He laid his pen down, surprised at the enormity of the thought, and the rightness, then a noise made him look up. Narrow camp beds were scattered around the room, some of the shift, both Auxiliary Fire Service and National Fire Service, were sleeping, some writing or reading, others playing cards, but that would change instantly when the bell went.

He folded the letter and placed it in the envelope, then dug out his diary with the address of Howard

House written in the back. He copied it out and had just licked the envelope and rubbed it down when Dodge stirred in his pit, shouting out, then jerking awake, before sitting up, sweat soaked. The sleepers slept on, the others took no notice because sometimes dreams worked that way, and if Dodge wanted to talk, he'd come across, pour a cuppa, and Steve would listen.

Dodge pulled up his braces, twanged them, scratched his head, and trundled across, his hair rumpled. 'You writing to the other coppernob?' he asked, going to the kitchen counter and pouring a mug of stewed tea. 'Yer want one an' all, Stevo?'

'No, you're all right, Dodge.' Steve stuck a stamp on the envelope while Dodge slopped in some milk and came and sat, taking a sip, and grimacing. 'Tastes like my old woman's when it's been brewing for weeks.'

'Stop with your moaning,' Steve said, patting the letter and handing it to an AFS woman who had just come in from the office and was heading for the counter where she poured two teas. 'Will you put that in the "out" tray, love?' Steve asked.

The girl, a blonde, grinned. 'Seems our Dodge think's yer've found yer love, Coppernob.'

Steve opened his hands to Dodge. 'Can't you keep that great big gob shut?'

Dodge grinned, slurped, and put the mug down. 'Seems not,' he said. 'So—' he began but the blasted bell broke into the room. Those asleep, all wearing their boots, sprang up, automatically dragging on their jackets. The card players threw their hands down, same with the books and pens. They rushed to the pole, where the sub waited at the bottom.

'V bloody 2, out Crewswall Road way,' the sub-officer yelled.

Dodge and Steve ran to the pump engine with some AFS, others headed for the towing unit with a trailer pump, while the rest pounded to the turn-table ladder unit and followed Steve out of the fire station, still dragging on their kit in the cab.

Crews were already at the scene when they arrived, including a turntable ladder from the other watch working about a hundred feet further up at the top of the street. The sub waved them to a halt. 'Get down the other end, it's a ruddy hospital.'

Flames were roaring skywards, patients and staff were evacuating. Steve drove the pump engine as close as he could, the others following until flagged down. The noise and heat roared – the paint on the appliances was bubbling. Steve jumped down in time to see a wall collapse on to the other watch's turntable ladder, taking it down and the firemen with it. He wouldn't watch. He couldn't, he had work to do. The heat took his breath away. Gas? They'd have to find the valve. He swung round to the sub. 'The valve, guv?'

'AFS is on to it. Tell that bloody hose-layer to get back, Dodge, he's far too bloody close.'

Dodge ran towards the lorry and there was an explosion. It took out the lorry, and Dodge. Steve stared, then started to run, but was grabbed by the sub. 'No, you can't do anything. Get back to your pump, sort out the AFS wallahs.'

Automatically Steve obeyed, running to his appliance. There were two divisional officers on the scene and four superintendents, and several AFS women who had driven them in staff cars. The only good thing about the bastard rockets was the light from the fires. It had been the same in the Blitz, but then the fires had also guided in more bombers. At least the ruddy rockets were pilotless.

At the pump engine, the AFS were rolling out the hoses and the firemen at their turntable ladder were doing what they should. He spun round but couldn't see the sub. 'Where's he gone?' Steve yelled.

'To the roof,' Sonny Jim called back, directing his hose at the fire. 'AFS has cut off the valve.'

'Right you are. But the whole bloody lot's caught, so it'll go on, whatever.'

Steve was directing his hose at the flames. The stream of water seemed pathetic against the massive soaring flames and the screams. The nozzle sprayed out the water. He was so damned hot even though it was January. There had been frost this morning, but the sun had come out for a while this afternoon. They'd been out all the previous night too, just an ordinary fire. How could anyone leave a pan on a cooker, and burn down a whole terrace? His mind was full of fragments of thoughts. It's what happened, it kept them sane. He wouldn't think of Dodge, not yet. The job had to be finished.

The staff and patients were filing past him, and then the wall to the left of him collapsed. A section of the Rescue Squad was directed to it because there had been patients and staff passing along the street to safety as it fell. He thought of Sylvia, safe. Thank God, thank God. And the girls. He wasn't going to think of Dodge's missus and her stewed tea. He'd have to go and see her, course he would. He directed the jet higher. Was the sub still up there? Quite right too, working out what the hell was happening. Not sure he'd like that burden. Give an order and be left wondering whether it was right or wrong.

Another wall fell. The ground shuddered and the bricks flew through the air. They hit him, one on the mouth. He tasted the blood. He directed the water higher – the flames were roaring from the window, there was so much dust.

So much noise. Was she coming to the reunion? He had to think of that, not Dodge his mate, his mentor, who'd had him in his home for meals, to stay, and been a father. Yes, that was right. Dodge was like a dad – or was he? He didn't know what a dad was. Like the priest? He barked out a laugh. A dad didn't sit the other side of the confessional grille.

He felt a hand on his shoulder. Sub shouted in his ear: 'Step back. If that wall comes down, you'll be done for.'

He'd been given an order so he stepped back. The heat was more than heat. It was sharp, deep, and the appliance was still blistering, his face was so hot it would blister too. It wasn't the first time, and it wouldn't be the last. Who would take Dodge's place? Someone, because someone always did. But not for the missus. Who'd work his veg plot at the back of the long, thin garden, and the shared allotment? Well, he, Steve, could.

His hands seemed stuck on the nozzle, like claws. Sometimes the watch were like this all night, and as the fire died they would start to feel the cold and their hands would freeze even more solidly in place. He looked at the AFS bloke who'd taken Dodge's hose: it was Alfie, who nodded. Yes, someone had taken Dodge's place, because they always did; it was a chant in his head.

As the turntable ladder blokes turned their hoses on the upstairs windows Alfie called, 'You 'ear that, Steve?'

Steve looked across. 'Hear what?'

'I heard someone crying.' He nodded towards a wall that had plummeted to the ground, the bricks sprawling across the kerb, skidding from the heap of rubble at their centre.

Steve looked for the Rescue Squad. No sign of them. 'Take me hose under your other arm, I'll have a dekko.'

'Righto.'

Steve dragged the hose across and pinioned it beneath Alfie's arm. Alfie directed both nozzles at the fire which, Steve saw, was waning just a bit. He headed towards the rubble and saw an arm and the starched cuff of a nurse. The fingers were moving, as though she was waving. They were so small, so white. He felt sick. He didn't want to remove the rubble to see what he feared.

'Hang on, Miss,' he said. 'We're getting to you.' He pressed her fingers, she pressed his, and he heard her weeping.

Piece by piece he lifted the rubble and was joined by a Rescue Squad lad. 'Quick, quick,' the boy said.

'No, careful, careful,' Steve replied, wondering how he could sound so calm, so normal, when inside, he was sobbing. His dad was dead. His real dad from years ago, and now Dodge. Two dads. Careless, not careful. He barked a laugh and it sounded parched and strange.

The boy looked at him. 'You all right?'

'Course I am. What's yer name, son?'

'Tim, and yours?'

'Steve.'

They picked at the rubble, dug into it, then shoved a great wedge of it over to the road with a crash.

The heat from the fire was beating on them. 'Not long now,' Steve said to the nurse, who was quiet. Her fingers weren't moving now; even her starched cuff seemed limp and grubby. Steve felt for her pulse. It was thready but there. He yelled for the medics. Alfie passed on the call. An AFS bloke had taken Steve's hose.

Steve worked with Tim, tossing bricks and beams to one side, until finally they reached her. She was lying quite still, her uniform torn; only the cuff was complete, but by now without a vestige of white. 'On three,' Steve said. They eased the nurse out and laid her on the ground. Her hair had been pinned up, Steve supposed, but half of it now hung down, stained red. Her hat was nowhere to be seen. Or didn't you call a nurse's headgear a hat? Was it a cap – or perhaps a veil? He called again for the ambulance. He smoothed back her hair, saying, 'Why hello there, wake up, come on, lass.'

The Rescue Squad lad was feeling her limbs. She moaned. One leg was crushed. Steve smiled. 'There you go, good girl. Any minute you'll be on a stretcher and taken, not to your hospital, but to another. Nice clean sheets, kind nurses like you, busy doctors.'

Her eyes opened and she gasped, 'Thank you, but what about the rest?' Her eyes closed again. Steve's heart sank. They'd been busy all night, and now there were others. Tim looked at him. 'How old are you, son?' Steve said, as the ambulance blokes ran up.

The lad said, 'Twenty-three.'

Steve shook his head slightly: they were the same age. 'New to it?'

'A bit, but it doesn't seem it.'

Steve sighed because a sub was pointing at him to keep digging and leave his hose to the AFS bloke. 'Come on, then.'

The two of them worked on. It took two hours to clear the rubble, and everyone else was dead. It wasn't unusual. Steve left Tim to it now that others from the Rescue Squad had arrived. He dusted off his hands. The sub ordered, 'Take back your hose, Steve. We'll be here for hours yet. Just so you know, the ambulance crew thought the nurse would make it. That's something.'

Steve supposed it was. 'Tell the lad, would you?' He nodded towards Tim, who was sweeping up the road, then took his hose and directed the jet at what had once been a hospital. The rocket had actually come down further along the street, so this end was blast damage, gas and fire, and so it went on day after day. Vengeance bloody rockets, Herr Hitler, eh, keeping on until your last gasp, and until your own bloody empire is in ruins as the bombers come over because how else can we stop you? And how the hell was any of it going to be rebuilt?

The turntable ladder had been moved along to Steve's sector, which meant the far end was under control, but here it would still take some time. He took up his stance, gripped the nozzle tighter, and held his jet of water steady. The heat was still intense, the smoke billowing, the air choking. He and Alfie were coughing. Alfie spat. Steve laughed. 'That's disgusting.'

'No manners on the bloody hose. You should know that.'

They stood together, working the hoses as initially the water seemed to feed the flames, not douse them, but in the end, the hose would win. It was hypnotic, and Steve was glad, because when this was over he'd have to make the trip to Dodge's missus. He slid to thoughts of Sylvia, instead. He wondered if she felt a bit different too, adrift, always hoping they wouldn't upset their friends, afraid of losing them, and wanting someone to be loyal to when perhaps they should be looking for someone who was loyal to them.

Dodge had been loyal, yes, he had, but Steve had realised that long ago, just hadn't put it into words. Some friends though . . . Well, some friends seemed to guess you were scared they'd drift away, and asked more and more of you. But not Dodge, not the watch, not Harry his band mate, and not Sylvia; the two of them were just together, and she was the person he hadn't even known he'd been looking for, his 'someone', his 'everyone'. Just like that, out of nowhere – or out of a puff of smoke, as Dodge had said, as he'd puffed away at his Woodbine.

The sub came up. 'Bertram and Pete are taking over your 'oses, you two. Go and have some cocoa. The canteen women are here; bloody angels, they are.'

Bertram took Steve's hose. 'Off you go, lad,' he said. 'They've found Dodge. Best his missus doesn't see him, so the sub's done the identification.'

Steve walked to the canteen that had been set up, Alfie's arm slung over his shoulder. He thanked the elderly women, held the mug between two hands and drank, feeling the steam of the drink on his scorched face, which had a heat blister the size of a grape. Still Alfie stayed close, but that's what the watch did, looked after their own, just as the sub had looked after Dodge's missus.

Yes, there were some things best not seen, but she'd be told that Dodge had saved countless lives and was one of the best. But what should he, Steve, say to her? That Dodge had been like a dad to him and his death was like a dagger to his heart? Did that sound stupid? Well, it was bloody well true.

He stared at the dregs of the cocoa. Alfie nudged him, 'Back to work, eh? We still got a fire to douse, whatever else 'appens.'

They walked back, and again Alfie slung his arm round Steve, who could still taste the cocoa, though the lump in his throat seemed too large for him to have swallowed any. But the world never stopped. Someone just came and put his arm across your shoulders, and you drank cocoa and got on with the job, knowing you were not alone.

Steve took his hose back from Bertram, and Alfie took his from Pete. Pete shouted above the roar of the fire, and the clatter and crash of the emergency vehicles, 'It's on the wane. Might not be an all-nighter.'

Bertram slapped his back. 'Not an all-nighter, eh? Back before dawn? Stranger things have happened, old son.' Bertram was from Westminster School, a toff down to his boots, and a good sort. He strode away, heading for the next hoses to relieve. Pete laughed, his teeth white in the grime of his face. 'Too true, me old son.' He winked at Alfie and Steve, and followed.

As Steve played the hose on the top flight of windows, from which flames licked, he was thinking of his letter to Sylvia. He wasn't sure if he should have written, but he had to try to build something with her. Would she reply? Well, it was done now and in the post. He moved his hose further to the left, knowing he'd have to wait and see but in his bruised heart he hoped she'd welcome it.

Chapter 13

The recuperation continues at Howard House

It was Wednesday, the fourth day of their Dorset recuperation and at last the three girls felt like walking from the garden out to the ha-ha. Their joints seemed looser and their stitches were tightening, which Mrs Holmes had decreed meant that they were healing. Dr Havers had appeared again this morning and agreed with her.

Polly snorted, 'But how could he not?' They were all smiling as they walked along one side of the ha-ha while a two-man patrol marched the opposite way along the other, their eyes probing the fields and their whistles swinging round their necks.

'Hey, you.' Henry's voice reached them. The patrol halted. 'So sorry, chaps,' he shouted again. 'Not you. Do continue your patrol if you will, and thanks indeed for it. It's you girls we're after; just wait for us oldies.'

Henry, Thomas and Simon Rogers were following the girls, with walking sticks tucked under their arms. 'For the sticky bits,' Rogers muttered as they reached them. They each carried a letter. Thomas Holmes said, 'We thought we should bring your letters to you, or you'd give us a roasting on your return.'

Verity looked at the other two, then at the men. 'Could it be that you were actually sent by a trio of women, who'd give you a roasting if you didn't reach us?'

'Oh, I say,' said her father, as Thomas and Rogers grinned, and agreed, 'Got it in one.'

They handed over the letters and walked along while the girls tore the envelopes open. They read as they walked, and Sylvia smiled, 'Dear Coppernob,' Steve had written. His handwriting seemed open-hearted with its rounded vowels, and strong blue ink. He talked of a long night on duty and said it was nothing unusual. Of his relief that all three of them had not received life-changing wounds, and how he hoped that he would see her at the reunion in a few weeks' time. He had signed the letter, 'Yours ever, Steve'.

If only he meant 'Yours ever', Sylvia thought, folding the letter carefully and tucking it into her pocket. She thought about the words as she walked along, her hand open against the letter that had his imprint upon it in smoky smudges. He had kept his word and written, and her heart seemed to expand with happiness. She looked up at the sky as a flock of pigeons flew over. The patrol took pot shots and brought a couple down.

They fell on to the sheep field. 'We should train Pup to "fetch",' Polly said.

Henry muttered, 'Indeed for that'd be a couple for the pot, and two fewer to eat the crops when the time comes.'

Rogers said, 'I saw you walking Pup round on the lead, girls. How old d'you reckon she is?'

Polly said, 'Sam, the bloke with the sheepdog, reckons five months or so, which is why, except for tiddling on poor Sylvia on the train, she is more or less house-trained.'

Rogers had taken up position beside Sylvia, who said, 'She's a dear little girl, sort of skewbald like Maisie, but gentle. When she licks she doesn't have a real go, but . . .' She stopped as she saw the others grinning at her. Henry said, 'Ah, so she is already one of the pack. Not sure I've ever heard a dog's lick being quite so closely analysed.'

At the end of the ha-ha they crunched over the drive and opened the gate into the fenced-off wooded area. It had been planted with deciduous trees in the late eighteen, and early nineteen hundreds though conifers had clearly had the impertinence to take root and add some height to the proceedings. Over to the left they heard the sound of footsteps. Henry held up his hand. They stopped. Thomas almost ran to the front to stand next to him, and Rogers pulled Sylvia in front of him, waving the other two girls into a huddle with her, taking up position at the rear with his walking stick up and ready. Henry called, 'Who's that?'

'B patrol, Sergeant.'

Henry looked past the girls to Rogers, who nodded. Thomas called, 'Carry on, patrol.'

'Thanks, sir.' They heard rustling, and then silence except for a few hardy birds that seemed to think it could be spring in spite of the freezing January day.

The whole incident was unsettling, and Verity asked, as they walked on, 'Mrs B mentioned that the patrols were twofold, Germans and Leon. A "just in case" manoeuvre. Is this right?'

Polly said, 'Just a minute, is this why you're walking with us today? After all, it's the first time we've been up to doing anything but pottering about the immediate gardens.'

The three men flushed, looking anywhere but at the girls. Henry tied the scarf tighter around his neck. 'No, no, don't be silly. We were told to bring letters.'

The girls didn't believe him.

Polly said, 'What about you, Dad?'

'Along came the postman to the house, and then along came the women into the vegetable garden, bearing the letters with Rogers lassoed by their side, and along came the three of us, just as we said.'

Sylvia muttered, 'Maybe. So what have you really heard about Leon?' She could tell there was something wrong, some sort of alertness that surely couldn't be put down to the war.

The men shook their heads. 'We've heard nothing. Have you?'

The girls looked at one another, and they all walked on. They emerged at the far end of the rear gardens, near the ice house, which was dug deep into the ground. At the bottom of the descending steps was a new wrought-iron gate, with a lock. Verity stared. 'Why?' she pointed. 'It looks like a hiding place, a secure but cold hiding place. And we're not moving until you come clean. Are we, girls?'

Henry retied his scarf. Verity snapped, 'Do stop fiddling. You've tied it once.'

Henry muttered, like a naughty boy, 'There's no need to be sharp.'

'There appears to be every need,' retorted his daughter.

Polly wagged her finger at her own father. 'So, you, Mum and Joe have moved from the cottage to the big house, not to save on the heating or because you're great chums, but for safety. Is that it?'

'But we are great chums,' Henry muttered, kicking at the ground.

'It's foolish to keep two kitchens going,' Thomas added, hands in pockets. He started whistling.

Polly went to stand in front of him. 'You only ever whistle when you're caught out. Remember the time you'd forgotten Mum's birthday and picked flowers from Dick's allotment?'

Henry shook his head in horror. 'Really, Thomas. That's not cricket, old man.'

Verity snapped. 'Stop putting on an act and trying to prolong it, Father. Just come out with it. It's ruddy cold, but we're not moving until we hear what the hell's going on. All this prevarication is making me jumpy. What about you, girls?'

Sylvia, who had watched all this, realised that living in Howard House was a bit like huddling behind a barricade, with its few key players being brought into safety while outside were the patrols, and a sheepdog running around the grounds as though just exercising. And what about the closed curtains the moment the lights went on in the house? That could be explained by the dimout, but even so, what about the sudden starts at strange noises?

She said slowly to Rogers, who seemed to have set himself up as her guardian while she was here, 'You can't always be needing to go into the town for shopping when Joe goes on the bus for school. You know he doesn't like being babied, but there you are, two of you always sitting at the back so he can have his independence, but like watchdogs, nonetheless. And at home time there's one of you, or one of the patrol, just happening to get Joe's bus home.'

Polly looked at her admiringly. 'Oh, good point, Sylv.' Sylvia had given up trying to get them to use her full name and, in a way, rather liked the nickname. It reflected the change from her former late-entry difficult trainee to a full member of the pack.

The men exchanged a look, then Henry spoke. 'A chum of mine in the police – you remember him, Verity, Constable Summerton?'

'Yes, of course I do. He spanked me in front of all my friends when I scrumped Major Warburton's apples, and how does one forget that? But do get on.'

'There's just been a whisper that that bloody Leon, far from breathing his last, has been sighted in London a couple of times still on the run from the police, only to disappear again. Well, not disappear exactly. Summerton says there's talk he's still in London, up to no good but nothing concrete from any of their snouts. Do you remember Norton, who owned that sordid little club near the West End? He was going to give evidence against Leon for his wheeler dealing, and sabotage of the butty, until a bloody bomber dropped a load and caught him in his bungalow, putting an end to the case. Well, the whisper was that Leon might have made a move on that club, because it was a front for a lot of black market and who knows what.'

'Right up his street,' Polly sniffed.

The men nodded. Henry continued, 'The Metropolitan Police sent in a snout a few times but the club's barely functioning, and Dougie, the doorman, just shrugs, and says it's ticking over with the staff holding the fort. The police sent in a couple of coppers to have a look around. They found no trace of Leon, but he's somewhere in London, or so Summerton's rather large nose tells him.'

'How does this Summerton know all this, down here, and what does "who knows what" mean?' Sylvia asked.

'Ah, good question. His nephew works as a policeman in the Met, and shares things with his uncle,' Henry told her. They were walking on through the copse, and there was a rustle that turned out to be one of the pigs. 'This is where I put out the scraps,' Thomas said. 'That one's fattening nicely.'

'Don't change the subject,' Verity insisted, as they proceeded past bushes and some holly trees.

'If I might just interject so we can finally get to the point.' Rogers wasn't asking a question. He was leaning with both hands on his walking stick, looking incongruous in his black butler's suit and mucky green wellington boots. 'It seems, girls, that Norton, in addition to black market dealings with Leon, had quite an operation around the edges of the West End: protection, prostitutes, violence. So it's more than a perhaps that this leads to a gang business. The policemen who asked around are a bit "windy" Sommerton's boy thinks, but he doesn't actually know if they's on the take.'

The girls listened as Thomas took up the thread again. 'So, given the possibility that Leon might have taken Norton's place, we therefore keep an eye on

Joe; not that the lad realises, of course. He just thinks we're old fussers if he thinks anything about it at all.'

Sylvia nodded. 'Oh, I see now why you and Mrs B have joined forces, as it were. It's for protection.'

The answering silence was profound, as Sylvia realised she had spoken her thoughts aloud. Rogers looked at her, his eyebrows raised, saying finally, 'My dear, protection does not come into it. It is a . . .'

He petered out, smiling gently, his grey hair lifting in the wind, his faded blue eyes preoccupied with memories. Henry came close, and patted Rogers on the shoulder. 'These youngsters, eh?'

Sylvia found her voice then. 'I'm sorry, I was thinking it and then there it was. It was rude, unforgivable and not my business and it must seem I don't approve, but it's not that at all. I think love is rather wonderful, but it's just . . .' How could she say that they seemed so old?

She turned to walk on, anywhere. Rogers was quicker than he looked and caught her arm. 'My dear, what's to do? Good Lord, Mrs B and I are in a partnership, have been for years, not that young Verity would have noticed, and why should she? Mrs B's husband returned from the 1914 to 18 war and then took off, we know not where, so a wedding there is none. Does that cross your Ts, and dot your Is?'

Sylvia nodded, saying in a small voice, 'I didn't need them crossed, really I didn't. I just— Well, love, and families, and people and their lives, are so new to me, and I find it very wonderful that—'

Verity jumped in. 'It's so good to have the nitty-gritty. I mean about Joe, of course.' Rogers smiled slightly, while Thomas and Henry looked at Sylvia as though, Verity thought, they were seeing the girl for the first time. Finally, all three men followed the girls along, Verity with her arm around Sylvia, who muttered, 'I'm such a fool.'

Verity just said quietly, 'No, *we* are because we are all only just realising how it must have been for you, and is for so many others.' Finally they emerged through the gate and into the side garden.

Henry called, 'So for now, we would just like you to walk a little closer to the house. Had Dog been with you still, it would have been better. She would have given huge alarm if she had noticed any intrusion. But things are what they are, so it's up to you three to be sensible.'

The girls walked in the afternoon, but stayed within easy reach of the house, stopping, listening, and looking. The next morning they took their turn on the bus, carrying the men's walking sticks and explaining to Joe that they needed them in case they fell or felt odd. They told him that they were going into town to have a look in the shops.

'We'll sit at the back of the bus so no one knows you know us,' Sylvia promised as they waited at the bus stop.

He waved them away. 'Then do please be standin' over there, and there be no talkin' to me. I can get a bus, yer know. I'm good on the roads as well as I be good on t'cut.'

On the bus his friend Martin had kept him a place, and the girls walked firmly to the rear, but the whole way they took turns to glance behind, just to be sure. They were all decanted in Sherborne, and walked yards and yards behind, with the whistles Thomas had provided at the ready. He'd said the girls would be bugger all use in preventing a kidnapping, but they were to whistle as though the hounds of hell were around them, and it would bring the police.

The girls would do this, but they'd also use the walking sticks to whack a few heads, they'd decided as they talked in their beds the previous evening before sleep claimed them, stung by the remark that they'd be bugger all use. 'Best not burst our stitches, though,' murmured Sylvia. 'I'm more frightened of Bet being furious than of Leon, or your dads.'

The other two girls knew that she was lying, because Leon was a brute, and would in all likelihood bring others, after his defeat in the Holmeses' garden. But a few whacks could gain time and allow the police to get to the scene.

At the end of the eight days, they'd had their stitches removed, and were signed off fit for duty, by Dr Havers. They also knew now that Henry, Thomas and Rogers had everything under control, or everything that could be controlled.

On their last afternoon they sat around the kitchen table, having a cup of tea with Mrs B, Rogers, Henry and Pamela while Thomas and Joyce Holmes collected Joe. Henry said, stroking Pup who was curled up on his lap, 'So, you are getting the train tomorrow morning, and going straight to the depot office at Bull's Bridge for orders, with Pup. Will she really be safe with all that water?'

Verity said, 'She'll be chained as the boaters' children are, to the range chimney, and will toddle around the cabin roof until she is just a bit more reliable.'

Rogers said, half laughing, 'Perhaps that's what we should do with Joe.'

They all nodded. Mrs B said, 'Ah, but he needs his freedom. It's a tricky balance.'

Henry muttered, 'Life is. I'm wondering, girls, what you all think you will be doing after the war? I mean, the canal can't continue as a transport system in the face of such road and rail competition.'

The range spluttered in the silence that fell. Pamela placed her hand on her husband's and squeezed. She said, 'What Henry is trying to say, girls, is that Howard House must change. It's so big that even with us all here, we have still closed up almost two thirds, and there are the cottages, the grounds . . . It could be an hotel or a school, but it needs young people to make something like that work. We have money, but not the energy or hunger. Perhaps it's worth thinking about – along with your men, of course.'

Again there was silence, and again the range spluttered. Pup yelped in her sleep.

Polly said quietly. 'Our men might not come back.'

Henry said, 'I believe they will, but if the worst happens, you three will still need a life. We mention it only for you to keep in the back of your minds, because the war will be over sooner rather than later, you mark my words. Our forces are almost in Germany, the Russians are closing in on it, Japan will take longer but Hitler can't withstand the might of America.'

At that moment they heard Joe clattering down the steps from the yard and bursting into the kitchen without stopping to remove his boots, his face red from the cold. There was excitement in his every fibre. He was followed by Thomas and Joyce looking pale and stressed. Suddenly Sylvia felt sick. Leon? It was clearly what all those sitting around the table thought.

There was no chance for Joyce or Thomas to explain before Joe slung his satchel on the table and drew out a certificate. 'I won,' he shouted, dancing around, waving the certificate. 'I won the competition, and my story is going to be in the newspaper.'

Polly leapt up. 'Oh, Joe, that's so wonderful, let me see,' she said.

The girls clustered around the certificate, reading over the top of his head his name, J. Clement, and the title of his story, 'My Life on the Cut'. Sylvia felt sure her heart had skipped a beat. She looked round to see Joyce and Thomas whispering to Pamela, Mrs B and the other two men. Henry jumped up, thrust Pup at Rogers, who clung to the dog as though the old man's mind was full of imaginings about Joe, and what this piece could reveal about his whereabouts. Joyce had backed close to Thomas; her hat had slipped sideways and the feather was bobbing. Henry rushed to the telephone in the boot hall and was making a call, but his words were muffled. Could he stop the piece? Please, Sylvia pleaded silently, because what if Leon saw it?

He came back, pale, nodding, then opening his hands, as though to say that actually he wasn't quite sure. He walked to Joe, ruffled his hair, and sat back down as Joe stuffed a slice of cake into his mouth, while Polly, Sylvia and Verity seemed hardly able to breathe with anxiety.

Henry asked, 'So, tell us about your story. The reporter is going to print it, I gather. How exciting. But you know, the photographer that was coming to take your picture can't now, his editor says. He's just so busy.'

The relief in Thomas and Joyce's faces, not to mention those of Rogers and Mrs B, as well as Henry and Pamela, helped the girls relax. 'Have you got your story, Joe?' asked Sylvia.

'No, the reporter has it.'

Verity said, 'That's a shame, because we're off tomorrow. What did you actually talk about?'

'Oh, just 'ow yer get through bridges, how t'boats be loaded and unloaded, the cabins, how you women have filled the places of the men. How yer loved Dog and yer saved Jimmy. I didn't say anything about Uncle Saul, or me, so you can stop worrying about Da. I knows yer do worry, cos of all the sitting on buses, and the patrols. He won't know I is 'ere, course 'e won't. Besides, he can't read, or couldn't, less'n he learned in prison waitin' for the trial that didn't 'appen. So how can he read the newspaper?'

Sylvia saw the grown-ups push aside their worry with hearty smiles. 'We aren't worrying,' Joyce said. 'We're just so proud.' And they were, but if only he hadn't mentioned Dog, and Jimmy, and the women who ran the boats, because there were others who could read, and they might be Leon's friends.

In bed that night, the three girls went over the plans that the aunts and uncles had made the moment Joe had gone to bed: the patrols were to be tightened, and Henry was trying to find some sort of body-guard who could be paid for discreet surveillance. They knew of the contents of his phone call to the editor, a golfing pal, who had promised to cancel Joe's photo shoot, along with an article on the winners themselves. So, there was just the story, which had already been typeset and if that was pulled it would cause more gossip amongst journalists than if it was just left.

Verity said, after tossing and turning, 'After all, why would Leon's tentacles stretch as far as deepest rural Dorset? And if they did, why would they take any notice of a short story competition in a local newspaper?'

But none of them slept very well, jerking awake at the slightest sound.

In the morning, on the bus to the station with all the 'grown-ups', Henry told them that indeed there were to be more men hired, the expense to be covered by him of course, because no toe-rag was going to come and take their boy away.

Henry finished in a fierce whisper, 'All quite unnecessary, of course, for the wretched man is probably long gone, or blown to smithereens by a rocket with his name on. After all, why should it be the good ones who get blown apart? If he's elsewhere, and has friends in London, they won't read local newspapers from around the country. I know we're being absurdly careful, but one likes to cover all flanks. Summerton's words can't be erased from our minds and must be acted upon if we are any sort of guardians.'

By the time they reached London after trundling along for several weary hours nipping out at the stations to let Pup do what she had to on the flower beds, the girls had genuinely felt reassured by Lord Henry's measures. Good grief, it was enough that the V2s and a few V1s were still smashing into a London which was freezing in a bitter January. Smashing so that they blasted windows, bringing frostbite to those who had to live within their walls. And what about the tiredness that was sinking into people now that they were on the last leg?

On the top of the bus back to the depot they talked of Howard House because they had given no thought to the end; not really. Sitting on the back seat Verity leaned into Sylvia. 'You do understand, our Sylv, my father meant you, too, and whoever your man is. I mean by that Coppernob, what say you, Pol?'

Polly smiled, as Pup sat at her feet and tugged at her lead, yelping at the people who came on board. 'I say, just think, all the families together, because I rather think that Rogers and Mrs B have decided that you are theirs. We could all set to and make something – anything – work.'

Sylvia was more relaxed than she had ever been. As the convalescent leave had drawn on she'd felt she was no longer an extra in life. Steve's letters, which had continued arriving, and her replies had cemented that sense.

She had settled herself on the bedroom window seat to reply to his letters, pen in hand, writing of the view from their window, or of Joe and Maisie, and Joe's tin hat, and how he had corrected the drawing she had made of him standing with his hat on, preparing to mount. She had enclosed the drawing and Steve had replied, saying that he thought it was wonderful.

She had written back, to tell him that was because of Joe's efforts, but he had replied by return, saying that it was a joint effort, she and Joe together, which was the best sort of picture. Sylvia smiled to herself and touched all his letters, which she carried in her trouser pocket, and returned to the present in time to hear Verity discussing the future.

'We could have an hotel, but we could also have a place where men can stay who can't get rid of the nightmares,' Verity said. 'Even if our men can't be with us – for we have to consider it, girls – we could manage that ourselves. For heaven's sake, if we can get a load of aluminium to Tyseley and back, we can run an hotel.'

'But only with the help of the older ones,' Sylvia said. 'We'd need them, and they'd need to be doing something.'

Polly muttered, 'But I don't think Saul would ever leave the cut, and I'm staying where he is.'

The bus drew up at their stop and as they walked down the stairs, Pup in Sylvia's arms, Verity said quietly, 'The cut might leave them, you know, high and dry. Father was right, it's as though the war is the last real time that cuts will be needed, and a whole way of life will end.'

Chapter 14

Back on the cut at last

The girls walked towards the depot as the freezing evening fell, cloaking the leafless trees with yet another level of frost. Their steps quickened, and Polly lifted the flagging Pup and carried her under one arm, her carpet bag in the other hand as they swore to one another they could sense the cut. It was the longest they had been away, and it was only now that they truly realised how much they had missed it. They skirted the war memorial, not looking at the shrivelled Christmas wreath that had been placed by someone in memory of a son who would not come home.

They passed the pub, hearing the piano playing, the voices raised in song. It was 'The White Cliffs of Dover' and Vera Lynn's voice stayed in their heads as they walked along the lane. There was a bright moon; they could no longer call a bomber's moon, because the rockets were sent man-less from the Continent and it didn't matter how much light there was, or wasn't. One of their carpet bags contained clean clothes from Verity's wardrobe to share amongst them all, and knitted hats, scarves and gloves from Joyce.

Another bag contained spuds washed free of soil by Pamela, and sliced cured bacon from the pigs, enough to share with whoever *Marigold* and *Horizon* were moored between. The third had books for Jimmy Porter, the seven-year-old they had saved from drowning when they were trainees, and whose family had given them Dog, whom they could just about think of now without weeping.

At last they were at the entrance to Bull's Bridge Depot and could let Pup down. The guard came out of his hut tipping his hat. 'Well, by all that's holy, the girls are back, bloodied but unbowed. We 'eard 'ow you've been doing from Bet Burrows.'

The girls grinned as they passed, waving a hand in his direction. Pup danced about on her lead. 'Just tick us off on your clipboard, Vernon. We're not hanging around while you find our names, because you'll take all day about it, and give us pneumonia.'

His laugh followed them across the yard, busy with bustling men against a background of narrow-boats heading east and west. Polly said, as they headed for the Administration Office, 'Can you imagine this falling silent?'

'Stop it,' snapped Verity. 'Let's just take it a day at a time.'

Sylvia opened the office door, which caught in the wind and slammed back against the wall. Bob looked up from behind his counter, getting to his feet and grimacing. 'Might 'ave guessed it were you three. Put the bung in the 'ole, and bring your troublesome selves in.'

Sylvia walked up to the desk. 'Is that any welcome for wounded warriors, Bob?'

'Cain't see no warriors, 'ere. Just three lasses who didn't complete their ruddy run. There's no pay, yer know, and make sure that dog don't pee on me floor.'

Sylvia slapped her hand on the counter. 'She won't, and of course we know, and you needn't look so pleased about it.'

The other two stood either side of her. 'Just reporting for duty, you little ray of sunshine,' Verity said.

'Bet around, is she?' Polly was reaching across the counter, pinching one of Bob's sandwiches neatly stacked on greaseproof paper. 'Hey,' he said slapping at her hand. He missed, deliberately. Polly knelt down and gave Pup a crust, crooning, 'Enjoy this, it's the only thing you'll get off tight wad, let me tell you.'

They were all grinning, as he signed them in. Then they turned to leave, but he called them back. 'Hey, not so quick. 'Ere yer go.' He handed them one of his buff envelopes. 'What's this?' Verity asked. 'Make us happy and tell us we've been sacked.'

He shrugged, sitting back down and ramming a sandwich in his mouth. 'Just summat the lot of us put together. Can't 'ave yer going round with a beggin' bowl being more of a nuisance than you already are.' He splattered sandwich crumbs over the countertop, and wiped it clean with his hand.

Sylvia and Polly waited as Verity opened the envelope and looked in. She pulled out pound notes and coins. 'That's as much as our pay.'

Bob shrugged again. 'Bet and her two trainees 'ad yer pay, cos they did the run in yer boats, not that they wanted to 'ave it, but rules is rules. So the lads at the depot just put in a bit 'ere and there fer yer envelope, cos we knew yer'd be going on summat rotten the minute yer got back, and that were more than we could take. Best you go and find yer boats, and take that hound with yer before she christens me floor. Yer make sure yer take her to see Maud in the canteen afore yer go. Yer know 'ow she felt about Dog. Bet's at *Marigold* to do the handover and will tell yer the orders.'

With that he rose and walked into the rear office with his shoulders slumped and the girls remembered that Maud wasn't the only one who'd adored Dog. As they reached the door, Bob called from the rear office doorway, 'Glad yer back, girls. We was right worried, we was. Never bloody ends, do it?' He slammed the office door behind him.

The girls were almost overcome but Verity tucked the money into her pocket and they set off again, Verity waving the envelope, through the weaving men, who grinned, and shrugged off their thanks. The girls turned right at the canal frontage along the lay-by and it was as though Pup knew they were on their way home and strained at the lead, pulling them on. They passed all the narrowboats moored stern first against the kerb but no one was about. They arrived at *Marigold* and *Horizon*.

In the moonlight they could see that the holds were already loaded, and the tarpaulins tied down. The centre-line running boards were also in place along the top, linking to the metal stands spaced at intervals down the length of the holds. Smoke was rising from the cabins, and as they stared Bet emerged from *Marigold*'s cabin grinning and saying, 'Bob and the new orders clerk, Marty, felt it might be a kindness to have the trainee team run the Limehouse gauntlet to load up, just this once, blackmailing us because we nicked your fee. Just this once, mind.'

Bet jumped down on to the bank, and hugged them all. 'Timmo's rabbit is stewing in the range, we've tidied the cabins after our nightly wild parties. I suggest you eat, get to bed, and toddle on up to Tyseley early in the morning. For your information, the Bottom Road is no longer used, but you'll pick up coal from Coventry on the proper cut. Why? Because all the Idle Women put their combined feet down, plus numerous others, and now that arm is defunct.'

She grinned, then snatched at Sylvia, towing her forward by her carpet bag. 'Come with me to sign out on your cabin, young lady.'

Sylvia let herself be led, feeling much like Pup on her lead. Surely Bet knew that she wasn't fussy like she used to be? They leapt on to the counter of *Horizon*, then Bet entered first, waving her hand around. It was immaculate, and the range was spluttering, as a piece of coal dropped into the firebox. 'I just wanted to let you know that your fireman left me a message with Bob the moment you left hospital. I telephoned the fire station as he asked, to give him your address in case you didn't. He wasn't taking no for an answer, you see. Was that okey-dokey?' Sylvia sat on the side-bed smiling. 'More than okey-dokey, Bet. We've been writing to one another.'

Bet was grinning. 'Of course you have. Life can be short, Sylv. Grab happiness where you can. I also gave him Tyseley's address, so you never know, there might be a letter waiting for you at the office when you arrive. Come on then, don't know why you're sitting down, you layabout. You need to get back on to *Marigold*, eat, drink and be merry for tomorrow you work.'

Bet was scooting up the steps on to the deck. Sylvia laughed. Honestly, Bet was incorrigible. She followed, almost shouting, 'You didn't have to drag me here to tell me this. The girls know he wrote, and that I replied, and if I have to listen to any more teasing I will pull their hair out by the roots.'

Bet was standing on the bank. 'Not a bad idea. They have enough woollen hats to keep their bald heads warm, I presume, after a week or so with

Mrs Holmes and her clicking knitting needles. I do love that Joyce Holmes, salt of the earth. Now I have to toodle-pip to get back to my girls and make sure they're behaving. Guess what, we have two new boats. Well, not new, but would you believe they're *Swansong* and *Seagull*, Saul's old boats. Another reason for a quiet word. Break it to Polly, if you would. I don't want her thinking he's back, which would possibly lead to a bit of a do.' With that, she waved and headed further down the bank.

Over the rabbit stew Sylvia mentioned the news about *Swansong* and *Seagull*. For a moment Polly looked sad, but then she ate some of her baked potato. Eventually she said, 'Well, it's good that they're in Bet's care, but it'll be strange, and not just for me. The other boaters will look a bit sideways for a while.'

At last the meal was finished, the washing-up done, Polly and Verity smoked on the counter, while Sylvia walked Pup along the lay-by looking for the Porters' boats so that she could pass on the books in the carpet bag she carried.

Each time she passed a boat, it seemed that the boaters were back, just waiting to fuss over Pup, express sadness at the loss of Dog, and their concern about the girls, but also, as she was leaving, the women would say, 'We 'ears yer 'as a nice young man, we does. Bit of a fireman, we 'ears. Saved yer. Makes a bond, eh? Bet likes him, so she do.'

Long ago the girls had given up trying to work out how the cut telegraph worked, though this time, with Bet about the place, there was little need to look too far. By the time she found the Porters she had ceased to blush, and merely nodded, saying, 'Yes, we're all very grateful. His name's Steve, and I do rather like him.'

In this way she saved Mrs Porter the trouble of asking all the questions the others had hinted at. But this time, Mrs Porter, who had lifted Pup and was tickling her under the chin, said, 'I 'ears 'e be a coppernob an' all.'

'Well, yes.'

'I 'spect yer and his little 'uns'll dodge the hair, but their childer will be the coppernobs. Tends to go like that, it does.' Mrs Porter was handing Pup back. 'She'll be a good 'un. It were Ma Mercy who knew the litter were born a while ago near Buckby, but this 'un weren't took up. We knows why now, cos of yer need.'

Dazed at the information about any coppernob children, Sylvia was about to carry on when Mrs Porter crossed her arms and stood by the tiller, which had been turned round to make more room on the counter. 'Yer mark my word, young Sylv, that coppernob be a good 'un, steadfast an' true. I feel it in me water. Just right fer yer. You be thanking them at 'Oward 'Ouse fer the books, eh?'

Sylvia almost staggered back. Feel it in her water? Could she? Did she? When she saw Polly and Verity on *Horizon*'s counter, flipping their cigarettes into the cut, she carried Pup over to them. 'Pol, Dog slept on your feet in bed, so you should have her. If she's going to pee on anyone it should be her mum.'

Polly nuzzled the puppy's neck. 'Are you sure, Sylv? Mightn't you want her?'

'A share of her is fair enough, and now I'm going to crash into my bed.'

The other girls were too, but as she was about to step on to *Horizon*'s counter Sylvia said, 'Does Mrs Porter's water tell the truth?'

The minute she said it, she wished she hadn't, but the girls didn't turn a hair. Verity, who was half in and half out of *Horizon*'s double doors, said, 'I'd believe any of the boaters if they talk about their water. Mark you, if I talked about mine it would be a load of cobblers, because I really don't know what they mean, and if it's their bladder I don't even want to think of it. Here, take the carpet bag. We've taken our clothes out; yours remain.'

Sylvia took it and stepped across on to *Horizon*'s counter, laughing, but inside she was hugging the words to her. Steve and she would not only be happy, but have red-haired grandchildren, and for a wild moment, she wanted to rush back into London to his fire station and hurl herself into his arms. Instead she almost skipped down the steps into her cabin, lighting the oil lamp, and shaking out the cross-bed's double blankets to give them just another warm. She took his letters from her trouser pocket and slipped them beneath her pillow, hoping there would be another waiting for her at Tyseley, as Bet had hinted.

The next morning, at the break of day, they pat-pattered towards Cowley Lock on the Grand Union Canal. They were on a short tow because it was so cold that the ice would have collected overnight between the wall and the gates when they were opened, leaving no room to enter abreast.

As they reached the winding pound just before the lock, a lock which was the first in the long climb towards Birmingham, they all basked in the release of being on their boats, on the cut, and being back home. Verity was to lock-wheel today – opening and closing the locks – but Steerer and Mrs Mercy were coming through on their way back from Tyseley, so the lock was ready and in they went, the Mercys' ''Ow do' ringing in the girls' ears, and their thanks for Pup in hers, they hoped. As *Horizon*'s tow-rope was detached from the stud, and the butty's momentum carried it alongside until it nudged the sill, Pup, on the roof of the motor, barked. Sylvia called, 'Hello to you, too, little Pup.'

To Polly she said, 'She seems happy enough on the chain.'

Polly answered, 'Enough of that, young Sylv. Why were you asking about Mrs Porter's water?'

'Mind your own business,' Sylvia answered, dodging down into the cabin to pour an enamel mug of tea each. She brought them up, passing them to

Polly, and said, 'Put them on the counter. Pup will knock them over if you leave Verity's on the roof.'

Polly did so as Verity wound the paddles and the water gushed in and lifted the boats. Polly wouldn't let it rest and threatened to ask Mrs Porter, if Sylvia held out. So Sylvia told her, mostly because she wanted to share it.

Polly sipped her tea, looking over the top of her mug at Sylvia. 'I didn't need my water to tell me that,' she said. 'Crikey, it stands out a mile. He's such a good man with eyes only for you. In this day and age, unless you grab the moment, Sylv, it could all be gone. All those fires, the damned rockets. He's as much on the front line as Tom and Saul.'

Sylvia just stared at her, the tea suddenly losing any appeal. As the boats reached the high-water mark she said, 'Well, thank you for all of that. Now how do you expect me to sleep at night ever again until this war is over?'

Verity was shoving on the beams, opening the gates, and as Polly pat-pattered from the lock she leapt on board and grabbed her tea, getting ready to grab *Horizon*'s prow tow-rope, and sling it on *Marigold*'s stern stud. Sylvia called as she threw it, 'That friend of ours, Miss Polly Holmes, has just been explaining how every day could be Steve's last, and I should make every second count.'

There was a jerk on the butty as the tow caught, and out they all went. Verity stood on the cabin roof, alongside Pup. She cupped her mouth and yelled,

'Honestly, Sylv, Polly has no tact, unlike me. What she means is don't mess about. If you like him, spend time with him. As for every day being his last, he's a professional, he knows what he's doing. But yes it could be his last, but probably not. Have I helped?'

Sylvia seldom swore, but now she did. 'No you ruddy haven't.'

Verity's laugh soared, and joined that of Sylvia, who finished her tea, knowing the girls were trying to tell her to grab love because, after all, they were all in the same boat, and the two of them had done just as they were advising. She smiled. She'd sleep. They were adults, after all, and this was their life.

Chapter 15

Good time is made as they head for Tyseley Wharf

That same day they pat-pattered all the way through the rising locks of Watford and Kings Langley, with Verity lock-wheeling the first half, and then Sylvia the second until they reached the peace of the pound, which lasted until Berkhamsted. It was along here, on the towpath, that Polly jogged Pup, slightly overtaking their boats and lifting Pup when a cross old bulldog tried to eat her, alongside some allotments.

The equally old and cross owner, who closely resembled his dog, looked at Pup huddling in her arms, then at *Marigold* and *Horizon*. 'Young woman, aren't you the one who usually has a different dog – Dog I think was her name? Samson likes that one. He doesn't care for nippers.'

Polly looked down at Samson, and vaguely remembered him now. 'Our lovely Dog died in a V2 blast that buried us three girls a couple of weeks ago. Though she was hurt she sensed where we were and tried to dig us out. The firemen and Rescue

Squad took over when she died on the job.' She tried to keep her voice level but wasn't at all sure she succeeded.

The old boy stooped, pulling Samson's ears gently. 'You were on your way to Limehouse, I expect?'

Verity sounded *Marigold*'s hunting horn, two blasts, which translated meant 'Got a problem?' Polly waved to show she was all right. The boats chugged past, stlll on a short tow. 'We were,' Polly said, 'but we had to fetch Dog who'd taken off after something, and then had to find a telephone box, and so on; you know how these things go. You keep thinking, could we have done it differently, and perhaps she would still be alive?'

The old boy said, 'I did a lot of that in the last war, and the answer is – perhaps, but perhaps not, so it's fruitless. It happened, and now you have this little pup.'

He looked from Pup to Samson. 'Now, Sammy, be a gentleman and teach this youngster how to make new friends, if you please.' He held up a finger, then dug in his pocket for a small piece of toast. This he gave to Samson. 'Try letting the youngster sniff about Samson while still on the lead. What do you call her?'

'Pup.'

'Ah, as original as dear old Dog.'

Pup, now supposed to be sniffing around as instructed, started to be silly, leaping at Samson, who growled, then snapped. Pup sat still. 'There, you see, she's been told by her elder and better.' His chortle was disarming. He gave both dogs a piece of toast. This time Pup approached Samson more carefully, and they both had a good sniff around one another until finally Pup came to sit between the old boy and Polly. 'You're one of those lasses who's filled in for the boaters gone to war, I suppose. Bit of a change for you?'

'You could say that, and for the boaters. They've been kind; well, more than kind.' The wind was getting up. Polly snatched a look at the sky. Would it snow?

The old man was shivering. He had no scarf. She snatched off hers. 'Here, wear this; alarming colours but not too grubby yet. It's one of Mum's new ones. Fair exchange for Pup's lesson.'

She now noticed his threadbare coat and woollen gloves with holes. He refused the scarf, blushing, but tipped his hat. Polly insisted, 'Please, take it for my sake. I have a whole carpet bag full of them in the cabin and can't wear them all. Mum knits even more when she is worried, so over the last two weeks while we three've been recuperating it's been an avalanche of strange-coloured wool which has been clickety-clicked into something that at least keeps one warm.'

At this he half bowed, and said, 'Then, how kind, I will.'

Polly wrapped her scarf around him, and his rheumy eyes twinkled. He said, 'My wife knitted, it's one of the things I miss more than I ever thought possible. My name is Reginald Forsythe.'

Polly introduced herself and waited, but Reginald said no more. They just nodded. Polly stuck out her hand, covered in her own holey woollen gloves. 'We'll pass one another again,' she said.

'I do so hope so, and please, Miss Polly Holmes, and your two friends, don't waste time wondering, as regards Dog, whether you took the right turning, as it were. Who knows what taking another one might have brought. Celebrate the memories. It's that which keeps us going, isn't it, Samson, old man?'

Polly ran on with Pup, who leapt at the lead until Reginald's voice reached her. 'Tell her no, my dear, you must take control. Always remember that: take control.' Polly did, working with Pup until she overtook *Marigold* and entered a bridge little further on; snatching up Pup, she jumped on board as Verity steered alongside the towpath.

Pup was put on the side-bed and slept immediately in the warmth of the cabin. Polly made cocoa for the two of them; Sylvia called that she had just had one. 'I'll fill you in later,' Polly called back to *Horizon*. 'By the way, not sure Coppernob would approve of your cocoa moustache.'

Sylvia's laugh reached her.

Polly told Verity all about Reginald, then dug out another scarf for herself. She would telephone her mother from Tyseley and see if she could find something made of a more subdued grey or brown that she could re-knit for Reginald.

Polly lock-wheeled on the rise to Tring, which was easier because several of the locks were ready. Steerer Wise and his missus had passed through, heading for the south on *July* and *Midsummer*. The Wises had called "Ow do, had to lay back for Timmo, who be ahead o' yer and so be Steerer Mercy. Them'll be mooring up at Leighton, so get yer throwin' arms at t'ready, cos they'll expect to beat yer at darts. Been too long without yer.'

Once through the Tring locks they pat-pattered past the entrance to the Aylesbury Arm. It was Maudie's, Joe's mother's, favourite part of the cut and where she had finally been found, having escaped from Leon; out of her mind, and badly battered, without memory, but alive. She had been taken to a psychiatric hospital until a vestige of herself returned, and Granfer had received notification. Verity was smoking, hunched on the cabin roof, Pup beside her, covered by one of Mrs Holmes's scarves to head off the bitter cold. Verity watched the wind take the cigarette smoke, dispersing it almost immediately.

'Darling, I don't think I can bear to see Dog's burial place yet, beneath the apple tree in Bet and Fran's orchard. Call me feeble, but I just can't.'

Polly guided the tiller with her elbow, flicking her own cigarette into the cut. 'I feel the same, Ver, and I dare say Sylv does as well. Why don't we leave that for the return trip? We can mix it with seeing Maudie at Granfer and Lettie's. We do just need a quiet word with Granfer about Joe's story in the newspaper, and we must warn him to be extra vigilant on Maudie's behalf.'

Verity looked up, shaking her head, 'But . . .' But Polly waved that away. 'I know, I know Bet's told Fran, who will have told Granfer all about the newspaper, but I want to make sure he really understands that there's a vague possibility Joe could be traced. We must reassure him about the precautions our families are taking.'

Verity agreed. 'Good, we don't want him and Lettie in a flap, and we also need to see how much better Maudie is, and whether we can tell Joe about her yet. But *dare* we tell him until the business of Leon is confirmed one way or another? If Leon . . . ?' Verity sighed now, glancing behind her. 'Damn and blas—' She stopped. Then half laughed, 'That always reminds me of Solly, and the blast. I do hope the old devil is driving Jacob and his wife round the twist, because it'll mean he's getting back on top of things.'

The girls were still chuckling when Verity leapt off the boat to manage the locks on the descent to Leighton Buzzard before mooring up for the night. It was dusk before they made it, and wolfed down Spam fritters for their evening meal. Sylvia merely poked at hers. 'I was totally surprised when the nurses and doctors mopping us up weren't drowned by this stuff gushing out of our every nook and cranny. I'm so sick of it, more so after two weeks without.' She shoved it away. 'Oh come on, girls, let's get to the pub and thrash Timmo at darts.'

The pub was warm and bright behind its dimout blinds, the fire roaring as wind sucked the flames up the chimney, and the windows rattling. The table by the fire was theirs as usual, a reward for saving Jimmy's life what seemed a long time ago. Polly got in the half-pints of mild as Timmo called from the dartboard, 'Get t'beer down yer, for 'tis time t'be beaten. Bernie's do be taking t'bets tonight. But we do ask yer to be gentle with us.'

There were guffaws all round, and steerers stopped by the table to tell them they had been missed, and all were right glad they was back. Pup sat on Sylvia's lap until they finished their drinks, and then Ma Wise came and stood before her, saying Pup could sleep on her. They changed places, and Ma cuddled Pup close. As Sylvia was about to follow the other two girls, the boater caught her sleeve. 'Right sad about Dog, she felt like all of ours she did. But Pup should see you better from yer pain,' she said. 'So, too, yer fireman, eh?'

Sylvia shook her head. 'It's set in stone now, isn't it Ma, the whole cut knows that Ma Porter felt it in her water?'

'Course 'tis. Some things is, ain't they, they just is.'

Ma Wise settled Pup on her voluminous lap, brought out her crochet from her bag and stretched out her legs before the fire. Sylvia grinned, letting the boater's words run through her head: '. . . they just is.'

Happiness soared as she joined the other two, who were tossing with Timmo for who should throw first. The girls won the match, beating Timmo, his brother Peter and his uncle Trev easily. As Polly said, accepting a Woodbine from Timmo, 'It's like taking candy from a baby.'

'What's candy?' Timmo said, grinning, and lighting both cigarettes.

'Ah, Verity and I learned that from some GIs we met in London ages ago. Sweets, those rare things these days, Timmo.' She dropped her voice, holding his arm. 'How are you without Thomo?'

Timmo's face grew sad. 'Fair to middlin', our Polly. We does miss 'im something sore, so when we heard a damn rocket might 'ave got yer three lasses, it were just too much. Yer 'appy with Pup?'

She reached up and kissed his cheek. 'More than happy. It's given us someone else to love but we do still miss our Dog. We're calling in on Fran on our way back to see where she is, and then on to Granfer and Maudie.'

Timmo blew his smoke up into the air. The ceiling was stained almost brown between the beams. 'I had heard tell the bastard might be back in London. I also heard tell there might 'ave been summat in a newspaper. If'n you need the boaters at yer back, girl, yer only 'ave to say. Saul ain't 'ere to fight fer the boy, and Maudie, but we is. All of us is.'

The pub had fallen silent, and behind her Verity and Sylvia came close as the men lifted their glasses to them, their faces grim. Steerer Wise said, 'He were never one of us, that Leon Arness, just turned up on the cut when a youngster, and t'was clear 'e were black to 'is 'eart and worse. What's more 'e 'urt Maudie and Joe frequent, 'e did, and they *is* ours. We says nothing to no one about where Maudie be. But we is 'ere, should he start his games again, yer 'ear us, lasses?'

They said, together, 'We hear you, and thank you.'

As though a conductor had moved his baton, things fell back to where they were, and there was laughter, talk, and now the piano was being played. If Saul was here, Polly thought, he would be singing, perhaps with Sylvia who had the voice of an angel. Against this background, the bets were divvied up. The girls won nearly £2 for the darts kitty but put it over the counter for drinks all round. Bernie, the publican, was pleased. Everyone was pleased, and the girls had a further pint or two.

In the morning they headed up the Grand Union Canal, though they were not happy, because not one of them was without a headache, so the moaning was loud and long. The worst was from Verity until Sylvia, who was lock-wheeling as they headed towards Fenny Stratford, yelled as the boat sank down to the lower level, 'Enough, Ver, you're making my head worse.'

'Ver?' groaned Verity.

Polly shrieked with laughter. 'Oh, good girl, Sylv. You've kept using it, and so shall I. Sylv, Pol and Ver, what could be better.'

Sylv shouted down at them, panting as she opened the lock gates, 'Quite, and it's still all for one and one for all, and don't forget, we are still four. We may have lost Dog who was given to us by boaters but the boaters have given us Pup now. We're really lucky people.'

'If mucky, calloused, with sore hands, sore heads and ruddy cold's lucky,' moaned Verity.

'Oh, shut up, Ver,' shouted the other two.

The next day they headed further north. There were fewer locks, and they relaxed as they pat-pattered through the long Blisworth Tunnel, then, just past the Buckby turn-off they made it through the Braunston Tunnel before mooring up for the night. Timmo had left some rabbits and pheasant on the back of the cabin, and they had let them hang in the cold, to coax more flavour.

They had hoped to make it to Tyseley, but perhaps tomorrow? At dawn, though, they had to hack their way out of the ice which jammed them into their moorings, and then it was a slow trawl. They put up at Hatton, and finally made Tyseley Wharf at midday the next day, sighing with relief and feeling more grubby than ever before. They weren't, of course, it was just that they'd forgotten during their recuperation how awful they usually looked and smelt.

Chapter 16

Renewing Tyseley friendships and saying goodbye to others

They liked mooring up at Tyseley because the water was on a level with the wharf, unlike Limehouse, where you had to climb up wall ladders. Otherwise the chaos was the same, with lorries revving and taking away loads, or bringing them. Men bustled, the workshops were busy and above it all was the screech of steel being worked, or wood being hammered.

Ahead were cranes swinging loads on to queuing boats, the boaters' wives heading off to the shops with their string bags, or perhaps washing down their cabins while the men found out the details of their new loads. The main relief was that there were no V2s, and hadn't been since the London environs. On the quay they peered round, and up, and there was Alf Green in the cab of one of the cranes. His wife was Alice Green, an attendant at the public baths and in whose guest house they stayed if they were held overnight. Alf yelled down as they headed for the lavs, 'The missus 'eard you was on yer way, and 'as three rooms ready for yer, and three cubicles at the public baths. We're glad you made it through yer troubles.'

Their spirits lifted. They waved and rushed on to the lavs because using the bucket kept in the store at the back of the cabin was the worst part of their job. Afterwards they rushed back, calling in briefly for any letters. The clerk shook his head. 'Post ain't been yet. Try tomorrow, 'cause you'll be off to the baths now, won't yer?'

Sylvia pushed her hand into her trouser pocket, touching Steve's old letters, disappointment swamping her. But at least she had these, and would post those she had written to him on the journey up. But should she? What if he had forgotten her; out of sight, out of mind?

The other two called her to hurry, and the three of them headed back to the quay. 'Don't be disappointed,' Polly said. Verity added, 'He's busy, so let your heart cut him a bit of slack, eh? Look how he's written up to now, and never ever forget Ma Porter's water.' They all three grinned, Sylvia most of all.

On the quay they found the foreman looking speculatively at *Marigold* and *Horizon*'s holds, and then at his schedule. Polly whispered, 'Oh no, he's not going to order it to be done now, surely? We won't get clean, or have a night on shore.'

'Not if I can help it, darling,' said Verity sidling up to him. 'Oh, Mister Roberts, we would be so very pleased if our steel isn't offloaded until tomorrow.

We've been injured, just look at this arm, still in a sling, and it's our first trip back and we must bathe, we simply must. The danger of our wounds becoming infected . . .' she sighed pathetically.

He tucked his clipboard beneath his arm, staring at her. 'You can toady up and whine all you want, Miss Verity, but how much do you expect to alter my schedule when the rest of the time you call me rude names?'

The girls' hearts sank. Sylvia wanted to kick Verity because she had called Roberts a lazy arse a month ago, and a few other choice words, after which he had told her to shift her own arse and be quick about it.

Then he smiled. 'But on pain of death from Alice Green, I have scheduled you in 8 a.m. tomorrow, but no later, mind.'

Verity flung her arms around his neck and kissed his cheek. The other two raised their eyebrows and all three rushed off to collect a change of clothes, and then tore for the tram, then tore back for Pup, accidentally left in the cabin. Would Mrs Green allow her in? Would she be safe on the tram or would she pee?

Mr Roberts was watching their antics from the quay, shaking his head and sighing as they stopped near him, Pup under Sylvia's arm. He shouted, 'Leave her in the office, for Pete's sake. We have newspaper we can put on the floor. We'll need her lead because I'll take her home with me at the end of the day, and if she chews the furniture, it's not just her guts that will be garters, the missus will have mine an' all. After which, Miss Verity Clement, I will have yours, with mustard on 'em.'

Verity made as though to throw her arms round his neck again, but he held her off with his clipboard. 'That's quite enough for one day. Go and drop her in at the office.'

They did, and flew once more for the tram, finally arriving at the baths and running in because early afternoon had become late afternoon.

Mrs Green was in the foyer, talking to the receptionist. She opened her arms to hug them all, seemingly uncaring for once that they would besmirch her starched white overalls. She said, as she held them close, 'The starch'll have to cope this time but let's not make it an 'abit. Seems we might not 'ave seen you all again and that wouldn't have done at all cos yer our cross we must bear, so there.'

She led the way and Sylvia was given No. 3, 'because yer clean yer bath proper'.

Sylvia smirked at the others, who pulled rude faces as she entered, shut the door, and filled the bath to the eight-inch line. It was the biggest bath cubicle, with a mirror, which wasn't altogether a plus as none of them were exactly oil paintings. She stripped off her clothes and checked her wounds. They were all healed, or as good as, and quite clear of infection. But then they had made sure they had a stand-up wash every evening, just as a precaution. Whereas normally they just tipped themselves into the cabin beds and slept.

She heard Verity sink into her bath with cries of relief, which changed to, 'What a swot you are, Sylv. A nice clean bath indeed, and that cubicle isn't that much better than ours anyway.'

Sylvia leaned back, letting the water cover her body, feeling the muck disperse, not to mention the way the aches and pains eased in its warmth. 'Oh, Ver, it is, though. It's got a mirror, and such a lovely young man to towel me down.'

Verity hooted with laughter. 'I will tell Coppernob.'

But Sylvia was already sliding down beneath the water, feeling happier and more sure of herself than she had ever done in her life. He might not have had time to write, but she would see Steve at the reunion, she was sure she would, and the mere thought of it made her want to sing, and, anyway, there might be a letter from him when they returned to the dock in the morning.

She surged out of the water and broke into the song 'You'll Never Know Just How Much I Love You'.

There were groans from the other two girls, until they joined in.

Later, hair washed and bathed, they walked to the Bull and Bush pub on the corner of Mrs Green's road. Nothing had changed. 'Most peculiar,' muttered

Polly. 'I feel we've been away for ever, but somehow, not, if you know what I mean?'

Sylvia said, 'I think it's because we nearly died, then had to recover so we *have* been away further and longer than it seems.' She stopped. 'I'm talking rubbish.'

Verity slipped her good arm round her friend's shoulders and almost hung there. 'No, just for once you're not, dear heart.' They entered and watched as Frankie and Old Cedric played dominoes with their friends, while Boris wiped down the bar with what seemed the same grubby cloth as always. This he tucked in his apron, as always, whistling as he so often was, until he saw them. 'Well, well, 'eard you three had a lucky escape but Dog didn't. Gettin' on with Pup, are yer?'

Sylvia braced herself, but surely out here they wouldn't have heard of Steve? She rushed to say, 'Yes, she's a sweet little thing. What's on the menu today?'

He took his pencil from behind his ear, licked the lead, then brought out his pad from his apron pocket. 'Well, we have fish 'n' chips, or sausage and mash, but the fish is orf.'

Polly as always said, 'Ah, hard choice, girls. I suppose it will have to be the sausage and mash, Boris.'

Boris laughed. 'You girls crack me up.'

They smiled, because no, nothing had changed. He turned away, then back again. 'No coppernob fireman with yer, then?' He was looking at Sylvia.

She sighed, giving up. 'Unless he's invisible, no, Boris.'

He laughed again. 'Killin' you are, you girls.'

He took the order through to the kitchen, came back and poured three half-pints of mild without waiting to be told. They took the drinks to a table near the fire. The same dingy print of ancient Birmingham hung on the wall. The coals gleamed red in the grate. The same three women as always sat across from them, wearing hairnets. They nodded at one another. ''Ow do,' the women said. 'Better, are yer?'

The girls smiled. 'Almost perfect,' Polly said.

One of the domino players called, 'We knows that, but are yer better?' The men cackled.

While they did so Verity whispered, 'I'll bet a bob on Gladys's ash falling on our very own coppernob's sausages.'

The other two took her bet. Gladys arrived with the tray, her cigarette stuck in the corner of her mouth, the ash as always an inch long. It fell. She put the plates of food in front of each girl, and a large plate of bread and butter. She retreated to the kitchen. Sylvia looked at her plate. The ash had fallen on her mash. Verity, crowing, held out her hand. Sylvia shook her head. 'You said the sausages. It fell on the mash.'

Verity looked stung. 'But you know I meant *your* plate, not ours.'

Polly winked at Sylvia. 'You said the sausages, so cough up.'

Verity did so, grumbling as she ate her meal.

'Yes,' said Polly. 'Everything's just the same, even misery guts Ver.'

When they had finished, they passed the table of domino players on their way to the door. 'Yer take care,' said Frankie, still wearing his black armband in memory of his son's death just a few months ago.

'You too,' insisted Verity.

They slept like children in Mrs Green's bedrooms, ones that didn't rock, and around which no wind blew and no owls hooted. They had forgotten how tired working on the cut made them feel, and how sore it made their hands, shoulders and back, especially when their wounds were healed but echoes of them remained. And how the chilblains itched, created by standing on the counter steering in the bitter winter winds.

They ate scrambled egg and toast for breakfast in the dining room, looking at the photos of the repertory theatre actors who stayed here when performing. They paid and rushed out along the street for the tram, to be back at eight. They were, and even had time to check for letters at the office and pick up not just those that waited for them, but Pup from the foreman's office. Apparently, her behaviour had been exemplary, and he hoped they'd learn from their pet.

Polly stood on Verity's foot as her mouth opened for a sharp riposte, so she closed it again, and smiled sweetly. 'We really are very grateful, Mr Roberts,' she insisted.

Mr Roberts looked worried. 'Get out of here. I feel as though you're softening me up for something. Probably to eat me, raw.'

They placed the half-dozen eggs they'd bought from Mrs Green on his desk, blowing him kisses as they left. He grinned, throwing a screwed-up ball of paper after them. They shut the door just in time. 'Thanks for the eggs,' he yelled.

'Thanks for having Pup, Mr Roberts,' Verity called back through the door. 'Really, you're a pal. Thanks so much.'

His voice followed them down the corridor. 'I'm not your pal, don't ever think I am. You three are more trouble than all the other Idle Women and boaters put together, so help me.'

They were all laughing as they hunched their shoulders against the freezing wind of the yard, but they didn't care. Each of them had a letter from their man and their parents, or sort of parents, for Sylvia's was from Rogers and Mrs B. They tucked them away on the bookshelf the Grand Union Canal Carrying Company had installed in all the IW's cabins, to read once they were ready to go again.

The next hour or so was spent untying the hold tarpaulins so the loads could be heaved out by crane, then brushing out the empty holds, counting their blessings that they were to be loaded with a clean product – wood, here at Tyseley – and so they did not have to go to Coventry for coal, just this once.

At last they were on their way south back down the Grand Union Canal, not the Brum Bum where they'd have to haul the butty by hand through the short pounds because the banks were too decrepit to deal with the wash, and the locks, which couldn't cope with two boats in them at once. Instead they pat-pattered along, tied up abreast so they could at last relax, and read all the news from their men, and Howard House.

They shared this over several cups of tea, huddling on their counters, Polly and Verity smoking, Sylvia not. Apparently Tom and Saul were taking a few deep breaths and relaxing at a village they had captured, and were guarding some very old, and very young, Germans who had held it. These young and old warriors were still defiant, certain that Germany would win the war, that their Führer would subdue or kill the British with his Vengeance rockets, and sure also that their Führer had another weapon to unleash on the pathetic Britishers.

Verity drew on her cigarette. 'Vengeance for what, one wonders. Being beaten by the nations who have real cause for vengeance?'

They had not told their fiancés of their own meeting with a V2 and had no intention of doing so. Why worry them unnecessarily?

Sylvia told of Steve's battle against the hospital fire and numerous others, and the loss of Dodge.

She said nothing about the reunion, which he called the bright spot on the horizon in his last letter and how he longed for her to return to Bull's Bridge in time to make it. His words had made it real, and the thought jangled every nerve in her body, because what if Harriet . . .? She shut her mind. Slam, bang. Shut away. Just think of Steve, not where you will be seeing him, she urged herself.

They read their letters from Howard House, and all said much the same: apparently the paid guard was working well, but they had added another couple of men so they each did an eight-hour shift. The remnants of the Home Guard were perfectly happy to patrol and poach the odd pheasant. Joe was well, there had been no more articles, and the one on the competition had been buried near the back amongst the advertisements, so was not obvious.

Sylvia lock-wheeled them towards the Braunston Tunnel and as they finally travelled through its darkness Verity muttered, 'Oh, for more of these on the dash to Limehouse. It would be smashing to have a roof over our heads every few minutes on that particular bit of the cut.'

Sylvia called loudly, enough for her voice to echo, 'Must you say smashing?'

'Quite,' Polly agreed. 'It's a blasted nuisance.'

'Shut up,' yelled Sylvia, 'I will tell Solly of you, and he'll slap your leg.' But even she was struggling not to laugh.

Once out in the open air of the dull grey afternoon, they turned left along the Leicester Line, stopping before Crick Tunnel, and mooring up for Buckby. They dragged poor Pup out from the warmth of the motor cabin, clipped on her lead and set her down on the bank where she barked at some ducks who flapped their way to lift-off along the cut. The girls set off down the rutted track to Fran and Bet's house. Once they had seen Dog, they would go on to Granfer and Maudie, because the letters from Howard House had also asked them for an update on Maudie's condition, with reference to Joe.

They walked alongside grass verges still spiked with frost and the track puddles still frozen just as they were between the ploughed furrows of the fields either side. Winter wheat was showing green, but struggling to survive in this harsh weather.

'Our poor boys,' Verity murmured. 'They'll have to bivouac in this hard earth, I expect. At least we have the cabin and the range fire to keep us warm.'

Pup skittered about as they walked. Sylvia said, 'And at least Steve has his fires to keep him warm.'

There was a pause, and then they all laughed so loudly that the sparrows in the hedges flapped up into the air in a rush.

'Oh, Sylv, you are such a hoot. Thank heavens you're in love, because you'd be wasted in a nunnery, eh Pol?'

Polly frowned at Verity. 'I'm sure nuns laugh. Sometimes they seem very jolly if you see them walking along the street.'

'Oh, I know, but it's surely not for our Sylv? Not now she has a mirror coppernob. Not now she's so happy. Look at her, she's glowing, and we'd never see her and I couldn't bear that. We have an hotel, or a school, or something to run, perhaps even an orphanage, all of us. One for all, remember.'

Sylvia walked at their side, listening to them chattering on like the sparrows that had returned to their hedges. She wished they'd said nothing because it had been growing easier to concentrate all her thoughts and dreams on Steve, on Ma Porter feeling it in her water, on a life with children.

She rubbed her face, feeling her filthy woollen gloves rasping against her skin. The other two girls fell silent and she could see them snatching a look at her, and then at one another, worried.

'How much further?' Sylvia asked, to pretend she was quite all right.

'Five minutes or so.' Instead of discussing Sylvia's life, the other two girls switched to Joe, wondering how Maudie really was, because Granfer's painfully written letters were few and far between. He had not long ago learned to read and write, which wasn't surprising when most boaters couldn't. They wondered how Joe would feel to be returned to his mother, in Buckby, when the time came, and how Howard House would cope with losing their adored boy. And then there was Leon, who cast such a long dangerous shadow. Leon who must never know where his family were because they all feared he would destroy them, much as he would pull the wings off a butterfly. But at least it was clear from what he had said when he attacked Polly's father that he thought Maudie was dead, so perhaps she was safe, but what if Joe came to Buckby, and what if subsequently, Leon heard that Maudie lived?

Polly said, 'I remember when he attacked Saul outside that pub, after he and Granfer had rescued Joe from the cabin where Leon had beaten him and locked him in. You know, after Leon thought he'd killed Maudie. And then again, what about when he found Joe at Mum and Dad's . . .'

'Don't, Polly,' murmured Verity.

'But he would have killed Dad if Mum hadn't beaten him off. His sort survive to hurt us all again, because he won't let Joe go. I know it. I feel it. And what about him arranging to fire *Horizon,* and trying to kill Dog . . . Just being here makes me realise how vulnerable Buckby is and I'm frightened for them, for us all.'

Sylvia thought the same, and saw that Verity was nodding. Sylvia said, 'At least Howard House gives Joe some protection, but is it enough? What if Leon does see that story Joe wrote?'

Polly shrugged. 'Your dad did his best to kill it.'

Verity groaned. 'Oh don't say kill. And yes, he did, and who reads local newspapers unless you live in the area? Surely we'd know if he was in Dorset. He's more likely to come back to Buckby, and let's face it, the boaters can't keep an eye on them all the time.'

Sylvia whispered, 'But why would he come to Buckby? He thinks Maudie is dead, and Buckby is too obvious to settle Joe here. But if Maudie wants him . . . Oh, it's all so difficult.'

They fell silent again and Sylvia barely noticed the chattering of the birds any more as they walked the final hundred yards to Spring Cottage. Beside them Pup had settled into a walk.

At last they were at the rear of Fran and Bet's cottage, walking alongside the white picket fence, opening the gate, and making their way down the crazy paving path. They knocked on the back door.

Verity whispered, 'She'll be teaching at the school, surely.' There was indeed no one in, so they dropped a note into the letter box in which they explained that they had actually managed to get there, as they had asked Fran if they might, to see Dog. They had also reiterated the concerns about Leon. They stressed that should he become aware that Maudie was still alive, and they heard of it, they'd be sure to let her know, so she could warn Granfer. But in the meantime, she should warn the villagers, and Granfer of course, to be on the lookout – just in case.

But now it was time for Dog, and they banished Leon from this place, breathed deeply and together they walked round the cottage to the orchard, wondering how they would know where their friend was buried. But at the third apple tree Dog's collar hung from a branch, swinging in the breeze. One after the other they reached out and touched it.

Polly swallowed hard, and lifted Pup to sniff the collar, then set her down near the mound beneath the tree. Weathered branches had been tied into a cross, with the name Dog burned into it with a poker. 'She would have been your friend, Pup.'

The girls waited while Sylvia said a prayer, almost in a whisper, as their memories came and went, much as the light flickered through the apple tree leaves in the fullness of summer. Eventually Pup yelped, and pulled at her lead. The girls smiled, and followed her, walking around the cottage and back on to the crazy paving path where, in the summer, the camomile plants recovered from the winter frosts would come again, and lift their scent to the skies.

Once in the lane they walked into Buckby, hurrying now because they hadn't too much time to spare, what with the load to deliver at the paper factory, which was one of their favourite stopovers, and the collection of their orders at the depot. As they hurried round the last bend, down on the right they could see Granfer standing in Lettie's front garden by the fence, looking towards them. He waved and they broke into a run. It seemed so long since they'd seen him, though it wasn't.

He clicked the gate shut behind him and limped towards them. He had never limped. They ran faster, reaching him, hugging him. 'Why are you limping, Granfer?' asked Polly, fear at once gripping the girls: Leon?

As though he guessed their concerns, he shook his head, and hurried them back to the house, pointing up to the eaves. Pup was barking in Verity's arms as he told them, ''Twas a darned cat that seemed stuck by the chimney. So I took meself up on t'ladder. Darned cat took one look at me ugly mug and leapt down yon roof, into t'ivy, and on to t'garden. I slipped on darned ladder 'alfway down, and fell. Didn't 'alf twist me knee. Our Lettie said to stop mithering, cos at least the cat was right as rain.' He dropped his voice. 'So it weren't that bugger, Leon, so stop with the long faces.'

He opened the front door and led the way in; they followed, relief making them laugh. Lettie came from the kitchen, flapping Granfer aside with her tea towel and hugging the girls, as well as stroking Pup. She smelt of scones, just like Mrs B always did. 'Come through, do 'e be tellin' yer of the cat? You'd think 'e'd charged the army single 'anded and earned himself a wound and a medal, silly old bugger.'

Granfer was already sitting down, settling himself nearest the scones. Verity snuggled up next to him, because Granfer had a reach like no one else's and this way she'd be offered the scones first. She looked up at Sylvia and winked. 'Might not clean my bath like you do, Sylv, but I know what side my bread's buttered.'

Granfer looked from one to the other, then nodded to the remaining chairs. 'Sit yerselves down, lasses. Verity, put the pup down. She'll have a sniff and settle.'

They did, and Pup did as Granfer had thought, until the back door opened and Maudie stood framed in the doorway. Pup yelped then, and Verity snatched her on to her knee, fearful that she would alarm Maudie's fragile psyche. Maudie's dark eyes, so like Saul's and Granfer's, were bright, though, her long black hair glossy, falling free in great swoops of curls. She kicked off her boater's boots, lining them up at the side of the doorstep, and entered, shutting the door carefully. The girls waited for her to turn around, keeping their voices low and steady, to avoid frightening her.

'Hello, Maudie. Do you remember us, you came on our boats to help us when you were a bit poorly?' It was Polly.

Sylvia and Verity merely smiled because too much talk or activity had frightened Maudie when she was released from the hospital. Released specifically to help on *Marigold* and *Horizon* as part of her recovery by re-enacting happier times, or so the doctors had thought. It had worked

'I does,' Maudie said, slipping on to the chair Lettie pointed to. 'I does remember yer. I 'ave marks like yer does.' She pointed to her shoulder and hands, where the girls had the callouses from hauling the butty.

But what struck all three girls was that she said 'remember', when before she had said she 'knowed' but didn't know why she 'knowed'.

Almost without daring to interrupt her, Sylvia took a scone proffered by Granfer, who winked, and mouthed *remember*. So, he had noticed the progress too. Well, of course he had, he was her grandfather. Polly must write to Saul and tell him. But had Maudie remembered she had a son? Up until now she had said, when she realised that she knew Granfer and wanted to stay here in Buckby with him and Lettie, 'I knowed there is someone, not he who hurt me, but someone else.'

Should they ask?

It was as though Lettie had read her mind, because as she reached over to place a cup of tea at the side of Sylvia's plate she laid a warning hand on Sylvia's shoulder, a hand that Verity and Polly also noted. Well, the three of them had a shared thought process, after all. It wasn't everyone who toiled all day and then had stand-up washes and shared the pain of an ablution bucket. It was bound to bring about some sort of invisible semaphore.

Granfer was pushing the butter from one to another.

'Heavens, Granfer, it looks as though this is rather more than your coupon allowance.' Polly took a little off the corner of the block, which still had beads of moisture on the top from the patting of the wooden paddles.

Lettie sniffed and sat down, straightening her flowered pinafore. 'Who does yer think taught our Saul his poachin' skills? Even the farmer likes a bit of pheasant or rabbit.'

Maudie smiled shyly, 'And it be t'farmer's mouser an' all, our Granfer saved.'

Granfer smiled back at her, then turned and said to Polly, 'Yer can tell our Saul that, when yer writes to 'im. I 'ad an letter today, so I did and I will write a bit of a note back and I will tell 'im that. How they gets the mail, Lord knows. Bloody marvellous, I call it, but our Saul said if there's someone coming hurt off the front line sick they takes the letters with them if there be time in the mayhem, as well as it getting through in other official ways.'

Maudie said, 'I remember Saul, he be my brother.' She was spreading the butter carefully on her scone and no one said a word; they just waited, but Maudie said nothing more.

Lettie pushed a jar of plum jam across to Sylvia. 'You be trying this. Not a lot of sweetness, but some. The WI do make some with sugar t'authorities gives us, to sell on t'others to help the war.'

Sylvia said, as she spread a thin layer of plum, 'I've just remembered, before the war, at the orphanage we had cream one Founder's Day. It was a treat. We put the cream on top of the jam, but some put it beneath. I suppose it depends what you like. I've never forgotten the taste, and when the war is over, I'm going to buy cream, and make jam with loads of sugar, and bake scones, and sit with a cup of tea and eat a whole plateful, you see if I don't.'

She was talking to herself, really, and could suddenly taste that scone, and saw that everyone was looking at her, longingly.

Verity said, 'I can taste such scones too, I really can. You are a pest, Sylv, because now we'll have to wait Lord knows how long just tasting the memory, until we can have cream again.'

They were all smiling. Lettie rose, and from the fridge drew out a small jug. She placed it by Sylvia and said, 'There you be, lass. No need to taste the memory, have some o' this. 'Tis special from t'farmer, because of the cat, but there be enough for us all.'

There was a reverential silence as Sylvia poured a little of the thick cream on to her jam, and then it was passed around. Polly said, 'On three. One, two, three.' As one, they lifted the scones and took a bite, and Sylvia shut her eyes, remembering the hush that had fallen on the orphanage dining tables as Mother Superior had indicated with a downward gesture that they might all begin.

The taste then was, as this was now, so delicious that Sylvia had thought on that Founder's Day that heaven must be something like it; quite different to everything she had known before.

'Heavens,' sighed Verity, 'you might need to nip up a ladder again, Granfer, but how to entice the cat up first, eh?'

Granfer held a finger to his nose. 'Been thinkin' on that, I 'ave.'

They were laughing as Maudie said, wiping her mouth gently with one of the napkins Lettie was handing round, 'I remember my boy Joe does like cream. He do like butter and jam, too. Leon hurt him, but Saul helped him, and took him from the pain.'

Sylvia felt as though she must hold her breath and make no sound, and the other two girls were the same. Granfer and Lettie were the only two who seemed relaxed. Again Granfer winked at them all.

Maudie put her hands in her lap. 'Yer see, I does know, and remember my boy. But 'tis too soon to see 'im, fer I am not quite well. Some days I forget almost who I is still. Some days things is amazing clear. Today it is that day when things is bright with remembrance, and I thank yer fer 'aving my boy in the 'ome of one of yer, but I fear that when I is well, he will not know me enough to want to stay where I am.'

Again there was a silence, except for the burbling of the range and the clock. For a minute Sylvia thought of Henry's Rolls-Royce and its ticking clock. She heard her own voice then, measured and as calm as her thoughts: 'I didn't have a mother, Maudie, but if I found she was alive, I would be so joyous my heart would surely break. And my life would be complete. Your Joe will feel as I would. We know him well, you see, and I tell you that is the truth.

He is a fine boy. He teaches me to draw, for his drawing is like your brother Saul's. Saul taught him to paint kettles in the way that boaters like. Do you remember those – red background, with a bird, and flowers?'

Maudie looked at her, her expression thoughtful. Finally she said, 'I does remember. The kettle paintings is like when the sun is out and the colours of the earth shine bright. I is glad you share drawing with my boy. I did too, when he were young.'

As one, Verity and Polly reached forward and held Sylvia's hands. 'Oh Sylv,' whispered Polly. Another reached forward across the table – Maudie. She placed her tanned, hardened hand on all of theirs. 'I will be his ma again, but he is not to know it this moment, for I is not mended enough, and my boy needs me to be mended every passing day, don't he, Granfer?'

Granfer nodded. 'If you say so, sweet Maudie.'

He slurped his tea then, while Lettie stood and bustled around, dragging her handkerchief from her apron pocket as she went to the range to top up the teapot. Granfer said, 'One more cup, my dear girls, then you must get on to the depot.'

The hands were released and another scone was eaten; without cream, but that didn't matter, the memory remained, as did the memory of Maudie recapturing the colours of a bright day, and Joe. As Sylvia listened and chatted, her mind was busy thinking of Joe. She hadn't realised before just how important Joe was to so many people. Heavens, he was crucial. How on earth would all this be resolved? As she gazed around the table she and Polly shared a look, and Polly's concern for her parents was obvious. How on earth would they feel when Joe returned to his mother? The loss would be profound.

It was then that Sylvia pondered yet again the question of safety, and again came to the conclusion that if all these people – the boaters, Granfer and his family, Polly's parents, Verity's, the three girls, the men – were all in one place, how much safer it would be. She nodded to herself.

'Oh look,' Polly said, smiling. 'Our Sylv's got her thinking cap on.'

Maudie stared hard at Sylvia's head, so then it had to be explained, while they gulped down their cup of tea and, pulling Pup behind them, hurried to the door, making rushed farewells, with Polly quietly warning Granfer that some thought Leon might be in London, he might read the newspaper, that perhaps it would be better if they came down to Howard House. There, it was said.

The old man merely nodded. 'The boaters been telling us the same thing. They heard yer at darts.'

'Of course they have,' Polly said. 'News travels on the wind, doesn't it?'

'Summat like that, and don't yer worry, we is being so careful, with so much boater and Buckby kindness the bugger won't get near us,' Granfer muttered, winking in a way they didn't understand, but there was such certainty in his voice that they found themselves reassured.

The girls had to run to make up a bit of time, with Pup darting in and out of the tractor ruts along the lane. Once on the boats, they cast off and finally headed south, climbing the locks until a clouded dusk fell along the cut as they headed for the Blisworth Canal. They moored for the night near open fields crisp with frost, and Sylvia thought again of Joe, and the many who loved him, and Saul away at war, and Granfer and Lettie, and all those at Howard House. And, of course, Maudie. How wonderful to be loved by so many; what must it feel like?

On that thought she slept. At first her dreams were full of a life at Howard House, all of them together, until that was torn apart by fragmented, tormented pieces of Leon's darkness, and then, finally, the reunion and those she would meet very soon.

Chapter 17

The St Cecilia Orphanage Reunion looms

Somehow the tiredness always started to overtake them the closer they came to the depot because it meant they would soon be at the end of this journey but probably at the start of another, with barely a beat in between. And even worse now, they'd be pat-pattering back into London, towards the lions' den of rockets, and perhaps Leon, who had come to dominate their thoughts since their trip to Buckby and Maudie's improvement.

But that wasn't quite yet. The motor hold had to be unloaded at the Aylesbury Basin, which was at the conclusion of the Aylesbury Arm, a mere six miles of cut through unspoilt countryside, and then the butty would be unloaded at one of their favourite wharfs, belonging to the paper factory.

Later, as they approached the paper factory, Verity blew two blasts on the hunting horn, which had become a tradition: it meant that hot mugs of tea would be summoned up for them by the foreman. When they moored up, Arthur the foreman was already there to supervise the unloading, whistling down the tea from the office. His black band in remembrance of his daughter was still on his arm. As they stood with him the girls wondered when he could remove it without seeming to dismiss her very existence.

''Ow you lasses doing?' Arthur said, the icy wind doing its best to tug off his hat. 'Yer got out from under, then?'

Verity sipped her tea as Polly replied, 'Indeed we did, guided by our Sylv's red nose. Do you need her to light up any dark corners in the factory, Arthur?' Sylvia dragged her scarf up and over her nose, then realised she couldn't drink her tea, so slipped it down again.

Arthur smiled gently. 'Don't yer pay them no mind, little miss. Yer brighten up lives, you do. Just like yer all do.'

Sylvia almost whispered, 'And you, and your family, now your daughter's gone?'

'Oh, we just get on with it, but I does just think that to be killed by a doodlebug towards the end of the blasted war is . . . Well, you know, cos yer nearly copped it from the V2. Then I 'spect the bloody Nazis will bellyache that they're being 'ard done by now we're movin' in. I'll "hard done by" 'em, if I ever get me hands on 'em. Look at the bloody mess they've made of the bloody world.'

Polly and Sylvia took the mugs back to the office, handing them to the clerk. 'Okey-dokey, are yer, gals?' he asked. 'Bit bruised and battered, but—'

'Unbowed,' Polly finished for him. They laughed together. 'Thanks for the cuppa.' She opened the door.

He said, as they left, 'Not long now, lasses, got to be over by Christmas, eh? Then a land fit for 'eroes, if there's anything left of it, the beggars.'

They headed on, approaching the south, waving as Bet and her girls headed towards them on *Swansong* and *Seagull* well north of Cowley Lock. It seemed so strange to see Saul and Granfer's pair out and about again. Verity gave them a couple of blasts on the hunting horn, then yelled, 'We said goodbye to Dog and put a note through the door for Fran. Granfer's family is coming on well, but not quite 100%.' Everyone was very careful not to name Maudie except at boater venues.

At the Cowley Lock they waited for another pair to come through, and it was now that the thought of the reunion gripped Sylvia by the throat. This time it refused to be shoved away but hovered just out of her control. She was torn between longing for Steve and dread at being back.

She made herself concentrate on the pair that were approaching. They were crewed by women as well, ones they barely knew. They all called, ''Ow do,' and waved. Had Bet trained them too? Probably. Finally Verity lock-wheeled them through Cowley Lock, and then the Bull's Bridge lay-by was in sight, but their day wasn't over. They moored up stern first, as the sun was setting behind the clouds, and removed the tillers before dragging out brooms from the store. Sylvia was glad, for it kept her busy. She was about to head down into the butty hold to start the clear-out when the other two girls grabbed the brush from her.

Verity wagged a finger at Sylvia as though she was a five-year-old. 'Certainly not, you make a cuppa, or take Pup for a walk, and we will do the dirty work. Then you will nip to the lavs, use the depot's hot water for a proper wash and we will stand guard to repel boarders. The workforce can wait. After which, we will help you put a seam line down the back of your legs and some slap on your face because you have a reunion to go to, friends to see, and a bloke to meet.'

They pushed her off the boat, so she walked Pup along the kerb, chatting to the boaters who were boiling up their wash or returning from the shops, though they'd be shutting soon as the day was wearing to a close. She felt peculiar. Seam lines? Slap? She hardly ever bothered. What would Sister Augustine think? What about Harriet? Sylvia and Pup carried on to the end, and back, but she was too nervous to enjoy the puppy's antics, though young Jimmy Porter made up for her as he leapt off his motor. Taking Pup's rope lead from her he ran ahead, then stopped, making Pup sit. 'See, Sylv, 'tis what you must be doing. Train 'er or she'll end up in the cut, and it be dirty. I can remember that, afore Verity and Polly got me out again.'

She smiled but it was as though she was walking two feet above the earth, with her head all fuzzy and a tremble throughout her body. She returned to *Horizon* with Pup, then took her towel and headed for the yard, the girls strolling with her, making idle chatter. They stood guard while she took over the sink, washing, again and again, seeing the memory of Harriet, the one she kept trying so hard to repress, the one of Harriet walking from the dormitory towards her postulancy at St Cecelia's Convent, alone, looking back at Sylvia who had shaken her head, calling, 'I'm sorry, I know I promised I would come with you when we were younger, but I'm just not sure enough.' Disappointment and accusation had shown in every move of Harriet's body at *her*, Sylvia Simpson's, betrayal.

The girls took her place while she returned to the butty, where she sat, hoping the boat would sink and so it wouldn't be her fault that she was unable to go to the reunion. The girls arrived fifteen minutes later and made Spam fritters, which they all ate as usual in the motor cabin. Sylvia dressed in the butty, and they met up in *Marigold*'s cabin. The girls, who were dressed in skirts too, explained that they were coming with her to north London to make sure she actually entered the portals of the orphanage, and what's more, stayed there.

Sylvia sat down suddenly on Polly's side-bed, defeated. She had intended to spend the evening walking around, anywhere but near the orphanage, despite Steve saying that he would be there. Because so too would Sister Augustine, Harriet and Father O'Malley and she was frightened she would let the whole thing drag her back, away from her happiness.

'Don't worry, please, please,' pleaded Polly. 'Steve will come, he saved your life, remember that. He will come.'

They didn't understand, Sylvia thought.

Verity said, getting her make-up case from the bottom of the cupboard, 'Darling, we can see you are nervous, and we're not having you doing a runner, my girl. We know you once thought of being a nun, but we also know that Sister Augustine said that you must make sure it wasn't imagination. One has only to see your face with Steve to know where your happiness lies, so you're not doing a bunk on our watch, is she Pol?'

Polly gripped her hand. 'It doesn't mean you don't love God. You do and can go on doing so. But love has many forms . . .'

Verity put some rouge on Sylvia's cheeks, a little lipstick, a smudge of Joy perfume behind her ears, and held up her mirror. 'Look, you're quite divine.'

Sylvia stared. She *was* different: her eyes seemed to sparkle, her lips were more obvious. The other two were busily applying a bit here and there to their own faces. 'We're going off to visit Solly at Jacob's once you are delivered and the door shut behind you. We telephoned dear Solly after our ablutions, and he and Rachel will be delighted. Or so they said, so naturally we choose to believe them.'

The last thing was to put a seam line down the backs of their legs with the remnants of Verity's eyebrow pencil and then they set off.

They didn't arrive until eight o'clock, and the reunion was to start at 7.30. Sylvia stood across the road at the church, behind and to the side of which the orphanage seemed to tower, with a narrow entrance on to the street. To the rear of the orphanage was the convent. It was small but active, and it was here that Harriet was a postulant, before becoming a novice, and finally a nun. Sylvia pointed. 'We'd come out from that door and head for school in a crocodile.'

She looked at the church and could smell the incense as though she was there. She could hear 'Hail Mary, full of grace'. She could see Father O'Malley. She so seldom went to Mass; churches were hard to find along the cut. But not that hard, a small quiet voice said.

'Come on,' Polly said, slipping her arm through Sylvia's. Together they walked across the road. Polly pulled on the bell. A small sliding peep-panel opened, then slammed shut, and the door opened immediately. Sister Augustine said, 'You came. I'm so very pleased. Girls, will you come in too? The more the merrier.'

She held out her hand, beckoning to them. Verity said, 'That's so kind, but we have to see Solly, who was buried beneath rubble with us. Ah, but you met him in the hospital. Be gentle with our Sylv, we're all still a bit pale and interesting, if you get my meaning.'

Sylvia flushed; no one asked Sister Augustine to be gentle. But the head of the orphanage merely laughed, her white wimple juddering along with her chins. 'Oh, I'm not sure about that, Verity. It is Verity, isn't it? I might run your friend and mine round the play area a few times, don't you think, to make sure she behaves appropriately.'

Sylvia realised that in her panic she had forgotten Sister Augustine's normality, and her humour. She turned to her friends. 'You go on to Solly, give him my love and tell him I'll see him another time, would you?' She followed Sister Augustine into the darkness, or so it seemed to her, but turned to wave. They still stood there. Verity blew her a kiss. They were worried, and Sylvia wanted to hug them both in thanks for their love for her.

A novice nun was in control of the door, and now it closed, shutting Verity and Polly from view. This was what it must be like if one took the step to postulancy, Sylvia thought. She shivered. Sister Augustine seemed to glide ahead, while Sylvia's court shoes clipped on the flagstones. Sister Augustine said, 'The reunion is being held in the refectory, which you will remember from your years with us. This time though, my dear, the tables and chairs have been pushed back, and we even have a little band. One hundred years is quite a cause for celebration, or so Father O'Malley feels, as do the sisters. I do hope you agree?'

They were at the double doors that led into the refectory, and Sylvia heard laughter, music and loud chatter. She had remembered life here as a murmur. The doors seemed to magically open, but in fact they were being handled by two postulants wearing black dresses and short white veils. Was one of them Harriet?

But no, she didn't recognise either and breathed a little easier.

Sister Augustine stepped to one side, ushering her forward. 'In you go, my dear. You will find your dormitory friends in a group near where your dining table was. Strange how we cling to familiar things, isn't it?'

She didn't wait for an answer but glided back down the corridor to receive whoever was ringing the doorbell. Sylvia entered into the light, remembering the bell that had rung at the start of the meals, and the scramble to finish before the next one sounded. At which point, finished or not, the plates must go to the monitor at the head of the table, to be taken to the trolleys.

She expected that like everything in the convent, the reunion had been organised to the sound of bells.

Sylvia shut away the thought, and walked to the table that had been reserved for Dormitory St James, looking all around. He was not here. Would he come?

There were religious pictures on the walls: Jesus Christ as Light of the World, and another of Him knocking on a door, bathed in light. She could almost hear Him say that He was standing at the door and that if she heard His voice and opened the door, He would come to her. She dragged her eyes away. She wanted Him in her life, but not to be her life. Please, not.

She wouldn't look at the postulants who stood behind a table where cups of tea were being served.

Instead she moved on to the Dormitory St James table where a small group of girls stood, and though they had become young women, she recognised a few. She waited until the group made room for her, and Rosemary, the tallest girl, in a WAAF uniform, smiled. 'Well, it's Sylvia. How's life? Do you still talk in your sleep? I remember you waking the dorm with that nightmare you were having. I didn't understand a word.' Sylvia had no time to answer or collect her thoughts, because her dream was the last thing she had thought anyone would remember. Nora, who wore the uniform of the WRNS, smiled. 'You doing all right, Sylvia?' she asked. In fact, they were all in uniforms of some kind, including Dawn, who wore that of the Auxiliary Fire Service.

Dawn asked, looking her up and down, 'So what are you doing for the war effort? Not a lot, from the look of it.'

Dawn had always been spiteful, wanting to get one up on everyone, Sylvia thought.

She said, 'I was recruited for the Inland Waterways to take over from the men who went to war. We carry supplies in all weathers. I am a bit late, so sorry, just back from Tyseley Wharf; I probably smell in spite of the dab of Joy.' She realised that she sounded much as Polly and Verity would in the same circumstances. Heavens, they really had become as one.

Dawn sniffed, and Sylvia said, 'I wouldn't sniff. You might get more of a whiff than you need or want.' Heavens, she *was* Verity.

Just then Sylvia felt a hand on her shoulder and heard the words, 'Hello, Coppernob.' She smiled, overcome with relief, and turned to meet her Steve, the man who had saved her life and who she knew, without any shadow of a doubt as their eyes locked, that she loved beyond all else. And without whom there would be no light or joy in her life. Lovely Steve, who with one touch had caused her fears to melt away and leave her free.

They smiled at one another as though there was no one else around, and something more happened, something that took the breath from her body; not like the blast – something warmer, sweeter. He reached out to her, and she took his hand.

Dawn gasped, 'Steve, what on earth?'

He wrapped his arms around Sylvia, pulling her against him. She had never felt so cherished. He said, 'This young woman was one of those we dug out of rubble south of the canal when a couple of V2s came down close to one another. You might remember hearing about it, Dawn, from the safety of your office.'

The girl flushed. Steve continued, 'Sylvia and her two crew members, with the lovely Dog, were making a phone call to their depot because another boating pair had been caught in the blast on the canal. Dangerous lives these girls lead, but I'm sure you all know that. They just don't have a uniform to prove it, only scars and exhaustion, and grief for other boaters who haven't been so lucky, and for Dog who died saving them and others.'

There was a general shuffling, particularly from Dawn, who disappeared to collect a drink of tea from the urn. The others clustered closer and really began to chat. Sylvia found herself sipping tea that Steve brought them on a tray, longing for half a pint of mild instead. Heavens, she really had changed, just like all these girls. Rosemary whispered, 'Lord, I could do with a smoke, and a shandy.'

Steve, his arm around her, whispered in Sylvia's ear, 'That Dawn needed to be put in her place, I hope you didn't mind me having a go. Her watch has been under a lot of strain with her gossip and tittle-tattle.'

The music had become louder and Father O'Malley called, 'I think it is time everyone took a partner – any old one will do – and sort of shimmy a bit. Or shall I get Sister Augustine to show you all how? Now, that would be a sight to take home with you, I dare say.'

As they all laughed, Sylvia couldn't remember Father O'Malley being anything other than rather frightening.

'Oh come on, let's make the old boy happy, and sort of shimmy,' Steve grinned, and led her into the centre of the room. They were alone for a moment, and Sylvia didn't know where to look as people stopped talking to watch, so she just stared at the top button of Steve's uniform. He saw her looking. 'I'm going straight on shift after this, so have to leave at ten,' he said.

It was a waltz of sorts; the band were ex-orphanage boys, not professionals, so it was a bit patchy but nothing mattered as they danced and others took to the floor. Steve said, 'I'd forgotten the humour of the staff.'

'I had too. It took me by surprise,' Sylvia replied. As they executed a turn, his grip around her waist tightened. She confessed, 'I didn't want to come.'

He just nodded, then after a pause, murmured, 'It's not somewhere I wanted to come again, it reminded me too much of what I am, but it's all right, now I'm here, with you. Everything always will be, with you. But can you smell the cabbage they had at lunchtime?'

They both roared with laughter, and it was then that Sylvia saw another postulant taking over from a novice behind the tea urn. It was Harriet and as she scanned the room she saw Sylvia, and cocked her head to one side. Steve whirled Sylvia away, back into the throng. He spun her, and she clung to him, but each time they turned there was Harriet, and the warmth ebbed from Sylvia and the fear was back, along with the guilt and the confusion. She made herself listen to Steve, who was talking of Dodge's missus who had been waiting for such sad news since the war had begun. 'He was like a dad,' Steve was saying. 'Not sure I know what a dad should be, though.'

Sylvia knew, because they must be like Henry and Thomas, and even Rogers. She focussed on the 'family' at Howard House, and Steve's hand on hers. Did he mind the callouses? Would they remain for ever or would her hands soften again after the war as someone said. Who was that, perhaps Dr Havers? She couldn't remember. And would she and Steve stay together, would everything be all right, as long as they were? Had she even answered him? If not, the words he had uttered had come and gone.

They were dancing in step now, closer together. She saw Father O'Malley then, his black-rimmed glasses slipping down his nose as they always had, weaving through the dancers, stopping for the odd word, until he tapped them both on the shoulder. 'This is not an "excuse me" dance, but an "excuse me" to ask you to help the floundering band, dear Sylvia. Just sing us a tune or two, to help them along, won't you? They're getting a bit hot and sweaty with the stress of it all, don't you know. Harry's all right, of course, on the ivories, but the other two are reluctant conscripts to the stage. Your help would be magnificent too, Steve.'

It was posed as a question, but after her time on the waterway Sylvia recognised an order when she heard one. So did Steve, obviously, because he raised his eyebrows, and muttered, 'Our master has spoken. Harry and I have a band – or had. Been too busy recently.'

He stood at the side of the stage, waving to the piano player, who grinned, and mouthed *could murder a pint*, as Sylvia suggested to the band 'Begin the Beguine'. The players searched through the music resting on the stands, to no avail, so instead she sang unaccompanied, remembering how she and Saul would sing in the pubs, and even at Verity's snooty club in Jermyn Street; singing for their supper, that time. What would Sister Augustine think of that? She realised that Steve was dancing with a WAAF. They didn't talk, and he was as stiff as a board. Had Father O'Malley 'excused' them into a dancing pair? She sang on, and every time Steve turned he had eyes only for Sylvia.

The song ended, and while the applause rattled round the room, Harry, the piano player, suggested 'A Nightingale Sang in Berkeley Square', and with his accompaniment and the uncertain saxophone, but not the drummer who had taken his chance and done a runner, it worked well. As she held the last note, she could see Steve heading towards them and she held out her hand for him to help her down. Instead he leapt up, patted Harry on the back, then took over the saxophone from the older man, who wiped his forehead with relief, saying that Father O'Malley was a beggar for dragging people in when they had a cab they should be driving, or just when rescue was in sight, asking the rescuer to go and dance with a lonely girl.

The cabbie went on, 'You're a mate, son. I need to get on, yer see. I remember you coming here, Coppernob. Just a babe, but what a little terror you grew into. Glad yer seem 'appy. It takes time to get yersel' sorted in yer 'ead, don't it? Probably same for you, the girl coppernob that is.'

Steve and Sylvia looked at one another in agreement as Harry played a solo on the piano. Steve and Sylvia stood together nearby tapping their feet and Steve said, 'If you aren't an orphan, you don't know how it is.'

Sylvia thought for a long moment, then said, 'Yes, but there is love here, and laughter, and I realise there's much to be grateful for. If we're lucky we get that one person, as you had Dodge, and perhaps I have Rogers and Mrs B, and Polly and Verity, of course.' She paused and took hold of her courage. 'And there's us.'

His arm slipped around her and he pulled her close, saying into her hair, 'I'm so glad you said that.'

She sang again now, with Steve on saxophone. This time it was 'Tea for Two', and then 'Boogie Woogie Bugle Boy', and laughed as the room erupted into jive dancing, to the consternation of Father O'Malley, who was spoken to by Sister Augustine, and even received the dreaded wag of the finger. Father O'Malley wiped his forehead, and Sylvia thought at any moment he would cross himself.

She swung round, to see Harry standing and thwacking the keyboard, while Steve's saxophone was pointing to the ceiling as he blasted out the notes. She conducted them to a halt at the end, all three of them together. They bowed to the applause, panting, laughing. When they lined up the only ones missing were Saul and Tom, Polly and Verity.

Over the noise Steve said, 'It's ten o'clock, I have to go, but come with me. We can travel part of the way together and I'll leave you where I can get a connection and you can carry on. It'll just give us a little longer together. Say yes, because I can't bear to miss a moment of "us".'

The musicians bowed again, then Father O'Malley leapt on to the stage and hustled them off, saying, 'Wonderful, wonderful, not sure what the sisters really thought of all that American dancing but they will recover.'

Steve said, 'And so will you, Father. But look, we have to go. Shifts.'

'I've others to take over the stage now, but my thanks, both of you.'

Harry made for the hall with them and the boys lagged behind, chatting, as Sylvia headed along the dark corridor. There was a movement to her right, and Harriet emerged from the shadows. Sylvia knew she should stop, but every part of her wanted to brush past. Harriet took all decision from her and walked alongside, hands clasped in front of her and whispering, so quietly that Sylvia had to strain to hear, 'Dear friend, you seem happy. Remember that you can always come back. After all, lives change, and realisation comes that the selfishness of personal happiness counts for nothing in the face of God's love and purpose. Never forget that I am here, alone, when that wasn't what we promised.' She reached out and held Sylvia's arm, shaking it, just as Sister Augustine, standing at the door into the street, turned. Harriet hurried back into the refectory.

For a moment Sylvia let the darkness of the corridor and her guilt smother her but then Steve was by her side, walking with her to the door, saying, 'You know, bugger it, I was going on shift early, but why? Tonight I'll get there on time, so I'll come all the way to Southall with you.'

They thanked Sister Augustine, who looked at Sylvia closely, taking her hand and pressing it gently. 'You look happy, and that is all we want for you,' she said. 'Remember my words, dear Sylvia, not those of everyone with an opinion they wish to force upon you.'

Steve said, as they walked down the street, 'I hadn't realised that Sister Augustine is such a good woman, but what did she mean by everyone with an opinion, and so on?'

Sylvia said, 'I don't really know.' But Sister Augustine had clearly seen Harriet's intensity, the shake of her arm, and probably guessed that it could add to the confusion that she knew Sylvia had experienced over her relationship with God.

As they continued, Steve's arm came around her and he said, 'You are my everything, Sylvia. I know it seems ridiculous – after all, one minute I didn't know of your existence, and now I feel I have known you all my life.' He half laughed. 'Well, perhaps in a way I have, both of us living here, but in different houses, and separated by – what, five years?' They walked on in silence. She said tentatively, 'You make me so happy, and I feel so different since we met, but I'm scared . . .'

She stopped. She didn't want to talk about a broken promise, about the selfishness of love, because she feared Harriet could be right. Was happiness selfish? Would she, they, pay? Steve was talking over her thoughts now, as they reached the underground station, where the bus stop stood too, and it was his voice she listened to. 'Don't be scared. Nothing's going to happen to me, or you. We just have to remember to live the day to its fullest. After all, what happens, will happen.'

But that wasn't what she had been scared of.

They took a couple of buses, until finally she was within walking distance of the depot. Steve got off with her, and for a moment she wanted to cling to him and never let him go. The clouds had built, few people were about, and she didn't have to cling because suddenly he was holding her tightly. They kissed, and kissed again, and again, and he said, against her mouth, 'I never ever want to let you go, never. But I must. There are houses to hose, lives to save, you to miss when you go on to Limehouse, and if you ever, ever get in the way of a V2 again, I will never forgive you.' He pulled away. 'Do you understand, Sylvia Simpson? Because I love you more than life itself.'

She whispered, 'I understand.' She pulled his head down and kissed his eyes, his cheeks and finally his mouth, saying against it, 'I love you, Steve Bates. Love you until the sky falls in. Do you understand?'

They were smiling as he straightened, saluted, and turned away, almost singing, 'I understand, oh I do so understand.' He ran then, to catch the bus heading towards the east. She watched him go and knew that Harriet was wrong, for love wasn't selfish: she would give her life for that man.

At Golders Green in the sitting room of Jacob Fisher's apartment, Verity and Polly checked their watches as the chiming of the grandfather clock in the hall reminded them that they should be leaving. Solly sat to their left, in a comfortable armchair, with his son Jacob and daughter-in-law Rachel ranged in a worn settee to their right which Solly had just told them had come from his Furniture Emporium. Polly bet he had only given them a small discount. She asked. Solly tapped his nose. 'Mine to know, yours to find out.'

They all laughed.

Polly nudged Verity. 'It's well past ten o'clock, we should go, Solly, or we will turn into pumpkins, and I for one don't want to. But neither do I want to go. It's just been so fine being here, seeing you so well. Grumpy but well, and to tell you too much about our worries. Leon Arness in particular. Very boring.'

Jacob leaned forward and said, 'This isn't Dad being grumpy, young Pol. He's on his best behaviour in case you drag him under some more rubble. And you have not been boring. There is much darkness simmering that has nothing to do with the war.'

But Rachel was looking confused. 'Pumpkins you said? Why would you turn into such a thing?'

Polly said, 'Ah, don't tell me, Jacob, that you haven't introduced your wife to the story of Cinderella? Well, I insist that you do so soon, but briefly Rachel, it's all about a scullery maid, who isn't really a maid but the daughter of the Baron who has married again. His wife is horrid, and so are her daughters . . .' She stopped, seeing Rachel looking all at sea.

Verity took over. 'What Pol's trying to explain is that all is well in the end and Cinderella marries her prince. But as Pol said, it's up to Solly or your husband to fill you in on the details, because we really must go.' She started to rise, as Polly said, 'Meanwhile, talking of scullery maids finding their prince, our own boater has, I hope, found hers.'

She rose too.

Solly reached forward, gesturing to the girls and his son and daughter-in-law. 'If, as you said earlier, it is that young fireman, nothing bonds like the saving of a life, and if they are both without parents, then they will know to cling together.' He looked at Rachel and Jacob. 'It is what *we* do, after all, my children, and will do even when we discover news of Emmanuel, and so many others of our family.'

The girls were moved by his intensity, and Verity said, 'You sound so worried, Solly. Is there still no news, and here we were, grizzling on about a horrid little crook?'

'One minute our Emmanuel, my beloved papa, was here, the next he was gone, pouf.' It was Rachel speaking as the two of them also rose. Jacob held her hand, stroking it, saying, 'But Father is right, we have one another, whatever news we receive of him or the many members of our family in Hungary.'

Verity said, 'You have us, too. For whatever you need, you have the three of us and always will.'

Solly was struggling to rise, but Verity leaned down and kissed his cheek, pushing him back and telling him, 'No, you sit here and guard your will against all comers, dear Solly.'

She made way for Polly, who lifted his hand, and kissed it. 'You take care, and a second kiss from Sylv. She loves you very much.'

They left, with Jacob seeing them to the door. Polly said, 'If we can help, tell us, any time.'

Jacob half bowed. 'That is what I wish to say to you, and dear Sylvia. Any time, you understand. Do not worry alone. None of us should, and I will be alert for someone called Leon Arness.'

They left, but Jacob remained standing at the door. He called softly, 'My gratitude knows no bounds, for the presence of you three saved my beloved father. I repeat, please, if you need me, come, and meanwhile I will report if I find anything on Joe's father.'

Chapter 18

In the Blind Weasel plans are being laid

Leon sat in Norton's former chair, in his former office at the back of his former club, the Blind Weasel, on the edge of the West End which looked on its last legs, but weren't, not really, but it were a good front. Leon loved the word 'former'. He had heard it from one of the two coppers he had on his books. It sounded important. He looked around Norton's *former* office slowly, so slowly. There were no windows in the office, and only a little lighting. Had Norton's former bungalow been t'same, before the V1 got him, and took him out? Vengeance rocket, eh? Well, he'd got what was coming to him for trying to put him, Leon Arness, away.

Norton were going to show the judge his books, even though 'e'd been happy enough to buy his black market booze from Leon, but it hadn't worked out so well for 'im, had it?

But for Leon Arness, now known as Lionel Harkness – what was the point of having a road sign that would point the cops to him? – it had proved a way into something better than t'cut. He swung round, scanning the room again, its dark panels, the rugs under which was the main safe. Best to have no window, he preferred it that way. It was safer: no point in having the Met crashing through the window to take him out, or some other gang moving in on his territory. That's always supposing they got past Dougie, and if they did the lamplight made him a poor target. Yes, he reckoned he'd thought of most things.

He looked at Norton's fish tank, more like a whole wall of 'em buggers behind him. As he watched the fish he thought about Mario Babbaro, head of the Babbaro family, who ran a gang near Limehouse Basin.

It were amazing what the Italian shifted from t'Basin off the merchant ships that moored up, stuff that he sold on at a goodly price. Babarro should have been interned and his sons with him but weren't, and now the internees were mostly back home anyways. That's cos the war were winding down but, thank God, weren't over yet. Leon nodded to himself. He had plans, and those plans meant taking over Mario's Limehouse.

He spun round, reached into the top drawer of Norton's old desk and drew out the fish food. As he rose, the chair seat moved, catching his leg. He cursed. Bloody Norton had been so damned fat he had strained the shock absorber in the joint between the seat and the pedestal, giving it a will of its own. Leon's laugh was harsh; the key was not to let anyone or anything around you have just that – a will of their own.

He lifted the lid, took a pinch of food and spread it over the surface of the water, then another, as though he were their king. He watched the fish bobbing up, snatching at it, hating the stink of the food. He slammed on the lid and returned to his chair. As he threw the food into the drawer and slammed it shut, he shouted at the fish, 'There yer go, I starves yer for a few days and then I watches to see who wins, so don't yer forget who owns yer. And who can kill yer, or keep yer living.'

The smoke from his cigar rose straight up from the ashtray. He reached for it and rolled it between his fingers, feeling for any movement of the tobacco leaves. There was none. Who'd a thought he'd like 'em? Well, he weren't sure he did, but they were Norton's so why not? He laughed slightly. What'd them stinkin' boaters think of him now, as they dragged their arses from Limehouse Basin, slogging along t'cut, freezing and hauling for a few ruddy pennies a run? What was the matter with 'em? They could sell off some of the load, easy as winking, or buy up some goods off the ships and sell them off along the way.

Who'd win between him and Mario? Well, he would, but that's because he weren't going to move until he were good and ready, then Mario would be fish food. 'Yer 'ear that?' he flung over his shoulder at the fish. 'Too big fer yer, but a few in the Basin'll be glad of 'em.'

There were three taps at the door, then another two. He checked that his revolver was on the shelf over the kneehole of his desk as he sat upright, one arm on the desk, the other on his lap and the gun handle towards him. The signal were right, but you couldn't be too careful.

The knock came again, as it should. 'Who it be, Dougie?' he barked.

'Tony Burrowes, boss.'

Leon smiled, 'Let 'im in. Stay put t'other side.'

'Right yer are, boss.'

The door opened, and the accountant came in, with the books under his arm. The one thing Leon had learned in the clink, or remand as they called it, was his numbers and his letters. His men didn't know that; all they knew was that someone checked the books on the heels of the accountant. He'd inherited Manny from Norton and thought he were skimming the books, and when Manny disappeared they knew something was amiss – but not that Leon had checked the figures himself, and then killed 'im.

Of course, his men suspected Manny were feeding the fish in the Thames, but Leon shrugged. No one could talk if he did the dirty work himself. So far, Tony was playing the figures straight. But when it came to it, so had Manny when Leon rechecked, but that were water under the bridge. He sniggered cos he were so funny.

The old man Burrowes placed the books on the table. 'Profits up again, Mr Harkness. A steady rise, which is what you want.'

Tony Burrowes waited to be allowed to sit down in the hard chair opposite Leon. Norton had shortened the legs, so any visitor was lower than the boss. Leon kept the chair because he remembered how small it had made him feel. He leaned back in the chair, his eyes as hooded as his thoughts. 'Ain't what I want, though, be it? I want big profits, and quick. War's ending, could all come crashing down.'

Tony said, 'Not necessarily.' He waited. Leon finally nodded, and Tony sat and looked up at Leon, who snapped, 'I ain't goin' to give yer an invite, Tony. If you've summat to say, say it. I ain't got all day, 'tis like 'olding a lock for some bugger, which only puts yer behind on yer run.'

Tony swallowed, holding his homburg by the brim and turning it round and round. 'Look at it this way, boss. War costs a pretty penny, so the country borrows but it has to be repaid. How do we do that? By not spending much. If the Labour Party get in, they've these plans to spend and spend on ... what d'they call it, the welfare or something; a war against poverty, on top of the debt. That'll mean more borrowing, and more cuts where they can. So, we're talking about rationing going on, p'raps even more severe, maybe for a couple of years, maybe more. The black market's still yours for the taking.'

Leon took up his cigar again, then reached down into his bottom drawer and pulled out the wooden box containing the Cubans. ''Elp yourself.' He threw a box of matches across the table, and watched Tony take one, sniff it, roll it between his fingers. He toasted it, holding the match beneath it, rolling the cigar over and above the flame. Once the tobacco had dried, Tony placed it in his mouth and, still with the flame beneath but not touching, drew the heat in until it lit.

Leon leaned back. Norton had taught him all that, and it made him laugh to have passed on the lesson ter both his accountants, who must think he were a man of the world. 'So,' he mulled. 'Still time to expand.'

Tony looked puzzled. 'Don't know about that, this area's pretty established. Got a few families working it.'

'Be there anything that says it 'as ter be a family, Tony?' Leon heard the ice in his own voice, and so did Tony, who sat up straight, his hand trembling as he removed the cigar from his mouth, coughing slightly. 'Course not, Mr Harkness. You are surrounded by the equivalent of a family; after all, what is a group likes ours if not a family.'

Leon shrugged, and waved him away. 'Send in Dougie on yer way out.' That was it. Leon had things to think about.

Tony looked from his cigar to the ashtray. Leon waved again. 'Tek it with yer, but don't drop ash on me floor.' Tony scuttled to the door, and tapped four times, then again. The door opened. He rushed through it. Leon heard him yammer, 'Quick, he wants you.'

Leon roared, 'Who be 'e, the cat's doo-da?'

Dougie entered and closed the door on Tony's frantic apology. Dougie was huge, and muscle-bound. He'd been a bare-fist fighter and was still useful, and though he had once been Norton's man he'd the sense to put down his knuckledusters when Leon invaded the premises out of hours. That had been after that Mrs Holmes beat him off the old man and away from his son Joe, his own property. Just like that Polly she were, and whatever that Tony do say, you needed a family to build an empire to make you like a king. He glanced back at the tank. 'A king,' he roared.

It were all the boy's fault. He could have come quiet out of the school playground after he'd paid a couple of blokes to find where he was. He'd travelled all the way down to Woking himself, he had, thinking the boy would do as he were told. But he'd said, 'No, Da' and run back into the building. His own lad said no. Leon still couldn't work it out, the ruddy toe-rag. So he'd had to go to the Holmeses' house.

He shook his head, remembering the hammering in his head, the blood dripping down the back of his neck when that Polly's ma had whacked him with the frying pan, again and again. He felt the rocking of the train when he took off from the garden. He'd gone to London, course 'e had, cos where else did he know. He'd gone there from the 'ome for kids with no folks when he were fourteen, and then to t'cut, but this time as he walked from Waterloo to nowhere in particular, he'd thought how Norton had kicked the bucket, so why not take on his place, and his men?

He'd stopped in a pub, hired some loafers, promising them jobs if they did well. They'd all gone in, whacking with clubs, but it were half empty, with almost no booze behind the bar. It was so easy it were like a knife going through a slab of butter. Norton's men had put down their clubs, and fists, no problem. Leon had told them their boss was dead from a bomb on the bungalow. And he'd told them he'd see to 'em if anyone squealed to the cops about him being back in town, but if they stayed they'd get their wages, just the same. No one had squealed, or if they had, no coppers had come. Mark you, it cost a bit to keep those two cops on Norton's payroll sweet, but it were worth it.

Dougie moved slightly, bringing Leon back from the past. 'We got a lot of work to do, Dougie, cos the game ain't over yet, cos though the war might be soon there'll be rationing for many a day for'ards. Now, what about me boy, Joe? Any news from any snouts? He ain't in Woking cos the Holmes house is shut. Got anything on the Holmes name yet?'

'Not a whisper, boss. But I 'ad a thought. Shirley's ma sent her the local paper from Hastings way. All sorts in that, about school things, and the like. What say we ask ones we know with folks about the country to send in the local rags? Might be summat.'

Leon was nodding. That weren't a bad idea. 'You'll see to that, then, will yer Dougie cos I've other things on me mind. Now, I been thinking about the scheme o' things and I got to make a plan, I have, Dougie, cos why pay a wholesaler when I could take over that end for meself, eh? Think on, Dougie. What if I get rid of me middleman at t'docks . . .'

Dougie nodded, his eyes sharp, but shocked. 'Mario's got a bloody army, boss.'

'Then that's what we'll get an' all. I'll need a bit of a one to get me boy back when we do find 'im, anyway. And I needs 'im back as we get big.'

Leon was thinking his Joe could read proper and his mind were quick with figures, and family were family, when all were said and done, and the gangs that had them were stronger by far. After all, the lad'd take over the business one day, so he would keep his mouth tight shut and loyalty sharp, he Lionel Harkness'd see to that. 'So, yer get thinkin' about how to find 'im.'

Dougie said, 'Right you are, boss.'

He paused and Leon could almost hear his thoughts grinding like wheels in the big bloke's head. Dougie finally said, 'Maybe I'll get Shirley, the club hostess, to talk to everyone she knows and them in the club as she takes the fags round. She might get her personal punters, if yer know what I mean, on to it too. Bit of blackmail works well. Get 'em to ask round about his name. Harkness, right?'

'Try Holmes, cos that's bloody Polly's surname, and 'Opkins.' Try Woking. Try Buckby way but they wouldn't be that stupid to hide 'im there. They'd know I'd ask, and I damn well have already. But try again. Try places along the cut. Maybe Tyesley. Ask if anyone knows the name, eleven year he be. Haul in them papers too and I'll pay Shirley a bit extra to read 'em in the day before the club really opens for business.' Leon looked thoughtful. 'Tell 'er to thin 'em out for me. I'll get me reading up a bit to recognise them names in the ones she puts on me desk. You keep on with the narks in the cop shops too, and around the bazaars, eh?'

'There are the evacuees registers too, boss. But it'll be a needle in a haystack.'

'Yer think I don't know that?' Leon smashed his fist on the table. Dougie braced himself. Leon thought for a moment. 'All right, tell yer what. You're going to try and get the other names, the last names of the girls on that damned boat that Polly Holmes runs. I'll get that private investigator bloke on that too, make it a race. Who finds 'em first gets a bottle of Scotch. We can check where them girls are from an 'all, and get 'em papers specially, and check for the last names that match them girls' at the schools. How's that for bloody brilliant. Someone should 'ave thought o' that before.' Leon glared at Dougie.

Dougie nodded. 'I should 'ave, I'm right sorry, boss. I'll get on now.'

Dougie turned, and left. Leon sat back in his chair, pulled the accounts towards him, and started to go through the figures. He weren't sure how long to go on paying the coppers in the bloody sticks for news. It hadn't worried him that much before cos he'd been so busy, but now he were building up his empire it more than mattered that the boy was here. It were weak for a bloke to let his boy 'ide.

He looked at his cigar in the ashtray. The smoke was curling in the slight draught from the door. He hurried over and banged it shut. He worked on the figures for a couple of hours and they were all kosher. He rose, pulled back the rug, lifted the boards and opened the safe with the new combination.

Leon placed the books in. Back went the boards, and the rug, and then he poured himself some whisky and sat looking at his fish, working out just how all that the Babbaro family at Limehouse had could become his and Joe's. Then they'd be known as the Harkness Family, and they'd bring the money flooding in, which would show those who'd seen him off from the canal just who they'd been dealing with, just as he'd shown Maudie when she'd talked back once too often. He wondered what lock she were laying in, or what pound. Then shrugged. What did it matter?

Chapter 19

Mid February and the girls' work on the cut continues

Sylvia's butty, *Horizon*, was tied abreast *Marigold* as they headed up the cut with holds full of aluminium. She thought she'd dream for the rest of her life of tying up tarpaulins, then untying the wretched things with fingers scraped raw by the rope, and blistered, calloused and frozen. Would she also dream of the chilblains on her fingertips, her calves and toes? It wasn't so bad while everything was numb, but in the warm cabin at night, as the three of them ate supper, the itching and throbbing drove them nearly insane.

She had mentioned in a letter to Mrs B, at the start of February, that they hadn't been bothered by chilblains so badly before, and Mrs B had sent wintergreen from the medicine cupboard in the Butler's Pantry, saying that everyone was tired from the war so things were catching up with them. That evening they'd rubbed it in, and the itching seemed worse as the heat rose, but after a while there did seem to be an improvement, or enough of one to be worth the stink of wintergreen in both cabins.

Verity called from the counter of *Marigold*, 'Cocoa, Sylv?' She was holding a steaming mug, her woollen hat pulled down, her scarf up.

'Oh please.' She clambered on to their counter, took it and returned to her tiller though she didn't need to, because *Marigold* could steer for both. As she sipped her cocoa she wondered what the end of the war would mean. Would she and Steve still be together in London, as he continued in the Fire Service, or at Howard House to start afresh? She thought yet again of the feel of his kisses, of the words they had said, and knew that wherever he was after the war, she would be. But what about the other two? Would they go to Howard House with Saul and Tom, and leave her and Steve behind? The thought troubled her.

Verity was saying, as they headed along the pound between Fenny Stratford and Stoke Bruerne, which was an area blissfully free of locks, 'If only we knew where our two men actually were.'

'Well, we don't, so that's that,' said Polly, ever the practical one.

Verity pouted. 'Yes, but ...'

Sylvia joined in, 'Would it help to worry about specifics? If you knew they were trying to find a way over the Rhine as our Allied armies seem to be doing, while the German rearguard fights to delay them every step of the way, wouldn't it get to you even more? I don't want to know every fire or every V2 that explodes in Steve's neck of the woods.'

The two girls looked at her. Verity grimaced. 'Heavens, she's slopped her cocoa, the little firebrand.'

Sylvia shrugged, grinning a little. 'Well, I can't bear it when you're both so worried.'

'You are too, about Coppernob,' Polly said quickly, ducking as two swans seemed to sweep low over the cut. They heard the swish of their wings over the pat-patter. That was the only annoying thing about being towed abreast, thought Sylvia. If she was on a short tow behind she didn't hear the motor. She laughed. Honestly, how ridiculously fussy they were all getting. Was it because they were so close to the end?

Just then they heard Bet's hunting horn ahead, and slowed. Yes, there she was, approaching as she headed south. She hailed them from fifty feet away. ''Ow do,' Bet called. 'How did it go at Solly and Jacob's?'

'Crikey, haven't we seen you since then?' It was Polly, who had finished her cocoa and was now rolling a couple of cigarettes. 'Hey, moor up for lunch, there are studs either side of the cut here.' As she said this there was activity in the sky to the right. 'Fighter escorts for the bombers,' Verity said. 'Why, oh why, won't Hitler surrender?'

Bet called, 'Good idea. What have you cooking? We three'll scoot across the bridge with our Spam fritters, or have you got enough in your pot? And, Lady Verity, the Russians have found Auschwitz, such a terrible death camp apparently and quite beyond imagination. They came upon it as they approached from the east, so the German hierarchy will be trying to get rid of more camps and the evidence of their crimes, so that's one of the reasons they won't surrender, and of course, because they're insane, the lot of them, they probably still think they can win.'

The girls moored and all squashed up in *Marigold*'s cabin. Bet, Evelyn and Mabel added their Spam to the *Marigold*'s carrots, gravy and baked potatoes. Meat would be a treat they'd have tomorrow. Verity, Bet and Evelyn sat on the cross-bed, their enamel plates on the pull-down table; Mabel sat on the end of the side-bed. Polly and Sylvia squeezed up on the side-bed too, resting their plates on their knees. The talk was desultory, until Bet smiled across at Sylvia.

'I hear from Mrs Green that Coppernob has booked in for a night at the guest house when you girls arrive, all freshly bathed and smelling sweet. It sounds serious.'

'I love him,' Sylvia said. The others looked up in surprise. She had never said it before but she did, with all her heart and soul. Bet looked anxious. 'What about Coppernob?'

Verity poured water from the jug into their enamel mugs. 'Of course he loves her, you can tell it a mile off. Perfect, all of it. Two coppernobs together; such sense to it.'

Sylvia was nodding, because there was.

Mabel was thirty, an actress who had decided to do her bit, though she wasn't keen on the callouses, because, as she had explained, they could so affect her career. Now she said, 'There's not a lot of sense to love, but it makes the world go around, and everything worthwhile.' She looked at the others and smiled. 'The line from a play I was in.'

The others weren't sure quite how successful her career had been but no one dreamed of asking; after all, what business was it of theirs?

Bet ate the skin of her potato, then said, 'Evelyn, stop poking yours about. I know you don't like it, but the skin contains some vitamin that's supposed to be good for us, and it's roughage, which helps—'

Mabel cut across her. 'Must we have another reminder of your thoughts on the use of roughage, oh trainer of ours? I want to get back to how your meeting with Solly and Jacob went, Verity. I hope the old reprobate is recovering well?'

The talk continued as Sylvia brewed tea, half listening to the account of Verity and Polly's time with Solly and Jacob while she'd been with Steve at the reunion. Every letter Steve sent, every night she lay in her cross-bed, brought him back to her, the feel of her hand in his, the telephone calls she made to the fire station when they had finished playing darts at the stop-over pubs. And now, there was to be a meeting in Tyseley, which was Steve's first four-day leave for over a year, taking advantage of what seemed like a lull in the rockets, as the Allies took over sites set up in occupied countries.

She passed the mugs around, knowing they'd all light up cigarettes. Even a few months ago she'd have scooted them up on to the counter, but not now. Now, nothing like that was important, and she wondered afresh at the tense, unhappy, fearful girl she had been.

She listened, concentrating on Verity, as she told of Solly.

'As you probably know, Bet, he lives with Jacob in Golders Green now, and was very perky on the whole, wasn't he, Polly?' She went on to tell them of Jacob's wife, Rachel, who adored Solly. She was from somewhere near Budapest, in Hungary, and had arrived in Britain in 1937 with her parents, when they had decided Hitler was turning his anti-Semitic rhetoric into actions and wouldn't stop at Germany's frontiers. Her father had helped for a while in Solly's shop but there was little enough work for one, let alone two.

Polly said, 'Oh, poor Solly, do you remember his face, Ver, when Jacob said that it was a gift to the world when the V2 made such a bonfire of the whole lot?'

Verity was tapping her cigarette against the ashtray. 'I know, but Solly was playing along, wasn't he? What was it they were saying about Rachel's father, Mr Teller? He'd gone missing, or something? They didn't dwell on it because it was clearly too raw.'

'Yes, they think it must have been a V1 or 2 that got him,' Polly continued. 'I know they've asked around, and left his name, Emmanuel, with the Red Cross, but we should all keep an ear open just in case we see it on a list of – well, found people, or missing people, I suppose. But in spite of their worry they insisted we were to ask for help as regards Leon, should we ever need it, which was typical of them. I expect they'll keep an ear to the ground for him as well.'

Bet was shaking her head. 'They seem lovely, and as for Emmanuel, the trouble is that with a V1 or V2 people sort of get blasted to smithereens, just like Timmo's brother Thomo so . . . Was it Emmanuel's office that was hit?'

Verity couldn't remember if he even had an office. 'He'd picked up what work he could, apparently, since leaving Hungary. His English was good, and he'd been an accountant in Budapest, and worked from home I think. They've tried telephoning those clients who were in his address book, just in case they could pinpoint where he was, but with no luck, and often no answer. So many have closed down, or moved away, or been hit.'

It was all so sad, because Emmanuel had been Solly's friend. Not that Solly was from Budapest; indeed, he had been born in the East End, but most of his family were still over in Hungary. Sylvia said, 'We're going to see the three of them again, perhaps when we get back from this trip. I mean, when you've spent a few hours in the dark with a man, you have a sort of bond.'

She knew perfectly well what she'd said, and waited for the hoot of laughter, which duly came and lifted the moment, but then Polly grew serious. 'I will bring up Leon again when we see them. You never know.'

As they puffed away and sipped tea, busy with their own thoughts, Sylvia smiled at Verity and Polly. The three of them could so easily transfer to Howard House if the men agreed, or at least this was what the three of them discussed in the evenings, when the day's work was done, and Granfer, Maudie and Lettie could too. But would they all agree? She sighed, and put all such worries aside, because they could do nothing like that for the men until the end of the war, but if Leon wasn't found, they could perhaps persuade the Buckby family to move at least. She fed Pup who sat beside her on the side-bed with a piece of leftover potato skin.

Later, as they echoed their way through Blisworth Tunnel, they discussed whether to call in on Granfer and see how things were with Maudie. Bet had said that Fran still wasn't sure that Maudie was 100%, when they nipped in on their way back from Coventry just now.

Polly screwed up her face, squinting into the lowering sun as they exited. 'Let's leave it for our return. That'll give her just a couple more days, and who knows, we might at last be able to tell Joe.'

The others didn't reply, just nodded, because none of them dared to think how Joe would react. Or anyone else, really, when it came to Joe leaving Howard House.

They made Tyseley Wharf in Birmingham two days later, and as they clambered on to the quay there was the foreman, Mr Roberts, his clipboard in his hand.

Verity murmured, 'I feel he should have a stop-watch, to click us in, and click us out, and time us, particularly when we remove the tarpaulin so they can get at the hold.'

Polly nudged her. 'He has ears like a bat, just like Bet.'

Sylvia stood the other side. 'Quite, so shut up.'

'Well, well,' said Mr Roberts. 'If it isn't the three musketeers again. I've 'ad Sylvia's young man pestering the life out of me, wondering when you was getting in. Worse than Pup, he is, yap yap. I says, d'yer see my crystal ball I happen to have on my person? He says, no. I says, quite, cos I ain't got one. I told 'im though that since it's almost dusk it won't be till the morning, so he's gorn off. Alf Green tells me he's booked into Alice's guest house. He'll be in a room a floor down, and she'll 'ear every blessed footstep, you mark my words, so no 'anky-panky.'

The girls just stared. They'd never heard Mr Roberts talk so much. Sylvia knew that she had blushed bright red. Steve had been here, he'd been wanting to see her so much that he'd yap-yapped.

She couldn't suppress the grin on her face. Mr Roberts just looked at Pup at their feet. 'Dare say you'll be wanting me to take the mutt to the missus again. Well, since the lad is the one who hoiked you packets of trouble out of the rubble, dare say we can manage that. All that training lost under a load of bricks'd be a crying shame. You best be off, then. I have you booked in first thing.'

The girls shut Pup in the cabin, dashed to the lavs, then back to the boats, grabbing clean clothes and Pup's blanket. Tying her lead on, they led her to the office for Mr Roberts, who was on the quay supervising the final unloading of Timmo's boats. They rushed for the tram and now they laughed, and laughed, Polly spluttering, 'Honestly, is there anything at all the cut doesn't know about our lives?'

They said the same to Mrs Green who showed them to their usual cubicles, and said, as she stood outside before walking back to reception, 'Ah well, women on the cut are summat to talk about, and you three are something else, an' all, what with Saul being yer man, Polly, and Tom being on the boat fer a bit, Verity, and the coppernob being saved by another coppernob. Couldn't make it up, could yer? Mark yer, Bet's special too.'

Washed, and tidied, they walked from the baths to the Bull and Bush. Sylvia's heart was thudding. The idea had been that he'd meet them here, and join them at Mrs Green's. They entered the fug of the pub, and there, sitting with dear old Frankie still wearing his black armband and the other domino players, was Steve. The girls stood inside the door and waited for just a moment, then, in the hush, Steve turned and looked, his face breaking into a smile. He touched Frankie's shoulder, and stood, then headed towards them. He looked different in mufti, Sylvia thought, starting to walk towards him, then they clung together. The pub regulars applauded.

Into the chaos Boris called from behind the bar, 'Oh, lawks, is 'e going down on one knee too?'

Sylvia buried her head in Steve's shoulder, as he kissed her hair. 'It's wet,' he said, 'and smells of shampoo. I do love you so, you know. Is it too soon to propose? Frankie, our stalwart domino player, says it's not.'

She laughed up at him. 'What do you think?'

He slipped through her arms, on to one knee, looking up at her. 'I haven't a ring, and I haven't known you for long, but actually, I feel like I've known you for ever but you already know that. So marry me whenever we can, eh?'

Sylvia was scarlet, the heat beating in her face. 'Do get up,' she whispered. 'Everyone's looking.'

Verity, who was alongside now, muttered, 'Let them look, and put the poor beggar out of his misery. What does length of time matter?' Sylvia looked from her to Polly, and saw the underlying anxiety in their eyes, and for a moment she saw Harriet, and pushed her aside, saying in a rush, 'Yes, yes, of course. I love you too, so much.' The last bit was whispered.

Steve grinned, and sprang up. 'Thank the Lord for that, my knee was killing me.' The pub was watching and waiting. He kissed Sylvia, and the feel of his lips was gentle, and exciting, and she wanted to hold him, and be held for ever. She drew away, and the regulars were still watching, and waiting. Polly sighed, and whispered, 'You, kind sir, are going to have to buy everyone a drink. You walked right into that, as did our Tom and Saul, who got down on their knees here too. I reckon it's Frankie's little game to up Boris's takings.'

Steve looked round and laughed. 'What are you all having?'

A babble of voices answered, and he went round each table taking orders, while the girls asked what was on the menu. Boris was leaning on the bar, grinning as Steve tried to remember the drinks. He yelled, 'Don't yer worry, lad. I knows 'em all by 'eart. Come and choose yer meal.'

Verity said, 'Well, come on, Boris, out with it. What's on, and what's off tonight?'

He took his pencil from his ear, and the pad from his apron pocket, licked the end of the pencil and said, 'It's fish 'n' chips, or sausage and mash.'

The three girls waited, while Steve returned to the bar. Verity conducted as Boris said, 'The fish is orf.'

All together the three girls shouted, 'Oh, a hard choice, girls. I suppose it will have to be the sausage and mash then, Boris.'

Boris laughed until he coughed. 'Oh, yer girls crack me up.' It was these things Sylvia would remember for the rest of her life, and suddenly she was glad, so very, very glad, that Steve had proposed here, where Saul and Tom had done the same.

Steve left Boris to dispense the drinks, having done his bit by coughing up the money, and carried three half-pints of mild and a pint to the fireside table. He sat down, just as Verity said, 'So, where's it to land this evening?'

'Steve's plate, on the mash,' Sylvia and Polly said as one.

'You're on.' Verity spat on her hand and held it out to be shaken. 'You're disgusting,' Polly said. Sylvia just sighed. 'Put it away.'

Steve held up his pint. 'Cheers, girls. I'm really glad you didn't shake her hand, sweet Sylv.' He took hers in his and kissed it. 'Did you mean it?' he asked.

The other two girls waited. Sylvia smiled, drew in a deep breath, because to say she would marry would close all the doors finally, on betrayal and guilt, and confusion of any sort. 'Of course, but only if you stop calling me Sylv.'

'I didn't know you preferred Coppernob.' He kissed her hand again, winking at the other two girls. Polly whooped. 'Oh, he'll do, indeed he will, Sylv.'

Gladys was approaching, and the girls sat very still. The tray was loaded with four plates this time, and Steve leapt to his feet and said, 'Allow me.' He took the tray. Gladys's ash fell on the floor. Verity's face was a picture.

The girls stayed in the pub until closing time, and a bit beyond. They knew where Mrs Green's key was and none of them wanted the evening to end; somehow having Steve amongst them was almost like having Saul and Tom too. The talk was a bit about the war, a bit about Boris's missus who none of them had ever met, and about Gladys who must be seventy and was still at work. Then they moved to Dodge's missus, who was working his allotment because the plants had a right to grow whether Dodge was there or not. She'd added, 'And he is here, in the fact that he planted 'em.'

They tiptoed up the outside guest-house steps, while Verity felt for the key under the plant pot to the right of the front door. 'It's not here,' she hissed.

It was freezing. Steve rummaged too, and while he was bent double, the front door opened and Mrs Green stood there, in her dressing gown, with her hair pinned up. 'Boris called, he said yer were celebrating so I knew to keep yer fires burning in yer rooms, and I wanted to be here for yer. Good news is always worth staying awake for.'

They trooped in, the cold hanging around them like a blanket. Mrs Green held Sylvia's face between both hands and looked hard. 'The shadow 'as gone from yer eyes, and not before time. Yer treat her right, young man. Yer room's on the first floor, the girls' is on the second, cos I'm not 'aving any hanky-panky under my roof.'

Verity was mouthing the words. Sylvia remembered them from the night Tom had stayed.

'We promise,' said Steve, looking like a rabbit caught in the headlights. They all followed Mrs Green to the first floor, where she pointed to the second room on the left. 'Alf and me is in the first, and there's a couple of creaking floorboards outside our room, and I have ears like a—'

'Bat,' the girls chimed in.

Steve stood his ground for just a moment, stooping, and kissing Sylvia on her lips, eyes and hair. 'Thank you,' he said, 'for agreeing to be my wife.'

He walked away, and two floorboards creaked on the landing as he tiptoed past the bedroom where Mr Green was sleeping. Mrs Green followed him, opened her door, waving the other three up the stairs, whispering, 'Usual rooms. Breakfast at seven.' The door shut behind her.

The three girls smiled and crept upstairs, letting themselves into their rooms quietly, though Polly popped back out for a moment as Sylvia entered hers. 'We so want you to be happy, right through to your heart and soul, Sylv, so that the shadows lift completely, and the confusion. If he can do that, then we love him.'

Sylvia smiled as she shut the door and leaned back against it. The coal fire was low in the grate – rationing made a fire a small thing but it gave warmth, and a flickering light. She raised her eyes to the heavens. 'Thank you,' she said. 'For giving me this love.'

She slept and dreamed, not of the cut, but of the picture of Christ knocking on the door, which hung on the refectory wall. She heard the words: I am here, at last. It was Steve's voice and it woke her. She looked around, and smiled. 'At last,' she whispered. She slept, and woke again and this time thought of Solly, looking for his friend, the accountant. She slept and dreamed and woke again to a knocking. It was Polly. 'Come on, lazy-bones. Can't be late for Mr Roberts and his stopwatch.'

She sat up, shouting, 'He hasn't got a stopwatch.'

It was Verity's voice this time. 'Oh yes he has, in his head. Come on, I can smell toast, and scrambled powdered eggs, and there will be Steve, not to eat, but to sit next to.'

She hurried. She had a fiancé, she had someone to love, and a family in the girls, and Steve, and would one day have her own children. It was in Ma Porter's water.

Steve rushed from the guest house to catch his train, and they rushed for the tram to untie their loads, and within an hour everything was back to normal except for the fact that soon Sylvia would wear a ring and belong with someone.

They headed off within three hours to pick up coal from Coventry. Once there, the coal train came along the quay, and the team of men offloaded the dusty black lumps, their faces as black as the coal. They did it quickly in return for copious cups of tea, and then *Marigold* and *Horizon* set off again on a short tow, not covering the hold with the tarpaulins because they'd long ago decided the coal could withstand the rain better than the tarps could withstand the filth.

They kept going steadily, catching up with Timmo, Peter and Trev on *Venus* and *Shortwood* also on short tow, and settling down behind them, passing Steerer and Ma Mercy on *Lincoln* and *York*, who were heading north, and hailed them to ask if they were seeing Granfer and, if so, to say "Ow do.'

'We will,' shouted Verity. As usual there had been no mention of Maudie. To their surprise, when they approached the turn to Buckby, Timmo and the butty turned too. Even more surprising was when Timmo and the boys tied up at the Buckby mooring. The girls moored up behind and, with Pup, jumped on to the bank. Timmo came strolling along, with that walk that boaters had, which seemed to be going nowhere fast but ate up the miles.

''Ow do,' Timmo muttered, his face flushing. In his hand were a couple of pheasant.

Polly reached out for them, but he shook his head. 'These does be fer Granfer and the like. I is catchin' yer some on t'way on down.'

Verity said, 'Would you like us to take them for you, Timmo?'

He shook his head. 'I said to 'em last time, I'd bring 'em again meself. Seems it's a good idea, Granfer says. I knew 'er, yer sees, afore that Leon turned her 'ead. Poor poor lass.'

Verity nodded slowly, and Sylvia could see the abacus of her mind making two plus two equal fifty, or in other words, a love match where there probably wasn't. But as they walked together, and Timmo talked of growing up alongside his Maudie, she realised that perhaps Verity's counting had been accurate.

They passed Spring Cottage on the left, where icicles hung from the back eaves. Somehow it didn't seem that cold, but it was north facing. Timmo nodded. 'I nipped in an' paid respects, I did. She were a grand wee dog.'

Pup was leaping ahead on a long rope. Timmo said, 'She be fine too, you girls. Yer see, show's yer love can be replaced, d'ya think?' There was pleading in his voice.

The girls looked at one another as they neared Granfer's cottage. Polly said quietly, coming alongside Timmo, 'Oh, yes, Timmo, especially if the love is better. But it has to be a gentle and patient love, if you get my meaning.'

Timmo looked down at her. 'A waitin' love, yer means.'

Sylv said, 'That's exactly what she means, Timmo.'

They reached the picket gate. Polly opened it, but Timmo hung back. 'It would please me for yer to go first, cos my heart is in a flummox. And, rest easy, cos I knows her my life's length, and I cares, yer see, so I is used to waitin', and lovin' and lookin' after, for I does that from a distance. Always 'as, always will and that Leon won't come near 'er less I 'ear o' it first, cos Buckby looks after its own, it do.'

The girls walked down the path, Verity whispering, 'I don't think I have ever heard such a genuine and wonderful declaration of love.'

They knocked, happy that Maudie had a protector, but then, the whole of the cut, and Buckby, had already taken on that role by their very silence about Maudie's existence, and their awareness of the need to be vigilant.

Sylvia said, 'Now we'll see how she is but we shouldn't ever tell her that we worry about Leon when he's probably never going to emerge from whatever hole he's in. As we've said a million times, even if he isn't dead he thinks she is. Heavens, I'm muddling myself, let alone you two.' They heard footsteps coming along the flagstoned hall.

Polly whispered, 'You're not muddling us, we do that for ourselves.' They all smiled. 'I do just hope she's stable, and wants Joe to know of her survival. But what will happen then? Does he come here, or will she visit him at Howard House?'

Sylvia held Polly's hand. 'After that, will she take him away from the "parents" and life at Howard House?'

Verity leaned forward. 'I hardly slept last night, wondering how on earth Joe, and the grown-ups, will handle it all without disastrous pain? And even though the boaters and Buckby people are keeping a watch, how . . . just in case . . .'

She petered out, and Sylvia whispered, 'Just in case Leon is still . . .'

She too couldn't finish. Polly said, 'We mustn't keep going with the what if, and the in case . . .'

As the door began to open, Polly's whisper was harsh. 'Mum said she always knew the day would come, and that the important people were Joe and Maudie, so we'll just hang on to that and it'll all be fine.'

But all three feared that it wouldn't be and Sylvia couldn't bear for Joe to be caught in this confusing love, and perhaps . . . If only they knew if Leon still lived, and if so, where he was, Sylvia thought.

Chapter 20

Maudie's progress is revealed

Granfer opened the door, ''Tis yer girls, and little Pup. Oh, 'tis good to see yer on this cold and frosty day.' He seemed different – lighter, taller. 'Yer is to come on in.' He raised his voice and called over their heads, 'Yer planting yerself out by t'gate, Timmo lad, growing pheasant, 'stead o' apples?' Bring 'em birds in, and we'll 'ang 'em out in t'larder, or Lettie will, so don't be 'anging there, or our Lettie'll be out after you, beating yer in with her broom. She don't want t'heat letting out.'

He waved the girls in past him. They kicked off the mud from their boots first and made to take them off. 'No, lasses, see, 'tis newspaper on t'floor, so leave 'em on. She says that's the best place for all them little newspaper letters that a body can't be seeing but with a magnification glass.'

They were all squashed up in the hall as Granfer waited for Timmo, patting the man on his shoulder and talking of Fran's school play her little 'uns had performed, until Lettie called from the kitchen. 'Yer weren't born in t'barn, our Artie, so shut the door, do, and come on through. I want to put our Timmo's birds out in't larder, or might even put 'em hanging in t'shed. Nice and cold 'tis.'

Somehow they all untangled themselves and headed for the kitchen, then sat around the table. Lettie was by the range, topping up the teapot. 'I felt it in my bones you'd be coming in today my girls, but weren't sure about our Timmo. Sometimes he do, sometimes he don't. Sit down, lad.'

Sylvia hadn't realised Timmo made a habit of calling, and exchanged a smile with the other two. He was edging towards the back door, the pheasants hanging from his hand. Lettie smiled at him. 'Yes, I think, all things considered, we'll put 'em out in the shed, lad. Off yer go, and yer might give our Maudie an 'and getting the lunchtime veggies, if yer've a mind.'

The girls had never seen Timmo move so fast, and the door slammed shut after him. Lettie poured tea, looking at the clock above the sideboard. 'Yer'll be staying fer yer lunch. 'Spect yer'll miss yer Spam but some things yer 'ave to learn to go without, eh Artie?' She was laughing. 'We had a letter from our Saul this morning. All about yer, Polly, a bit about Maudie, and summat about a big old river they was eyeing for to get across, but a lot was blacked out.'Tis always blacked in parts.'

Verity said, 'I expect there're letters waiting for us back at the depot. That's the trouble with the boats, there's no letter box. Or perhaps we'll have to wait until someone is able to ship them home on the hospital run.'

Lettie pushed cups of tea across the table at them all, then she and Granfer sat down. Granfer fiddled with his teaspoon, stirring and stirring his tea until his elder sister snapped, 'Whisht, enough o' that, young Artie, yer goin' to tell 'em or is I?'

It was about Maudie, the girls knew, and all Sylvia could think was what would happen to Joe. Why was life so complicated? Granfer was talking, and she caught up on his words, which were about Timmo who'd taken to calling. 'With his pheasant, or rabbit, or just himself, though he knowed I catch the beggars an' all. On t'way up to Tyseley, and on t'way down to depot, he comes. Reckon Pete and Trev get a bit sick of his lovelornness, but they's good boys.'

Lettie sighed. 'Yer does go round that mulberry bush, our Artie.'

Granfer grinned. 'Well, he comes, and our Maudie starts 'membering more, yer see, not just shapes, or pain, or things she knows but don't know how she knowed, or things she remembers one day and not t'next. She 'membered Timmo for times gone, from when they was little 'uns, and she 'members kindness, yer see. I reckon she sees kindness all around her, and feels safe to remember that bugger Leon. But 't'weren't till Fran takes it upon 'erself to give us tickets to 'er childer's school play, and says it could do our Maudie a fair bit o' good, that we sees the window in her mind swing open. Bit o' a jerk, weren't it, our Lettie.'

Lettie, who was sipping her tea, looked over the cup and said, 'I'll be givin' yer a bit of a jerk if yer don't get yourself wriggling on a bit.'

Granfer chuckled. 'She likes the story an' all, so don't you be afeared of the bad wolf, yer girls.'

The girls were actually sitting gripping one another's hands beneath the table in an effort not to fall on the floor laughing at the double act, but they were also on edge. Where was all this taking them?

Sylvia could see the sky growing darker as the clouds built, sucking the light from the kitchen, and sighed; they would have rain for the onward journey today.

Granfer dragged his clay pipe out of his pocket, but it was snatched from him by Lettie. 'Only when you tell the tale.'

He sipped his tea instead, his eyes twinkling, and the girls knew better than to hurry Granfer 'Opkins when he held the stage. 'We goes to the play, but our Lettie and me was disturbed, we was. It had boys that was Joe's years and they 'ad a cardboard butty they was standing behind, on the counter. They was wearin' clothes like our Saul and me, and there were a bigger girl, dressed like our Maudie did. They did act mooring, they did act steering, they did sing a song, they did—'

333

'And Maudie?' interrupted Verity.

'She said naught, she done just sat on her chair, she did, sat and watched but were somewhere else in her 'ead. It finished. People clapped. She 'eld her 'ands to her head, like she couldn't stand such noise, and walked out, and walked and walked, and we follered, didn't we, Lettie? She wouldn't let us be near her, so yes, we just follered.'

Lettie was nodding. 'We were in a right fright. She went on though 'twas half raining, half sleetin' and cold, right on to the cut she tore, and we was feared she were to go in. So we ran quick as we could but we's old and might not have caught her, but our Fran were behind, and we didn't know that, and she tore on past us, and stood just by 'er on t'bank.'

Granfer had somehow taken back his pipe from Lettie and was furiously tamping down the tobacco he'd dragged from his pouch. 'We all just stood there, getting wet and cold and I was wondering where we go from 'ere, and 'oping we weren't all going in t'cut, when she said, "I have a boy. I have Joe, my 'ead 'as quite cleared, and I can remember all my life: Leon; my boy. All o' them, clear as day, and day after day, and Timmo, Saul, Thomo who is killed as Timmo said. You, Granfer, and you, Auntie Lettie. I knows yer, and I remembers yer."'

Lettie sat back in her chair. 'And she has, clear as day from then on. Our Fran were right to find that key to unlock it all and make it stay clear for her, instead of Joe and the rest comin' and goin' like a pendulum in her head. She remembers Leon, the beatings, and 'ow he 'urt his boy for the love of it, for the power o' it, and she remembers it all clear, and constant, she do, and the cut, and us.'

'Good old Fran,' cheered Polly. 'Good old Timmo, for putting his foot in the door.'

'But now, what about Joe? Do we tell him his mother is alive?' Sylvia asked.

At that moment, the back door creaked open and Maudie peered into the kitchen, her eyes lighting up to see the girls. She shook off her boots, to be followed in by Timmo who did the same, because his were inches deep in mud too. They had picked sprouts and cabbage, and gathered up carrots from the sawdust in the box in the shed.

As they all set about the vegetables, Maudie looked at Polly shyly. 'I remembers my boy, clear and long.'

Polly smiled, 'My mum will be really happy for Joe, and for you.'

Maudie cut up the carrot into slices on the wooden chopping board, taking great care, and clearly trying to say more. Timmo beside her said quietly, 'If yer 'as more to say, that is right, and good, ain't it, Polly?'

Polly reached across, and pinched a bit of carrot. 'Here, I've had some of your carrot, and let's have some of your words, shall we?'

How clever, Sylvia thought. Boaters understood a deal, but perhaps everyone did. They waited as Maudie put her knife down, while Timmo looked at her protectively.

Maudie said, 'I long to see my boy, but I fear to take him from his other families. For they's his families cos they have given 'im a home, and love, so Granfer tells me, cos them write weekly, one from your ma and da, Verity one week, and one from yer ma and da t'other, Polly, and Mr B and Rogers, t'other week. Auntie Lettie and Granfer reads them. So, I would like a letter from my boy, cos they tells me 'e is at school and knows his letters well. One day, I would treasure to see 'im, but not to cause him worry, nor yer ma and da. If you does see my meaning?'

They all saw exactly. Maudie continued. 'Granfer is learnin' me my letters, and p'rhaps I can read 'is letter myself, soon. I tries real 'ard, and Timmo says he do too, so he can help. My boy can't have a ma who don't know her letters, or her numbers.'

Sylvia said, 'He will love you as much as he always has, Maudie, whether you can read or not, but I think I understand why it is important to you. It helps to bridge the gap.'

Maudie looked at her now, her dark eyes as serious as the words were. 'You be right. It be like my boy is on one side of the cut, and I is on t'other, and we need to reach across it, and clasp our 'ands firm together.'

It was Timmo who spoke now. 'It be a time of waitin', it p'raps be?' He frowned, searching for words. 'It's to be patient, to be knowing that you will be together, but step by step on that bridge, till your Joe feels quite certain. And there must be thought, deep thought, as to 'ow it can be done, and mayhap that can be shared.'

The girls knew he was talking about a relationship between Maudie and himself too. Did Maudie know that? Sylvia wondered. Perhaps, because Maudie turned her hand upwards and let Timmo's rest on hers, her fingers lightly clasped around his for a moment, and then she began chopping the carrots again.

The girls toiled through the rain, behind Timmo, Peter and Trev, but the locks were with the boys, and the girls steadily fell behind, mooring up for the night at Cosgrove, happy to be alone; they still had so much to talk about, even though they'd been chewing it over all day. The more they talked, the less they knew. In the end Polly slapped the motor cabin table. 'Enough. We will just telephone Howard House with the news of Maudie's progress, and her wish that Joe be told, and the possibility of a letter from him to her at Buckby. It's not ours to decide how and when any of their worlds will change.'

Verity agreed. 'Then we'll follow up with the same letter to them all, and explain that Maudie

337

is learning to read, but that in the meantime Granfer will read for her, and that she is mindful of the situation, and only wants the best for Joe. That she has no fear that Leon will return, and best to keep it that way for now. Sylvia, what do you think?'

Sylvia sipped her tea. A coal dropped into the firebox, and settled in the ash. The range would be chuntering in her butty cabin, too. 'Yes, I agree to all of this,' she said. 'You see, it really is between Joe and his mother, with the support of the Howard House parents. There's no rush, I think is the thing to emphasise, but for now, let's forget about it, or if it keeps going around in my head I will take off, and with the cold, my red nose will light my way.'

They all laughed, a little, and headed for bed.

It took them two days to reach the depot, with the locks past Tring all against them. 'We're just out of kilter,' sighed Polly to Sylvia as they motored abreast.

Verity lock-wheeled all those from Kings Langley to Cowley Lock, with the red buses crossing the bridges the nearer they got to the depot. Sylvia took to counting them, and adding the few army lorries, and one civilian lorry, even a couple of ambulances hot on the tail of a racing fire engine. Sylvia also thought of Steve, but when didn't she?

She also thought of Timmo and Maudie, and she wondered if there was divorce in the boater world, for was Leon dead or alive? Had there even been a marriage or did they jump over a broom? She knew Romanies were said to do this, but boaters weren't the same.

She called across to the other two on *Marigold*. Verity replied, as Polly slowed for the lay-by. 'Sometimes there is a wedding, but sometimes not – they just live together, or so I gather. Much like on the land.'

As Polly reversed *Marigold* into a space, Verity and Sylvia took up the boat shafts and nudged Ma Mercy's *York* to one side, and Steerer Porter's *Oxford* to the other.

There was a slight bump as the stern of the motor eased against the lay-by. Sylvia jumped out, and moored up both boats, as Ma Porter came out on to her counter, standing on the top deck and not pausing in her crocheting in the failing light. ''Ow goes it in Buckby, my girls?'

'Granfer and the family are well, very well. All is nearly normal.'

Ma smiled, and then they heard from Ma Mercy: 'That be grand news.'

Verity nudged Polly. 'Go on, see if they know?'

Polly swallowed, and whispered, 'It's awfully rude.' She turned to Sylvia on the bank. 'It was your question and best you ask it.'

Sylvia stood with her arms akimbo. 'It wasn't that important, and by the way, you two are the absolute limit.'

Ma Porter came to stand at the stern of her counter. 'Best get it out, lass, or 't'will stick in yer throat.'

Sylvia walked the few paces to Ma's motor counter, just as Jimmy came to sit on the roof, calling to Polly that his homework was ready to be marked. Sylvia waited for Polly to praise him, then said quietly, 'We were wondering if a certain person had been married to another certain person or just sort of jumped over a broomstick.'

Even as she was saying it, she could hear Polly start to laugh. Soon all the women and Jimmy were at it. Ma Porter said, 'There be no jumping over broomsticks, or tillers or any somesuch, yer funny little lasses. And if'n I was to guess which certain person might be attached to another certain person I'd have to say they is like Steerer Porter and me who isn't, but Steerer Mercy and Ma is. Just what takes yer fancy, if yer see what I mean. It's what you do with the promise that be important, young Sylvia. You remember that, with your young fireman. 'Ear tell 'e went down on 'is knee like them two blokes of yer mates. So, the promise is made. Words on a sheet of paper don't make it stronger, nor weaker, does they?'

Sylvia thought to herself how she had said to Verity and Polly after they had accepted their offers in marriage that it was a sacred oath. So, of course Ma was right. The boaters' gods were the waters, the trees, the seasons, and their pledges to them and to one another were just as valid.

Polly was standing on the counter. 'Now you've got your answer, Sylv, we've the hold to clear of sawdust, and splinters, then we'll get off to the office and pick up our mail, and phone Howard House.

Sylvia jumped back on board the butty, grabbed the broom from Polly, knowing exactly what was going to happen, just as it happened every time.

Polly leapt for the bank. 'Meanwhile I'm going to grab the lav. I'll catch up with you soon.'

Verity called, as she always did, 'Don't take all day or we'll come and sweep you out, won't we Sylv?'

It was all as it always was, but at least a possible obstacle to a union between Timmo and Maudie did not exist. That was a good omen for the future, wasn't it? Sylvia jumped into the hold and began work too tired to think any more, but when she slept she dreamed of promising Harriet she would be with her when she left, and they would become postulants together. Sacred oath? Sacred oath was the phrase that was chanted over and above them.

The six adults drank brandy in the kitchen of Howard House once Joe was in bed. They needed it as they absorbed the girls' telephone call just after their supper of lentil and vegetable soup, with cheese, pickle and bread to be eaten alongside. Together, they tried to work out how to tell Joe of

341

his mother's existence, for a start, and that she would like a letter from him, before they even thought of a meeting between them.

Mrs Holmes said, 'That poor woman. When you think what she's been through and now she has to try and get to know her son again.'

They all turned, as the kitchen door creaked. In the half-open doorway, hanging on to the handle, wearing his slippers, pyjamas and dressing gown, stood Joe.

He said, his hair tousled, 'I thought yer were cross wi' me, at supper, cos Uncle Henry didn't eat his cheese and pickle, and he loves cheese and pickle. An' he didn't look at me, and now I's 'eard what you was saying, so is it that yer cross that my ma is alive, and that we will need 'spensive stamps if'n I write to 'er?'

Henry slid back his chair and came straight to the boy, hunkering down and holding him tightly. Joe felt the comfort of those arms, and they reminded him of the comfort of Saul's. All these people were like the comfort of Saul and so too them girls, and he couldn't bear the thought of leaving them, because on his da's boat there'd only been pain, and misery and shouts, and his ma wrapping her arms around herself, not him, because she was more pained than he, and more often and more bad.

Henry said, 'No, no, not the price of the stamp, but how to tell you the wonderful news that your mother lives. That she didn't die as we all thought. She loves you so much, young man, and she wants to meet you slowly, but she has a waitin' love, which is what she called it. So there is no rush to meet, to write, to do anything.'

Henry stood up, 'Lord,' he said. 'I don't know about the door creaking, but *I* certainly did just then.'

Joe looked up at him, and laughed aloud. 'I 'eard the crack in yer knees, too,' he said, then he leaned into Henry. 'I don't want t'leave yer comfort, 'tis a feeling I get with all o' yer. I have Maisie, I 'ave school, I 'ave my world on land while Saul be away at t'war. I know I is safe 'ere, from me da, should he still be alive, cos you have men around, you come wi' me on the bus, though you think I don't know why. But I do. But near the cut he can get me, if he do be alive, but we don't know, do we? The men is all just in case, so my thoughts tell me.'

Mrs Holmes called from the table, 'Heavens, Joe, and we thought we were being so clever. You are correct. It is all just in case.'

Joe continued, looking round all of them, 'But while I is 'ere, in the house wi' you all, I is safe, I feels safe whether he be alive or not, and I never is with me ma, and Da. You is all like my Uncle Saul and Granfer. Yer 'olds me close, and the girls do too. Yer know our Polly took a chair to me da when he were hitting and hitting Saul, with his men doing it too, and kicking 'im. She saw 'em off, she did. And Verity, she be there, strong and tall, and Sylvia, she writes and draws, and feels bad that she thought it were me who burned the butty, but I knows she made a mistake, and her heart is vexed, and for her I have a special caring love, cos she needs it an' all. She draws better'n she did, too.'

The six of them laughed a little, and let him talk until he was done. At last he began to slow, and to remember the sunlit times with his mother, when his da was away on 'his business', as he called it. Then they would laugh, and talk, and she would braid her hair so that it hung heavy down her back like a rope. Ma Ambrose had said it was her 'crownin' glory'.

'I had forgotten about Ma Ambrose. She were kind, and Steerer Ambrose come between me ma and da more'n once, and Timmo was there when he could be. He be kind, do Timmo. He watched over us, like Saul.'

Joyce Holmes slept on the side-bed in his room that night, so when Joe turned over, he could see her by the light of the little bedside lamp. The next night it was Uncle Thomas, and the next Mrs B, and so on, and so on. His comforters were always there for him, and they said, each of them as they kissed him goodnight, that his ma and granfer would be his comfort again. Well, he thought when these words were spoken; perhaps they would, but

344

this was his home now. Here at Howard House, and he didn't know how he could tell his ma and granfer that.

He was afeared he would have to use words that would hurt their hearts and he didn't care to hurt anyone, except his da, for he was the very devil.

Chapter 21

Mid March 1945 – the shadows deepen around Joe and his mother

Leon sat at his desk and took a newspaper off the top of the stack of ten that Cheryl had brought in. She'd taken over from Shirley after that silly cow had been hit by a V2 while standing on a street corner. He laughed. Bit ripe, really. She'd started by earnin' a living on a street corner, and waiting to cross the ruddy road she'd copped it. Mark you, the bleedin' Allies should have taken out the launch sites more than they had.

Cheryl had stuck her head round the door this morning, like the mouse she was, all brown hair, brown eyes, and twitchy. He'd looked up and shouted, 'Boo.' She'd disappeared. He'd laughed then heard Dougie call her back. 'You'll 'ave to toughen up,' Dougie had said. 'It's the boss's way.'

Dougie had opened the door, and she'd almost tiptoed in with the newspapers. 'I been through 'em, Mr Harkness. These are the ones I think might be about your boy, given the surnames your investigator found for you. I've been reading the local

346

newspapers from all the areas around Woking, Sherborne and London for that Sylvia Simpson too, and Buckby and Tyseley. Only might, mind. He's still checking the schools around and about.'

Darting across the room to place the local papers on his desk, she'd knocked his ashtray. She'd squeaked in alarm. His cigar ash had fallen, which was a ruddy nuisance because he liked a bit of ash on the end of his Cuban.

He'd growled, 'Bugger off.' She had.

He shook out the local newspaper from somewhere in Guildford, and settled back, reading the piece on page two she'd circled with a pencil which were the same colour as the type. She should o' done it in red. Do he have to think of everything himself? It weren't as if he had naught else to do. There was an army to raise to finish off Mario's base near Limehouse, and black market goods to find for the extra clubs he were supplying . . .

He scrunched up the paper. What did a farm boy have to do wi' him? This was a lad who'd saved his da from death. Didn't the mouse have eyes? Cos the da and t'boy looked like two peas in a pod, for heaven's sake, so how could t'lad called Holmes be a Harkness?

He checked the clock. The men would be here in a minute, but he had to work his way through these, just in case. All right, there were nothing yet from the snouts. He scanned the next, a local rag from the Dorset coast. Something about the pier, and a boy called Tom Simpson found there, dead. Didn't look like nothin' but a drowned fish, and what was he doing on t'pier if he had drowned? Didn't make sense. He found himself reading, and no one, not even the coppers, could make sense of it neither, except his hair were red. Well, his boy's weren't.

Dougie knocked at the door just as Leon scrunched up that newspaper too, throwing it to the floor. 'Got the boys 'ere, boss.'

'Let 'em in.'

Leon didn't get up. He reached for his cigar, which had built up a head of ash again, and watched as Sammy, Molt and Freddy came in. He could tell they were carrying, but he had his revolver on the shelf, and Dougie was on alert. You couldn't trust no one these days. Well, when could you?

Molt began. 'We got a bloke into Mario's. The eyetie's got to take one or two non-Italians cos the bank job cost him a few to clink. Some ain't come back from internment cos they're fascist to the core.'

Leon stared at him. 'I don't be needin' an 'istory lesson, I need to know how many you got on the inside o'his outfit, that be what I bleedin' need.' He was banging the table. He turned to check his fish. They didn't like vibrations.

'Now yer done made me upset me fishes, so get on wi'it.'

The men shuffled and he could see they were watching his hands, waiting for him to go for his gun. Even then no one would move, because they'd hope the bullet wasn't going to be for them. As he looked at them, Leon realised that being here, in the office, was like being steerer of a damn great motor, with a string of butties tied up behind on short tows, waiting for him to take 'em where he wanted them to go. Or maybe sink them.

He laughed, they laughed, but they didn't know at what.

'Freddy, 'ow many men you got now who can fight and take orders, and keep their mouths shut? We got to make a move before t'end of March.'

Freddy looked Leon in the eye, and slapped down a list. 'This lot so far. How much money you got, boss? That's the answer I got for yer. I've some who'll do it for more'n we're paying. We need ten more, at least, and the coppers needs more bunce, cos they has to get to a bloke on Mario's beat.'

'You'll 'ave yer money for another ten, plus the copper. Give the ones we've got more, an' all, or they'll be mithering and I 'aven't time for buggering about.' He turned to Sammy, slapping his hand on the pile of newspapers. 'What you got fer me on the boy?'

'I'm working tight with the investigator, as you said, boss, easier now he's come up with names of them girls' families. We've checked out the boaters, the boaters' pubs too and all stops in between for 'im, though as you said, that'd be too bloody obvious. We've asked around Tyseley, and Buckby, but no one knows naught. I think they've all got straw between their ears I do cos they all talk so stupid, and we're not asking, we just listen. We've got snouts looking at schools too, and hospitals, evacuation registers cos so many 'as left t'south for other parts. And Cheryl the Mouse of course, looking through those papers, glad to be off her back, or her feet for a while. I got ears everywhere, eyes everywhere. We'll get there, boss.'

Leon nodded. 'When us know where t'little tyke be hiding we'll plan it careful, just like we'll plan t'Mario snatch. Get the boy. Bring 'im 'ere. I'll up the coppers' bunce so they won't say a word when we get 'im here. Now get out, get on with things, and leave me to work me way through this lot.'

The men trooped out. Leon picked up the next newspaper, from Dorset again, and flicked through it. There was nothing ringed, silly cow. What was Cheryl playing at? He was about to scrunch it up, then saw an advertisement about a couple of blokes wanting work. He laid the newspaper on the table, and saw they were bookkeepers. Well, he had Tony who was scared stiff, so 'e'd probably sniffed what'd happened to Manny so he'd behave himself. But . . .

He saw it then, a piece about a competition winner ringed in pale pencil, silly stupid cow, and the story was about a narrowboat and three women, and it were by Joe Clement. Leon bit down on his cigar; it broke and fell on to the paper. He swept it off, leapt to his feet and almost ran to the door, yanking it open. Dougie was leaning against the wall reading

The Sketch. 'Get Freddy back in 'ere, at t'double,' Leon ordered.

It took Freddy a minute to arrive, sweating and panting. 'Sorry boss, we were just off out to round up—'

'Don't want ter 'ear it.' He waved the newspaper at him. 'This be my boy, so you and me needs to sit down and work out a plan. It got to be right, and it got to be quick. So lots of checking, then get someone inside the place. Maybe a gardener. Report back to me, first thing tomorrer. I need to know all about this school, this boy, where 'e be, and a photo. Get someone down there with a camera. Got it?'

Freddy rushed off. Leon sat down and read through the rest of the newspaper, getting a feel for the place, knowing it were his boy, one that could read and write, one that could help his business, and then he wouldn't need a Tony any more. It could just be kept in the family. Yes, it were Joe, got to be. How else could he talk about the cut like this lad did, and be named Joe, and this Clement bollocks would be stopped. It would all be stopped, because it were going to be Harkness and Son, and they'd spread out their net as wide as they liked, and his army would get bigger, and everyone would fear the family, so they would. That'd show the cut, who thought they'd chucked him out with the rubbish.

Sylvia hung out their washing on the line strung over *Horizon*'s empty hold. They were abreast, heading for Limehouse Basin, determined to get in and out as quickly as possible. There'd been a bad V2 rocket explosion in West Hampstead to spur them on, and the rockets were still hitting England and Belgium.

'Perhaps we'll be beyond range soon. Surely they'll move the sites as they retreat,' she called down to Verity.

Verity looked up from the bottom of the butty's hold. She'd drawn the short straw and was aligning the hold boards over the bilges before another load was plonked on top of them. 'I'm not a mind reader, sweet Sylv, so explain what's running through that active mind of yours.'

Sylvia did, just as Verity swore as the boards trapped her fingers. 'Damn, another black nail. So, who will get the damned rockets then, I wonder. France? Or will the Allies get across the Rhine in force, and run 'em to ground – or maybe our bombers'll wipe more sites out?'

Sylvia hunkered down by the store and called, 'I wonder if Polly ever thinks of her old friend Reginald in his bomber. They've lost so many, and the Americans too. And then there's the war with Japan . . .

Polly yelled from *Marigold's* counter, 'I have ears, I can hear, and yes, of course I think of Reggie, and of them all, but if I hold on to the thought I get so bunged up with worry I feel sick. So I just think about it ending, and then we can all begin again. Can you imagine eating an orange?'

Sylvia and Verity exchanged a glance. Polly was engaging in what they were all becoming experts in: diversion. Verity hauled herself out of the hold and leapt on to the cabin roof, Sylvia following, with the surplus pegs stuffed into her pockets. They reached the counter to find that Polly was reading the letter from Howard House yet again. It had arrived that morning. Bob from the office had run along the lay-by as they were about to cast off, waving it. 'Says it's urgent,' he yelled.

Now, Sylvia leaned back on *Marigold*'s cabin, crossed her arms, and asked, 'What do you think, Pol? Any different from the last two times you read it?'

Polly was pulling at her lip. Sylvia murmured, 'That's not a pretty look.'

Polly stuck out her tongue. 'Neither's that,' Verity said, now sitting up on the roof next to Pup who no longer needed to be chained, knowing better than to launch herself off the boat after doing just that when they finally got away this morning. They'd had to fish her out with the boat shaft and sluice her off with water before she was allowed into either cabin. She was still sulking.

Polly said, 'No, just the same. I repeat that Mum has copied what Joe has written and wants to know what we think.'

Sylvia said, 'Yes, we know. We listened the first two times.'

'Well,' snapped Polly, 'one more time for luck.' She began:

'Dear Ma, I is glad that I have heard that you is alive. Course I am. I is surprised, cos you seem to have been a long time dead—'

Verity interrupted as she rolled two cigarettes. 'I'm still not sure about that bit.'

Sylvia answered, 'It sounds a bit raw, I know, but as I said the first time it's how he feels. I think that Maudie will recognise the simplicity of it as being from her boater son and know he hasn't changed, or not much.'

Polly was steering off centre as Timmo's *Venus* and butty hove into sight heading back from Limehouse, fully loaded.

Sylvia muttered, 'Who better to ask. Let's flag him down.'

Polly grabbed the hunting horn and gave three blasts and they heard one in answer. Verity muttered, searching the sky, 'I don't want to stop for long.'

Sylvia was on the roof now, waving to him, calling, 'Don't moor, just slow right down. We need to ask you something.'

They heard his hail in reply: ''Ow do, right you is.'

Both pairs slowed, checking behind, but there were no other boats to hold up.

Timmo eased *Venus* along so that his stern counter was on a level with *Marigold*'s. Both pairs wallowed to a stop. 'Bet would be proud at our skills,' Verity murmured.

Sylvia laughed at her. 'Don't be daft, she'd give us a kick up the bum for cluttering up the cut.'

Timmo called, 'Is yer all right, yer girls?' There was a brightness in him, a bracing of his shoulders, as though the grief over Thomo's death had been replaced by a certain joy.

'We hope so,' shouted Polly over the idling motor. 'Don't want to stop you for too long, but Mum has sent me a copy of Joe's first letter to his mother. Do you think it's all right?'

She read the first two lines, and then continued:

But though I is surprised, I is glad too, and glad too that you is with Granfer and Auntie Lettie. They is family, like Saul. But I is with family too, cos they have become so. You would like them, Ma. They is comfort, just as Granfer and Auntie Lettie is to you. As I is writing this, I feel my heart becoming full that you is here, in the world again, and I would like that we should meet, but I am vexed because I have happiness here, and you have happiness there, so I is not sure how we put the two together to make us Ma and son again.

I will write again, cos I is so pleased you is in the world.

Your son, Joe

For a few seconds there was silence, except for the sounds of the cut, and the bank with its warehouses, bridges, and comings and goings; on a level with them a man sat fishing. For what? wondered Sylvia. He was staring at them, probably wondering what they were doing, just stopped, and talking here where the V2s could get them. Well, she thought, I could say the same about him, but he probably lives in London, so where is safe?

Timmo said eventually, "'Tis an honest lot of words and thoughts. His ma will see the sense in them, and the caring. 'Tis as you said, girls, 'tis a waiting love. That's all. And in the waiting, things will happen and all will be well, or not.'

He saluted, then said, as an afterthought, 'And I will be in Maudie's world, to hold her heart together should it crack, and 't'will be the same for Granfer and Lettie. 'Tis what it is, my girls.'

Pete called from the cabin. Timmo began to head away, while the girls continued towards Limehouse Basin. 'Oranges,' muttered Verity. 'Now there's a thought.'

At Howard House that evening, the telephone went. It was the girls telephoning from Sid's pub at Alperton.

Henry answered, as Rogers was out checking the patrols, and Thomas didn't like phones and couldn't quite get the hang of the fact that you only paid if you made the call. 'Howard House?'

'Father, it's me.'

Henry smiled. 'Good evening, Me.' He heard her laugh and it warmed him. He asked, 'Did you receive Joyce's letter, darling? What did you think?'

Henry listened as Verity explained that they had shared it with Timmo as they passed on the cut. He looked as though he'd picked up wood from Limehouse, because they'd noticed some had pierced his tarpaulin as he motored on. Henry tried not to rush her. 'Well, I expect he'll do a repair job. What was that? Oranges? Oh Lord—' He heard Pamela hiss, 'Oh, darling Henry, do get on.'

He pressed his hand over his ear and waved her to silence. Verity was now saying there had been a bloke fishing on the bank, but for what? she asked. Henry drew on all his patience, and it was the least he could do while his daughter was a sitting duck within range of the bastard rockets, and he was here, safe. She gave him no time to answer but rattled on.

'Timmo said that the letter was the truth, and that it was something that Maudie would understand, and that she knew it was to be, in Timmo's words, a waiting love. He also said that if the words were to cause Maudie's heart to crack, he, Granfer and Lettie would be there to hold her heart together, and he to hold all their hearts together.' On the last word Verity's voice cracked a little itself.

Henry swallowed; there was such simplicity, but also poetry, in the words. He heard Sylvia calling, 'Come on, Ver, stop waffling on, you're needed at the dartboard.'

That's my girls. He smiled to himself, but said, 'Bless you. I'll tell the others and we will send the letter.'

Verity said quietly, 'Father, will you all be all right if Joe decides to live in Buckby with Maudie?'

There was a long pause. She repeated, 'Father, did you—'

He answered now, 'Of course we'll be fine. We all have one another. What is it you three girls say? All for one and one for all, and perhaps he would visit . . .' He stopped. 'Or we could . . .' Again he stopped, then he grew brisk. 'But one step at a time, eh? The thing we need to remember is that Joe's needs come first. Must go, darling. Stay safe.' He replaced the receiver, rubbed his forehead. Yes indeed, that's what they must all remember.

Chapter 22

End of March 1945, on the cut

Marigold and *Horizon* had pulled in at Alperton as they had done so often. It was evening, and the girls sat for a moment, while Verity 'put her face on, darlings'. Sylvia was laughing. 'Why do people call it that? It's as though it's a mask to hide behind.'

Verity sniffed as she puffed up her hair and checked in the mirror. 'Perhaps it is, darling, who knows. I just think that if we're to meet Solly, Rachel and Jacob at the club in Jermyn Street I should at least have a vestige of make-up, given that so many of my old set are bound to be there, in their ship-shape togs.'

Sylvia watched her from the side-bed. 'Of course, sorry, Ver, I didn't mean to sound carping, I was just pondering aloud.'

Verity gestured her over to the cross-bed. 'You didn't. It just made me think. Put on a bit of Passion lippy, darling, and as we're meeting Steve as well, it won't be wasted.'

Polly snorted from the side-bed.

Sylvia dabbed a little on, ran her finger over her lips to eke it out, then threw the lipstick to Polly, who dabbed on a bit. Verity slipped the rouge and lipstick into her make-up bag, and snapped it shut. Polly put the mirror they'd been using into *her* handbag, saying, 'I still feel we should have bought Rachel a birthday present.'

The three of them paused for a moment, as the oil lamp flickered. 'Do you?' Sylvia muttered. 'Perhaps you're right.'

Verity stood up. 'My mind wouldn't be soothed by a gift. It's one thing after another for them. I mean, as though it isn't bad enough that they still don't know Emmanuel's whereabouts, there are these details about Auschwitz. They can't be true, surely. I mean, it's too unbelievable that a whole nation could do that. To millions?' They were silent for a moment, for what could anyone say? thought Sylvia.

Verity muttered, eventually, 'Oh well, let's try not to think about it, if that's at all possible.' She stood up, as Sylvia searched for something, anything, to get them back on track. In the end she said, 'It's so generous of your father to foot the bill tonight. That's a really good gift in itself and the Fishers were delighted at the thought. Anyway, with the shops empty, what would we get her?'

Pup was with Ma Mercy who was moored up further along, so they banked up the range, turned off the oil lamp, and headed out past the pub and up the road to the Tube. Sylvia rolled round her finger the engagement ring that Steve had presented to her when they'd last snatched a meeting at Limehouse in early March. The train lurched now, as it drew out of a station and rattled along while passengers hung from straps; the three of them had seats, for once.

Dearest Steve, he was her last thought at night and the first in the morning, and she didn't know what she had done to deserve such happiness. And now that the rockets had stopped, or so it seemed as the Allies stormed on into Germany, he would be safe.

She sighed, almost hugging herself with joy. Soon she would be Mrs Bates, and have children, and would have to wash and clean, and – heavens, even help to run the Howard House Hotel. Steve, bless him, was at last talking about getting a transfer to Dorset as the girls had talked so much about their futures there.

'Penny for them,' Polly teased her, clutching her hand. 'As though I don't know.'

Sylvia squeezed back. 'The hotel, and soon Tom and Saul will be back, and life can begin again, Pol.'

Verity, sitting on her other side, said, 'Do you remember how you used to say we must treat all this as a pause, Sylv? Well, please God, that is almost over.'

The woman opposite stood to follow the other passengers who were gathering at the doors as the train rattled into a station. 'Don't you be counting your chickens before they're hatched, pet. Tempting fate, that is.'

She left. The girls looked at one another, downcast, until the woman next to Verity nudged her, and said, 'There's always one who'll throw cold water on you. You count as many chickens as you like, the time for making plans is coming closer, and if no one grabs the nettle, a right mess we'll be in.'

The three girls smiled at her but sat with their own thoughts until they reached Piccadilly, where Steve had said he'd meet them. He was there, standing near the boarded-up base of Eros. Sylvia ran to him and clutched him close. He held her back, saying, 'Hey, what's up, Coppernob?'

Verity said, 'Some silly woman on the Tube poured cold water all over us, if you must know.'

Steve gaped as people bustled about them. Polly laughed, 'Not really, Mr Fireman. She just told us not to count our chickens before they were hatched, and it left us feeling ridiculously uncertain.'

Verity snatched the conversation back: 'But only for a moment because, girls and boy, we're off for a night out, with the Fishers, the ones with real problems, so buck up, all of us. Slap a grin on and leave the horrors at Eros, at least for tonight.'

Steve grinned all round. 'Well, if the old bag poured water on you, Ver's just given us a shot from the Fire Service hose, so best do as she says.'

Sylvia loved him at that moment so much that she would have died for him. Well, she would anyway, but . . . Steve was looking at her. 'Are you coming, or staring at where Eros was, hoping it'll magically reappear? Well, it won't come out of storage until this bloody war is finally over, and what's more, darling girl, the other two are striding ahead.'

They caught up, running hand in hand, heading down Regent Street in the dimout bustle, and soon, surely, even that would be lifted. Yes, Sylvia told herself, the war was almost over so there was every reason for spirits to lift. They dodged the traffic as they crossed the road and headed on to Jermyn Street and the club. The Fishers were waiting for them at the bottom of the steps and Solly hugged them all, calling them 'my girls'. He looked at Steve, 'And my saviour, Coppernob.'

He shook Steve's hand, then hugged him close. Sylvia heard him say, 'You're my boy. You need anything you come to Solly, you 'ear. You're my boy cos you saved my life, and them girls' lives too.'

Steve hugged him back, saying, 'Bad mistake, wasn't it, Solly? You'll be up to mischief in no time, causing mayhem. Because they already are.'

Jacob, Solly's son, was grinning like the Cheshire Cat as he shook Steve's hand and said, 'Oh, Steve, Steve, you failed me. You really should have left him in the rubble until he told me where that darned will was.'

Steve was laughing so much he could barely speak, but managed, 'Still hiding it, is he? Shame the rockets have stopped or we could have stuck him back in some rubble until he let on.'

Only Rachel was quiet, but smiling; a smile that didn't reach her eyes. They waited at the foot of the steps as Verity pounded on the door. 'Open up, the gang's all here.'

The hatch slid open. 'Ah, Lady Verity, we were expecting you and your party, and from the noise thought it might be you.' The door opened. A new doorman was laughing as he shook their hands and ushered them in. Though elderly, he was muscled enough to repel unwanted boarders. 'Pleased to meet you, I'm Stanley,' he said. 'Is there a Mr Saul to sing with a Miss Sylvia, as the band is hoping?'

Polly said, 'He's still storming the Germans, I'm afraid, but I'll tell him he's missed.'

At her words, Stanley stopped smiling. 'Please do, and wish him a safe return, and also for your Mr Tom, Lady Verity. Your father apprised us of the special nature of your booking this evening. You know the way, but straight ahead for the coats, if you would.'

He gestured them to the rear of the corridor. They left their shabby, rather smelly clothes with the checkout girl, who handled them as though she wished she had tongs. The Fishers' and Steve's were threadbare but clean. But weren't everyone's threadbare at the end of this long war? thought Sylvia as they followed Verity up the wide staircase, towards the music.

Once in the ballroom they wound through the tables and saw that clearly not everyone *was* threadbare, for there appeared to be several that the war had suited well enough. Jacob nodded to acquaintances, who were smoking cigars and wearing black tie, with wives in evening dress. 'And again we lower the tone, in our rather low-grade mufti, the Fishers and Steve excluded, of course,' murmured Verity, steering towards the head waiter, who indicated their table at the edge of the dance floor.

Jacob sat next to Verity, with Solly on the other side of her. Then Sylvia and Steve, while Polly and Rachel sat together. Refreshments were ordered, and the music seemed to grow louder as the drinks became more plentiful. Steve was watching the band, and in a break he slipped across. It was then that Sylvia saw the pianist was Harry, who had played at the orphanage reunion. 'We get everywhere,' she muttered. Solly leaned closer, his hand to his ear. 'Speak up, gal. Who gets everywhere?'

'Kids from St Cecilia's. The pianist is one of the old boys. He and Steve had a band for a while.'

'Ah, did he ever,' said Solly. 'You and our Steve make a good team, and you'll 'ave a family and tour the world as the Bates Family Singers and keep us all as we'd like to become accustomed.' He spread his hands, taking in the whole table. 'So 'ere we are, you girls, our Steve, and the Fishers, and the girls' families who have written, did you know, to say how pleased they is that we are all better, and that we are all such friends, and how precious friendship is, and then it becomes strong enough to be family.'

They hadn't known, and were so grateful that their parents had contacted the man they had suffered with, and who they had come to cherish from their rushed meetings. Solly was continuing. 'That's 'ow it should be, ain't it, eh? The world swirls and new patterns are made, and people come together, never to be broken apart.' Suddenly he fell quiet, and a darkness came over him.

Sylvia laid her hand on his as Rachel leaned across. 'When you wrote and told us the news of your engagement, Sylvia, we were all pleased, were we not, Jacob? From darkness of rubble, came light.'

Sylvia whispered to Solly, 'Rachel is right. Out of darkness can come light, my dear Solly Fisher.' The only answer was the squeeze he returned. Meanwhile Jacob was leaning back, listening to a man in evening dress who had stopped by his table. Jacob's face was serious as he listened to the whispered words. The man nodded to the table and left. 'Jacob?' Rachel queried. 'You did not think to introduce us?'

Jacob reached for his cigarette smouldering in the ashtray, and said, sotto voce, 'He is not one who cares for introductions. I have been sending out requests for information on Manny. It takes us into the world that is, shall we say, less than kosher. Accountants have many uses to many people who swim in less than pure water, and it is where men of a dark nature find their place.'

He whispered to Verity who was sipping wine to his left, 'I have also asked him to report on any Leon Arness.'

She whispered back, lifting her glass to him. 'You are very kind, Jacob, I—'

Polly interrupted from across the table, 'But, hang on, who's Manny?'

Sylvia turned to look at Rachel. 'I thought you were looking for Emmanuel?'

Rachel was running her finger around the edge of her glass. 'We still seek my father. Some know him as Emmanuel, some as Manny.'

Jacob said, very quietly, still fiddling with his cigarette and leaning forward, 'That man is one who knows him as Manny.'

Steve was striding towards the table now, gesturing to Sylvia. Reaching her, he said, 'Come, your glorious voice is needed, sweetheart.' They headed for the stage, Steve whispering that the band were primed for 'Happy Birthday', and the club had created a surprise birthday cake for Rachel, on the hey-ho from Lord Henry.

At the table Polly watched as Steve took up the saxophonist's instrument, and at a nod from Harry they soared into 'Happy Birthday, dear Rachel', as the waiter headed towards them with a small cake holding a tactful single candle. Rachel flushed, and patted her face with her handkerchief, while Solly, Jacob and the girls joined in the singing. Soon all the clientele was at it and then Harry eased them into 'Begin the Beguine', followed by a medley of dance songs. Polly and Verity exchanged a look, because Sylvia and Steve were alight with love, and it was still a great relief to them that Sylvia had reached a safe shore, away from all uncertainties.

Solly leaned forward. 'So, 'ow is the little boy Joe? Does he see his mother yet, or will he ever?'

Verity answered, 'Not yet, Solly. He knows that she's alive and with Granfer, and he has written to her. I'm sure he will want to see her, but he's confused. He has a life in Dorset and loves his school and though Fran teaches at a school in Buckby he's frightened, I think. Some of the boaters have heard that questions have been asked about a boy who used to be on the cut and is no longer. It could be just chatter but they are alert. The police know nothing, it seems, but Father's high-up friend just has a feeling . . . and so does a local constable's boy in the Met. Anyway, there's been nothing firm and the wretched Leon's probably been smashed to smithereens in a rocket attack.'

She faded out, knowing that Emmanuel had probably been caught in an attack too, but Rachel and Jacob were on the dance floor now, so she continued. 'Let's face it, it's wartime, and Leon's not a priority with the police – how can he be? My father has paid a private detective but his books are full of missing persons, so I suppose he does his best. We think perhaps Leon's changed his name. Well, I would if I were him, Leon Arness is something easy to remember, and he could grow a beard couldn't he, and anyway . . .' She lowered her voice. 'It's so kind of Jacob to have the word out for him.'

Solly said, 'He can, so he should, but we keep it all to a low voice, eh?' He lowered his voice too: 'Some here are, shall we say, private people.'

The girls nodded, and had no intention of asking just how Jacob and his father knew such 'private' people.

Verity's voice seemed overloud as she leaned back in her chair, saying, 'Incidentally, I phoned Father today when I went to the pub to use Sid's lav, and he's found a replacement for Barry, the bodyguard who was knocked down by some damned rogue on a motorbike on his way back from the pub. The replacement's a bloke called Dobbo, who knew Barry and heard he'd died and came to offer his services. He had good references from a bloke called Tony Burrowes who lives in Richmond. Dobbo did some work for him, so he says.'

Solly swung round, and stared, deep in thought. Finally he asked, 'Who d'yer say?'

Verity repeated the name, 'Dobbo.'

Solly said, 'Nah, not that one, the one who gave him 'is reference.' Verity repeated it, and Solly scratched his head. 'I don't know why but it seemed to ring-a-ding a bell, but no, it's gorn. Anyway, this bodyguard any good?'

Verity nodded. 'Seems so, and he has a dog which Joe loves, so that's even better. Father likes him because he was in the war; artilleryman, I gather. They talk of their times out there in the trenches, Mother says. She's not so keen, I feel, but that's probably because it takes Father away from her list of chores. So, anyway, Howard House has Dobbo, his dog, and Ken the old bodyguard, and the old boys and their patrols. Not sure what more they can do.'

They all looked thoughtful, until Verity stood, and hooked her thumb at the dancers. 'Come along, Solly, let's trip the light fantastic.' She wouldn't listen to his protests but dragged him on to the dance floor.

Polly was content to watch the swirling pairs, thinking of Saul, knowing she would feel deliriously happy when he returned and wished it was now, for then she wouldn't lie awake at night fearing for Joe quite so much. But it wouldn't help the fear she felt for the happiness of her parents should Joe leave, which perhaps he must, or her fear for the future of all the boaters. In fact, she realised she was a bundle of fear; for the lives of Saul and Tom, for practically everything which was absurd, because soon the war would end. But the words of that woman in the train had dug deep.

Chapter 23

Early April. Tom, Saul and Geordie with the Allies on the heels of the Germans

They had crossed the Rhine how many days ago? Who knew, Saul Hopkins wondered as they marched, or rather stumbled, mile after mile chasing the buggers, until they reached some woodland, which led to a hamlet a few hundred yards away. Lieutenant Morris flagged down his men and sent Sergeant Williams over to a barn off to the right, where another company had set up a rest stop. Morris then had a word with Corporal Jones before following Sergeant Williams.

'Looks like there'll be a bit of a conflab going on, lads, so shift yourself off the track into the edge of the woods, there's a clearing over there, and keep your eyes open, eh?' Corporal Jones ordered.

The men broke ranks and jumped the ditch into the clearing. Jones set up lookouts at all corners of the compass while Tom and Geordie hunkered down along with the others. Saul slipped off into the woods, his hessian bag on his back, to set a few traps, which is what Sergeant Williams often ordered after business was done. He returned ten minutes later, having set down a string guide to lead him back to them. They waited as fifty feet in front of them, on the bend in the track, Morris sent Sergeant Williams back to the clearing and remained in conversation with the lieutenant at the barn, gesturing, and pointing ahead to the hamlet, the woods, and the way they'd come. Even from here Saul and the others could hear the laughter and chatting of the men in the barn.

Saul and Tom sighed. 'Same old, same old,' muttered Tom. 'It'll be no fraternising, no pilfering, when there are all those bloody chickens running about the place and we're ruddy hungry. But there should also be a bollocking for that lot, hunkered down, a sitting bloody target cos I bet they haven't cleared the village.'

They heard Morris snap at Sergeant Williams on his return, 'Not good enough, not good enough at all. I told Lieutenant Border the village needs clearing, men need dispersing.' He looked towards the barn where nothing had changed, and said something quietly to Corporal Jones who nodded, and squared his shoulders as Lieutenant Morris and Sergeant Williams returned to the barn. Allied planes were flying over, probably giving a sense of security. But didn't that bugger Border know that was false?

At the edge of the clearing Corporal Jones was doing what he had been doing, looking to his left and right, peering through his binoculars at the hamlet, examining the roofs, the church, the windows, the shadows, not letting his guard down for a moment. He murmured, 'Bloody idiots, hunkered down in a bloody barn, ain't got the sense they were born with. Talk about a bloody hen coop, with foxes pithering round and about. Time that idiot Border, or I reckon that's what the boss said his name was, got some sense or I reckon it'll be shafted into him, if he don't listen.'

They didn't answer because he was talking to himself. They all seemed to do that these days. Tired, they were, Saul thought, bloody tired. Geordie hadn't learned, even yet, and replied, 'Aye, well, Corp, them Nazis were promised so much and instead of the riches o' the world they're at the bottom, and I can't say me 'eart bleeds, man.'

Corporal Jones looked at him. 'What the 'ell you talking about, Geordie?' he said. He posted even more lookouts, adding, 'Lieutenant Morris says it might look all right, but keep alert; that Border's fresh out, and inherited a ragtag of a company in that barn. I reckon any minute now the men'll be out and dispersed, and they'll all be on lookout two hours on and off. Our Morris might 'ave been a civvy in real life, but I'd 'ire him any day to get you lot slung into clink cos he covers the bases, unlike them silly buggers.' He jerked his head towards the barn. 'What good do Border think it'll do to post a couple of guards either side of the barn, when there'll be those in the bloody village champing at the bit to take a potshot before their world ends.'

Saul watched as they all heard Morris raising his voice over by the barn, and saw him stabbing his finger at Border's chest.

Tom raised his eyebrows. 'That's Morris's promotion out the window.'

As the rest of their platoon watched, Morris called across 2nd Lieutenant Green, who was checking a map near Corporal Jones. Green was a stuck-up twerp from Chelsea who hadn't thought a world existed outside his nice little London niche. That was until he arrived out here but his post was temporary, and no one really knew why they had been landed with him. They heard an order being issued at the barn, and the guards were doubled while others spread far out in suitable cover. Sergeant Williams returned shaking his head, saying to Corporal Jones, 'Not enough, the pillock. Still others left in the bleedin' barn. Gawd, talk about wet behind the ears.'

They watched as Morris strutted across to the track to scan the hamlet with his binoculars. He swept the top floor windows, then doubled back to one in particular, before striding across to Border and stopping so close they almost touched noses. Again, there was shouting, and Morris gripped Border's arm and showed him the windows. At last the bloody idiot nodded, and swung back to his NCOs, changing the order. They sprang into action and soon all the men filed out to disperse in the woodland further south, to the left of the village. Patrols would be formed to check the houses – that was clear from the words that reached them – but they'd go out as the sun went down, and therefore wouldn't be sitting targets.

Williams and Jones nodded to one another and then allocated duties, emphasising that there must be no pilfering or fraternising. Williams looked at Saul. 'A word, Saul 'Opkins.'

Saul stood, and followed Williams to the nearby fire that some were ready to light up when there was an all-clear. Corporal Jones posted more men, some facing outwards from the clearing and others sent deeper into the woods. 'Nice bit of woodland,' Sergeant Williams said. 'Fancy yer've already been for a stroll with yer poacher's eye. So off yer go, lad. No chickens, mind, but bound to be a few rabbits, maybe a bird or two caught in 'em traps, now the sun's going down. Reckon the lieutenant could do with a bit of meat to chew on, instead of Border. Take that lump of no good grumbling sidekick Tom with yer to watch yer back. Password, cockerel call, that cackling one you do, and then the reply will be "hen", so yer don't get your 'ead blown off. Geordie, if you get separated you'll just use "beak" and the reply will be same. I reckon this lot o' Nazis 'ere aren't as quiet as they make out. The lieutenant spotted a weapon o' sorts at the window. Jones verified it.'

Tom said, 'Do I have to, Sarge? Can't Geordie? Me feet hurt.'

The sarge just looked at him, then nodded. 'Geordie, yer go on point for Saul, then, while chummy joins the latrine dig instead o' yer.'

Tom groaned, 'Sarge?'

Saul and Geordie laughed, heading for the fringes of the clearing and hearing the sergeant call, 'Lookouts extend to fifty feet, Saul. After that, they're not friendly.'

Saul listened for footfalls as well as the rustle of wildlife as he followed the string, trusting Geordie, on point to his left, to watch out for him.

They travelled away from the noise, and as the canopy grew denser beneath conifers which were mixed with leafless deciduous trees and the darkness grew, he picked up an empty trap. Never mind, there were others. He didn't speak, and neither did Geordie. They just listened, because they had a long way to go before they reached Berlin, or until Germany surrendered, and they were determined to get home alive. Further on Saul gathered booty from the traps, putting the rabbits in one bag, the traps in the other.

He heard the noise at the same time as Geordie. They both froze. They were too far out for patrols, surely, but Saul made his cockerel call.

There was no response. Saul slashed the string, rammed the scrambled ball of it into his pocket as they doubled over and edged away. Was someone heading towards them? They'd known it before.

Saul could travel silently, and Geordie, almost, since he had also supplemented his parents' larder between pit shifts. They edged back towards a large oak, dropping to one knee, back to back, and letting their eyes and ears become accustomed to the area. An owl hooted, the wind moved the branches, some of the weaker ones rubbing together. There were no leaves to rustle, as they were still in bud. Small mercy, but a useful one. There was indistinct noise. They breathed through their mouths. Saul withdrew a Luger he'd 'found' as they fought their way to the Rhine, and kept the knife in his left hand. Geordie had done the same. Was it a German fellow poacher, or a rearguard Nazi platoon, or villagers out for retribution? Or their own outpost guards?

Off towards the hamlet they heard an explosion. Saul covered his ears. He didn't care what that was, he needed his hearing. He flashed a look at Geordie, who was doing the same. Again they listened, and the rustling was more distinct, and now they heard the snapping twigs, a guttural voice, quickly hushed. Geordie lifted his gun. Saul shook his head and gestured towards the clearing. They had to prepare the men for a flanking attack, though Morris and Green would suspect the explosion was a diversion cos it was the same old ploy. They were up now, but still doubled over, racing silently, heading to the clearing, just as poaching had taught them.

The rabbits were bouncing in the bag, and Saul held the traps tight against his body, so that they didn't clang. He cackled a cockerel call. 'Hen.' A loud whisper.

Saul whispered, 'Attack be approaching be'ind us. Attack, approaching.'

They ran on, and burst into the clearing. Morris had already positioned his men well into the brush, with some facing the hamlet, some the woods. Border's men were emerging from the woods, dashing towards the burning truck and the end of the imploding barn. Sergeant Williams muttered, 'Bloody idiots. Sitting bloody targets.'

But even as they watched, Border suddenly stood still, as though some sense had at last filtered through, and started issuing the right orders. His men disappeared into the shadows, behind buildings and trees, seeking out the attackers, who had started firing from the houses, and behind them. 'Thank Gawd for that,' muttered Sergeant Williams, again to himself. 'Corporal Jones, are the men ready?'

Morris was nowhere to be seen until he emerged from the woods to their left, clearly positioning his men; 2nd Lieutenant Green had been doing the same to the north. Morris said to those few who remained in the clearing, 'Get that fire lit. Let's have a bit of talk, laughter, as though you're not taking it seriously, eh? You're the bait, lads, we've got your backs. Get ready to dive out of sight once the messiness starts.'

Saul nodded to himself. Morris always made them dig in for just this manoeuvre, and so far it'd worked.

Morris was hurrying to Saul and Geordie now, who had hunkered down with Tom behind a fallen trunk of rotten tree, facing east the way they had come. Tom had their rifles ready for them; Saul placed his Luger on the trunk, his knife was back in his belt. 'How many, Saul?' Morris whispered as he came to crouch beside Saul.

'From t'sounds, it'd be a platoon, sir.'

Geordie nodded. 'Aye, but what's coming from the other direction, sir?'

Morris patted his shoulder. 'Just been out there. I'd say the same again.'

Saul raised an eyebrow at Tom as the lieutenant melted into the shadows, on the opposite side of the clearing to Williams, Saul whispered, 'I does reckon he likes it.'

Tom grunted, 'I don't care whether he likes it or not, I just want him to be the best there is, and he bloody well is.'

Geordie's lips were pursed in a soundless whistle, as always before a set-to, as he called it. But this time he un-pursed them enough to say, 'Aye, I always says, there's good bosses, and bad 'uns, and he's the bloody best, man.'

The firing began then, at the outer ring, and Sergeant Williams shouted, 'Steady now. Rifles, and Stens at the ready. Fire at will but don't waste your bloody time firing at shadows.'

Saul wondered what they'd do without that voice, always there, always steady. Didn't the man know fear? There were shouts, the crashing of bushes, the hurling of grenades which exploded behind them, throwing up earth and stones that cut through Saul's uniform. He swore, waiting, waiting. There was the sound of men rushing, a yelled challenge: 'Hen.' But no answering 'hen'.

They held fire and the lookouts leapt the fallen trunks of trees, taking position behind stacked wood. Germans were firing, and some of the fools hurled themselves into the clearing. 2nd Lieutenant Green's group took them out. The Sten guns were firing over the piled trunks, only for their fire to be reciprocated and now there was bloody chaos and they fired blindly at the oncoming attackers.

Over the noise they heard the revving and rumbling of their tanks, and the roar of their guns which were firing beyond the barn. Well, Saul hoped them were theirs but no one paused, they just kept firing until their barrels were red hot. Some of the buggers broke through, and they comprised both troops and civilians. Geordie was now whistling, which meant he was getting angry. Well, too bloody right, Saul thought, and as always, for some strange reason, whenever Geordie whistled Saul thought of Leon, and how he'd beaten Joe and had been happy to think he'd killed Maudie. P'raps it were because Geordie's rage was Saul's rage for that bugger. He pulled his finger even tighter on the trigger, and each bullet was for Leon, because until they knew where he was there'd be no peace for the Hopkins family.

'It's a bloody German Tiger,' the sarge called. Saul snatched a look. The Tiger was in the hamlet, roaring through, shelling the woods where the other company was, then swinging round, and now it was targeting them. A shell burst to the left. Trees shattered, men screamed and groaned. Saul was struggling hand to hand with a bloody great farmer, and all he could see was Leon, kicking him outside the pub, beating him with a club, and he fought back, clubbing the German with his Luger until he crashed to the ground, out for the count, but not dead. Saul swung round in time to see Border out in the open with an anti-tank weapon, firing at the Tiger. The men bailed out, hands up. Lieutenant Border drew his pistol and ushered them into the barn. God, he wasn't going to shoot them, was he?

The lieutenant came out and positioned his men inside the barn as guards.

Saul was relieved, and fought on, until suddenly it was over. The men surrendered. Sergeant Williams issued orders and the prisoners were marched to the barn and kept under an even heavier armed guard. Surely any renegades wouldn't attack a barn that contained their own people? Or would they? The actions of these bastards were beyond anyone's imagination because the Allied troops were beginning to hear about the concentration camps that had been discovered the length and breadth of Europe as it was attacked from east and west.

Patrols marched on the village, checking the houses, carrying out weapons while the radio operator hunched over his set. Sergeant Williams came from the woods, helping Lieutenant Morris into the clearing. Morris's blood was staining the front of his tunic. Williams was yelling for a medic. One looked up and rushed across, leaving others to tend the German and British wounded. The sarge issued orders. A German doctor was dragged from a house at gunpoint. The gun stayed fixed on him as he was rushed to the clearing. Border came with him, pale, drawn and shaking. Sergeant Williams looked up at him and said, 'Yer did a good job there, son.'

The lieutenant nodded, his smile brief, relief in his voice. 'About time, eh, Sergeant Williams. How's the boss?'

All the men waited. No one spoke as the doctor poked and prodded, and the medic hovered, watching carefully. Morris was stretchered to the doctor's house. The doctor's wife was a nurse, and she knew of one more. The medic stood over her while she worked on Morris, and her friend aided the medics tending all the others. Three of these were triaged and taken to the doctor's house as well.

Corporal Jones supervised the men, who hunkered down into groups within the clearings; those that weren't on watch, anyway. They watched and they waited. Saul skinned and cooked the rabbits.

They caught some of the chickens, too. If someone complained they'd bloody sort them, so they would, because their lieutenant was hurt bad.

Reinforcements arrived, some stayed, some marched away the prisoners. The houses were searched more thoroughly now and more weapons were found in the attics and basements, some even in the crypt of the church. They were all destroyed. And still the men waited, but they ate the rabbit and chicken. Lieutenant Border posted guards, and kept the men dispersed until dawn broke. A couple of ambulance transports arrived, their red cross glaring in the early morning sun, and the wounded were loaded by stretcher, including the Germans.

'What about Lieutenant Morris, Sarge?'

'Still with us. Going off in the ambulance. We'll be under Border, but he's come good. You all just stay at your posts, and that's an order.'

Their boss was taken from the doctor's house, the company medic walking beside the stretcher, holding a drip high in the air. Saul, Tom and Geordie looked at one another, grabbed their weapons and headed towards Morris along with the rest of the company. Sergeant Williams was heard to say, as they passed him, 'Stay at yer posts, I said. Talking to me bloody self, eh?' But within seconds he was leading the way, along with Corporal Jones, shouting, 'In full marching order, if you please. We don't want the lieutenant to become annoyed, and cause his blood pressure to boil, now, do we?'

The men shouldered arms and stood to attention in a line behind the ambulance with Sergeant Williams, Corporal Jones, 2nd Lieutenant Green and Lieutenant Border, as their boss was carried the final yards. They waited at attention until he was on board, though the doors were still open. There was a pause, and Sergeant Williams was gestured by a medic to the back of the transport. They watched as he ducked into the ambulance, and heard Williams bark, 'Yes, sir.'

He jumped down, about-turned, and spoke to the two officers. Lieutenant Border laughed. 'Give the order, Sergeant Williams, in those precise words, if you would.'

Sergeant Williams raised his voice. 'Get yourselves back to work, or the boss'll want to know the reason why. Keep your bloody heads down, clean your weapons, and get those latrines finished, and good show, the lot of you. You're men to be proud of.'

They set off the next day, leaving the remaining chickens in place, and the civilians to what was left of their lives, but they spared them no sympathy. The war had lasted for six years as these people fought tooth and nail for a madman who, not content with destroying country after country, had indulged in obscene crimes in his people's name.

They caught up with their own tanks a week later, and the fighting continued. Lieutenant Morris died, though, as their platoon was entering a large village. Still they had to fight on step by step in an almost monotonous way. There was some things that they would remember, Saul thought as they captured a boy of fifteen or so, who was dressed in a ragtag uniform, his rifle barrel hot from firing from his bedroom window and who was riddled with lice. They gestured that he go outside for delousing, but his mother held him back.

Tom had learned some German, and said that she must let him go. She wept. 'Töte ihn nicht.'

Tom shook his head. 'She thinks we're going to kill him.' He told her, 'Wir werden nicht.'

Geordie muttered, 'You should tell her we're not bloody Nazis.'

Lieutenant Border, who was passing, said, 'Enough of that, Geordie. He's only a boy, without the sense he was born with.'

'Aye, sir, but she ain't.'

Tom said to the woman, 'Es ist Typhus zu stoppen.' They stripped him of his clothes, dusted him with DDT to prevent him, and the village, dying of typhus, and sent him back in.

They moved on, and on. To the east the Russians were advancing fast and resistance to the Allies faded as refugees started heading towards the west, desperate to escape the Russians bent on revenge for the treatment and execution of so many thousands, probably millions, of their countrymen by the Nazis.

Saul, Tom and Geordie marched on, putting one foot in front of the other, still alert for rearguard lunatics. They stuck to the side of the road, not wanting to make any form of contact with Germans; not now, not after all they were hearing about the Jews. Somehow they had to keep hold of their humanity. On they marched, deeper and deeper into Germany, further from England, but nearer peace. But not quite yet; there were 'miles to go before they slept', or so Lieutenant Border said, as he walked amongst his men. 'That's almost a line in a poem by Robert Frost,' he told them.

They just smiled. He had a funny way with him, did Border, but as they couldn't have Morris, they'd have him. Saul thought of the cut, as he marched on. He already knew t'feeling of there being miles to go before he slept, but he'd been on water then. He said to Tom, as Border moved on, 'I reckon our lasses know t'feeling an' all. They be pat-pattering up the cut, and we'd 'ave 'eard if they'd been caught in a rocket in the mail that gets through from home. Wonder how Joe be? Wonder too if Maudie be well enough to see 'im? Seems years since she were found, but it's not.'

Tom shrugged. 'It is years, you daft old boater. Years, and bloody years.'

Geordie muttered, 'Oh Gawd, I hope we have a billet tonight. Sick I am of digging a bloody latrine.'

Tom said what he always said: 'Thought you'd be used to digging. After all, you're a pitman.'

And as he always did, Geordie pursed his lips in a silent whistle, which meant 'quite enough of that', but he wasn't as angry as he made out. Saul smiled as the rabbits and turnips in his hessian sack jolted on his back. Tom, Geordie and he were a team, just like the girls.

At Howard House Joe was by Mr Dobbo's side, with Rover at the other. They stood with their backs to the ha-ha, and Mr Dobbo handed Joe the ball.

'Right you are, Joe. Throw the ball, and I'll tell Rover to stay at me heel. We need to make sure he don't run after it, till I'm ready for him to do that. You got it?'

Joe turned sideways, as Uncle Henry had shown him when he taught him to bowl at a wicket. He preferred to take a run but Mr Dobbo had said to do it standing for the first time. Mr Dobbo said, 'You ready, then, Joe?'

'I am, Mr Dobbo.'

'In your own time, then.'

Joe drew in a breath, and then waited for a count of three to steady himself, which is what Uncle Thomas had said when he had the cricket bowling lesson. 'Three,' he whispered, and from a standing point, he threw the ball overarm. It went miles, he thought, pride making him smile. Mr Dobbo pressed his shoulder. 'Good throw,' he murmured. His voice changed as Rover stirred when the ball bounced on to the lawn, and then bounced again. 'Stay, Rover.'

When the ball lay still Joe waited, motionless, hardly breathing. Would Rover wait too? He saw Uncle Henry coming along the ha-ha now, but Joe wouldn't call, wouldn't wave, because this was dog training, and important. Now Mr Dobbo shouted, but not really. He just spoke sort of loud but with a fierce grating sound which must make Rover feel nervous, because it made Joe feel it. 'Fetch, Rover.'

The dog, an Alsatian, bounded forward, his legs pumping the ground, going so fast Joe knew he could never keep up with him, ever. The dog almost skidded on the grass as he snatched up the ball, turning. Mr Dobbo yelled again, 'Stand, Rover.'

Rover did, then on Mr Dobbo's command, he walked back, drool hanging from his mouth, and laid the ball at Joe's feet, for that's what Mr Dobbo told him to do.

Joe didn't want to pick the ball up, because it was slimy from the drool, and there were even strands of the stuff on it. Mr Dobbo said, 'The drool won't hurt you, and it's his gift, and I have told Rover to bring it to you. Perhaps you really should pick it up.'

Uncle Henry had come close now, but he stopped. Joe knew he was watching and listening. Mr Dobbo said nothing, just waited. Rover sat, his mouth hanging open, watching – and was he pleading? That's what it looked like, that there were pleading in his dark eyes. Joe bent and picked up the ball, and Rover's tail wagged, thwacking into the ground.

Joe looked up at Mr Dobbo. 'You is right, Mr Dobbo. I were rude and Rover doesn't deserve rudeness. He do look after me, so he do. Should I throw it again?'

Mr Dobbo was looking at him, strange, just for a moment, and his eyes had the same look that Rover's had, that sort of pleading, but then it were gone. Uncle Henry said, 'You're doing a good job all round Dobbo, replacing Barry, I must say. So glad you came, it's good for the boy to have someone to show him all sorts of things that perhaps us old codgers are out of the way of. Anyway, there's a cuppa in the kitchen for you both – if you can spare the time from your training, that is?'

Joe checked with Mr Dobbo. 'We could give Rover a biscuit, Mr Dobbo. Mrs B's are quite sugary from the honey she puts in them.'

He watched as Mr Dobbo seemed to be thinking, then he scratched Rover behind the ears. 'Best not, Joe. We'll get on round the perimeter, but don't let yours, and your uncle's, get cold.'

Mr Dobbo half saluted them both and called Rover to heel, moving on. Uncle Henry tousled Joe's hair. 'He's a good man, Joe. You could do worse than take a look at Dobbo as an example of how to be.'

'He be a bit like our Saul, and you, Uncle,' said Joe as they headed off back to the house. Then Joe remembered Mr Dobbo's ball, stopped, and called after his bodyguard, 'I'll throw the ball back, Mr Dobbo. You can do more training with Rover, and p'raps you'd let me help tomorrow after school, too. Or another time anyway.'

He threw it, Mr Dobbo caught it, tossed it into the air, caught it again, called, 'We'll do that, Joe,' then walked on.

Uncle Henry said, as though he was thinking aloud, 'Dobbo would be a useful man for the cricket team, Joe.'

'He would, Uncle Henry, but Rover would be better.' They laughed together, then hurried across the lawn, round the side of the house to the kitchen.

Chapter 24

It's a week later and Leon's various plans are coming along

Leon Arness, commonly known as Lionel Harkness, checked through the plans at his desk. He liked the roll of the words 'Leon Arness, commonly known as Lionel Harkness'. He could hear a tune when he said it. Right clever it were. Course, he owed it to Manny, not that he'd said that when the accountant had come the first time to do the books. The old bloke had thought he was a mate of Norton's who'd taken over the business. The old man was a bit deaf, and though Leon had said Arness, the old beggar writ down Harkness. Old Manny had even got Leon wrong and writ Lionel at t'top of his invoice. He can't 'ave checked through Norton's old invoices.

It were a sign. New name, new beginning.

Dougie knocked. Leon called, 'Do be getting in 'ere, don't 'ang about.' He checked his watch, and then the school timetable in the right hand corner of the A3 sheet of paper; the plan of the school and nearby roads took up the rest.

Leon stabbed at the playground. 'Dobbo got himself sorted? Built up a pretence of being a pal?'

'He 'as, boss.'

Leon stabbed at the road.

'We needs car, second snatcher and driver. Yer can vouch fer 'em? No point in grabbing t'boy and 'aving no getaway.'

Dougie nodded again. Leon muttered, 'So 'ow's Dobbo and the dog getting to the school?'

'Sid'll pick him up, drop him along the road before lunch playtime so he can be strolling past. Sid'll move the car up when Dobbo lets the dog get started. Then it should all go smooth, like.'

Leon looked up. 'It better do. Then yer'll bring 'im 'ere. I be takin' up the back stairs to me flat.' Leon checked his watch again. 'Sid's be down there, now?'

Dougie nodded. 'He called in from a phone box. Got another hour or so, then he'll pick up Dobbo, who got off the morning shift and ain't due on at Howard House again till three. He won't turn up, course. They should be 'ere by six at the latest, boss.'

Leon rolled up the plan. Beneath it was another. 'Yer sure we ain't got no more of Mario's men skulking about being barmen, flappin' their ears?'

Dougie flushed. 'Sorry about that, boss.'

Leon grunted at the great clod; he was all muscle and no brain. What were the point of having someone steer the butty on tow if they pitched it in t'bank? For a moment he was surprised, cos he didn't often think of the cut. Maybe it was because he was getting his boy back and the last time he'd seen him were on the butty. Family was family, and Joe would learn t'follow orders and would know better than to steer crooked. He grinned because Angelo had taken 'em for mugs, serving drinks and shaking cocktails, but they'd fed him what they wanted Mario to know, before Leon had done for him, good and proper. Leon said, 'It'll all go well, I can feel it in me bones.'

Dougie grinned at this. 'When do we make our move on Mario?'

'Fer me to be knowing, not yer. We've most of t'men we need, and some o' the dosh, but when we moves in we can get that quick enough. Tells me 'ow it goes.'

He flicked a finger to the door. Dougie hesitated. 'Goes?'

Leon growled, 'On m'boy, what else?'

Joe had swapped one of his cheese sandwiches for a jam one at school lunchtime. Martin's mum made good jam, and Mrs B said it was because she ran the WI jam-making for the war effort. He supposed that with the Allies chasing the Germans back to Berlin the war would end, except for the Japs, so would jam and oranges be in the shops again? He hoped so, because the girls talked about oranges a lot so he'd buy them one.

He asked Martin, 'What's an orange taste like?'

Martin was looking inside his sandwich at the cheese, and smiling. Eddie sat at the end of the table, and leaned forward. 'Me mam says they's sweet, and juicy, but they 'ave a skin with dimples. My auntie says the dimples is like my mam's thighs.'

Martin pulled a face. 'What's thighs? Something you put on the sideboard, like a vase?'

The boys didn't know. The hubbub grew as the children relaxed over their sandwiches. Tommy at the other end of the table had sausage sandwiches, and the smell made Joe's mouth water, but Tommy's dad was a butcher, and anyway, sometimes he shared. Joe would share the bacon from the pigs which rooted around in the copse, but he didn't want to be there when one was killed. He said, 'Mr Dobbo's dog Rover can't get the 'ang o' the pigs. He barks his 'ead off, but Mr Dobbo makes him sit. He's my mate, is Mr Dobbo. We been training Rover together.'

Martin had taken a bite of his sandwich, and asked, crumbs spattering across the table, ''Ow's t'other one who kept an eye out, the one who were 'it by the motorbike before Dobbo came?'

'Barry still be in 'ospital though we thought he were to die. Auntie Joyce and Pamela and Mrs B took me to see him, took 'im a bread and butter pudding, but he pulled a face. Mrs B were right annoyed and wanted t'bring it home for us, but 'e were sorry, and said it were lovely. So Auntie Joyce and Auntie Pamela teased him and said it would put 'airs on his chest. Or that's what they said. I haven't got hairs on my chest and I have bread and butter pudding.'

Martin shook his head, 'Neither have I.' No one round the table had, and they asked Miss Watson if she had and she went red and told them not to be cheeky. The boys looked at one another, and shrugged. Grown-ups weren't 'alf daft, they whispered.

As Miss Watson rang the bell for the end of lunchtime, they smoothed out their greaseproof paper, tipping the crumbs back into the OXO tins in which they carried their sandwiches, and tucked them under their arms to line up for playtime. At a word from Miss Watson they rushed to their pegs, tucked their tins on the benches and slung on coats, found their marbles and tore out of the boys' entrance into the playground. As they ran into the cold, Joe laughed and laughed, because he was just so happy. This morning his ma had written to say she understood, and would never drag him away, but would like to come and see him.

The aunties and uncles had thought that a good idea as a first step, and Uncle Henry had said that he'd go to Southall to bring her and Granfer back, if the girls would pick her up in the boats.

Joe, Martin and Eddie chalked a circle, moved back, and knelt in their short trousers, the asphalt 'crumbs' digging into their knees. Joe wondered what Uncle Henry meant as a 'first step'. He'd ask him when he caught the bus home, as it was Uncle Henry's day. It was Martin's turn to start and he flicked his dobber, the largest of his marbles, into the others which were collected in the centre. The dobber split them up, ramming several out of the ring. 'Ha,' Martin shouted, collecting up the outcast marbles and his dobber. 'I've got four. Your turn, Eddie.'

Joe watched Eddie carefully because he was a wizard at a marble flick, but Eddie was so fast he could never see how he did it. He wondered if Mr Dobbo would know. He'd ask. Eddie's dobber whopped into the remaining clump of marbles and they skidded one into another, and then out of the ring, Eddie's dobber skidding with them.

'Belter,' yelled Joe, looking despairingly at the few scattered marbles left. He tried to decide whether to aim for the one nearest the edge of the circle, but then his dobber'd come out too, or to go for the three together and get a spin on the marble, and whack them all outside but the dobber might stay inside the circle. He was just ready to flick when he heard a frantic barking, and a man, shouting above the laughter and chat of the children in the playground. He tried to concentrate, but just as he was about to flick he was nudged from behind, knocking his dobber from his hand. It crawled to a stop, nowhere near any other marble. He spun round, but then laughed. It was Rover, and he tried to lick Joe's face. 'Hey, what you doing 'ere, boy?'

Rover was pulling at his sleeve, turning round, scattering the marbles with his paws, and some children were screaming, and running away. Joe called, 'It's only be Rover, he won't hurt you. He does what Mr Dobbo says.'

He looked around and there was his bodyguard by the open school gate. How queer, cos it was always kept shut. Miss Watson was storming over to Joe, her handbell at the ready. Joe thought she were going to hit Rover with it, and stood up, grabbed Rover's collar, and scurried off to the school gate as Mr Dobbo called, and beckoned Joe. 'Bring him back, lad. I was out walkin' and 'e saw you, dashed in, and now he's confused. Rover, come.'

Rover pulled Joe to the gate, while Miss Watson called to him to return immediately, holding the clapper to keep the bell quiet. Joe was really proud as he walked Rover, and Martin trotted along a bit behind, saying, 'Coo, you knows what yer doing, Joe.'

It was then Miss Watson rang her handbell for end of playtime, and the children, including Martin, ran back to the boys' and girls' entrances, while Joe took Rover right up to Mr Dobbo, who smiled. 'That's the way, lad. Right up close, eh, so he don't run off again.'

Just along the road from Mr Dobbo, a car was parked with its engine running. It was a black one with a sort of statue on the bonnet. He turned, and Martin were looking at him while Miss Watson was calling the two of them to hurry, and ringing her bell like billy-o.

The back door of the car was swinging open. Someone called, 'Grab the boy, for Gawd's sake, Dobbo, what the 'ell are you 'anging about for? What'll his dad say if we bugger this up?'

Joe hesitated, suddenly thinking of the cut, of his da, of the fists. He stepped back, his legs wobbly, looking from Mr Dobbo, to Rover, to the car, all of them looking strange, suddenly. Big and dark and strange, and he couldn't work it out. Martin called, 'Come on, Joe. You can't go without your uncles at Howard House saying it's all right. We'll get ticked off; come on, Miss Watson's going bonkers with the bell.'

Joe was backing away now, wanting to be with Martin, playing marbles, wanting Eddie and Miss Watson, wanting his uncles and aunties. He saw Mr Dobbo's hand point to him, and now Rover leapt, grabbed his arm, hurting him. Joe lost his balance, Miss Watson shouted, 'Leave that boy alone.'

Joe turned, but Mr Dobbo grabbed him by his collar, dragging him through the gateposts towards the car. Joe called, 'Help me. Please, please someone.' He was lifted – it was so quick but he called, 'Mr Dobbo, what yer doin'? I don't like me da, and what about me ma? Don't let me da hurt me ma.' He was thrown into the back seat, and hit it with a thump, banging into someone else who was bony, and who grabbed him. Rover was leaping in after him, but

Joe could see the children racing through the play-ground towards the gate, with Miss Watson in the lead, ringing her bell, ringing and ringing it. He wanted to be with them. He leaned forward, pushing against Rover, who growled. The bony man hugged him; it hurt. The man yelled, 'Keep still, you little bleeder.' The man smelt of drink. It were like his da used to smell before he hit him and his ma.

Mr Dobbo leapt into the front seat but the car was already moving and the door swung on his arm, and he swore. Mr Dobbo hadn't sworn before, he'd been kind. Joe heard the screams of the children, and the screeching of the tyres, as something was put over his head: a cloth. It stank of sweat. He vomited. Sick filled the sack. It was cheese and jam. The man cursed and dragged the cloth off, winding down the window, throwing it out. Rover was sitting on the back seat, growling at him, but Joe had thought Rover were his friend, like Mr Dobbo. Joe said to the back of Mr Dobbo's head, 'I thought you be my friend, Mr Dobbo. I thought you wanted to keep me safe.'

The taste of sick was still in his mouth as the bony man tied something round his eyes. It was dark again. Joe said again, 'I thought you'd keep me safe, and now I'm not, and I've wet myself and I don't know what yous doing.' He was crying, and you didn't cry, not in front of grown-ups, or your friends.

Mr Dobbo muttered something, and the driver said, 'Don't go all soft on the lad. 'E won't thank you for it, Dobbo. Just think how it's goin' ter be when he's back with his dad, and 'e's the boss's son. Shut yer gob and do as yer told, that's all we 'ave to do, or it'll be the worse for us. Yer know what 'e's like. 'E wants his family back, so that's that.'

Joe fought the bony man holding him now, and shouted, 'You leave my ma alone, you 'ear me.'

The minute he said those words he sank back down into the darkness, because he knew he had made a worse mistake than he'd ever made in his life. He didn't think his da knew his ma was alive, and now he'd told these men. He started to really cry then, until there were no tears left, and the blindfold was wet. He could smell his wee, and the man who held him could too, and cursed him.

Chapter 25

That same day the hunt for Joe begins

After lunch at Howard House, Rogers shook out the tablecloth in the yard and headed for the steps past Henry and Thomas who were hanging out the washing. In the kitchen the women were laughing because they'd had a look and it was all higgledy-piggledy, but as Mrs B said, 'They do it deliberately so we don't ask 'em again, but we will, because many hands make light work.'

He folded the tablecloth and returned it to the drawer in the kitchen table as the women finished in the scullery. Lunch was only a vegetable flan but the amount of washing-up seemed ridiculous. Why did they have to use so many dishes? Then there'd be a cup of tea that would have to be washed, and he was on sink duty. The telephone rang. He shambled off. Who was it this time? Perhaps the butcher about the pig? 'Howard House resid—'

There was no time for him to finish because Miss Read, the headmistress of the school, shouted, 'It's Joe, someone's taken him. There was a dog, a big

Alsatian, and a Mr Dobbo? They took him. I've called the police. It was a big black car.'

Mr Rogers tried to clear his mind. What was the bodyguard doing at the school? What had he saved Joe from? Who was threatening Joe? He said, 'Dobbo took him to safety, you mean?'

Miss Read shrieked down the phone, 'Don't be obtuse, you absurd little man. He's taken Joe, the dog grabbed him by the arm in the playground, there were other men, he was dragged into the—'

Now Mr Rogers let the receiver dangle from the telephone on the wall, and rushed back into the kitchen and yelled, 'They've grabbed Joe. Get Henry and Thomas.'

He rushed back and snatched up the receiver as a plate crashed to the floor, and broke. There was the sound of the kitchen door slamming back against the wall. 'Miss Read, please tell me all about it, I'm so sorry, such a shock . . .' He trailed off, his heart racing.

Miss Read seemed in no better shape. 'Quickly then, but you must come because the police are here, and need statements. The boys were playing marbles, Miss Watson was on duty – you'll need to talk to her too, though the police already are – and the dog came into the playground. The gate shouldn't have been open, I'm so so sorry. But it was, and in came this dog.'

Mr Rogers felt his heart slowing as he breathed once, twice, coughed and thumped his chest. It was something he'd learned but couldn't remember where. He shook himself. 'So, the dog came in. It was an Alsatian?'

'Yes, Mr Rogers, according to Martin.'

Mr Rogers thought for a brief moment. 'Ah yes, Joe's best friend.'

'Yes, that's right. Then Mr Dobbo called from the gate and wanted Joe to return his dog. Martin said that when Joe got close to Mr Dobbo, a car door opened and someone told Mr Dobbo to get on with it, and he grabbed Joe. And dragged him to the car.' The headmistress stopped on a sob.

Henry rushed through, with Thomas right behind. 'What? Tell me?' Henry shouted.

Mr Rogers held up his hand and frowned at his employer. 'Please, Henry.'

Henry waited as meek as a lamb, panting. Mr Rogers waited a moment too, and when Miss Read had collected herself, he asked, 'Was anything else said, Miss Read? Anything that Martin or Miss Watson remember?'

'All that Martin really heard was some shouting about getting him to his dad, and Joe saying something like, 'Leave my ma alone.' Then there was a screech of tyres, but the police have come into my study, so I must go. You'll be here soon, won't you? I'm so sorry, so very sorry. We've tried to be careful. The gate is always locked but the chain had been cut. Oh, dear me.' There was a click, and Mr Rogers replaced the receiver, staring at the wall.

Henry stood at his elbow, with Thomas just behind him, and the women, who were holding the hem of their aprons to their mouths. Mr Rogers explained all that had happened, ending with Joe's words. Henry drew in a deep breath but his voice was shaking as he said, 'We've got to get there and sort out help from the police.'

The three men rushed back through the kitchen where Mrs B, Pamela and Joyce were scrambling into their coats. Mr Rogers said, 'Someone has to stay here, just in case . . .'

Mrs B stared at him. 'In case what – he walks in the door, safe and sound? We heard everything. Maudie is in danger, our boy is in danger from his bloody father, so don't be so bloody silly.'

Mr Rogers sat down at the table, out of breath suddenly. 'You never swear.'

Mrs B held her fist against her mouth. 'Henry is calling you. You are right, Simon. We will stay, and we will telephone the depot, and Fran, so she can warn Granfer, and we will find our lad, and try and protect Maudie, and that's that.'

Pamela and Joyce were already heading for the telephone as Rogers heaved himself to his feet and joined Henry and Thomas in the car.

The girls had just moored up at Tyseley, easing their limbs in the early afternoon while Pup leapt and skittered about, yelping. She seemed to love the spring as much as they did. The otters were busy;

and they'd seen a kingfisher, though it was early. The allotments were a hive of activity but there had been just a few rather sad sprouts for sale, though loads of early potatoes. They sighed as Mr Roberts the foreman ran up to them waving his clipboard. He must think they were late and so they'd get a ticking off, but they'd headed straight here with no stop at Buckby. They'd thought they'd leave that until the return journey.

Mr Roberts shouted, 'Thank God you're here.' Verity grinned and said, 'It's only four o'clock, and here is your load safe and sound.'

Mr Roberts shook his head. 'Never mind that, come here, all of you.' He waved them into a group in front of him and handed them a message. 'It only came through to the Bull's Bridge Depot just after lunchtime, and they phoned through to here knowing you were on your way.'

His face was sombre, and he was calling the crane to leapfrog Steerer Mercy's pair, *Lincoln* and *York*. 'We'll get you unloaded ahead of the rest, but I sent Timmo off quick smart in the fastest unload ever, and then the fastest reload there's ever been. He headed for Buckby and Granfer Hopkins to get there about one o'clock. Mark you, the office is phoning through to the police station there and all, and to Fran at the school.'

Sylvia read the message over Verity's shoulder, and wept, just like that. Wept for Joe, who she had blamed for setting fire to the butty last year, when it had been Leon's fault. Leon's men had tried to snatch Joe back then, but Dog had stopped them; she had misunderstood in all the kerfuffle and told the police of her suspicions, and they had put Joe into a remand home for the night. She buried her face in her hands, and Steerer Mercy came up, shouting, 'Why we been jumped for the unloadin'? What be wrong?'

Sylvia shouted back, 'For heaven's sake, shut up. Joe's been taken, we have to get to Buckby and make sure Maudie is safe. It's that bloody sodding bastard Leon.'

Everyone looked astonished. Polly said, pulling Sylvia to her, 'It's all right. We'll get unloaded and get straight off when we've taken on whatever needs transporting. Sorry, Steerer Mercy, she doesn't mean it.'

Steerer Mercy was looking sad. ''Tis no matter. She'll be thinking o' the time the lass accused the lad of firing the butty, when it weren't 'im, if you get my meaning, just that devil Leon's. 'Ow the 'ell do he be finding t'lad?'

As Alf swung the crane, the girls leapt down on to the motor, untying the tarpaulin over the steel ingots, rolling it up, and Polly shouted up to Steerer Mercy on the quay, telling him all they knew. 'Keep your eyes and ears peeled, please, Steerer Mercy, because Lord knows where Leon is, but the one sure thing is he'll hunt Maudie down, now he knows she's alive. Or he will know that when Joe reaches him.'

Sylvia listened to all this, working like fury on the tarpaulin, but inside she was desperate. Their boy had been taken. What would Leon do, and how would they ever find him? There had been no trace so far. Despair raged. They all worked more quickly than they had ever done.

Behind them Bet, Evelyn and Mabel were now moored up, but there was no time to talk as they moved to the butty and started to untie the tarpaulin over that load. Mr Roberts was telling Bet the news, though, so all three jumped down on to the counter, crossed the cabin roof and joined them on the gunwale, untying as though there was a hurricane driving them on. Leaving the five of them to roll it up, Bet took off across the yard, calling, 'I'll telephone Fran at the school. She'll get a guard.'

Mr Roberts yelled, 'The police are on it.' But already Bet was running to the office.

The girls were off, lashed abreast, within two hours, a record, and the locks were with them as the dusk seemed to hold off for them, but when they saw a telephone box near a warehouse at Leamington, Sylvia suddenly yelled, 'Moor up, we need to telephone Solly.'

Verity, who was steering, looked puzzled, shouting, 'We haven't time.'

Sylvia crossed to her counter and gripped Verity's arms, shaking her, shouting into her face. 'We haven't time not to. Don't you remember Solly half recognised the name Tony Burrowes, Dobbo's referee? If he could just try harder, perhaps they could find

Leon through Burrowes. After all, Dobbo must have been Leon's man, mustn't he?'

They pulled in immediately and Sylvia ran to the telephone box. She fed in the money, then asked for Jacob Fisher's number, which Polly had written in her diary.

In Golders Green, Solly was reading the newspaper, his mind half on the war news and how the Allied columns were racing across the German plain, closing in on Hanover, and half on the lilac tree in his son's garden, which went with the ground floor apartment. It was threatening to flower. It was that time of year. Rachel was working on her embroidery, silently. She had been silent more often than not as the days, weeks and months had gone by since Manny had disappeared. In Europe there were so many Jews dead; the news disclosed camp after camp as the Allies advanced, but it was Manny they concentrated on, because how could anyone believe that all their relatives had died in those camps? No, it was beyond imagination – but Manny was manageable.

The telephone was ringing. Jacob was in his study and would answer it. It was usually for him, after all. Solly looked out at the lilac tree again. The seasons held him together. They came, they went, and there was a sense and a peace in that.

'Dad,' called Jacob from the hall. 'It's Sylvia Simpson. You know, Sylv of the terrible trio.

Something's wrong; the boy, Joe, has been taken by his father. Come, they need to talk to you.'

Solly was already hurrying to the telephone, Rachel close behind him. He took the receiver, not wanting to hear such news on top of everything. 'Sylv, 'ow yer gettin' on? What's all this about the boy?'

He listened as Sylvia talked about his hesitation over the name of Tony Burrowes. She explained and ended, 'He was Dobbo's referee. Dobbo must have been working for Leon, so Leon must have seen the newspaper article and put two and two together to find out where Joe was. We need you to try and think of whether you really do know something about Burrowes. We've just phoned Verity's mother, who said that the police can't get anywhere, the car has just disappeared and there's no talk of Leon in London apparently, or anywhere else. They even tried the Blind Weasel club, but it's still half dead, and a bloke called Dougie who's running it didn't know what they were talking about. Their policemen and snouts are drawing blan—' She stopped, her voice breaking, and sweat broke out on Solly's forehead.

He heard Verity's voice now. 'I'm sorry, Solly, but we're so worried.' He felt his throat working because now *she* sounded funny. Polly's voice came next. 'We have to pull in before Braunston, in about an hour, perhaps two. Can we call you again, just in case? If you haven't remembered, we'll call you in the morning. Please, Solly.' Now *she* was sounding funny too. The telephone went dead.

Jacob took the receiver from Solly, and had to peel his fingers free. 'Blimey,' Solly said. 'Me fingers 'ave set hard.'

His son held him, saying, 'Let it go, Dad. You've not cried since you were buried. Let it go.'

An hour later the telephone went again, and Jacob answered it. He told Sylvia that Solly was working his way through Manny's books and diaries but so far, nothing. Sylvia said she would telephone in the morning.

Bet had caught them an hour out of Leamington, and moored up too, just before the locks. All six of them stood by the boats, smoking, even Sylvia, though inhaling made her feel sick. It was better than the whirling panic, though, and the talk was of Joe, of course. Sylvia's thoughts were prayers. She had once misjudged Joe and therefore felt obliged by a powerful love, just as she was obliged to Harriet, but that was because of betrayal. She dug her hands into her pockets and, just like a boater, she made a deal and hers was between herself and Him. She whispered, 'I will come to you if you keep our boy safe, but only if you do that, and return him to us, safe and sound. What is my life beside his safety?'

*

411

Joe was led through the corridor into a poorly lit room. A man with a beard and short hair sat behind a desk. Mr Dobbo gripped Joe's shoulder and Joe were glad, because his legs were all wobbles and had been since he got out of the car. He didn't need a wee, he'd done it in his pants like a baby, and the memory made him swallow with shame. It had only happened once because he'd had nothing to drink, and now he was really thirsty, but his head was swimming so much he feared he'd be sick again if he were given water. So he just stood beside Mr Dobbo, right up against his leg because he was afraid he'd fall down otherwise.

The man behind the desk said nothing, just sat smoking that big brown cigarette, looking at him, or at least it seemed like he was. The light was on a big stand behind the man and there were more above the fish tank, or were the lights inside the fish tank? Joe wasn't sure, and the light was swimming, or maybe wobbling like his head. It was a huge fish tank, and it made him remember the cut. There were fish in the cut too; the kingfisher caught them. He could smell the cut, see it, the way the sun sort of danced on the water and the boats made ripples. His Saul at the tiller, laughing, or painting his kettles with him, guiding his hand.

He could see Sylvia when she thought it was he who had burned the boats, poor Miss Sylvia, for she was right sorry she had done that, but he wouldn't be at school or sunk in the aunties' and uncles' world of love but for her. He was grateful to her from the bottom of his world and for all the love she had given him since. He could see Granfer polishing his pierced plates, Polly laughing and Verity calling him 'darling'.

He wouldn't see his ma, in case he said something about her again.

At that thought, the swimming in his head was sliced with fear, and the fear was getting larger and larger as no one were saying anything. Perhaps they were going to put him in the fish tank? One of the men in the car had told Mr Dobbo just before they stopped outside this dark place that Mr Dobbo had to be tough or he'd end up with the fishes, like that Manny.

The man moved now, putting his big fat brown cigarette in the ashtray. He leaned forward and said, 'Ain't yer got a hello for your da then, Joe?'

Chapter 26

Will Joe be saved, and Sylvia have to pay her dues?

Marigold and *Horizon* had been loaded with wood for the paper factory, but after a morning call to Solly an hour out from Leamington they moored at Buckby, where there were other pairs all tied up too. They tore along to Granfer's with Pup running on her lead. Verity banged on the door.

'Steady on, Verity, leave it standing,' Polly said.

It was pulled open, and Timmo stood there, his hands fisted. He relaxed when he saw them, and pulled them inside, checking up and down the road. In the kitchen were various boaters, taking orders from Granfer. It became apparent that those pairs that could manage with one adult and a couple of children had gone on, and left the second adult at Buckby. They were spread about the village.

Verity said, 'You need someone to keep an eye on the moorings.'

Timmo nodded grimly. 'We do 'ave them, but hid they be. They be all spread from here to there and

414

will pass the word back, should it be a bad 'un arriving.'

Sylvia asked, 'How will you know it's a bad one?'

Granfer, sitting at the table, with Maudie by his side, muttered, 'Cos them'll be strangers to the village.'

Polly told them then what Solly was trying to do, and that they'd telephone him from Fran's, because Bet was there now, just phoning around the area with warnings, and pleading for information from pubs along the cut.

Maudie looked up, her eyes full. 'Yer find my boy, that's all. I'll go back ter Leon, but find my boy and I'll stand in his place.'

Timmo stood behind her, his hands on her shoulders, shaking his head. Maudie gripped his hands, as Lettie began to pour the girls mugs of tea. They hadn't time to drink it, so they stopped her, listening as Timmo said, 'He wants yer both, Maudie, so if yer do that, you'll not free yer boy.'

Maudie whispered, 'But I be with him.'

The boaters and the girls just nodded, Timmo too, for what mother would not go? Verity said, 'Father and the others are paying for information, and waiting. They want to do something, but as Mrs B said, until they know what, all they can do is pray.'

They ran off again, back to Fran's, to call Solly. At Fran's, Bet, Evelyn and Mabel had yet more tea on offer, and sandwiches with ham. How? Verity wondered. Did they have access to a pig, as her father did? She gave one sandwich to Pup, but couldn't face food, and neither could the others. Bet made them sit and drink tea and so she and Sylvia sipped while Polly telephoned Solly. There was no reply. 'Damn it,' Polly yelled.

Bet said, 'Come and eat. I insist. Who knows what the next few hours will bring and you must keep up your strength. You all look like death.'

Verity took a sandwich, looking from Bet to Sylvia, hoping Bet would see what she was trying to say. Bet raised an eyebrow, but then Mabel said, 'Sylvia, eat.'

Sylvia just pushed the plate away. Mabel said, 'You're not punishing yourself, are you, for what's happened? I heard about the mistake with Joe, but that's what it was. No one could have stopped it, but somehow when things happen we blame ourselves.'

Sylvia merely shook her head. 'Is that a line from one of your plays?' Her smile was false.

Mabel said, 'No, from my heart.'

Sylvia whispered, 'I'm sorry for what I said. I'm sorry, too, because I'm just not hungry. I feel I can't eat, not while he's away and we don't know what he's going through.'

Verity stopped after one mouthful and put her own sandwich down. It tasted of sand, because underneath it all, that's what she felt too, and she couldn't get the picture of a scared Joe out of her head.

*

Sylvia needed air, and, outside, standing near the lavender, she looked up at the sky and repeated her promise to God. Bring him back safe, she thought, knowing He would hear her thoughts. She continued in a whisper: 'Dear Lord, there are so many whose lives depend on his safety, so many who love him, whereas it is only Steve who loves me, and he will learn to love someone more worthy.'

She smelt the lavender, heard the bees. Yes, Steve deserved better. Someone who hadn't broken promises, or reneged on obligations as she had done with the convent, with Harriet. Or inflicted hurt as she had done to lovely Joe when she had pointed him out to the police over the butty fire. The cut had been a lesson to her, because on the cut there were no thank-yous, just obligations repaid, which really amounted to a deal done, a line drawn. It was a lesson she had only just understood.

She returned inside and they tried to telephone Solly again. Again the phone rang and rang. They would wait and try again.

Joe leaned even harder against Mr Dobbo as his father approached, and his beard made him look like a pirate.

Joe stared up at him. 'I want to be 'ome,' he said.

He felt Mr Dobbo's leg stiffen, and his hand tap his back in warning. He closed his mouth but it was too late, Leon said, ''Ome with y'ma, eh?'

417

Joe shook his head. 'I don't want for to be dead, for she 'tis dead. I want to be with me aunties and uncles.'

Leon took another pace and loomed over him, and now Joe couldn't see the fish tank, cos his da's great body were blocking it. He waited and yes, it really were his da, for he was pulling off his great thick leather belt from the trouser loops. It were the belt he always used. Winding the end without the buckle round his hand, he lashed it through the air. The buckle glinted. 'Yer get a forked tongue if yer lie, boy. How often do I says that to yer?'

Joe didn't think he could pee again, but he did, right there, on the carpet, and his da was looking at it. His shoulders lifted and his arm came up. 'Where do yer ma be?'

'Up with the stars,' Joe said, 'Cos yer hit 'er so bad, and then me. She be up with the stars.'

His da looked at Mr Dobbo. 'Sid thought the lad said not to hurt his ma. Did yer 'ear it too?'

Mr Dobbo sighed, then muttered, 'I 'eard nothing. The boy's never spoken of 'er, all the time I've been there. 'Is home is the House, seems to me.'

Leon stepped up so close that the leather belt dragged on the floor. When he stopped he lifted it and it whipped into Joe's face. Joe wanted to cry out, but clenched his mouth shut. He did what Uncle Henry had said, and counted to three, to settle himself, but he were too wobbly. He tried again and it were better, a bit. Joe looked up: Leon was so close to Mr Dobbo's face that they were nearly touching. 'I don't believe yer,' Leon said, his voice soft, in the voice that Joe was afraid of. He wanted to warn Mr Dobbo, because he had said he hadn't heard, but he must have done, so somewhere there was goodness in him.

Leon said, 'Strange that, cos as well as Sid, t'other bloke 'eard 'im too, so yer see my problem, Dobbo. I paid yer for a job, and now I feels yer's lying to me.' His voice was still soft, and Joe wanted to cringe. Mr Dobbo just stood quiet, his shoulders back, and still his hand patted Joe calm.

Joe didn't understand why Mr Dobbo was helping him, cos Mr Dobbo had taken him, but then . . . and then . . . Well, he had stopped Sid from hitting him when he'd been a bit more sick. Were he sorry for causing grief, like Sylvia had been?

But that wasn't right. Sylvia had really really thought he'd fired the butty and was a menace, so she hadn't done it for pay and she hadn't sent poor Dog to grab him. He saw Sylvia's face, her red hair, heard the softening of her voice as time had gone. He thought about the letters she had written him and the drawings. While Polly and Verity's letters had made him laugh about all the boaters, Sylvia's writing had been of the voles, the otters, and the kingfisher, things that meant the world to him. She had even tried to draw a few, especially the kingfisher. He'd wanted to draw her a special one and teach her how to do it easier than the effort hers

419

took. How he wished he had now because perhaps he were going to die, and you couldn't show people 'ow to draw when you were up with the stars. Or he didn't think you could.

The blow that Leon landed right in Mr Dobbo's middle jerked Joe back into the room, away from Sylvia's red hair. The big man doubled over and knocked into Joe, which pushed Joe on to the rug. Mr Dobbo fell to his knees, gasping something horrid, his face pressed into the rug too. But that would only be the start, Joe knew, as he crawled away and down came the belt, and the buckle caught Mr Dobbo's head. There would be blood on the carpet but you couldn't see it because it were so dim.

He heard Mr Dobbo say, 'Yer a bastard, yer are, Mr Harkness. I thought yer wanted yer boy out of love, but yer don't. You'll destroy all the goodness in the lad, and there's a lot.'

Mr Harkness? Who be he? Joe thought, as he crawled to the desk, grovelling beneath the kneehole and out the other side. He pulled himself up in the light of the fish tank behind him, and still the fish just swam. Would his da put Mr Dobbo in it? But how could he fit? The water would gush out and the carpet would get wetter than his pee had made it. His head was filled with stupidity as he watched his da. He was kicking Mr Dobbo with his great steel-capped boots. Joe looked down and the light caught the gun on the shelf.

Saul had a gun, an airgun which he took out sometimes looking for rabbits, he did, and he probably had a bigger gun out at the war. Joe reached for the pistol. An air pistol wouldn't hurt his da much, but this would stop him. He'd heard Mr Dobbo's words and knew, like Sylvia, he were sorry, and that were good enough. It was what Saul and Granfer said. It was what his ma used to say about his da. 'Yer da's sorry, and he be right, I did something to make him bad, but I will learn.'

She were wrong, for he could see even then it was his da that was bad, to the core, and so could Saul and Granfer and the rest of the cut. But he remembered Mr Dobbo's eyes, when Rover brought back the ball, they was the same as they were now, looking at Joe as he hid behind the desk. They were full of pleading, and it were the pleading of sorrow.

As he picked up the gun there was a banging on the door, 'Boss, boss, yer needed. Yer copper friend is in the front, been sent to check, 'e says, cos the boy's been taken, and all the coppers are 'aving to go through 'oops, again and again. Needs a bit of a sweetener, I reckon, but we've all played dumb.'

Joe shoved the gun in his waistband at the back, where the boaters carried their windlasses. It were hid beneath his coat, but he were still shivering. As Dougie came in, Joe silently slipped through the kneehole to the front of the desk, and sank to the floor again.

Dougie looked from Mr Dobbo to Joe, to his da, shocked. Leon was threading his belt back through the loops. He kicked at Mr Dobbo. 'Get these two into the old storeroom. Leave 'em there overnight, or as long as it takes for the little tyke to tell me where his ma be. Let me know when he do, or I don't want to 'ear a word about it.'

He went to a picture of London Bridge that hung on the wall, pulled it open like a window, and fiddled with a round thing. Joe heard *click click click click*. His da pulled the door open, and took out cash, pushed the door closed, slammed the picture back and strode from the room. Dougie looked from Dobbo to Joe, then hauled Dobbo to his feet. Dobbo looked at Joe and winked. Joe scrambled to his feet, winking back. Dougie said, 'What yer doin' with yer eye, boy?'

'It hurts. Da banged into it with his belt.'

Dougie slung Dobbo's arm over his shoulders, and hauled him out of the room, shoving Joe before them. All Joe could feel was the gun. He couldn't believe that Dougie couldn't see it, but soon his da would know it were gone. 'Get a bloody move on,' Dougie growled. 'Straight down the corridor, turn left at the end, if yer know yer left from yer right.'

Stung, Joe said, 'Course I does, I'm from t'cut.'

'Well, big bloody deal.' But his voice wasn't right for the words. It was kinder, almost embarrassed.

Joe turned left, hearing Dougie's heavy breathing behind, and the stumbling footsteps of Mr Dobbo.

They stopped at a door, and Dougie fiddled with a bunch of keys on a ring on his belt, grumbling, 'Why the 'ell you had to get yerself into this mess, Dobbo, I don't know. Now we'll all 'ave to put up with his bellyaching. Get the boy to tell 'im what he wants to know, for Gawd's sake, and yer own and the lad's.'

He opened the door and pushed Joe inside, but it weren't a hard push. He then helped Dobbo down on to the concrete floor, slamming the door shut behind him. In the darkness Joe heard Dobbo moving, and finally heard him say, 'Sorry lad, I didn't know it'd be like this.'

Joe sat, holding his knees. 'I know yer sorry, just as I is sorry fer me da 'urting yer. 'E'll do it to me ma, yer see, so I thanks yer for holding silent. It were my mistake to say it, so we's square, I reckon.'

Dobbo laughed softly, then fell silent. Joe said, 'Mr Dobbo, what about Rover. Be 'e dead? I felt him beside me on the back seat, but where be 'e now?'

Dobbo was silent, but after a while he moved. 'Say again, lad.' His voice was weaker. Joe repeated himself.

'Oh, don't yer fret. Rover is with a mate who was outside the club. 'Spect yer didn't see 'im in the shadows. I had half a thought this would happen, but I should've done a runner then, or had him take you as well, and faced yer da by meself. My mistake is a mite bigger than yours, but I'll do what

I can when he talks to yer again. But yer might have to tell him the truth, yer know. He has ways, he has.'

The silence fell again.

Leon finished with the cops and hurried back into the office, rubbing his hands. The youngster, a constable, had looked pale and his frown deep as he said, 'If you've got him, you ain't 'urt him, Mr Harkness, or sent him to Scotland with that Manny?'

'Course not,' Leon said, pressing another ten quid into his hand. 'Ain't got a clue where he be. Come and look around if yer don't believe me.'

The copper had shaken his head, knowing better than to disbelieve someone like Harkness. He had turned on his heel and left.

Leon straightened the rug that Dobbo had rucked up when he were on the floor. He only used the wall safe when the men were in the room. They knew nothing of t'real one. He called Dougie into the office. 'Any news?'

'I been waiting for the copper to go, boss. Vlad's called from Buckby. No one says anything, but there's so much coming and going to the cottage, and them girls from *Horizon* and *Marigold* is at the old grandpa's cottage that I reckon something's up. They went to that Bet's place as well, their trainer, who has a phone, Vlad says. Vlad thinks there's so many boaters around and about he reckons yer wife is definitely there with her grandpa.'

Leon roared, 'Well, what be Vlad doing? Tell him to get in there with his blokes, and see. If she is, grab 'er. If she ain't find out from the old man where she be. We shouldn't be hanging back waiting for an invitation.'

Dougie said, standing firm and thrusting out his chest, 'You thought the boy would tell you, that's what we're waiting for. We don't want to cause a ruckus for nothing.'

'Well, he bloody didn't, so it's time to have a go at the old boy. I never bothered, cos I thought her were dead, but if that's what Sid and the bony lad who went along said they heard Joe say, we got to follow. If she be there, well and good, we'll grab 'er, then my boy'll soon be biddable.'

'Vlad asked about casualties.'

Leon looked at Dougie as though he was mad. 'What does I care about such? Get him in there, I be 'aving enough now.'

He stormed past Dougie and rushed down the corridor. He beat on the door, shouting through it, 'I've men in Buckby, so you got anything to say afore we 'it yer granfer's?'

There was silence. Then the boy yelled, 'No, and damn yer, she ain't there, I tole yer, she's up wi' the stars.'

For a moment Leon faltered. Were she really dead? Well, let Vlad find out, it were no skin off his nose, one way or the other. It'd give the old boy a fright, which wouldn't be a bad thing. He kicked the door and returned to the office, but once there he hesitated. He'd best show his face in the club for a while and get set up for the night, or he'd be fretting on his own. He'd feed the fish first, though, and see 'em fight for it. That always gave him some cheer.

Solly closed the books at last, and sat back in his chair, exhausted. He was alone. Rachel was at work in a nearby solicitor's office, and Jacob in his office in the City of London. He wrote all that he had discovered on a scrap of paper. It wasn't much, but it was enough.

He telephoned Jacob on his direct line, a line that a few of his customers had, but only a few.

'Yes,' Jacob said.

'It's me, son. I have found Tony Burrowes. He did work for Manny sometimes, when he were overloaded, but only for one person; well, two.' Solly was becoming confused.

Jacob said quietly, 'Take your time, gather your thoughts, I'm not rushed.'

But he was, Solly knew. He was busy but Solly didn't rightly know doing what. Something about buying and selling and sorting things for people.

Solly breathed deeply. He said again, 'Burrowes worked for Manny, 'e did. And the figures he double-checked for Manny were for someone called Norton, in a club in the West End or near called the Blind Weasel. Then Norton was crossed out in the book. Then a while later this Burrowes audited

Manny's figures for the same club, but the name on the book was Lionel Harkness. I reckon this Burrowes took over from Manny as the main man, so if we can get to 'im we'll know about not just Manny, but who this Lionel Harkness really is, cos I reckon those girls is right, that Leon Arness would change his name to summat similar. So compare the two.'

There was silence at the end of the line, then Jacob said, 'You've done well, Dad. If – no, when – the girls telephone again, tell them—'

Once more, Solly interrupted, because he'd been reading his scrappy note again. ''Ang on, son, this is important. Next to some of the names and clubs there's this P and an amount. Right at the back of the diary is a list. P means police. I reckon this Norton, and then Harkness, was paying off the coppers, or a couple anyway.'

Jacob's voice had tightened. 'Reckon you're right. Tell the girls this news too but make sure they don't inform *any* police. It'll just be a couple of bad apples, but if they get to think they're rumbled ... Have you the Howard House phone number? Let me have it and I'll tell them as well. I reckon there's a damned good chance Joe is with Harkness. Where else would he be? I need to find out for certain, though.'

Solly shook his head, 'But 'ow, son?'

Jacob said, 'You leave that to me, eh. I'll have it sorted in a couple of hours. Make sure the girls keep close to Maudie, in case Harkness has already sent out a team. He won't go himself. He's building an army.'

Solly said, 'A what? 'Ow do you know that?'

'One hears things, Dad.'

Solly put the telephone down, wondering how one heard such things. He was feeling more and more tired. Almost immediately, the telephone rang. It was Verity, saying they'd tried just now, but he was engaged. He explained some of what Jacob had told him, and about the police. 'Jacob says to make sure Maudie is protected, and he'll handle this end, and he's going to telephone Howard House to tell 'em to keep shtum with the coppers, cos who do you trust and who not? Probably just a couple of bad Met apples, but yer never know, he said. Yer got that?'

Verity said, 'We can't thank you enough, really. God bless you all.'

Solly smiled, but tiredness had progressed to exhaustion. Even as she was saying that he feared in his heart that Harkness must have done something to Manny. He returned to his chair by the window and watched the lilac, as he needed hope. But for what? In his heart he knew Manny must be gone. For going on, he almost heard Manny say. It was what he always said.

All six girls rushed back to Granfer and they didn't have to bang on the door, because this time Steerer Mercy opened it. 'Get yerselves in,' he ordered.

As Sylvia led them down the corridor she told Granfer and Timmo all that was happening, then they sat with Maudie, Lettie and Pup, while the men demarcated their troops. Verity smiled at them all. 'Well, looks like Leon's men have a surprise waiting for them, girls,' she said.

Lettie handed each of them either a pan or a rolling pin. Polly laughed and laughed, and as Maudie looked on, shocked, she explained how her mum had whacked Leon when he attacked her dad at their house, hitting him again and again with her frying pan. Heedless of her bravery, she was only mollified when her dad replaced the rivets and made it serviceable again.

Granfer returned to the kitchen. 'Timmo's on lookout at a bedroom window with his club, but they won't all get this far, not through the boaters, they won't, but we'll split yer all up and spread yer over the rooms for the ones that might. Just get crackin' if they gets in. 'Tis only after we catch the buggers that we call the police, and the newspaper. We need 'em to witness it, to be sure the beggars gets put away. They might well talk about who set 'em on, too.

Chapter 27

Can Jacob find out all he needs to know?

Sylvia took one of the back bedrooms and peered out from the edge of the curtain. The window was ajar so that any signals received by Timmo from the lookouts could be transferred to the boaters waiting in the shed. Timmo walked round the rooms from time to time, checking on everyone, his red-spotted kerchief at his neck. Finally, as he brought in a mug of tea for her, brewed by Lettie, he stood for a moment beside her.

Sylvia had until then been transferring her weight from foot to foot, unable to be still, but with Timmo so near, she calmed. In doing so she remembered that the sisters at the orphanage were always still, seeming to glide when they walked in an atmosphere of such containment and quiet that all in their path grew so too. Would she ever achieve that devotion, that state of being, when all she wanted to be was here, out in the world, with all these people, and Steve?

Timmo said nothing, just placed his hand on her shoulder for a second before moving on again.

It was then that she realised that gliding on the cut was also a sort of devotion, creating a similar peace and stillness. Was this why she had found she loved it? Was her 'deal' in fact something that she wanted, and not just something she had to do to save the lives of so many from loss? Would a deal work with Him anyway? It had to, or . . . But what about Steve? It wouldn't just be her loss. The pain was suddenly sharp. The girls? The pain grew . . .

She saw the bushes move, then they were still. At the same time Granfer called from the front bedroom, 'They's movin' in on this side.'

Sylvia watched the back closely; the bushes moved again. She called, 'And from the back, or I think—'

Timmo flew into the room, to stand with her. 'All that kingfisher watchin's made yer eyes keen. I knows yer saw it, and never fear, we're ready.' He made the pigeon call they'd all agreed on.

'There,' breathed Sylvia, slopping her mug of tea as she slammed it on the windowsill. 'Amongst the silver birches.'

'Got 'em.' Timmo made the call three times. Steerer Wise opened the shed door a crack. Timmo was gone, down the stairs two at a time, checking the boaters in the hall and those in the kitchen. Steerer Ambrose was in charge of those placed 'who knew where' outside, and the boaters would have picked off some of the marauders as they approached. They weren't silent poachers for nothing.

Sylvia heard a harsh whistle, like a policeman's, and then Leon's men, carrying clubs, were charging from the back. Granfer yelled, 'They're charging the front.' Maudie was in the bedroom now and so too were Polly and Verity with Timmo who had appointed himself bodyguard, as had the girls, and they would fight any who came up here, to the death. As she watched, Steerer Wise burst from the shed with his boaters, including two youngsters from the flyboats, which wouldn't normally stop for anyone. They caught the intruders, tackling them to the ground, as the curses were hurled, and blows. Two escaped and kept going to the house.

Sylvia heard the crash of the back door, but there were boaters the other side of it, and the intruders didn't get far. Some escaped and ran from the back garden into the woods, but two of the boaters were after them, with no need for clubs. There were shots from the attackers then two more boaters broke off from the melee and, roaring with rage, took off into the woods, too. Sylvia pressed her face against the window as Bet tore into the bedroom, and they all watched.

Bet said, 'The police and the newspaper have been called.'

Sylvia's laugh was veering on the hysterical, as she said, 'It doesn't seem real, any of this.'

Bet muttered, 'What does at the moment, anywhere?'

Evelyn and Mabel flew in. 'We're needed, Bet. You too girls. Timmo is to stay with Maudie. The hooligans are tied up, but everyone seems to have cuts and bruises.' They tore downstairs as Leon's men were led, dazed, to the front garden, and made to sit. Bet yelled, 'Evelyn and Mabel, sort out the Dettol and bandages. My girls, to the front with me. We'll start fixing that lot of toe-rags.' With Sylvia, Verity and Polly, she ran out of the front door, picking up her hessian first aid bag from the hall table. Slamming the front door, she nearly tripped over four of the men forced to sit on the path, their hands bound together, linked by rope to their bound feet.

The boaters stood guard while Timmo hurtled down the stairs, shouting, 'Where's yer leader?'

Bet shouted, 'Where is Maudie?'

'In the kitchen with your girls. Don't yer worry, some boaters are inside the back door.'

One of the men muttered, 'Out in the woods at the back, with the gun. He'll bloody use it too, but we don't want no part of that.'

The police were arriving, some cycling, but there were also four in a car. They piled out and up the garden path, handcuffs at the ready. First they rounded up the boaters, and only then did they haul Leon's men to their feet.

'You're all under arrest,' called a plain-clothes detective who was strutting down the path, having leapt from a squad car. He snatched off his hat, slapping it against his leg. 'I'm not bloody having this

London gang stuff on my patch. You're a load of bloody ruffians, the lot of you.'

Bet stepped between the Inspector and the men, pointing to Leon's lot. 'These men attacked Mr Hopkins's house.'

The Inspector said, 'They all entered, did they?'

Timmo, who was struggling with a policeman who had snapped handcuffs on one of his wrists, yelled, 'Not all, but that were only cos we be 'ere. They was after Maudie.'

The Inspector snapped, 'You took the law into your own hands instead of contacting us.'

Bet grabbed the Inspector's arm then as the journalist, who had crept closer, took notes. She hauled him a few yards away, explaining something which appeared to owe much to gestures and four-letter words. She was more furious than Sylvia, Polly and Verity had ever seen her. It was they who stood between the police and the boaters now, ready to . . . well, fight, Sylvia thought.

The Inspector was arguing with Bet, who said something that stopped him in his tracks. He stared at her, and at last nodded. He walked back, slowly, with Bet. A police van was arriving. The Inspector said, 'Release the boaters, get the others into the van.'

He turned on his heel and sulked off. More of Leon's men were being hauled struggling around the side of the house by boaters led by Steerer Ambrose, who had tied the ruffians' arms behind

434

their backs. Steerer Ambrose held a pistol between his thumb and forefinger. He called back the Inspector, whose strut was no longer in evidence. Steerer Ambrose pointed to a blond hatchet-faced man and said, 'You'll need this. He winged one of t'fly boys, and we boaters don't take kindly t'guns, we do not. He be named Vlad, strange sort o' name.'

The Inspector sighed and came forward. 'Neither do we. Get over there.'

He pointed to the van. Steerer Ambrose hauled the man to the nearest policeman.

All the girls sat in the kitchen after the boaters had left to hitch lifts back to their boats on any passing pair that came through the Braunston Tunnel. Granfer had not thanked them; neither had Maudie, because the boaters didn't thank others – they merely obliged in their turn, for these cut people looked after their own, it was a code, there was no need for thanks. Sylvia said thoughtfully, 'It truly is an obligation, a sort of deal, isn't it?'

Bet nodded. 'That's exactly what it is, Sylv. And it works well, and is understood by everyone.'

Sylvia just looked at her, then glanced out of the window at the sky and the clouds which were being blown on the wind, until she was brought back into the kitchen by Polly asking Bet what she had said to the Inspector. 'I know his father. I mentioned this, and said that there was a policeman, or two, helping the man who arranged this, and he'd muck up the plan to rescue the son of the woman they were trying to grab today if he started to fanny about saying things and doing things he shouldn't. Did he want that on his conscience or his subsequent job application? I also drew his attention to the journalist.'

Granfer was pouring brandy, which they all downed in short order, wondering what was happening in London.

Jacob sat at the back of the darkened bar in Piccadilly. He was tired, but then he'd been on the telephone for hour after hour, using his contacts to dig deep into Harkness's world, and Norton's before him. He'd taken to the streets, pulling in favours, making promises that he could just about keep, and of course money had changed hands, but what was money when the Nazis' death factories had consumed his people in Europe, and broken his father's and his wife's hearts? What was it when a boy had been stolen by a man who beat him?

He sipped the warm beer. Life had moved on from the barrow, then the textiles, and widened into the world of a middleman, someone who finds what people need, which, after all, was what he had learned from his father. 'You want a sofa? I'll find someone who wants to sell one.' Business was the same, the world over; it was just a matter of degree.

He forced himself to drink, to hold his hands steady, because he had not been a middleman in such as this, ever – but needs must. How would he recognise Mario? How would Mario recognise him? How would he start with the gang leader? Would he even come? He'd said he would, but if he felt that Jacob was lying and there was nothing of interest, it would be the worst for Jacob.

The door of the bar opened. A small Italian entered, his coat over his shoulders, and he wore a homburg at a slight angle. Behind him were two larger Italians, or Jacob supposed they were because they were similarly dark. Jacob rose. One of the bodyguards noticed Jacob and whispered in his boss's ear, but Mario was already making for him. The bodyguards were looking to left and right, but no one took any notice.

Mario arrived at the table, and Jacob stood, holding out his hand. It was ignored. Mario sat, Jacob too. Mario looked at him, his eyes hooded. 'So?'

Jacob swallowed, gripping his hands together. He explained what had happened in Buckby. He had received the telephone call that Bet had promised and explained about Joe, who they guessed was being held at the Blind Weasel, perhaps upstairs in the flat, or somewhere on the premises.

'Guessed?' Mario's tone was flat.

Jacob swallowed again. 'More than that. Someone is looking after a dog that belongs to one of those involved. He responded to payment from a contact of mine. So we know Joe was, and hopefully still is, held at the club. Ten of Leon's men have been arrested—'

'Leon?'

'Perhaps you know him as Lionel Harkness. He is actually Leon Arness, wanted by the police for the assault of Mr Thomas Holmes, amongst other things. He took over the business from Norton, who was killed by a bomb.'

Mario was nodding. He lifted a finger to one of the bodyguards, who drew out a gold cigarette case from his breast pocket, and offered a cigarette to Mario. The bodyguard lit it with a gold lighter. Jacob was not offered one.

Mario inhaled, exhaled, and still without emotion said, 'So?'

'This friend of Dobbo, who owns the dog, told me that there is an attack to be made on the Limehouse organisation by Harkness. He has built his army, which has now lost ten men.'

Mario said nothing for two long minutes. Jacob could feel the sweat running down his back. His mouth was dry, so he sipped his beer, but his hand was trembling so much the beer slopped on the table and ran out of his mouth. Jacob drew notes written on a sheet of paper from his pocket and placed it on the table before Mario. 'Here are his plans, as far as my contacts can tell. But Harkness is obsessed with his son and wife. Now is the time to strike, while he is thinking of them, if you wish to turn the tables and expand into his territory, rather than let him expand into yours. He will be expecting a report from Vlad, his man on the raid. It will not have arrived yet, but he has no cause to fear it will not succeed. I repeat, now is the time.'

Mario looked at the plan then nodded. 'I have similar information.' He leaned back, his cigarette smoke wafting. 'Though I did not know the Vlad scenario, or that Harkness is distracted.' He stood, and stubbed his cigarette out in the ashtray set in the centre of the table.

He spread his hands. 'And from me you want?'

Jacob could hardly speak. His heart was beating so hard that he could hear it in his ears, and it was taking his breath away. Finally he said, 'To save the boy. I will be outside the club to receive him. Then I will leave and I want to know nothing more . . .' As Mario turned, Jacob spoke again. 'There is a policeman in his pay, or two. I don't know who.'

Mario smiled a little now. 'Ah, but I do.'

As he began to leave, Jacob spoke yet again. 'Vlad, captured by the police, might well give up Harkness, so I repeat, perhaps be quick.'

Mario raised an eyebrow. 'Yes, I had arrived at that thought. Finally, and this is the end, is there anything else I can do for you?'

'Find out what happened to Manny Teller, as he is known here.'

'He is dead, left near Limehouse in the canal by your friend Harkness, to insult us.'

Jacob's flare of pain was so deep it scared him. 'He is no friend.'

Mario left, his coat swinging, and no one looking after him but Jacob who felt sick and too tired really to find his way to the club, but he must. Someone must wait in case Joe was freed. In case, he repeated to himself as he, in his turn, left.

Joe was so thirsty he could only think of water, and the hardness of the floor, though Mr Dobbo had taken off his jacket for him to sit on, and now he were the one shivering. Mr Dobbo said, 'We shivered in the trenches, lad, so this is nothing.'

Joe had slept, and then woken, and slept again, and each time he dreamed of water, and woke thinking of it. He remembered Polly, Verity and Sylvia talking about being so thirsty under the rubble that it was hard to think of anything else. It made him feel more like one of them, if a boy could be like girl boaters. He told Mr Dobbo about the girls, and how Dog had shown Steve the fireman where they were, but how Dog had died. Mr Dobbo said, 'I wonder if Rover would do that for me?'

Joe looked at Mr Dobbo, who didn't seem so strong and big now, just sad and ashamed. 'I 'spect so, cos he'd be doing what you want, won't he? He does that day after day so he must love yer and want to please. He pulled me out of the playground cos you told him, after all.'

Dobbo hung his head. 'I wish to 'ell I hadn't told 'im. I don't know what come over me. I were greedy, I suppose, but I knew it was wrong, but I didn't think your dad would 'urt you. Never would I 'ave—'

Joe interrupted, leaning his head on his knees: 'It don't matter, Mr Dobbo. No one would know what he were like less'n you saw 'im at it.' Joe thought it was strange how much you could see when you got used to just a tiny slit of light coming in under the door. ''Ow long d'yer think we been in 'ere, now?' he asked.

Mr Dobbo said, shrugging, 'I don't know, and best not to keep asking, because it makes it seem worse.'

'Is my da going to let us out?'

Mr Dobbo sighed. 'He said last time he wouldn't 'less you tell 'im where yer ma was, and now he's found out t'other way, from the shouting we've been hearing, but 'e's waiting for summat else. I think he's going to bring her here. It might make it better fer yer, to be together. 'E might be glad enough, and it could change him.'

Joe shook his head. 'It won't, Mr Dobbo, but what'll he do to you?'

'Don't you worry about that. It's me own fault, and I deserves it. Not at all something a soldier should be about.'

They fell silent again, then they heard a crash, shouts, and the sound of running feet. Joe shrank back into the corner, and Mr Dobbo found his way over to him. 'Stay behind me, y'ear. You stay behind me, and keep yer mouth shut.'

Joe whispered, 'You got the gun, Mr Dobbo?'

'Yes, lad, cos no one's goin' to 'urt yer, I'll try and see to that, and neither will you be the one firing it and living with that stain on yer heart and in the eyes of whoever finds us.'

They waited as the noise got worse, and Joe heard his da shouting and yelling, but he couldn't hear what words he was saying. There were voices coming nearer, with heavy accents – and was that a groan? 'Is they quarrelling, Mr Dobbo?'

'I don't know, lad. P'raps Vlad's brought yer mum 'ere. 'E has an accent.'

''T'weren't me ma groaning, that were a man.'

Big heavy footsteps approached. 'Mr Dobbo, I be scared,' Joe whispered.

'Try not to be. I will stop 'em and you must go quiet if they get past me, and try and make it clear away later. You got that? If questions is asked about any shots fired, you never touched the gun, you never brought it from the study, it were me. I've wiped it on my shirt, so there're none of your fingerprints. If they've brought yer ma, try and get 'er away too. Yer understand. Don't yer worry none about me.'

The footsteps were closer still. Lots of them, and now raised voices. Dobbo sat up straight. Joe heard the click as he cocked the pistol. Dobbo said, 'If you was my boy, I'd be proud of yer. Yer just remember that. Get well, get strong, and get away.'

The footsteps had stopped outside the door. They heard the sound of the key in the lock. Dobbo whispered, 'Yer be still.'

'Dobbo.' It was Dougie. 'I'm opening the door, and I'm coming in. They're taking Joe back to his aunties and uncles, you understand?'

The handle was moving. Dobbo shouted, 'I've got a gun. I took it from the bastard's study, I took it and I'll bloody well use it, if you 'urt an 'air of 'is head.'

Joe was leaning on Mr Dobbo, his head resting on his back, and he patted him as Mr Dobbo had done to him when he were afraid as he stood in front of his da.

'No one's going to hurt him, Dobbo. Mario's men have taken the boss, and they're letting me get you out safe and sound, and the boy to Jacob, who's waiting outside. Then I can scarper, they say, though whether they mean it, who knows.'

Joe sat up. 'Jacob? That's Mr Fisher's son. What about me ma, Mr Dobbo?'

The handle was moving again in the dim, dim light, and squeaking. 'The lad's ma?' Dobbo asked.

'Safe. The boaters were waiting for Vlad and the cops have the lot of them. Come on, Dobbo. Rover's waiting for yer.'

Mr Dobbo said to Joe, 'Yer want to go with Jacob?'

'Only if you come too. We can all go home together and Rover can come too.'

Dobbo laughed slightly. 'Ah well, I think that door's closed for me, lad. So let's see if we can get you out safe, eh?'

'I'm coming in, Dobbo. You got that.'

The door opened slowly, and light shafted in, dazzling them, and they could see nothing. Joe waited for the shot, because there was a big man with something in his hand. But nothing happened. Joe saw a shape come forward and take the gun from Mr Dobbo's hand. Joe's eyes were used to the light now, and he saw Dougie put the safety back on, and the keys he had been holding in his pocket.

Dougie reached over Dobbo and picked up Joe. Joe said, 'I be awful thirsty, Mr Dougie, and I peed and I smell.'

Dougie said, 'Well, that's Jacob's problem. Up you get, Dobbo. We're finished 'ere. We best get out and away, quick like.' But Dobbo didn't move. 'You go, I'll take what's coming. Get the boy away.'

Joe said, as Mr Dougie carried him to the door, 'Mr Dobbo helped me, 'e did. 'E wouldn't let me da 'urt me good and proper, and he paid fer it. Don't 'urt 'im no more. I wants him to come 'ome with me.'

As Dougie carried him past men whose eyes were dark and deep sunk and hard, a small man wearing a homburg said, 'It is a good thing we do today. It is a good thing your Dobbo did, too, because I have been listening. Let him go with the boy.' The man flicked his fingers at someone behind Joe.

Joe peered over Dougie's shoulder and watched as Mr Dobbo were pulled from the old store. He looked like an old man. Joe wondered if he himself did too, because that's how he felt. The man with the homburg was saying, as he blocked the corridor, a strange smile on his face, 'And you, Dougie, give me that gun, and don't you ever come back. Just find another patch. You, Joseph, you live your life away from the cesspit of this world, and take your guardian with you too. I will give you nothing of your father's, but you should want nothing of his. You have friends who have worked hard for you for nothing more than love, which makes you blessed.'

He stood aside, his face so sad. Joe, carried by Dougie, with Mr Dobbo walking along behind, called, 'Thank you, sir.'

They passed along the corridor and through the club and Joe saw many men, some with guns, spreading out into it, and through it. But he never saw his da, and he hoped he were gone for good.

Mr Dougie carried him up the stairs and out through the doors, into a London where red buses and cars were buzzing about, and pigeons were landing on roofs. Somewhere a car horn hooted, and on a corner, a man in a red scarf was selling papers and calling out the headlines. It was like it always was, when he thought it would be black and grey, and changed. Opposite was a man who crossed the road, removing his hat. 'Joe, I believe,' the man said. 'I'm Jacob Fisher, Solly's son. Your mother is safe in

Buckby. I can take you to her, or to Howard House, it's your choice. But should we take you to our home, to bathe and dress you first? Would you like that? Then I can telephone everyone and tell them that you have returned.'

Dougie put him down, but Joe's legs couldn't feel and he crumpled. It was Mr Dobbo who picked him up. 'I reckon 'e'd like that. I will help you with him as far as that.'

But Joe clung to him, saying, 'Mr Dobbo 'as saved me. He made a mistake, but 'e has saved me, and I would wish 'im to come home with me. And please, Mr Jacob, we'd very much like a drink o' water.'

So, with Joe safe in the arms of Mr Dobbo, whose dried blood was caked on his face and head, Jacob hailed a taxi to Golders Green while Dougie hurried off and was lost in the crowd. When they had almost reached the Fisher house, Jacob asked, 'So, where is home, Joe?'

Joe was almost asleep in Mr Dobbo's arms, and he said, surprised that such a question should be asked, 'Howard House, with me aunties and uncles, and the girls, o' course. Cos I need to show Sylvia how to draw a kingfisher, proper. Ma can come and see us there when she wants, cos that's what we said.'

Chapter 28

Tuesday, May 8th 1945 – VE Day on the cut

The girls moored up at Alperton well before the sun had even thought of going down. They could have pat-pattered on, but what was the point – now? Polly dusted off her hands and let Pup romp along the bank. The women were out washing as always, and Polly sauntered along, keeping an eye on her dog, which Maudie called an old cut dog, now. 'Cos,' she said, 'yer 'ad to grow up fast, or drown.'

Maudie wasn't one for too much of a laugh yet, though she'd smile. It was good of her to join them and run the butty. Polly dug her hands deep in her pockets, and stopped by Ma Porter, who was wringing out Jimmy's trousers. Polly took the end tossed by Ma. Together they twisted away from one another, and the water gushed on to the grass. Polly found herself watching as some of it sank, and some of it dribbled along and into the water.

Ma Porter said, relieving her of the trousers, folding them up and placing them in the wicker basket by her side, 'Yer Saul is safe now, that's a blessing. And young Verity's Tom. All safe, Maudie and her Joe too. Happy an' all, though only a fool asks for 'appiness. What we need is a roof over our 'eads, a good family and something to get up for every morning, and as we go on, to leave a footprint.'

Ma Porter was dipping into the rinsing water with her tongs and hauling out Steerer Porter's trousers. She raised an eyebrow. Polly nodded. 'So, that's what we need, is it, Ma Porter? It makes sense.'

She gripped the trousers and these they wrung out too. Ma said, 'Saw a kingfisher I did on t'way 'ere. Jimmy saw it first. 'E said yer Sylvia woulda liked it, mayhap even drawn it.'

Polly kept twisting, and it was like her heart. Why? Why had Sylvia gone into the convent without a word to them?

'Steady, lass. You'll twist t'legs right off, yer will,' Ma Porter said.

Polly saw that her knuckles were white from the gripping. She grinned and tossed the legs back to Ma Porter. 'I hear from Joe that Jimmy's writing to him at Howard House?'

Ma stood with her arms akimbo. 'Wouldn't be able to do that, would he – write, I mean – but for yer teachin'. Reckon we'll put 'im in the boarding school, so he 'as something he can do when the cut runs down, which it surely be doing, now t'war is over. Not today it won't, nor tomorrow but some time not far off. Your Maudie's going down to Dorset, I hear, to visit Joe, who 'as chosen his 'ome.'

Polly wiped her hands down her trousers and took the roll-up cigarette the woman offered. They stood and smoked together for a while as Pup sniffed round and about. Polly said, 'It's complicated. Joe feels safe there, he has friends at school, and he doesn't want to come back to the cut. I think perhaps Maudie will work with Timmo on his pair soon, now Trev is thinking of leaving, and visit her boy regularly.'

Ma Porter led the way on to her counter and sat on the stool while Polly perched on the cabin roof. 'It be like our putting Jimmy in boarding school. Maudie knows we 'ave to do what's best for them we love. And after all, she loves Timmo too. Who knows, they might do summat near Howard House when the work on the cut runs out. P'raps he could drive a lorry, like yer Saul in t'war, an' do transport on roads, instead o' the cut?'

Again they fell silent. Polly looked along the bank and could see Maudie polishing *Horizon*'s chimney brass, and Verity just sitting on *Marigold*'s roof staring at the tiller, her cigarette smoke and the range smoke rising in the late afternoon air.

What would Sylvia, the postulant, be doing right now? Polly felt her throat thicken and she swallowed. She smoked her cigarette down to its stub, then tossed it into the water. 'She never said goodbye, she just left a note. Didn't she like us at all? Was it just a lie?'

She knew she might have said it before, but didn't care, because she still couldn't bear it. 'We miss her, she's part of us. Why didn't she say goodbye? We went to the convent, but she wouldn't see us. She never said she was even thinking of it and we thought she had Steve and was happy.'

Happy? Only fools wanted happiness, Ma Porter had just said.

Ma Porter produced her crochet from beneath the stool, and her fingers were busy. Her wrung clothes were folded neatly in the basket on the bank, her second boiler was simmering next to it, the smell of soda filled the air. The steam rose straight up. Ma Porter said, 'P'raps you's thinkin' too much of yerselves not of 'er. 'T'ain't why didn't she say goodbye, is it? More why did she go at all, so sudden like? That's what yer should ask yerselves.'

That night in the pub the air was as smoky as ever from the cigarettes and the fire, the chatter was loud, and over everything was an air of heady relief that VE Day had arrived. Those with men at war could breathe again, as long as they weren't in the Far East, of course. Relief also that the Limehouse run was quiet, and there'd be no more rockets or bombs, but how the hell were they going to rebuild the country? Bet, who was with her two girls and Maudie, by the fireplace, bought the first round. Bet, Polly and Verity played Timmo, Trev and Pete at darts and the girls lost. Timmo gloated, and they laughed, along with everyone in the pub. They sang the national anthem and then fell silent as they thought of those who wouldn't come home, and felt joy for those who would.

Long before closing, Verity and Polly walked back to *Marigold* and *Horizon* arm in arm, past the drinkers, some of whom had moved out into the garden which faced the cut. They were followed by Maudie and Timmo, who were talking quietly. They heard Maudie laugh. Verity said, 'She needs to be with Timmo, not with us two miseries.'

'Granfer says she feels she owes us a debt for Joe's safety.'

They walked along the towpath past Ma Porter's resting boiler, and Polly said, 'Talking of miseries, Ma said today that we're looking at Sylv's decision from our own point of view, instead of asking why she went.'

Verity stopped dead. 'What have I just said?' She slapped her forehead. 'Just listen to me nattering about Granfer saying Maudie feels she owes us a debt, so what about Sylv? Perhaps it's not belief, but obligation. Do you remember that she used to feel she owed it to the orphanage, and something about a Harriet, to become a nun and serve the order, and God? It made her the grumpy-guts she was when she first joined the waterway girls, but once on the cut she found another way of thinking, helped by Sister Augustine's advice.'

Polly heard Pup barking from *Marigold*. 'She's heard us, come on – and of course, yes, yes, she did say something like that, and we knew how she felt. What the hell is the matter with us? But no, hang on, she had Steve, she was in love, that was all in the past. Anyway, why act on it now? Joe's back, the war is over, and everything is safe, including Steve, who only has ordinary fires to deal with.'

They looked at one another. 'Perhaps that's why,' said Verity slowly. 'She feels she can leave now, because her war work is done. We've got to stop thinking that she left just us, Pol. I mean, she knew she'd get questioned if she told us her plans, which is bloody cheeky of us, really. She knows her own mind, and who are we to think we're more important than a calling?'

Polly vaguely saw the sense, and was too tired and upset to think about it any more. Pup barked again, and she called, 'We're coming.'

They went to bed early and couldn't sleep, but since Sylvia had gone that was normal, so they made cocoa and talked, running through all the possible scenarios, but this time, rather than concentrating on how they felt, they looked at it from Sylvia's side, moving from obligation to the decision that she had a real calling, and back to . . . what? They talked of her past guilt over dobbing in Joe over the butty fire, and the bond she and Joe had subsequently built up. Polly muttered, 'Look at all the letters, the drawings, the relationship between the two. Has she moved her sense of obligation from the orphanage to Joe?'

They smoked, shoving the double door open to air the room. Instead of another cocoa they drank tea, wishing it were gin. 'If it was a sense of obligation to Joe, how far would that go?' mused Verity.

Polly dropped the stub of her cigarette into the dregs of her mug of tea. It hissed. Verity scowled. 'That's disgusting.'

'Shut up.' Polly carried her mug up on to the counter and shook it over the cut. The stub dropped, floated, sank. She leaned against the cabin, staring up at the stars. Verity called from the cabin, 'Do you remember her thinking it was rude that no thanks were given on the cut, and then much later understanding the boaters' unwritten obligation to repay? She said it was a sort of deal, and one that drew a line under the matter.'

Polly eased herself on to the roof. The cool breeze made her shiver, but there was a slight heat from the chimney. Pup bounded from the cabin and leapt up to sit with her. A deal? she thought. A deal? When does an obligation become a deal? She said, raising her voice a little, 'Do you remember when Sister Augustine told Sylvia that there was no obligation to repay the orphanage by becoming a nun when Sylvia was so confused? So, thinking about that, does Sylvia still feel an obligation, but not to the convent; instead to Harriet for that promise she says she made and didn't fulfil, but why now? And why rush off? So perhaps instead it was a deal to help Joe stay safe. But a deal with who?' She rubbed her forehead. Why couldn't she and Verity just accept that it was Sylvia's calling? Because they loved the damned girl, and the girl loved Steve, and had come alive, and had talked of a future at Howard House if Steve got his transfer, because . . . Well, just because it didn't damn well make sense, and yes, they didn't feel it in their ruddy water.

Verity was scrabbling from the cabin on to the counter now, standing there, wagging her finger, almost shouting. 'Yes, yes, but go back to a sense of obligation, or rather, don't go back but take it further. Do you remember how we came across Sylvia praying when Joe was taken? She was so fierce. What if—'

Polly interrupted. 'So what are you saying?'

Verity was shaking her head, pacing the tiny counter. 'I'm not sure what I'm saying, but . . . What if her deal was with her God? Perhaps she made a promise to do what she thought she should have done in the first place, which was to fulfil her promise to Harriet, and her obligation to the orphanage and to Him, and would do so if Joe was all right?'

Pup yelped. Polly hushed her. Verity stopped in front of her. 'Pol, think of it; how much more obliged would Sylv feel if someone she absolutely loved was saved. What if she – oh, I don't know, promised to sort of sacrifice herself for Joe's safety?'

Polly sighed. Verity shoved Polly along, and sat between her and the chimney, and they huddled together, feeling the breeze stiffen and hearing the accordion playing in Sid's pub garden. Clearly there was to be dancing till dawn, but not here, on *Marigold*, not until they believed that Sylvia had left for the right reason; for her, not them.

Verity shook her head. 'We're probably being totally selfish. What if she is "home"? What if she has willingly and wholeheartedly chosen that world over us, and all the future plans, not to mention poor Steve?'

Saul and Tom had marched tired mile after mile as the battalion headed towards the Baltic to cut off the Russians heading for Denmark, and as May 8th passed and became May 9th German troops marched in the opposite direction, in step, shoulders back, rifles borne correctly as they escaped the Russians. Their women hurried too, and they ignored the British, just as Saul and Tom ignored them.

Tom and Saul talked of the future, and the past. Geordie had been wounded and returned to Britain as a casualty, taking letters with them in reply to the girls, which they had received in a package from Sir David McDonald, who was the father of a canal girl Verity had saved from drowning last year, and brought by a Lieutenant Wilberforce who had joined the company. As they marched they talked of Howard House as an hotel, or a school, which the girls had mooted. They thought an hotel, but what did the girls really think?

'We can ask them,' Saul replied.

'Best leave it till they've grown used to Sylvia running off to the convent.'

'But soon, when we're home.'

Saul said, 'Demob is slow.'

'I bet Leon's also finding life a bit slow in clink, but bloody lucky just to be dobbed into the police and not floating in the Thames. OK, he was found with a packet of evidence linking him to the murder of Manny. Strange, that,' Tom muttered, as they kicked up the dust. 'He'll probably hang.'

'Lord, I'll be glad to be back, with the Channel between us and this lot. I've had enough of sorting out the filthy, vile bloodiness of their mess.'

Steve had become used to the absence of bombs and rockets, which was something he thought would never happen. He held his hose on the house fire, started by a candle falling on to papers. He wished he'd never been a fireman, then he'd never have come to her rescue, her, his ex-fiancée, Sylvia Simpson, who could have been Sylvia Bates by now.

He worked alongside Terry and missed Dodge so much. He missed Sylvia so much more, with her red hair, dancing eyes, calloused hands, and kindness. What bloody kindness was it, though, to send a note saying that she had a vocation to fulfil and that she was sorry, so very sorry, and had loved him so much? Had? That's right, had.

The water was fizzing from the nozzle and soaking his hands. But at least he was alive, whereas Sylvia had buried herself behind walls. Buried, that's what she was. So why had he saved her in the first place? She should have sent him away then.

'You all right, Stevo?'

'Course, Terro,' he joked.

'You look a bit . . . Oh, I don't know.'

'We're alive, Terry, so what more do we want? Over three hundred of us firefighters aren't, and Gawd, thousands of our blokes are injured. Why the hell should I be fed up, eh?'

Terry aimed at the next burning window. 'I don't know, lad. You tell me. Something about your "to be missus" doing a bunk into a nunnery. It would fair break me up, so you sure you're all right?'

Steve couldn't stand it any longer, and said, 'No, don't think I'll ever be all right again. I loved her so much, and I don't understand it. It was so sudden, and I hate the bloody nuns, and that Sister Augustine – they've got to her.'

He looked up as the sub called out, 'You've drowned that one good and proper, lad. Wake up.' Steve shifted his aim to the next. Terry said nothing, just muttered, 'You'll have to light a few candles for that remark, lad.'

Steve shook his head. 'I know, I'm an idiot. There's just something not right, something . . .' He trailed away. 'I'll go and bang on their door again, I need to speak to her, I've just got a feeling about it. If she

457

was really called I think I'd know, and I'd accept it, but it's all wrong.'

The flames were dying and black soot was staining the brickwork. Poor buggers, thought Steve as he heard the wife sobbing. He said to Terry, 'They dodged the bombs, and got smacked by a bloody candle. There's no sense in any of it.'

'That about sums it up, all of it,' muttered Terry, as the hoses died on the heels of the flames. 'But getting back to you, you have to make sense of it, so go and see them again, and again, until you do. Or shut up and just accept it. What about her friends on the canal?'

'They're as confused as me, they think there's something ... But they say they could be quite wrong. They're going to try and see her again.'

At Howard House, Joe rode Maisie around the schooling ring but he couldn't concentrate because he'd never got to teach Sylvia to draw a kingfisher easily, and now he wouldn't because she were somewhere else, behind a wall, loving God more than the girls and more than him. She hadn't even waited to say hello, but had written a note, saying she was glad he was safe, and to make something good of his life.

He called to Auntie Pamela, 'I don't want to ride any more; I just want to go to my room.'

Auntie Pamela came to him and held Maisie's bridle. 'That's all right, but you'll have to put away the tack and rub her down first. It's a shame, though, it's such a lovely day for celebrating the end of the war.'

Joe shrugged. 'I don't care about the war, I just want to go to my room and get the kingfisher really right. Then I can send it, and she might miss the cut enough to come out of the convent, then I can see her and tell her she was someone I thought of when I was in the dark because she watched the kingfishers, the otters, and the whole world, really.' Suddenly he was crying, because she was one of the girls and he loved them all, and it wasn't the same, nothing was, and she hadn't said hello, and she hadn't said goodbye.

Sylvia rose at 5.40 on May 21st at St Cecilia's Convent attached to St Cecilia's Orphanage and church, dressed in her black dress, placed her short white cotton veil on her head, and fixed it in place. She was here, Joe was safe, and her God was with her, just as He always had been, but now there would be no one else, as there had been before. It was what she'd promised.

After meditation there was the first Mass in the beautiful chapel. The windows streamed early summer light on to the marble floor, staining it blue, red and green. She knelt, sat, stood and knelt. She breathed in the incense, she listened to the Latin, which was truly beautiful and God given. At 7.30 there was breakfast. She couldn't eat, and there was no need to speak because talking was as bad as eating. If she talked she thought, and she mustn't think, because she loved God with so much of her being, but not with all. There were others she loved more.

She knelt, stood, sat, for second Mass and at 9.00 helped in the laundry. It always made her think of the steerers' wives boiling their clothes, wringing them out. Of course, they – the girls – hadn't done it often enough. She could smell the soda, feel the hot wet clothes as she and Verity wrung them out between them. She could feel the wind from the cut, and see the kingfisher diving and creating barely a ripple to break the surface. Did Joe still have her drawing? She mustn't think, the pain was too much. He was safe.

At 10.30 there were elevenses. She couldn't take more than a mouthful of tea.

She dug in the garden because it was spring and she must dig up the roots of the dandelions as Mrs Holmes and Joe had done before they had moved to Howard House. Did they still? But no, it would be Henry and Thomas. Would Howard House become an hotel? Would the girls marry their men? Would Steve . . . ? She stared at the worm squirming in the earth, and lifted it out, and watched it contracting and elongating on the palm of her hand. It seemed to grow too big, then too small, so small. So very tiny, just as she wanted to be tiny, and then to disappear.

At 11.45 it was Examen and with the other postulants she used prayer to reflect on the events so far today to detect God's presence and discern His direction for her. So, why are you making me think of the cut, or am I forcing myself past You to reach them? To reach Joe, Steve and her beloved girls?

She rose for lunch at noon. She sat with Harriet, and two of the new postulants. The other three were to wait on the Mother Superior, the sisters, the novices and the postulants. They all ate but she couldn't, because she must continue to disappear. She lifted the glass of water, merely taking a sip. They all talked, she did not, because with words came thoughts.

At 12.30 there was the Midday Office, and the hour was sanctified with prayer, psalms, hymns, readings . . . She felt the blessed blackness grow, the breath ease from her, the nothingness envelop her and the coldness of the floor flood her. It was over.

Sister Augustine sat opposite her old friend, the Mother Superior. They smiled at one another. 'She's in the sickbay?' Mother Superior sat with her hands hidden by her sleeves, like a muff.

Sister Augustine nodded. 'She shouldn't be here. When she arrived I knew that really, in my heart, but she was so determined, I thought we should allow her to enter as a postulant, to show her that God needs her life to be with those she loves. She has a determined sense of obligation, a need to sacrifice, but God doesn't expect that, as you and I know. She has spoken just now, as I held water to her lips, of how she had made a deal, of all things, Mother Superior, with God, and promised she would serve Him if Joe was safe. I explained that God does not require such sacrifice, He doesn't make deals, He just loves, and that she is already deserving of that love. I gather that memories of Harriet have been reinforcing her need to sacrifice. They made a promise, which was reinforced at the reunion. I should have guessed when I saw Harriet with her.'

Mother Superior's smile was strained. 'We need to talk to Harriet, with compassion, but firmly. But to return to our dear postulant, Sylvia: her response to *your* words?'

'Relief, and doubt. I think that your wisdom is needed at the bedside because she is so malnourished, so fearful that the boy, Joseph, will be in jeopardy if she reneges. She's a dear little thing, and was a shining light at the orphanage. She loves another shining light, our Steve Bates. Do you remember? A bit of a pickle, but with a wonderfully good heart. He was her fiancé, and I believe still is in his heart, as he calls weekly, as do the two girls from the canal. There is much love for her so she would be released from her postulancy into good hands, but still be under His care, because of course He is all that's good in the world.'

The Mother Superior was already rising. Sister Augustine followed her out, and they walked in perfect companionship along the dark corridor. Mother Superior stopped by a window overlooking the playground of the orphanage. She said, 'We do all we can but the life of a child in an institution might perhaps lead to a fear of a personal relationship. This is not recognised by the child, and the mind plays tricks to prevent that commitment, such as forcing oneself to accept a role which is, in fact, not called for. I feel that frequently there is a fear that those they love will leave, and then what? Or, as you say, she genuinely fears retribution on the child if she does not follow her imagined obligation. It's all rather complicated, but then life is. Either way, I will talk, listen, and decide, but, my dear, I am sure with your experience, you understand exactly what is necessary.'

Sister Augustine looked out at the orphanage, feeling sad. 'It's never enough.'

'Ah, my dear, but often it is, because there is love here, when otherwise there would be none, except God's, and how is that to be known?'

The *Marigold* girls received a tannoy message when they returned from Tyseley in early June. It was from Steve, telling them that Sister Augustine had contacted him. Sylvia had spent time addressing her concerns about her future and had made a decision to return to the outside world. The Mother Superior would not permit this until her three friends were able to receive her at the door. The girls telephoned

Steve at the fire station and said early the following morning they would meet him at the convent, because it was already dark, and they must first release Maudie from the butty.

'Where will she go?' Steve asked.

'Oh, don't worry about that, she'll skip to Timmo's pair, which will suit them both because Trev has left to train as a lorry driver, and Timmo is set to head for Limehouse tomorrow.'

They brought Sylvia home to Bull's Bridge Depot the next day, with Steve stuck like glue to her side. He had taken leave, and would travel with them on the pair.

'Just as Tom did,' Sylvia said, looking thin, pale and wan.

As they headed through the depot gates they were checked off the clipboard, and then walked through the chaos of the yard, with the men tipping their foreheads at Sylvia, as though she'd been off for the day.

She walked along the lay-by, breathing in the smell of the cut, the soda from the women's boilers, the cooking of the lunch. She waved at Ma Porter, who smiled, and Ma Ambrose and Ma Wise, and everyone else. They merely said, ''Ow do, lass.' It resonated, it warmed and it made her feel stronger.

Steve gripped her hand. 'I'm never going to let you go again.'

She knew he wouldn't and she knew that she wanted to be with him. She wasn't scared any more.

She hadn't even known she was until the Mother Superior had soothed her forehead, her face filled with God's love, and explained so many things.

Polly and Verity, who had waited with Steve, had hugged her before Steve could get near her, saying to him, 'We love her too, Steve. You must wait. For us it's all for one, and one for all, isn't it, dearest Sylv?'

The words were music, they sang to Sylvia as the three of them clung together. Verity whispered, 'We will always be together, do you understand? You, Steve, the boys and us. We are family. Mrs B and Rogers have been pulling their hair out, they are quite bald, darling.'

Sylvia had laughed but she couldn't really hear it. She was back, she was a good person. She was able to love God and all these people. She felt at peace. Then Steve had been allowed to approach. He had held her as though she was porcelain, and whispered into her hair, 'I will always love you, always.'

She whispered, 'I couldn't tell you, any of you.' She looked at the others. 'I wouldn't have been able to pay, as I thought then, for Joe's life because I wouldn't have been able to leave you.'

Verity had said, 'Well, that's sorted, and Joe says that when you come again to Howard House he will show you how to draw a proper kingfisher, so with that promise to look forward to, let's get on, we have orders to deliver.'

Now she stood by *Marigold* and *Horizon* just as Timmo and Maudie passed on *Venus* and *Shortwood*, travelling abreast to the east. They hooted, each standing at their tiller. Sylvia waved, and called, 'I'm back, I'm home.' It was only a whisper, though, one that drifted on the wind as she felt she also drifted.

Timmo hooted again and all the narrowboats moored along the lay-by hooted too. Polly laughed, leapt on to the counter, and hooted back with Bet's hunting horn. 'Yes, Sylv,' she called. 'Everyone's happy because Maudie's with Timmo, and you're back with us, at last.'

Sylvia felt the lay-by beneath her feet, and stepped up on to her butty, *Horizon.* She stood, feeling the movement. She balanced. She stepped forward and ran her hands along the cabin roof. Pup barked and leapt from *Marigold*'s roof to hers in one bound, then sat, eye to eye with Sylvia. Sylvia whispered, 'I miss Dog, but I love you.' They looked at one another for just a moment and it seemed as though Pup nodded.

Sylvia lifted her head to the wind, and the sun. The sky was blue and the cut rippled as a pair went past. Sylvia knew that she really was home.

Chapter 29

August 1946 at Howard House Hotel

The bustle in the kitchen was escalating into near hysteria as Mrs B and Rogers held open the door for Dobbo and his wife so they could carry the two-tier wedding cake out unhindered and up the stairs. It was destined for the marquee on the front lawn. 'You are to lay down your lives rather than let this cake fall to the ground, is that quite clear?' she instructed Henry, as he and Thomas followed them out of the kitchen carrying bottles of champagne cooling in buckets of ice from the ice house.

Mrs B called, 'Never you mind issuing orders, just concentrate on getting those bottles to the marquee too.' As the four of them climbed the steps to the yard, she blessed Dobbo for resurrecting the ice house in the cold of winter.

Still standing at the door to the boot hall, Mrs B turned and surveyed the kitchen. The table was heaped with food acquired with saved-up coupons, as austerity bit deep. Well, there were debts to repay and a country to rebuild and their survival, then and now, was worth it and she'd deal with anyone who grumbled and grizzled.

In the scullery the girls from the village were ferreting out the tea towels with which to cover the pork pies, sandwiches, ham vol-au-vent cases, the . . . 'Oh,' sighed Mrs B. 'There'll just have to be enough. Come along, girls, or you'll miss the show.'

Myrtle laughed as she rushed out with the tea towels piled high in her arms. 'Oh, you shouldn't call a triple wedding a show, Mrs B, but I suppose it is. Even though, I suppose, it's a double and single wedding really. One Catholic, two Protestant. It's all so exciting, with the Howard Hotel about to open an' all. Come on, Sally, quick. Got the confetti?' They laid the tea towels over the food while beside her Rogers pulled at his starched collar. 'It really is most extraordinarily stiff, my dear.'

Mrs B kissed his cheek. 'Ah, but our Sylvia doesn't get wed every day, and you looked so proud escorting her down the aisle of the church. Though I have to say, the incense got in my tubes, and didn't half make me cough. Now it's just Polly and Verity in the Hall chapel, then the hordes will need feeding. I'm right worried there won't be enough.'

Rogers slipped his arm around her. 'You know there will, and I bet that the guests slip a bit of food on to the table too. We just need to make sure that it's brought through from the kitchen to the marquee before they actually leave the chapel. You've—?'

'Yes, don't you fret, Dobbo and Sarah have got that all set up.' She dragged her notepad from her pocket, checking her list. 'Dougie is at the bottom of the drive, with the dog cart, waiting to bring anyone up who can't struggle over the gravel if they've come by bus. The nuns just somehow glided up after Sylvia and Steve's ceremony. I don't know how they do it.'

There was a clatter of feet on the steps down from the yard, and a yelp. 'Oh sorry, Pup.'

Pamela and Joyce ran into the kitchen, and almost screeched to a halt at the side of Mrs B. 'Come on, all of you. Round Two is about to start; the chapel bells are about to be rung, our lovely girls are lurking in the entrance, the boys are standing in front of the altar with Joe propping up Saul, and Steve patting Tom's back, though so damned hard I reckon he's in danger of being sick. I feel that's not necessarily the job of a best man, but who am I to judge. Just hope they've checked they have the rings.' Joyce was wearing a hat of gauze and feathers she and Mrs B had dug out of the attic and remade, and the feathers were dancing like berserkers.

She beckoned the two girls who were just putting the final coverings over the food. They all hurried up the steps, heading past the stables which now housed several ponies for St Cecilia's Orphanage children who came to stay several times a year, taking up the smartened attic bedrooms.

The chapel nestled behind the stables in amongst a copse of silver birches and had been ignored and unused for too long, Sylvia had decided when she and Steve joined them at Howard House at the end of 1945. She had explained to Lord and Lady Clement that a house of God, of whatever persuasion, should not be allowed to fall into disrepair, or, in fact, disuse.

Henry had said, with a slight salute, 'Fair point, Captain. Will get on to it right away.'

Mrs B nudged Pamela now, as they all began to walk along the crazy paving path towards the chapel door, saying, 'Oh, do you remember how Henry passed on the task to Steve and Dobbo to sort out, which you sniffed at, so he, with appalling grace, also got sawing and painting, while Thomas took the bulk of the gardening on his shoulders?'

Joyce and Pamela were laughing, and as they slowed, puffing and panting, Joyce added, 'Thomas has found gardening help from those who came looking for work on demob, and the vegetables have become quite a money earner at the market. He thinks he's some sort of tycoon, I believe. Poor Jacob will be roped in as a middleman if he's not careful, to flog them in Covent Garden or some swish hotel. That's if there's any left, because Mrs B gets first dibs.'

Pamela murmured, 'Perhaps we should turn some of the pasture over to more vegetables, if Jacob does think he can do something with them. And there are still the pigs in the copses, of course.'

'My word, do I hear the makings of another tycoon to my left?' Joyce said, nudging her.

They neared the chapel steps hearing Harry, Steve's friend, playing the Wedding March. The three 'aunties' had decorated the entrance at dawn this morning, scared that it might rain in the night, leaving everything bedraggled. The parachute silk strips all three of them had cut and sewn fluttered in the soft breeze, anchored and looped to short poles banged in by Granfer. Bunches of roses and lavender were tied to the posts.

Mrs B slowed before they climbed the step into the foyer. 'Do you think Granfer will stay on, now Lettie has passed on?'

Pamela sighed. 'I do so hope he does. Joe and Saul would be thrilled, and then there is only one family that Maudie and Timmo have to visit when they can get away from the cut.'

Sylvia waited in the foyer, fingering her wedding ring, running 'Mrs Bates' through her mind, smiling, smiling and unable to stop. The day was balmy, the sound of a distant harvester hung in the air, which then became drowned by Harry's organ. She watched the three women approaching, laughing at something. She slipped from the lobby to meet them. She too wore elegantly fashioned parachute silk, and had removed her wedding veil, for now she was to be the matron of honour to her two friends, who had just been her bridesmaids.

She looked at the three of them, as they stopped talking and opened their arms to her, hugging her. She smelt their perfume: it was Joy, as hers and Verity's was. 'Darling girl,' Mrs B said. 'You were so beautiful this morning.'

Verity called from the entrance, 'Isn't she any more, then, Mrs B?'

Sylvia called, 'Oh shut up.'

Joyce muttered, 'Nothing changes.'

Sylvia linked arms with Mrs B, and with Rogers, and they hurried in, while he yanked at the collar Mrs B had double-starched. Sylvia had asked why. 'Because I'm not having him letting his head droop. It does, you know, and it makes him look old, and as I say, I'm not having it.'

Polly, now standing next to Verity, called, 'Come on, I thought you'd never get a move on.'

Rogers muttered, 'Darned collar, cutting into me chin, it is.'

Mrs B snapped, 'That's why you're wearing it, so keep your head up.'

Sylvia smiled. These were the parents she had never had and, of course, Rogers had given her away, Mrs B had helped her with her dress, both had helped Steve and her sort out the rear Lodge Cottage which was to be the Bateses' home.

Sylvia grinned at Polly and Verity. They wore parachute silk too, but the three mothers had woven their magic and each had its own identity. Polly reached out a hand and clasped Sylvia's, saying,

'Ah, you, as an old married woman, will follow *us* down the aisle this time. Did Father O'Malley think he was seeing double when both Saul and Tom stood as best man to Steve, I wonder, Sylv?'

Sylvia grinned. 'Quite probably, but he was really pleased that Father Murphy had allowed him to officiate.'

The organ started the Wedding March yet again, and all the girls shared a smile. Polly muttered, 'He'll be out here, hauling us in soon. It seems to me he's a bit louder than the first time.'

Henry and Thomas arrived hotfoot from the marquee, to take their place beside their daughters. They had set up the buckets, and reported that the girls, Dobbo and Dougie were well aware that timing was crucial and they must rush from the chapel when the photographs were taken, to get the food to the marquee for the ravening hordes.

Organising these weddings had been like planning a battle, Saul had said, when they'd all met for drinks in Howard House Hotel bar last night, and Henry had shaken his head, whispering, 'Oh my, you'll live to regret those words, you see if you don't once our Pol gets hold of you. Imagine calling a wedding a battle plan, oh my.'

As they had sat and chatted, Timmo, Trev and Pete had been playing Bet, Evelyn and Mabel at darts while in the lounge Sister Augustine talked to Solly about the vagaries of the world, and the need to go on when one's whole family, village or shtetl had disappeared, while Maudie talked to Rachel of children, because Rachel's baby was expected in two months.

That night the girls had retired as usual to their room, still with its three beds, still with Pup lying on Pol's feet, talking of the work they had already done on the hotel, and all that still needed to be done. Talking of the renovation of the gardener's cottage that Dobbo and Dougie, who had left London saying he had a hankering for something better, were handling. It was almost ready for the ex-soldiers in need of a break, or help. It only needed the ramp to the front door, and the lowered sink and so on in the kitchen, then it would be finished. Two more bedrooms had been built on the back, while there were three upstairs for the able-bodied.

They lay in bed talking of the cut, which they still missed, of the gift that had arrived today from the McDonalds, whose daughter Verity they had saved from death in the lock, which seemed like years ago. It had been a surprise, because Sir David McDonald had already given them the huge gift of arranging a prompt demob for Tom and Saul. It was only then that the girls had resigned from the Inland Waterways Scheme, which was winding down anyway, and returned the GUCCC boats to Bull's Bridge, eager to start on the hotel project they had all decided upon.

As the stars filled the sky they talked of the brave gamble of the Holmeses, who sold up their house and invested the proceeds in the hotel as long as one of the hotel lounges was called the William Lounge, after their son, Polly's twin brother. They and Lord and Lady Clement each had an apartment on the second floor, though Mrs B and Rogers wouldn't budge from the Butler's Pantry, because, as Mrs B said, they would be in overall charge of the catering and let no one forget it.

Tom had grunted, 'No one would dare.'

Sylvia reminded them, as Polly tossed and turned, 'After which Tom had not been allowed second helpings for two days.'

The laughter and chat had continued until they tried to sleep, but Polly couldn't sleep and Verity had thrown a pillow and told her to stop wriggling. Polly had complained, 'I can't help it, I'm so nervous, so happy, and I love him so much.'

'Oh, shut up,' the two others had yelled together.

In the end they had crept down to the kitchen and sneaked a bottle of wine from the fridge, and five glasses, and were on their way out when they saw Rogers peering at them from the Butler's Pantry. Verity put her fingers to her lips. He nodded, and they went on their way, tapping lightly at Bet and Fran's door.

All five of them had sat up until the early hours slouching on the three beds, talking about Sylvia getting to the church on time in Henry's Rolls-Royce which he barely used now, having bought himself a motorcycle and sidecar as being more suitable for a time of austerity.

Sylvia had said how Pamela refused to sit in the sidecar without a helmet because he was such a dreadful driver. Fran was laughing so much she had to bite on a pillow or wake the household.

Verity had explained that the Rolls-Royce would be kept and used for the wedding receptions the hotel would provide. Tom would be the driver, as well as doing many other things.

They had then talked of the flat above the garages where Verity and Tom would live after the wedding, and which they had spruced up no end, while Saul and Polly had been doing the same with the small house behind the stables where the grooms had formerly lived.

Dobbo and his wife, and Dougie, were in apartments of similar sizes. And Pup and Rover spent most of the time foraging for burglars and eyeing up the pigs in the copse, trying to work out if they were friend or foe.

Finally they had grown quiet, and as she was allowing herself to fall asleep Sylvia had heard the click of the door when Bet and Fran tiptoed out, and it had all been as good as the cut, or almost, for here there were no kingfishers, or otters. But her final thoughts were that perhaps there would be, when the second stage of the renovation was completed. For then the clearing of the small lake in the north corner would be complete, and Joe could perfect her drawings of wildlife.

In the morning, as the girls helped to zip up Sylvia's dress they talked of the kingfisher that Joe had painted for her and Steve, and which Saul had framed. 'Where will you put it, Sylv?' Polly said, standing back and smoothing down the folds of Sylvia's dress.

'Above the mantelpiece, it's so beautiful.'

'You know that Joe has hung the one you did for him on your return from the orphanage above the fireplace in his room, in between the two parents' quarters on the second floor?'

Sylvia laughed slightly. 'Yes, he showed me.'

Verity muttered, 'Dreadful though it is because, quite frankly, darling, I have never, ever seen a kingfisher that shape, but they say beauty is in the eye of the beholder. It just shows how much he loves you.'

The other two were screaming with laughter and pretending to beat her as they heard a vehicle driving along the gravel. They sneaked a look from the window, and saw that it was the boaters arriving, having hired a charabanc to get them to the wedding, with just time for the reception, and a few pints, as Sid had written to say. They'd also brought the old bulldog, Samson, and Reginald Forsythe who the girls had first met on the towpath with Dog, and then Pup. They'd all go back the same day, and a boater would take Reginald on, after they'd stayed the night with Sid.

Sid had said he and the missus could only afford one day away from the cut. During the reception, Henry and Thomas were going to talk to them all about possible jobs with people he knew on the river when things really became quiet on the cut, though Sid and the missus would always be welcome to run the bar at Howard House Hotel. Samson and Reginald Forsythe would be welcomed as residents in return for an advisory role as keeper of the guests' pets.

And now, Sylvia thought, as the double doors into the chapel opened and the brides' mothers slipped into the church, while their men waited at the altar, there was only Maudie and Timmo to settle in a place that was right for them, but she knew it would be here, because she felt it in her water. She smiled at Ma Porter, who sat with Steerer Porter and Jimmy in the back row. Ah, yes, she felt it in her water.

She held Verity and Polly's trains, and murmured, 'Come on, girls, get a gallop on, our men are waiting and we have a future to live.'

Polly and Verity turned and smiled at one another. 'Oh, shut up,' Verity whispered. 'Lovely Sylv.'

Polly shook her head. 'We just have to remember it's one for all, and all for one.'

Harry was thumping out the Wedding March for the third time, but later he would be playing at the reception with Steve on saxophone, and probably

Sylvia and Saul singing. Henry with Verity on his arm said, 'For goodness' sake, let's get on with it, we've all waited long enough for this day, and, what's more, the champagne will be warming.'

Thomas said, as they started down the aisle, in step as they'd practised, 'We seem one bottle of wine short. Anybody know anything about it?'

The girls just smiled, and he said, 'Yes, I thought so. No headaches though, that's my girls. Trenchermen to the last.'

They were all laughing as they reached the altar, and Saul and Tom only had eyes for their brides, and Steve for his wife.

They had moored up at last, thought Sylvia. Home and dry, and full of hope for the future.

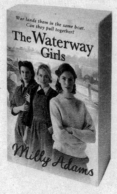

March 1944, West London

It's been five months since **Verity Clement** fled home for a life on Britain's canals and she could never have imagined how tough it would get. Yet hauling cargo between London and Birmingham is far easier to face than the turbulence she's left behind.

When Verity's sweetheart returns unexpectedly from the front line, she dares to dream of a brighter future. But life aboard the *Marigold* is never smooth sailing. New recruit **Sylvia** is struggling with demons from her past while crewmate **Polly** must carry on in the wake of devastating news. Verity does her best to help, but a shocking discovery is about to turn her own life upside-down.

As the realities of war begin to take their toll, the waterway girls will have to pull together if they are to survive the uncertain times ahead.

arrow books

'Would anyone ever think of her with real love?'

It's July 1942, and twenty-three year old nightclub singer **Kate Watson** has made a home for herself in bombed-blitzed London. A motley crew of friends has replaced the family she's not spoken to in years. That is until the evening Kate's sister **Sarah** walks back into her life.

Sarah has a favour to ask: she needs Kate to return home to Dorset for one month to look after her daughter, Lizzie. Reluctantly Kate agrees, even though it means facing the troubled past she hoped she'd escaped.

Kate is confronted once again by the prejudice and scrutiny of the townsfolk, including the new village vicar. As the war continues, Kate must fight her own battles and find not only the courage to forge a future but perhaps, at long last, love.

Hear more from

Milly Adams

LET SLEEPING DRAGONS LIE

Here be Knights! Fights! Bats!

Garth Nix & Sean Williams

Piccadilly
PRESS

First published in 2017 by Scholastic Press,
an imprint of Scholastic Inc., New York, USA

First published in Great Britain in 2018 by
PICCADILLY PRESS
80–81 Wimpole St, London W1G 9RE
www.piccadillypress.co.uk

Text copyright © Garth Nix and Sean Williams, 2017

A CIP catalogue record for this book is available from the British Library.

ISBN: 978-1-84812-687-9
Also available as an ebook

1
This book is typeset by Perfect Bound Ltd
Printed and bound in Great Britain by Clays Ltd, Elcograf S.p.A.

MIX
Paper from
responsible sources
FSC® C018072

Piccadilly Press is an imprint of Bonnier Zaffre Ltd,
psrt of Bonnier Books UK
www.bonnierbooks.co.uk

To Anna, Thomas and Edward,
and to all my family and friends.
- Garth Nix

To Amanda, and all our friends and family,
with gratitude and love.
- Sean Williams

ONE

'Bilewolves!'

'Help us!'

'Help me!'

'Aarrgh, no, no –'

The shouts and screams grew louder as Sir Odo and Sir Eleanor raced towards the village green, their magical, self-willed swords, Biter and Runnel, almost lifting them from the ground in their own eagerness to join the combat. Well behind them came Addyson and Aaric, the baker's twin boys, who had come in a panic to tell them the village was under attack.

Above all the human sounds of fear and fighting, a terrible howling came again, from more than one bestial throat.

'Slower!' panted Odo as they reached the back of the village inn, the Sign of the Silver Fleece, or the Grey Sheep, as it was nicknamed, since the sign had long since faded. 'We must be clever. Stay shoulder to shoulder, advance with care.'

'*Nay, we must charge at once!*' roared Biter, even as his

sister sword snapped, 'I agree, Sir Odo.'

'I do too,' said Eleanor, slowing so her much larger and less fleet-of-foot friend could catch up. When he was level with her, she moved closer so they were indeed shoulder to shoulder, their swords held in the guard position.

Together, and ready, they rounded the corner of the inn.

A terrible scene met their eyes. Some forty paces away, four enormous, shaggy, wolflike creatures, each the size of a small horse, stood at bay facing a man and a woman. The people were hunters or trappers, judging by their leather armour and well-travelled boots, although they were quite old to be in that trade. Both looked to be at least fifty.

The man had a cloth of shining gold tied around his eyes, which perhaps explained Addyson's panicked description of 'a blind king' being attacked by the bilewolves. The cloth *did* give the impression of a crown.

Blind or not, king or not, the man wielded his steel-shod staff with a brilliance that made Odo gasp. The weapon was a blur, leaping out to punch one bilewolf's snout, then jab another's forefoot. The woman was equally adept, though she wielded a curved sword, the blade moving swiftly and smoothly as she danced with it, the bilewolves slow and clumsy partners. Close to the inn on the edge of the green, three villagers lay dead or seriously wounded, their torn and jagged clothes still smoking from the bilewolves' acid-spewing jaws. Eleanor's father, the herbalist Symon, was bent over the closest victim, frantically trying to stem the flow of blood from a wound. He looked up for a second at his daughter, but did not speak, turning instantly back to his work.

Odo grasped the situation immediately. Only the two old warriors kept the bilewolves away from the wounded and the rest of the defenceless villagers. But they were outnumbered and, despite their skill, overmatched by the sheer size and ferocity of the animals.

'Forward!' Odo shouted, and he and Eleanor marched together.

'For Lenburh!' shouted Eleanor.

Odo knew from the slight tremor in Eleanor's voice that she was afraid, though no one else would be able to tell. He was afraid as well. They were only twelve years old and had been knights for little over a month, but he knew the fear would not stop her, and it wouldn't stop him either.

They did not expect their war cries to be answered, but off to the right came a shout: 'Forward for Lenburh!' A horse came galloping across the green, the ancient warhorse of Sir Halfdan, who, like the master who rode it, had not been in battle for twenty years or more. True to its training, the warhorse held straight for the bilewolves, despite their terrible stench and formidable snarls. Sir Halfdan, despite age and infirmity, was rock-solid in the saddle, a lance couched under his arm. He had not had time to put on any armour save his helmet and a gauntlet. He still wore the nightgown that was his usual garb these days, and his one foot was clad in a velvet slipper.

A bilewolf turned towards the galloping horse and charged, leaping at the last moment to avoid Sir Halfdan's lowering lance. But the old knight knew that trick and flicked the point up, taking the beast in the shoulder, the steel point punching deep. Bilewolf shrieked, lance snapped, and then horse, knight and dying bilewolf collided and went flying.

At the same time, one of the three remaining bilewolves bounded up on the back of one of its fellows and leaped high over the head of the blind staff-wielder. The man jumped upon his companion's shoulders and punched up at the bilewolf's belly, but the beast had launched itself too well. The staff merely struck its wiry tail, severing it midway along as the bilewolf flew past them.

Odo and Eleanor rushed across the green, expecting the falling bilewolf to attack them and the unprotected villagers behind. But it ignored them, spinning about as it landed to strike at the two warriors once again, dark blood spraying from its injured tail. The blind man jumped down with the deftness of a travelling acrobat and stood back to back with the woman. Together they turned in a circle, staff and sword blurring to hold the bilewolves at bay.

Odo slowed and edged cautiously closer, wondering how the blindfolded man had struck so precisely with his staff.

Meanwhile, Eleanor narrowed her eyes, seeking a way into the battle.

'Take the one to my right!' shouted the swordswoman to Odo and Eleanor, her voice strong and well used to command. 'It is already lamed!'

'Sixth and Fourth Stance!' said Eleanor. 'You high, me low.'

They moved in perfect synchrony, as they'd practised, Odo stepping left and out, Biter held above his head to strike in a slanting downward blow, as Eleanor stretched out low with a lunge at the bilewolf's right front leg, which it already favoured.

The bilewolf bunched itself to leap up at Odo, choosing the bigger target. But Runnel's sharp point cut through its leg even as it sprang. It fell sideways, yelping, and Biter came down to separate its massive head from its body, the sword twisting to avoid a spray of bile from the snapping jaws. Both young knights struck again to be sure it was dead, and then swung about to move to the next target.

But the remaining two bilewolves were already slain, one with a crushed skull and the other with a sliced-open throat. All four carcasses lay steaming, the grass beneath them turning black and smoking where the acidic drops fell from their jaws.

'Sir Halfdan!' cried Eleanor. The old knight lay motionless upon the ground, the haft of his broken lance still couched under his arm. His warhorse lay near him, unable to get up. It raised its head and whinnied, as if in answer to some trumpet no one else could hear, but the effort was too much. Its head fell heavily back and did not move again.

'Wait!' Odo called as Eleanor started towards the fallen knight. 'Do you see any more bilewolves?'

The swordswoman answered him. She and the man still stood back to back, their weapons ready, as if they expected another attack at any moment.

Or they didn't trust Odo and Eleanor.

'There will be none,' she said. 'They hunt in fours and are jealous of their prey. You are knights of the realm?'

'Uh, we're knights, but not . . . exactly of the realm, I don't think,' said Odo. 'I am Sir Odo.'

'And I, Sir Eleanor.' It gave her a small thrill to say that, although there were more pressing matters to consider. 'If there are no more bilewolves, we must help Sir Halfdan while my father attends to the others –'

'One moment, Sir Eleanor,' snapped the woman. 'How are you knights, but *not exactly of the realm?*'

'It's a long story,' said Odo. 'We were knighted by the dragon Quenwulf –'

'Quenwulf?' asked the woman. Her expression shifted to one minutely more relaxed. 'Was it she who gifted you with the enchanted swords you bear?'

'No!' said Biter. He was still not entirely convinced he shouldn't be a dragonslaying sword.

'Uh, no,' said Odo. 'We found them. Like I said, it is a long story –'

'Best saved for later,' said the blind man. His voice was even more used to command than the woman's. 'Take me to the fallen knight, Hundred. Sir Eleanor, did you say he was Sir Halfdan?'

'Yes, Sir Halfdan holds the manor here,' Eleanor told the man as she studied the woman more closely. *Hundred* was a very strange name, but perhaps it was apt for a very strange person. In addition to the curved sword she still held at the ready, Eleanor noticed she had a series of small knives sheathed along each forearm, and unusual pouches on her belt. The backs of her dark-skinned hands were white with dozens of scars, like Eleanor's mother's hands – not wounds from claws or teeth, but weapon marks. A sign of many years of combat and practice.

'Sir, we should go on at once,' protested Hundred.

'No,' said the man. He turned to face where Sir Halfdan lay, and began to walk towards him, using his staff to tap the ground. After a moment, Hundred went ahead of him, and the man stopped tapping and followed her footfalls.

'He must have amazing hearing,' whispered Eleanor to Odo.

'I have *well-trained* ears,' said the man without turning his head.

Odo and Eleanor exchanged a glance, then hurried after the odd duo.

Sir Halfdan lay on his back, not moving. His helmet, too big for him, had tipped forward over his face. Hundred knelt by his side and gently removed it. The old knight's eyes opened as she did so, surprising everyone, for he had seemed already dead.

'Sir Halfdan,' said the blind man, bending over him.

Sir Halfdan blinked rheumily, and his jaw fell.

'Sire,' he whispered. 'Can it be?'

The old knight tried to lift his head and arm, but could not do so. The blind man knelt by him and closed his own hand over Halfdan's gauntlet.

'I remember when you held the bridge at Holmfirth,' said the blind man. 'In the second year of my reign. None so brave as Sir Halfdan. You remember the song Veran wrote? She will have to write another verse.'

'That was long ago,' whispered Halfdan.

'Time has no dominion over the brave.'

'I thought . . . We thought you dead, sire.'

Eleanor mouthed 'sire' at Odo and hitched one shoulder in question. He shrugged, unable to explain what was going on. But looking at the blind man in profile, there was something familiar about the shape of his face, that beaky nose, the set chin.

'I gave up the throne,' said the man. He touched his golden blindfold. 'When I lost my sight, I thought I could no longer rule. I was wrong. Blindness makes a man a fool no more than a crown makes him king.'

At the word *king*, Odo suddenly remembered why the old man's profile looked familiar.

It was on the old silver pennies he counted at the mill.

Eleanor had the same realisation. They both sank together to the earth, their hauberks jangling. Odo went down on his right knee and Eleanor on her left. They looked at each other worriedly and started to spring up again to change knees, before Hundred glared at them and made a sign to be still.

'My time is done, sire,' said Sir Halfdan. There was a rattle in his voice. He glanced over at his horse. 'Old Thunderer has gone ahead, and I must follow . . .'

He paused for a moment, the effort of gathering his thoughts, of speaking, evident on his face.

'I commend to you, sire . . . two most brave knights . . . Sir Eleanor and Sir Odo. They –'

Whatever he was going to say next was lost. At that moment old Sir Halfdan died. Egda the First – for the blind man was certainly the former king of Tofte, who had abdicated ten years ago – gripped Sir Halfdan's shoulder in farewell and stood up, turning towards the kneeling Odo and Eleanor.

'He was a great and noble knight,' he said. 'The Hero of Holmfirth Bridge, and even then he must have been over forty. To think of him slaying a bilewolf at the age of ninety!'

'We didn't know he was a hero,' said Eleanor uncomfortably. She was thinking about some of the names she had called him because he was slow getting organised for their journey east, to be introduced to the royal court. And how some people in the village had mocked him behind his back for having only one foot, though they would never dare do so to his face. 'He was just our knight. He's been here so long . . . um . . . sorry, should I say "sire", or is it "Your Highness"?'

'I am not a king,' said the blind man. 'I have been simply Egda these last ten years.'

'*Sir* Egda,' said Hundred sharply. 'You may refer to his grace as "sir" or "sire".'

'Now, now, Hundred,' said Egda. He smiled faintly, exposing two rows of white, even teeth. 'Hundred was the captain of my guard and has certain ideas about maintaining my former station. I wish to hear how you were made knights by the dragon Quenwulf, but first there is work to be done. The bilewolves must be burned. Are the wounded villagers attended? I hear pain, but also gentle soothing.'

Eleanor looked over to where the wounded were now being lifted to be carried inside the inn. Her father was assisted by several other villagers, including the midwife Rowena, who often worked with him.

'They are being tended to by my father, who is a healer and herbalist, sir,' she said.

'I'll gather wood to burn the bilewolves,' said Odo. 'Addyson and Aaric can help, if it please you, sir.'

'I do not command here,' said Egda mildly. 'Who is Sir

Halfdan's heir? Has he a daughter or son to take up his lands and sword? Or, given his age, grandchildren perhaps?'

'There's no one,' said Eleanor, frowning. She looked across at where the wounded and dead were being taken into the inn. 'Only his squire, Bordan, and I think he was one of the three other people the bilewolves –'

'They sought to help us,' said Egda. 'Would that they were less brave.'

'I warned them away,' said Hundred harshly. 'If they had kept back, they would have been in no danger.'

'Only if the bilewolves were after you in *particular*,' said Odo, made curious by her comment.

'This is not a matter for you, boy,' said Hundred. 'Sire, we must be on our –'

'No,' interrupted the former king. He didn't seem happy with the way Hundred was addressing Odo's enquiries. 'We will rest here tonight, not camp in the wilds. Sir Halfdan was my father's knight before he served me. We must show proper respect, see him put to rest. Also, I want to hear the story of these two swords – who are strangely quiet now, though I heard them in the battle.'

'I merely wait for my knight to introduce me, sir,' said Biter. He sounded aggrieved. 'He is new to his estate and I am still teaching him manners.'

'Oh,' said Odo. He held up Biter, hilt first. 'This is Hildebrand Shining Foebiter. Often called Biter.'

'And my sword is Reynfrida Sharp-point Flamecutter, or Runnel for short,' said Eleanor.

'𝕲reetings, sir,' said Runnel.

'𝕬nd welcome, sire,' added Biter, not wanting to be left out.

Egda nodded. 'Well then. Sir Odo, to the burning of the beasts. Sir Eleanor, if you would introduce me to your father and other notables in the village, we must order . . . that is, *suggest* the arrangements to lay Sir Halfdan to rest. Hundred, cast about for any sign of other unfriendly beasts.'

'Sire!' protested Hundred. 'I cannot leave you unprotected.'

'Sir Eleanor, would you give me your arm?' asked Egda. 'Sir Odo, would you take care to listen, and come should I call for aid?'

'Yes, sir!' said Odo and Eleanor together.

'You see,' said Egda to the frowning Hundred, 'I have two knights to guard me. Come, let us be about our business!'

He strode off confidently towards the inn, tapping once more with his staff and hardly holding Eleanor's crooked arm at all. Odo stared after him. When he looked back to see what Hundred was doing, he was surprised to find himself alone. In just a few seconds, the elderly warrior had disappeared from the middle of the green!

TWO

'Sire, the good villagers of Lenburh are assembled.'

Hundred's soft voice broke the breath that Eleanor had been holding as she waited for Sir Halfdan's burial rites to begin. The knight's body had rested all night in the manor house's great hall, wrapped in his best cloak with his shield across his chest and his sword at his side. Eleanor had volunteered to sit with him, and Odo had joined her, relieving her at the old knight's side when she grew tired. The two times she slept, she dreamed of her mother, who had once lain in that very spot. It seemed an age ago.

Now it was Sir Halfdan's turn. Reeve Gorbold relinquished his position at the head of the funerary procession to Sir Egda and joined the others bearing the body. Even though he was already one of the strongest villagers in Lenburh, Odo suppressed a grunt of effort as they raised Sir Halfdan high. What the old knight had lacked in a complete set of legs he had more than made up for in girth.

A lonely bell tolled as the solemn procession made down

the hill to Sir Halfdan's family crypt, past the small fenced-off area of the estate where Eleanor's mother was buried.

Eleanor wondered if she would join her mother there one day. Someone would need to assume the mantle of Sir Halfdan's estate, and Odo was the most likely to settle here when he attained his majority. Eleanor herself would prefer to be adventuring and seeing the world.

Deep in these thoughts, Eleanor walked into Hundred's back as the procession came to a halt. The bodyguard clicked her tongue.

'Brave in heart,' said Sir Egda, tapping one end of his staff softly against the earth, 'and noble in death, we farewell this good knight and remember his deeds.'

He stood aside to let Sir Halfdan's bearers into the darkness of the crypt itself, to the stone plinth that had long ago been prepared by Borden, Sir Halfdan's loyal squire, who had gone to his own grave earlier that day. Odo stooped to avoid banging his head, and tried to ignore the stories he'd heard about carnivorous barrow bats inhabiting such places. He had avoided asking Biter if they were real, in case it turned out that they were. When his hauberk snagged on the sculpted foot of a knight's effigy protruding from another plinth, he freed himself with a quick tug and a reminder to concentrate on moving quickly but respectfully. Being a funeral bearer was a great responsibility.

Ahead of him, holding Sir Halfdan's foot, Symon turned

and bent forward. Odo followed, and together the bearers settled the fallen knight on his final resting place.

When that was done, Odo stepped back and bowed.

Outside, Runnel twitched. Eleanor drew her from her scabbard, raising the sword in sad salute. A grey light shimmered along the blade, reflections from the cloudy sky.

'Be at peace, knight of Lenburh,' said the blind old man. He turned and tapped the way to the village hall, following the sound of the bell. The villagers followed him, grim-faced. They had much to discuss.

'Our lands cannot stand unprotected!' cried Gladwine, whose sheep grazed the southeast meadows. 'Without a steward, we are vulnerable to any passing thief or brigand!'

'How will we find a new one?' demanded Leof the woodworker.

'Who will guard us?' went up the cry from several people.

'Not these *children*,' scowled Elmer, Addyson and Aaric's father. His sharp eyes took in Eleanor and Odo where they sat to either side of Egda and Hundred at the front of the hall.

'We'd do a better job than a baker,' muttered Eleanor, resenting the implication that they wouldn't be good enough. They were knights. They had fought serious enemies and had stared down a real, live dragon – or at least they'd survived an encounter with one, which was more than most people could say, Elmer included.

'I have sent word by pigeon to Winterset,' said Symon across the restless crowd's murmuring. 'My colleagues in the capital will report to the regent, who will appoint the next steward.'

'How long will that take?' asked Swithe the leatherworker, who had wanted to skin the bilewolves before burning but found the hides too foul-smelling for any purpose. 'What if more of those terrible creatures come?'

'There will be no more,' said Hundred in a clear and steady voice. 'I traced the pack's spoor to a hollow where a craft-fire recently burned. This fire was lit to summon the bilewolves and send them against my liege.'

This was news to Odo, who struggled to keep the shock from his face. Someone had *deliberately* called the beasts that had killed four of his fellow villagers? As well as Sir Halfdan and squire Bordan, Lenburh had lost Halthor, an apprentice smith, and Alia, who had moved from Enedham last year to look after her sick aunt.

A flame of sudden rage burned in his chest. 'Can we track the person who lit the fire?' he asked in a pinched voice. 'They must be brought to justice.'

'They will be long gone from here by now,' Hundred said with finality. 'Our best hope of finding them is to wait until they try again.'

'We'll be ready when they do,' said Eleanor, patting Runnel's hilt. The swords had stayed silent during the meeting, knowing that some in the village were still unnerved by their enchanted nature.

Elmer snorted. Egda's beaked nose swivelled to point directly at him. The baker swallowed whatever further comments about the young knights' competence he might have offered.

'You will be ready,' Egda said, 'and Lenburh will be safe, for I am leaving at tomorrow's dawn.'

A gasp rose up from all assembled. Only Hundred was unsurprised.

'So soon, sire?' asked Reeve Gorbold, whom Odo had overheard making plans to profit from Egda's presence by charging villagers in the area a halfpenny to see the former king in his new home.

'Word of trouble in the capital reached me in my self-imposed exile,' Egda said. 'Winterset is my destination. Besides, I cannot remain here and put innocent lives at risk. Better to continue on my journey north and east and cut the source of our troubles from the kingdom once and for all.'

Eleanor felt a stirring of excitement in her gut. After a month of waiting for something to happen, an adventure had come right to her doorstep.

'We must accompany you, sire,' she said, leaping to her feet and drawing Runnel in one swift movement. 'We will be your honour guard!'

'If you would have us,' said Odo, doing the same, but more cautiously. Biter clashed against his sister's steel with a ringing chime over Egda's head. 'We do not wish to impose.'

A flicker passed across Hundred's face. Was it a smile? If so, was it of gratitude or amusement?

'My liege needs no honour guard,' she said. 'He has me, and we travel fast and light into unknown danger –'

'That's why you need us,' Eleanor insisted. 'Because it's unknown.'

'Numbers are no substitute for experience, knightling.'

Eleanor ground her teeth. Were they always to come unstuck on this point? 'But there's only one way to gain experience, and if you won't let us –'

'Your place is in Lenburh,' Egda pronounced. 'I must return to Winterset and see what my great-nephew Kendryk has wrought.'

Odo frowned over this piece of information, wondering at its import. If the old king was displeased with his heir and tried to take back the throne, could that lead to unrest in the court, perhaps even civil war? Tofte had been peaceful for many generations, all the way back to King Mildred the Marvellous. The thought of villager fighting villager again was a terrible one.

That was reason enough to accompany Egda, to ensure no trouble came to the young Prince Kendryk. After all, Odo and Eleanor ultimately owed their fealty to him, the heir to the throne, not to Egda or even to their home . . .

Before Eleanor, following the same reasoning, could find

a diplomatic way to press for their inclusion in the party journeying to the nation's capital, a horn sounded outside the guildhall, then a rapid patter of running feet came near. The doors burst open.

'Strangers!' cried a wide-eyed lad half Odo's age. 'Lots and lots and lots of them, on horses!'

'*More* strangers?' gasped Reeve Gorbold. 'What are the odds of that?'

'Very small, I hazard to say,' said Symon with a thoughtful expression. 'Lenburh has never seen such a flood.'

A babble of speculation rippled through the gathering, and Egda rapped the end of his staff against the floorboards for silence.

'Reeve Gorbold, perhaps you should invite them in.'

'But name no names,' warned Hundred. 'We are not here.'

'Of course, sire, uh, madam, of course.' The reeve bowed in confusion and hurried from the hall.

Odo and Eleanor exchanged a glance and followed as fast as their armour allowed, holding their swords at the ready.

'What if it's the people who sent the bilewolves?' Odo whispered at Eleanor's back.

'I don't hear any howling or snarling, do you?' she cast over her shoulder.

'𝔚𝔢 𝔞𝔯𝔢 𝔞 𝔪𝔞𝔱𝔠𝔥 𝔣𝔬𝔯 𝔞𝔫𝔶 𝔟𝔢𝔞𝔰𝔱!' Biter declared.

'𝔅𝔢 𝔴𝔞𝔯𝔶, 𝔩𝔦𝔱𝔱𝔩𝔢 𝔟𝔯𝔬𝔱𝔥𝔢𝔯,' Runnel cautioned. '𝔖𝔬𝔪𝔢𝔬𝔫𝔢 𝔴𝔦𝔱𝔥 𝔱𝔥𝔢 𝔰𝔨𝔦𝔩𝔩 𝔱𝔬 𝔩𝔦𝔤𝔥𝔱 𝔞 𝔠𝔯𝔞𝔣𝔱-𝔣𝔦𝔯𝔢 𝔦𝔰 𝔞 𝔴𝔬𝔯𝔱𝔥𝔶 𝔣𝔬𝔢. 𝔑𝔬𝔱 𝔱𝔬 mention the person who commands them.'

Eleanor gripped her sword tightly and hurried out into the light, where she came face-to-bridle with a band of some eight travellers on horseback, all sporting the royal seal on their breasts – a blue shield, quartered, with a silver sword, a black anvil, a red flame, and a golden dragon, one in each segment. All the new arrivals were armed, although none had unsheathed a weapon. At their head rode a tall, thin man wearing an unfamiliar red uniform with silver piping, topped by a wide-brimmed cloth hat, which he raised on seeing the reeve's chain of office, and then again for the two young knights.

'Well met, bereaved citizens of Lenburh,' he said, holding the hat now at his chest, revealing a pate of fine, white hair, brushed in a spiral descending from the top of his head. 'Rest your troubled hearts, for I have come to give you ease.'

'And you are?' Reeve Gorbold asked.

'Instrument Sceam,' said the man with a brisk bow from his waist.

'Your name is "Instrument"?' Eleanor repeated in puzzlement.

'Instrument is my title. I have been sent to assume the mantle of responsibility so recently vacated by Sir Halfdan.'

'Sent by whom?' bristled the reeve.

'By the regent, of course,' said Sceam with another bow.

'So you're to be our steward?' Odo asked.

'Not steward,' the man said. 'Instrument. Of the crown.'

'But we don't know you,' said Eleanor.

'That hardly matters, does it?'

Reeve Gorbold straightened with a sniff. 'Only people whose families have lived in Lenburh five generations can be stewards. That's the rule.'

'The rule has changed. May I come in and explain?'

'You'd better, I suppose. Your horses will be attended to.'

'My thanks, Reeve Gorbold.'

'You know my name?'

'And those of your young companions also – Sir Odo and Sir Eleanor. I know everything about you.'

'But . . . how? What are you *doing* here?'

Instrument Sceam dropped lightly to the ground and produced a rolled-up parchment from one pocket. It was crumpled and stained brown at one end, as though by blood.

'Why, I received your note.'

The message-carrying pigeon informing the capital of Sir Halfdan's death had travelled only as far as Trumness, a town on the mountain road east of Ablerhyll. There it had caught the attention of one of Instrument Sceam's companions, a keen-eyed archer, and been immediately shot down.

'You shot,' Reeve Gorbold spluttered, 'my pigeon?'

'Of course,' Sceam replied.

'But . . . *why?*'

'It was white.'

'So?'

'White pigeons are no longer authorised to carry messages to Winterset. Only the speckled variety. This is another of the many changes I have been sent to inform you about.'

'What are these changes, exactly?' asked Symon.

'Well . . .' Instrument Sceam placed his hands on his knees and scanned the crowd. He was seated in the place Egda had occupied a moment ago, alone on the raised dais. The former king was wearing a hood that covered the upper half of his face and standing well at the back. Eleanor recognised his nose and the stubborn jut of his jaw, but only because she was looking for it.

Of Hundred there was no sign at all.

'The pigeons, for one.' Sceam was happy to have their full attention and showed little sign of letting it go. 'All communication with the capital is now limited to official channels, from Instruments such as myself to the Adjustors and the Regulators, who take the messages to the highest level. I have cages of the speckled breed in my baggage for that very purpose. They are not to be used without my express permission.'

'Let me see if I understand this correctly,' said Symon. 'Instruments report to the Adjustors.'

'Yes.'

'And Adjustors report to the Regulators.'

'Yes.'

'To whom do Regulators report?'

'To the regent.'

'And the regent – Odelyn – reports to Prince Kendryk, the heir?'

'Why, yes, of course. It is only proper that the regent keeps young Prince Kendryk informed for . . . ee . . . educational reasons at the least.'

Sceam's smile was wide and seemingly sincere, although there was something in his eyes that made Eleanor's hackles rise. Perhaps it was the familiar way he referred to the regent, the old king's sister, and the dismissive tone he used for her grandson, the young heir who had not yet been crowned.

Or perhaps it was something more immediate.

'Where do knights fit in?' Eleanor asked.

'Ah. As traditional stewards of the estates of Tofte, these honoured individuals will of course be found a role in the new system.'

'What kind of role?'

'It's not my place to say. Something ceremonial, I imagine, such as standing by doorways in the capital to make them look more regal. You will be told in due course.'

Odo felt Biter stirring in his scabbard in response to the word *ceremonial*. No sword wanted to end up on display, doing nothing but growing dull with time and dust. No knight either.

'There must be some kind of mistake,' Odo started to say, but was cut off by a frail-seeming but penetrating voice from the back of the room.

'Forgive me, I am an old, blind man, and hard of hearing to boot . . . This new system I believe I heard you speak of . . . is it the work of Prince Kendryk himself?'

'Of course,' Sceam said, not recognising his interlocutor. 'The regent made the announcement on his behalf three months ago. Implementation throughout the kingdom is well under way, although outlying regions such as this one are naturally behind schedule. We will soon make that up, now I that am here!'

The Instrument clapped his hands in eagerness to get started.

'My collectors will move among you over the coming week,' he declared, 'collecting this month's tithe.'

'But Sir Halfdan paid the crown just *last* week!' spluttered Reeve Gorbold.

'I'm afraid there's no record of that in the capital,' Sceam said. 'Also, from this month, tithes will increase by five silver pennies per household.'

'What?!' the reeve exclaimed, but he was far from the only person in the room to think it.

'To cover the costs of instituting the new system. Prosperity has its price!'

'This is preposterous –'

'It is *progress*, Reeve Gorbold. Now, I am weary. I will retire to the manor house to rest. No need to show me. I know the way.'

With that, he stood and pressed through the dumbfounded crowd, flanked by two of his well-armed aides. Eleanor went to step into his path, unwilling to let the matter of this 'new system' go so readily. She hadn't spent her whole life dreaming of being a knight only to end up standing around in a doorway holding a pike!

Before she could take half a step, however, a small but very strong hand gripped her elbow.

'Discretion,' whispered Hundred into Eleanor's ear, 'is our best stratagem at this time.'

Eleanor frowned at the old woman. How would saying nothing be of any use to anyone?

'We will talk around the back,' Hundred reassured her, nodding to where Odo was being led off by Symon, with Egda bringing up a close rear.

Under cover of Sceam's departure, the five of them slipped from the guildhall by the tradespersons' door.

CHAPTER
THREE

'This cannot stand,' said Egda.

'*Never has a truer word been spoken!*' exclaimed Biter, lunging out of Odo's scabbard and flashing about the smithy in which they huddled, well out of earshot of Sceam and his cronies. The furnace was cold out of respect for the dead apprentice. '*My siege, let us slay the upstarts while they rest, before their unrighteous hold on the estate is established!*'

Odo expected the former king to scold Biter for being too rash, as Odo himself always did, but he was surprised.

'Yes, Biter, I believe you are half right, at least.' Egda leaned on his staff, looking all his years but no less determined. 'Slaying should not be necessary, but it is time for direct action.'

'Sire,' said Hundred, 'you must not openly declare yourself.'

'That would be unwise,' Symon agreed. 'If the crown is truly behind this strange new system –'

'It is not Kendryk,' Egda interrupted with surprising venom. 'This must be the regent's doing. Odelyn was ever ambitious. I hoped she would be true, but it is clear she is loyal to nothing other than her own desires and ambition.

'Kendryk's coronation has been delayed long past his turning sixteen, and treacherous efforts have been made to keep this news from me, and from all at the Temple of Midnight where I formerly made my home. Now I must help Kendryk claim his proper birthright. Odelyn cannot prevail against both of us.'

'If it is not too late,' observed Hundred. 'We have perhaps tarried here too long already.'

'You can't leave us with Sceam, that . . .' Eleanor fought for a fittingly cutting phrase. '. . . that slimy cumberwold!'

'We will not,' Egda promised her, reaching out to pat her shoulder. 'He will be dealt with tonight, once the moon has set.'

'𝕯𝔬 𝔶𝔬𝔲 𝔥𝔞𝔳𝔢 𝔞 𝔭𝔩𝔞𝔫, 𝔰𝔦𝔯𝔢?' asked Runnel, standing point-down at Eleanor's side, her ruby gleaming a soft bloodred. '𝔐𝔬𝔯𝔢 𝔡𝔢𝔱𝔞𝔦𝔩𝔢𝔡 𝔱𝔥𝔞𝔫 𝔪𝔶 𝔟𝔯𝔬𝔱𝔥𝔢𝔯'𝔰, 𝕴 𝔪𝔢𝔞𝔫.'

'I do. We need six able-bodied volunteers. Master Symon, can you enlist them to our cause?'

Eleanor's father nodded. 'I could find a dozen without taking as many steps.'

'Very good. Light footfalls would be valuable also.'

'Understood, sire.'

'Hundred? Settle on a rendezvous point while I address our knights and their swords.'

Egda turned to Odo and Eleanor as Symon and Hundred conversed in hushed voices.

'Sir Odo, Sir Eleanor: tonight, we fight for Lenburh, as you have fought bravely once already. I have no compunction concerning your courage when called upon to act in the teeth of the moment, but with forethought . . . and in consideration of your tender age . . . I wonder if you might prefer to watch this battle from the gallery.'

'Not fight with you?' Eleanor couldn't believe what she was hearing. 'Don't be mad – I mean . . . sorry, sire . . . but we're knights, not shirkers!'

'Our place is by your side,' Odo agreed with a vigorous nod.

'It is kind of you to worry, sire,' said Runnel. 'Although they may be young, Odo and Eleanor have drawn blood against beasts with two legs as well as four.'

'The dragon Quenwulf herself decreed them knights in truth,' agreed Biter, sweeping back into Odo's hand and lifting his arm in a salute. 'We are your eager servants!'

Egda nodded, the corners of his lips turning up in a smile. 'It seems I have little choice in the matter. Against noble hearts, one rarely does. You will follow Hundred's lead as we advance together on the manor house. Together, we will do what must be done – and quickly, ere Instrument Sceam and his lackeys recover from their long journey. Those who break the rules of chivalry do not deserve chivalry in return.'

He paused, then added, 'We must refrain from killing

anyone, if we can. They are in some sense servants of the crown, and though greedy varlets, they do not deserve to die.'

At sun's fall, Eleanor's father and the others gathered behind a hedge near the Dry Well. Hundred kept watch as Symon made introductions. He had brought along the six largest men and women in Lenburh, Odo's mother and the baker among them, all with their staves. Odo wondered at Elmer being there, but decided that against a common enemy, all were united. Besides, the baker was as strong as Odo from carrying sacks of flour.

'Sir Odo, Sir Eleanor, Hundred and myself will lead the assault,' Egda explained. 'We will enter from the rear, subduing and restraining any guards we find. You have your lengths of rope, Eleanor, Odo? Good. Symon, you and your stout allies will take positions in the grounds to ensure all exits are sealed from within and without. Reinforcements must be stalled, and none must escape to spread the word of what happens here. Remember, knock them down, but refrain from killing if you can.'

'Understood, sire,' said Symon.

'Four against seven?' said Elmer. He had the good grace not to add, 'one of them blind and two of them children?' which Eleanor gave him credit for. 'What if you run into trouble?'

'Then your aid will be invaluable. Listen for Hundred's horn. If you hear it, come running.'

'Aye, sire.'

Symon daubed his face black with charcoal to better hide in the darkness, and in a few moments he had attended to the others.

Hundred returned. 'All clear,' she whispered, her breath little more than a breeze in the night.

'Very well,' said Egda. 'We begin.'

Biter and Runnel slipped silently from their sheaths and joined their knights in readiness. As Symon and his six strong-arms slid off into the darkness, Hundred took the lead, moving in a rapid crouch towards the estate. Odo followed, watching his tread carefully to avoid dry twigs. Eleanor came after him, nearly as quiet as Hundred, and behind her, last of all, Egda, moving with confident stealth, his hood tugged low over his face, well used to the darkness that impeded the others.

An owl called 'Who!' as the four humans passed beneath her branch. Swivelling her head from side to side in case their footfalls disturbed any cowering mice, she suddenly froze, then launched with deadly speed into the air. An instant later there came a tiny, short-lived squeak, and she flew to her favourite perch to eat her first snack of the evening.

There was a guard posted to the rear of the manor house, a long-limbed woman who had nodded off with her chin propped up on the cross-bar of her boar spear. Eleanor looked around for Hundred, but she had disappeared.

Seconds later she darted out of the trees and brought the guard down with one hand across her mouth and a forearm tight against her throat.

The guard struggled for a minute, then fell unconscious. Odo and Eleanor bound her limbs while Egda tied a gag across her mouth. Hundred took the boar spear and the guard's dagger away and hid them in the bushes.

'Gag, bind, remove weapons,' she whispered.

Odo and Eleanor nodded. Hundred made it look easy, but both knew it wouldn't be. Odo felt Biter shift in his hand, and held the sword tighter. Biter might well need to be restrained from delivering killing blows.

With all the sound of a shadow, Hundred opened the door and eased inside.

Eleanor went next, wishing her mail didn't make so much noise. Odo could hear nothing over the sound of snoring that issued from the interior of the manor. The main hall, it quickly became clear, had been taken over by Sceam's entourage. Six sleeping figures sprawled on their bedrolls, lit by flickering candles and the remains of a fire. Sceam was the closest to the warmth, curled into a ball.

Odo tallied up the numbers and concluded that there must be another guard at the front door.

Hundred held a finger to her lips and tiptoed among the sleeping figures, removing weapons from their owners with the dexterity of a pickpocket. The collection of daggers and swords she quickly accumulated went behind a tapestry that lapped down to the flagstones behind the front door.

Then she pointed Odo at one guard, Eleanor at another, and made a clicking noise with her tongue next to a third, which Egda followed to position himself close to that sleeper. They all sheathed their weapons and readied lengths of rope.

With everyone in position, Hundred held up three fingers, closed one, then another, and then, with the last, suddenly seized the sleeper in front of her as the others did the same to theirs, swiftly trussing them up like livestock, wrists tied to ankles.

This was done so quickly that by the time their confused shouts had woken the last two guards, Odo and Hundred had already finished their first lot and were onto them. One guard sprang up with a dagger, but Hundred gripped his wrist and twisted his arm until he shrieked and fell to his knees, dropping the weapon. Odo simply clapped the one who came at him on the shoulder blade, sending him straight back down again. Both were tied up in a moment, as Eleanor and Egda closed in on Sceam, who had got wrapped up in his cloak and was struggling to free himself.

Eleanor bent down and pulled the cloak away. Sceam's head popped out, his expression outraged.

'How dare you! Guards! Guards!'

The front door burst in, admitting the single remaining

guard. But Odo and Hundred were ready. Hundred tripped the guard and Odo fell on him, one knee pinning him to the ground as Hundred removed his sword and they both tied him up.

'You can't do this!' screeched Sceam. 'I am an Instrument of the Crown!'

Hundred drew a shining leaf-shaped blade and held it up in front of the Instrument, moving the knife slowly back and forth.

'Who . . . who are you?' asked Sceam nervously, his eyes following the glint of the blade. 'What do you want?'

'Remind him who you are, Sir Odo, Sir Eleanor,' Egda said.

'We're the knights of Lenburh,' said Eleanor, drawing herself up to her full height. Possibly this was less impressive than she intended, as she was shorter than Sceam.

'And we don't take kindly to being told we're no longer needed,' added Odo.

'D-did I say that?' Sceam said, nearly babbling. 'I'm s-sorry I gave you that impression —'

'*Ceremonial, you said.*' Biter leaped out of his scabbard, evading Odo's attempt to grab him. The sword swung in a lethal arc until his tip pointed directly at the Instrument's fast-beating heart. '*The word leaves little room for ambiguity.*'

Sceam's eyes widened at the sword's short speech, but he seemed less afraid of the sword than he was of Hundred. His sharp eyes had spotted that his guards were tied up, rather than lying dead. Clearly his enemies were afraid of doing any real damage to persons of his importance.

'You don't know what you're dealing with,' he spat. 'The times are changing, and you can't fight it – not with steel or spells or other old-fashioned notions. This is the age of opportunity, where anyone can rise, regardless of birth or wealth. Stand in our way and you will be trampled.'

'Is that what Regent Odelyn tells you?' Egda asked. 'Her age of opportunity applies only to herself. And she does not have the right to do what she has done.'

'Bah!' Sceam tried to sit up straighter, but quailed back as Biter shivered in front of him. 'The regent has done only what *must* be done! Prince Kendryk is weak. He is not fit to rule. His hours are spent in the palace, idly doodling. The boy has lost his mind! The regent does not want power for herself, but to take it away from a madman for the good of the people –'

'Take it away?' Egda interrupted. 'Do you mean Odelyn intends to crown herself? To be king and not just regent?'

'The prince is unfit to rule,' said Sceam sullenly. 'The king – *Regent* Odelyn – is doing only what is necessary. Now, you yokels have had your fun. Regulator Ardrahei has twenty . . . no, *fifty* guards with him, and if he doesn't receive a pigeon from me soon after dawn, he'll come looking, and then you'll all be locked up in irons! If you disperse now, I will be merciful. Go!'

No one moved.

'You think you've won,' snarled Sceam. 'You are wrong. Regulator Ardrahei and the regent will hear of what has happened here –'

'That I doubt very much,' said Egda. 'And even if they do, they will simply know what happens to people who ignore the ancient customs.'

'Regulator Ardrahei will come, with his *eighty guards* –'

'And we will fight them. The four of us, who dealt so easily with the eight of you.' Egda gestured with one hand, encompassing the roped-up fighters. 'Have no fear on our account. Hundred? It is time.'

The woman nodded and drew out a small gold-banded horn and sounded it, its harsh call echoing through the hall and beyond.

A minute later, Symon and the other six burst into the manor through the front and back.

'What is this?' Elmer asked, looking about him in confusion at the disarmed men and women tied up on the floor. 'Where's the fight?'

'Temporarily delayed,' Hundred told him.

'Take this man to the lockup,' Egda instructed the baker. 'He's to be treated well but denied access to writing materials and pigeons, be they speckled or otherwise. Lock the others in with him. Keep them there until you receive word from Winterset. Hundred, give them a gold noble for the prisoners' upkeep.'

'No need on that score,' Elmer said, taking a protesting Sceam about the collar and lifting him with strong arms. 'I think I have some mouldy loaves left from last week, perhaps a pot of rancid butter or two . . .'

'Does this mean you're our new steward, sire?' asked Odo's mother, with a surprisingly humble tug at her forelock.

Egda inclined his head in regret. 'You do me a great honour . . . but I think Master Symon would fit the role better than I.'

'Me, sire?' Symon looked momentarily startled, then bowed deeply. 'Until the prince is crowned king and appoints a proper replacement for Sir Halfdan, I will serve . . . if the others will have me.'

'Aye,' said Elmer. 'You'll do. You're fair, even if you do think too much.'

That was as close to a compliment as the baker ever came, and Eleanor was amazed to hear it. Symon bowed again, and Elmer dragged Sceam out of the manor and down the hill, shaking him all the way. Odo's mother and the rest retied the Instrument's crestfallen guards into a hobbled line and quickly followed, encouraging them with taps from their staves.

When they were gone, Symon turned to Egda with a wry smile.

'You never had any intention of us fighting, did you, sire?'

The former king swept back his hood and straightened

it. 'No. I merely wished to see if people would follow you. And they did. Therefore, you would make a good steward. I would appoint you permanently were it my place to.'

Eleanor beamed in pride. Her father, acting steward of Lenburh!

'What next?' asked Odo. 'First the bilewolves, and then this lot –'

'They are not necessarily connected,' said Hundred.

'Perhaps,' said Egda. 'Although I suspect both actions do arise from the same source.'

Hundred nodded thoughtfully, then turned back to the others. 'My liege and I passed through Lenburh only because it's on the river road, so we might have missed Sceam entirely if the master of the bilewolves had chosen a different moment to make their move. A mixture of fortunes for both of us.'

'I hope that rescuing you from one problem makes up for bringing another to your door,' said Egda.

'Think nothing of it,' said Symon. 'If we can be of assistance, you have but to ask.'

'I beg only for provisions,' said the former king. 'My intention remains to leave at dawn.'

Dawn! Eleanor sensed an opportunity slipping through her fingers. She couldn't bear the thought of just wishing for adventure, as she had been only yesterday, instead of having one.

'You must let us come with you!' she exclaimed. 'Especially

now you know it's probably the regent who sent the bilewolves. You need us to protect you!'

'Eleanor is right,' said Odo heavily. He really didn't want to leave Lenburh again, not so soon. He could tell from Eleanor's shining eyes she was looking forward to adventure, where he only felt the weight of responsibility. But like stacking sacks of flour at the mill, this was an essential task that wouldn't just happen, and more hands made lighter and safer work. 'We can't let you go on your own.'

'With two knights,' said Symon, 'and two enchanted swords, you would better your odds against the prince's adversaries.'

'What about your daughter's safety?' Egda asked him. 'By helping you restore peace to the kingdom, she will ensure that she has a home to return to. The same goes for Odo and his parents too.'

'You are wise, Steward Symon,' said Egda, with a gracious nod at the two young knights. 'Now that I know you two follow orders as bravely as you rush into battle, I would be grateful to you both if you will join me on this quest as cadets in the royal – no, I suppose I must call it the former king's guard.'

Eleanor gaped in surprise, momentarily lost for words. She had expected an argument, but it turned out the old man had been one step ahead of everyone again . . .

'Sire, it will be an honour,' said Odo with a quick bow to cover his feelings of apprehension. He wasn't frightened of any adversaries he might meet along the way, but being thrust into the world of Winterset and the court was daunting. Sir Halfdan's original promise to take them there had dragged on until it seemed likely never to happen. Now it was about to become a reality, and he didn't feel ready to leave his home.

'On foot, it will take a month or more to reach the capital,' said Symon. 'You should take the horses – two each, plus two for baggage. Sceam won't be needing them.'

'And you will send the speckled pigeons to Winterset,' said Hundred, 'with false reports that Sceam is securely installed?'

'Of course. That will gain you some time.' Symon took Eleanor in a quick embrace and nodded at Odo over her shoulder. 'Travel safely and fight well. Remember what Quenwulf told you.'

'Knights be true,' she said, nodding. 'And swords . . . ?'

Biter flew out of Odo's hand. '𝔇o not grow rusty!'

'𝔍n min𝔡 or steel!' Runnel finished in more measured tones.

FOUR

Dragon, dragon, heed our call . . .

From within the uppermost spire of Winterset Castle came the sound of a young man humming.

Come to aid us, one and all . . .

'I know that tune,' said the young man's grandmother. 'Don't think I don't know what you're singing in here.'

The young man paused at his work, concentration broken. A long shadow reached across the wall in front of him, a silhouette anyone in Tofte would recognise, thanks to its nose. Proud and angular, it had graced kings of Tofte for three hundred years. She had it, her brother had had it, and the young man had it too.

He looked down at his crimson-spattered hands and attempted to gather his thoughts. If he could just complete the next section of his mural by nightfall, his mind would feel so much more at ease.

Dragon, dragon, heed our call . . .

His beaky-nosed grandmother had other ideas.

'I've just come from the Privy Council,' she said, her voice smug. 'They've voted unanimously to put off the coronation indefinitely.'

She paused, her mouth curving back into a smile, before continuing.

'*Your* coronation, that is. However, the *next* coronation has been brought forward and will take place in three days. Mine, that is. Can't leave the kingdom without a proper ruler any longer. I will be king. How does that make you feel?'

Prince Kendryk hung his head. Red was plastered all down the front of what had once been an extremely fine robe featuring a tiny, recurring motif of the royal seal. Now it was stiff and, frankly, not terribly comfortable. He kept it on though. Clothes were much harder to do without than sandals. His last pair had worn out and he had given up asking for them to be replaced. His grandmother enjoyed enforcing such petty deprivations.

'Leave me alone, Grandmother,' he said. 'I'm busy.'

'Ah, it speaks. I was beginning to wonder if you'd forgotten how.'

'I have nothing to say to you.'

'But you'll sing that nonsense children's song in the hope that the old fool will come rescue you – the one who left a baby heir behind in swaddling clothes because he lost his nerve? I know that's what you're doing: "Old Dragon" nonsense. I think he was always more of a lizard, my oh-so-great brother

Egda. I suppose he couldn't bear the thought of people calling him "Old *Blind* Dragon" . . . old *fool*, more like –'

Prince Kendryk closed his eyes and concentrated to block out her rant. The song was his lifeline, a shining thread leading to a future where he was no longer badgered by the woman who had driven his mother to an early grave and would be only too happy to see him in his.

Dragon, dragon, heed our call . . .

'Pah,' she exclaimed. 'You're as mad as they say you are if you think a song will bring that sightless dullard here. And if it did, what could he do? He's blind and useless. Probably dead now, for all we know. A sudden attack of bilewolves, perhaps . . .'

She smiled again, waiting briefly for a response that never came, then walked away with a snap of her fingers for her shadow and chief servant, a black-haired man who did the regent's every bidding with a smile that was too wide for any sane person's liking. A massive sword hung at his waist, brutal and cruel, with an empty setting where a gem had once been fastened.

'Let us leave this half-wit to his idle pastimes, Lord Deor. We have important affairs of state to attend to.'

'Yes, Your Highness.'

'Grandmother?'

She stopped and turned, her heels squeaking on stone.

'Yes, Kendryk? You've changed your mind? You will

officially abdicate and resign any claim to the throne? It isn't necessary, of course, but it would be . . . convenient.'

The young prince tilted his head back and pointed into the uppermost gloom of the spire.

'There are bats up there,' he said. 'I hear them squeaking.'

'What of it?'

'They're trapped. I would like the porters to open a shutter or two so they can escape.'

'And why should I do that?'

'Maybe I will sign the paper. If the bats are freed.'

'Bats and daubing paint! I should put you in a cage and hang it from the city gates so everyone can see your idiocy!'

Muttering irritably, the regent stomped off, slamming the door behind her.

Prince Kendryk lowered his gaze to the wall in front of him. The mural was incomplete, but he was free to resume now. He had made great progress in recent months. The end was at last in sight. Perhaps a week and it would be done, if he wasn't interrupted again.

Stooping to place both hands in the bucket of red paint, he began once more to daub thick lines on the ancient black stone of Winterset, humming all the while.

Dragon, dragon, heed our call.

Come to aid us, one and all.

Half an hour later, as the city bells tolled seven, he paused briefly, hearing the slow grind of the shutters opening overhead. The bats were being set free.

That meant his grandmother did need him to sign the abdication papers, no matter what she said.

But he wouldn't, Kendryk told himself. He wouldn't do anything she wanted. He turned back to his painting.

From a cruel and dreadful fate,
Save us now, ere it's too late.

CHAPTER
FIVE

Both Odo and Eleanor had ridden horses on occasion, usually farmer Gladwine's old nag Pudding, who had a good nature provided there were plenty of apples on offer.

Never in their lives had they ridden like this, on fine riding horses, leading fresh remounts.

Both were weary, having slept restlessly, albeit for very different reasons. Odo had tossed and turned, imagining the many obstacles that might stand between Lenburh and Winterset, until eventually his two nearest older brothers begged him to get out of bed and leave them to their rest. As a result, at dawn he had not just been packed and ready, but the earliest to arrive at the rendezvous point by the stump of Lightning Tree, and thus gained the first choice of mount.

Eleanor's restless night had come from imagining the very same things as Odo, only to her they were not obstacles but opportunities. She imagined herself following in her mother's footsteps, battling monsters, defeating villains, and gathering more fame and glory with every mile. The simple act of seating herself a-horse made her feel very grand, which was a good start.

At Hundred's cry of 'Let us hie hence!' they set out from Lenburh along the river road, heading north, alternating between a steady canter and a walk. None of them was wearing armour; this, plus sufficient supplies for one week, was carried by the two baggage horses. When the steeds they rode grew tired, they would swap to those that ran unburdened alongside them. That way they would make maximum progress without dangerously exhausting any of the animals.

The road was good and the weather fair. In the slower stretches, Egda asked them about Quenwulf, and they told him the story with only occasional theatrical interruption from Biter. With astonishing speed, they came to the turnoff to Ablerhyll Road and followed it northwest, into territory Eleanor and Odo hadn't visited before. Near a small hamlet called Gistern, they stopped at a swift-flowing brook to stretch their legs and water the horses. Odo's thighs ached; he wasn't used to riding and tended to grip too hard with his legs. Eleanor had an easier time of it, being both more practised and lighter. Hundred gave her the task of changing the saddles and checking the packs containing their armour and supplies. Nothing appeared to be loose, but it still had to be done.

As Odo stretched his aching legs, he studied Egda. The

old man had a new, tense set to his jaw, and he stood alone, facing silently back the way they had come. He looked regretful, almost angry.

'Is Egda all right?' Odo whispered to Hundred. 'Does he think we've left something behind?'

'Only ghosts,' she said, not looking at him.

Odo glanced at Eleanor, but she hadn't heard. Then he looked back at Hundred. Did she mean actual ghosts? he wondered. Surely not . . .

Soon they were up and riding again, and so it continued until dusk, when they halted for the night. This time both young knights were given chores to perform as they made camp in a tidy copse bordered by blackberry bushes. They brushed down the horses and gave them feed, then lit a fire, caught two rabbits, dug a necessary trench and made dinner.

The meal left them feeling heavy and sleepy, but there were more tasks to perform. Bedrolls had to be laid out, dirty clothes aired and checked for fleas and other unwanted passengers. Neither Odo nor Eleanor had gone to such lengths on their one other epic journey; former kings clearly required better treatment.

'Who cares about the best way to lay out a blanket?' Eleanor muttered under her breath. 'We're knights, not inn servants. We should be practising swordplay!'

'The best knights are humble and consider no skill beneath them,' Runnel chastised her. 'For instance, Sir Hollis, my

47

first knight, was an excellent carpenter. Sir Faline could cook to make a gourmand weep, and Sir Treddian's stitches were ever tiny and neat –'

'You're not helping, Runnel,' Eleanor complained.

Biter made a rasping noise that Odo had learned to equate with clearing his throat. 'I hate to disagree with my more experienced sister –'

'Really?' said Runnel. 'That's never stopped you.'

'But I do feel that Sir Eleanor raises an excellent point. Our knights have much yet to learn. How are we to teach them when every waking moment is taken up with chores?'

'Being a knight isn't all about fighting,' Odo said. In fact, in his opinion, the less fighting, the better.

'No, but we have to be ready to fight when we need to,' Eleanor grumbled. 'Sometimes I really think we got the wrong swords . . .'

When it was finally time to settle in for the night, they found Egda in his bedroll with Hundred keeping watch nearby, patiently sharpening one of the many blades she kept in her pockets.

'Is the fire high enough, sire?' she asked.

Only it wasn't her voice. She sounded like a man, deep and husky.

'Aye, Beremus. It is well stoked and raging.'

Eleanor and Odo hesitated on the edge of the campsite,

wondering what was going on. The fire was banked, only coals being kept for the morning.

'Even the coldest night will pass with a tune to warm your heart.'

That was Hundred again, in yet another voice, this time a woman's, but younger than her own and more musical.

Egda sighed. 'Peg, your lute would comfort a dead man. Give us a round of "Drunk Eyes Fair See What Fair Not Be," would you? It'll put Beremus in the mood for a laugh, and by the stars, he needs one.'

Hundred hummed a few bars of the bawdy song, but her voice was rough and there was definitely no lute to accompany her.

Egda sighed again, and this time raised his cooling tea in a mournful salute. 'To all the friends we've farewelled down the years,' he said.

'To all the friends,' Hundred echoed. 'Where have those knightlings got to?'

Eleanor cleared her throat and stepped into view. 'Yes, well,' she said, sensing that they had interrupted something private and pretending that she and Odo were too deep in conversation to have noticed, 'I maintain that Clover Gorbold is the only girl in Lenburh fit to marry a knight. She may be three years older than you and interested only in geegaws, but she is the reeve's daughter. I'm sure her collection of polished stones would grow on you in time.'

Catching on, Odo joined in. 'What about you? The acting steward's daughter *and* a knight? You'll have to leave town to find an available prince – or maybe a number of them will duel for you on the green.'

'They'd be fools then. As if I would be impressed by anyone who wasn't duelling with *me*.'

Eleanor folded herself on top of her bedroll, shifting her weight onto one hip to spare her aching backside. Perched on a flat stone in front of her, she found a steaming mug that smelled like heaven after a long day in the saddle. A second sat in front of Odo, and he sipped gratefully from it.

'You are young to think of marriage,' said Egda.

Neither Odo nor Eleanor saw the twinkle returning to his eye.

'We're not!' they both protested.

'Just joking about it,' said Odo.

'Not much else to joke about in the village,' said Eleanor.

'Perhaps it's as well to begin to think about it, even so,' mused Egda. 'As knights, you will be attractive partners to many. One purpose of the court is to make matches between far-flung families, and many young folk – not quite so young as you two – come to the court to seek a suitable match. If we survive, I expect you will both be sought after at the many dances and balls and flirtations and whatnot.'

Eleanor and Odo exchanged horrified glances.

Hundred surprised Odo and Eleanor with a smirk. 'More

for you both to learn! There are at least twenty different dances, not to mention the language of flowers – you know what the different coloured roses mean, don't you?'

Odo was far too aware of where they were headed, if all went well and they weren't captured by the regent's Instruments, Regulators and Adjustors en route. To the royal court – and not just the court, but the castle of Winterset and its surrounds, a city of many thousands.

'I can't imagine it,' he said, his voice suddenly weak and small. 'So many people in one place. So many strangers.'

'𝔥𝔞𝔳𝔢 𝔫𝔬 𝔣𝔢𝔞𝔯, 𝔖𝔦𝔯 𝔒𝔡𝔬,' said Biter, nudging the sharpening stone and oil closer to him. '𝔌 𝔴𝔦𝔩𝔩 𝔱𝔞𝔨𝔢 𝔠𝔞𝔯𝔢 𝔬𝔣 𝔶𝔬𝔲 𝔞𝔰 𝔶𝔬𝔲 𝔱𝔞𝔨𝔢 𝔠𝔞𝔯𝔢 𝔬𝔣 𝔪𝔢.'

'Oh, I'm not worried about that,' Odo said, taking the hint and beginning to clean his sword. 'It's just . . . everyone will be *looking* at us.'

'You won't be the object of their attention,' said Egda. 'The court will be watching the people *around* you, to see whose favour you have won. If you are alone, you will be perceived vulnerable. If you attract a crowd, they will think you strong.'

'Crowds are like dragons,' Hundred said with a sniff. 'Half as smart as they think they are, and not nearly as powerful. Pay them no heed.'

'Do you miss the court?' asked Eleanor, stifling a yawn.

'Never,' said the old woman, but Egda was silent. He

seemed to have gone to sleep, or was maintaining a determined pretence.

'If you're tired, Biter and Runnel can keep watch,' Odo said to Hundred, thinking that she must be as exhausted as he and Eleanor were, probably more so, given her age.

She shook her head. 'They're welcome to stay up and keep me company if they like, but I'll not trust the life of my liege to ancient swords, particularly when one of them can't remember how he ended up at the bottom of a river and the other once thought she was cursed. No offence, either of you. You're good in battle, but I cannot bring myself to trust you.'

With that she closed one eye and went very still.

Odo waited a good minute before concluding that Hundred was literally half asleep. That way she could keep watch all night and still get some rest, albeit half that of someone sleeping normally.

'What's the river got to do with anything?' muttered Biter, quivering gently under Odo's oiling rag.

'She's saying you're unreliable, little brother,' said Runnel. 'Or are you being rhetorical?'

'Ancient, she said!'

'Be glad she didn't mention that nick you've got as well. You don't remember how you got that either.'

'It is no impediment to my performance!'

'Careful, Biter,' said Odo, pulling his hands away. 'If you

52

get any more worked up, you'll take my fingers off!'

'I am sorry, Sir Odo. She does my nerves no service by being so provocative!'

'Who, me or Hundred?' asked Runnel.

'Both!'

'All right, that's it,' said Odo, packing up the oil and rag. 'You two can keep arguing if you want, but I'm going to sleep.'

'Me too,' said Eleanor, surrendering to another yawn. She tugged open her bedroll and slipped inside, feeling disappointed that their first night on the road wasn't filled with stories about the old king's adventures. She had been looking forward to that. Maybe tomorrow morning, when Egda was rested. This was her chance to learn about what her future life would really hold.

Biter and Runnel took positions on opposite sides of the campsite, dividing their time equally between watching the night, watching Hundred and watching each other.

To Eleanor's continued disappointment, the second day began with more chores, and then they were riding hard for Ablerhyll, changing horses every hour or two. It was too tiring for Egda to talk, or so Hundred maintained. The terrain grew hillier and the road snaked left to right and up and down, crossing rivers and streams on narrow bridges and passing through woods draped with vines and cobwebs. The landscape was dry but heavily farmed, with crops, cattle and cottages in evidence everywhere they looked. There were few hamlets or villages, however. All roads led to Ablerhyll, it seemed.

The sun was high as they neared the large town, smelling smoke and unwashed humanity in equal measure. Eleanor gazed ahead with something very much like awe. This was the biggest town she had ever seen in her entire life! A dozen spires were visible over the fortified walls, and the smoke from hundreds of chimneys rose up as one and drifted off in a grey fog. It made Lenburh look like a hamlet in comparison.

One of the spires had an odd addition attached near its top, a flimsy-looking cross made of fabric stretched over a wooden frame. It turned slowly in the breeze like a water wheel or the blades of a windmill, but horizontally. Odo, well versed in how both wind- and water-driven mills worked, wondered what it could possibly be.

This curiosity was not his only emotion. He felt nervous, almost as if they were going into battle, even though they were just planning to pass through the town and continue out the other side. They weren't stopping even for supplies, since Lenburh had provisioned them well, and the lighter they travelled, the better. They would have gone around the town entirely, except it was surrounded by market gardens, irrigation ditches, and walled orchards with no easy way through, so the road through the town was by far the quickest way to proceed.

'Remember,' said Egda, lifting his cloak to his chin and tugging his hood forward again, 'do not use our real names.

I am your grandfather Engelbert, and this is your great-aunt Hilda. You are Otto and Ethel, and we are taking you to be apprenticed in Winterset – Otto with the miller, Ethel with the herbalist.'

'Say it back to us,' Hundred requested.

They did as they were told, feeling more vulnerable without their real names than they had without their armour, which was still stowed on the baggage horses. Biter and Runnel lay concealed under the saddle blankets of their horses, out of reach but ready to fly forth at the slightest provocation.

It annoyed Eleanor to be hiding the fact that they were knights after so long dreaming of becoming one, although she could see the sense in it.

'Remember,' Hundred went on, 'there is likely to be an Instrument here, since Ablerhyll is closer to the capital. If we encounter one, act humble and cooperate. Our aim is to pass through unnoticed.'

The town gates were open, but there were guards watching all who passed through them. Eleanor felt their hard, suspicious gaze sweep over her and her companions as they approached.

'Do you think they'll recognise us?' she whispered to Runnel.

'Unlikely,' said the sword, her voice slightly muffled by the saddle blanket. 'Even if they've been alerted about the king, they'll be looking for an older couple on foot, not what looks like a family group on horseback.'

'Oh, I hadn't thought of that.' Still, she sat ready in her saddle as the guards approached, pikes held at an angle so they crossed, blocking the way.

Egda started telling the guards the story about heading for Winterset to establish his grandchildren in their proper trades, but he told it in a voice that was much lighter and higher-pitched than his own, and included so many unnecessary details – the weather they'd supposedly left, the meals they'd eaten on the way, what people had told them about the road ahead – that the guards soon became restless.

'Cease this blathering, Engelbert,' said Hundred in a crone's harsh snap. 'Give these good men the toll and we'll be on our way.'

Making a show of unhappiness, Egda reached into his saddlebag for a purse. Then, with great reluctance, he proffered each guard a silver penny. They snatched the coins and waved the party on.

'Never fails,' said Hundred once the guards were out of earshot. 'One good thing about getting old is that nobody takes you seriously any more.'

'Same with being young,' Eleanor said.

'True enough.' The old warrior turned in her saddle to look at Eleanor and, to Eleanor's utter surprise, winked.

Keeping a close eye on the town's inhabitants, they proceeded along Ablerhyll's crowded main thoroughfare, Hundred in the lead and Odo bringing up the rear. He kept his horses on a tight rein, wary of slippery mud and loud noises that might see him unseated. The horses were calmer than he was, well used to people and their activities. His anxious gaze soaked up tradespeople hard at work, children playing, stray dogs running between them, and rats eking what living they could from the scraps. There were tiny flies in abundance, and over all a fug that reminded him of his crowded home after a long winter. Over a constant rabble of voices, he could make out what sounded like dozens of cracked bells ringing in the distance.

They passed a market, and the smell of mutton pies made Eleanor's mouth water. She yearned to stop and try one, but there was no room in their mission for dallying. Maybe later, she told herself. When they had defeated the regent, there would be time to eat all the pies she wanted . . .

'Something is not quite right,' warned Egda.

Odo nodded. He felt it too. Ever since entering the town, his hackles had been raised, like someone was watching him behind his back. He turned his head both ways, but couldn't see anyone acting out of the ordinary. No one was looking at them at all, as far as he could tell.

'You are perilously exposed,' said Biter, the tip of his pommel poking out into view. 'I do not like it. An assassin could easily reach your position with a blade thrown from an open window, or from a nearby rooftop with an arrow, or even a dart tipped with aetrenbite poison –'

'Be quiet, little brother,' said Runnel. 'You will give us away.'

Biter subsided, grumbling.

Eleanor looked around her, eyes and ears alert.

'Birds,' she said. 'I can't hear any.'

'Ah, yes,' said Egda. 'There should be pigeons, sparrows, all the winged scavengers. But the sky is silent.'

'Otto and Hilda, look up at the tops of those spires, but carefully, so you won't be noticed,' Hundred instructed.

Odo scratched his head and glanced up under cover of his hand.

Perched on the very top of the nearest spire was the largest raven he had ever seen, head crouched low into its feathery blue-black shoulders.

Its gleaming eyes turned to follow them.

Odo glanced to another spire, and another. Each had its raven, and each raven was watching them with a soundless, chilling intensity.

A slight movement caught his eye. There was another raven, much closer, perched atop an eel-seller's stall. It met Odo's gaze, and he saw with a shudder that its eyes were not the normal black of a raven's, but a smoky grey.

Eleanor saw it too.

'The person who sent the bilewolves . . .'

'Yes,' said Hundred. 'Somewhere, a craft-fire is burning.'

'How do they know we're here?'

'They may not. They may simply be watching every traveller on this road.'

'So what do we do about them?' asked Eleanor. 'Go inside where they can't see us?'

'No,' said Egda. 'We must not be trapped here. The best way to avoid an ambush is to move fast, before the jaws can close.'

Eleanor wished he had chosen a different metaphor. The poisonous ferocity of the bilewolves was still fresh in her mind.

'We just keep going?' she asked. 'And hope nothing gives us away?'

'Precisely,' said Hundred. 'The road is open ahead. Let's trot. That should not be too suspicious. Simply travellers anxious to make the most of their time.'

Eleanor nudged her mount with her knees, and the horse obligingly broke into a trot. Eleanor grimaced as she lifted herself off the saddle in time with the rhythm. The clip-clop of the horse's hoofs made a martial drumbeat on the cobbles. Odo fought the urge to look at the birds and concentrated instead on making himself as inconspicuous as possible. He tried whistling nonchalantly, but that only made the lack of birdsong even more obvious. Everyone seemed to be looking at them now, through barred windows or over half-empty barrels, around companions or across tables strewn with wares. With every minute, Odo felt the tension in the small of his back grow.

Finally, when he felt he could take no more, he caught a glimpse of the gate on the far side of the city through a gap between two tall houses whose upper balconies overhung the road. It was so close, just around one more corner and then straight. He felt a surge of relief.

Hundred saw the gate too, but also something else. She raised her hand and everyone reined their mounts back to a walk. They clustered together as they slowly continued.

'The gate is closed,' she said quietly. 'It shouldn't be closed during the day.'

'Show no alarm,' said Egda. 'When we turn the corner, we'll come to a stop. Odo, act as if your horse has taken a stone in its shoe, while Hundred looks to see what is going on at the gate.'

'What if it's closed to keep us in?' asked Eleanor.

'They have no reason to suspect –' began Hundred.

But she was suddenly interrupted by a loud voice from behind them.

'Sir Odo! Sir Eleanor! Stop!'

CHAPTER
SIX

Eleanor's right hand lunged down the flank of her horse. Runnel was already moving. Barely had the sharkskin grip touched the palm of her hand than she was wheeling around, sword upraised and ready, Odo matching her speed precisely. Runnel and Biter caught the light brilliantly, sweeping forward and down to point at the throat of a man running full tilt towards them.

The man gulped and skidded to a halt just out of reach of the deadly steel. He was old and muscular, with wild white hair sticking out in odd tufts from under an acorn hat. He stopped so suddenly his hat tipped off and landed in the dirt at his feet. He went to pick it up, then froze as Biter twitched warningly.

'It's me!' the man cried. 'Old Ryce. Surprise!'

Odo squinted. It was true. The last time he had seen the ancient machinist – who had been held captive by the false knight Sir Saskia and made to fake a dragon's fire – Old Ryce had been a filthy, ragged figure hurrying up the river road for places unknown. Now he was clean, dressed in a smock covered in pockets and wearing a new hat. Which was getting muddy on the road.

'Oh, sorry,' said Odo, withdrawing Biter. 'I didn't recognise you.'

'What are you doing here?' asked Eleanor.

'Oh, you know Old Ryce. Working, building – no dragons this time. Never again!'

'You are certain you know this man?' asked Hundred, two jagged throwing knives held at the ready. 'He has a look of someone who has experienced evil.'

'We definitely know him – and yes, he has,' said Eleanor, face pink at the thought of how close she had come to skewering their old friend. 'We rescued him from a false knight and he helped us survive a terrible flood.'

'Old Ryce is very glad he did too,' stammered the old man. 'That's my name, and good friends we all are. Hello, Sir Eleanor and Sir Odo! I saw you but you were moving so quickly I almost missed you, your honours. But I didn't, did I?'

'Indeed, you did not,' said Egda. 'However, perhaps now is not the best time for a reunion.'

With a furious squawking and flapping of wings, a dozen black shapes converged on them from all sides, claws and beaks reaching for their eyes. Odo ducked and covered his head with one arm. Eleanor lunged her horse forward, out of the cloud of birds. Egda spun his staff overhead, knocking a raven to the ground. Hundred produced a whip and cracked it twice. Three birds fell dead, instantly slain.

That left eight, climbing up to regroup before they dived again.

'We are too exposed here,' Hundred said. 'More will come!'

None of the birds had attacked Old Ryce, who stood stock-still with his mouth open, dumbfounded. At Hundred's words, he woke from his shock.

'This way! Old Ryce knows where the birds won't go.'

He headed off down a narrow side alley at a surprising clip, all elbows and smock flapping around his knees. The others dismounted swiftly, leading their horses. Odo was the first to follow, almost dragging his horse along. She was a headstrong bay with the name 'Wiggy' branded into her halter. Where she went, the others would come too – and they did, down the narrow, washing-draped lane, the rapid chatter of their hoofs echoing from all sides.

Eleanor peered up, keeping a sharp eye on the birds. The ravens tracked the fleeing party in a ragged flock from above, occasionally ducking lower to see their quarry through obstructions and cawing for the others to catch up.

Old Ryce took a series of tight turns deep into the warren of Ablerhyll, the alley darkening as the upper levels of the houses grew closer and closer together, blocking out the sky. Occasionally one of the people or a horse slipped in the muck underfoot, but none of them fell, and even as the smell of filth and rubbish rose up to choke them, the birds became scarcer, unable to get through the overhanging rooftops, upper storeys, washing lines and bird nets hung by pigeon hunters.

'This way,' called Old Ryce over his bony shoulder. 'Nearly there!'

Through the narrowest of gaps between two lurching, irregular balconies that almost met above his head, Odo caught sight of the spire with the strange windmill. The blades were turning sluggishly in a faint wind, each lined with metal chimes, so the entire construction made a constant racket as it rotated, the same racket that Odo had noted earlier. The birds that hadn't been put off yet were scattered for good now, retreating with a series of indignant cries from the incessant metallic noise and the four giant blades threatening to smash them into a cloud of feathers.

'Through here,' said Old Ryce, opening a large double door at the rear of the structure and waving them inside. Once they were all under cover, he dropped a bar down to seal the doors with an echoing slam.

The base of the spire was as big as a barn, with a high, arched ceiling and walls covered in mysterious pipes and gears leading up into the shadows. Over the sound of the chimes came a steady, mechanical clanking and gurgling. The horses whinnied nervously, and Eleanor sheathed

Runnel in order to soothe hers by patting it on the neck as she caught her breath.

Egda's expression was pained, the sounds clearly an affront to his sensitive hearing. 'What is this cacophonous place?'

'Ah! This is the answer to Sir Eleanor's question. What is Old Ryce doing here? Well, when he was released by the real dragon, who thankfully didn't take offence at the making of a fake one, he didn't know where to go, so he went where things needed fixing. First an axle on a wagon that broke in a ditch. Then a water wheel with a wobble. Then a village clock that was stuck at midnight. Finally, this. Honest work!'

'I don't doubt it,' said Hundred, dismounting, closely followed by the others. 'But what is it?'

'A backwards weather vane. Ain't it marvellous?'

'A weather vane that runs backwards?' asked Odo. 'What for?'

'Good question, your honour. You really ought to ask the clever chap who built it, only he's dead now. No one really knows how that happened – they found his shoes in a mud puddle in the cellar but nothing else – or understands the machine, but I can fix what seems to be broken. Indeed, I think I *have* fixed it, at long last. Funny how things don't seem to stay fixed around here. But all Old Ryce has to do now is pull the lever and see if it works.'

'How will you know?'

'It'll rain. That's what it does. It brings rain to wash out the streets and feed the farms . . . and whatever else rain does.'

Eleanor understood then. Ordinary weather vanes measured the weather. A backwards weather vane *created* the weather. Remembering the dry fields on the way to Ablerhyll, she could well understand why the town would want one.

'Such devices were known of old,' said Egda heavily. 'But they were prohibited, with good reason. Interfering with weather is all too like the craft-workers who twist and change good animals into beasts like bilewolves.'

'The Instrument hired me himself,' said Old Ryce nervously. 'Have I done wrong? Old Ryce means no harm, but if this is like that dragon engine –'

'Let us not be distracted by talk of the device,' interrupted Hundred. 'We are now trapped. How are we to escape Ablerhyll with ten horses in tow? We cannot leave them behind. We need them to get to the capital quickly.'

'We are safe here for the moment,' observed Runnel. 'The birds cannot get in.'

'The fiend who lit the craft-fire will be seeking other beasts even as we speak,' said Biter. 'One of us should go on a sortie to seek the smoke and deal with him once and for all.'

'Craft-fires don't smoke – it all goes into the creatures they control,' said Hundred. 'But a sortie, all of us riding

66

out at once, might work, if the gate is opened by someone first. I can sneak – wait, what's that?'

Over the ringing of the chimes and the clanking of the backwards weather vane, they heard one dog howl, then another. Soon a whole pack was raising up an unnatural chorus.

'From birds to dogs,' said Hundred grimly. 'Even if the birds have lost us, the dogs will sniff us out.'

'We can fight them off,' said Eleanor. 'Old Ryce, do you have any weapons?'

The old man looked fearfully around. 'Just tools. And my lunch, your honours. But I want to help . . .'

'If we're going to make a stand here,' said Odo, 'it'd be better if you got out while you still can. This isn't your fight.'

'Old Ryce has to help his friends. That's what friends do. Particularly when it's his fault they found you.'

'It's not your fault,' Eleanor said. 'It's not Odo and me they're looking for. You just got caught up in this by accident.'

'Indeed, and I will not have another innocent life on my conscience,' said Egda. 'Old Ryce, in the name of the authority I once bore, I command you to leave immediately.'

'Authority?' echoed Old Ryce, blinking at Egda. 'Command? Oh my, that nose . . . I thought I recognised it, but never dreamed . . .'

He went down on both knees, joints cracking loudly, and prostrated himself.

'Get up and run, man,' said Hundred. 'Before it's too late!'

Outside, the dogs fell silent, only to be followed a moment later by a heavy pounding on the huge doors.

'Open! Open!' boomed a voice. 'By order of Instrument Umblewit!'

'**O**h dear,' said Old Ryce, raising his eyes.

'Get rid of them,' Hundred hissed. Old Ryce nodded and went to the gate, putting his head close to the bar.

'G-go away!' he shouted. 'I'm busy!'

'Too busy for Instrument Umblewit? Don't forget who pays you, tinkerer.'

'Um, Old Ryce is conducting a dangerous experiment. Oh, yes, very dangerous!'

'It'll be very dangerous for you if you don't let us in right now,' came the retort, followed by renewed pounding. Fortunately the doors were extremely solid and sounded as if they could withstand anything short of a battering ram.

'What can we do?' asked Eleanor. 'We can't fight the entire town, can we?'

'We can fight our way through,' said Hundred, testing her sword's edge with one thumb.

'Why don't we try to talk to them?' Odo asked, seeking

another way. They had barely begun their mission and here they were facing certain death at the hands of the Instrument and his minions! 'They're not really going to attack two knights, are they?'

'They will once they see us,' said Hundred. 'I am sure the orders have gone out to kill anyone who happens to be blind and has an impressive nose.'

Egda's expression soured at that description, but he said nothing to contradict it.

'There has to be *something* we can do,' said Eleanor, gripping Runnel tightly in frustration.

'There is a way out,' said a pale-skinned, child-sized figure that stepped out of the deepest shadows. It had green hair the colour of an old bottle, and skin so thin that silvery veins could be seen pulsing beneath. Long fingernails tapped a stoneencrusted belt keeping its dark smock clinched about its waist. It was flanked by two just like it, but taller. Six black eyes regarded them with wary and not entirely welcoming calm.

'Urthkin!' barked Biter, jerking into a guard position.

'Where did you come from?' asked Odo, tugging his sword back down to his side. They had met these underground creatures before, and he remembered very well how dangerous they could be if provoked.

'From the earth,' it told him, as though he had asked a stupid question.

'Stone make you strong,' said Egda. 'Darkness clear your sight.'

The ritual greeting seemed to please the urthkin. 'Wide be your halls. Tunnels guide you true.'

The others joined Egda, bowing deeply to make themselves look as small as possible. Among the urthkin, height was deemed a disadvantage.

'What are you doing here, Urthkin?' asked Odo.

'The earth will offer you safe haven,' the urthkin told Eleanor, who was the smallest, 'if you agree to our terms.'

'And, uh, what are your terms?' she asked.

'This machine must be destroyed.'

'No!' Old Ryce exclaimed. 'That is . . . dark ones . . . why? I don't even know if it works!'

The urthkin leader glanced at Old Ryce, whose head bobbed at a point significantly higher than hers, and again did not reply directly.

'We have tried to ruin this abomination many times,' it told Eleanor. 'Always we have failed. The knowledge of its making and breaking is beyond us, and its key parts lie too high from the earth. But it is not beyond the tall one here.' Another contemptuous glance at Old Ryce. 'If he will end its terror, we will help you escape this place.'

'Terror?' echoed Old Ryce, his mouth hanging open. 'Has Old Ryce done it again? But there are no dragons this time . . . I promised!'

Eleanor soothed him. She didn't really know what was going on, but she recognised an opportunity for escape when she saw one.

'Could you destroy the machine if you had to?' she asked him. 'Would you, if it was hurting someone?'

'Well, yes. But all it does is make rain. If it does. It hasn't been tested –'

'We know of such things from long ago,' the urthkin told Eleanor. 'And the tall one believes.'

'Old Ryce does think it will work,' said Old Ryce slowly. 'Old Ryce has laboured very hard, has puzzled out many strange things, has done work such has not be seen for –'

Clearly it mattered to the old man whether he had succeeded or failed.

'It must be destroyed,' pronounced the urthkin.

A louder pounding on the door suggested those outside had found a battering ram of some kind.

'I suggest a fair trade,' said Egda over the sound of the ram slamming into the door. 'Let Old Ryce start the backwards weather vane, but not let it continue very long, to see if it works. Rain will also distract our enemies outside, gaining us time.'

'Does it work like that?' asked Eleanor to Old Ryce. 'I mean, if you stop it and then destroy it, the rain will also stop?'

'Yes, yes,' replied Old Ryce. 'Little rain, then more rain, then lots more rain.'

'How about a little rain, just for a few minutes, to see if it works, and then Old Ryce will destroy it?' Eleanor proposed to the urthkin.

'Very little rain,' said the urthkin.

'Yes, not too much,' she told it, wondering why that was so important. 'Old Ryce will wreck it once the skies open – isn't that right, Old Ryce?'

The old man nodded.

'And then you can show us how we can escape,' she said. 'How the earth can save us.'

The urthkin inclined its head, but only minutely. 'On my name, Shache, I swear it as scortwisa of Ablerhyll, scortwisa-that-was of Anfyltarn.'

Eleanor blinked in surprise, understanding the urthkin term for leader. 'You recognise me?'

'Yes, and your champion.' Shache didn't glance at Odo, but he knew it meant him. The duel he had once fought and very nearly lost against an urthkin still haunted him.

'Is that why you helped us?' Eleanor asked.

'No.' Shache bowed. 'Proceed. Remember, very little rain. Too much, and we will leave you to your enemies. Or slay you ourselves, as oathbreakers.'

Old Ryce glanced at Eleanor, and then at Egda. They both nodded, so he scampered off to a bank of levers and counterweights that occupied an entire wall. Grabbing the largest lever, he pulled with all his might.

When it failed to move, Odo joined him and added his considerable strength to the endeavour.

With a slow grinding noise, the lever came down, down, down, and then locked into its lowest position with a definite click, followed by a sound like thousands and thousands of bees buzzing inside the walls, a sound that slowly faded upward.

Old Ryce stepped back and looked around, rubbing his hands eagerly. 'Hee hee, now we see.'

'What's going on in there?' bellowed the voice from outside.

'Stand back!' Old Ryce called. 'Big experiment about to begin!'

Even as he spoke, the backwards weather vane was picking up speed, growing noisier with every second. Potent oils bubbled through pipes. Wooden cogs spun faster and faster, until they began to smoke. Dust rained down from far above, where the axle driving the four blades turned, rapidly becoming a blur.

Odo gathered the reins of two wide-eyed horses in each fist, stopping them from rearing in fright, the others restraining their horses too. The entire structure shuddered so violently around them that it seemed likely to collapse. There was nowhere within to take shelter.

'Is it working?' Eleanor asked Old Ryce, shouting over the deafening roar of machines. He was grinning like a madman.

'Let's find out!'

He tugged her to the base of a long pipe that snaked up to the very top of the spire and pressed her eye against it. Through it, via series of cunning lenses, she saw the sky above. It was no longer blue. Thick, black clouds were gathering.

Even as she watched, a bolt of lightning leaped from one cloud to another with a sudden roar of thunder loud enough to drown out the backward weather vane.

Old Ryce clapped his hands and performed a capering dance.

'Any rain yet?' bellowed Hundred into Eleanor's ear.

She shook her head.

'Wait for the rain. It'll put out the craft-fire.'

Eleanor pressed her eye back to the tube, understanding now why Egda had pressed for that particular condition. The urthkin might have driven a stiffer bargain had they known the humans were to gain more than just a simple distraction from the shower. It was so dark outside now that an urthkin wouldn't have been troubled by the sun. The pounding on the door had ceased as people looked skyward in wonder, waiting to see what would happen next.

No less than three lightning bolts cracked at once, and the deluge began.

With a deep-throated roar, torrential rain began to pour on Ablerhyll. Heavy drops fell on roofs and dripped through the spire's ancient eaves. Long trickles snaked under the barn doors, approaching the hoofs of the nervous horses. The air smelled dense and heavy with moisture, and of a stranger tang, like lightning itself.

'Enough.' A tiny, sharp-clawed hand gripped Eleanor's shoulder.

'Not yet,' said Hundred. 'A few more seconds.'

'*Enough!*' declared Shache after the briefest of pauses, its black eyes following a particularly thick rivulet across the floor.

'Yes!' declared Eleanor. 'Old Ryce, make it stop – for good!'

The aged mechanist stopped dancing midstep, looked sad for an instant, then nodded. Crossing once more to the bank of controls, he pulled several more levers and turned the screws on two wide pipes open to maximum. Then he stood back, dusting his hands on his tunic.

'What'll that do?' asked Odo.

'Make it go faster,' said Old Ryce, looking up nervously. 'Until it tears itself apart.'

'How long?' asked Eleanor.

'About a minute.'

'Then I think it's time you met your side of the bargain,' Hundred told Shache. 'Or we'll all die together.'

'The earth will save us,' said the urthkin. It walked several paces away and slapped the ground with its hands.

There was a rumble beneath their feet, the horses shifting nervously, and then the earth fell away to reveal a wide tunnel that sloped down into darkness.

The urthkin went ahead, a pale glow emanating from its skin, just enough for the humans to see the way.

'Let's go!' said Eleanor, ushering her horse forward. It needed little encouragement, spooked by all the noise above. One by one the party led their steeds into the welcome dark and quiet, even as the rainmaking machine behind them began to shudder itself to pieces.

CHAPTER

EIGHT

Odo had never been so deep underground before. All around him he felt the weight and pressure of stone and earth. It was like nighttime, only a thousand times darker, save for the faint glimmer of the urthkin's skin ahead and a little light from the room behind. It was noisy though, very noisy, with the footfalls of many people, plus ten horses, plus the racket of the backwards weather vane echoing from above.

However the urthkin had opened the ground, it closed up behind them, just as the last packhorse made it in. With that sealing, off went the very last of the lantern light from the chamber. A minute later, the ground shook and there was a terrific bang from above, the sound of the giant machine rending itself from top to bottom, the pieces falling in on themselves. It sounded like the world ending. Odo stopped for a full ten seconds with his hands over his head, half expecting the ceiling of the tunnel above him to collapse. Old Ryce stood above them with his hands pressed upward against the stone, as though prepared to hold it in place single-handedly.

The ceiling held, but the sound of small impacts echoed through the tunnel for some time. He hoped no one had been hurt. When it was over, Old Ryce sighed and sadly let his hands fall.

'There can't be anything of the spire left up there,' said Eleanor in awe.

'Good,' said Hundred. 'They'll think us dead, crushed under the wreckage.'

'Hurry,' said Shache. 'This road will not remain here long.'

'What is this place?' asked Eleanor as the procession got moving again. Blinking, she realised in amazement that even though there were no obvious lights, she could still see. As well as the urthkin themselves, there were thin veins of moon-white light snaking through the stone walls, where something like fungus grew. The light was just enough to make out the shapes of those around her, so she could avoid stepping on anyone's toes, or being trodden on herself.

'You are in our lands . . . you have no words,' the urthkin answered. 'It is the home we have beneath your human home. An undercity perhaps?'

'You mean you live down here?' asked Odo in horror. His words emerged as a choked squeak. Although he had known the urthkin lived in the earth, he had imagined vast caverns big enough to hold entire villages, not this narrow tunnel that wouldn't be here long.

'We live in many places,' said Shache enigmatically. 'Many of them are unknown to humans, who are forbidden here, just as we are forbidden in your cities.'

'The ancient pact that has existed between urthkin and humans for hundreds of years allows urthkin to build under our towns whenever they like,' Egda explained. 'For the purposes of trade mainly. It benefits both sides.'

'We would never break that pact,' Shache told them, 'but human sometimes do. Humans like Instrument Umblewit.'

A strange sound echoed along the tunnel, that of many sets of urthkin teeth grinding together. Eleanor looked back and was surprised to see more than a dozen urthkin bringing up the rear.

Shache continued. 'A foolish man brought the device that is now destroyed to Instrument Umblewit, hoping for reward. He had found it, hidden away, with a book that told of its use. Including how the machine could bring drenching rains – not to clean the streets or water the fields, but to drown urthkin, to flood us out of our undercity. This is what Umblewit threatened, because we would pay her no taxes, would not obey her commands to bring gold and gems and precious things of the earth. We, who have only ever brought prosperity to Ablerhyll in fair trade! If we could have slain her, we would have, but she is too cautious, too well guarded. We could only attempt to harm the lower parts of the machine.'

'It was you!' exclaimed Old Ryce out of the darkness. 'You're the reason the machine kept breaking down! Umblewit was going to punish me if I couldn't get it to work!'

'The urthkin had a right to defend themselves, since that device was intended as a weapon,' said Egda, which seemed to Odo a fair summary of the injustice of the situation.

Old Ryce harrumphed a couple of times, as though he had something caught at the back of his throat, but a couple of solid pats on the back from Eleanor soon cleared the obstruction.

'We have many machines in the undercity,' said Shache. 'Machines for the digging of tunnels and seeking of gems. Perhaps the tall one would like to see them?'

Eleanor couldn't see Old Ryce well enough, but she could imagine the look of delight that crossed his face.

'The tall one would like that very much!' he exclaimed.

'It shall be so,' said Shache.

They came to a junction in the tunnel. Odo could hear echoes vanishing off into two directions ahead, and even though he still wasn't breathing properly, he could tell that the air from one to the left was much fresher than that to the right.

'Here we part ways,' Shache told them. 'Follow the tunnel that leads upward and it will open on a hillside out of sight of humans . . . *other* humans. The tall one will come with us, if he so wills. We will collapse the tunnel behind you.'

The party split into two unequal parts, and the urthkin made moves to head on their way, deeper into the earth.

'Wait,' said Egda. 'Umblewit has broken the pact here, and perhaps others have done so elsewhere, but I would see it fixed in Ablerhyll and throughout the kingdom. You have my oath that everyone who suffers at the unjust hands of the Instruments will receive recompense.'

'With darkness comes wisdom.' Shache bowed. 'I see that it is so with you, old one. Tunnels guide you true.'

'Goodbye, Old Ryce!' called Eleanor. 'Until we meet again!'

'Goodbye!' Odo managed to squeak out. He really didn't like being all closed in. Glowing urthkin veins and thin lines of mould on the walls simply did not compare with a well-trimmed lantern – or, even better, the bright sun.

'Goodbye! Goodbye!' echoed back to them from Old Ryce, and then they were alone.

The urthkin were as good as their word, as Odo had known they would be – a fact that gave him great comfort as they proceeded up the twisting, turning tunnel, leading the horses behind them. Within half an hour, there was a hint of greenish sunlight ahead, and then they were suddenly outside, in a stand of dense bushes that hid the tunnel opening from sight. Stepping through the bushes, Odo took a deep breath of deliciously fresh air and reacquainted himself with the vistas of the surface world. The sky was heavy with clouds and the ground damp underfoot, but the rain had ceased with the destruction of the backwards weather vane and the air was still.

Hundred looked at the sun and declared them slightly south of the road they had intended to follow from Ablerhyll. Despite the turns and winding of the tunnel, they hadn't ultimately strayed far from their path.

'The sun is setting, sire,' Hundred told her liege. 'I would argue for travelling by night, but all are weary, the beasts no less than us. Perhaps a short respite is in order?'

'You are right, Hundred.' The former king wearily inclined his head. He had been perfectly spry during their troubles in Ablerhyll, but now seemed once again to show his age. 'We will make camp until moonrise, then continue on our way along the road, for that will be fastest.'

'Why *does* he call you "Hundred"?' Eleanor asked as they tethered the horses and began unloading them. She had often asked herself this question, wondering if it was perhaps the number of battles the old warrior had been in, or the number of people she had killed in battle, or the number of ways she knew how to kill people . . . or some other grisly fact entirely, as befitted a warrior of Hundred's experience.

'I come from a large family,' was all Hundred said on the matter that night, before giving Eleanor a long list of chores to ensure she was too busy to ask again.

'Why is she always so mean to us?' Eleanor grumbled under her breath as she and Odo hurried to complete their tasks before darkness fell. 'Aren't we knights too?'

'I like her,' said Odo, although he mainly just liked knowing what he had to do. Being a knight had often felt like stumbling around in the dark, trying not to break anything valuable, and it came as a great relief to be told how to behave. Mostly, though, he was glad to be no longer underground – that was something he hoped never to have to endure again. 'We're apprentice guards,' he added. 'It's our job to be bossed around.'

'Many great knights have begun their lives as apprentice guards,' said Biter. 'Sir Winchell, for instance, spent a year emptying latrines before slaying the Vile Beast of Esceanda –'

'The two tasks were not unrelated,' said Runnel. 'One lived in the other.'

'But the fact remains, sister: all must begin their journey somewhere.'

'*Swords* don't start out at the bottom,' Eleanor complained, then snickered at her unintended joke. 'Like Sir Winchell did. You're just made . . . and enchanted . . . and off you go to see the world. I wish I could be like that.'

'We are more than metal and magic,' Runnel told her. 'We learn just as you do.'

'By our deeds are we known,' Biter added with some

finality, suggesting that the time for idle chat was over. 'As are true knights.'

Odo sensed that there was a lot more to the story of the swords than this. He knew little about how Runnel and Biter had been forged – but how much did he himself really know about how he had come to be? His father had told him bedtime stories as a young child about the courtship between him and his mother, but they were surprisingly light on details.

'Every day we see something new,' he reminded Eleanor, thinking of backwards weather vanes, urthkin tunnels and bespelled ravens.

'Yes, but it would be better if we were learning new things as well,' she grumbled, disinclined to be satisfied.

Finally the horses were cared for and the camp was prepared for the night. Odo and Eleanor wearily reclined on their bedrolls and listened to Egda and Hundred once again pursue a brief exchange with people who weren't there, including two whose names they had not heard before. Odo wondered how long until they started repeating their lost friends, and whether it made either of them any happier.

Hearing Egda and Hundred talk to the dead made Eleanor feel surrounded by ghosts lurking in the shadows. She shivered.

'Your education proceeds apace, my young knights,' Egda told them, returning to the living with a scratch of his proud nose. Eleanor wondered if he had overheard her complaint about not learning anything. 'My father always said that nothing compares to putting a person right into the affairs they wish one day to manage. "Errors made in ignorance are lessons always learned," he liked to tell me. At this pace, you will surpass Hundred and me in wisdom before you are half our age.'

Warmed by the encouragement, Odo felt bold enough to ask something that had been on his mind all evening.

'This pact between humans and urthkin . . . who started it?'

'Ah, that would be Acwellen the Sage, many kings ago. He brokered a peace after a long history of squabbling between our two very different peoples. It turned out that, provided certain provisions were made regarding trade, we really had very few reasons to fight, except for occasional acts of pigheadedness on either part. It saddens me that we are in such a time at present.'

'What will happen if the pact is permanently broken?' asked Eleanor, not wanting to fight the urthkin but thinking of the many battles — and the demand for brave knights — that might arise if it was.

'War,' confirmed Hundred, the gleam of long-ago fires in her eyes.

'It will not come to that,' said Egda. 'Not while I live.'

Odo had his doubts as to how much four people could do against the entire might of the Regent and her Instruments, Adjustors and Regulators, but he had faith in his betters, as he had been raised to, and suppressed his misgivings for now. Presumably the former king had allies he could call on, or at least favours to call in.

'Are there pacts with any other creatures?' he asked.

'Many,' Hundred said in her brisk way, for Egda had fallen abruptly silent again, as was his wont at night. 'Dragons, for instance.'

'There's a pact with *dragons*?' Eleanor asked.

'Of course. Otherwise they might have eaten us all long ago.' Hundred stood. 'I'm going to cast about to see if anyone is looking for us from Ablerhyll. I won't be long. Swords, keep watch, and knightlings, rest, for we ride again in three hours.'

'Yes, sir,' said Odo and Eleanor as their enchanted swords took up position at either end of the camp.

Eleanor tried to calm her thoughts, but they were busy from the day and what lay ahead. She was beginning to appreciate that she occupied a small place in a very strange world full of very strange things, but that only made her want to see it all.

'Who do you think negotiated the pact with the dragons?' she asked Odo. 'I wonder how it works.'

But her friend was already asleep, and the swords didn't answer either. Soon, lulled by the chirruping of a nearby cricket or perhaps a lone lost bat, she was asleep as well.

CHAPTER
NINE

They rode all that night and slept the next day, granted a reprieve from all but the most basic of chores as they raced the sun to form a camp. There was no conversation that morning, just grateful collapse into sleep for all but Hundred, who took the first watch. Odo was next, and he was not easy to rouse. Knowing that Eleanor was tired, he gave her an extra hour before waking her up in turn.

'No troubles?' she yawned.

'Three bees,' he told her. 'But luckily your snoring scared them away.'

'Ho ho. Get some rest, Jester Knight, or I'll let the bees sting you when they come back.'

Eleanor perched on a log near Runnel, rubbing her eyes and wishing there was a fire so she could make some tea. This was the worst part of being a knight, she thought, sitting around waiting for something to happen. And when something *did* happen, it was often horrible and entirely out of her control. She had greatly preferred it when she and Odo had been off on their own adventures, answerable to only themselves, even though there were times the errors she'd made in ignorance had very nearly cost her life or the lives of others. At least back then she hadn't been expected to do chores all day and dig other people's toilets and ride until she ached in every joint.

Still, it was better than staying at home and doing nothing. Of that she was completely certain. She was seeing the world, albeit slower than she would have liked. And every now and again Egda let something slip about the life in court that awaited them.

The sun sank slowly towards the horizon, painting the western sky in brilliant reds and oranges. Her instructions were to wake the others when the fiery disc touched the distant hills. As the shadows lengthened, she thought she heard the high-pitched cries of the lost bat again, but she put it out of her mind in order to do as she had been instructed.

'Hundred?' she said, shaking the old woman's shoulder. This time the warrior had both eyes closed, properly asleep. 'Time to wake up.'

The next thing Eleanor knew, she was on her back with a glittering knife at her throat. Then Hundred's eyes cleared and she came fully awake, letting Eleanor go with a grunt. She stood up and replaced the knife into a pocket at her side in one fluid movement.

Behind her, floating in the air like a giant silver mosquito with an emerald eye, hovered Runnel, caught between saving her knight and respecting Eleanor's superior.

'That can be tonight's first lesson,' Hundred told Eleanor, who got nervously to her feet and brushed herself down, feeling as though a dozen small rocks had embedded themselves through her tunic into the skin of her back. 'Let sleeping knights lie, or at least rouse them gently, if you want to see another sunrise.'

'Yes, sir.'

'Get the other knightling to his feet and we'll start on another lesson . . . if I haven't put you off?'

Eleanor nodded, face burning. Hundred too had obviously heard her complaint about not learning anything. She would have to mind her tongue more carefully.

'𝔇𝔬 𝔫𝔬𝔱 𝔟𝔢 𝔡𝔢𝔰𝔭𝔬𝔫𝔡𝔢𝔫𝔱,' whispered Runnel as she returned to Eleanor's side. '𝔍 𝔣𝔬𝔯 𝔬𝔫𝔢 𝔯𝔢𝔩𝔦𝔰𝔥 𝔱𝔥𝔢 𝔠𝔥𝔞𝔫𝔠𝔢 𝔱𝔬 𝔩𝔢𝔞𝔯𝔫 𝔞𝔩𝔬𝔫𝔤𝔰𝔦𝔡𝔢 𝔱𝔥𝔢 𝔤𝔯𝔢𝔞𝔱 𝔨𝔫𝔦𝔤𝔥𝔱 𝔶𝔬𝔲 𝔴𝔦𝔩𝔩 𝔲𝔫𝔡𝔬𝔲𝔟𝔱𝔢𝔡𝔩𝔶 𝔟𝔢𝔠𝔬𝔪𝔢, 𝔲𝔫𝔩𝔦𝔨𝔢 𝔱𝔥𝔢 𝔬𝔱𝔥𝔢𝔯𝔰 𝔍 𝔥𝔞𝔳𝔢 𝔰𝔢𝔯𝔳𝔢𝔡.'

But it wasn't combat Hundred taught them, it was how to scratch together a healthy breakfast from roots and berries found in the copse nearby, supplemented by insects attracted to the light of a small fire. Boiled and mashed together with a small amount of water, then fried as a paste on a blackened iron plate, the mixture was not nearly as revolting as either Eleanor or Odo feared. In fact, it had an almost-pleasant nutty taste and left them feeling full and energised for the night ride ahead.

'There's a bat flapping around the camp,' commented Odo as they packed up. 'I've seen it fly over three times in the last minute.'

'How can you tell it's the same one?' Eleanor asked.

'It's small, but really fast. Like a mouse with wings.' Not at all like the legendary barrow bats, which were rumoured to be as fat as rats, with wingspans as long as his arm. He was glad it wasn't one of those. 'Do you think the same person who sent the bilewolves and ravens sent this one too?'

'I've never heard of craft-workers using bats,' said Eleanor. 'What can we do about it anyway?'

'I'll tell Hundred,' said Odo. 'Best to be careful.'

Eleanor forgot about the bat as Odo wandered away to talk to Hundred, and focused on reviewing strikes and blocks. If she wasn't going to learn anything new, she would at least remember everything she'd learned already.

They rode quickly, following Hundred, with Egda safely protected between them. The sky was clear, with stars so bright it seemed sometimes they were about to fall. When the moon rose it was half full and painted the road with ripples of light. The horses made a driving, percussive rhythm as the party climbed steadily higher in altitude, broaching the shoulders of a mountain range that Hundred called the Offersittan, which stood as a barrier directly across their path.

'The usual way to cross the Offersittan is at Kyles Frost,' she said as they dismounted to walk the horses for a while, before changing to the fresher ones. 'However, that will be impossible for us because it is closely guarded. When you see the twin peaks Twisletoth and Tindit standing on the horizon like the horns of a giant beast, you will know that we are close and need to be wary of other travellers on this road.'

'Do you have a plan?' Eleanor asked.

'Perhaps to go around it, although that will take us much longer. I believe in preserving all possibilities, as long as my name is Hundred . . . Ah! Our stealthy companion has made its move at last!'

The bat had dropped out of the sky with a leathery flapping and grasped a branch directly overhead, emitting an impatient series of squeaks and chirps. It was thin and shivering, as though very weak.

A small throwing knife appeared in Hundred's hand. Runnel and Biter joined their knights as all three of them took up positions around Egda, who asked, 'What is it? Another bird attack? But this sounds different.'

'It's a bat,' said Eleanor. 'And it's been following us.'

With so many blades pointing at it at once, the little creature squawked back into the air and resumed circling.

'It was searching for us the night we escaped Ablerhyll,' said Hundred, who had not needed Odo's warning, 'and found us this morning. I have watched it closely ever since, awaiting a third approach from our enemy, the lighter of the craft-fires, but there has been no sign of any other animal adversaries. I believe that this is something different. No less a threat, perhaps, but not of an immediate nature.'

'What made it land now?'

'I believe, Sir Eleanor, it was because I said my name.'

The bat flapped around them three times, occasionally coming closer, then darting away. It was indeed very small, and presented no obvious danger to them. Eleanor was sure Hundred could have downed it with a knife, and as she hadn't, was forced to conclude that Hundred intended more from the encounter than a swift end to the creature.

'Let it approach,' Egda told them. 'If its intentions are perfectly natural, or at least peaceful, we will soon know. Perhaps our enemy wishes to treat with us.'

'Aye, sir.' Hundred lowered her hand to her side, but kept the blade at the ready. Odo and Eleanor did the same.

The bat circled one more time, then swooped in to grasp the same branch as before. Gripping the tree tightly and tucking its wings against its sides, it regarded them from its upside-down position with eyes as black as jet.

'Its eyes aren't smoky,' said Eleanor. 'It's not some craft-worker's servant.'

The bat's ugly muzzle twitched as it started squeaking again.

'Sounds like it's talking to us,' said Odo.

'But bats can't talk, can they?' Eleanor, cocking an ear,

could make no sense of the string of tiny sounds. 'Not like dragons.'

'What's it doing?' asked Hundred. 'Talking, you say?'

'Can't you hear it?' Odo glanced at the puzzled face of Hundred and knew his answer.

'I hear nothing,' said Egda. 'The pitch of its voice must be too high for my old ears.'

'I hear it, but can make no sense of it,' said Odo slowly.

'I hear nothing,' said Biter with a puzzled shiver.

'Listen,' said Eleanor, concentrating hard. 'It almost sounds like . . . like letters . . .'

Odo frowned. She was right. The tiny bat wasn't saying words, but spelling them!

'– r! y! k! u! r! g! e! s! h! a! s! t! e! p! r! i! n! c! e! k! e! n! d! –'

'What's it saying?' Eleanor said. 'I can't string it together quickly enough.'

'I can,' said Odo. 'Hang on.'

His mouth moved as he followed the rapid stream of letters, supplying spaces and punctuation where they seemed likely to fit. Soon he realised that the bat was repeating one message over and over.

'"Prince Kendryk urges haste,"' he said. 'It's a message from Prince Kendryk!'

'From the heir himself!' said Egda. 'Even as a boy, my great-nephew had an unusual bond with animals and kept many pets.'

'Wait.' Odo held up a hand. 'The letters have changed.'

'I'm getting it now.' Eleanor listened closely. 'The message says, "Imprisoned. My coronation cancelled. Regent to be crowned king. Only the old dragon can save Tofte now." Who's the old dragon?'

'My king,' said Hundred to Egda, who huffed impatiently, 'he means you. Kendryk must indeed have sent this missive.'

The bat fell silent, message delivered in full, and watched each of them closely as they spoke, enormous ears seeming to take in every word. Its strange features were screwed up in a state of permanent anxiety, and Odo felt a pang of sympathy for it. This poor animal had flown all the way from Winterset, across mountains and plains, probably lost them in Ablerhyll because of the underground tunnel, then found them a day ago only to be unsure who they were until it heard Hundred's name. This wasn't a message that could fall into the wrong hands after all.

'Do you have a name?' Odo asked it, wishing he had a bug or something to offer it.

't! i! p!'

'Tip?'

'm! i! s! s! e! d! t! h! e! c! a! v! e! m! o! u! t! h! b! y! a! w! i! n! g! t! i! p!'

'Tip will do.' Odo reached a hand up to where the bat clung to the branch. It eyed him warily for a moment, then stepped across like an inverted parrot. Its feet were sharp-tipped and clung tightly to him, but not painfully because it was feather-light. It was shivering less now, as though getting used to them.

'Well, you've always wanted a pet.' Eleanor smirked.

'But now what do I do?' Odo asked, standing awkwardly while Tip looked trustingly up at him.

'Interrogate it while we ride,' said Hundred. 'Learn everything it knows. Then we will decide.'

'But how . . . where do I put it?' He waved his arm back and forth. Tip's feet shuffled from side to side, maintaining their tight grip.

'Affix a scarf around your throat. Let it cling to that.'

'It's a *him*, I think,' Eleanor said, helping Odo with the scarf.

When the woollen collar was in place, he brought Tip closer and the bat swapped his grip.

'There, a bat necklace.' Eleanor tickled Tip on the top of his head, which hung down almost to Odo's belly button. He blinked up at her and might have smiled. She found it hard to tell exactly what that ugly face was doing, but in manner he wasn't unfriendly.

'Mount up,' said Hundred. 'Let's away. If everything this creature tells us is true, we have even less time than we thought.'

Odo found it hard to ride and follow Tip's spelled-out

squeaking at the same time. Luckily his horse, once again the intelligent Wiggy, knew to follow Hundred's even when its rider was distracted. To make matters even more difficult, what Tip told him was filtered through the intelligence of a small bat, so much of it was about the moths that lived high above throne rooms and other meeting places, cracks that led to caves underneath the city, and which guards disliked bats to the point of trying to skewer them on pikes. Only where Prince Kendryk had instructed the bat specifically did he have information of use to another human.

One message was very clear: if the Old Dragon didn't appear in time, all would be lost.

'Why are you called the Old Dragon?' Eleanor asked Egda as they rode.

Hundred barked a laugh. 'Be careful what you say, Sir Eleanor. He never liked the name, no matter how well earned.'

The former king grimaced. 'I was dubbed so upon defeating the giant Fylswingan of Brathanad – although truthfully it is an inherited title, passed down along my line for three hundred years. Every long-serving king tends to earn it eventually, even the most placid.'

'So Prince Kendryk will be the Old Dragon one day too?'

'Yes, if he is given the opportunity to become king in truth – and to grow old, as so many have been denied.'

Egda descended into a funk, bringing the subject to a close.

They rode on as the road became ever steeper, winding

through valleys and over ridges, past forests and beside rivers Eleanor had never heard of. Occasionally Tip launched himself from Odo's throat to seek out a tasty snack, but mostly he stayed in place, spelling out his messages and resting after his long flight.

'He says the regent's coronation is in three days,' Odo told the others as they watered the horses in a stream and swapped mounts. 'That's enough time for us to get there, is it?'

'Not unless we travel day and night,' said Egda. 'Perhaps not even then.'

'Or cross the Offersittan at Kyles Frost,' Hundred said.

'I thought you said we couldn't do that,' said Eleanor. 'It's too well guarded.'

'I said it's impossible, not that we couldn't do it.'

'Hundred eats the impossible for breakfast and hunts the inconceivable for supper,' Egda commented with a weak smile. 'As Beremus used to say.'

Eleanor and Odo exchanged a glance. The dead were dead and likely to stay that way – unless talked about too much, as some in Lenburh believed. Though neither of the young knights believed this, they were a little alarmed when Egda and Hundred talked about their dead friends, particularly when Hundred assumed their voices.

'Is it only impossible to cross at Kyles Frost as ourselves?' asked Odo.

'A disguise!' agreed Runnel eagerly. 'Something more than fake names.'

'Or we could draw the guards away from the pass,' said Biter, 'with a spectacular diversion. It would be easy to arrange an avalanche.'

'Easy to get us all killed too, foolish sword,' said Hundred, tapping her chin with one gloved finger. 'Before we formulate any kind of plan, we must obtain information. On nearing Kyles Frost, we will send Tip ahead to scout for us. What he sees from the air will greatly aid us in our passage.'

'Oh,' said Odo. 'I thought we'd send him back to Winterset with a message for the prince, so he knows we're coming.'

He'd be safer there too, he thought to himself.

'Later perhaps, but not now.' Hundred dismissed that suggestion. 'He is more use to us here. At this pace we will be close enough to put him to work by midnight or thereabouts tomorrow. Tip must be ready by then. The winds blow powerful and cold over the pass at all times.'

'How did the prince put the message in Tip and make him talk in the first place?' asked Eleanor. 'Perhaps we could do the same to another bat, or an owl or something.'

'It is a great skill,' said Egda. 'His father, Prince Aart of Gelflund, had the knack of it, and clearly he taught young Kendryk. I do not have that skill, and neither does Hundred. The only gift old soldiers like us have is experience.'

'And plenty of it,' said Hundred, mounting in one smooth

motion. 'Time passes. We must make a good distance yet before dawn, if we are to meet this new deadline. I see craft-fires and bilewolves in my waking dreams.'

They mounted and rode on, trading avoiding potholes and low-hanging branches for the larger concerns waiting ahead.

CHAPTER

TEN

Tip stayed at Odo's throat for the rest of the journey, blinking up at him with tiny black eyes and snuggling into the scarf for warmth. Odo quickly became accustomed to his presence and on occasion completely forgot he was there, particularly as the road wound like a snake around hills and along increasingly steep-sided valleys, requiring him to take more care with Wiggy's footing. They had long bypassed the town of Trumness, where Reeve Gorbold's pigeon had died, and were now entering the foothills of the Offersittan. The mountains themselves loomed like vast black storm clouds directly before them.

Eleanor strained through the darkness to catch sight of the sentinels of the pass that led between Twisletoth and Tindit, vast stony fangs she had read about in accounts of the deeds of mighty knights. They were so high, it was said, that snow never melted at their summits, and ice trickling down their sides carried strange relics frozen many centuries ago.

Imagine, she thought, what it would be like to skate those

ice rivers from the summit all the way down to the bottom. She was a good skater, having learned the two times in her life that the river had frozen over. What a thrill that would be!

Glancing behind him, Odo saw by moonlight that Eleanor was grinning, and wondered what new thought was running through her mind. There was always something. At least she was happy.

The strange sensation of a tiny bat burrowing into his throat and a series of small squeaks distracted him.

'What's that, Tip?'

'o! w! l! s!'

'Owls?'

'h! u! n! t! i! n! g! i! h! e! a! r! t! h! e! m!'

'Where? I can't see them.'

'f! a! r!'

Tip burrowed even tighter into Odo's chest, as though trying to make himself invisible.

'Tip hears owls,' Odo told the others, and Hundred immediately reined in her horse so he could tell her what he knew.

'Owls hunt bats,' Eleanor said.

'And when directed by a craft-fire,' Hundred said, 'they might hunt people too. And there are pale owls in the mountains, as big as large dogs. Quickly, head for that stand of trees.'

They galloped under cover and tied the horses to the

trunks, giving them an early feed to keep them quiet. Dawn wasn't far away; Eleanor could see it in the sky even with the mountains cloaking the eastern horizon. She stared westward, where she imagined any pursuit might originate, and within moments her attention was rewarded.

Two huge white birds, flapping in tandem, came into view. They flew high above the road, carefully following its tight-wound twists, heads turning from left to right to scan every inch. There was no doubt what they hunted. Or who.

'Quiet now.' Hundred's instruction was barely a whisper of air.

Odo and Eleanor crowded into each other under the stand of trees, listening as flapping wings came closer, passed overhead, then went on up the road. Eleanor didn't realise how tightly she had been holding Runnel, or even that she had drawn her sword at all, until the owls had flown by them.

'Two more breaths, to be sure,' Hundred instructed.

Odo counted three, then dared move again.

'Will they come back?' he asked.

'Not in full daylight,' Egda said. 'Our pursuer might use other birds, I suppose, but they do not know for certain that we are on this road, or we would have been assaulted in force. But we must be wary of any animals acting in concert or behaving strangely. Still, for now I think we will be safe to emerge from cover.'

'Tip has proved his worth most handsomely,' added

Hundred. 'Would that I had such sharp hearing!'

Odo tickled the bat between his enormous ears and Tip chittered ordinary bat noises in response.

'Dawn is upon us,' Hundred went on. 'Let us make camp here. Build no fire, knightlings. Even with Tip, we will take no chances.'

The day passed slowly, the coldness of the air becoming apparent to all in their turns to sit watch. The sun, when it finally appeared over the crest of the mountains ahead, was weak and watery. A belly of cold provisions hardly helped.

Odo sat thinking with Tip curled up at his throat, sleeping as bats do naturally during daylight hours. Before turning in, he had listened to Egda and Hundred once again conversing with their fallen friends, and again found reason for disquiet. Honouring the dead was one thing; keeping grief and sorrow alive was quite another.

All through his watch, the last before waking the others to resume their journey, he pondered a plan to put the past to rest. Once he had it, the question was only whether he had the courage to put it into effect.

'What weighs on your mind, Sir Odo?' asked Biter when he faltered in the middle of some quiet practice on the edge of the campsite. 'Your strokes are heavy and your eye is off by a good yard. Were that tree a bilewolf, you would be torn asunder!'

'I wish I was more like Hundred,' Odo said. 'She doesn't have any doubts. I keep telling myself that I'm a real knight. That I, uh, eat adversity for an afternoon snack. But all I can think about is how things could go wrong, even when I know what I need to do.'

'I am sure many things have gone wrong for my knights in my past, although in truth I can't remember what they might have been,' said Biter, slipping out of Odo's hand and coming around to face him, emerald flashing in the dappled light. 'Knowing what one must do is the hardest lesson for some knights to learn. Though it is generally better to do something than nothing.'

'For once my brother has wisdom,' said Runnel, darting from Eleanor's side to join them. 'What is it you know you must do, Sir Odo? Perhaps we can help you find the means.'

He told them, which was a trial in itself, but they did not think him foolish or rash. It seemed mad to him to try to tell a former king what to do, but they did not think so. For the rest of his watch they formulated a plan, and when it was time for Hundred and Egda to wake, they put it to effect.

'My liege, the sun is setting.' Odo woke Egda first, knowing what had happened to Eleanor the previous day when she'd woken Hundred.

'Thank you, good knight.' Egda sat and threw off his bedroll in one motion. He might already have been awake, for all Odo could tell. There was no way to know behind the blindfold whether his eyes were closed or open. 'Today we ride in earnest.'

'What is this?' asked Hundred, who had definitely been asleep a moment ago. She was on her feet, staring at the fruits of Odo's labour on the edge of the camp.

'I mean no disrespect,' he said, nudging Eleanor's bedroll with his toe, not entirely sure which way up she was lying under it. No part of her was visible. 'But there is something we must put behind us. That is . . . I believe we ought to . . . if you agree, my liege . . .'

He executed a clumsy bow, hoping he wasn't making a grave mistake and overstepping himself.

'Speak, Sir Odo,' said Egda.

'You were good to us in Lenburh,' he went on. 'We were grieving for Sir Halfdan as well as Bordan, Halthor and Alia. You took charge and helped us put him to rest. That was a kindness we all needed. Now I think . . . that is, if you don't mind me saying . . . it's nothing to do with ghosts or the like, honest . . .'

'What the big stampcrab here is trying to tell you is that he'd like to do for you what you did for us,' said Eleanor, struggling to her feet and quickly grasping the line of Odo's reasoning. 'You've lost many people. Good people, and friends. You've been lamenting their loss in the wilderness for a long time. Maybe it's time to set down that task, now you're coming back into the world. There's no good in dragging the dead around when they haven't asked you to. They don't take kindly to it, or so the stories go.'

Odo looked gratefully at his oldest friend, who always had words when he did not, even when she was only half awake. He wondered if her father had told her something similar when her mother had died. 'I thought we might . . . lessen your sadness. Not forget your friends, but let them rest.'

The former king didn't respond. He looked older than ever, and his expression was impossible to read.

Odo glanced at Hundred, who inclined her head in the tiniest of nods.

'The lad has built a grave, sire,' she told Egda in a soft voice. 'There are twigs and berries – an old Karnickan ritual, I believe. A stick for the body, a seed for the soul? To put grief to rest and let the happy memories thrive?'

'That's right,' Odo said.

'How did you – ?' A crack in Egda's voice prompted him to stop and clear his throat. 'Of course. The good swords have been continuing their education of our young knights while our backs are turned.'

Odo swallowed. 'Are you angry, sire?'

'Not at you, and not for any of this. You are right. I must shed my present load in order that my shoulders can adopt another. You are my guide, Sir Odo. I place myself in your hands.'

He held out his own hands and Odo took them gently, with

utmost respect and kindness, and led the former king to the long trench he had dug, where they both knelt. The trench was a foot across, a foot deep and four feet long. Biter and Runnel stood at one end with their sharp points in the soft earth. Two piles of twigs and berries lay next to the trench. Foraging for them while keeping a careful eye on the camp had taken Odo his entire watch.

'Take a twig in one hand and a berry in the other,' he said, guiding Egda. 'Say a name. Then Hundred will take the twig and Eleanor will take a berry. They'll put them in the hole, one by one. When we're done, I'll cover them up all up and you can say a few words if you'd like to.'

Egda nodded. Drawing a deep breath, he did as Odo instructed, clutching a twig and berry, one in each hand.

'Beremus,' Egda said.

Odo and Hundred reached to take the twig and berry from his fingers. He resisted for an instant, then let go. Hundred snapped the twig and placed the pieces in the hole. Eleanor pressed the berry into the exposed soil, where it might release its seeds and grow.

'Beremus,' they repeated, and Odo and the swords said the name too.

'Peg.' Another twig, another berry. 'Peg.'

'Sir Sutton.'

'Sir Sutton.'

And so it went until the two piles had dwindled almost

to nothing, and Odo began to wonder if he had gathered enough. How many close friends was it possible to lose in one lifetime? How had Egda borne so much grief for so long?

Finally, with just three twigs left, Egda raised shaking hands to the golden blindfold and slid it up and over his head, revealing red-rimmed milky eyes. Tears trickled down his cheeks and gathered in the furrows at the corners of his mouth.

'I am done,' he said.

Odo used his big hands like shovels to fill in the hole, and Eleanor and Hundred helped him pat it down, making a miniature barrow. Then they knelt back and waited in silence. It mattered to none of them that night had fallen and a strenuous journey awaited. Tip watched them with sombre eyes, sensing that this was human business that he didn't need to understand and was best to stay out of.

'When I was king,' Egda finally said, 'I was surrounded by many who called me friend. I soon learned to recognise, and hold in the highest regard, those whose friendship was true. They are more rare and more precious than jewels. In the wilderness I held their memories tightly, feeling that I was poorer for losing them than the entire wealth of the kingdom. Now I see that I was doubly a fool: a fool once for thinking a blind man cannot still be king, and a fool twice for thinking a man who has been rich in friends and lost them can never regain that wealth. Today I am made fivefold richer, for now I have Hundred, and Sir Odo and Biter, and Sir Eleanor and Runnel. I thank you, friends, from a heart that beats stronger already.'

They inclined their heads, Odo blushing furiously. He had expected Egda to talk about Beremus and the others, not about *him*.

'It was all Sir Odo's idea,' Eleanor said. She didn't dare blink, for fear of releasing a tear from the fullness of her eyes. She was thinking of her mother and imagining how proud she'd be to know that a king had said such fine things to them. She also promised that she'd bury a twig and a berry for her and Sir Halfdan when she returned to Lenburh. It was a lovely thing to do.

'You do each other credit,' said Egda, replacing the blindfold and rising resolutely to his feet. 'And I have no doubt that you will return the honour at the first opportunity, Sir Eleanor. Now, we must ride like the winds of Gelegestreon to reach the approach to Kyles Frost before sunrise. Spare no horses and give no quarter! Are you with me, knights?'

Odo and Eleanor leaped to their feet and swept up their swords.

'Yes, sire!'

Hundred made a show of rising more slowly. 'Let's at least save some of the horses in the event we need them again. And perhaps we should pack up the camp first, before rushing off into the night? I for one would miss my bedroll.'

Egda, a grave man whom Eleanor and Odo had hardly ever seen smile, amazed them both by roaring with laughter.

'The mighty Hundred, dragging her heels to enter the fray? Thought I'd never see the day!'

Pack up the camp they did, eating nuts and stale bread as they went, but when they mounted and set off, Egda riding close at Hundred's heels, it was all Eleanor and Odo could do to keep up.

ELEVEN

It grew colder and colder, until Eleanor and Odo shrugged into the cloaks packed in Lenburh but never needed previously, and the steel of their swords grew icy to the touch. The horses' breath steamed as they strained up the ever-rising slope, while the foliage around them grew gnarly and stunted as if here even plants hunkered down against the chill.

The moon was behind them when they passed under a sleeping hamlet that grew out of a cliff wall like some strange forest fungus. Few candles flickered around tightly sealed shutters, but still the party of four, ten horses, two swords and one bat slowed their pace to a stealthier trot and kept their faces carefully obscured.

No one halted them. Glancing over her shoulder at the hamlet receding into the night, Eleanor saw no sign that anything living had observed their passing.

The memory of the pale owls kept pace with her however. She felt the gaze of their invisible master in the space between her shoulder blades like a physical pressure. It never slipped any of their minds that they were being hunted.

One hour before dawn, they pulled off the road into a sheltered alcove, a hollowed-out cave with just enough room for all of them.

'Before we proceed much further along this road,' Hundred told them, 'we must determine what we face. It is time to send Tip on his mission.'

The little bat stirred eagerly at the sound of its name. Odo held out his arm, and Tip walked along it until he could see all four of them equally well. The willingness of his expression touched Odo's heart. He had no doubt their new friend would do anything they asked – but what if there was an archer ahead the equal of the one that had killed Reeve Gorbold's pigeon over Ablerhyll? What if a flock of ensorcelled owls tore him into tiny pieces?

Odo stilled his fears as Hundred gave the bat his instructions in the plainest possible terms. Tip was to fly along the road up to the pass, counting guards as he went. He was to note any archers and unusual animal behaviours as well. Then he was to fly back to them as quickly as possible. If he was seen aloft after dawn, their craft-fire-lighting pursuer might follow him to where Egda and the others awaited his return.

'y! e! s! y! e! s! y! e! s!'

The little bat nodded, which was a strange gesture to see upside down, then opened his wings and flew off, chirruping happily as he went. Odo hoped he would take the opportunity to eat some insects along the way. Hundred had said that the winds blowing over the pass were strong. He would need all his strength to survive them.

'Don't fret,' said Eleanor, patting his shoulder. 'Tip must have flown through the pass once already – on the way here, remember?'

'Oh, yes, of course.' That did make Odo feel better.

He rubbed down Wiggy and swapped his saddle over to his second mount, the dun Salu. Hundred inspected his work with the horses, as she often did, and Eleanor's too. There was still much for them to learn about caring for the beasts. Until they had squires, they would have to look after their horses themselves, if they ever had horses of their own. That was assuming they survived the bitter chill in the air . . .

Winter in Lenburh wasn't half as cold as they felt they were that night, and Eleanor was actually grateful for the chores Hundred gave them. Even sheltered from the light predawn snow that settled on the valley road, and even with the body warmth of the horses around them, she was soon shivering. Seeing this, Odo loaned her a spare woollen hat that went over her own and came down almost over her eyes. It helped, but she was too cold to stay still. The chores kept her moving, and moving kept her warm.

'Shame there's not enough room under here for us to practise,' she said through chattering teeth. One swing of Runnel would likely cut two horses in half.

'Here, catch,' said Hundred, taking something that glittered from behind her back and tossing it to her in an underarm throw.

It moved so quickly Eleanor didn't realise it was a knife until it was halfway into her hand. Only at the last instant did she twist and catch it by the handle – and only then did she see the tiny scabbard that protected the blade. Her fingers had never been in any danger.

'And here, one for you.' A second blade crossed the distance to Odo. He fumbled with one hand, lunged with the other, and after a quick juggle finally snatched it out of the air. When he looked up, Hundred held two more knives, one in each hand, and Egda was grinning.

'Attack me,' Hundred said. 'Expose your blades if you wish. It will make no difference.'

Odo didn't doubt that, but Eleanor was willing to accept the challenge. She had practised for hours with one of her father's old scalpels, as blunt as a stick but well balanced and perfectly effective against the gnarled apple tree in her backyard back home. She dropped into a fighting crouch and inched forward, watching Hundred's hands. When she saw her chance, she lunged.

Hundred let her get close, then twisted on her heels and moved in such a way that left Eleanor disarmed and with a knife at her throat.

'You are dead,' the old woman whispered into Eleanor's

ear before letting her go. 'Pick up your knife and try again.'

Eleanor grinned and did as she was told. This was exactly what she had been waiting for!

Odo came to her aid, circling around so they were attacking Hundred from opposite sides. Again, however, Hundred repelled their lunges with dizzying ease.

'Now you are both dead.'

Odo took that as both a caution and a challenge. 'Any suggestions, Biter?'

'I fear my advice would be useless, Sir Odo.'

'This is itself good advice,' Egda said. 'An enchanted sword can only teach you how to *defend* against a knife, using a sword. There is no such thing to my knowledge as an enchanted knife, so you must fight Hundred the hard way.'

With that, Hundred lunged at Odo, but it was a feint, and a second later Eleanor was 'dead' again, and Odo soon followed. Even though he tried hard just to stay alive, it was impossible to keep out of Hundred's reach. She was too nimble.

'Never suppose that sword and armour make you invulnerable,' she told them. 'One day you may be without either, and this lesson could save your life. Now watch closely and I will show you the disarm I used the first time.'

Eleanor soaked up this new knowledge like Swithe the leatherworker soaked up his ale, not even noticing the cold any more. In fact, she soon shrugged out of her cloak in order to free her arms, although she kept Odo's hat to spare her ears.

'Now against each other.' Hundred watched as the young knights sparred. The horses seemed to be watching too, or at least not shying away when the scuffle occasionally came near them. The small stable formed a ring around the two fighters, flicking their ears and tails as though in amusement.

'Enough,' said Hundred finally. 'It will be dawn soon. Best spare your strength for Tip's return.'

Eleanor studied the knife as she handed it back to its owner. The blade was one she hadn't seen before, slender, with a grip worn into the shape of Hundred's fingers. There were no jewels or any other adornments on the blade, handle or sheath. It was what it was: a well-made weapon that had seen a great deal of service.

'How many knives do you carry?' Eleanor asked. 'I've counted at least eleven.'

'That many?' asked Egda with an amused look. 'Are you sure they're all different?'

'Yes,' Eleanor said, listing all those she had seen since the fight against the bilewolves. 'Plus the sword. There can't be many more or you'd jangle.'

'I would indeed. And I would be very heavy.' Hundred didn't smile, although that could have been a joke. 'Weapons are tools. I like to keep one for every eventuality. Estimate the number of eventualities, and you will know the number of my blades.'

A flutter of wings came from the opening of their shelter. They turned as one to see Tip flapping furiously. He emitted a series of excited calls on seeing them, and caught Odo's outstretched arm in a tight grip. Tip wrapped himself in his wings, shivered and breathed heavily.

'Welcome back, little friend,' said Odo, beaming in relief. 'I was beginning to wonder.'

'Well, I didn't doubt you for a second,' Eleanor said, handing him a piece of dried fruit she had saved from supper. Tip gulped it down – or up, as the case was.

'Tell Sir Odo and Sir Eleanor what you saw,' said Hundred. 'All of it.'

They crowded around to hear. Tip had a lot to spell out, and frequently he was asked to go back and repeat short passages where their interpretations differed. It soon became clear that a considerable force lay ahead of them, with thirty soldiers and six archers protecting the pass from every approach. The gates were closed and barred, and anyone nearing was stopped. A small camp had formed beside the road, temporary home to those who had been turned back. Rather than descend all the way back down, it appeared they were willing to wait until those the guards were looking for had arrived and been caught, and the gates opened again.

Odo's mood flagged as Tip's account came to its unhappy conclusion. There was no way through the pass that didn't involve a fight – a fight they were likely to lose, against such numbers . . . and archers too. At least they still had the advantage of surprise.

'Thank you, Tip,' said Egda to the tiny creature. 'You have served us well.'

Tip wriggled with pleasure and burrowed into Odo's scarf, blinking exhaustedly.

'So what do we do now?' asked Eleanor. Even she was daunted by the odds. 'Turn back and find another way around?'

'We press on,' said Hundred. 'All is not lost.'

'𝔏et us make a war council,' said Biter, 'while we camp here for the daylight hours. I am certain we will devise a plan.'

'No camp today,' Hundred said. 'As exposed as that makes us, standing still for too long would be worse. I have faith that snow and fog will obscure us from above. If we make good time, we will be at the gates around nightfall.'

'And then we will see,' said Egda. 'That is, you will see and I will listen. If we encounter anyone on the road, remember our aliases: Engelbert, Hilda, Otto and Ethel. Swords, stay hidden, ready if needed. Great peril lies at Kyles Frost, but there is danger enough on the approach for all of us.'

They were back on the road in moments, having never truly unpacked in the first place. The snow had eased off, but thick mist clung to the steep cliffs like white veils to a tearful cheek. Shapes loomed out of the mist as they rounded each tight bend – rocks every time, but making Eleanor's heart race all the same. She expected discovery and threat at any moment. The only thing that worried her more was the steep drop-off where the road met the open air. One missed step in the flowing fog could be her last . . .

An hour into their ascent, Egda surprised them all by starting to sing. In a clear if slightly cracked voice that vanished into the muffling fog, he began the first line of 'Fools and Kings' and sang it all the way through to the end.

'What's he doing?' Eleanor hissed. 'If people can't see us, they'll hear us for sure.'

'I believe that's the plan,' said Hundred. 'If you were looking for someone travelling in secret, and you heard this racket, would you ever suspect?'

'They might shoot us just to shut us up.' But Eleanor grinned and joined in on 'Green Leaves,' followed by 'The Soldier's Song' and 'Meat, Mead and Mother.' Where she forgot the words, she simply sang the notes. Odo knew them all – one of the dubious benefits of belonging to a big family that enjoyed regular sing-alongs – and he had a sweet, light voice that belied his size. Had he been higher-born and not found a sword while looking for eels in a dying river, Eleanor reflected, he might have become a troubadour.

At that moment, both of them were happy that he hadn't. There was something about singing in the face of danger that swept away all concerns, apart from keeping to the path and holding the pitch. Everything else could wait . . . except when it couldn't.

Twice they encountered parties going back the other way, both on foot. Odo and Eleanor kept their hands near their hidden swords in case they posed a threat.

The travellers all warned them of the blocked pass ahead and advised them to turn back.

'More snow coming,' said one, a barrel-maker with bright red cheeks, possibly from drinking too much of the wine his wares contained. 'And no sign of relenting among the ironheads at the gate. Never seen such stubbornness in all my days. You'd think an army of rebels was on its way to storm the gates of Winterset itself!'

'Is that what they're saying?' asked Hundred with carefully manufactured alarm. 'An army? We don't want to get caught in a fight.'

'They're not saying anything, no matter who asks. One of those newfangled "Instruments" is up there. Called Colvert. She's been there three months, acting as afraid as a lamb in a wolf den. I hear there's an Adjustor up there as well, sticking their nose into everything, although why one of them would bother with Kyles Frost is beyond my ken. It's just a road with a door. Everything worked better when Sir Jolan was in charge . . . ah, that is to say, I thought it might . . . ah . . . forget what I've said, would you?'

Hundred thanked him for the warning, but said that she

and her wit-addled father and ingrate grandchildren would try their luck all the same. They couldn't keep the pass closed forever, could they?

On his well-meant warning being ignored, the barrel-maker and his entourage went on their way with a shrug. As they rounded the next bend, the singing that had caught their ears resumed as carefree as before. They'd soon learn, the barrel-maker thought.

None in the travelling choir was as carefree as they sounded. *An Adjustor*, the barrel-maker had said. They'd had trouble enough with Instruments, and only escaped one of them by extremely good fortune. What new troubles – and additional forces – might this higher official bring?

It was a fear they didn't voice aloud, in case less friendly ears were listening.

After a long rendition of the round-song 'My Merry Wife', Odo declared his voice too hoarse to go on. Hundred agreed, saying that the pass was close anyway, so perhaps observant silence was preferable. Tip unfolded his delicate ears and went gratefully to sleep.

Before they had gone much further, Eleanor became aware of a rising rumble from ahead, with a strange hissing laid over the top of it. It reminded her of the sound of the Silverrun in full flood, but oddly different.

'What's that noise?' she asked.

'The Foss,' said Hundred. 'It is a waterfall that plunges

one thousand feet from the lake that fills the pass and becomes the Suthgemare River, which wends all the way to the Southern Ocean. Our road leads over it.'

'Won't we get wet?' asked Odo.

'No.'

'That's a relief,' said Eleanor with a shiver. 'And what about the lake? Is there a bridge?'

'One challenge at a time. To gain the lake, we must first pass through the gate.'

Eleanor and Odo returned to fretting. Surely there was no possibility of passing undiscovered. One glance at Egda's nose and eyes would reveal his identity. All the guards had to do was pull back his hood and everything would be lost.

'You must have come through here plenty of times,' said Eleanor to Runnel. 'How would you do it?'

'My knights have always been in the service of their king and therefore had permission to pass,' the sword said. 'Under present circumstances, one knight alone might bypass the guards in stealth, but not four, with horses.'

Odo was having a similar conversation with Biter. 'If a frontal assault is out, a diversion is too dangerous, we can't sneak past and we don't have very good disguises, I just don't see how we can possibly get through.'

'We can only trust that our liege has a plan that doesn't involve leading us to certain death,' the sword advised him. 'In that unlikely event though . . . promise me that I won't end up in the water. I could not bear to sleep with the eels again. I would rather be melted down for a cart brace than lose still more of my memories.'

With Hundred unwilling to reveal her thoughts, all they could do was fidget and wait.

CHAPTER
TWELVE

The road led between walls of sheer stone that blotted out the sun. To their left, a steep drop plummeted into darkness, from which emerged the sound of churning water. As the road became narrower, the thunder of the Foss grew louder until it filled their senses. Finally, the waterfall itself appeared, revealed as the cliff walls parted in sweeping curves to form a giant bowl ringed with craggy, snowtopped peaks, the two largest, Twisletoth and Tindit, vanishing into a dense roof of clouds.

Ahead, the road crossed a natural rock bridge spanning from one side of the pass to the other. Out of a ragged hole under this bridge spewed forth a torrent of water wider and more violent than any Odo or Eleanor had ever imagined. Foam sprayed in white flecks and became a mist that painted their faces in chilling damp. With a roar that rocked them to the bones, the torrent vanished into the chasm below, beginning its journey to the far-off sea.

Wordlessly — for what was the point in even trying to

talk? – Hundred waved them forward, onto the bridge. The stone was slick and slippery, the violence of the water so great Odo feared the bridge might shatter under them at any moment.

But Hundred did not hesitate, so he followed resolutely, looking neither to the left nor the right, concentrating only on Wiggy's footing.

When he reached the other side, he felt as though his bones had turned to jelly. He reached down to pat Wiggy on the flank, grateful for the mare's steady footing and nerves.

Egda came next, then Eleanor, looking as shocked as she felt. Only when she was safely on the other side did she stick her tongue out to taste the spray. It was cold and clean – pure water from glaciers higher up the mountains. It made her feel very much alive, and grateful to be so.

Hundred led them on, through a dense cloud that covered the road, hiding what lay ahead. When they passed safely through it, their challenge was laid bare before them: another rock bridge much larger than the first, topped with a heavy wooden wall with gates midway, leading further into the hills. The gate looked impregnable, studded with iron bolts and braced in holes dug deep into the rock. Below, where the road joined the bridge, several wagons clustered, covered and uncovered, waiting to proceed. Some had pitched tents and lit fires. Odo's stomach rumbled at the thought of hot food. Or was that nerves? It was hard to tell.

A dozen armed guards stood in front of the gates. Eleanor's sharp eyes picked out the gleam of helmets on ledges high above, undoubtedly the archers that Tip had described.

On a narrow balustrade above the gates stood a tall figure dressed entirely in red. Eleanor couldn't see this person's eyes, but it was clear they watched the road and all who proceeded along it. Fortunately snow still fell, obscuring them from close scrutiny. The sun had long disappeared behind the mountaintops and would within half an hour set completely.

Instead of leading them directly to the gate, Hundred turned to join the wagons.

'The chill sits heavily in my bones,' she called back to them, adopting her 'Hilda' voice. 'Let's rest here a while and see what causes the delay. At the very least we can avail ourselves of a fire, if these good people will make space for us.'

Her cry was heard over the roaring of the Foss. Two young lads scampered from the wagons to help with their horses in exchange for a copper farthing each, and soon they were gathered around a campfire, warming their hands and hearing the story about the Adjustor's blocking of the pass once more.

'Aye, madness it is indeed,' agreed a carpenter clad from head to waist in what looked like one thick brown scarf, wrapped many times around him. His hands stayed hidden, held close to his body for warmth. All they could clearly see of his face was his mouth. 'I have a shipment of doors due in Wohness tomorrow morning and I won't be paid if they don't arrive on time.'

'And I've a herd of goats that won't survive another night without forage,' grumbled another traveller. She passed around a flask of warming spirits that made Odo's eyes water just sniffing at it. 'We're going to lose our livelihoods, and who will help us? Not those wretched Instruments, and not that Adjustor neither. They only care about making us follow the rules — rules that make about as much sense as a partridge in a pie shop!'

The grumbling became a steady rumble from the dozen or so people gathered around the fire. Odo and Eleanor had been enlisted into a game of knucklebones played by the other children gathered there. Odo deliberately lost and was cast out of the ongoing competition, so he could pay attention to what the adults were saying. Eleanor was more competitive and rose steadily through the ranks, beating one after another of the local champions.

'Has anyone ever considered standing up to them?' asked Hundred, speaking in a low voice in case any guards were in earshot.

'What can we do?' asked the goat herder. 'We're just honest folk trying to turn one penny into two. The prince tells the Regulators what to do, they tell the Adjustors, the Adjustors tell the Instruments, and the Instruments and their guards do what they will.'

'I hear it's not the prince at all,' said the carpenter very softly. 'It's the regent who's brought in all the new nonsense and sent away the knights. All these money-grubbing new officials answer to *her*.'

'That sounds like dangerous talk to me,' said 'Hilda' as her ancient, hooded father poked at the end of a protruding stump with a booted foot, making sparks fly up from the fire. 'If word were to reach the Adjustor of what you were saying –'

The carpenter's eyes narrowed and his hand closed on a chisel in the box at his side.

'I've already lost everything,' he said grimly. 'Or at least I will have if those doors don't arrive tomorrow. And I doubt anyone here will betray me to the guards. They'd better not try anyway.'

'Peace! Your loss is my loss, friend.' Hundred leaned closer and spoke so softly that Odo could only make out a fragment of what she said. 'Perhaps . . . you and I . . . solution to both our problems . . .'

The carpenter sized her up with a long look, then nodded. Together, they moved out of the firelight to talk in private.

Odo watched them go, wondering what she was up to.

'Yes!' Eleanor clapped her hands in triumph, then reached out to shake hands with her fallen opponent, a boy her age who accepted defeated with a surly grimace. 'Shall we play again?'

A chorus of disillusioned nays was the reply, and gradually the other children wandered off, leaving Odo and Eleanor alone.

'If you'll keep an eye on, uh, Grandfather here,' he said, 'I'll go check on the horses.'

'Right you are, Otto. I'm happy to stay here in the warm.'

Odo walked off through the ring of wagons to where the ten horses were hobbled in two close lines, each mount under a warm blanket. They whinnied and shifted restlessly as Odo approached, their hoofs crunching and squeaking on the snow. The night was bright from the moon and stars, but very cold, Odo's breath billowing out in soft white clouds. There was no sign of Hundred. Whatever she was doing, she had to do it soon if they were to pass Kyles Frost in time to save the prince.

He raised both hands, as though warming his fingers on his breath, and spoke softly through them.

'All quiet out here?'

'Nothing to report, Sir Odo,' said Biter from his hiding place.

'If anyone comes too close,' said Runnel, 'we'll do our best talking-horse impersonation to scare them off.'

'You'll do no such thing!' snapped Biter. 'A talking horse is hardly less conspicuous than a talking sword –'

'Obviously. Let me have my joke. It is boring out here with no one but you and the horses to listen to. They are

130

pleasant creatures, but one can only bear so much on the subjects of oats and eels.'

With a flutter of wings, Tip dropped out of the sky and clung to Wiggy's bridle. Half a moth protruded from his mouth.

'Any movement around the gates?' Odo asked him.

Tip gulped down the moth. 'n! o!'

'Do you know where Hundred is?'

'b! e! h! i! n! d! y! o! u!'

Odo turned and there she was, coming out from between two of the wagons and walking towards him.

'We need to shed six horses,' she told him in a low voice. 'I'll leave you to choose. Have the remaining four ready to leave as quickly as possible, but do so without making it look obvious. Wait for me here.'

'We won't be able to carry all our supplies.'

'We don't need them. Where's your sister Ethel?'

'By the fire, with, uh, Engelbert.'

'Good. I have a job for her too.'

With that, Hundred vanished back into the dark, as though she had never been there.

Eleanor was playing with Egda and marvelling at how he could catch the knucklebones he couldn't see when Hundred suddenly appeared next to her.

'Father,' she said to Egda, 'you're looking unwell. This cold is not good for you. Our new friend Wilheard has generously offered us shelter in his wagon. This way.'

She lifted Egda by one elbow and Eleanor took the other. He played the weak, old man with aplomb, shuffling listlessly away from the fire. Those remaining in the warmth offered their sympathy while at the same time wishing that they too had the opportunity to find protection from the freezing night.

'Wilheard is the carpenter,' Hundred whispered to Eleanor and Egda. 'His caravan is the covered blue one – you can see the pile of doors poking out the back. Knock twice and do as he says. I will meet you there in a moment.'

She disappeared again, leaving the two of them to wind their way through the wagons and horses forming the temporary camp.

'What's she up to?' Eleanor wondered aloud.

Egda tapped the side of his nose, but said nothing.

Odo had just finished choosing the horses and reorganising the supplies when Hundred returned. He had picked Wiggy among the four. With Tip securely hanging from her bridle, he turned at the sound of footsteps.

'Bring them all,' Hundred said, taking the reins of her preferred horse and leading him after her. The rest trailed obediently along, with Odo and Wiggy alert for stragglers. They came around the camp to a long wagon with a blue canopy covering the front third and a high load of rectangular doors securely roped into the back two-thirds. Four worn but worthy nags were hitched to the back of the wagon. Hundred rapped twice on the side.

The carpenter opened a flap in the canvas. Past him, Odo could see Eleanor and Egda sitting at a narrow table, still warmly dressed despite the heat of the small travelling stove next to them.

'We're ready,' said the carpenter from within his thick, looping scarf.

Odo blinked. It wasn't the carpenter's voice. It was Egda's – and the person sitting at the table wearing Egda's hood wasn't Egda at all, but a man similar in size whose face Odo had never seen before. The girl wasn't Eleanor, either, but a woman in Odo's spare woollen hat. They had switched places!

The real Eleanor peered out past Egda. She was wearing different outer clothes too, most notably a huge, brightly coloured scarf wrapped many times around her neck and over most of her face.

'I'm much warmer now,' she said with a grin. 'Got the horses?'

Hundred nudged Odo inside and shut the flap behind her.

'Six horses, as per the arrangement,' she told Wilheard. 'Fair trade for the wagon and your clothes. We will do our best to deliver the doors, or see that you are paid for them in full at a later date. If you go back to Ablerhyll, we will send word to you there.'

'If not,' the carpenter said, 'the horses will fetch a good price. They are fine beasts.'

He spat in his palm and held it out to Hundred. They shook.

'Don't forget to carry on the act until the morning,' Eleanor said. 'Offer to play knucklebones with the other kids. That'll scare them off.'

The carpenter and his wife left the wagon, doing a passable impression of an ancient old man and his great-granddaughter. It was just possible, Eleanor thought, that this plan could work.

'What about me and Hundred?' Odo asked. 'There's no disguise for us.'

'You and your grandmother have to get through in search of mountain wort to cure her joint fever, and we're simply helping you along.'

'But why would they let a granny and her grandson through when they won't let anyone else?'

'Because the grandmother will have something that will convince them to do so.'

'What?' asked Odo.

'Leave that to me,' said Hundred. 'I heard something promising from the others who've tried to get past, and I can be very persuasive when I have to be.'

Egda chuckled. 'Wasn't that what you told Headstrong Harold at the siege of Dysig?'

'It was indeed,' she said. 'That's how he got his new nickname – Headless Harold.'

THIRTEEN

Eleanor didn't feel nervous until the wagon started moving, drawn by their four remaining horses up the road towards the gate. She sat inside with Hundred, peering out through a hole in the canvas while Odo drove, Egda sitting comfortably at his side, disguised as the carpenter. Both swords were hidden again, this time in a long storage space under a seat, Biter grumbling about being constantly kept in the dark.

'Fear not, little brother,' Runnel reassured him. 'If this plan goes awry, you will have your time in the light.'

The gate was brightly lit by many torches set in iron stands along the road, as well as two big lanterns above the gate. The guards must have heard the wagon before they saw it, because half a dozen had already turned out, archers with arrows notched.

The wagon trundled onto the rock bridge and stopped as one of the guards held up her hand. Tip circled overhead, invisible in the gloom.

'Go back!' yelled the guard. 'Go to sleep!'

'We've got papers now!' Egda shouted back in a surprisingly good imitation of the carpenter's voice.

The guard looked over her shoulder. A moment later, an officious-looking woman in the red-and-silver uniform of an Instrument, with a huge bearskin cloak thrown over it, emerged from a sally port in the main gate. She stalked over to the wagon, chin up and nose wrinkled as if facing something highly unpleasant and much beneath her.

'You again, Wilheard? I've already told you you're not going through.'

'I beg your pardon, Instrument Colvert,' Egda said, keeping his head down as if being extra humble but really to keep his face hidden under his hood, deep in the shade of the canopy. 'The thing is, this young lad and his grandmother have special dispensation from the regent to pass through, and I've volunteered to drive them.'

'Dispensation? What are they, spies?'

'Not our business to know. I suppose the regent has her reasons too.'

'And I suppose you thought you could deliver your beloved doors into the bargain, I bet.'

'Ain't no harm in turning a good turn into a profit, is there?'

'I suppose not.'

Instrument Colvert chewed the inside of her lip uneasily. Odo tried to look superior and threatening in a non-knightly way. He had never met a spy before, but supposed they looked much like ordinary people, or else they wouldn't be much use as spies at all.

'Dispensation, eh? Well, I guess they've got a letter to prove it. With the proper seal. Let's see it.'

Egda fished under his winding scarf. 'I've got it here. Seems in order to me, but you'd know better than a humble tradesman.'

A leather scroll case passed from Egda's hands to the Instrument's. She opened one end and tipped it up. Blank parchment slid into her waiting palm – and so did six gold nobles.

She looked at the coins, eyes widening in surprise, then up at Egda and Odo.

Odo held his breath. A bribe! A massive bribe. Six gold nobles was more than a simple carpenter could make in a year, maybe two! But this was where everything could go entirely wrong. If Instrument Colvert's loyalty to the regent was fierce enough, she could expose them with a word, and then the arrows would fly.

Her eyes gleamed as brightly as the coins, then narrowed in speculation.

'Do you feel that chill?' said Egda with a shiver. 'Must be hard up here, night after night, listening to the likes of me complaining. At least we can turn around and go home whenever we want. How long since your family saw you last, eh? A week? A month? Longer? If only you could offer them comfort until you return . . .'

Instrument Colvert's hand closed over the coins and slipped them into her pocket.

'These look in order to me,' she said, replacing the paper and the lid of the scroll case and handing it back to Egda. 'I will order the gates opened.'

'And our friend the Adjuster?'

'The Adjuster is asleep. I'll let him know in the morning. Who are we to interfere with the regent's business?'

With that she turned and reentered through the postern door. A moment later, with a great clunking and groaning, the gates swung out, revealing the road beyond.

Odo kept his face carefully neutral, praying his relief was perfectly concealed. So far, so good, but there was a way yet to go.

Inside the wagon, Eleanor, who had followed the conversation but not seen the coins, marvelled at the ruse.

'How – ?'

Hundred explained. 'I had heard this Instrument was open to bribes, but the others waiting simply couldn't offer enough. These Instruments are lackeys brazenly seeking advantage in a new regime; greed is the one thing they all share. Let us hope that the Adjuster is no less greedy, and they share the bribe and keep their mouths shut.'

The wagon rocked over uneven flagstones through the

gateway. It was more than twenty paces deep, with a portcullis at the far side that was raised by the time they reached it. Odo flicked the reins, willing himself not to look back, and urged the horses out into the open air.

The moon had risen higher and now lit up the land ahead, including the teardrop-shaped lake Hundred had described to them. It was as large as Lenburh, a tarn fed by glacial meltwater from the surrounding mountains. This, then, was the source of the Foss, the waterfall he could still feel rumbling underfoot. And yet, as he approached the lake, following the snow-covered track that led down the rock bridge to the nearest shore, he could see that it was frozen. Obviously the ice didn't penetrate entirely down to its depths, otherwise there would be no water to flow anywhere.

'Keep going,' said Egda, 'onto the ice. It is very thick and will carry us. Aim for that spur of rock on the far side, the one that looks like a flag. It marks the road down.'

'Is there another gate to get through?' Odo asked.

'No, but there will be a small garrison stationed on the other side. They do not normally stir, as the gate is the main defence. With luck they will pay us little heed.'

Odo urged the horses warily onto the ice. It held, as promised. Many other wagons had come this way, and their iron-shod wheels had scored a rough road across the surface. Even so, horses and wheels slipped from time to time, and they could only move slowly across the ice. Tip swooped down to fly alongside them, wings flapping hard.

Eleanor came out of the canopied cabin and sat next to Odo on the driver's bench. With a whoop of delight she marvelled at them heading across a lake of ice in the middle of the mountains, under the moon! She couldn't wait to tell her father when they got home.

'We made it!' she cried. 'I thought we were going to have to fight our way through for sure.'

'Do not tempt fate,' cautioned Hundred, sticking her head out between them to look ahead. 'We are not safe yet.'

'What can they do now?'

Odo told her about the garrison on the other side of the lake.

'Just remember that you are supposed to be Wigburg,' said Hundred. 'She has likely been this way many times and is no longer prone to whooping.'

'How could anyone ever get tired of this view?' Eleanor craned her neck to take in the complete moonlit vista. Looking behind them, she asked, 'Do they always let off fireworks when people come through the gate?'

Odo risked a glance over his shoulder. A bright red light was shooting up into the sky, dripping fiery sparks and casting a bloody pall across the snow.

'No!' exclaimed Hundred. 'That is a flare alerting the garrison ahead that we are to be stopped. The Instrument has betrayed us!'

Odo instinctively flicked the reins to drive the horses faster, but Hundred reached out and made him loosen them again.

'We cannot risk speed,' she said. 'If a horse falls or we overturn, then all is lost. Keep up the pace.'

They were perhaps halfway across the lake.

'Who gave us away?' fumed Eleanor. 'It couldn't have been Wilheard or Wigburg, could it? And the Instrument took your money!'

'Unfortunately, those who can be bought do not always stay that way. I think this proves that the Instruments are more afraid of their superiors – and the regent – than we expected.'

Odo concentrated on the horses. The pretence was done. All that mattered now was escape. Eleanor called for the swords, and they instantly appeared, Runnel joining her knight as she clambered up onto the top of the load of doors at the rear of the wagon, following Hundred, and Biter floating in the air next to Odo like a giant dart. Egda came to join Odo on the driver's bench, staff at the ready.

'Hurry the horses as we leave the ice and pass the garrison fort,' Hundred told Odo. 'Trust in speed to throw off the aim of the archers and the horses' hoofs to deter any guards who try to bar our passage.'

At speed, the gate was barely a minute away. Already he could see the wooden palisade of the guardhouse, torches flaring and metal helmets shining as guards raced to get onto the walls.

Suddenly, Tip was flying next to him, chittering urgently.

'What's that you're saying?' he asked.

'l! o! o! k! l! e! f! t!'

He glanced in that direction and saw a large shape loping across the ice. It was a bear, such a dark brown it looked almost black in the night, and it was running right for them.

'a! n! d! r! i! g! h! t!'

Two more shapes, larger even than the bear and with long, lethally sharp-looking horns and teeth. Also running.

'Gore yaks!' cried Hundred. 'It seems we have craft-fire to contend with too.'

'Look,' said Eleanor, pointing in the rough direction of Twisletoth, on whose flanks a green spark flickered, sign of a craft-fire. 'That flare wasn't just to alert the guards ahead.'

'Would that we were up there rather than here,' Hundred growled. 'Then we would see a match! How do we go, Sir Odo? Will we outrace these creatures before reaching our human enemies?'

'I . . . I don't think so,' he gasped, panting with the effort of controlling the horses. They could smell the bear and were anxious to flee from it. Both the bear and the gore yaks were running along such a path as to cut them off some distance from the top of the road, where the guards awaited them. 'They're going to get to us first.'

'You and I will take the bear, Sir Odo,' said Biter. 'It will be no match for our combined strength.'

'And we are no match for the rain of arrows that will inevitably fall on us if we stop,' said Hundred grimly.

'Our options are sorely limited,' Egda declared. 'There is, however, one we have not discussed. A more direct route to the bottom than any winding road.'

'The Ghyll?' Hundred's expression turned to alarm. 'Sire, that would be madness.'

'Where madness blinds, inspiration may find.' The old man gripped his friend's shoulder. 'It is our only chance.'

'Who or what's the Ghyll?' Eleanor asked, made extremely nervous by Hundred's reaction.

'It lies through that notch yonder,' said Hundred, pointing at a triangle segment cut of the surrounding mountainsides, not far from where the guards waited. 'Once, there were two waterfalls leading from this lake to the plains below. One was the Foss, which you have already seen. The other, by far the more dangerous, was the Ghyll.'

'We can't swim down a waterfall!' exclaimed Odo, thinking of the horses as well as themselves.

'That would indeed be impossible,' Egda said, 'if the Ghyll had not frozen solid, long ago. And it is not a single vertical fall, but a series of many low falls.'

Eleanor gaped at him, remembering her desire to skate down a glacier. 'My father always says, "Be careful what you wish for." Now I know why!'

'It is madness,' Hundred said again. 'We will never survive.'

'We can go around the yaks at the last minute,' said Odo, calculating distances and times. 'We'll surprise them.'

'That is only the first of our trials. The ice will smash us to pieces!'

'Not if we ride the doors!' exclaimed Eleanor. 'Wilheard's doors! We can take one each, use them as sleds. If we hang on tight and brake where we can –'

'Madness,' said Hundred for the third time, but her teeth were bared now. It was almost a smile. 'Move quickly! We have mere moments to prepare.'

She looked after Egda while Eleanor prepared for Odo. His armour and pack were heavy, and so was the door she unshipped for him from the stack, but weight was no concern. She didn't even notice it. Her heart was pounding, and the night seemed alight. Urgency kept her thoughts off what a frozen waterfall might look like, one even more violent than the Foss.

When she looked up with a cry of 'Ready!' she saw that the bear and gore yaks and guards were now frighteningly close. The animals' eyes were smoke-filled from the sorcery of the craft-fire. Archers drew back their bows.

Odo wrenched the reins hard to his right, and the horses reared up in protest, throwing slivers of ice from their hoofs. Then they found their purpose again, along with their purchase, and began to gallop for their lives. The wagon bounced and lurched, almost overturning, newly loosened doors falling off the back. Everyone held on for grim life, Odo cursing as he now tried to hold the terrified horses back.

The wagon lurched onto two wheels, nearly tipped, then steadied on a new course, heading past the snarling yaks and directly for the top of the Ghyll. Arrows flew, but all fell short or were chopped out of the air by Eleanor and Hundred. Two struck the beasts, who howled in rage as they skidded on the ice to follow their quarry.

'Steady!' urged Egda, crouching beside Odo and pointing his staff forward as though he could see the way ahead. 'Steady!'

Shouts went up from the guards. A score or more emerged from the guardhouse waving swords and pikes, their spiked boots giving them ample purchase on the ice. If the Ghyll proved unpassable for any reason, Eleanor thought, they would have to fight humans as well as beasts in order to survive.

Her heart was in her throat as they reached the notch. Odo put every tiny scrap of strength he possessed into hauling back on the reins, as Hundred slammed on the brake. The horses saw the drop too and turned violently, breaking their traces and running free. The wagon sped on, teetering on two wheels, bouncing and skidding as everyone on board screamed or shouted, including the swords, before finally hitting a ridge of ice and slowly toppling over.

'Move!' cried Hundred, tossing her door and Egda's from the top of the wagon. Eleanor obeyed, with packs and armour to follow. She ignored the roaring of the beasts and the shouting of the soldiers. She put everything out of her mind except for the plan, their one and only chance of survival, quickly lashing her pack to the door and testing the looped handholds she had made for herself and Odo.

But when she glanced down the Ghyll, she faltered.

A narrow, jagged ravine led down the side of the mountain. Sandwiched between those lethal stone walls was a dragon's tongue of pure white, curving and twisting into savage bends and turns, surrounded on every side by knife-sharp edges and bone-smashing boulders, any one of which might kill her.

Odo joined her to carry the door to the very edge of the frozen waterfall. The first part of it was an almost vertical drop of a dozen paces or more, before it levelled out for a while and then went into a series of frighteningly steep curves.

But the bear and the gore yaks were almost upon them. There was no time to waste.

'Race to the bottom, Sir Eleanor?'

'Race, Sir Odo? I believe we will!'

The two knights lay full-length on their door, swords hovering overhead, and gripped the rope handles.

'Three, two, one – go!' they cried together.

They pushed off, Hundred and Egda hot on their heels. Then all was ice and speed and falling – and screaming, definitely screaming – as they raced for death or the bottom of the Ghyll, whichever came first.

CHAPTER
FOURTEEN

Prince Kendryk hardly ever slept these days. Finishing the mural, and finishing it quickly, was all that mattered. He could tell from the gloating in his grandmother's voice that time was running out.

When he did sleep, he dreamed of the earth shaking and splitting open, and huge gouts of flame blazing forth, as though the very world was ending.

He was in the middle of one of these dreams when a rough hand shook him awake. He was confused for a long moment. Was the ground shaking, or was he? Had he finished the mural at last and brought his plan to completion, or was it all unfinished and the outcome still unknown? Sometimes he wished he could simply let it go, and maybe if the outcome for Tofte wouldn't be so awful, he would have. Personal gain wasn't what he craved, and never had been.

'Look at him, sleeping on the floor like some common drab,' the regent muttered. 'Wake up, grandson! I have better things to do than attend to madmen in belfries.'

Kendryk sat up, rubbing his eyes. The person shaking him was Lord Deor, the Chief Regulator. Kendryk flinched away from his rough touch, and Lord Deor stepped back, executing the merest sketch of a bow as he went. The scabbard of his heavy sword dragged along the ground with a harsh scraping sound.

'He is awake, Your Highness.'

'About time.' She took Lord Deor's place at Kendryk's feet, not deigning to stoop. She towered over him like the throne she coveted, a tall structure of wood and gold that made anyone sitting in it look simultaneously very small and extremely self-important.

'I have news of your great-uncle,' she said without preamble, 'the *former* king. You must brace yourself.'

Kendryk placed his outspread hands on the stone floor. 'I am as braced as I will ever be, Grandmother.'

'He is dead,' she said. 'I received word this morning. There can be no doubt.'

The news, though half expected, was still shocking. Kendryk's eyes flooded with tears, and he sensed the world crowding in around him like the walls of a prison. Was he truly alone now? Did he have no one to turn to but himself?

Dragon, dragon, heed our call . . .

He looked up, past his grandmother, to the mural. It was so nearly finished. He had hoped for more time, but now, perhaps, there was none.

'I see that you are as shocked as I was,' Odelyn said without any trace of shock at all. Egda's sister, the regent, the architect of everything that had befallen Tofte in recent months, had no love lost for her brother. 'Knowing that it would be your wish, I have declared a state funeral for three days from now. The kingdom will pause in his honour and bid a final farewell to a great king.'

The slight emphasis on *great* was all for Kendryk.

'Yes,' he said through his grief. 'That is a good decision.'

'I thought you would be pleased, although . . .' She took three steps in a half-circle, coming around so he sat between her and a wide-smiling Lord Deor. '. . . I do hate to tread on my brother's memory. My coronation is of course scheduled for *two* days from now. I considered a delay, but why, when the nation is in need of succour? What better time for a new beginning?'

Coldness spread from Kendryk's heart through the rest of his body.

'You think you have won.'

'I have, grandson. Did you really think you would ever wear the crown? You are not fit to be king, and you know it.'

There's only one way to find out, he thought but did not say.

'I will accept your congratulations at a later date,' she said. 'You are grief-stricken at the news of your great-uncle's fate. We must remember that the last Old Dragon lived longer than anyone expected, and console ourselves with the knowledge that the kingdom will be well cared for in his wake.'

Kendryk could take no more of her gloating. He had but one question for her, and then she could be gone.

'Will there be a viewing?' he asked.

Her lips tightened under that proud, jutting nose. 'Why do you ask?'

'I wish to pay my respects.'

'There will be a coffin, but no viewing. The body is too . . . damaged.'

'You have seen it with your own eyes?'

'I have not,' she admitted, 'but there can be no doubt. No doubt at all. I have it on the word of no less than three Instruments and one Adjustor. The old man is dead at long last . . . so thoroughly dead that not even his most loyal supporter could doubt it.'

He had heard her slight hesitation, and wondered at it.

'How can anyone be more thoroughly dead than just . . . dead?' he asked.

Lord Deor's smile slipped off his face like blood off a burnished shield.

'There have been an abundance of royal deaths,' the regent said. 'I am informed that Egda died defending a nowhere place called Lenburh in the jaws of a bilewolf. I am also informed that he died in a town called Ablerhyll after a terrible accident. I am further informed that he died at Kyles Frost while foolishly attempting to sled down the

Ghyll. He can't have died in all three places — but he is sure to have died in one of them. Lord Deor is looking into it. I expect he'll have it resolved before the memorial. Won't you, Lord Deor?'

The Chief Regulator bowed, shooting Kendryk a murderous look. His right hand never strayed from the hilt of his sword.

'We will leave you to your grief, grandson,' the regent said. 'Rest assured that your troubles will soon be over. The crown that would sit so heavily on your tortured brow will soon sit on mine, and you may spend all your days daubing paint on walls, knowing the kingdom is well cared for. Who would not be satisfied with such an arrangement?'

She gestured dismissively at the mural, its sweeping lines and jagged points, and he was left with no illusions as to his fate. Yes, he might live beyond the coronation itself, but how long until he was found at the foot of a ladder with his neck broken? Or subtly poisoned by something slipped into one of his paints?

Not that there would be any point painting once Odelyn was crowned king of Tofte. If he didn't finish the mural before then, all his efforts would have been for naught.

The regent and the Chief Regulator swept out of the tower room without so much as a glance behind them. They saw no threat in him, and that was exactly as it should be.

Two days. Time hadn't quite run out yet. There was still a chance.

Looking up into the shadows high above, he sought the black, flitting shapes he knew would be there. One, the smallest, swooped down to catch his outstretched arm.

'Do you have a message, Tip?' he whispered.

The tiny bat shook his head and looked up at him with sorrowful eyes.

'All right then, little friend. You'd better tell me what happened.'

CHAPTER
FIFTEEN

The last thing Eleanor remembered was the sound of ice crunching against wood and being battered back and forth like a ball in a barrel, with Odo at her side and Runnel and Biter swooping in to try to lever their makeshift sled away from the most obvious dangers of the icy slope. That memory of the terrifying ice slide seemed to stretch on and on, but finally there had been an obstacle that could not be dodged, a sudden flight into the air, Odo shouting, the swords screaming – and then a blow to her head that flung her into darkness. It echoed as though it meant to go on forever.

Waking was much worse.

Eleanor sat upright and clutched desperately at her face. Something – a furred hand? – was pressed tightly over her mouth and nose. She was suffocating!

Her fingers found purchase, pulled, and suddenly light and air returned. For a moment, all she could do was gasp in breaths. She barely saw the dappled light of the clearing in which she found herself, or the splintered ruin of the doors that lay around her, or the tumbled disorder of packs and armour.

The first thing she truly noted was Odo, who lay struggling on his back next to her. There was a giant moth over his face. It was as large as a dinner plate, a match for the one that had been attached to her.

'Ugh!'

Fighting dizziness, she crouched over him and tore at the creature with both hands. It was surprisingly strong, with long legs that hung on tightly to his ears and hair, and curling antennae that batted at her eyes. Finally she ripped it away and it fluttered angrily off into the trees.

'What was that thing?' Odo wheezed in revulsion, catching his breath. He looked around. 'Where are we?'

'Giant moth,' she said. 'And I have no idea.'

But they were alive – and the immediate priority was finding Egda and Hundred. Eleanor staggered uneasily to her feet, red blotches still dotting her vision. There! Another ruined door, and Hundred grappling with her own smothering moth. Nearby lay Egda, his gold blindfold off and face tightly wrapped up in grey-and-brown wings. He wasn't moving.

'Gah!' Hundred freed herself the moment Eleanor reached their liege. They took one wing each and pulled with all their might. The moth tore in half and came away with a ghastly ripping sound. Egda fell back on the mossy ground, eyes half open, insensible even to Hundred's firm slap across his cheeks.

'He can't be dead,' Odo said. 'He can't be!'

'He isn't,' said Hundred, resting her head against the old man's chest. 'But his heart is slowing down. We must restore its rhythm – somehow.'

'I saw my father do this once.' Eleanor frantically cast her mind back, clutching at details that eluded her. 'Old Osgar . . . at the fair . . . one punch to the chest . . .'

'A slap to the sternum might well do it,' said Hundred, beginning to look frantic as the seconds passed and still Egda did not stir. 'With the heel of the hand, if it were powerful enough. But it could also kill –'

'We have to try,' whispered Eleanor.

They all looked at each other. No one wanted to be the one who killed the king, even if it was in an attempt to save him.

'Let me through,' said Odo after what seemed like minutes, but was only seconds. He bent down, raised his right hand, and brought it down hard where Eleanor indicated.

Egda flopped like an eel, coughed three times and opened his sightless eyes.

'My liege,' said Hundred, her voice betraying such relief that Eleanor had never imagined she could possess.

'I dreamed,' he said in a ragged voice, 'of sliding down the refuse chute at Winterset . . . and landing in a mountain of old pillows . . . feathers rose up to choke me . . .'

With uncanny accuracy, he reached out to clutch Hundred's wrist.

'We survived!'

'Indeed,' she said, patting the hand gripping her. 'We would not have, but for the quick thinking of these two young knights.'

Eleanor caught Odo's eye. *Knights*, not *knightlings*.

'But are we safe?' Egda went on. 'Were we followed? We must move quickly, ere we are discovered –'

'We will, my liege. First we must ascertain where we are. A forest of some kind . . . probably the upper reaches of the Groanwood. There were smother-moths.'

Egda rubbed his throat and sat up. 'The work of our enemy?'

'Most likely happenstance, or else worse would have come by now.'

'It may yet be on its way.'

Odo looked around him, at the close-packed trunks and the shadows beyond. There could be anything out there.

Feeling suddenly vulnerable, he reached for Biter but found his scabbard empty. So was Eleanor's.

'The swords,' he said. 'Biter and Runnel – where are they?'

Hundred checked her side. The curved blade that usually hung there was present.

'Inspect the wreckage!'

The three of them scrambled through the broken doors,

but found nothing but Egda's staff.

'This is most mysterious,' said Hundred.

'They wouldn't just leave,' said Eleanor. 'Would they?'

A twig crunched in the undergrowth. They spun to face it. Odo reached down to pick up a branch and hefted it in one hand, wishing he was at least wearing his armour. Eleanor did the same.

'Who's there?' she called. 'Come out where we can see you!'

An enormous hooded figure parted the bracken – a man easily a foot taller than Odo. He raised his hands to tug back the hood, revealing a scalp that was utterly bare of hair; deep, hooded eyes; and a face pockmarked with scars, like burns made by fiery sparks.

Craft-fire, thought Eleanor in alarm. Perhaps the moths hadn't been natural after all.

'To me!' cried Hundred, and Eleanor and Odo moved at the same instant, putting themselves in front of Egda. Without swords, without even knives, they would defend their liege to the death.

As the giant moved towards them, two familiar voices cried out from the bracken.

'Sir Odo!'

'Sir Eleanor! We are here for you!'

Their hearts leaped as the swords rocketed towards them.

Barely had the familiar pommels met their hands when their assailant gestured and tiny darts hissed out of the trees, striking them each in the throat. Odo felt a sting of pain, followed by a rushing, clouding sensation as darkness swept over him once more. The last thing he saw as he dropped to the ground was six more hooded figures stepping out of the trees, and Biter sweeping up to meet them.

Eleanor's second awakening in as many hours took much longer than the first, arriving in fits and starts like Pickles the cat approaching a stranger. She didn't even realise she was awake until she caught herself wondering if the smothering moths had just been a terrible dream . . . and Egda's near-death experience . . . followed by the giant figure approaching them from the heart of the forest . . .

None of it had been a dream. It was all real.

Eleanor came to full wakefulness with a sudden jerk, sitting bolt upright and flinging what felt like a blanket from her legs. She was lying on a rush bed in a long stone room lit only by a fire at one end. By that flickering light she made out a high, vaulted ceiling, tapestries of dragons in flight down the walls and three sleeping figures lying on beds next to hers: Odo, Hundred and Egda, all three snoring heavily.

She let out a sigh of partial relief. They were alive, somehow. But where were they? And what was going to happen to them next?

Her eyes adjusted further to the firelight and made out

a sword stand in front of the fire. In it were two swords, conversing in low tones.

'Runnel!'

The topmost sword leaped from its rest on the stand and rushed to her. 'Sir Eleanor! You have awoken at last.'

'Yes, but I don't know . . . anything. What's going on? Where were you when we needed you?'

'That is either a very short or a very long story, depending on how you tell it.' Runnel balanced on her tip and leaned close, so her ruby touched Eleanor on the arm. 'My brother and I, we thought you were safe in the forest at the bottom of the Ghyll. We did not know about the moths, otherwise we would never have left you.'

'But then that man in the woods . . .' Eleanor rubbed her neck, where a numb, upraised patch marked the spot the dart had struck her. 'He attacked us.'

'There is much we did not know.'

A door opened and closed, and a hooded figure stepped into the room. Eleanor stood and raised Runnel before her.

'Stop there. Come not one step closer!'

The figure raised its hands straight up into the air. 'I'm Adelind,' it squeaked in the high-pitched voice of a startled girl around Eleanor's age, 'third apprentice to Master Knucius. I mean you no harm.'

Now that Eleanor studied the figure more closely, she could see that it was much shorter and more slender than the one she had seen in the woods. And when Adelind hesitantly tugged back her hood, revealing a thick mane of golden curls, messily tied back in a knot, she knew for certain that they were very different people. Adelind had a long, pointy nose and sprightly blue eyes, and though she had small spark scars on her face, far fewer than the huge fellow in the forest.

'Where are we?' Eleanor asked her.

'C-Clynan Smithy. Your swords came to us for aid.'

'And so you attacked us?'

'We only did as our charter demands. None but those who serve the forge – the true smith and apprentices – may know its location. Not even knights. We are honestly and terribly sorry to have frightened you.'

'I . . . I wasn't frightened,' said Eleanor. 'I was just confused.'

'Understandably so. All will be explained, I promise. Can I put my hands down now?'

'Yes, of course. Sorry.'

'Are you feeling well? Your sleep was long and very deep. Can you stand?'

Eleanor, as yet unwilling to let go of Runnel, tested her legs. Her knees held.

'Good,' Adelind said. 'Would you care to eat with us? We are about to have our evening meal.'

'I'll wait for the others, if it's all the same to you.' She still didn't entirely trust the situation and wasn't about to leave her friends alone for a second.

'They will wake soon. The fire in your veins roused you first, as Master Knucius predicted.'

Eleanor checked on Odo, then Egda, then Hundred. They all seemed to be sleeping soundly. On the floor next to Egda's bed lay his staff and the small blade he used to cut up his meals, the only weapons he carried. Surrounding Hundred's bed . . .

Eleanor blinked, doubting her eyes.

All about Hundred's bed was a sea of silvery metal. Fixed blades, folding blades, blades that could be concealed in a collar, cuff, hem or epaulette, or in the heels and toes and sides of boots. Knives for stabbing, sawing, slashing and throwing. Needles, spikes, barbs, prickets – every deadly shape imaginable was present in unimaginable number.

'Ninety-nine,' said Adelind, catching the direction of Eleanor's gaze.

'What?'

'That's how many weapons your friend was carrying. We have never seen such armament on a single person – all fashioned from the finest steel too. She is truly a bodyguard fit for a king.'

Eleanor studied Adelind closely and was relieved to find nervousness and restless excitement, but no sign of ill intent. Still, it unnerved her to understand how exposed they were.

'You know who we are?'

'We told them,' said Runnel. 'We had to, in order to obtain their help.'

'You mean they wouldn't have helped us anyway?' asked Odo from behind them. 'They would have just left us there, maybe dying, because we weren't important enough?'

He rose to his feet and Biter swept into his waiting hand. He had woken a moment ago, and pretended to snore while taking stock of his surroundings. It didn't sound as if Eleanor was in any danger, but it paid to be cautious. Who knew what sort of callous band they had fallen in with?

Literally *fallen*, he thought, remembering all too clearly the headlong plunge down the Ghyll. They had been lucky to survive twice that day already. He wasn't going to risk their fortune turning now.

'Oh dear,' said Adelind, putting her hands up again. 'You do not understand.'

'So explain,' said Hundred, also rising to her feet. She held her sword in one hand. 'We are listening.'

Adelind took a step back with another squeak.

'We mean only good, not harm!' she said.

'If that is so,' said Egda with quiet authority, 'then you have nothing to fear from us.'

Adelind took in the four companions and their weapons with one nervously assessing glance, then lowered her hands.

'Perhaps . . . yes, it's almost certainly best that Master Knucius talk to you now. This way.'

Turning quickly, she led them towards the door, which opened before her and guided them deeper into the smithy.

Master Knucius was the giant they had seen in the forest. He was no less impressive sitting at the head of a broad wooden table lined with steaming dishes. When Adelind brought the smithy's guests to him, he stood and indicated that they should sit in the empty positions around the table. There were five out of eleven. The rest were filled with men and women ranging from Adelind's age to around forty winters.

'These are my apprentices,' said Master Knucius in a voice like ancient trees falling. 'Snorri, Theudhar, Vragi, Childa and Jorunn. Adelind you have already met. Welcome to Clynan Smithy, the last remaining true smithy in the Groanwood.'

He bowed, and both Odo and Eleanor felt compelled to bow in return. Though these were the people who had shot them with darts and carried them to places unknown, there was something about the giant man that demanded deference. Hundred bowed too, although not so deeply. Only Egda remained upright, though he did bend his head.

'Please, sit,' Knucius implored them. 'Eat. You must be very hungry after your ordeal.'

That was true. Odo's stomach rumbled at the scent of fresh bread, roasted meat and numerous fragrant herbs. He glanced at Eleanor, who nodded tightly. Unless Hundred or Egda said otherwise, there was no obvious reason to be sceptical – of the food, at least. They would all be eating it.

Adelind poured ale. Knucius returned to his seat when Egda was in his. Odo felt the bright eyes of the apprentices watching him closely, and sensed a thousand questions waiting to be put to them.

'Why are you being so nice to us now?' he asked, getting in first. 'After putting us to sleep with poison darts?'

'The smithy is secret,' said the oldest apprentice, the man named Vragi. 'No one can know where it is.'

That accorded with what Adelind had said, but it wasn't the end of the issue. 'Couldn't you have told us about it? Maybe you could have just blindfolded those of us who can see.'

'There wasn't time,' said the apprentice called Childa. 'Guards were descending along the road at an unprecedented pace. Any hesitation would have been disastrous for all of us.'

Hundred nodded as though she had expected this answer. 'You covered your tracks well, I presume.'

'Very well indeed,' said Adelind with a grin.

'And how did you convince the guards that they found what they sought?'

'Four fresh pig carcasses,' said Knucius in his bedrock-steady tones, 'mangled beyond recognition. What the ruse did not require, we eat tonight.'

He gestured at the bowls of meat. Odo identified trotters, ears, tails and other parts of a pig that could not be mistaken for human no matter how 'mangled' they were.

His stomach turned. Suddenly he wasn't hungry. The apprentices, however, seemed delighted by the unexpected feast.

'Are you really Egda the Old Dragon?' asked Snorri, the youngest male, as he scooped a couple of choice cuts onto his plate.

'I was.' Egda sniffed. 'Now I am just Egda.'

'*Sir* Egda,' Hundred firmly corrected him.

'And you're on your way to Winterset to thwart Regent Odelyn's plans to oust Prince Kendryk and finish getting rid of the knights and stewards?'

'You are well informed of the kingdom's affairs,' Egda observed drily. 'Would that I'd had your knowledge sooner.'

'We send patrols all about us, to keep the smithy secret, and so learn the news from intercepted wanderers and the like,' said Knucius. 'Also, the farmsteads from whom we source provisions have all had Instruments imposed, with their greatly increased tithes, taxes and tolls. They suffer, as all will suffer if Odelyn secures her grip upon the realm. Please, Jorunn, pass our guests the greens.'

Eleanor took the bowl.

'What's a true smithy?' she asked. 'And why is it so secret?'

The six apprentices went to answer at once and were silenced by a raised hand from their master.

'That is a harder question to answer than you realise,' he said. 'Much of the world's knowledge is dangerous and should not be shared widely. On the other hand, knowledge that is hidden is in constant danger of being lost. I am charged with preserving a pact that has existed for many centuries, ensuring that certain techniques do not fall into the wrong hands. One of my apprentices will carry on the tradition when I am gone. Thus Clynan Smithy has endured the ages, and will endure ages to come.'

Odo glanced at Eleanor. She raised an eyebrow. The smith's reference to a pact had not gone unnoticed.

Knucius continued, 'Suffice it to say that your faithful swords sensed the presence of Clynan Smithy in your time of need, and came immediately to us. They could have guided you here, through the Groanwood, but you were incapacitated. Once we learned who you were, we rushed to your aid.'

That brought Odo back to his earlier concern. 'And if we had not been knights and an Old Dragon and his bodyguard? Would you have left us there to die?'

'We would never have known you were there. Only your swords – magical swords that only knights can wield – could have found this place, and except in direst need we do not stray beyond our doorstep. This, in part, is how we have remained undiscovered for so long.'

Eleanor supposed that made a kind of sense, although it troubled her if she pondered it too deeply. Had no one ever stumbled across the smithy by accident and told others of their discovery? How could something be so well hidden that it absolutely never could be found? Perhaps it was underground, or invisible . . .

'I think I met you once,' Hundred told Knucius around a cheekful of gristle. 'In Aern, after the great revolt. You were blacksmith to the king's guard.'

'For a time, yes, I was. You have a good memory. That was many years ago.' His deep-set eyes twinkled with fond recollections. 'Your name was different then.'

'I never put much store in names.'

'No, I see that now.'

Biter was buzzing at Odo's back, as though he wanted to ask something.

'Yes, Biter, go ahead.'

'𝔈xcuse me, 𝔐aster 𝔖mith, but you have healed my knight and our siege. We will be forever grateful.'

'I am honoured to be of service.' Knucius inclined his head. 'Would that I could do more, but my duty lies here, not in the world beyond.'

'𝔓erhaps there is something else you could do . . . for me . . . if it is not too much to ask.'

'I know the boon you seek,' said Knucius, and suddenly Odo did too.

Biter's nick, the sword's one tiny imperfection – no one knew what had caused it, and the smiths at Anfyltarn had been unable to repair it. Perhaps a *true* smith possessed the skill to make Biter whole.

'Only two things can harm an enchanted sword,' Knucius said. 'A dragon's tooth or another enchanted sword. Do you remember which caused your nick?'

'No,' said Biter forlornly. 'But I have long suspected that I was once a dragonslayer. If only I knew!'

'Does the nick itself plague you?' Knucius asked. 'Or is it the mere thought of imperfection that causes you pain?'

It was a question that Biter did not immediately answer.

'Both, or so I believe,' supplied Runnel. 'My brother is undoubtedly vain, but he also suffers from ignorance. This might be connected to the nick, or to the centuries he spent at the bottom of a river –'

'Eels.' Biter shuddered. 'Would that I could forget them.'

'I believe he would be a happier sword,' Runnel concluded, 'if he could remember.'

'Would it please you for me to grant this boon?' Knucius asked Runnel. 'Would it ease your burden?'

'I am no longer the Sorrowful Sword, Master Smith,' she told him. 'My curse is lifted. I serve Sir Eleanor, who I know will one day be a great knight, and my liege, but I do also care for my brother's well-being. We are siblings of the true smithy in Eathrylden. We are bound forever.'

'Nobly said,' the smith told her. 'Very well. I will inspect the wound this evening, after our meal, and repair it if I can. This will bring me a rare opportunity to teach my apprentices more of the art of such blades.' Heads bobbed eagerly around the table. 'I would say one thing however, in caution. Sometimes we forget things for a reason, humans and swords alike. Dragons too, although they would never admit it.'

'The mighty Quenwulf charged us with learning more of our true natures,' Biter said.

'Did she? Well, she has her reasons, I suppose.'

He spoke with such familiarity that Eleanor asked, 'Do you know her?'

'Distantly,' he replied with a faint smile. 'I owe my livelihood to a boon from her father.'

On that subject he would say no more. They passed the rest of the meal in conversation about smother-moths, barrow bats, gore yaks, bilewolves and many other strange creatures awaiting the young knights in the wider world. If even half of the ones she hadn't met yet were real, Eleanor decided, the world was a very exciting – and dangerous – place indeed.

CHAPTER
SIXTEEN

'Wait here until I come back,' Adelind told them upon returning them to their room. 'All except Biter. If you will come with me, good sword.'

'Can't we watch?' asked Odo.

'No, the master said so,' she said with calm finality. She seemed to have overcome her earlier nervousness. Odo wondered how often she saw strangers. Possibly rarely. 'The secrets of the smithy can only be known to anyone sworn into its service.'

That was a blow to Eleanor's curiosity, but not entirely unexpected. When Adelind and Biter were gone, she restlessly paced the room, tapping the four walls with the toes of her boots.

'What is it with this place?' she wondered for the hundredth time. 'Have you noticed that there are no windows? Just lots of musty dragon tapestries.'

Odo nodded. 'I haven't seen any doors either. Not to the outside.'

'Plenty of chimneys though. I guess that's to let out any smoke from the forge.'

'You guess correctly,' said Egda. 'I have been in one such smithy before. I was very young. My mother, the king, sent me to learn something of this secret tradition, just as I learned a little about many other secrets in the kingdom. That is one of the principle duties of a ruler: to know one's kingdom more thoroughly than anyone else.'

'Which makes me wonder how young Kendryk has ended up where he has,' Hundred said. 'He was trained, wasn't he?'

'As well as any heir.' Egda looked glum. 'We either missed something, or the regent had her own secrets that she kept from us.'

'My coin is on the latter.'

Hundred began putting her many blades back into their pockets, while Eleanor watched in fascination.

Odo lay back on his bed, listening to the fire crackle. He wondered what was happening to Biter. Knucius would have to soften his steel in a furnace in order to repair the nick. He hoped they wouldn't have to melt him down completely and reforge him. Surely then he would be an entirely different sword, and it would take a long time.

'𝕯o not be afraid for my brother,' said Runnel, coming to hover next to him. '𝕿he smiths will do nothing to harm him.'

'But what if he comes back . . . different?' asked Odo, voicing deeper fears. 'What if he remembers something important from the past that he has left undone and doesn't want me to be his knight any more?'

Eleanor crossed the room to punch his shoulder. 'Don't be such a lubberwort. You're the one who woke him up, remember? He'd still be at the bottom of the Silverrun if it wasn't for you. He's not going to leave you behind just because he remembered a . . . I don't know, a girlfriend or boyfriend or something. Do swords have girlfriends or boyfriends, Runnel?'

'No,' her sword said. 'It is not in our natures to associate solely with our own kind.'

'There you go then. You're his knight, Sir Odo. He's not going to leave you for anyone.'

'I hope not,' he said, with a feeling of relief that surprised him. Although Odo hadn't wished to be a knight, he had learned to like the sense of accomplishment that came with it. He loved the satisfaction of doing a good day's work, as he had learned in the mill. Now he had new work, and he wanted to do it well.

'Hope for something more useful,' Eleanor told him, 'like a quick road to Winterset before the regent has her way.'

Hundred started to say something, but was drowned out by a sudden roar. All eyes turned to face the door, half expecting a monster to burst in, but the door remained firmly shut. The roar persisted for several seconds, then subsided to a deep hiss through which loud pounding sounds could be heard. Hammers, Eleanor thought – but hammers unlike any she had ever known – followed by a screech of metal on metal that made her ears ring.

'It is the forge!' cried Egda over the terrible sound.

'What are they doing in there?' bellowed Odo.

'I do not know. Some things are secret even from kings!'

There was no point talking any longer. They lay or paced or polished their weapons, as their individual temperaments dictated, and waited for the din to subside.

When, with one last earsplitting screech, the forge finally fell silent, Odo took the pillow off his head and sat up. The smithy seemed to shudder in the sudden absence of noise. He caught Eleanor's eye, hardly daring to breathe.

A thump at the door made them both jump. They were on their feet when it opened, eager for news of Biter's fate.

It was Adelind. 'Come, Sir Odo,' she said, gesturing for him to follow.

Her expression was unreadable, which only made the butterflies in his stomach worse.

'I want to come too,' said Eleanor. 'Odo's my friend. He might . . . need me.'

'And I,' said Runnel. 'Biter may be something of a fool, but he is my brother.'

'Very well,' Adelind told them, 'but no more. Swear that you will speak to no one of what you see.'

'I swear,' said Odo.

'And I,' Eleanor said.

Adelind turned and led them out of the room, into a section of the smithy they hadn't visited before. Here too the ceilings were high and the spaces lit by blazing lamps or the occasional glowing stone, but the flagstone floor was appreciably older, with slabs bowed in the middle by the passage of many feet. The walls were stained black as though from blasts of fire and smoke. The only tapestries they saw were threadbare and partially burned. Apart from the roof high above, they saw no wood, and as elsewhere, no windows.

Adelind guided them to a workroom that was so hot Odo instantly broke into a heavy sweat. Benches lining the walls were stacked with what looked like large, dull grey trays in various semicircular shapes, many of them rather like kites, narrowing at one end to a near point. Bundles of long, curved sticks that might have been sled runners hung from the beams nearby. There was a powerful smell of charcoal and iron.

Biter lay on a broad, stone table surrounded by Knucius and the apprentices. He wasn't moving.

'Is he . . . ?' Odo had to stop to swallow. 'I mean, did you . . . ?'

'The nick is gone,' said Knucius, and indeed there was no sign of it at all. The blade shone as though newly forged. Biter's emerald gleamed, and even the small dents in his golden hilt had been polished away.

'*he looks . . . brand new*,' said Runnel, with something approaching jealousy.

'In many ways he is,' said the smith. 'He has been washed in sweet oils, bathed in three fires, hammered by a master smith. This will profoundly alter a sword. Is it any wonder he has not woken yet?'

'But he will, won't he?' asked Eleanor.

'I believe so.' Knucius motioned them closer. 'Calling to him may hasten his return. That is the reason I had you brought here.'

Eleanor could see the sense in that. It reminded her of the time Farmer Gladwine was kicked in the head by Pudding and, despite all her father's salves and balms, would only open his eyes when Mistress Nant offered him one of her legendary tarts.

She pressed through the apprentices and leaned over the sword. 'Can you hear me, Biter? If you can, you'd better come back quickly. Sir Odo is forlorn without you. It's all I can do to get him to eat, and you don't want him to starve away to nothing, do you?'

Biter didn't stir.

Runnel tried next. Slipping out of her scabbard, she flew above the table, so her hilt pointed down towards Biter's.

'*Little brother, awaken. You have slept long enough. If you're not careful, the eels will get you again!*'

Biter shivered minutely. The rattling sound of his blade

on the stone gave them momentary hope, but he quickly fell still and did not move again.

Finally Odo moved forward with a heavy heart, for what if Biter failed to wake no matter what he said? Sir Odo would be swordless in a world where knights were sorely needed.

'Biter, please wake up. The regent is taking over the kingdom and we must get Egda to Winterset so he can stop her. We can't do it without you. Everything started with you, remember? I wouldn't be here if we hadn't found you in the river. You can't leave us now.'

'Not just when it's getting interesting,' added Eleanor. 'You'll miss out on all the fighting!'

Biter lay still and heavy on the stone slab, as though none of them had spoken.

'I am sorry,' said Knucius. 'I believe he will awake, but perhaps not in time. I can provide one of our ordinary swords for you, if that would serve your purpose. A pallask, perhaps, or a more elegant rapier?'

'Wait,' Odo said, still thinking of Biter's long resting place at the bottom of Dragonfoot Hole. 'There's one thing we haven't tried.'

Reaching across the table, he ran the pad of his thumb down Biter's exceedingly sharp edge. Instantly, his skin parted and blood began to drip onto the stone.

Wincing, he raised the hand and squeezed his bleeding finger so crimson drops fell onto the repaired blade, running down the gutter just as they had when Odo had woken him the first time.

'Flee, Sir Nerian! Flee! I will save you!'

With that sudden cry, Biter swept up and off the slab. Smith, apprentices, Odo and Eleanor dived for the floor as the sword slashed and stabbed empty air overhead as though fighting an invisible opponent. Biter recoiled from powerful blows in return. Sparks flew. He seemed to make ground, but then suddenly, propelled by nothing anyone could see, he flew across the room, ricocheted off the wall and fell to the floor with a clatter and a ghastly cry.

'Noooooo!!'

Then all was still, and Odo, simultaneously hoping and fearing that the sword had lapsed back into sleep, crept closer to pat Biter's sharkskin grip.

'Don't be afraid, Biter,' he said. 'You're safe.'

'Sir Odo?' said the sword, as though waking from a powerful dream. 'For a moment, I thought you were my former knight . . . returned from the dead.'

'Do you remember him now?' Eleanor asked. 'Do you remember what happened to you?'

'I did . . . but it is fading quickly.' Biter stirred in Odo's hand as though he might fly out again. 'I see a terrible knight, clad entirely in black. She wields a terrible sword. We fight, Sir Nerian and I together. He is strong of heart, mighty of arm. I am fast. It seems that we might defeat our

179

foe, until . . . behind the black knight I see an even darker shape . . . a shadow that grows taller . . . and wider . . . No!' cried the sword. 'I can see no more. No more!'

'It's all right, Biter,' Odo soothed. 'You're fixed now. You don't have to remember any of this. It doesn't matter any longer. The only thing I care about is that you're back with us again.'

'Your young knight speaks the truth,' said Knucius. 'Whatever you recall or don't recall, it is unlikely to have any bearing now.'

'There is one thing,' Biter told them in a steadier voice. 'I remember the name of the sword I fought – the sword that killed Sir Nerian, I can only assume. That sword's name was Tredan Falconstone. Perhaps you know of him, Master Smith? If you can tell me that he has been lost or melted into slag, I will rest easier.'

Knucius's ruddy face lost some of its colour.

'I do know this sword,' he said. 'I know him very well. The smith who prenticed me was charged with erasing a similar injury to yours, a nick in the Falconstone's edge, but one that had grown worse with use over many years. My master knew the sword by reputation and attempted to melt him in the forge, but her ruse was discovered before she could complete the task. Still glowing orange with heat, Falconstone slew my master and escaped along with his knight – an equally damaged and dangerous individual. I have never seen either since, but I have heard of both, although they have changed their names. The sword is called the Butcher Blade of Winterset now, and his knight is Lord Deor, Chief Regulator of the realm, and the regent's right-hand man.'

'Winterset, you say?' Biter's emerald gleamed brilliantly in the firelight.

'Yes, your destination.' Knucius nodded. 'But be wary, should you encounter the Falconstone. My master, before she died, was able to wrest free the black opal that adorned his hilt. I smashed that stone myself, hoping this might end the sword's grim intelligence, but all I achieved was to rob him of his voice – an act that appears to have driven him to even greater cruelty and malice. No sword that I know of, anywhere in the world, is more dangerous.'

With that grim pronouncement he crossed to one of the shelves lining the walls, took down four of the kite-shaped plates and handed them to his guests. Odo and Eleanor realised that what they held were actually shields, shields that looked like leather but were metallic to the touch and incredibly light. They were big enough to shield Eleanor from throat to knee, and Odo from throat to thigh.

'Take these,' said Knucius. 'You will need them if you encounter Falconstone. They were made from single dragon scales and will turn even the most deadly of blades.'

Dragon scales? Eleanor examined her new shield in wonder. What were dragon scales doing in a smithy?

Odo was asking himself similar questions. Did that mean the tusklike shapes lining the walls were dragon claws, or even teeth?

'Thank you, Master Smith,' said Biter on their behalf. 'We will find the Falconstone and end his butchery.'

'Your true quest is to stop the regent,' Knucius reminded the sword firmly.

'One will likely demand the other,' said Runnel.

'Indeed.' The smith wiped his hands on his apron. 'Return to your liege now and rest. You leave in the morning. I have arranged a sailing barge to take you to Winterset, ultimately along the Hyrst. You will arrive before nightfall.'

He clapped his hands and the apprentices filed from the room. Eleanor and Odo followed Adelind back to their quarters, where they put a light bandage on Odo's thumb and relayed the events that had occurred.

'I remember Lord Deor,' Egda said. 'But the one I knew must be dead by now, and the title inherited by a cousin or some other relative, since he had no children. Or perhaps the regent simply chose to grant a stranger the title, rewarding them for their services. Or to secure those services.'

'And those of the Falconstone,' said Hundred.

'Yes, it would not be the first time a sword ruled its knight, rather than the other way around.'

'Impossible!' said Eleanor, nudging Odo. 'I can't imagine it.'

Odo wasn't in the mood for jokes. The following night

they might be in Winterset, and Biter was bent on a rematch with the sword that had notched him. Odo could tell from his sword's brooding silence that it was all he thought about. And if they survived that encounter, they would still have the regent to deal with. She sounded dangerous enough without a sword.

'Don't worry, Biter,' he said. 'We'll do everything we can to set things right for you. And if you remember anything else, you'll let us know?'

'Thank you, Sir Odo. Yes, I will. I still do not know how I ended up in the river for so long.'

'At least you know now that Sir Merian didn't cast you aside,' said Runnel. 'That is one fear you can put to rest.'

'But I could not save him,' Biter said with some bitterness. 'Surely he would have prevailed against any ordinary knight!'

There was no reassurance to be had on that part. Sometimes knights died, as Runnel knew well. She had lost three in a row. Eleanor could only hope that the runs of bad luck for both swords would end now.

CHAPTER
SEVENTEEN

After breaking their fast the next morning, Knucius and the apprentices took their visitors down a series of winding ramps deep, into the earth. At the bottom, Eleanor and Odo were amazed to find a wharf carved from the stone, alongside which rushed an underground river, moving so quickly it was flecked with foam. Moored at the wharf was a barge with elegant orange sails, furled, onto which they loaded their armour and a small amount of supplies donated by the smithy. Its sole crew member, introduced as Captain Gnasset, welcomed them aboard with a grunt and gestured for them to stay out of the way. Vragi untied the mooring ropes and the other apprentices pushed the barge away from the dock while they said farewells over the echoing roar of the river and gave their thanks. But for the help of Knucius and his apprentices, they might have fallen into the hands of the regent, or much worse.

'Come back and visit one day!' Adelind called to Eleanor as the barge wallowed away. 'It gets lonely here.'

'I don't even know where "here" is,' said Eleanor. They hadn't once seen the outside of the smithy.

'Just send Runnel into the Groanwood to find us. She'll show you the way.'

'Will you shoot me with a dart again if I do?' asked Odo, still grumpy about that.

'Only for fun.' Adelind grinned and waved, then followed Knucius and the rest of the apprentices back up the ramp.

Eleanor waved back, then turned to look over the barge, staying well clear of Captain Gnasset, who stood at the stern, tiller in one hand. The long, flat-bottomed boat was called *Photine* and there was a cabin towards the stern for passengers, the deck at the front dedicated to cargo. It was stacked with boxes and barrels and sacks, covered with tarpaulins and roped down. No one would think it anything but a trader on a regular voyage down the river.

Photine was slow to get going, but once the current had her in its grip, she soon got up to a speed something akin to a slow walk. Gnasett rarely broke what appeared to be a vow of silence, at one point directing them gruffly to use poles to fend the barge off. The underground river ran through an artificial passage that had suffered several rockslides and the way ahead was lit only by a lantern hanging from *Photine*'s snub-nosed prow. After several close calls, Odo was glad to see daylight ahead, then a diamond-shaped exit from the tunnel.

They rushed out of a mountainside on a raging swell of water that carried them rapidly under a thick canopy of trees. Branches met and tangled overhead like grasping fingers, hiding the sky above from view – along with any chance of seeing the secret underground river to the smithy. With a rattle and snap, the mainsail rose and filled, Gnasset hauling on the halyard from her steering post at the stern. The barge was rigged to be sailed alone, and judging from her rare speech and general lack of interest in the others, Gnasset liked it that way. Probably the smiths had chosen the most reticent bargee they could find, one who would have no trouble keeping their secrets.

'This river is the Hyrst,' said Egda, filling his lungs. 'I have not smelled its fresh, cool scent for too long. My friends, now at last I truly feel as though we are coming home!'

Eleanor resisted the impulse to tell him that Winterset wasn't home for them, but a far-off place they had only heard about in stories. Still, she too felt excitement rising at the thought that they would soon stand where knights of old had been dubbed and had duelled each other, where heroes had lived and died, where wars had begun and ended. Her mother had passed through here, on the way to the battle that had earned her both honour and an honourable ending. Time would tell what fate had in store for Eleanor and Odo, but at least they were going somewhere *important*.

Odo measured the space between the cargo on the forward deck. There was a narrow lane between boxes, perfect for more knife practice, where they could stay hidden as well.

'Bored already, Sir Odo?' Hundred grinned as she tossed them each a blade.

Eleanor remembered all of Hundred's weapons laid out in the smithy. 'Why ninety-nine weapons,' she asked, 'not a round hundred, since that's what you're called? Have you lost one?'

'Never. They only counted ninety-nine.'

'You mean there's one they didn't find?'

'In a sense. There is one nobody can ever take from me.'

'Short of killing you,' said Egda.

'No one's managed that yet, my liege.'

'The day is young.' Egda smiled to himself as he turned into the cabin, leaving the hatch open so he could hear the knifeplay of the young knights and the rush of river water from *Photine*'s passage with equal clarity.

Eleanor worried at the mystery of Hundred's missing weapon while she and Odo reviewed the moves they had learned on the road to Kyles Frost. Did she have a spell she could call on in direst need? Or some kind of supernatural creature she was able to summon just once in her life? That would be a fine trick.

It was Odo who guessed the truth. He had been considering possibilities much nearer to his experience, such as Hundred's intelligence and knowledge of combat, her cunning and her wit.

'It's you, isn't it?' he asked her while recovering his breath from a particularly close bout with Eleanor. 'You're the hundredth weapon.'

Hundred bowed. 'At my lord's service.'

'Who gave you that name?' Eleanor asked, kicking herself for not guessing before Odo.

'A master of fighting with only one's body. She trained me in the desert for three years, without weapons of any kind, except for the ones that I possess by nature. She taught me that what makes the knight is not the sword . . . no offence,' she added for Biter and Runnel's benefit. 'But the spirit. If the spirit is strong, no enemy can defeat us.'

'Even those armed with bows and arrows?' asked Egda, poking his head out to play the sceptic with wicked pleasure. 'Or dragons?'

'My liege knows full well the difference between death and defeat,' she said, unfazed. 'That is why we are on this mission, is it not?'

Eleanor and Odo practised all morning, getting used to their new dragon-scale shields as well as the knives. They broke off only when other vessels neared, or there were travellers on the riverbank who might catch a glimpse of them. Though Knucius had taken steps to make it look like they had died in the fall down the Ghyll, it wouldn't pay to advertise the presence of any knights sparring on their way to Winterset. So a family of traders they became again, eating lunch in the afternoon sun and taking turns watching from the bow of the barge for any debris or newly formed sandbanks. Save Egda, who stayed in the cabin, thinking deep thoughts.

The river became steadily wider as the day wore on, joining other tributaries rushing down from the mountains. Occasionally they saw huts or small boating communities and waved at the children who took delight in their passing. There was little traffic on or between either bank, and only one bridge, which required the mast to be unstepped and lowered, Gnasset dismissing the offer of help from Odo, skilfully using a mechanism of gears and pulleys to bring it down and raise it again.

Hundred remarked on the lack of traffic on both river and riverbank, putting the blame on the regent, who had clamped down on the movement of Tofte's traders and raised tolls that made travel uneconomic. The state of the Hyrst River reflected the state of the kingdom as a whole, she feared, where short-term gain for the regent would be paid for by long-term disaster.

Once they spied a trio of disconsolate-looking knights hacking through an overgrown path on the eastern bank of the river. Their markings declared them to be from Nhaga, a prosperous province half to the east of Winterset as Lenburh was to the west. They looked tired and dusty.

'Nhagese knights,' Hundred said to Egda. 'They were ever among the most loyal, sire. Should we . . . ?'

'Do you recognise any?' asked Egda.

'One has the look and stature of Sir Haelf the Tall,' replied Hundred. 'A daughter . . . granddaughter, perhaps.'

'Yes,' said Egda, answering Hundred's unfinished question. 'We may have need of them.'

'Can you bring us closer to shore?' Hundred called to Gnasset, who shrugged but obeyed. 'Within arrow-range but outside the reach of a throwing-knife. There.'

Hundred stood up and waved her arms as the barge slowed, both wind and current weaker near the bank.

'Good knights!' she called. 'Where head you?'

'Winterset!' called out a very tall woman with an accent that emphasized her *r*'s. 'Spare us your offer of passage. We can't afford it.'

'A knight short of coin? You must have fallen on hard times.'

'Hard times indeed, for we have lost our lands and our livelihood. We go to petition the prince to reconsider his recent actions.'

'Are you the rebels I've heard rumours of?'

'We are no rebels!' exclaimed one of the other knights, a man with a vivid scar under his chin, like a second mouth. 'Our loyalty to the crown is unquestioned!'

'Well then, penniless knights, would you consider a boon?' Hundred called back. 'My father was a soldier. He had that same footsore look as you on returning from a campaign. Rest on a barge headed in the direction you're going will gain you much and cost me nothing.'

The knights quickly conferred as the *Photine* grew nearer.

'Very well, we accept your offer with thanks,' said the tall woman. 'I can't deny it would be a blessing.'

Gnasset brought the barge in to gently touch the shore. Odo helped the three knights aboard, and gave them their aliases: Hilda, Otto and Ethel. The knights introduced themselves as Sir Uen (the scarred man), Sir Talorc and Sir Brude (the tall woman). Sir Talorc had the breadth of a man but the voice of a woman, so Eleanor decided to think of her that way. They were road-worn, shedding dirt where they sat. When Uen removed his helmet and mail coif, a shower of pebbles rained to the deck.

'Sorry,' he said. 'We had to sell our horses and our march has been long, without a doubt. Your hailing us is the first bit of luck we've had for a week.'

'Charity does not sit well with us however,' said Sir Talorc. 'We would earn our way to Winterset, if you'd allow it. Find us a chore, or allow us to defend you if the pirates that have been known to ply the Hyrst River put in an appearance –'

'Rest assured,' said Hundred, raising one hand for silence, 'if the need arises, we will ask. Tell us what has befallen you. We are eager for news from the east.'

The three knights spun a familiar tale: the arrival of

Instruments from Winterset bringing new rules and demands for increased tithing, backed up by official documents and force. Unable to break her oath to the crown, Sir Brude had capitulated first, then joined forces with Sir Uen and Sir Talorc from neighbouring estates as word spread of similar misfortune. They had accordingly set forth to put their plight to Prince Kendryk himself, though they had also heard the rumours that he had been supplanted by his grandmother.

'Knights have been stewards of the land and its people for countless generations,' said Sir Talorc. 'We have served in peacetimes and war. We have given our lives countless times! Who are these Instruments to tell us we're no longer needed? On what grounds do these Regulators overturn centuries of tradition? By what right do the Adjusters plan to rule?'

'Some might say,' said Hundred in a tone that made it clear she was playing devil's advocate, not espousing a true position, 'that this system will be fairer than the old. It sweeps away the privileges of knighthood and replaces it with a hierarchy that is more accessible to all.'

'Whoever said that would be spouting nonsense!' exclaimed Sir Uen. 'I was born of peasant farmers, and gained my knighthood on the field of battle, as so many have done, or by adoption. Knights are present for all in need, and obey the ancient laws and customs. These Instruments follow no laws but new ones they make to their sole advantage, and they have the backing of either the prince or the regent to do it. If it is the regent, then she shall pay for . . . that is . . .'

He stopped talking, realising he might have gone too far.

'There might be many other knights like you,' said Odo. 'If you all gathered together, you could form an army.'

'A dangerous strategy,' said Sir Brude. 'One that would plunge the kingdom into civil war.'

'Sometimes even a civil war is merited,' said Sir Talorc glumly. 'We hope it is the regent behind all this. If it is Prince Kendryk himself – the rightful king – I do not know what we can do. Leave the kingdom and become mercenaries, to die in the far south, I suppose.'

'Your loyalty to the king is commendable,' said Hundred. 'What if we could prove to you that he is innocent, and it is indeed the regent who plagues the kingdom with these Instruments, Regulators, new taxes and tolls?'

'I wish you could,' said Sir Brude warily. 'But where would you find such proof? What do river-plying merchants know of affairs of state?'

Hundred reached into a pocket and tossed her a silver penny. Sir Brude caught it and turned it over in her hand.

'What is this?' she asked.

'The proof you require,' said Egda, emerging from the cabin.

He looked as regal as anyone could after a long trip through mountains and forests, battling beasts and enemies as he went. His gold blindfold, now facing outward again, was as straight as his back. His expression was as proud as his nose. Beside him, jewels gleaming, hung Biter and Runnel, floating points-up like a supernatural honour guard.

Sir Talorc gasped and lunged forward onto one knee. 'Highness!'

The other two knights were quick to follow.

Egda waved them onto their feet. 'A king no longer,' he said. 'I abdicated the throne, and I have sworn the same oath to the crown as you, as a simple knight. My abdication was foolish, born of an excess of pride, as might also be said of my self-exile to the Temple of Midnight. But though I have been slow to return, I now go to mend matters and ensure my great-nephew sits upon the throne, not my treacherous sister. Are you with me?'

The three knights drew their swords and cried, 'Yes!'

'Need I remind you, my liege, that we are being hunted?' Hundred said, but with a smile. 'Pray resume your seats, friends, and let us make proper introductions.'

CHAPTER
EIGHTEEN

Biter's plan, of course, was to storm the palace as soon as they arrived. But only he believed that deposing the regent would be so simple. There was Lord Deor and his evil sword to consider, and the lighter of the craft-fires, not to mention a kingdom full of the regent's underlings.

Matters only became more complicated when, with a flutter of wings, Tip dropped out of the sky above, sensitive eyes blinking in the daylight.

'd! a! n! g! e! r! d! a! n! g! e! r!'

The three knights, seasoned by the return of the former king with two young knights and their magical swords, took a talking bat in their stride. The news Tip brought, however, gave them all pause.

The coronation of the regent was scheduled for dawn the next morning. In the name of security, Lord Deor had ordered the Hyrst River gate closed and all visitors searched. There would be no entrance to the city by barge, not for Egda and his three friends.

'Roads too will be watched,' said Hundred. 'We won't get in that way either.'

'Overland, perhaps?' suggested Sir Brude.

'That would take too long,' said Egda. He pressed his hands together and tapped the tips of his index fingers to his chin. 'There must be another route . . .'

An idea occurred to Eleanor that she almost immediately dismissed.

'What about . . . no, that would be too dangerous.'

'Tell us anyway,' said Hundred.

'She eats danger for dinner, remember?' said Odo.

'Well, I was thinking of how we got out of Ablerhyll,' Eleanor continued. 'Through the urthkin tunnels. Shache said there were tunnels under every city, but then I remembered her telling us that humans aren't allowed in the undercities without permission, so unless we're going to fight the urthkin as well . . .'

She shrugged. It had seemed a good plan for an instant, but now everyone was staring at her with wide eyes, like she had gone mad.

'The pact does indeed forbid humans from entering urthkin territory uninvited,' said Egda. 'But the pact is broken. The normal rules do not apply.'

'We can enter through the Shadow Way,' said Hundred, 'and petition the Monarch Below herself. If she grants us passage, we will avoid Lord Deor's precautions entirely.'

'And come up on the regent from underneath,' said Odo, clapping Eleanor on the back. 'That's brilliant! Oh, except for the going-underground part,' he added, remembering how awful it had been the last time. 'But apart from that, good thinking!'

Eleanor beamed at the praise.

'We would gladly accompany you into the undercity,' said Sir Brude, speaking for her companions as well. 'Might I suggest, however, that instead we provide a diversion at the river gate, to ensure your safe passage through the Shadow Way? Both will certainly be watched.'

Egda nodded. 'That is a wise plan.'

'The barge will reach the Hyrst River gate in an hour.' Hundred looked up, taking in the darkening sky to the east. 'Night will fall at the same time. We have that long to prepare. Eleanor – next time you have a good idea, do not keep it to yourself.'

'Yes, sir. I mean no, sir, I won't. I promise.'

Sir Brude winked at her. 'Remember this day, young knight. A superior may never ask you for advice again.'

The hour passed quickly. Odo and Eleanor donned their armour for the first time in days, and darkened its sheen with mud drawn from the riverbank, as did the others. Tip, after a fond welcome from Odo, scouted the way ahead, returning frequently to assure them that there were no obvious observers on either side of the river. Ahead, they could see the lights of Winterset proper, twinkling in the dusk. Each slow twist of the water brought them nearer to the capital.

Homes began to crowd the water, and *Photine* was joined by many other boats, the likes of which Odo had never seen. People of all shapes and colours swarmed the decks, calling to each other in unfamiliar accents. The speech of some of them was impossible to decipher. They might as well have been talking a different language!

'There,' said Hundred, pointing at the port shore. Gnasset guided *Photine* towards the bank.

Dimly through the gathering gloom, Eleanor made out upraised pillars and partial arches standing out above thick undergrowth: the ruins of an ancient stone building, long left to neglect.

Photine bumped ashore and the two parties bade a soft farewell. Sirs Brude, Talorc and Uen would go with Gnasset to the river gate, to sneak in and distract the guards watching the area around the Shadow Way. Odo hoped they would get through safely and Gnasset and *Photine* would safely reach her normal berth. He liked the silent captain, and the knights were good, brave people he hoped to see again soon.

Hundred led the way along a narrow path through the undergrowth as the barge pushed off, its sail catching the evening breeze with a snap. The way ahead was still and quiet. There was no sign of watchers of either species, human or urthkin, but Eleanor didn't doubt they were there. The Shadow Way was the entrance to the secret undercity: people weren't going to be allowed to just wander in.

At a dense stand of bushes, Hundred silently urged them to stop and wait. Tip joined them, finding a handy branch at eye level. He quietly chirped that he too had seen no one nearby.

They sat and waited, making as little noise as possible, for perhaps an hour.

Then, suddenly, from the south came the warning blast of a horn, three times. Eleanor and Odo turned to face the source of the sound, although of course they could see nothing. The Hyrst River was much too far away, and by now the night was as dark as a tomb. Faintly, though, they thought they could hear shouting.

Egda alone had cocked his head in the opposite direction. Moments later, they heard what he heard: a crunching of twigs and leaves as two people moved away through the undergrowth. Guards, drawn to the aid of the river gate by the blowing of the horn.

The four of them shrank back into deeper shadows as the guards went by. Once they were safely past and their footfalls could no longer be heard, Tip fluttered off to make sure there were no more. He returned a moment later with the all-clear.

'Follow closely,' Hundred whispered to Eleanor and Odo.

'Keep your swords sheathed. We leave our enemies behind us.'

The ruins rose up to enfold them, and slowly the vegetation fell away. Their boots crunched on pebbles and flakes of slate. Hundred surrendered guidance of the party to Egda, who needed no light to follow the path. Sometimes he stopped to feel his way forward with the tip of his staff, or perhaps employ other senses, such as sound or smell. Once he dropped to one knee and tasted a pinch of the earth. Satisfied, he led them on, Tip flying silently above.

Out of the ruins, a gaping archway appeared, the only intact structure Eleanor had yet seen. It had to be the Shadow Way itself, for Egda led them unhesitatingly inside.

Darkness swallowed them. Even sound seemed to fade away into nothing. Odo held his breath, not knowing if the walls were yards or inches away. Either way, the air itself pressed close and still, and he felt as though just opening his mouth might put him at risk of drowning.

Egda led them ten paces, then stopped.

'Stone make you strong,' he said, bowing low. 'Darkness clear your sight.'

Four silver-veined figures, glowing from the inside out, stepped from the impenetrable shadows.

'Wide be your halls,' said one. 'Tunnels guide you true.'

Instead of Shache's pleased tones on hearing the traditional honorific, this urthkin's response was thin with suspicion.

'Turn back, human travellers. This is not your path.'

'But it is,' said Egda, still bowing low. 'We humbly seek an audience with the Monarch Below.'

The urthkin hissed. 'The scortwisa supreme takes no visitors of your kind, not after the breaking of the pact.'

'It is on this matter I wish to speak with her.'

'Your wishes are not her wishes, sky-dweller.'

'They were once,' said Egda, bowing deeper still. This was the urthkin equivalent of standing taller. 'I am Egdalhurd Begimund Coren Theothelm of House Chlodochar, once King Above of the Human Realm and keeper of the pact between my people and yours. I do not demand audience, but I hope and believe that my old friend Thrieff will see me when she knows I am here, if you would be so good as to inform her.'

The urthkin shifted anxiously and whispered among themselves in their thin voices. Eleanor kept her hand on Runnel's hilt in case things went badly, but she told herself that she had no reason to feel anxious. The urthkin had always treated them honourably in the past.

Something moved behind her and she felt a tiny pinprick at her neck.

'Move, tall one, and I will spill your lifeblood to the dirt,' said the urthkin holding the curved knife to her throat.

Eleanor froze, and her gaze flicked to her friends. Odo and Hundred too were each standing with an urthkin blade at their throat, visible in the glow of the hands that held them.

'Biter, no!' cried Odo, struggling to keep his sword from bursting free. 'We are the intruders here. We stay or leave at their – what's the word?'

'Behest, I think,' said Eleanor.

'Mercy might be better,' said Hundred through gritted teeth.

'They dishonour you,' said Biter. 'You are knights of the realm!'

'This is not our realm,' Runnel reminded him.

Egda stood straighter, but not so straight that his head was higher than any of the urthkin.

'We await the Monarch Below's pleasure,' he told them calmly.

'You will come with us,' said the leader of the urthkin guards. 'Say nothing unless spoken to. Touch nothing.'

'We understand,' said Egda. 'Lead on.'

Odo let himself be shoved forward. The urthkin at his back was so small she practically had to stand on tiptoes to reach his throat, but that didn't lessen the danger. It would be all too easy to kill them and bury the bodies where they would never be found.

As they shuffled forward along the Shadow Way, he felt the walls close in around him . . .

'w! i! t! h! y! o! u!' chirped a familiar voice from above, and he felt the band about his chest loosen a little. Tip was watching, one of many bats flying back and forth, snapping up cave insects – probably his family, left behind to seek out the former king. He would know if something happened to them now. That was some comfort in the dark.

They walked for what felt like hours, always downward, but sometimes turning left or right. Glowing patches in the walls enabled Eleanor to make out the rough edges of things around them, such as buildings fashioned from hollow stalagmites, doorways, even windows. Breezes touched her face from odd directions, sometimes tickling with the scent of far-off spices, sometimes slapping her with smells more foul than fair. She saw urthkin coming and going, and heard their soft voices along with rhythmic cries and banging that might have been music. Whereas the tunnels they had seen under Ablerhyll had seemed cramped and empty, Winterset's undercity was a thriving subterranean metropolis.

They came at last to a vast space that could not be measured by the eye. When Eleanor strained to make out the walls, she sensed only that they curved to her left and right without end. The ceiling rose up in a dome that never seemed to come down. Soft, echoing sounds filled the air. Pale light glimmered. Somewhere nearby were many, many urthkin.

'Approach,' called a sharp-edged voice from somewhere in front of them.

Odo's urthkin guard nudged him forward. He supposed that they had reached their destination, perhaps a throne room of some kind, and therefore expected to head up a flight of steps or another ramp to where the Monarch Below might be sitting. Instead he stumbled as the way ahead sloped sharply down.

A faintly shimmering crowd of urthkin hissed as the humans passed among them. Eleanor stubbornly hung her head, determined not to stand straight.

'That is close enough,' said their guide. 'Wait here.'

Their guards melted away into the crowd, and Odo felt a thousand eyes staring at him, waiting for him to make a mistake. Remembering the stern instructions they had been given, he kept his mouth tightly closed, and hoped Eleanor would find the patience to do the same.

A single flame flickered into life several yards below them. It was tiny, dancing atop a narrow white candle, but it seemed so bright it made them all blink.

By its light, they saw that they were standing in a barred cage on the edge of a wide, circular space at the very bottom of which sat a tiny urthkin on a low stool, a long crystal shard held upright in one hand, like a spear. She wore no crown, but Eleanor knew instantly that she was the Monarch. She sat at the lowest point of the throne room, perhaps the lowest in the city.

'I offer you the gift of light, old friend.'

The Monarch's voice was thin, but strong.

'Would that I could accept it,' said Egda, bowing his blindfolded head. 'But my friends will be grateful.'

'Your words are as fine as ever. Long has it been since you brightened our halls.'

'The loss is mine. In darkness I sought wisdom, but some would say I found only further foolishness.'

'That remains to be seen. What brings you here? The pact offers no protection any more; you have placed yourself in grave danger.'

'I seek only safe passage through your realm.'

'To what end?'

'To halt the coronation of my sister, tomorrow morning.'

'You believe you are up to the measure of this task? You and your three companions?'

'I believe so.'

'Then you are indeed a fool. Prince Kendryk could not stop her, and he was wiser than you, if too tall for any urthkin's liking.'

'He inherited his mother's height, along with her birthright,' said Egda with a fond smile that faded as fast as it came. 'While Kendryk lives, I will hold out hope.'

'And if he doesn't? My spies report that he survives, but a sly hand with a knife could easily fix that overnight.'

'Odelyn would never kill her grandson. The future of her line depends on him producing an heir that she can control.'

'Lord Deor might not see things so reasonably, and orders can so easily and tragically be misunderstood.'

'You comprehend my haste then.'

The Monarch pondered Egda's words with her chin on one wrinkled hand, examining each of her visitors in turn. Odo tried not to fidget when she looked at him. There was something incredibly penetrating about her dark eyes.

When she spoke again, it was clear that she had made a decision. Unfortunately, it appeared to be the wrong one.

'I cannot interfere in surface affairs. The pact forbids it.'

'But the pact is broken!' Eleanor cried out.

'Silence!' One of the guards reached into their cage and gripped her wrist tightly, yanking her arm so her face was mashed against cold iron bars.

Runnel was instantly in her other hand, and Hundred and Odo were close behind her with weapons drawn. Tip swooped down and flapped at the guard's face, but was batted away with one sharp-nailed hand.

'Harm any of us, and you will pay dearly,' Hundred hissed in a fair impersonation of an urthkin's chilly tones.

'Desist at once!' The Monarch's command rang out through the vast bowl, echoing off distant walls and seeming to come back at them from all sides. The order was not just directed to the humans in her presence. Eleanor's arm was instantly released, and she fell back into the cage as suddenly as the guard who had held her retreated. Tip walked on his feet and wingtips to the base of the cage and climbed up to the top, where he hung, glaring angrily at any urthkin who approached.

'We are urthkin,' the Monarch Below rebuked her fellows. 'We do not injure those who come to us in honest supplication. Even if they are disrespectful. Human girl, step forward.'

Eleanor obeyed, blushing furiously.

'The pact is indeed broken,' the Monarch Below said. 'Humans no longer trade fairly with urthkin. They talk of flooding the undercities. They creep into our tunnels to steal treasure they think we hoard. What would you have me do?'

Eleanor glanced at Hundred, who gestured encouragingly.

'I would listen to Egda,' she said, 'and give Prince Kendryk another chance. I don't know him . . . but he can't be that bad, can he? From what we've heard, it is the regent who has done everything, even when it has been in his name. He has never done anything directly himself.'

'His time runs short,' said the Monarch. 'And my spies tell me he spends all his time finger-painting. How will that save his kingdom?'

Eleanor had no good answer to that. Finger-painting didn't sound very promising.

'We destroyed the backwards weather vane in Ablerhyll,' Odo said, braving the wrath of the urthkin to add the weight of his opinion to Eleanor's. 'You know we honour the pact. Let us through and we'll do everything we can to set things right.'

'Harm above means harm below,' said the Monarch. 'Isn't that what we used to say, old friend?'

Egda bowed. 'It has ever been so. War between our peoples benefits no one – and there will be war if Odelyn becomes King Above. She cares only about herself.'

'Then I am decided,' said the Monarch. 'Your kingdom is in danger, humans. We will come to your aid. Our tunnels lead all under the city. You have but to tell us where you wish to go, and you will be taken there.'

'We must be atop Old Dragon Stone by dawn tomorrow,' Egda told her.

'That stone, of all stones?' she said.

'It is where our coronations take place. He or she who is to be crowned takes the royal sword and, crying out the ritual words, plunges the blade into the Stone. There is a niche for that purpose, carved long ago, some say by a dragon's tooth.'

The Monarch Below nodded. 'Our hammers cannot penetrate this rock. We can, however, take you to the base of Old Dragon Stone before night's end. Will that suffice?'

'It will do us very well, Majesty. Thank you.'

'Thank me by putting a proper ruler on the throne you relinquished. If the young finger-painter is not up to the task, find another.'

CHAPTER
NINETEEN

The Monarch Below gestured, and her guards opened the cage. Darkness descended once more with the snuffing of the candle. Odo felt strong hands urging him along, more respectfully than before, and he let himself be led, hoping that sooner rather than later he would be in the open air again.

They left the throne room and followed another complicated series of tunnels through the underground city, Tip flying patiently along with them. Occasionally they stopped to rest, eating what little remained of the fruit, nuts and bread the smiths had given them. At the second rest stop, Tip flapped around Odo's head, hinting that he was hungry. Odo put some pieces of fruit in one palm and held them out so the little bat could snatch them carefully with his claws.

There wasn't enough light to be sure, but Odo sensed his urthkin guide watching him closely, and when she spoke he was certain of it.

'The winged mouse . . . we call them Friends in the Dark . . . he is your pet?'

'Tip? Not really. I guess he belongs to Prince Kendryk, if he belongs to anyone. He's helped us a lot though.'

'His kind help us too. They eat the eight-legs that plague us, and we use their droppings to grow crops.'

'You have plants down here?' Odo couldn't believe his ears. How could anything grow without light?

'Yes, we have many. You should see the forests of – I do not remember your word.'

'Mushrooms,' Egda supplied.

'Yes, mushrooms. Some of them grow thirty armlengths high!'

'That sounds amazing. I wish I could see them,' Odo said, with some honesty. 'But how could I? There's no light.'

'Ah, that is a sadness. Perhaps one day our monarch could make an exception for you, as she has made an exception today. You should bring your dark friend with you.'

Odo held out some more food for Tip, who pounced on it with gratitude.

They walked until they were footsore and weary, through caverns and halls immeasurable to the human eye. They had no way of telling the time, which only made the thought of what lay ahead more unsettling. Would they have time to rest before taking on the entirety of Tofte's army, if it came to that?

'I do not expect we will face anything more than several dozen or so, without bows,' Hundred said. 'Although this coronation is real, we saw no banners on our approach to the city and heard no call for the population to celebrate. The regent will risk no public fuss until Prince Kendryk is safely dealt with.'

'That's sneaky,' said Eleanor.

'Many monarchs have been,' said Runnel. 'Gisila the first crowned her son in secret the moment he was born because she knew her uncle was trying to depose her. By the time he succeeded, the boy was grown into a man who knew the secret, that he had been king all along, and ordered his uncle executed.'

'King Addlebert was crowned seventeen times,' said Biter, 'in order to confuse his enemies.'

'Some would say that he was more confused than they were,' said Runnel. 'Permanently.'

'It is difficult to be wise,' said Egda, 'when the whole world is watching you.'

Eleanor could appreciate that. She didn't like it when even her father verbally quizzed her on her schooling. Answers she knew perfectly if she was on her own fled her mind with the ease of eels the moment he demanded them. That was why she left the judgment part of being a knight to Odo, whenever she could. How could she possibly know on the spot what the right answer was?

He told her once that he didn't really know for sure, but he did know what felt right, and he trusted his instinct.

That was the kind of instinct a king needed, she supposed. And a willingness to trust one's ally in the dark.

At last they came to the end of their long subsurface journey. The smell of fresh rain wafted from an opening up ahead, and their guides slowed to a halt, calling out in their strange voices to the guards there. The urthkin parted before them, bowing, and Odo and Eleanor and the others crawled cautiously out of a narrow split in the earth and found themselves once again on the surface world, where they belonged. Even by starlight, everything seemed brightly lit, making them blink.

Odo let out a huge sigh of relief, which startled a sleeping parrot in a palm tree nearby. It squawked and irritably raised its brightly covered crest. Odo shushed it with an upraised hand.

'Where's the palace?' whispered Eleanor, taking in the forest of bizarre plants surrounding them. This didn't look anything like the capital as she had imagined it. Some of the plants were long and skinny, with a tuft of radiating leaves at the top. Others were squat and many-trunked, like lots of trees merged into one. The air smelled of flowers, of which there were plenty, and damp, which the ground underfoot definitely was. Slippery mud squelched as they moved for denser cover.

'Look up there,' said Hundred, pointing. 'That shadow? It's Old Dragon Stone.'

Odo and Eleanor peered through the foliage. 'That shadow' seemed to take up half the sky, an imposing, angular shape with a flat top. It was much higher than they had pictured.

'The palace is behind us. This is the Royal Physic Garden,' said Egda, holding a star-shaped blossom to his sensitive nose. 'If my mother had known that it contained a door to the undercity, she would never have let me play here as a child!'

'Doors go both ways — and I imagine this one will be sealed ere long,' said Hundred, cautiously guiding them from tree to tree, closer to the base of the Stone. Their progress was slow and stealthy; they froze at the merest sound that might herald a human guard coming near. They could not be caught now, not when they were so close.

Even as Eleanor followed Hundred's gestured instructions, treading as lightly as a leaf in the older woman's footsteps, she marvelled at the fact that they had arrived. They were in Winterset at last!

She couldn't see anything, and was sure that not every new knight dreamed of overthrowing a plot to take over the kingdom on their first day in the capital, but few people were as fortunate as her. That was for certain.

When they were just a few paces from the base of the Stone, which now loomed like a wall of utter blackness blocking out nearly all the sky, they stopped for a council of war.

'Our objective is simple,' said Egda. 'To stop Odelyn from being crowned, we must reach the top of Old Dragon

Stone by dawn. Unfortunately, there is only one way up to the summit, and that is via the Long Stair. Given that large swithorm tree we just passed, I believe we are on the opposite side of the Stone.'

'That is so, my liege,' said Hundred.

'The Stair will be heavily guarded, which works to our advantage. No one will think to watch this side.'

'But how does that help us?' asked Eleanor. 'If the Stair is on the other side, that's where we need to be.'

'A tricky approach by stairs,' mused Biter. 'Uphill all the way, confined to a narrow space so only one can fight at a time –'

'With enemy reinforcements constantly coming from above and below?' said Runnel. 'I believe it would be nothing less than suicide.'

'Perhaps we could stagger our assaults,' Biter went on. 'Our fiercest fighter first, the remaining three at the base of the Stair to fend off reinforcements, retreating as needed.'

'You are forgetting arrows, little brother.'

'Then we remain in pairs, with the second knight on the stairs to deflect shafts fired at the first. Our knights' new dragon-scale shields should be equal to the task. Why do you only see problems, sister, when I see opportunities for valour?'

'There is no valour in dying needlessly,' said Hundred. 'I would rather we all survived *and* the right person was crowned. To that end, we need another plan.'

'Tip can fly up to the top,' said Eleanor. 'Does that help?'

'Sir Drust, it is said, once used a trained pigeon to break a castle siege,' replied Egda. 'The bird carried a thread to the top of the wall, passed it over a crenellation, and then carried the end back down to the knight. Attached to the other end of the thread was a rope. As he drew the thread to him, the rope ascended, then descended, and once affixed to a tree stump gave him access to the battlements.'

'Tip could do that,' said Eleanor. 'Or one of our swords.'

'I have rope in my pack,' said Hundred. 'It should be long enough. Thread we can pull from our cloaks.'

'Is there something Tip or the swords can loop it around?' Odo asked.

That question drew nothing but silence from those people who'd been to the top of Old Dragon Stone. Neither Egda nor Hundred could recall any extrusion strong enough to take the weight of an ascending knight, not in the form that a being without hands could manage, anyway.

'I'll go up the Long Stair on my own,' said Eleanor. 'I'm small. People don't even see me half the time.'

'I doubt that would be possible,' said Hundred, but Odo could see her calculating the odds. Unless he came up with another plan, that might be the only choice available to them.

'What about climbing the Stone on this side?' he asked.

'Much too difficult,' Egda said. 'I tried to scale it once

when I was a limber lad. The cliff is too sheer. A laden knight couldn't climb ten feet.'

'But what if we cut steps somehow?'

'The stone is too tough for hammers and chisel.'

'I know. You said only a dragon's tooth could mark it. But what about our swords? They can only be chipped by a dragon's tooth. Doesn't that make them almost as tough?'

'It does.' Hundred pondered this further. 'So one person ascending via handholds carved by the swords carries the rope, or a thread tied to their belt. When they reach the top, they can find an anchor point, tie a knot and the rest can follow. Is this your suggestion, Sir Odo?'

'Yes,' he said. 'And I should do it, since it's my idea.'

'No, you are too heavy,' Hundred countered. 'It should be me.'

'It can't be you,' said Eleanor. 'You need to stay here with Egda in case something goes wrong.' She took a deep breath, imagining the gulf of empty air below her at the top of the Stone. 'It has to be me. I'm the smallest, and therefore the lightest. I'll drag the thread behind me. I'll leave most of my armour here, but wear the shield on my back in case anyone sees me and tries to shoot me down. It's the only way.'

Odo was amazed that his friend's nervousness didn't show in her voice. He knew how wary she was of heights, but all he could hear was determination.

'I believe this plan is not only the best we can come up

with,' said Egda, gripping her by the shoulder, 'but I also firmly believe you can do it.'

'Well done, Sir Eleanor.' Hundred grinned. 'Now, let us make haste. If we are to win the day, we must arrive before Odelyn does. And we have no way of knowing where she is right now.'

TWENTY

Prince Kendryk swayed on his feet, staring blankly up the Long Stair like a man in a dream. The way was lit by torches, flickering and yellow. What was he doing here? Something important, he was sure of it. It had, however, momentarily slipped his mind . . .

'Get him moving,' snapped a sharp voice. 'I don't care if you have to carry him, Lord Deor, but we can't have him holding us up every time his thoughts wander. If he didn't have to sign his abdication, I'd have left him in the palace with his doodles.'

The jagged hilt of an old, gore-stained sword jabbed him hard in the spine.

'Start climbing,' growled the Chief Regulator in his ear. 'Or I swear I'll push you in the back on the way down.'

Oh yes. Kendryk remembered now. He was ascending Old Dragon Stone with his grandmother for her coronation ceremony. How could he have forgotten that?

As his legs began to move, resuming his climb one stair

at a time, more memories stirred. He hadn't slept for three straight days. That was why he had forgotten. And why hadn't he slept? Because he had been painting, painting furiously in the desperate hope of finishing in time.

Had he?

Had he finished?

Doubt became hope, which turned into certainty when a vision of the completed mural flashed into his mind.

He *had* finished. The great work of his life so far was done.

It was almost over.

Up and down his knees went as he ascended step by step, following a man he didn't know, a hairy behemoth wearing a wolfskin cloak and carrying a brand whose flames were green-tinged. Ahead of *him* was the woman carrying the crown in its ceremonial sack. There were four hundred and fifty-seven steps in the Long Stairs, a number he remembered learning from his great-uncle, who had taught him everything he needed to know to be a good king, except how to contain his grandmother's ambition. Nothing would satisfy her once she'd set her heart on the throne.

Well, Kendryk had soon thought, let her try. She'd quickly realise what a mistake it was.

There was nothing glamorous about ruling Tofte, as her procession of humourless, grey-faced Instruments, Regulators and Adjustors proved. They had no life to them, no heart or imagination. Not like the knights they sought to replace.

His first move, were he king, would be to recall all of those she had sent out into the kingdom. He would have to find other uses for them, of course; it wasn't their fault she had deluded them with false dreams. They could help run the palace accounts perhaps, or assist the lawyers negotiating trade deals with neighbouring countries, while the knights went back to the manors. Yes, that could work.

Prince Kendryk's weary head spun with plans that utterly contradicted the reality he was caught in. He knew very well that he would never be king.

Step. Step. Step.

His hands were tender where an apologetic attendant had scrubbed them with a wire brush while two others dressed him in attire fit for the ceremony. There was still paint under his fingernails though. When he raised his hands to his nose, he could smell the orange, the red, the gold . . .

'Remind me of the words, Lord Deor,' he said.

'Which words?' came the gruff reply.

'Of the ritual. The ones my aunt will utter when she pierces Old Dragon Stone with the Royal Sword.'

'You don't need to know,' spat Deor.

'No matter,' replied Kendryk dreamily. 'I learned them too. "Let Aldewrath object." The great Aldewrath, who crowned the First King. What do you think would happen if he were alive now?'

Deor laughed. 'Aldewrath was never real. Just a legend, a

story for children. Like your daubs.'

'I wonder if a legendary dragon ate my great-uncle,' muttered Kendryk. 'One old dragon eating another. Any more true tales of his death come along?'

'I'll feed *you* to a dragon, if you don't shut up,' said Lord Deor. But Kendryk was no longer listening. He was going up, up, up in the wake of a man who smelled of moss and rabbit droppings, while thinking of Egda and hoping the old man had somehow survived his third reported death. There was a smithy near Kyles Frost, one of the old ones. They would have helped him if he lived, Kendryk was sure of it.

Perhaps he was nearby, awaiting his chance.

Kendryk hoped so. He knew his great-uncle would want to be there.

Dragon, dragon, heed our call.

Come to aid us, one and all.

His lips forming the words of the ancient song, Prince Kendryk climbed grimly and in silence to a fate he could not avoid.

TWENTY-ONE

Just keep climbing, Eleanor told herself. *Don't look down. Don't even look up. Just reach for the next handhold and . . . pull.*

Her shoulders hurt, and so did her calves. Even the light cord she was dragging up tied to her waist had become heavier than she expected. But that was nothing compared to how it would feel if she fell. Briefly.

Fortunately, or perhaps unfortunately, there wasn't much light to see by. The city provided barely a glimmer as she ascended Old Dragon Stone, so even if she had looked down, she couldn't have estimated her height. She couldn't see the top either. It blurred into the black sky and seemed an infinite distance away. All she could do was search with her fingertips, seeking the notch that Biter or Runnel had hacked into the stone for her.

'l! e! f! t!' chirped Tip, and she adjusted her hand accordingly, found the spot. The bat's guidance was essential in the night; it was all too easy for Eleanor to drift sideways instead of going straight up to the next handholds.

Pull.

Her feet followed suit below, occupying the notches that had held her fingers not long ago. Periodically, one or other of the swords descended to tell her that she was making excellent progress, but she tried not to think about that either. She felt as though she had been climbing forever. It was easier if she accepted it and just kept going.

'r! i! g! h! t!'

Something tickled her face. Instinctively she blinked and twisted, while at the same time clinging tightly, afraid for an instant that she might lose her balance. It felt like a bug, perhaps even a spider!

Pull.

'If we make it to the top in one piece, it'll all be worth it,' Eleanor told herself.

'𝕭𝖗𝖆𝖛𝖊 𝖍𝖊𝖆𝖗𝖙, 𝕾𝖎𝖗 𝕰𝖑𝖊𝖆𝖓𝖔𝖗!' called down Runnel, followed a second later by a shower of rock dust. '𝖄𝖔𝖚'𝖗𝖊 𝖓𝖊𝖆𝖗𝖑𝖞 𝖙𝖍𝖊𝖗𝖊!'

'Don't tease me,' she said. 'You've told me that before.'

'𝖄𝖊𝖘, 𝖇𝖚𝖙 𝖙𝖍𝖎𝖘 𝖙𝖎𝖒𝖊 𝖎𝖙 𝖎𝖘 𝖙𝖗𝖚𝖊,' Biter declared. '𝕺𝖚𝖗 𝖊𝖓𝖉𝖊𝖆𝖛𝖔𝖚𝖗 𝖍𝖆𝖘 𝖕𝖗𝖔𝖛𝖊𝖉 𝖍𝖎𝖌𝖍𝖑𝖞 𝖘𝖚𝖈𝖈𝖊𝖘𝖘𝖋𝖚𝖑.'

'Well, don't talk too soon. I'm not there yet.'

Reach. Pull.

Far below, Odo strained his eyes to keep his friend in sight. Eleanor had long ago vanished into the dark bulk of the Old Dragon Stone. He reminded himself that this was a *good* thing. If neither he nor Hundred could see her, then neither could anyone else.

Fortunately for them, the sun would rise on the far side of the Stone. They hoped to climb in the predawn shadow, if only Eleanor reached the top in time.

The cord danced loosely in his hands as Eleanor took another step up. Odo carefully spooled it out, making sure it didn't tangle. As long as it kept going, he knew Eleanor was climbing.

'She must be near the top,' whispered Hundred. 'How much cord is left, Sir Odo?'

'A few fathoms. But she's still climbing.'

Even as Odo spoke, the cord jerked back and forth in his hands. His heart froze, thinking Eleanor was about to fall, but then the cord began moving upward at a much more rapid pace. The spool uncoiled and then the heavier rope it was tied to began to rise, the great coil near Odo steadily unravelling.

'It's her!' Odo cried. 'She's pulling up the rope!'

'Very well done, Sir Eleanor,' said Hundred, beaming. 'The hard part for her is over. Soon it will be our turn.'

'Yes, of course.' Odo checked the rope to make sure it too would rise without hindrance. 'I should go last, just in case I slip. Not that I will, but I would hate to drag you two down with me if something went wrong.'

'Very well.' Hundred accepted the sense of his suggestion.

'I will go first, then my liege. Unless he would like to be lifted up in a sling? There will be enough rope to form a rudimentary basket.'

Egda barked a laugh. 'You are mistaking me for our old friend Beremus. He was the one who had to be carried with his eyes tightly shut across Cheerless Chasm! Compared to that worn-out old rope bridge, this will be easy.'

Odo grinned with them. It was good to see Egda remembering his old friends with happiness, not grief.

The rope ascended rapidly at first, then slowed as the weight of it increased. Odo was glad they had tested Eleanor's strength before sending her on the mission, otherwise he would worry that it would be too heavy for her to haul. The rope, fortunately, was thin and light, while at the same time incredibly strong. Odo had tested that element too, tugging on a length with all his strength. The rope hadn't so much as twisted.

They watched the rope ascend steadily for some minutes until, at last, it stopped. Odo gave Eleanor a minute to tie the knot, then gave it a firm tug, twice.

Two tugs came back down to him: the signal to ascend.

Hundred dusted her hands, gripped the rope and began to climb. Odo watched her as she went up the side of Old Dragon Stone much faster than Eleanor had. The rope below her twitched violently in his hands, and soon it was Egda's turn to follow. He too was much spryer than an old person had any right to be, but Odo wasn't surprised. He had seen the pair in action too many times to be fooled by their looks.

When Hundred vanished from sight, the rope twitched two more times – a message relayed by Egda. A second later, Tip was with Odo, flapping excitedly to signal that it was his turn to join the aerial humans.

Saying a brief farewell to the pleasant greenery of the Royal Physic Garden, and trying not to notice an ashen shade to the sky, as though the first hint of day was already appearing on the other side of the Stone, Odo took the rope in both hands, placed his booted feet against the rock and began to climb.

Above, Eleanor watched anxiously as her friends inched towards her. She was glad she didn't need to pull them up. After firmly knotting the rope around a sturdy-looking nub of rock shaped roughly like a horse's head tucked inconspicuously into a hollow in the stone, she had bound her hands up in cloth to spare her scraped skin any further abuse. Just holding Runnel made her palm and fingers feel like they were on fire, even though the sword promised to be gentle. Eleanor wished she had some of her father's healing salve, but that was in her pack, which Odo was carrying, along with her armour.

She had a fine view of the western wing of the palace, a tangle of pointed spires and buttresses that defied easy navigation, but her attention wasn't fixed on it. Instead, every minute or so she leaned out as far as she dared, to see how Hundred was faring. When she arrived at the top of the rope, Eleanor lent her a hand to come up into the hollow, where she dusted herself down and took a drink of water.

'Excellent spot,' Hundred declared, craning her neck to look out of the hollow at the rippling surface of the top of the Stone. It was ridged like a giant fingerprint pressing up at the sky. 'No one will see us until we want to be seen. Wait here for the others and I will scout around. Biter, with me.'

'Yes, sir.'

With that, she was gone, scampering like a four-legged creature up to the very top of the Stone as easily as if she hadn't just climbed anywhere at all. Odo's magical sword followed like an obedient pet.

Egda was next, his staff tied securely at his back next to his shield, and Eleanor called down to him to let him know he was almost there. The former king needed no assistance joining her, however. He found his own security by hand and under foot, and stood with only slightly less flexibility than Hundred had.

'Hundred is scouting, I presume?' he asked.

'Yes, she told me to wait here.'

'I have no doubt she will be back soon.' He looked to the east, as though momentarily forgetting that he was blind. 'Where stands the day? Is dawn far off?'

The sky was turning straw yellow over the bulge of the Stone's uneven summit. 'Not long now,' Eleanor told him. 'Odo better get a move on, the lumpish . . . uh, knight.'

Egda laughed. 'No need to watch your tongue around me, Sir Eleanor. I have heard far worse on the battlefield.'

'𝔥e speaks t𝔥e trut𝔥,' said Runnel. 'If wor𝔡s coul𝔡 woun𝔡, I've 𝔥ear𝔡 some t𝔥at woul𝔡 take a 𝔥ea𝔡 clean off.'

Hundred and Biter returned at the same time Odo and Tip completed their ascent. Odo had barely a moment to catch his breath while Eleanor quickly put her armour back on, with Hundred's help, and salved her hands. They needed to hurry.

'The royal procession has reached the top of the Stone,' Hundred explained. 'I do not see Odelyn yet, but there are Instruments gathering at the summit of the Long Stair. I have no doubt that she will arrive shortly.'

'An𝔡 I 𝔡i𝔡 not see t𝔥e falconstone,' said Biter, sounding faintly disappointed that his nemesis wasn't immediately available to fight.

'𝔓atience, little 𝔟rot𝔥er,' Runnel cautioned.

'The ceremony will begin when they reach the proper place,' said Egda. 'Who is closer, them or us?'

'We are, by a fraction.'

'Then we can afford to be cautious. They will move slowly, as one; we will disperse and be stealthy. In pairs, we can get close before they see us, and attack from two sides.'

'Odo and Eleanor, together,' said Hundred. 'I will stay with my liege.'

They nodded, relieved to be fighting at each other's side.

'Will you give us a signal?' Odo asked.

'We will use Tip, if he can bear the sun when it rises,' said Egda. Tip chirped his assent. 'He will deliver word that our attack is about to begin. Otherwise, use your best judgment – and ignore what anyone says before or during the ceremony. The words are mere tradition and mean nothing. Your task is to keep the crown off the regent's head.'

'Get it to Prince Kendryk if you can,' Hundred added. 'We might as well crown him while we're at it.'

'You saw him?' asked Egda.

'No, but he will be here. She will need him to formally abdicate his claim in front of witnesses.'

'Indeed.' Egda sighed. 'Also, Odelyn loves to gloat.'

'So then, you have your orders,' said Hundred to Eleanor and Odo.

'Stop the ceremony . . .' said Odo.

'Prevent the coronation of an impostor . . .' Biter said.

'Get the crown . . .' said Eleanor.

'And restore peace to the realm,' said Runnel. 'A fine day's work!'

They split into pairs and headed off in opposite directions, Eleanor and Odo to the right with their magic swords, Egda,

Hundred and Tip to the left, staying crouched to avoid being seen too soon.

None of them noticed the eagle hovering high above, watching the humans scurrying, its once sharp golden eye now clouded with smoke.

TWENTY-TWO

'How many do you think there'll be?' asked Eleanor as they scrambled across the top of Old Dragon Stone, sword in one hand, shield in the other. Her raw hands were of no concern now. All she felt was anticipation for battle.

'In her honour guard? Your guess is as good as mine.' Not too many, Odo hoped, but he wasn't going to be put off by whatever he saw when they came into view. He had a job to do, and he would do it, or try to.

'Hundred made it sound like a lot.' Eleanor was thinking strategy. 'If they're only Instruments, like she says, that's a good thing. They're not the old king's guard – which is who we wanted to be, remember? When we were waiting for Sir Halfdan to introduce us to the court? Imagine if we had to fight them.'

Odo hadn't thought of that, and felt relief flowering through his battle-ready nerves. If these Instruments were as hapless as the ones they had already met, the fight would be quickly over, no matter how many they had to face.

'They are still fellow Tofteans though,' he said. 'Just like the people we fought in Lenburh. It would be better not to hurt them too badly, if we can avoid it.'

'𝕱ortunately for that plan,' said Runnel, '𝕴 lost much of my edge hacking at stone so 𝕾ir 𝕰leanor could climb.'

'𝕴 do not call being blunted an asset,' grumbled Biter. '𝕴 eagerly anticipate a good sharpening afterwards.'

'You'll get it,' promised Odo. 'But until then, please try just to knock people on the heads, if you can. And not *too* hard, even if they are the bad guy –'

'Wait,' said Eleanor, holding up a hand. 'I see someone.'

She dropped to her belly on the stone, and Odo did the same. He inched up beside her, straining to see what had caught her eye.

It was a pair of Instruments in red and silver, each holding their wide-brimmed cloth hats tightly to their heads. A strong breeze was making them awkwardly flop around. Fortunately their animated brims had prevented them from seeing either of the knights creeping up on them.

'Back up,' Odo whispered. 'We're too close to them to get a good view of the whole party. Until we know where the regent is, there's no point attacking anyone.'

Eleanor nodded, and together they shuffled around until the two Instruments were safely out of sight. They moved as quietly as they could, given armour, swords and shields.

As they swung around, relative to the wind, they began to hear voices carried on the breeze.

'Hurry that fool up, will you, Lord Deor?' a woman's voice commanded, taut with impatience. Surely the regent, Eleanor thought, but she couldn't see her yet. The voice could have come from just over the next ridge or from a great distance away. Maybe Egda could pinpoint them better.

Thinking of the other two, she looked up to see if Tip was visible. That might give her an idea of what progress Hundred and Egda were making.

There was a black dot some distance away. It *looked* like a bat in the predawn light, but it was behaving oddly. Instead of flying towards them or following someone below, it was corkscrewing up and down in a series of spirals, like it was drunk.

'Look,' she said, pointing. 'Something's going on.'

Odo squinted. The light was getting steadily brighter. Dawn couldn't be far off now.

'That *is* Tip,' he said. 'But what's he doing?'

'It could be a sign of some kind, something we're supposed to figure out.'

'It isn't anything I recognise,' said Runnel.

'Nor I,' said Biter. 'Although bat signals have never had a traditional place in warfare.'

'Wouldn't it be easier just to fly over and tell us?' Odo asked.

They puzzled over the problem for a frustrated second or two, weighing the mystery of what might be happening with Egda and Hundred against the need to get to the regent before the sun rose.

'We could split up,' said Eleanor.

'No, I think we have to keep moving together,' Odo decided, coming up on his hands and knees to peer ahead. He could make out a gathering directly in front of them, just a short dash away. Among two dozen or so Instruments were a handful of people in brighter garb, including a woman wearing an ornate sword on her hip. She had Egda's nose, marking her as a relative, and her purple robe featured the royal seal, so she had to be Regent Odelyn. Next to her was a strange-looking bearded man holding up a burning brand. Its fire was greenish around the edges and seemed to shed no smoke ...

'Craft-fire!' Odo hissed. 'That's what's interfering with Tip!'

'He *is* trying to signal to us!' Eleanor's heart leaped into her throat. 'They want us to attack!'

'At last!' Biter was ready in Odo's hand as he jumped to his feet, Eleanor and Runnel beside him.

'Shields forward,' Eleanor said. 'Charge!'

'For the prince!' Odo cried.

Eleanor grinned widely. 'For the prince!'

Heads whipped around to gape, but they didn't run

more than two paces. From above and below, a swarm of animals attacked the two attackers.

An eagle and dozens of sparrows and rooks and pigeons swarmed from the sky. Scorpions, spiders and ants issued from cracks in the rocks, crawling and thronging. They snapped. They screeched. Wide, ensorcelled eyes saw only their enemy: the two children in their midst.

For a terrifying instant, Eleanor felt as though she had been plunged into a nightmare. She raised her hands, covering her face with her shield and leaving Runnel to guide her blows, scattering the birds in a shower of feathers. Feeling crawling legs and furred bodies massing up her legs, she danced frantically to shake them off.

Odo was doing the same, but he knew that it was a losing strategy.

'Run!' he gasped. 'Leave the small ones behind!'

They ploughed through the swarm, and indeed the slowest of the creatures couldn't keep up. That left only the birds to worry about – and the Instruments who were already closing in with swords drawn, taking advantage of the young knights' distraction.

'Charge!' cried Eleanor again, thinking to use the birds to her own advantage. They were a blunt weapon, surely, unable at close range to tell the difference between knights and the Instruments. 'For the prince!'

'For the prince!' Odo cried again, although he was mainly thinking of the four people the bilewolves had killed – Sir Halfdan, Bordan, Alia and Halthor.

Eleanor and Odo ran into battle side by side, aiming right for the centre of the pack. The birds came with them, angrily flapping and calling. Half the Instruments immediately turned and ran away, throwing their weapons aside, leaving just six to fend off the attackers. They braced themselves.

'For the prince!' came an answering cry from the other side of the royal procession.

And then a second. 'For the prince!'

Hundred and Egda burst out from cover and attacked the backs of the watching Instruments. Two fell with throwing knives buried deep in their shoulders. Another two dropped with tendons cut in their ankles. Egda's staff spun, knocking black-clad men and women down in all directions while Hundred's sword cut graceful arcs through the air.

'Hold them back! Call reinforcements!' cried the regent, standing tall in the middle of her honour guard, with Lord Deor and the beast-master on either side. A lank-haired young man in a red tunic nearby had to be the prince. He was looking around wildly, startled by this unexpected development.

'Yield now,' cried Egda, 'and your treachery will be forgiven!'

'You're supposed to be dead, you old fool!' Odelyn responded. 'How many times does it take?'

Eleanor and Odo concentrated on their own battles. Odo lowered the shield from his face long enough to block a wicked slash to his ribs from a skinny woman with surprising strength in her arms. The blow jarred every joint in the left side of his body, but he was ready with an answering blow. An upward swing of the flat of Biter's blade broke three of the fingers on her sword hand, and she fell back with a cry.

Eleanor had two opponents, one of them seemingly more afraid of the birds than he was of her. She soon showed him the error of his ways. A quick stab to his knee sent him to the ground, and she still had time to dispatch the eagle pecking at her ears.

'Think you're so clever, eh?' her remaining opponent goaded. 'Anyone with a sword can be a knight. I had to pass an *exam*.'

'Yeah? Well, examine this.' Thinking of all the things Hundred and Egda had taught her on the road to Winterset, Eleanor thrust Runnel at his face, and he fell back in surprise. She took advantage of his momentary distraction to disarm him and then knock him out cold.

Stepping over his supine form, she batted away the birds long enough to take the measure of the battlefield. Hundred and Egda were on the far side, and Instruments were dropping all around them, felled from knives Hundred threw by the handful. Egda was advancing steadily on the regent, who was herself still moving, drawing a long tail of her honour guard behind her. She remained intent on her mission.

'I see the falconstone,' Biter said in a determined tone, tugging at Odo to go fight him.

'Wait,' Odo said, pulling him back. 'We have to stop the coronation first. I don't see the crown.' Wings and claws flapped at his face. 'Ugh, these wretched birds! If only we could do something about them!'

Even as he said it, one of Hundred's blades caught the craft-worker. The bearded man went down with a cry, and his green-flamed torch went out. The animals were instantly released, including the scorpion Eleanor hadn't noticed raising its pincer to strike her throat. It dropped to the ground, turned a circle in confusion and scurried away.

Odo gave a cry of triumph and raised Biter high.

'For Lenburh!'

'What?' Eleanor looked around and realised that Tip and the other beasts were no longer slave to a supernatural will – a will that had been permanently ended. 'Oh yes! For Sir Halfdan and the others!'

'The battle is far from won,' Runnel cautioned as a furious Lord Deor shouted at the Instruments to attack and called for reinforcements from below. Those reinforcements came running up the steps roaring, and Odo found himself separated from Eleanor despite his best efforts to get back to her. Hundred and Egda had also been driven apart.

'Divide and conquer – an obvious tactic,' Runnel observed

as Eleanor leaped over the supine form of another challenger.

'That's a game two can play,' growled Eleanor, driving hard through the throng to where the regent and her pet lord stood. She was so quick charging through the lines of Instruments that only two managed to interpose themselves, and they were so startled to see a young girl charging them, wielding a magic sword, that the best they could manage was a token defence. She knocked them both down, and suddenly Eleanor found herself facing a much deadlier foe.

'Foolish girl,' said Lord Deor, raising his heavy sword. The hiss of its steel was as deadly as his smile. 'You will pay for your insolence.'

She didn't waste breath on words. Adopting the Third Proper Stance, she used the matching Deadly Strike, Angry Fox, to thrust Runnel towards the gap between Lord Deor's pauldron and gorget. This was one life she would not spare, if she could avoid it. But the Falconstone was faster than it looked, and swept across the Chief Regulator's body in a blur to block the blow. The deflection was so keen and swift that she hardly felt it. All she knew was that her momentum shifted and suddenly she was exposed down her right side and fighting for her life.

One blow she narrowly blocked, then another. Thankfully her shield proved up to the task, taking the force of the Falconstone without shattering, although her arm felt badly bruised and it took all her effort to remain on her feet. Cold sweat dripped into her eyes. Perhaps, she thought, she and Runnel had taken on more than they could handle, although she would never admit it. Grinding her teeth, she turned aside Lord Deor's next thrust and came in low for one of her own. Again the Falconstone deflected Runnel with almost sinister ease, like it was toying with her, and she fell back under a rain of blows.

Lord Deor's smile grew wider still.

Eleanor squared her feet, and in the process looked down. Seeing one of Hundred's knives between her feet, inspiration came to her.

'Be ready,' she told Runnel in a whisper.

'Always, Sir Eleanor.'

She lunged forward and at the same time let go of Runnel and dropped into a roll, scooping up the knife as she went. Runnel completed the strike, which was blocked by the Falconstone. That left Lord Deor open on his right flank.

Eleanor leaped up and stabbed, adapting the Sixth Deadly Strike to work with the knife, as Hundred had shown her. The tip of the blade slipped through a gap in Lord Deor's armour, but he twisted away quickly enough to avoid a lethal injury. *Worth a try*, she thought, even as he landed a blow on her shield that would have split her in two like firewood had she not successfully blocked it; as it was, it completely numbed her arm. She raised the knife, knowing it was little use to her now. The

Falconstone knocked Runnel aside as Lord Deor wound himself up for a blow that surely not even a dragon-scale shield could resist.

Then Egda was between them, his staff spinning a protective whirlwind around Eleanor, enabling her to catch her breath and her sword. Grateful, she squared up once more, and together she and Egda drove Lord Deor back.

'Where is the regent?' Egda asked her.

Eleanor didn't dare take her eyes off Lord Deor to look. 'She was here a moment ago . . .'

'We must find her! She must not complete the ritual!'

Eleanor dropped back a pace, letting Egda defend her, and glanced around. The regent was hurrying away from the battle, dragging the unresisting prince along as a hostage.

'Behind, to the right!' she told Egda.

'Go!'

Eleanor broke off, and Egda drove Lord Deor back several paces. In response, Lord Deor roared in anger – he was used to enemies fleeing, or trying to, not to being forced back. And then Egda added insult to injury by turning and following Eleanor!

But even as Lord Deor started to lumber in pursuit, he was distracted by Hundred, who threw a knife that glanced off his shoulder without doing any harm. Another narrowly missed his ear. The third bit into his neck, and he turned with a snarl to see the small old woman running towards him, sword held high. Her battle cry was wordless, a pure shriek of rage and blood.

Meanwhile, another voice triumphantly proclaimed, 'Let Aldewrath object!'

The shout drew Odo's attention. In shock and dismay he saw the regent standing astride the hilt of a ceremonial sword buried deep in the Stone, raising a golden crown high, ready to make herself king of Tofte.

TWENTY-THREE

It was all happening so quickly Kendryk could hardly keep up, particularly in his exhausted state. First a swarm of birds and other creatures had descended on Old Dragon Stone, summoned by the unnatural fire carried by the hairy man. Then the honour guard had come under attack by none other than Egda and his loyal retainer, the legendary woman with one hundred weapons. Kendryk could have cheered, but then his grandmother had grabbed the small bag made of woven gold from a nearby Instrument and dragged him away from the fight, still pursuing her quest to make herself ruler of all she could see.

She could see a long way from the top of Old Dragon Stone.

'It's here somewhere,' she muttered, eyes searching the well-worn stone ahead. 'Ah, at last!'

The notch could have been a perfectly innocent crack caused by years of weathering or a lightning strike, but for the ring of symbols surrounding it. Kendryk couldn't read them – no one could, not even the scribes who had recorded their secrets in the royal library – but to his feverish eyes they had the look of a warning. Or a promise.

'Stand still,' she said, releasing him. He didn't run. This was exactly where he needed to be.

She approached the hole in the stone, drawing the crown from the golden bag and the Royal Sword from its scabbard. They had once been plain but valuable things, the products of a simpler time. Both had since been decorated by less secure dynasties with jewels, filigree and etchings proclaiming the worth of the bearer – all of it unnecessary for the purpose they served. *The righteous ruler makes the crown*, someone had written in a book only Kendryk had read for hundreds of years, *just as the true knight makes the sword.*

'This is wrong, Grandmother,' Kendryk told her wearily.

'This is statecraft. Weaken your enemies and take what ought to be yours.'

'You have only made your enemies stronger. Don't you see? Your Instruments are hated across the land.'

'They do not need to be liked. They just need to be loyal.'

'They are – as long as you can pay them. What happens when you run out of money, or their greed rises to match yours?'

'Pah! I don't have time for this. We can argue politics in your dungeon cell – if I can spare the time from being king.'

She raised the sword and slid it one-handed into the stone, completing the first part of the coronation ritual.

'Let Aldewrath object!'

Kendryk's breath caught in his throat. So quickly. All it took now was for the crown to descend on Regent Odelyn's head. Then she would be king in all but right and the land would tremble under her.

Unless something stopped her, at the very last.

Closing his eyes, Kendryk opened his throat and began to sing.

Dragon, dragon, heed our call . . .

The prince's mellow, surprisingly deep voice cut through the moment of shock that spread across the battlefield. Eleanor was caught midstep as she realised that the regent was about to win. Odo had just felled his last opponent. Hundred would have thrown a knife to stop the regent, but the only blade she had left was her sword, and that did not throw well.

Egda cocked his head at the sound of his great-nephew's voice, and listened.

Come to aid us, one and all.
From a cruel and dreadful fate,
Save us now, ere it's too late.

Old Dragon Stone raised no objection to the sword or to Regent Odelyn's words.

She raised the crown higher and cackled triumphantly. The prince kept singing, louder.

DRAGON, DRAGON, HEED OUR CALL.
COME TO AID US, ONE AND ALL.

His voice rang out across the battlefield and across the city. Bakers stopped with their hands in their ovens at the sound of it. Children stirred in their sleep. As dawn touched the slender spires of the palace, Kendryk's voice followed.

FROM A CRUEL AND DREADFUL FATE,
SAVE US NOW –

Out of the palace came the sound of bells ringing, glass smashing and stone blocks shifting in their ancient seats. Heads turned to look as a cloud of colour burst from every window and crack, rising up into the sky. There it swirled and stirred, a mix of reds, oranges and golds, painted gloriously in the light of the rising sun. For a moment it looked as though it might disperse, but then it steadied and took shape.

A dragon . . . in the exact shape of the prince's mural.

Kendryk smiled to see it. All these weeks of labour had not been for naught!

His creation's ethereal wings flapped once, twice, driving the magically animated paint towards the top of Old Dragon

Stone. Everyone seeing it quailed, thinking the magical beast might open its giant jaws and eat them, or wrest them up into the sky in its claws.

Even Odo and Eleanor, who had just a month ago braved the stare of the mighty Quenwulf, felt their jaws open in amazement and fear.

Odelyn paused, staring herself, a look of horror on her face as it seemed she was to be thwarted at the last moment by the grandson she had considered a fool and a dragon she had believed to be mythical.

But this dragon was flying too low. The broad wings flapped almost carelessly one third and final time. Then, with a soundless crash that somehow made the stone quiver faintly underfoot, it struck the vertical cliff face and became a mural once more . . . a portrait of a dragon big enough for all the city to see.

All was silent again.

A moment later, Odelyn released a short, barking sarcastic laugh.

'Thank you, grandson. A . . . a noble display,' said the regent. 'Truly fit for a king.'

Kendryk did not reply. He stood there calmly, as if he was still waiting for something else to happen.

Odelyn began to lower the crown onto her own head, beaming a triumphant smile.

A smile that suddenly faltered as the stone shook beneath

them, far more powerfully than it had the first time.

The regent stumbled and missed her head. Quickly she raised the crown to try again.

Old Dragon Stone rocked a third time, even more strongly, as though struck by an impossible blow.

The regent staggered. Everyone did. It was as though the world moved beneath their feet.

'What's happening?' Eleanor gasped.

Odo shook his head. 'I don't know. Maybe something to do with that . . . ghost dragon or whatever it was . . .'

'Look at the prince!' She pointed.

Kendryk had exploded out of his patient pose. He was turning circles in place, dancing a jig that took him nowhere. His robe flapped around him as he clapped his hands in delight.

'What have you done?' the regent shouted, crown momentarily forgotten. 'What have you done!'

'Called for help,' the prince replied. 'And it worked!'

Odelyn roared with anger and lifted the crown again, but before she could settle it on her head, Old Dragon Stone kicked like an egg with an impatient chick. A crack opened up between the regent and her grandson, and both staggered back from a jet of potent heat that issued from it. Pale blue flames leaped high into the air. There came a roar like the Foss in full flow.

'Who summons me?' The voice was so deep and forceful

just the sound of it opened more fiery cracks in Old Dragon Stone. 'Who disturbs my slumber?'

'It is I, oh Aldewrath!' cried Kendryk delightedly, even though the hem of his robe was on fire. He stamped it out. 'It takes a dragon to summon a dragon – and you are the *original* Old Dragon. Awaken and repel the usurper!'

The crack at Kendryk's feet broadened, gaping many yards wide. He fell back with one arm upraised to protect his eyes. The regent stood gaping as the snout and chin of a giant, red-scaled creature rose up out of the crack and sniffed the air.

'It *is* a dragon!' Eleanor cried.

'Not just any dragon,' said Hundred with awe in her voice. 'That's Aldewrath himself!'

'I thought . . . I thought he was a myth,' whimpered a nearby Instrument, who had dropped her sword in shock.

'Apparently not,' said Odo. 'Your prince just summoned him.'

The Instrument turned tail and fled, taking with her those few who remained standing.

Aldewrath's giant nostrils opened again, sucking in mighty lungfuls of air, staggering everyone but usefully starving several fires of oxygen, so they went out. The entire top of Old Dragon Stone was covered in cracks now, and all of them radiated heat in waves.

'None of you smells true,' Aldewrath declared, his vast

head rising on a long, sinuous neck so one golden eye could take in Kendryk and the other his grandmother. 'What has become of the kingdom?'

'There's nothing wrong with the kingdom,' objected Odelyn, drawing herself up and once again raising the crown. She did not lack courage. 'The only thing it lacks is a king – me!'

Aldewrath narrowed his lips, and his sinuous forked tongue whisked across and wrenched the crown from her hands and sent it tumbling across the top of the Stone. Egda's head turned to follow the metallic ringing sound it made. A quick thrust with his staff stopped it from rolling off the edge and falling to the earth far below.

'Only descendants of the First King may hold the throne,' roared Aldewrath. 'That is the pact I made with her, long ago. I can be roused to protect the kingdom, but only by one of the First King's descendants. I carefully check when they follow the ritual during their coronation. In return, I am allowed to sleep in peace, without fear of disturbance from wandering knights and the like. As I am being disturbed now. Who must I punish for breaking the pact?'

Kendryk went down on his knees before the great dragon, but quickly sprang up again because the stone was too hot.

'To punish the person responsible, you would have to travel back in time,' he said, 'and I fear that might be beyond even you, great Aldewrath! King Brandar the Wise lived and died three hundred years ago. He lied about being an illegitimate son of the previous king, and won a war to prove it. When he came up here to be crowned, you, great Aldewrath, didn't object, because you were even more deeply asleep than usual. King Brandar was a powerful sorcerer who tricked his way onto the throne and made certain you never woke up to reject his claim – and then he convinced everyone you were just a myth!'

'A myth? For three hundred years? That is sorcery indeed. And treachery. But it does explain your unexpected scent.'

'What nonsense,' the regent scoffed. 'Don't listen to him, Aldewrath. He's a madman. He's concocted this story merely to put himself on the throne –'

'Don't you understand, Grandmother?' Kendryk said. 'I'm no madman – but if you can't rule, neither can I. None of our line can. We're all pretenders – even Great-uncle Egda!'

Eleanor glanced at the former king, who held the crown reverently in his left hand, perhaps remembering when he had once worn it. His face was ashen.

'Not . . . king?' he said.

'You were crowned,' Hundred reminded him firmly. 'You ruled. What does a bit of blood matter?'

'Ask the dragon!' he snapped. 'Maybe the First King's courage would not have failed, as mine did.'

'I have no opinion under the pact I made,' said Aldewrath. 'If I have slept three hundred years and missed the end of my old friend's line, I see no reason to stay awake now.'

The giant head began to sink back into the rift.

'You can't go back to sleep,' said Kendryk, aghast. 'You have to put *someone* on the throne!'

'*I can't? I have to?*' the dragon roared, eyes widening in outrage. Thin lips pulled back from teeth like long knives, and Aldewrath opened his mighty jaws wider, as though considering snapping Kendryk up. 'The pact has ended. I care not how you decide now. Let it be the person who first wears the crown, for all it matters to me!'

With that, Aldewrath retreated into Old Dragon Stone, which shook and complained in response. Flames and smoke spurted out of the cracks.

All eyes turned to the crown held limply in Egda's hand.

TWENTY-FOUR

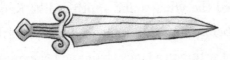

'**G**ive it to me, brother,' said Odelyn, advancing with a murderous look.

Eleanor and Odo closed ranks in front of Egda. Hundred moved to intercept Odelyn, and was confronted by Lord Deor. For a moment there was a stalemate, with Kendryk standing helplessly to one side.

'This isn't what I planned,' he despaired. 'Aldewrath was supposed to honour the pact and choose a new monarch. Surely there's someone left in Tofte with the royal blood!'

'What does it matter?' his grandmother snapped at him. 'Blood is no substitute for ambition.'

'And ambition is no substitute for ability,' Hundred retorted. 'You are sending your Instruments out into the kingdom knowing nothing about the people or the lands they are to be stewards of.'

'What's there to know? My subjects are the ones who need to understand that things are different now. The old ways are gone. No one believes in them anyway.'

'That's not true!' Eleanor declared. 'I believe in them. I've spent my whole life dreaming of being a knight, and now I am one, and you're not taking that from me!'

'See?' said Odo. 'You know nothing about Tofte. You've never visited the villages and smithies like Kendryk has, and Egda before him. You've lived *your* life in the palace, dreaming of sitting in a fancy chair and believing that made you king. It doesn't. You have to earn it.'

'I *have* earned it.' Odelyn lunged forward, pointing at Egda. Odo and Eleanor crossed swords to prevent her coming any closer. 'I stood in *his* shadow and watched him grow weak and cowardly. What kind of king just gives up?'

'She's right,' said Egda. 'I was not a good king.'

'My liege,' said Hundred. 'Don't listen to her –'

'But Odelyn would be a worse king still.' Egda raised the crown over a seething crack next to him. 'I should drop this right now and let it melt!'

'No!' cried Kendryk and Odelyn at the same time. Lord Deor lunged, knocking Hundred back into Egda – whose fingers snapped open accidentally, letting the crown go.

The impact knocked the crown away from the crack. With a penetrating chime, it struck the rock and bounced across the top of Old Dragon Stone, rolling at a rapid speed.

Everyone moved at once: Odelyn and Kendryk for the crown, Hundred to save Egda, who was teetering on the edge of the crack, Eleanor to protect Kendryk, and Odo to block Lord Deor. Only Odo wasn't the only one choosing his direction. Biter was pulling him too, hoping for a chance to even the score against Falconstone, the Butcher Blade of Winterset.

'Out of my way, boy,' Lord Deor growled. He was bleeding from a wound in his side, but it didn't seem to slow him.

'𝔖𝔦𝔯 𝔒𝔡𝔬 𝔴𝔦𝔩𝔩 𝔫𝔬𝔱 𝔟𝔢 𝔰𝔭𝔬𝔨𝔢𝔫 𝔱𝔬 𝔱𝔥𝔞𝔱 𝔴𝔞𝔶,' Biter responded, ready to fight.

But Odo reined him in, thinking fast. He didn't fancy his chances against an experienced knight and his equally vicious sword, although he would fight to protect Egda. He was about the same size as Lord Deor.

'It's in your best interest to stay back, good knight,' Odo said, watching the Falconstone closely for any sudden lunges. 'You and I, we're just following orders. In a moment this'll all be sorted out, without bloodshed, and we can go back to being on the same side, like we were before.'

'I'm not a knight, and I'm not on your side,' Lord Deor said, his brows darkening. 'I'm the Chief Regulator!'

With that he struck, the Falconstone's black tip slashing horizontally through the air. Biter and Odo moved as one to defend themselves with the fourth Certain Block. Metal rang against metal, and then again as Odo struck in return. He was used to fighting Eleanor, who was faster than him. Lord Deor was faster still – and Odo was very conscious of the fact that the Regulator was only the second person he had ever fought armed with a magical sword. Ædroth, sword of the false knight Sir Saskia, had been perfectly ordinary, and still she had beaten him.

That, however, was a long time ago and far away. Then, he had fought for his honour. Now he was fighting for the entire country – and for his life.

Ninth Deadly Strike, he told himself, drawing Biter back for another series of blows and adjusting the weight of his dragon-scale shield. Chief Regulator or not, Lord Deor was just another knight, and knights could be beaten.

Eleanor saw Odo fighting Lord Deor but had no time to feel more than a flash of concern. At least she had weakened him for Odo.

Her outstretched fingertips had just touched the rolling crown when a strong hand gripped her trailing leg and she fell over, almost landing face first. Eleanor cursed and lashed out as Odelyn ran by, but succeeded only in tearing off a handful of purple robe. Using a word that she'd never thought to utter in the presence of royalty, she looked around for Kendryk. He was too far away.

Odelyn had caught up with the crown. In a moment she would scoop it up and declare herself king. They had all heard the dragon's decree. Putting the crown on her head really *would* make her king.

A black shape descended from the sky. Tip caught the

rolling crown with both feet and furiously flapped his webbed wings. Eleanor cheered, but her relief was short-lived. The crown was too heavy for the little bat, and Odelyn too speedy. The regent got one hand on the circlet, sending Tip tumbling away and ripping it free.

With a cry of triumph, she raised it high.

Scrambling to her feet, Eleanor drew back her swordarm and launched Runnel in a wild, desperate throw.

The sword flew true, darting with a whistle betweenOdelyn's upraised hands, and caught the crown against Runnel's cross-guard.

'Cursed thing!' Odelyn snatched at the sword and almost lost her fingers for the effort. Runnel swooped around her, intending to bring the crown to Eleanor.

'No, to Prince Kendryk!' she cried.

Runnel changed course, and Kendryk raised his hands and ran backwards to catch the crown as it dropped down from on high. At the last moment, a fallen Instrument who had been feigning unconsciousness rose up onto hands and knees behind the prince and tripped him. The crown landed in front of her, and she snatched it up in both hands.

'To me!' cried Odelyn, opening her arms. 'Throw truly and I'll reward you with a hundred gold nobles.'

'Only a hundred gold nobles?' the Instrument said with a sneer. 'I heard what that dragon said. Anyone who wears this thing can be king – so why not me?'

'Why not you? Because crown or not, I'll have you hung, drawn, and quartered, you treacherous cur, that's why!' Odelyn bared her teeth and began to run.

Startled, the Instrument turned and fled, the crown dangling in her left hand.

Odo blocked another powerful blow from Lord Deor. The Falconstone's keen blade skidded down Biter's blunter edge, stopping at the cross-guard with the force of a punch. Gasping for air, Odo pushed with his shield and forced Lord Deor onto his back foot. That was the most ground he could gain, but surely the older man's strength would have to ebb soon. Blood still flowed freely down his side, and his smile was looking forced. What Odo couldn't win by skill alone, he might yet take with superior endurance.

Distraction came from an unexpected quarter. 'Leave this one to me,' cried Hundred, kicking Lord Deor in the knee and breaking the stalemate. 'Go after the crown. You have longer legs!'

Odo shook sweat from his eyes and looked around. Egda stood alone but out of harm's way, for the moment. Eleanor, Kendryk, Odelyn and Tip were chasing an Instrument who was running for the Long Stair, dodging and weaving around smoking cracks as she went. Her current path took her not far from him, and in her hand was the crown!

Lowering his head and roaring like a bull, he ran, wishing

for Eleanor's speed. But intimidation might do, and the sight of him had the desired effect.

The Instrument squeaked and changed direction, regretting ever getting involved.

'Here!' she said, throwing the crown at him. 'You have it!'

He hadn't expected her to go that far, and he flubbed the catch with his shield-arm, flicking the crown up into the air and twisting in midstep to turn and try again. Instead his left toe caught on a lip of stone, and he fell, spread-eagled. The crown came down, striking him on the head – where it stayed.

'Odo?' cried Eleanor.

Shakily he sat up.

Everyone was looking at him.

Everything was suddenly quiet.

He raised his hands. Yes, the crown was definitely on his head, which, according to the dragon, made him . . .

King of Tofte.

TWENTY-FIVE

All eyes were on Odo. *King* Odo, thought Eleanor in amazement. She couldn't believe it. Who could have guessed when they found Biter in the mud that his journey would lead him here?

Jealousy, this time, was the furthest thing from her mind. She felt only pride for her friend, who she thought would make a very good king indeed.

Lord Deor was the first to recover from the shock. He launched a surprise attack against Hundred, and she blocked too late. Her curved sword spun far out of her reach.

Empty-handed, she stood facing him, apparently helpless. He laughed, gloating, and drew back his sword to strike her down.

She launched herself under the blade, which swung harmlessly overhead. Using her weight in exactly the right way, she tipped him off balance, forcing him back one step, two steps . . .

Lord Deor took no third step. With a cry, he fell into a

fiery crack and disappeared. There came a sound like giant jaws crunching, and he was gone.

Out of the crack shot a black streak.

'𝕿𝖍𝖊 𝖋𝖆𝖑𝖈𝖔𝖓𝖘𝖙𝖔𝖓𝖊!' cried Biter, instinctively going to follow.

But as the Butcher Blade of Winterset rocketed off into the distance, heading south and west away from the sun, Biter stayed his flight. His knight needed him. The *king* needed him. Perhaps to slay the dragon, if it chose to stir again.

Odo barely noticed. His thoughts were a whirl – but he knew what he had to do. Although being a knight was something he had learned to like, he knew he still had a great deal to learn. Being a king was an even tougher job than being a knight, and he simply wasn't ready for such a task. He was a boy from a village who knew right from wrong, and liked knowing what he was supposed to do. He didn't have the first idea how to rule an entire country.

Eleanor saw all this pass across her friend's face, and understood completely. She would have been the same in his shoes, but for different reasons. She wanted to see the world, and kings mostly stayed at home and argued with people who wanted things from them. That sounded about as much fun as helping her father lance Old Master Croft's boils.

She could have cheered when he lifted the crown off his head.

'No,' he said. 'I am not ready to be a king. Perhaps I never will be.'

'I'll make you the richest man in Tofte,' said Odelyn, sensing victory within her grasp once more, even though she stood alone among enemies. This knight was just a boy, and boys were easily convinced to act against their own better interests. 'You'll marry the prettiest woman in Winterset.'

'I don't want that either,' he said without hesitation. 'And besides, it's not my place to choose.'

He tossed the crown to Egda, who heard the rush of air and caught it expertly.

'It's a wise man who knows his limitations, Sir Odo,' he said, weighing the crown in his hands. He laughed softly. 'As I believe I now know mine. I didn't give up the throne because I was blind. I abdicated because I no longer had the desire to rule. I was tired, frustrated and –' he forced himself to utter the word he had resisted for so long – '*old*. But there is no shame in that, just as there is no shame in being blind. I accept the truth now, and tell you with all honesty that I still don't want to be king.'

He laughed again, more loudly. 'And judging by the quaking underfoot, I suspect the great Aldewrath doesn't want me to be king either!'

He paused for a moment, everyone watching, everyone listening.

'But I do know someone who I think is suitable,' he continued. 'Someone whose clever planning, patience and humility shows he is fit to be king.'

There was complete silence for a moment. Egda raised the crown and said the name:

'Kendryk.'

Kendryk slowly walked over to Egda, placed his hands on the old king's shoulders and knelt before him. Egda lowered the crown on his head. Just as it settled there, Odelyn made a sudden lunge, only to be prevented by Eleanor and Runnel.

'There,' Egda said, tapping the crown lightly on top to make it sit securely. 'By the will of the dragon, it is done.'

As Kendryk stood up, Egda went down on one knee, as did Hundred and Odo. Eleanor stayed standing, but only because she didn't trust Odelyn not to run at Kendryk again.

'I might have the crown,' said King Kendryk as the rumbles of protest subsided, 'but I'm still only a pretender. Our whole family are pretenders!'

'All kings are pretenders,' came a rumbling voice from below, and the dragon's head rose out of the rift again. 'All human kings . . .'

'No!' shrieked Odelyn. She ducked under Eleanor's grasping hands, dodged Runnel's sudden swipe and ran at Kendryk, only to be caught and wrapped several times around by Aldewrath's lightning-fast tongue. The dragon held her like that for a few seconds, then whipped his tongue back, sending the regent spinning dizzily away until she fell over a stone and lay there, sobbing angrily.

Kendryk looked around in amazement, taking in his great-uncle, grandmother, three knights, and a dragon, all looking at him at once, the only person standing on Old Dragon Stone.

This was his moment, he told himself, after everything he had worked for during his long imprisonment at the hands of the regent, seeking a peaceful way to stop her from becoming king, pretending to be mad so she wouldn't think him a threat. Still, Kendryk had never dreamed that he himself might end up on the throne. That, surely, would fall to someone of the right bloodline. Yet here he was, the start of a *new* bloodline . . .

There was so much to think about.

He lengthened his spine, raised his chin, adjusted the crown so it sat straight across his forehead, and said, 'Are you proposing a new pact, great Aldewrath?'

'A modification of the original pact,' said the dragon. 'This time I will be wary of sorcerers desiring me to sleep overlong.'

Kendryk bowed, holding the crown with one hand so it didn't fall off. There had been too much kicking around of that crown already, and he could see several of the gems that had fallen off lying on the ground.

'On behalf of . . . of my people, I apologize for the actions of Brandar the decidedly un-Wise and the forgetfulness of Tofte. It will never happen again.'

'I sincerely hope not. Not too often, anyway. I sleep, but waking has its pleasures too. The dawn in particular. I will dream of this one while I await the next.'

Aldewrath's glassy eyelids flickered and he began to sink back into Old Dragon Stone.

Eleanor's breath caught in her throat. She had a question, but did she dare ask it? Only the thought that she might never get another chance forced her to try.

'Excuse me, Aldewrath?'

The dragon stopped, his snout just visible.

'Harrumph. Yes, little knight?'

'The person who started the pact between humans and dragons — was that the First King?'

'Between all humans and all dragons? I cannot answer that question. But between me and the people of Tofte, it was indeed her. Now, she truly had fire in her veins . . . and many exhausting questions of her own. Goodnight, and goodbye.'

Aldewrath's eyes closed and he disappeared for good. Old Dragon Stone grew silent and still. The cracks healed up. The fires went out. With a steely hiss, the Royal Sword slid out of the rock as though pushed from the inside, and fell flat with a clatter.

King Kendryk gingerly picked it up in his right hand, but it wasn't hot at all. He raised his left hand for Tip to land on and then transferred the bat to his shoulder. The little bat settled gratefully there, closing his eyes and falling almost instantly asleep. It had been a long night's work, with many surprises. What happened during the daytime was the humans' responsibility.

'Please, stand,' said the king. 'Sir Odo, Sir Eleanor – I feel as though I already know you from Tip's testimony. You have served my great-uncle well, and by serving him, served me and Tofte as faithfully as any royal guard.'

'It was our duty,' said Odo.

'And a pleasure,' added Eleanor.

'My gratitude is undying and . . . well, I don't know the proper words, but I'm sure I'll find them some day. Let us call your apprenticeship complete, shall we? I pronounce you the first members of the re-formed royal guard. Which means, unfortunately for you, there's still much work to be done. We need to tend the wounded and bind the unrepentant, starting with my grandmother.'

Odo bowed and went to fetch the rope they had used to climb the Stone.

Kendryk continued. 'Hundred, I believe there are loyal knights in the city. Could you gather them to attend me?'

'Yes, sire. I know three at least who will be eager to serve.' She hurried off to summon Sirs Brude, Uen and Talorc, who were certain to have made short work of the Instruments at the river gate.

'Great-uncle?'

Egda approached Kendryk, using his staff for support. He knelt before his great-nephew and bowed his head. 'I doubt you have any need for a blind old fool, but whatever I have to offer is yours.'

'You *are* a fool if you think I don't need your help.' The younger man beamed. 'Good kings have good advisers. Perhaps you will be mine, until the kingdom is secure once more?'

Egda bowed. 'It would be an honour, sire.'

'A madman and a fool in league?' scoffed Odelyn. 'I will laugh at you when things fall apart.'

'I hardly think that is going to happen, Grandmother,' Kendryk said as Odo finished tying her wrists together. 'Not while I have such loyal knights and swords at my side.'

Odo expected Biter to launch forth in an enthusiastic salute, but none came. The sword's tip kept nudging in the direction the Falconstone had fled, and Odo knew what preoccupied him.

Bowing to accept the compliment, Odo joined Eleanor in checking to see which of the Instruments had woken, and which of those had experienced a sudden and unexpected change of heart.

TWENTY-SIX

'I still don't understand how you talked Kendryk into letting us go home,' said Odo two weeks later.

Eleanor and Odo were in the royal stables, seeing to their horses. Wiggy had arrived several days before from Kyles Frost, along with Eleanor's favourite mount – Belbis, a strawberry roan with a distinct snowcap blanket on her croup and fierce curiosity for everything that lay off the beaten path. In that, she very much reminded Odo of her rider.

'I didn't,' said Eleanor in surprise. 'I thought you must have done.'

'No,' said Odo. He scratched his head. 'I did say I'd like to go back to Lenburh to see my family sometime . . .'

'I sort of feel we . . . I . . . might have disappointed him,' said Eleanor, 'and now he's getting rid of us.'

'What? No . . . I don't think so,' said Odo. 'You mean because of what you did to Lady Scrift?'

'Lady Scrift said we were the real rebels and traitors and should have our heads chopped off! Besides, I wasn't going to hurt her. If she'd stayed still she'd never have broken her leg.'

'Kendryk . . . the king . . . told me she deserved everything she got,' said Odo firmly.

Eleanor sighed as she brushed Belbis down. 'I guess I'm just not suited to seeing wrongdoers get away with things. Lady Scrift *volunteered* to be an Instrument.'

Odo had nothing to say to that. Though the regent herself had been decreed a traitor, and would spend the rest of her days in Winterset's highest prison cell, Kendryk had pardoned most of the Instruments, Adjusters and Regulators, though they would all be replaced.

'They should have all been locked up,' said Eleanor. 'Or had their heads chopped off.'

'I think the king was right to be merciful,' said Odo. 'And I do not think he was worried about you scaring Lady Scrift. He's not sending us into exile or anything.'

'No,' said a familiar voice from the stable door.

It was Egda, and Hundred was with him. Odo and Eleanor put their brushes aside and hurried to greet their friends. They had hardly seen one another since the coronation, what with exploring the city and learning their duties as royal guards, while Hundred and Egda had been often closeted with the king, offering advice.

'Where have you been?' Eleanor demanded. 'I haven't seen you since the feast three days ago.'

Odo nudged her warningly. 'There's been a lot to do, I bet.'

'Indeed,' said Egda, but not without an affectionate smile. 'Not all Instruments have obeyed the instruction to return to the capital, the pardon notwithstanding. Not all the former stewards have been located, nor knights who held other important posts. And we have only just set in train the Great Reckoning, the census that will keep many of those former Instruments busy, as we count and record all the people, holdings and other minutiae of the kingdom. Kendryk intends to rule with knowledge, not force.'

'As befits a sorcerer-king of the first rank,' said Hundred. 'I believe a ballad is already circulating through the taverns. It also names two young heroes with a bright future ahead of them.'

Eleanor blushed with a mixture of delight, embarrassment and frustration.

'If our future is so bright,' she said, 'why is the king sending us home now?'

'He knows you are too valuable to waste your time standing guard outside the throne room, or pacing the sentry-walk of the palace,' said Egda. 'Though I daresay you will have your turns at that in the future.'

'But why send us home?' asked Odo. On the one hand, he dearly wanted to see Lenburh again, but on the other it did seem surprising the king wanted them to go. Part of him wondered if it was a mistake and they'd be called back, just when he was starting to think about home again, and the way the river burbled beneath the mill wheel, and the birds sang in the morning . . .

'Hard to say,' said Hundred. 'There are many such decisions for the king to make.'

'Oh,' said Eleanor, unable to hide her disappointment. 'It just seems, I don't know, odd.'

'You thought being a knight was going to be one long adventure?' Hundred asked. She looked at Egda, who smiled. Even though he couldn't see the smile on Hundred's face, he must have heard it in her voice.

'What?' asked Eleanor.

'We must return to the king's side, but before we do, I just want to say what a pleasure it has been serving with you both,' said Egda. He was still smiling. 'The new ballad does not lie. The future of Tofte is in good hands.'

Both of them blushed at the former king's praise, but Eleanor frowned as well. There was something else going on here. Odo also sensed it, and looked at her in puzzlement.

'Oh,' Egda said on the threshold, 'a word of warning: we have received reports of a renegade sword heading west – an enchanted sword that slays anyone who approaches. Fortunately the king is sending two of his best knights to deal with it, while on their way to Lenburh.'

With that, he and Hundred were gone, and Biter was suddenly out of his scabbard and hissing about the barn, startling the horses.

'A renegade sword?' he cried. 'Slaying people? It has to be the Falconstone. It must be stopped! We must join forces with these knights.'

Odo started to laugh, soon joined by Eleanor.

'What?!' shrieked Biter. 'There is not a moment to be lost. We cannot allow these other knights to vanquish our foe!'

'Biter,' said Odo, quelling his laughter with difficulty, 'we are those knights.'

'Oh,' said Biter. Odo held out his hand, and Biter returned to it.

'You had better practise your moves, little brother,' said Runnel, leaping into Eleanor's hand. 'I believe you may still be a little rusty.'

'Never!'

Joining the swords in the joyous playfight, Eleanor and Odo danced back and forth through the sawdust and straw. Whether the future was in good hands or not, they couldn't say, but they could at least feel that it was mapped out with some degree of certainty. One magic sword wouldn't stand a chance against two, not to mention their knights . . .

Could it?

EPILOGUE

Without breaking step, the lone traveller stared up at the mountains in exhausted resignation. She had reached the flanks of the Offersittan and knew what lay ahead: a long and dangerous climb. Already haggard and thin after weeks of walking, clad only in filthy quilted gambeson and hose, she doubted she would live to see the other side. But she had no choice. She had to continue.

'Help! Save me!'

The desperate cry came from over a low hill directly ahead. Unhesitatingly, the traveller started to run. She was going that way anyway, and helping a stranger in need could bring her a meal, perhaps even shelter for the night. She was allowed to rest at night.

What she saw brought her very nearly to a halt. A bearded peasant armed only with a pitchfork was fending off a sword that chopped and slashed entirely of its own volition. An *enchanted* sword!

The traveller hissed through her teeth. Now this was a

predicament. She had experience with such swords, recent experience. She knew how deadly they could be.

Even as she approached, the sword lunged, killing the peasant with a single stab to the throat.

The traveller slowed, though she could not stop. This was an even more dangerous sword than she had supposed. Enchanted swords did not usually act without a wielder, and they did not kill peasants.

The sword withdrew from the body and turned in the air towards her, taking the measure of this new arrival. The traveller noted that it had an empty setting where a gem once might have been. It was strange, too, that it did not speak. Maybe it had nothing to say.

'Let me pass,' she told the bloodied weapon, her mouth curled. 'Or slay me. I care not. I am cursed by a dragon and must walk on.'

The sword answered, but not in speech. It came straight at her, and the traveller forced herself to keep her eyes open, to brace for the killing blow. No one could say she had died like a coward, with her eyes shut.

But at the last second, the sword spun in the air and the heavy pommel struck her a powerful blow directly above her heart.

She gasped, thrown backwards to the ground as though the earth had been pulled out from under her. A terrible pressure spread from the left side of her chest, down her left arm and up her throat. The sword had stopped her heart! With a single blow! Blackness crept in around the edges of her vision and she hissed out a curse, unable to do more than feel an incredible wave of anger and futility at dying like this, so pointlessly, and without enacting a terrible revenge on those who had wronged her . . .

The world turned black. She felt herself rushing down a tunnel as long as a dragon's throat . . .

And then she felt a second blow to the chest, one that brought her back to life. She drew in a ragged breath, feeling her heart resume beating with a lurch, then a stagger, then a furious racing, driven by panic and relief.

Her vision returned. The sword was hanging over her, mute and deadly.

It had brought her back from the dead!

Why?

An even stranger discovery awaited her on groaning to her feet, her treacherous feet that were condemned to walk east one thousand days. She had endured the dragon's curse barely one tenth that time, but now . . . now her feet were still.

Experimentally, rubbing her bruised chest, she took a step to her left, then her right, then behind her, away from the mountains. Nothing impeded her.

She could walk anywhere she wanted!

The sword watched her deliberations with patience and, she sensed, no small sense of expectation.

It had broken the curse. She had no doubt of that. By killing her and then restoring her to life, it had freed her from a fate worse than death for any knight, false or otherwise. Humiliation had once been her only destination. But now . . .

Now she had other prospects.

The sword was still watching her. She had no doubt that it could kill her again, in a moment, if it chose. Furthermore, she supposed the sword would kill her the moment she outlived her usefulness to it, whatever that might be.

She would be sure, in all things, not to give it reason to.

She went down on one knee.

'I am Sir Saskia,' she told it, 'at your service.'

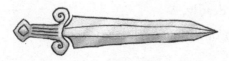